I0731906

The Roots Trilogy

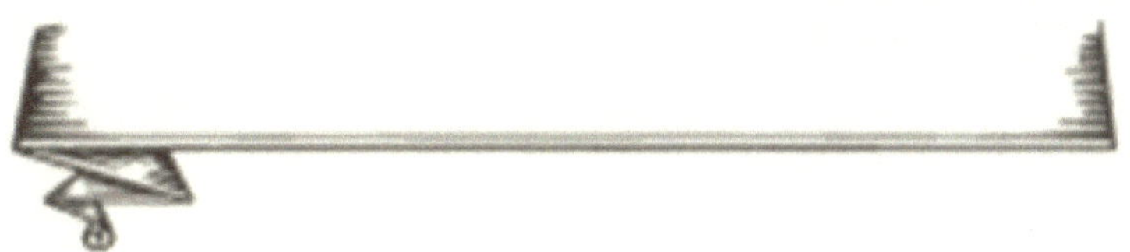

Katie M. Thornton

KMTK
PUBLISHING

This is a work of fiction. Names, characters, places, and incidents are products of the author's imagination or used fictitiously and are not to be construed as real. Any resemblance to actual events, locales, organizations, or person, living or dead, is entirely coincidental.

Published by KMTK Publishing.
Copyright © 2024 by Katie M. Thornton
Cover art Copyright © by Katie M. Thornton
ISBN **978-1-7381489-0-5**
Dumbledor 1 Font by Gem Fonts

All rights reserved. No part of this book may be used or reproduced in any manner whatsoever without written permission, except in the case of brief quotations embodied in critical articles and reviews.

CONTENTS

The Pirate Wars
A Roots Short Story

PART ONE

Chapter One

An Orphan Named Kavan

The Capital of Ellsgrove bustled with noise and people as the small caravan entered the city gates. A young boy with dark blonde hair stared up from his seat next to the driver, grey-blue eyes wide with wonder at the height of the city wall. The driver was a man in his late forties, wearing brown breeches, a white tunic, and brown robes overtop cinched at the waist by a belt.

"Here we are," Master Raymond spoke to Kavan for the first time that day. They had been on the road for several days. "The Capital. Your new home."

Kavan remained quiet as the soldiers at the gate checked Master Raymond's papers and then ushered them along. Three covered wagons followed behind them driven by older orphans; the soldiers allowed them to pass through as well. Kavan looked back at the other covered wagons that they had met up with just outside of the Capital that morning, each of them coming from a different direction. How many more orphans were there?

Kavan was nervous about being in such a big city. The village he had grown up in had maybe a hundred people; the din of the city was already starting to give him a headache. He watched from his seat as the wagon went along the city streets, going through a large marketplace where hawkers tried to sell their wares. He could smell food cooking somewhere and he felt his stomach rumble.

Ahead in the distance, he saw a palace on a hill looming over the city. He had heard about the king who governed Ellsgrove but had never seen him before. Now as an orphan, he would be a ward of the king. Would the king come to meet him?

Finally, the wagon stopped in front of a large brown stone building, its main door made of wood. Kavan noticed that the windows were covered with blankets. There was a plaque above the door that read 'The Boys' Orphanage of the King'. Across the street was a similar building that was for girls only.

"And here we are," Master Raymond said aloud as another man came out of the orphanage and took hold of the reins of the horse that had been pulling their wagon. "Come on boys, gather your things and line up at the door."

Kavan jumped down from the wagon and went to the back to grab his packs. At least twelve other boys also exited their wagons with their packs and headed for the walkway up to the door to the orphanage. Kavan was the sixth in line.

Master Raymond opened the door to reveal a small desk on the other side, another man sitting at it with some parchment in front of him, along with a writing utensil in his hand.

"This is Master Henry," Raymond told them. "You will register with him and then he will assign you your rooms. One at a time now."

Kavan waited, trying not to fidget. He balanced from one foot to the other as he got closer to the door. He stared at the back of the boy's head in front of him, a boy with black hair and dark skin.

"What is your name?" Master Henry asked the boy in front of him when it was his turn.

"Oscar, sir."

"How old are you?"

"Eleven, sir."

"And where are you from, Oscar?"

"Trelling, sir."

Kavan knew the village of Trelling, it was only a couple of villages away from where he was born.

The Master scratched something down on the parchment before asking, "And what did your parents do?"

"They ran the flour mill."

Again Master Henry scratched something down. He looked up at the boy with a small smile. "You can go to room six on the second floor. The room numbers are marked on their doors. Claim any of the empty beds and a locker for yourself. Once up there, you will be instructed on what to do next."

Kavan watched Oscar head towards the stairs with his packs before he stepped up to the small desk and the man sitting behind it.

"Your name?" Master Henry asked him.

"Kavan."

"How old are you?"

"Eleven."

"Where are you from?"

"Yulkin."

The Master scratched something on the parchment and then looked up at him again. "What did your parents do?"

"Ma ran the inn," he told the man. "Da was a soldier stationed there."

"Ah." Again, Master Henry scratched something down. "Too many of you boys were orphaned from the war in the southeast. Thankfully the king has negotiated peace now and there will be no more battles with Emberstine."

Kavan remembered his father talking about the war with Emberstine over dinner. The inn had been empty for a while because of the fighting, and they were mostly living on their chickens and whatever animals Kavan could trap in the woods. That day his mother had butchered one of the chickens to roast for the evening because they were expecting his father home. It had been one of the last meals they had had as a family before his father's captain had brought them the news: his father had been slain in a skirmish.

The fighting had started coming closer, and one day while his mother was out tending the chickens some Emberstine soldiers had attacked the village. His mother had died the same way as his father, by an Emberstine arrow.

"You may go up to room six on the second floor," Master

Henry told him. "Claim a bed and locker. You will get further instructions once there."

Kavan nodded to the man and looked around as he headed for the staircase that Oscar had ascended. There were oil lanterns on the walls that lit the way, and paintings of men wearing crowns that he assumed were kings of Ellsgrove.

The stairs creaked a little bit as he walked up them. He reached the landing and looked up the next set of stairs, curious as to what was up there. Then he looked down the hall at the eight doors, each of them with large numbers on them. The walls were plain whitewashed wood, with some scuff marks here and there. He looked at each of the numbers on the doors, and finally stopped in front of the one with the 'six'. He opened the door and walked through it, looking at the eight beds in the room. He was glad to see that the windows had glass in them, though they were mostly covered by blankets still. There was a lit fireplace on the outside wall of the room.

The boy who had been in front of him, Oscar, smiled at him from one of the beds. They were simple beds on wooden frames, the mattresses made of straw and cloth. At the end of each bed was a wooden locker. Two other boys who had been in the line ahead of Kavan were also in the room. They all looked to be around the same age.

Kavan put his packs on the empty bed next to Oscar.

"Hello," Oscar greeted him. "I'm Oscar. What's your name?"

"Kavan. I grew up in Yulkin."

Oscar's brown eyes darkened a little bit but then he smiled and told Kavan, "I know where that is! I used to go with my mom to the market there."

The other two boys introduced themselves, Elliot, and Matus. Kavan had been right, they were all eleven. Elliot's village had been a little further east than Yulkin; Matus' village was further west than Trelling.

They stowed their belongings in the lockers at the foot of their beds. There was a small blackboard on the front of each locker, and a piece of chalk, for them to write their names on. No more boys came to the room.

There was a knock on the door and another man dressed like Raymond and Henry opened it.

"I am Master John," the man told them. He had darker skin and hair like Oscar and looked younger than the other two Masters. "I hope you are settled in. I will show you to the bathing rooms and then the mess hall, if you will follow me."

The four of them followed Master John down the hallway to another stairway heading down to the main floor again. The hallway they found themselves in was made of stone, more oil lanterns lighting their way. At the end of the hallway were double wooden doors with old metal handles on them. Master John pushed the doors open and Kavan let out a gasp as he took in the steaming pools of water. There were other boys of varying ages already there washing themselves, but they did not stop to look at the newcomers.

"This is where you will bathe," Master John told them. "Once you are done, you will go through here," he pointed at another set of doors that he headed for. He opened these other doors and ushered them into a room with benches that were well-lit by both windows and lanterns. Kavan looked out the windows to find a garden with lots of trees.

"You will get dressed here, leaving your old clothes to be washed. Master Henry will have new clothes for you tomorrow morning, but you will get new bedclothes tonight after you bathe. Once you are done in here, it is this way to the mess hall," Master John talked as he walked, leading them through the changing area and another set of doors. This set of doors led them to another hallway that seemed to curve around, taking them back the way they had come in the first place. They reached another set of doors that John opened, revealing the large mess hall with lots of tables and benches. There were several tables with boys of varying ages sitting and eating, and Kavan could see where the kitchen was on the other side. He

could also smell the food, making his stomach rumble loudly.

John smiled down at him and said, "Go ahead and get your breakfast, boys. You will need the energy for your day."

***

He could smell mouldy straw that reminded him of his mattress at home. He tossed and turned in bed, fitfully sleeping.

In his mind he could see his mother outside of the inn, throwing feed for the chickens, a smile on her face as she laughed. She had been wearing blue that morning when the Emberstine soldiers had attacked their village. It had been her favourite colour.

As her screams echoed in his dreams and memories he shot up out of bed, his heart racing. The room was dark save for the fire in the hearth, and Kavan heard Oscar stir in the bed next to him.

"You OK?" Oscar whispered to him.

"Yeah," Kavan lied, wiping his brow of sweat. "Just nightmares."

"Of your mom?"

Kavan nodded before realizing that Oscar could not

see him in the dark. "Yeah," he whispered.

"I have nightmares about my parents too," Oscar whispered back.

Kavan laid back on his bed and rested his hand under the back of his head, peering up at the dark ceiling above. "What do you want to be when you grow up?" Kavan asked Oscar. "They are going to train us with useful skills so we can make a living once we age out, but what would you want to do?"

"I want to be a soldier so I can protect people," Oscar told him without hesitation. "You?"

"I want to be a soldier, too, so no other enemies tear families apart," Kavan told him.

"So we train together then," Oscar said as he laid back down too. "We will be soldiers together."

"Brothers in arms," Kavan whispered, and Oscar echoed him. They both fell back into a fitful sleep.

Chapter Two

The Boy's Orphanage of the King

Five years had passed since Kavan had come to the King's Orphanage. The war with Emberstine had come to an end a couple of years before, with Emberstine calling a truce and giving Ellsgrove a very large reparation. The King had chosen to give a portion of the money that Emberstine had given them to displaced families, further supporting the orphanages as well. They got new clothing allowances and were even given some money to spend in the marketplace on things of their choosing.

Kavan's sixteenth birthday had come and passed, celebrated by the boys who shared his year and the Masters. Kavan excelled in his classes, learning to read and write, and in the trades they were taught. He and Oscar had stayed true to their pact, training the most in the way of fighting. They trained every day, starting their mornings with a run around the city wall with some of the City Watch, and then with weight training.

The fencing director was most impressed with both youths and soon he had them helping with the younger boys. They also helped with the horses, cleaning the stalls every night, feeding and brushing them down. They had a greenhouse that they grew vegetables in to sell in the marketplace, and they worked hard to keep those plants growing well. Kavan and Oscar, as well as a few other older boys, were responsible for taking the vegetables to the market to sell once it came time to harvest them.

It was there at the marketplace where the boys interacted the most with their female counterparts from the Girls' Orphanage across the street. Along with vegetables, they both sold eggs from their chickens, but the girls also had quilts and baskets to sell.

With Kavan and Oscar were Elliot and Matus, along with two seventeen-year-old boys named Mikael and Ricko. The girls had their booth next to the boys', their quilts hanging up on racks behind them on display. There was Rachel, a petite blonde girl who was Kavan's age; Damaris, a dark-skinned dark-haired seventeen-year-old who was as tall as Kavan; and twins Eryn and Jolynn who were both brunettes and almost eighteen.

All four girls wore peasant dresses of varying colours, their bodices cinched modestly. The boys all wore trousers and tunics, and they all wore leather boots or shoes.

"What do you think you will do once you turn eighteen?" Mikael asked the twins as they stood around waiting for buyers. The market had just opened for the morning and it had yet to get busy.

"We have apprenticeships awaiting us with the city dressmakers," Jolynn informed him. "What do you think you will do?"

"With rumours of war with the Pirates of the Archipelago, we might have to fight," Mikael answered. "They will need soldiers."

Kavan and Oscar looked at each other, thinking the same thing. They were both leaning on the counter of their booth, listening to the conversation. Kavan shooed some flies away from their vegetables.

"But if it does not come to war?" Eryn wanted to know.

Mikael shrugged and said, "I have been learning how to be a blacksmith, they are always in need of apprentices."

"What about you two?" Jolynn asked Kavan and Oscar.

"We will be enlisting as soon as we can," Kavan informed her. "We will be soldiers, like our fathers before us. We want to help protect the people."

"What a waste of good potential," Eryn scoffed. "Why die for a king you have never met?"

"It's not about the king," Oscar told her, standing straight now. "He said it was about protecting the people. People like your family, and our own, who were killed in a war. We want to stop other families from being torn apart. What can be more noble than that?"

The girls were silent as they thought about it, Eryn looking uneasy.

"Sorry," Eryn said finally.

"We have seen a lot of boys head into the army and not return," Jolynn explained.

"And you know for certain they died?" Kavan asked her. She shook her head.

"There you have it," Kavan commented, ending the conversation as someone came up to their booth to get some fresh vegetables.

"Where will you live once out of the orphanage?" Mikael asked the twins once the customer had left.

"The dress shops have apartments above them for the apprentices," Eryn informed him. "We spend a few years there and then we can either go start our own shops in the city or move to another city, or get married and start a family."

Ricko chuckled and inquired, "Does every woman think of having kids?"

"No," Jolynn told him. "But it is expected of us."

"So you don't want kids?" Ricko asked her.

"I remember our mom struggling with so many kids, and then when dad died…things just got worse. Mom died in childbirth," Eryn told them. "There was us two, and four more girls."

"Sorry to hear that," Ricko told her. "You should be able to make your own choices."

"Tell that to the old men who only care about their progeny," Eryn said. "They don't care how much their wives struggle. Do you know the violence rate against women? You hear things in the market, especially around the washer-women. Men don't respect their wives enough. If I did get married, and he ever hit me, he would be dead the next day."

"Remind me not to get on your bad side," Ricko commented as another customer came up to them. A few women approached the girls' booth for some eggs, and one of them wanted to look at the quilts behind them.

Kavan thought about what Eryn had said. He looked at Damaris and wondered what she was going to do.

"What?" Damaris asked him, seeing him looking at her.

"What about you?" he asked.

She shrugged and said, "I have no idea. I'm not that great at most things. Gardening is fine and all, but I cannot sew to save my life, and I hate quilting."

"What does that leave for you then?" Kavan inquired.

"I don't know," Damaris told him. "I really do not want to talk about it right now. I have nearly a year to figure it out."

Kavan shrugged and turned away, focusing on another customer. The market picked up after that and they were too busy for the rest of the day to talk anymore about it.

They closed up their booths at the end of their allotted time, both having sold their produce and the girls their quilts. Together they loaded up their respective wagons with the now empty crates and headed back to the orphanages.

As they neared the orphanages they noticed young men dressed as squires and messengers running or riding through the streets, heading to seemingly important places in quite a hurry.

"What do you think that is about?" Matus asked Kavan and Oscar.

"Something big at the palace, no doubt," Oscar said with a shrug. "We will probably find out by morning."

They parted ways with the girls the street before the orphanages so they could take the carts and horses to the back stables; Kavan had realized long ago that the two orphanages were both built with the same blueprints and had their greenhouses and stables in the exact same places.

Kavan and the boys got the horse cleaned and put in the stable and then put the empty crates at the back of the greenhouse before going inside. Ricko had the coin purse and he left them at the back door to take it to Master Raymond. Though they had gotten some food from street vendors they were all more than ready for supper, so they went to go clean up.

They were heading to the dining hall when Ricko found them, and from the look on his face they knew he had found out what was going on.

"Well?" Matus asked him.

"The Pirates made their first move against the continent," Ricko told them. "They attacked the East Port, and one of Telemerachus' port cities."

Kavan and Oscar looked at each other before looking at the other boys.

"It's happening," Oscar said, slightly perturbed. "I can't believe it."

Chapter Three

The Price of Being a Soldier

Oscar turned eighteen two months before Kavan.

Kavan walked with Oscar to the city barracks where he was going to sign up to be a soldier. The war with the Pirates had started out slowly two years ago and had escalated only recently. Mikael and Ricko had joined the war effort the year before after the call for more soldiers had gone out. Every available man who was of age had flocked to the recruiting offices, with only the farmers being turned away.

"I will send word once I know where I am to be stationed," Oscar promised Kavan. Kavan looked at his friend and sighed inwardly, secretly hoping that his friend would not be stationed anywhere dangerous. "Maybe you could request to be sent to the same place."

Oscar had grown tall over the last two years, but so had Kavan; they were pretty much the same height. Oscar had grown his hair out into dreadlocks, using a leather thong to keep them out of his face. He had also grown a beard, something that Kavan was envious of. Kavan kept his hair neatly trimmed, and he barely had any stubble on his tanned face.

Oscar slapped him on the shoulder before hoisting his bag with what little belongings he had over his shoulder. He had a sword at his waist, a dagger on the other side, and a quiver with a bow over his other shoulder.

"I cannot wait to see you out there," Oscar told him. "I will miss you."

"And I you," Kavan said, grasping his arm in farewell. "Don't do anything stupid till I get there, okay?"

With a laugh Oscar gripped his wrist and then let go, turning to walk into the barracks. "I will try," he called back before disappearing inside the large metal doors.

Kavan looked up at the palace on the hill above the barracks, wondering if the king ever talked to his soldiers. With a shrug he turned and walked away, making his way slowly back to the orphanage.

***

The wagon Kavan rode in bumped around on the uneven road, jostling him and the other recruits around. The canvas had been pulled up over the wagon to cover it since the skies were threatening rain. In the distance, he could see giant storm clouds that flashed now and then with lightning. He could hear no thunder though.

They were nearing the East Garrison which was situated at the mouth of a river that ran inland quite close to the Capital. It was a strategic position because of this.

The East Garrison was also where Oscar had been stationed, and Kavan was eager to see him again.

Kavan thought about when he had left the orphanage. The Masters had seen him off, as had the other boys and the handful of girls he knew. It had been a bittersweet parting; he was heading out to do what he wanted to do, but he was also leaving the only place he had called home since his parents were killed. He barely had any personal belongings, just a chest with a handful of books and clothing. What would become of his things if he were to die in this war? Would they get sent back to the orphanage, or would they be discarded?

The wagon came to a halt and Kavan could hear the portcullis of the Garrison being opened. They passed through the gate and into the courtyard on the other side. Kavan could see the soldiers milling about, and wondered where Oscar was.

Kavan and the other recruits were instructed to leave the wagon and gather their belongings from the other wagon that had trailed behind them. Kavan had just pulled his chest out of the wagon when he heard someone shout his name. He turned and looked around, finally spotting Oscar on the walkway above the portcullis.

Oscar had his dreadlocks pulled back out of his face, and he wore light armour. At his waist was a sword, and there was a crossbow slung across his shoulder as well as a quiver with bolts in it. Oscar smiled broadly at Kavan and ran for the stairs that would take him down to the courtyard. Kavan met him there and embraced his old friend.

"Look at you!" Kavan exclaimed as he pulled away. "A true soldier!"

"You will be soon, my friend," Oscar reminded him. "Come, let me show you to your room and give you a tour. You will be expected to meet with the Commander later tonight."

Oscar took hold of the other side of Kavan's travellers chest and directed him to the doors to the garrison. Inside he led him up several flights of stairs lit by oil lamps until they reached the fourth floor.

"I'm on the floor below," Oscar informed Kavan as they stopped at a door with Kavan's name written on a chalkboard. "This is you. Privy is at the end of the hall, and yes there is actual plumbing." He pointed to a plain wooden door down the hallway. "The bathing room is downstairs though, I will show you where it is on our tour."

Kavan opened the door to his room and looked inside. There was a bed in the corner, a window above it, a desk against the other wall, a dresser, a weapons rack and an armour stand. He walked over to the window and found that he had a good look at the battlements and the ocean beyond. He placed his traveler's chest at the end of the bed and looked up at Oscar.

"Well, at least I don't have to share with anyone," Kavan told him with a slight chuckle. "It's not as small as
I thought it would be."

"I know, right?" Oscar said with a laugh. "Come on, let me show you around now."

Oscar took him down to the dining hall first and introduced him to some of the other soldiers that were around their age. They were all dressed like Oscar, each from different parts of the kingdom by the looks of it.

"We have the brothers Broderick and Brom," Oscar said as he pointed to the two young men who had dark skin and hair like Oscar. "Then there's Hansen, Korbin, and Marv."

Hansen was a tall broad shouldered young man with stark white hair and chiseled features. Korbin was more lanky, his skin tanned nicely, and his red hair tied back with a leather string. Marv was shorter and stouter than the rest, but he had muscles; his head was shaved bald.

"Welcome," Hansen greeted him and offered him a seat at the table they were at. "You are from the orphanage as well?"

Kavan nodded and took the seat, Oscar sitting down as well.

"How are things back in the Capital?" Marv asked him. "Any news about the war?"

Kavan shrugged and accepted a plate of food from Korbin. "Simple soldiers don't hear the important news," Kavan told them.

"Fair enough, but how about rumours?" Broderick inquired as he ate from his own plate of food.

"The Pirates are taking heavy losses from what I hear," Kavan admitted. "I heard about a ship that was smashed to pieces in a storm last week during an attack. No survivors."

"They haven't tried hitting here in a while," Oscar commented.

"Don't say that!" Brom demanded, continuing with, "You'll jinx it!"

Oscar shook his head and dug into his own food. Once he and Kavan were done eating he took Kavan to meet the Commander of the garrison. Commander Leon was a man in his late forties who looked like he needed a good night's sleep; there were bags under his brown eyes, and his face looked drawn. The Commander's office looked like he needed a secretary: there were papers strewn over his desk, maps and other documents by the looks of it.

"I assume your friend has shown you around most of the garrison by now?" Commander Leon asked Kavan after he had stood at attention.

"Yes sir," Kavan replied.

"Good. I hope you find your room acceptable. There will be a schedule of duties drawn up for the new recruits, all of the soldiers take part in different aspects of keeping the garrison running, from the horses in the stables to the meals in the dining hall. Understand?"

"Yes, sir."

"Good. The schedule will be posted on the landing of the stairs on your floor. Tomorrow morning you will report to the quartermaster–Oscar can show you where that is–for your gear. You are dismissed."

Kavan bowed his head lightly and exited the Commander's office with Oscar.

"The quartermaster is on the way to the bathing room," Oscar informed him as he led him away from the Commander's office and towards a set of stone stairs that went down. "It's this way."

***

The weeks went by as Kavan settled into life at the Garrison. The morning routine was weight lifting or running at dawn followed by breakfast. Kavan was on the late afternoon watch, so until his watch started he did chores in the stables or helped prepare meals in the dining hall. Oscar and Brom were on the same schedule and watch as him so they spent a lot of time together.

There were lookout parties who would ride up and down the coast to watch out for the pirates, and several of them had small skirmishes but none of them came close to the garrison yet. Kavan had been on one of those lookout parties that met with the enemy and he thankfully came away unscathed. Brom had taken a gunshot to the leg, however, and was laid up in the infirmary for a while. Kavan and the other young men would visit him every morning after their workouts to keep his spirits up.

Kavan awoke one morning with a feeling of unease. He swung his legs over the side of his bed and looked out the window to find a heavy fog had descended on the garrison. He could not even see the battlements, the fog was that thick. He changed from his night clothes to his workout ones and went to go meet with the others in the training yard.

The fog was as dense on the training yard as it was everywhere else. The soldiers were all on edge, for the lookouts had not returned yet and they could not see out to the ocean. When the fog still had not cleared after they had washed up and eaten, the concern grew even more.

Kavan walked out onto the battlements with Oscar and the others of their group to find the Commander and his Second-in-Command Kesse standing by one of the canons. Commander Leon had a spyglass in his hand and was trying to use it to see but the fog was just too thick.

"I want a message sent to the other forts," Commander Leon told his Second. "Our fastest horses. Ring the bell to muster as well."

"Right away, sir," Kesse bowed slightly before hurrying off to do as ordered.

"Sir?" Oscar was the first to stand at attention when the Commander looked at them.

"If this fog is natural, I'll eat my saddle bag," Commander Leon said as he shook his head. "I wish we had mages stationed here, they might be able to do something about it."

Kavan had to keep himself from laughing at what the Commander had said; if *he* was worried, they all should be. This was what they had signed up for though.

A bell ringing nearby made them flinch, but it was the call to muster. They would need to go get their armour and weapons in order to answer that. They dismissed themselves and went to do that. Since Brom was still laid up in the infirmary it was just the six of them in their group who helped each other get their armour on faster. A lot of the other men had their own groups as well, people they could each rely on and had trained together to do so.

Kavan was putting his sword belt on when he heard scuffling in the hallway. He looked up to find Brom using crutches to help him walk, and the fellow soldier had a determined look on his face.

"Oh no you don't," Kavan chided him. "Get your ass back in bed now!"

"Help me get my armour on–" Brom started to say but he was cut short by his brother who had heard him from the next room.

"Absolutely not," Broderick told him. "You will not only jeopardize our safety but everyone else if you go out there injured, and you know that. Go back to the infirmary."

Brom lowered his head and hobbled back down the hallway, his brother and Kavan watching him go, both shaking their heads. They waited till Brom had gone back down the stairs before they continued getting ready. Once they were all done they headed out to the courtyard where the rest of the soldiers were gathering. Commander Leon was waiting for them there, and once they were all gathered he gave them their orders. Half of them were to get the cannons ready, and the other half were to go to the river to make sure no one was trying to sneak past them. Kavan and his friends were part of the cannon group.

The fog had not thinned or lifted at all during the time they had spent donning their armour and grabbing their weapons. On the battlements they adjusted the cannons and loaded them; Kavan had his spyglass though he could not see through the fog to aim at anything. All Kavan could hear was the sounds of the calibrations occurring, until finally everything was quiet. It was eerily silent as they stood there in the fog, just waiting.

A high pitched whine split the silence and Kavan heard someone yell out, "Cannonball!" He felt the cannonball hit the side of the battlements below where he was standing and he swallowed hard. The pirates only had to adjust their shot before they could hit the soldiers on the battlements. *If only they could see through the fog*! Kavan thought to himself.

"Where do you think that came from?" Kavan asked Broderick as he started to adjust their cannon.

"You are seriously going to just aim in this fog and hope for the best?" Broderick asked him incredulously.

"Yes."

Broderick sighed and pointed in a direction he assumed the cannonball was fired from. Kavan adjusted the cannon a little more and then pulled the cord, stepping back as the cannon kicked as it fired the cannonball. Broderick quickly reloaded it as they waited, hearing the unmistakable sound of it hitting something made of wood and the shouts that followed.

"Aim there!" Oscar shouted as they heard the enemies shouting, and other cannons were aimed at the same area and consequently fired.

They could hear the sounds of a ship being torn apart and splashing sounds, but before they could celebrate their victory they could hear more cannons being fired at them. How many ships were down there? Had they all had enough time to calibrate their aim?

"Duck!" Kavan had to yell to Broderick as a cannonball whizzed towards them through the fog. They both moved out of the way and had to jump down the walkway to avoid the debris as the cannonball hit the stone wall behind them. Others on the battlements weren't as lucky; one cannon further down had been hit full on, causing chaos as some of the powder exploded.

Kavan stood and felt a breeze pick up into a gale, taking the fog out to sea and finally revealing the attacking ships. Kavan inhaled sharply as he saw longboats heading for both the shore and the river, each one full of enemy soldiers.

"Reload and fire at will!" someone shouted as an alarm sounded. Kavan could see his fellow soldiers riding to meet the enemy at the river.

Kavan and Broderick worked together to reload the cannon and adjust it before firing again, then again, at another ship as the others did as well. Kavan was vaguely aware of the fire being put out down the walkway as they worked.

A hook appeared on the side of the battlements near where Kavan was. He heard the sound of metal on stone and stopped to look around sharply.

"They are climbing the walls!" Kavan called out as he drew his sword and went over to the hook. He had to jump back as a man vaulted himself over the wall and aimed a flintlock pistol at him. Kavan struck the gun out of the man's hand with his sword and ran him through, pulling his sword out and kicking the man aside. He grabbed the gun and aimed it at the next man who was coming over the side, firing it. The man was hit full in the face and he fell back down into the water. Kavan threw the gun at the next man, missing entirely, and had to block a blow from a sword.

This new enemy managed to make it over the wall and was now squaring off against Kavan. Kavan could see Broderick fighting against the men coming up his section of the wall and noticed that he was struggling to keep up. Kavan dealt with the man he was fighting and went to go help Broderick, slashing one of the pirates from behind. None of the pirates wore heavy armour since they would sink if they went overboard, just light leather armour that was no good for close quarter fighting like this.

"There's too many of them!" Broderick yelled as they worked together to push the pirates back. They had killed a handful of them together, but more were indeed coming over the wall. Kavan looked at Oscar and the other soldiers on the wall fighting against the pirates as he heard gunshots coming from the river. Were they all going to die here?

"Somebody needs to ring the bell!" Oscar yelled. "Alert the countryside of the attack!"

Kavan glanced to the stairway that led to the warning bell at the top of the fortress–he was the closest soldier to it.

"Go," Broderick told him grimly. "I will hold them back."

Kavan broke free of the fighting and headed for the stairs, taking them two at a time. After a moment he heard someone else coming up the stairs and he risked a glance back to find a pirate coming after him. He swore to himself, knowing that fighting on the twisted stair would be no good, he had to get up to the top first. That urged him on and he ran faster, reaching the top where he clung to the rope and pulled as hard as he could, wincing at the loud sound of the warning bell. Then he faced the top of the stairs that the pirate was just reaching.

"You're too late," Kavan told him, but the pirate attacked him with his curved sword. He was no match for Kavan though, who quickly dispatched him and then rang the bell several more times before going back down the stairs. He found Broderick injured at the bottom of the stairs, holding back two more pirates. The dead were strewn all around the battlements, more of them soldiers than pirates. Where was Oscar?

"I'm here," Kavan said to Broderick, and he could see the relief in his friend's face when he heard his voice. Together they finished off the two that Broderick had been holding back, but as Broderick took hold of him to balance himself they heard a cannonball whistle through the air.

Kavan did not have the time to move as the cannonball hit the side of the walkway and burst through the stone, hitting them both with debris. He felt a searing pain in his back as he tried to move, and then his vision went dark.

***

Kavan awoke slowly, confused at where he was. He was laying on his stomach on a cot, and his back felt weird. He tried to get up, but hands held him down.

"Stay still, soldier," he heard a man say, and he recognized the surgeon's voice. "I'm almost done here."

"What…what happened?" Kavan managed to ask as he wiped his eyes.

"You were injured in the attack," he heard the surgeon say. "I am sewing up your wound. I'm sorry I am not a mage. There will be a considerable scar on your back, and once the freezing balm has worn off you will be in a lot of pain."

"The pirates?" He had to ask.

"Commander Leon routed the pirates at the river, and General Hayes arrived with his men to fight the rest back. I have heard we have you to thank for ringing the warning bell, which is why General Hayes showed up," the surgeon informed him.

"My friend, Broderick, where is he?"

"Don't worry about that now," the surgeon told him quietly. "Your friend Brom will tell you after I am done."

He could feel the tugs in his back slightly as the surgeon continued, and he tried to look around the room. He could see a handful of other injured soldiers in the room being attended to, but there were fewer than he hoped to see, and none of them were his friends. He started to get a sinking feeling in his stomach.

"All done," the surgeon told him. "One of the nurses will be by soon with some pain relief before the freezing balm wears off. Stay on your stomach as much as you can today, and get someone to help you up. That's an order, soldier."

Kavan nodded and tried to adjust his pillow to make himself a little more comfortable. That was when he saw Brom hobbling his way over to him with a grim expression on his face.

"You're awake," Brom commented as he pulled a chair over to sit next to Kavan's cot.

"Where are the others?" Kavan asked him. He could see Brom's eyes darken at the question.

"You are the only one left alive from the battlements," Brom told him.

Kavan jerked his head up and felt his back twinge. "No, that cannot be true," Kavan found himself saying as he tried to get up. He pushed through the pain to do so, much to Brom's chagrin; he vaguely heard the surgeon yelling after him as he staggered to the window of the infirmary that overlooked the courtyard.

In the courtyard all of the bodies of the soldiers who had died were laying there in neat rows, their bodies covered in their personal blankets from their beds. Each blanket had their names sewn into them so it made it easier to identify the bodies, and each soldier was encouraged to add colours or designs to their blankets as well. Kavan knew each of his friends' blankets because he had helped them with them, and now he stared down at them covering his friends' bodies.

Kavan fell to his knees against the wall. Oscar, Broderick, Hansen, Korbin and Marv, all gone.

Brom reached out and touched his shoulder. "You had better get back on your cot before you ruin the stitches," Brom told him quietly. Kavan vaguely remembered nodding before Brom helped him to his feet and back over to his cot where he fell down on his stomach and gave in to the tears.

Part Two

Katie M. Thornton

Chapter One

Heath

A boy ran along the rope bridge, taking care not to get his feet stuck between the wooden rungs. Not far behind him trailed two other boys, one older, one younger. They each had the same dark hair and green eyes, and they all dressed in breeches and tunics, their feet bare.

The first boy made it across the bridge to the smaller island that was on the other end and glanced behind him as the other two boys reached the bridge on their side. He shook his head and continued running, passing through a few small groupings of houses, disturbing chickens and scaring pigs as he went. Finally he reached the next bridge that led to the main island of the archipelago.

"Heath!" the older boy following behind yelled after him. The boy called Heath finally stopped next to a grouping of cedar trees along the path that led to the capital of Mast.

"You two need to run faster," Heath told them with a slight smirk, dimples showing in his cheeks.

"You got a head start on us," the older boy retorted. He was nearly a youth, whereas Heath was almost ten.

"Oh come on Graydon, you've got longer legs than me, if you weren't trying to keep pace with Everett you would have caught up with me," Heath told him.

"You know mom wants us to watch over our little brother," Graydon replied, putting an arm around their younger brother, Everett, who was seven.

"Where do you think it's happening?" Heath asked Graydon as they continued to walk towards the buildings in the distance.

"It'll be at the Commandant's House, of course," Graydon told him. "Every new Commandant is sworn in there."

Heath thought about the Commandant's House: it was the largest building in the centre of the island, several stories tall and built of both stone and wood. The top
of the building was shaped like a ship, and there was a lookout at the top of it.

The boys ran past the harbour on their way to their destination, each of them slowing down slightly to take in the sight of all of the ships that were there and the different flags that named the tribe they belonged to. The Tribes of the Archipelago were separated into at least fifteen tribes that spanned over all of the forty-five islands that made up the archipelago. For the naming of the new Commandant of the Tribes all of the respective leaders had come to witness it, for the Commandant ruled over all of the Archipelago.

The last Commandant had died of old age, so a new one had to be chosen. That it was someone from their own Tribe, the Tribe of the Sea-Dragon, and in fact was their uncle, made it more exciting for the boys–even if they were not supposed to be there.

There was a crowd of people outside of the Commandant's house, and the boys pushed their way through to the front. They hid behind some water troughs for horses as they watched.

Their Uncle Nikko was their mother's brother, and he stood at the top of the steps to the house in front of the large double doors that were inlaid with mother-of-pearl designs of ships on the sea. He was a tall man, well over six feet, with golden-wheat coloured hair that he had held back with a leather thong. Heath always thought that Graydon got their uncle's high cheekbones and his height from their mother's side of the family, for their father–who stood just behind Nikko–had way darker features. At least Heath had gotten his mother's green eyes, and her dimples, though he had inherited his father's dark hair and slightly darker skin that looked like a perpetual tan.

Heath watched as his uncle knelt and one of the Sea Priests, those in charge of crowning the new Commandant–who was wearing a rather ridicu-lous looking blue robe–place a crown made from coral on his uncle's head. The priest muttered some words while everyone watched, and then when the priest bade Nikko to stand everyone in the crowd cheered.

Heath looked at the leaders of the other tribes, all fourteen of them who were standing at the bottom of the stairs watching, and wondered if they were angry that they had not been chosen. From what Heath understood, the priests sequestered themselves for several days on the beach where they communed with the sea about who should lead them next; he had no idea how their magic helped them choose, but they had chosen Nikko.

Heath noticed their father looking at them, anger in his eyes that they would dare to be there when he told them to stay home. He elbowed Graydon in the ribs, the older boy yelping in response and glaring at his younger brother.

"Dad sees us," he whispered, just loud enough for Everett to hear as well. As one, the three of them turned and pushed their way back out through the cheering crowd. They started to run back towards their home island hoping that their father would not be able to leave the celebrations quite so fast and they had time to hide before he could discipline them.

When they reached home, which was a cabin-like house surrounded by cedar trees on the Island of Mast, their mother was waiting for them with a dinner that had gone cold. She looked at them, hands on her hips, with exasperation on her face.

"I have been calling you boys for an hour," she scolded them. "Where did you miscreants run off to?"

"Sorry mother," Graydon said as they sat down at the wooden table in the kitchen. "We forgot what time it was."

"Likely story," she said with a sigh. "I knew you could not resist going to see Uncle Nikko named the new Commandant."

"Why were you not there?" Heath asked her.

"Because I was here, making *you* food," she reminded him. "Food that has now gone cold!"

"Sorry, mother," Heath said as he looked down at his hands in his lap.

"Did your father see you?" she asked quietly. After a moment of hesitation Heath nodded.

Their mother sighed deeply. "Okay, well, take your cold food and go hide in the barn, I will deal with him when he gets home. We do not need you getting another lashing so soon."

Heath winced as he thought about the beating his father had given him several months ago, lashes on his back. He did not want to go through that again. He nodded to his mother and took his plate of food–as did his brothers–and together they headed out to the barns where the livestock stayed.

Heath settled into the mow of the one barn where the hay was stored, nestling himself in amongst the barn cats that tolerated him. He ate his cold food, sausages and mashed potatoes, in silence. He looked around the barn, noticing that his brothers had chosen to hide in the other barns. He shrugged, knowing that the cats would help keep him warm through the night.

Chapter Two

The Choices of War

"Heath!" Graydon yelled for his brother as he waded through the crowd of sailors at the tavern. He searched for him, looking for a tall man with dark hair, and found him at the dart boards on the other side of the room. Heath glanced up at him and smiled in welcome.

Heath was eighteen now, Graydon in his early twenties. Graydon had grown taller, like their uncle Nikko, and it seemed that Heath had gotten the height from their mother's side as well, for he was not much shorter than his older brother. Heath was wearing his sailor's outfit, his tunic untucked for a relaxing evening of drinking and throwing darts with his friend Maeve and her brother Lorenzo.

"How were the seas today?" Graydon asked them as he joined them, sitting in one of the empty chairs next to them.

"Unusually calm," Heath told him. "The Continent were absent."

The Continent were what they called the several different kingdoms that made up the single land mass to the east. The other continent to their west was one single kingdom of Jay'Al, one that was full of magic and danger with the orc parties that lived there almost side-by-side with the humans. Heath knew there was a lot of contention between the orc clans and the humans, that was why they rarely went there.

"I can tell you why," Graydon replied, "but I will need a drink first. This is a doozy."

Maeve looked at him sideways. "That can't be good," she said, shaking her head and making her wavy golden brown hair dance slightly around her face. "*You* needing a drink before telling a tale."

"You will understand in a minute," he assured her as Heath beckoned to one of the serving wenches for more drinks. It did not take long for three more ales to be brought to them. Graydon grabbed one for himself and took a hearty gulp from the cup.

"Uncle Nikko and father met with some of the ambassadors from the Continent today," Graydon told them. "Father shot the ambassadors from Ellsgrove and Raistminestine."

The three of them stared at Graydon in shock.

"Father said the ambassadors had a weapon, but you and I both know that he wants a war with the Continent," Graydon continued. "Uncle Nikko was wounded in the rebuff, but he is alive."

"Holy shit," Heath finally said. "What in the Hells was father thinking?!"

"Like I said, father wants to go to war with the Continent," Graydon told him. "You know how he is. They won't trade all of their resources with us so he wants to take them."

Heath swore, taking a long swig of his ale. "I will have to prepare my men for war," Heath whispered, thinking about his friends who were also the sailors on his ship. Maeve, and Jackson who had chosen to stay at home that night. He never thought it would come to that, to war with the Continent. Hijacking ships on the seas was one thing, but an all out war on the several kingdoms that made up the Continent? That was insane.

"I don't like this," Heath muttered. "Not one bit."

Maeve looked at him through her thick eyelashes, understanding why he was worried. His sailors were not just sailors to him, they were his friends. He had never lost one of them yet.

"Captain Heath," she spoke finally, "We will follow you whichever way you choose."

"Good luck with that," Lorenzo commented. He was not one of Heath's sailors, but one of the gunsmith apprentices of the Archipelago. "From what I have heard of Matteo, your father, he will have you right in the thick of the fighting out of pure spite."

Heath knew that was true; he was not the most favoured son. That was Everett, the golden child who got the most use out of his water magic. His father had never beat Everett like he had Heath. Matteo had a temper, but he would direct it at certain people and most of the time Heath found that he was one of his father's favourite targets.

Heath shook his head, trying to think. "I won't let anything happen to my crew," he said finally. "I will make the final decisions for us, not my father."

"I know," Maeve whispered, putting a hand on his shoulder. "We trust you."

That made it harder for Heath, knowing that his sailors trusted him. His father was to blame for the coming war; his father would be to blame for any of his sailors dying. Heath could not allow that. He had to think of something.

"I think I am going to call it a night," Heath told
them. "Graydon, will you be at breakfast with mom in the morning?"
Graydon nodded.

"I will see you then," Heath told him.

The tavern was at least on the Isle of Mast, so his walk home was not far. He was not going to sleep inside though, for he found the hay mow a lot more comfortable than his bed lately. He climbed up the ladder to the mow and found himself met with a very pregnant cat who was definitely in the midst of giving birth.

"Oh, Winnie," Heath said with a sigh. He had known that the tortoiseshell cat was pregnant but had not realized how close it was. She rubbed up against his legs and meowed at him in an urgent way before leading him to the spot she had picked to have her kittens. She was breathing heavily now, and Heath wondered if she had waited for him to come home in order to have her kittens, which made him feel bad for staying out so late in the night.

The first few kittens were born rather quick, and Winnie took care of cleaning them up right away. Heath laid down next to her in the mow and watched as the newborn kittens started to nurse before he fell asleep.

In the morning he found that she had given birth to five kittens in total, only one of them being a tortoiseshell like herself; the others were either calico or straight black. They mewed as they moved to nurse, and Heath helped them each find a teat. Heath watched as they drank their fill, marvelling at their round bellies and how adorable newborn kittens were.

He left the loft and went to the house, finding his mother Sofia in the kitchen at the wood-fired stove making breakfast. Graydon was there at the table, holding his head in his hands. Everett stood leaning
against the doorway to the other room, a cup of water in his one hand.

"Good-morning," Sofia said to Heath as he entered the house. "Has that cat had her kittens yet?"

"During the night, yes, five kittens," Heath told her. "Should be some nice mousers for the barns."

"You should take one for your ship," Sofia told him. "I remember the rats onboard our ships, it was a nightmare at times."

"I might just do that," Heath told her as he sat down next to Graydon. "What's for breakfast, mom?"

"Bacon, eggs, fried sausages, fried potatoes," she told him as she stirred something. "Grab a plate and come here."

"Grab me some, please?" Graydon asked him without looking up or taking his hands away from his face; he was definitely hungover.

"Yepp," Heath told him, and he grabbed two plates, letting their mother portion out their food for them. He returned to the table with the steaming plates, and Graydon started picking at it.

30

Everett got his own food and sat down with them, not saying a word. He ate heartily, cleaning his plate up before Heath was even half done his own.

"What do you make of what our father has done?" Heath asked Everett. "You were supposed to be there with him at the meeting."

Graydon looked up at him with narrowed eyes, shaking his head slightly as to dissuade Heath from
his topic of conversation.

Everett sighed and looked at his older brother. "He did what needed to be done," he told Heath.

Heath stared at his younger brother, the one who looked most like him, and wondered how they could be so different. Everett *was* their father's favourite, for whatever reason, but could Everett not see the danger this would bring to the people of the Archipelago? Apparently not.

"We tread in dangerous water, brother," Heath reminded him. "The Continent is made up of several kingdoms, each with magic users like us. Yes, they do not possess the guns that we have a monopoly on, but their magic is still a huge asset and can deter bullets. They have healers, we do not. What is so important to be worth a full out war with the Continent?"

"Resources," the words came from the door to the kitchen, where Matteo stood now. "We need more resources, and the Continent has refused to give them to us."

"What resources?" Heath asked him. "We can grow lumber here in a sustainable way, and we have animals for food. What else are we missing?"

"Different meat, more wood, clothing resources like silk," he told them. "There is so much out there that we do not have here."

"So you would risk everyone's lives for a war with the Continent?!" Heath asked him. "What you have done has endangered us all!"

Matteo grimaced at his son's words, but he did not back down. "This is happening, Heath, whether you like it or not."

"So be it," Heath commented, standing up from
the table. "But I will have you know that my sailors are not canon fodder, they are my friends, and I will *not* take them to their deaths."

He did not wait for a response, he turned and walked out. He ran to Maeve's house, one island over, where she, Lorenzo, and Jackson were having breakfast. Jackson was his other lieutenant, a tall, slightly darker skinned young man with similar dark hair and eyes.

"We cannot go through with this war," Heath told his two lieutenants. "Too many people will die."

"What do you want us to do?" Maeve asked him.

"Do you trust me?" Heath asked her and Jackson. They both nodded. "Then leave that up to me."

***

Heath scratched the chin of his cat, Selene, as he watched his old ship sink to the bottom of the bay. Selene had been one of Winnie's kittens, the only tortoiseshell kitten that she had had; Selene had long hair though, which must have been a trait from her sire since Winnie was a short haired cat. She was almost a year old now.

Behind him on the beach were all of his sailors, including his two lieutenants Maeve and Jackson.

"This must be hard," Maeve commented. "Your family ship is about to smash up against the rocks."

"It would have been harder burying any of you," Heath replied. "You are part of my family, all of you. I will not have any of you die for the choices my father made."

"We know, and we appreciate you," Maeve told him. "Thank you for keeping us safe."

"I have made contact with some spies of Ellsgrove," Heath told her. "The king is interested in our magic, and might have good use of us."

"Such as?"

"They are looking for a safer way to get to Jay'Al, since it is not safe to go through the Archipelago, and with the whirlpools on their other side…"

"So what are you suggesting?"

"We go north, through the Sea of Ice," Heath told her. "I can get us through the ice."

"Are you sure?"

"Yes."

"I suppose it is worth a try," she told him. "We follow your lead."

"Then let us meet with King Knox," Heath told her. "Let's see where this takes us."

Epilogue

Where Fate Has Them

Kavan stretched his back, very aware of the scars on his back that were still somewhat taut. He looked out over the Summer Palace from the ramparts, where the King and the Royal Family chose to stay in the summer, and wondered what the next year would bring him.

It had been a couple years since the Pirate Wars had ended, and he had healed well. He had been sent to the Summer Palace in the south of Ellsgrove as one of the head guards and he had a prominent position that he maintained by continuously demonstrating how good he was at his job.

There had been a sickness further north in Ellsgrove recently, and thankfully the south had not been affected. From what he heard though, the capital had been hit hard and the king, along with his family, had succumbed to the illness. A new King had been crowned, King Lucius, cousin of King Knox.

Kavan was called by a messenger to the Commander's office. He went, curious as to what the meeting could be about. He found his Commander, Zeke, standing at attention in front of a man in his late forties with blond hair, dressed impeccably well for a nobleman.

"You asked for me, sir?" Kavan asked his Commander.

"Yes, this is King Lucius," Zeke introduced him to the man standing there. "He was asking about you."

"Your Majesty," Kavan said as he took a knee, bowing his head down. "To what do I owe this honor?"

"I was hoping you would accompany my eldest daughter on a quest, if it turns out," Lucius told him. "I will not know for a few months still."

"I would be honoured to hold such a position, Your Majesty," he answered, and he felt his heart beating hard in his chest. The King wanted *him*?!

"Thank you, Kavan," King Lucius responded. "I would have you move to The Capital now though, so you can reacquaint yourself with the city."

"Of course, Your Majesty," Kavan responded, almost at a loss for words. "Thank you, Your Majesty."

***

Heath shivered, recuperating from the cold of the ice shelf he had to move through. His magic was good with the water, but staying warm was another thing.

The land of Jay'Al lay ahead of them, a kingdom full of magic that they had dared not go to for a long time. What would they find there? Heath had no idea, the records of the Tribes of the Archipelago did not have much on Jay'Al. Why, though? Was their magic *that* powerful?

They made landfall at dusk, and set up their tents. They kept their braziers lit as much as they could in the cold. In the morning they awoke to visitors.

The woman who approached them was in her early forties maybe, with dark brown skin and bright red hair. Her eyes were different colours, one blue and the other green.

"I am the Shaman of the Wolf Clan," the woman spoke, surprisingly in the Common Tongue. "What business do you have here?"

"King Knox of Ellsgrove has sent me here to make contact with you, after the last unsuccessful mission," Heath told her. "We look forward to working with the people of Jay'Al."

The woman gave him an interested look before turning to look at the warriors around her. One of them nodded and so she turned back to them with a large smile.

"It is good to have Ellsgrove back," she told him. "I believe I have the perfect spot for you. Please, follow me."

A Quest for Her Roots

Book One

Prologue

The sign of the tavern swung in the wind, the streets below it mostly empty of people coming and going. The tavern was a large four story stone building built into the wall of the city of Wardgrove. The tavern itself was mostly empty but for a handful of people eating or having drinks. In one back corner at a table sat a dark skinned young woman with bright red hair, wearing a simple cotton tunic and breeches. She sat with two other men playing cards, one of them another dark skinned young man who had black hair and the other a man with pale skin and dark blonde hair; both young men were dressed in fine velvet dark red breeches and fine cotton tunics, the rings on their fingers naming them as wealthy people.

"Roz, do you need another drink?" the dark skinned young man asked his female companion.

She nodded and focused on cutting the deck of cards as her friend signalled to the serving wench to bring over some more drinks for all three of them.

"How did you get so good at this?" the pale skinned man asked her.

"Oh, Oswick and a few other merchants have shown me some tricks," Roz told him. "Are you intimidated, Master York?"

The young merchant named Master York snorted with a laugh as he shook his head. "Just deal, Roz."

Roz dealt the deck out between them and accepted her new pint from the serving wench, thanking her by name.

"Do you know what's going on down south?" Roz asked the merchants.

"Some sickness in the capital apparently," York told her. "A lot of people dead. It seems to be staying in the south though."

"I've heard of a few people sick up here," Oswick added. "My family has been up here for months thankfully. I would hate to think of what it is like back home."

"It's fall, at least most of the trading season is over," Roz commented. "With winter coming in things will slow down more. I guess we can blame the sickness for how slow Wardgrove is right now."

Usually the large northern city would be teeming with merchants and buyers, but the Earl of Wardgrove had not really been surprised when the turn out for the Fall Market was half of what it usually was; Roz's father had heard the news from the south long before and knew it would affect the trade. At least some of the merchants had made it north, like Roz's good friend Oswick and their mutual acquaintance Master York.

Just then the door of the tavern opened, the street dark behind two men with swords at their waists who walked in. Roz recognized their insignia as knights of Ellsgrove and wondered what they could be doing up north.

Usually the knights were busy along the borders of the other kingdoms, and especially on the west coast where the Tribes of the Archipelago--more like pirates—were known to cause trouble ever since the tentative ceasefire of The Pirate Wars a few years before. Her own father had sponsored some young men to become knights, and her younger brother had had to do some training as part of his 'heir to the earl' training.

As the knights took off their hooded cloaks and sat down at a table Roz looked at them closely with her mismatched blue and green eyes; she recognized neither of them, though they were both handsome men.

Roz caught the serving wenches' attention and nodded towards the two knights. The young woman nodded with a smile and went to go take their orders for food and drink. Roz and her friends continued to play their game of cards, placing higher bets every now and then, as she watched the two knights.

One of them was tall with broad shoulders and curly blonde hair, with ice blue eyes. He had not stopped smiling and joking with his comrade since they had arrived. The second knight was shorter by a head and more lithe looking, with dark brown hair and freckles. He too seemed to be in a good mood.

When the serving wench brought them their food she also brought two pints of their finest ale. When the young woman told the knights that the drinks were courtesy of the young woman sitting in the corner they both looked at Roz with interest and raised their pints in a toast to her as a thank you.

Oswick raised an eyebrow at his friend but continued to play and drink. Roz was winning most of York's coin, much to the young merchant's displeasure and Oswick's amusement. Finally York announced he was done for the night and he headed up to his room rather solemnly. Oswick and Roz shared a laugh and she started to gather up the coins on the table.

"Lottie, my dear girl, another round," Roz called to the serving wench. She turned to look at the two knights who had just finished eating and were appraising her again.

"Care to join our table sirs, and share some news from the south?"

"We have not been south in months, miss. We have come from the north western garrison on our way south," the curly haired one answered.

"Well, come join us anyways," she said with a laugh. "Drinks are on me tonight."

"May we know the name of our beautiful host?" the curly haired knight asked her as he and his companion joined her and Oswick.

"Call me Roz," she told them. "This is my friend Oswick."

"I am Sir Sullivan, but you can call me Sully," the curly haired knight introduced himself. "And this is Sir Graeme."

"Welcome to Wardgrove," Roz told them. "What do you think of the city?"

"Different from what I remember," Sully told her. "On our way up to the garrison the fall market was thriving. It seems so empty now."

"Hopefully next year will be better," Roz told them. "The market is one of our biggest attractions."

"You are both merchants?" Sir Graeme asked them.

"Oswick is, I live here," Roz told them.

"You just play cards all the time?" Sully teased her.

"I do a lot of different things," she told him. "Care for a game of cards?"

"I should be heading out," Oswick spoke up, giving Roz a knowing look. "Behave yourself, Roz, don't empty the knights' purses hm?" She stuck her tongue out at him as he got up and walked out of the tavern into the night.

Sir Graeme yawned, making Sullivan laugh. "Maybe you should go to your room my friend," he told Graeme with a friendly pat on the back. "I do not feel tired yet so I will stay and play a game with you Roz."

"From the looks of how unhappy that other merchant was I am glad I am keeping my coin," Graeme said with a wink before bidding them goodnight and going up to the large wooden staircase to his room above somewhere.

"From where do you hail, Sir Sullivan?" Roz asked him.

"You speak exceptionally well for a commoner," Sullivan commented.

"Who said I was a commoner?" she asked him slyly. "I am a mage," she told him. "I have gone to school."

"Ah, I guess that explains it. Do you work for the Earl of Wardgrove?"

Roz smiled and nodded. It was not exactly a lie.

"What shall the wager be?" Sully asked her as she dealt the cards. "Shall we start with a few silver?"

Sullivan nodded with a smile and threw a few silver pieces on the table between them. Roz added her own.

"So where do you come from?" Roz asked him again.

Several minutes later Roz was laughing at the look on the knight's face as she won once again. She had kept him talking about where he came from--a small estate of a lesser noble lord in the east--and had distracted him enough by flirting with him.

"How old are you?" the knight asked her. "How can you play cards so well?"

"Old enough," she told him with a chuckle. "I graduated from the Mage's University this past year."

"Fresh out of the University and you already have a job? You must be powerful indeed."

Roz shrugged and told him, "I suppose."

Sullivan laughed and said, "So modest."

"Tell me about yourself, Sully," she implored him, signalling Lottie to bring some more drinks. "Do you have any siblings?"

"Two younger sisters. And yourself?"

"Two younger brothers and two younger sisters. When I am not out working I am at home with them, my father and stepmother."

"My sisters live on my small estate with me; my father died a few years ago and they help me manage the estate while I am out working for the Crown. They truly are amazing at it. I fear I would bungle things up if I were managing things."

"Ah, it is nice to see a knight who knows the true worth of a woman," Roz noted as she raised her cup in a salute to him.

"What do you do in your free time?" Sully asked her.

"Well I spend time with my merchant friends and make money playing cards, or teach some of the local women self defense. I also like to sit in an abandoned corridor and read until someone comes looking for me. And you?"

"You intrigue me, Roz. I too enjoy a good book, but I have not found the time lately to read. Maybe when I go home next I will do so."

"How about we up the ante?" Roz said this time as she took a drink before shuffling the deck. She looked at him coyly under her long lashes. "You take me out to dinner if I win."

Sullivan laughed and nodded his head, agreeing to the new terms of the game. Roslyn had started cutting the deck of cards again when the doors of the tavern burst open. In rushed her younger brother Edmond, along with two of their father's guards.

"What do you think that is about?" Sullivan asked her.

"Must be serious if he comes with guards," Roslyn said aloud to herself as she stood up.

"Brother, what's wrong?" she asked him as he and the guards approached their table.

"The king is dead," her brother told her. "The sickness killed his whole family."

Roz's face went as white as it could. "There are several people between us and the throne brother--" She stopped talking when she saw him shake his head. "What is it?"

"They were all in the south," Edmond replied. "Cousin Louise and the rest of them. They are all dead. Father is going to be crowned King of Ells-grove."

Roslyn looked at Sullivan to find him staring at her with his mouth open slightly.

"My lady," one of the guards caught her attention. "Your father sent us to make sure you get back to the castle tonight. The Priests of the Crown will be here tomorrow."

Roslyn turned to Sir Sullivan, "Sir Sullivan, I am sure you will be called with all haste back to the capital. Maybe we can continue our game another time. Safe travels."

Roslyn followed her brother and the guards out of the tavern, looking back at Sullivan who was gathering up his things hastily before heading up to awaken his comrade.

Chapter One

Roslyn stared up at the palace looming over the city from the carriage she rode in with her step-mother and siblings. Her step-mother Elle sat beside her, elegant in her fine gown of robin's egg blue velvet, her hair perfectly coiffed. Her younger brother Edmond sat across from them, looking a little ridiculous, Roslyn thought, in his fine velvet breeches and silk tunic, his hair slicked back like she had seen in the nobleman fashion of late. Her younger sisters, Eliza and Poppy, wore simple yet elegant gowns that matched their mother's. Her youngest brother Robert wore an outfit just like Edmond's.

Roslyn herself wore black leggings with a long dark blue tunic overtop, the sides split a little so she could have more movement. Dark brown calf-high leather boots adorned her feet. She wore her black mage's vest--with its many hidden pockets--and dark blue cloak as well. Her step-mother had only frowned at her outfit but had not said anything. Elle was used to Roslyn going against the tide, especially when it came to suppressing her just because she was a woman. She was a mage and a warrior first, princess second. She was not going to let her new status get in the way of all that she had earned in college or her arms training.

"We are almost there," twelve year old Poppy stated, bouncing a little bit in her seat with excitement as their carriage was ushered through the main gates of the city. Some of the King's royal knights rode around them, guarding them to the palace that was to be their new home. Behind them trailed wagons with some of their belongings, mostly clothes and books.

Roslyn had not been to the palace since she was eight, ten years ago. She remembered feeling very restrained, for her father had raised her very differently from the rest of the nobility. He had raised her as her birth-mother, a woman named Amelia, would have wanted her to be raised. Amelia came from Jay'Al, where the Clans were matriarchal, and women had way more status and voice there than they did in Ellsgrove. Her mother had died in childbirth, and her father had brought her home to raise her there. Since then the Tribes of the Archipelago had taken over the routes between the continents and no one had been able to return to Jay'Al. Roslyn wondered what it would have been like growing up there with her mother's family instead of in Ellsgrove. She always felt like there was something missing, some part of her incomplete. One day she hoped to be able to travel to Jay'Al and hopefully find what she was missing.

***

Elle looked at her step-daughter and hoped the capital would not be too much for her. She knew how cruel some noblewomen could be and wanted to save her step-daughter from experiencing their mockery. She also knew, though, that Roslyn could handle herself so she hoped that maybe, just maybe, Roslyn could make some headway with the noble courtiers and find a place there.

Elle looked at her eldest son and she noticed the worry in his eyes. He was now crown prince, not just a lord. He had a lot more to learn about ruling a kingdom instead of just an earldom. She knew he would do well under his father's guidance. Her husband Lucius had once been an ambassador, and had been trained by his grand-father the king. The old king had made sure all of the men in his line had the proper training, even though only one of them would become king. It was good that he had had the foresight to do so, though she expected he could not have imagined so many of the royal family wiped out by a sickness.

Lucius had met Roslyn's mother while on a mission as ambassador to Jay'Al, where they hoped to open a trading route. He and Elle had met later after he had returned with his daughter, a marriage at first of convenience and then of love: Elle was the heir of a large estate in the north and he needed a mother for his daughter. Elle had cared for Roslyn as if she were her own and had won Lucius' love along the way.

Lucius had wanted to raise Roslyn as her mother would have wanted, and Elle found freedom along with it. She had a huge say in the way their estate was run, an equal partnership with her husband that she knew many noblewomen in Ellsgrove did not have. Elle looked forward to being able to help Lucius change how things were done in Ellsgrove.

The carriage finally entered through the wide metal gates of the palace grounds and made its way up to the main entrance where King Lucius awaited the arrival of his family with many nobles in attendance.

***

King Lucius watched the carriage pull up to the main entrance of the palace with apprehension. He ran his fingers through his dark blonde hair and adjusted his belt again. His butler stood just behind him, stoic as ever, and behind them arrayed on the stone stairs leading up to the great double doors of the palace were some of his nobles. A lot of them were younger nobles who found themselves heads of their houses after the sickness killed their parents.

Only a handful of the nobles were Lucius' age, but they were of a more conservative nature. He had already butted heads with a few of them when he had brought up some of the reforms he had wanted to make, mainly the ones that gave the women of Ellsgrove more freedoms.

The younger nobles were more progressive but the pressure of the older nobles was something that held them back. Lucius hoped he would be able to give the progressives more of a voice in the months to come, especially with the help of his daughter.

A footman ran forward as the carriage came to a halt, opening the door and offering a hand to the new queen. Next came Edmond, followed by Eliza, Poppy and Robert. Roslyn exited the carriage last, and Lucius found the nobles behind him abuzz with whispering.

"Who is that? The exotic looking one?" he heard some-one ask another.

"Looks like she is a mage," came an answer, before someone said something else and he heard a few gasps.

"A bastard child?"

"He lets his daughter dress like that?" That sounded like one of the older noblewomen.

"You are talking about our new princess," someone spoke up, and the whisper's quieted. "I think she looks beautiful and practical. She is a mage, and quite frankly I like her style." Lucius turned to find the speaker, a tall red-headed young noblewoman who was smiling at Roslyn. There, maybe there was a foothold already.

Lucius was still glad that Roslyn was not in earshot to hear the comments. He went down to greet his family as his royal guards closed in around them.

"Welcome to your new home," Lucius greeted his wife with a kiss on the cheek. "Let's get you all settled in, shall we?"

Chapter Two

Roslyn quickly shut the door of her new solar behind her and locked it, effectively leaving her new ladies-in-waiting on the other side. She sighed in relief as she heard their muffled complaints from the other side until they eventually walked away. She sank into one of the heavily cushioned sofas in the room and stared up at the ceiling with her mismatched blue and green eyes. She smoothed her tunic out and adjusted her belt, glad that she had not given in to the pressure of wearing gowns around the palace. Many of the older noblewomen had voiced their displeasure at her way of dress but she had ignored them. She hoped her standing up to their dress norms would help some of the other younger noblewomen ease into the different style of dress that would give them more freedom.

Roslyn looked around her solar. It had been her cousin's, the Princess Anna, before she died. Everything in the palace had been taken out and burned after the sickness, and the current furnishings had been in storage for at least fifty years--they looked extremely outdated but at least they had furnishings. She had a few flowers in pots sitting around the room, special plants that she used in certain spells. She had inherited her magic from her mother's side, but she was able to find teaching here in her father's realm. None of her half-siblings had magic.

Large bookshelves lined the one wall opposite of the door, filled with her books from home and some of her magic tomes from the Mage University. In the corner behind the door was her desk, laden with documents her father had wanted her to go over and give her feedback to him.

There was a light knock on her door. With a sigh she asked who it was.

"Roz, it's me," replied a familiar voice.

With a flick of her wrist the door unlocked and swung open to reveal her younger half-brother. He smiled at her shyly and entered her solar. The door closed of its own accord behind him.

"Did father send you?" she asked him as he took a seat in a wicker chair opposite of her sofa.

Her younger brother looked completely different from her. She had inherited her mother's black skin, and her special heterochromatic eyes--one blue eye, one green. Her hair colour was a striking red shade, so very unlike most dark skinned people that lived in the southern deserts of their continent. Her brother Edmond, however, had porcelain-like skin and fair hair, with light blue eyes.

"Mother, actually; she asked Father for some time with me today. We are all adjusting to this new status, and she knows you feel restrained here."

Roslyn snorted, a very un-lady-like thing to do.

"Three months ago, do you know where I was?" she asked her brother.

"In the tavern in Wardgrove, drinking and playing cards with some of the merchant's sons," he responded with a laugh.

"I haven't seen my friends since; I was good friends with their sisters too: Maisie, Ellora, and Ginger were really good to me. Now I am stuck with these snobby ladies-in-waiting who were only sent to serve me because their families want them to garner status for them with the new royals."

"Have you tried getting to know them?" Edmond asked her. His eyes were serious.

"Some of them have made it quite clear that they do not like the way I dress, nor that I sell my magical potions like a commoner. Only one of them, Lady Theophania, has spoken up for me. As soon as I can I am asking father to let me leave the palace. Someone needs to oversee Wardgrove and our estates."

"I see. So you wouldn't want to be here at the palace with us?" Edmond looked hurt, but he had to know that the palace was a challenge for her.

"It's so different from home. Back there the noble families have known us since birth and accepted how our father raised us. Here? I've heard the whispers of my being a bastard child, and yes it hurts."

Edmond sighed and rubbed his eyes. She suddenly realised how tired he looked.

"How have you been adjusting to this?" she asked him, reaching out to take his hand. He took her hand in his and squeezed it briefly before letting go.

"All of these meetings, and everything we need to go over...Father has me with him on everything, teaching me. It was a good thing he was an ambassador and knows a lot about what it means to be a ruler. Our great-grandfather did good by making sure all of his grandsons had training, even if only one of them would rule. That was why father made such a good ambassador. I guess we have great-grandfather to thank for you, sister."

She laughed at that and waved a hand at him to tell him to stop. "Have you told Father you are tired?"

"I think I've been hiding it well," Edmond told her sheepishly. "I don't want to seem weak."

Roslyn swore, making Edmond chuckle. "No, he needs to know that he is pushing you too far; you are not weak, you are human and he does understand that. Do not give in to the societal expectations of men, my brother; you are so much more

than that and Father knows it. Let me talk to him."

Edmond laughed harder, and as he wiped tears from his face he said, "I came here to check in on you, and now you're taking charge of my welfare."

"Is that not how older siblings work?" she asked him. "Go back to your rooms and take this," she handed him a vial from the pouch that hung over her shoulder. "It will help you sleep."

He took it and thanked her. "I cannot remember the last time I had to take something to help me sleep."

"The stable fire a few years ago," she whispered, remembering his screams in the nights that followed.

"Ah, yes. Thank you, Roz."

"Go sleep, brother," she told him as he stood up. "I will come see you in the morning to see how you feel."

He nodded sombrely and left her alone in her solar.

***

Roslyn went to look for her father. It was the end of the month so he would be meeting with the provincial leaders. They came to him for help with problems in their provinces, as they had once done with his cousin. This meeting only happened once a month, so she knew it would take some time. She went to the library and grabbed a book before going to the Throne Room. She found a nice bench out of the way and sat down, opening her book and starting to read. With the book covering her face passer-by's paid her no heed and she was able to read in peace.

A short time later she was interrupted by someone's sword blade pushing her book down out of her face.

"Defend yourself," the man on the other end of the blade told her as he backed up. He was a handsome looking man in his early-twenties with very tanned skin and dark blond hair that was streaked by the sun. He wore a light blue tunic over loose breeches, with a sword belt around his waist. There was no one else in the hallway now.

"Excuse me?" Just who did this man think he was?

"Are you deaf, girl? Defend yourself."

She had no weapon on her, so she quickly looked around and saw some blades mounted on the walls. She reached out with her magic and called to one of the sabres on the wall, it flew through the air where she caught its hilt in her hand. She set her book aside and stood to meet the stranger, glad that she was wearing her leggings so she had more freedom of movement.

Their blades met, the ringing sounds echoing down the hall. Roslyn defended herself, using everything she had been trained in through the years, not just what her father's head guard had taught her but the merchant's guards as well. She blocked the man's blade and his fists, and even his legs when he resorted to that. Finally after several minutes he broke off with a grin and lowered his blade.

"Your father said you would surprise me, though I have to admit I did not believe him until now. Well done, princess."

"Just who the fuck are you?!"

Someone clearing their throat nearby made her stand straight to attention and look around. Sometime during their duel the doors to the Throne Room had opened and several people, including her father, stood there watching her.

"Roslyn," her father spoke, chastising her with a look, "I would like you to meet Kavan, your new Master at Arms."

"Honestly, Your Majesty, I do not think there is much more I need to teach her. She had good teachers, whoever they were," Kavan told his king with a bowed head.

"That was incredible," another man said behind the king. "Did you see how she moved?"

Roslyn blushed as the king turned to give the man a look.

She looked at the young man behind her father and recognized him as an Earl from the province of Harken which was on the east coast. What was his name again?

"My Lord Broderick, it's as if you have never seen a woman fight before," Roslyn's father commented. "Did you not know how graceful they could be?"

"Truly, Your Majesty, I did not," came the reply, much more quietly than his first outburst.

"I suggest you get used to it, Lord Broderick, for all of my daughters know how to defend themselves."

The man nodded and bowed before excusing himself. Roslyn's father turned his attention to Kavan. "I still would like you to help keep her skills honed, and her eldest brother as well. I know I can count on you, Kavan."

Kavan bowed deeply. "You honour me, Your Majesty. I will do what I can." Kavan turned to Roslyn, "Meet me in the Training Yard tomorrow morning at the seventh bell, along with your brother Edmond."

Kavan straightened and sheathed his sword before turning and walking away. Roslyn watched him go, admiring his behind as he walked. Her father cleared his throat, making her blush as she looked at him. All the other councillors had left, with her father remaining.

A Quest for Her Roots

"I need to speak to you, Father," Roslyn said as she returned the sabre to its spot on the wall.

Her father raised an eyebrow at her but indicated with a gesture that she follow him into the throne room. He sat down on his throne with a sigh and indicated that she sit in the empty Queen's chair beside him.

"It's Edmond," she spoke first, "He is very tired from everything and needs some time away from meetings."

"I thought he looked out of sorts yesterday but I was distracted..." her father looked away from her and back again, a look of fatherly love in his eyes that made her feel comforted.

"One of my cousin's expeditions returned the other day. They left over a year ago to try to find a different route to the continent of Jay'Al."

Roslyn sat up straighter at that name. The continent she had been born on, her mother's people.

"And?"

"They did indeed find another route," he told her in almost a whisper. "It avoids the pirates who have taken over the Eastern Ocean, and takes longer, but there is a way."

"You're certain?"

"Very. I want you to lead an expedition there in order to establish an outpost and a colony," her father told her. "You will leave in six weeks."

"Father, are you sure?"

"I am sending you because you were born there, and I know you have questions about your mother's family that I cannot answer. I had wanted to send Edmond as well but he will be needed here. I will be sending with you a company of my best soldiers, and your Master at Arms Kavan will be going with you as well."

"I feel safer already..." Roslyn commented with a smile, earning a laugh from her father.

"I will be talking to Edmond about it next," her father told her.

"You might want to wait until morning: I gave him a sleeping potion just a little while ago."

"Will you talk to him in the morning when you go to check on him?"

Roslyn looked at her father more closely now, and she saw new grey hairs in his dark blond hair at his temples, and the new lines around his blue eyes. For a man in his early forties he looked older now, and had he gotten thinner?

"Are you eating properly, father? You look thin and drawn."

"It is just the stresses of this new change," he answered her, putting a reassuring hand on her shoulder. "I need to go to my study to finish signing a few things now. Speaking of which, have you finished going through those papers I sent you to look at?"

She shook her head, chuckling inside on how he was changing the subject.

"Would you have them for me by the end of the week?"
"Yes, father."
He leaned over and kissed her on the cheek, saying, "That's my girl. You run along now."

***

King Lucius watched his oldest daughter walk out of the hall and collect her book from the bench. He was so incredibly proud of the young woman she had grown to be and of what she had accomplished. He had encouraged her to learn different styles of fighting, as her mother would have wanted. In Jay'Al the women carried their weight in the hunting and the defence of their people. He would have expected nothing less from any of his daughters. He knew the way he raised her was very different from the expectations of the nobility of his kingdom but he thought she was managing things well.

Now that he was king he hoped to impart that forward thinking on his sub jects. He knew it would not be easy but he still hoped it could be.

As for the journey to Jay'Al...he would have to tell Roslyn the truth about her mother's death before the voyage. He just was not sure he had the heart to relive it to her.

Leaving the throne room, the two guards who had been waiting for him outside of the throne room during his talk with Roslyn fell into step behind him. He headed for his office down the hall, walking past several statues and paintings of his relatives and ancestors. He remembered growing up in this palace with his cousins, all of whom were now dead from the sickness.

He had not wanted to be king before, but since the mantle had fallen to him he felt obligated to uphold it. His cousin had done a fine job ruling before, and Lucius had worried that he could not do as well, but thankfully his aides assured him that he was doing just as good as his cousin had. They had both had the same training in leadership after all. He felt that his cousin and grandfather would have been proud of him.

Thinking of Edmond, he now saw the signs of his son's weariness. He felt ashamed for not seeing it sooner. He also knew that his daughter was right and that he was indeed being too hard on both himself and Edmond. The kingdom had taken a bit of an economic fall after the sickness but thankfully with his merchant ties and knowledge he had been able to pick things back up again.

Maybe he could finally take a step back and let the Provincial-Governors take over that. It would free up more time to be able to relax.

Sitting down to write a letter, Lucius felt a weight off of his shoulders. Then he remembered that he still would need to tell Roslyn the truth and his shoulders sank again.

Chapter Three

Roslyn opened the door out to her balcony and stepped out into the coolness of the morning. The sky was still mostly dark, with only a hint of dawn colouring the sky. Birds in the Royal Forest to the east of the palace were waking up and singing their songs to welcome the sun. Roslyn closed her eyes and breathed in the cool winter air, relaxing a little bit. The only good thing about being further south on the continent was that there was barely any snow and it never got cold enough to freeze anything during the night.

This morning she had her hair in a braid that hung down her back and wore loose breeches and a light tunic for her meeting with Kavan. She was going to stop at her brother's room on her way down to the Training Yard to check in on him, and inform him of their father's plans.

Her light shoes made no noise on the fine carpets as she walked out of her suite of rooms and into the hall, closing her door quietly behind her. Her ladies-in-waiting, who slept in adjoining rooms to hers, were not up yet and she wanted to avoid them as long as possible this morning. The guards who stood watch at intervals down the hall bowed their heads in greeting and put their right hands over their hearts in their salute to a royal.

She knocked gently on her brother's door and waited.

After a moment the door was opened by one of Edmond's valets who bowed to her as she entered. The man was one of their former groomsmen from the Wardgrove estate and had been promoted to Edmond's valet upon their arrival at the palace.

"Good morning Rupert," she greeted him with a smile as she walked by him. "Is Edmond up yet?"

"Only just, your highness."

"Would you tell him I have come to check on him please?"

Rupert nodded and went into Edmond's bedroom, retur-ning a moment later to inform her that Edmond would be out as soon as he was dressed. He offered her a seat and asked her if there was anything he could get her for refreshment. She declined the offer as she took a seat on one of the sofas in the lounge of Edmond's suite.

"Good morning Roz," Edmond spoke as he left his bed-room.

"You might want to change your clothes," she advised him upon seeing his fine trousers and silk shirt. "Father wants us to do some weapons training this morning with a new Master of Arms."

Edmond swore and went back into his room, coming back out minutes later dressed in clothing like his sister was wearing.

"Is this better?" He turned around for her to inspect, and she laughed and told him it was better.

"Are you better this morning?" she asked him as she stood up and led the way to the door.

"Much better, thank you again."

"Oh don't thank me yet, I have more to tell you."

As they walked down to the training yard she filled him in on what their father had told her the day before about the expedition he wanted her to lead.

Edmond did not say anything the whole time, but she could tell he was thinking.

"I am both excited and nervous," she told him as they got to the door to the training room. "I will miss you though."

"Did he say anything else?"

She shook her head, "I imagine the meeting he wants with us after training will tell us."

Inside the training room Kavan waited for them dressed much the same as they were.

"I am satisfied with the way you held your own yesterday," Kavan told Roslyn before he turned to look at Edmond. "Show me what you can do, your highness. Choose a weapon."

***

Roslyn held the door for Edmond as he limped out of the training yard an hour later. She could tell that Kavan had enjoyed testing the prince's knowledge on self-defence, and before she followed her brother down the hall she turned to look at the slightly older Master of Arms. His shirt was drenched in sweat and sticking to him, and he was in the process of removing his shirt. She saw an old scar on the man's back, ranging from his left shoulder down to his hip.

"Can I help you with anything?" he asked her, folding up the shirt. There was another scar on his chest from his collar bone down to his navel.

A Quest for Her Roots

"We'll see you tomorrow morning," she told him before closing the door and hurrying after her brother.

***

From the Training Yard Roslyn and Edmond separated to their own rooms to wash up before going to meet their father. Roslyn put on a clean pair of dark blue leggings and a silk tunic. Across her shoulder she slung her leather purse that contained a few phials of potions and a book. She barely wore any jewellery, just a necklace around her neck that her father had given her when she was young: it had been her mother's, he told her. She only took it off that morning for the training session because she did not want anything to happen to it. It was the shape of a wolf's head cast in bronze, with silver eyes; her mother had been of the Wolf Clan. Her father had once told her that there was an identical piece done in silver with gold eyes that her mother had kept: it had been part of their marriage ritual.

Leaving her room Roslyn closed her door and turned, only to stop short as she found all four of her ladies-in-waiting standing there waiting for her.

"Your Highness," they said simultaneously with a low curtsy, their dresses making a fine swish as they went low and straight again.

"We need to have a discussion, I believe," the one Lady, Eleanor of Yurk, stepped forward to address her. "We were sent here to serve you, but we cannot do so if you do not want us here."

"Well, I don't," she told them with honesty. "I am not used to being treated like I cannot do anything myself. I do not need maids, I need friends. No gossips, no backstabbers, no one who is only here because their family sent them. If you find this too much for me to ask, you may leave. I myself will be leaving in six weeks on an expedition for my father across the ocean, and I doubt any of you want to go with me on that adventure, so shall we just save the trouble now? You are dismissed."

Roslyn walked around them, noticing that most of them looked distraught; Theophania, the tall redheaded young woman looked thoughtful. It was Theophania who followed her and stopped her by calling out her name.

"Theophania, right?"

"Please, call me Tiffany, your highness," she said with a curtsy.

Roslyn put her hands on her hips and regarded the woman in front of her seriously. Tiffany was older than her by a few years, whereas the other women had been either the same age or younger--but all of them were unmarried noblewomen. Tiffany certainly looked attractive, with her fine skin and curly red hair, so why was she not married yet?

"Why did you come to serve me as a lady-in-waiting? Why are you not married yet?"

"I do not want to get married, your highness. My parents indulged me, since I was the youngest, but I believe I have become a hindrance to them. So

53

when you came here, and I found out that you can fight, I asked my parents if I could come here to serve you."

"You actually wanted to be here?" Roslyn asked her.

Tiffany nodded and said, "My cousin went to the same mage school as you, and told me about you. I would not have come if my cousin had not liked you."

"Who is your cousin?"

"Lady Jessica of Lake Orila."

Roslyn remembered the girl, who was younger than her and had been her friend during their time at the school.

"The expedition will be dangerous. You will need to learn how to fight," Roslyn explained to her.

"I am willing to do it, your highness."

Roslyn sighed and noticed the determined look in the woman's eyes.

"Okay, fine. Have you ever handled a weapon before?"

Tiffany shook her head.

"You should start with exercises that will strengthen your arm muscles in order to hold a sword. I will come to you after I see my father and show you the exercises."

Tiffany nodded and went back to her room; the hall was now empty because the other ladies had already gone to pack their belongings.

"Everything alright?" Edmond asked his sister, noticing the thoughtful expression on her face.

"I dismissed my ladies, but Theophania wants to stay and come with us on the expedition. I was not expecting that, but I find myself intrigued now."

"Indeed, she sounds interesting," Edmond commented as they walked. They did not say anything more as they walked to their destination, which was across the palace and up a couple of flights. When they reached the large double door of red wood, which was guarded by two of the knights who made up the King's Guard, Edmond knocked on it.

Their father opened the door and bid them to come in with a hand gesture. Sitting at one of the chairs in front of the king's desk was a man dressed very differently than the courtiers of the palace. He had knee high boots on that looked very weathered, though they were clean. Brown and black stripped breeches were tucked into the boots. A creased white shirt with a brown leather vest over it was worn over the man's broad chest. Roslyn wondered how the man's arm muscles did not break his sleeves open. Her eyes went up to the man's top hat and his incredibly straight black hair that hung to his shoulders. Dimples showed in the man's young but weathered looking face as he smiled at her in greeting, his incredibly green eyes showing his amusement.

"Captain Heath, this is my eldest daughter Roslyn and my eldest son

Edmond," their father introduced them to the man. "Edmond will be helping to plan the expedition, and Roslyn will be accompanying you back to Jay'Al."

"Your daughter looks like one of the natives of Jay'Al," Captain Heath commented as he rose to bow to them.

"I was born there," Roslyn told him. "My father brought me back here."

Captain Heath took his seat again with Roslyn and Edmond taking seats in the other two chairs on either side of the man. The king took his own seat and indicated to the map on the desk in front of him.

"Captain Heath was just telling me the route that he took," the king told them. He indicated the strings and pins on the map that started at East Port-- the closest port to the capital--and headed north, through the ice of the northern sea and to the continent on the other side.

"You are going north?" Edmond spoke up, a little incredulous. "The ice has to be as dangerous as the Tribes of the Archipelago."

"Captain Heath succeeded, twice," Roslyn told her brother.

She turned to look at the man that sat beside her and asked him, "What makes you so special that you survived the ice where hundreds of other captains and explorers did not?"

"My heritage, your highness," he told her. "As your magic comes to you from your Clan, I am of the Water Tribe that sail the greatest ships."

"I thought all of you were pirates," Roslyn answered pertly.

He smiled at her wickedly and said, "I was a pirate, your highness. Better opportunities came my way so I found my out, and a respectable job."

Edmond snorted at the expression on his sister's face and turned to look at his father.

"You trust this man for this expedition?" Edmond asked the king.

"My cousin did," his father answered. "I trusted my cousin with my life, so I trust this man. He has proven himself."

Edmond nodded to show he understood and looked to his sister who was biting her lower lip in thought.

"What is your ship like?" Edmond asked Captain Heath. "Since you will be taking soldiers with you and builders--"

"There will be three ships," Captain Heath interrupted. "Mine alone cannot take everyone for the expedition. My lieutenants will be taking charge of the other two ships."

"Roslyn, I would like you to work with Kavan and the quartermaster Master Juvani to supply the expedition with food and weapons, and building supplies. One of Juvani's apprentices will be going with you, his name escapes me at the moment but Juvani assures me he is ready," her father said as he handed her some documents that she put in the bag she had slung over her shoulder.

"I trust your opinion, father," Roslyn told him. "Where can I find Master

Juvani?"

"I will have my butler Roland show you the way once you are done here." He motioned to the older man dressed in black standing near the door. When had he arrived? Roslyn wondered. "Captain Heath tells me it does get incredibly cold in the ice sea so you will need to prepare for that as well."

"Of course, father."

"It will be winter when they get there," Edmond commented as he looked at the map.

"Yes, the orcs that live in the northern area of Jay'Al will be in the south, which will make it safer for us to be there," Heath told him. "We had several encounters with them while we were there."

"I will not be home for my birthday," Roslyn said next, feeling a little disappointment, but she realized that she might be able to celebrate with her Jay'Alian family.

"We will miss you on your birthday but it is the best time to go," her father assured her.

"Edmond, I would like you to stay with me to go over a few things," the king told his son as Roslyn stood up to leave. He looked at his daughter again and said, "I hope to see you for dinner tonight, Roslyn."

She nodded and said, "I will be there." With a last glance at Captain Heath, who was watching her closely, she turned and left her father's study, Roland following her out. In the hallway Roslyn turned to the manservant.

"How are you so quiet?" she demanded to know, though she was smiling the whole time. Roland had served her father at Wardgrove but this was a first for her seeing him sneaking around.

The older man smiled back at her and indicated they should walk towards the main hall of the palace, all the while saying nothing.

"You never used to be so mysterious," she teased him.

"Your highness," he scolded, "It's just a trick of the trade that I cannot reveal."

Roslyn laughed at that and followed him down to the first basement level under the palace where the quartermaster worked out of. Roslyn thanked Roland for bringing her down there and assured him she could find her way back up. Roland left her there with a nod, and so she turned to address the door into the domain of the quartermaster.

She opened the door in front of her and was met by the sound of silence and the smell of paper and ink. The three apprentices sitting at the desks looked up at her in the dim light with squinted eyes. The walls were lined with bookshelves laden with books and scrolls.

One of the apprentices stood up and quietly went to a door on the other side of the room. He opened the door and went inside, emerging again a moment later with an older man in relaxed robes of muted colours.

The older man was the quartermaster, and he greeted her with a bow and a smile. Using both his hands he started to sign words to her.

With a slightly shocked expression Roslyn looked at the apprentice standing next to the quartermaster for help.

"Sorry," the young apprentice told her, "Not a whole lot of people know how to speak to deaf people. Master Juvani is really good at what he does, no matter his disability. That's why it is so quiet in here, we are used to it."

"What did he say?" she asked the apprentice.

"He greeted you, and...said that he heard about your beauty but 'hearing' it was miniscule to seeing it. He also saw your bout with your Master of Arms yesterday and he says you were very graceful."

Roslyn blushed at that and waved a hand to dismiss the praise, saying, "I was just using what I had been taught." The apprentice translated in sign language to Juvani.

The Master smiled and signed some more, with the apprentice translating again: "Let's get to business. Apprentice Aidan is the one who will be going with you." The young apprentice's face paled a little, but he continued, "So he will help you come up with what you need."

"Yes, right, the expedition," Apprentice Aidan said with a sigh.

Roslyn really looked at the apprentice now, instead of just looking at robes. He was not much older than her, with short cut blond hair and blue eyes. He was thin, his robes hanging off of him. She had seen that in a lot of palace workers who had survived the sickness—many of them had yet to regain the weight they had lost.

"Let's get to it, shall we?" Roslyn inquired of the apprentice.

The apprentice smiled and nodded, and he signed to the Master who agreed with a nod and a smile before going back to his office.

"How many people will be going with us?" Aidan asked her as he motioned for her to follow him to his desk.

She produced a list from her bag that had all of the names, with a tally at the top of each page.

"Two hundred and fifty in total," she told him.

"And do you have the blueprints for the outpost we will be building?"

Roslyn took out the blueprints from her bag and showed him. He took a few minutes to look over it.

"This is a considerable size, your highness."

"I know, it will take a lot of lumber, and nails."

"We will need a couple of blacksmiths," Aidan told her. "It will help to have as many nails for this as possible. The soldiers can bring the trees down easily enough, but we will need nails."

"Okay, do we have a list of blacksmiths who will be able to come with us?"

"There are a number of blacksmiths with apprentices in the city, I am sure we could get some of them on this expedition," Aidan mentioned.

"We need to send out requests for them, can you do that for me?" Roslyn asked him.

"I can draw up the requests once we're done and have them sent out. Next we need food rations. The voyage will take two months, so we need rations to last more than that just in case."

"Can we not fish for food?" Roslyn asked him.

"Yes, to a certain extent we can."

"So we still need to plan for that part, to make sure. I am sure people will get sick of eating fish." Roslyn made a face at that and continued, "Yes, it is easy to get sick of fish."

Aidan laughed at that and said, "Things will be better once we are on the continent, we should have access to more food." Aidan paused thoughtfully, before adding, "If the natives help us."

"I am sure we can hunt for ourselves," Roslyn commented.

"Maybe, but we should plan for such events."

"All right. Do you have another chair so I can sit?"

Roslyn looked around them for another chair. "Then we can get the numbers figured out."

Chapter Four

Later that day, Roslyn was sitting in her solar going over the names of the people who would be going on the expedition. Her father had already sent out orders and gotten responses from the soldiers, and now she had to add the names of the three black-smith apprentices that were going to be coming with them. As she perused the list, she realized there were two names that she knew well: two certain young merchants that she had grown up with. A note was written beside their names mentioning that they had volunteered to represent their families in the expedition, since the outpost would be a trading outpost as well. Roslyn thought it was interesting that they had chosen to go, but knew she would be in good company with them along. She would make sure they were on the same ship as her for it would be nice to play cards and drink with them again.

There was also the matter of figuring out where every-one was going to sleep. The soldiers were already used to sleeping in the hammocks, and the few horses would be secured in another section of the ship, so she only had a handful of people who she thought would want actual rooms: herself, Tiffany, Aidan, the two merchants, and the blacksmiths. She figured Kavan would not care where he slept either. She would put the blacksmiths on the second ship together, and she and Tiffany would probably share a room. She was pretty sure the two merchants would be fine with sharing a room with Aidan as well. That would leave rooms for the several head soldiers that were going with them, if they wanted to.

Roslyn's stomach grumbled and she realized it was close to dinner. She had promised her father she would eat with him, so she put aside her papers and went to get changed for dinner. She met her brother leaving his room and asked him to wait for her while she got changed.

"Are mom and everyone else joining us for supper too?" Roslyn asked her brother when she joined him in the hallway, wearing a light blue cotton tunic over black breeches, her hair pulled back in two braids.

"As far as I know, yes."

They reached the doors to their father's suite and the servant standing at the door let them in with a low bow. They thanked him for opening the door and proceeded inside.

They turned into the dining room and found their father sitting with Edmond's mother next to him, and their young siblings sitting around the table. Fourteen year-old Eliza had her long blonde hair pulled up in an elegant design like her mother's hair, but she wore a simple gown for the family dinner. Twelve year old Poppy had her blonde hair cut short because she hated having to fuss with it as much as her older sister did with hers. Ten year old Robert had his blonde hair cut short like his father's.

"Ah, there you two are," their father looked up from the paper he was reading and smiled at them. "I could hear Robert's stomach growling from here!"

"Lucius, darling," his wife put a hand over her mouth to stifle a chuckle. "No need to embarrass the lad."

Robert's face had indeed turned a little pink, so Roslyn went over to him and hugged him around the shoulders. "My stomach grumbles too when I am hungry, little brother," she assured him. "So does father's," she added with a whisper.

Robert chuckled at that and smiled warmly at his older sister.

"Mother Elle, how are you doing today?" Roslyn asked as she went over to her step-mother and kissed her on the cheek.

"I am well, darling, thank you. How are you doing today?"

"My one lady-in-waiting, Theophania, has chosen to go with me on the expedition. All of the others have left."

"Indeed? Theophania of Triewell is from a large family, and I was somewhat surprised when her application to be your lady-in-waiting came in since she was older, but her parents assured me it was for her benefit to come to court finally. Now that she is going with you though..." Elle looked to her own daughters and broke off, thinking.

"She has expressed the desire to learn to fight as well, so she will not be a hindrance," Roslyn added. "I showed her some muscle building exercises earlier, and I think she will do well."

Elle nodded, knowing that Roslyn's experience and intuition were hardly wrong when it came to such things.

"How are the preparations coming along?" her father asked. At that moment some servants came in to serve them their meal. One of the servants placed a plate of roasted lamb with potatoes and carrots on it before Roslyn.

"Is there gravy?" Roslyn asked the servant who nodded and told her that it was coming. A moment later another servant put a small decanter filled with steaming hot gravy in front of Roslyn's plate. She picked it up and drizzled it over the food on her plate.

"They are going well," she answered before putting a large piece of meat in her mouth. Her father took that as a cue to ask Edmond about his side of the arrangements.

"I went and spoke to all of the soldiers who will be going. The majority of them are young and want the adventure, but some of the older soldiers dread the ice. It should go relatively fine though, so long as they do not, you know, get stuck in an iceberg or something."

"I know you are worried about the cold, especially on the ships," their father said to them, "but I assure you, Captain Heath's men survived."

Roslyn swallowed finally and asked her father, "Was he really a pirate?"

The younger children looked up at their father with interest, since they were not privy to most of what was going on, especially not the former jobs of a certain sea captain.

Lucius smiled at his children and looked Roslyn in the eyes and said, "Yes, he was. Grandson of the notorious Captain William. Captain Heath and his crew were shipwrecked on our southern shore during the war when they decided to take the chance to get out of the family business. My cousin hired him for the expedition because of his knowledge and his magic."

"And his Lieutenants, they were pirates too?" Edmond asked next. Their father nodded with an amused smile as he watched his two oldest children.

Elle chimed in by asking Poppy about the classes she had that day, and for the moment the fact that three of the top leaders of the expedition were former pirates was forgotten by most of the people in the room.

Chapter Five

Earlier that day...

K avan peeked through the door and watched as Roslyn walked away down the hall. It had been interesting testing her the day before for he had never had to train a woman. He honestly had not expected her to hold her own even though the king had told him she knew how to handle a blade.

He winced as he felt the scar on his back tighten. He had not meant for her to see the scars--he had thought she had walked out of the room and kept going without shutting the door. The last thing he needed was her asking him about the scars; he did not want her pity.

After putting on a fresh shirt he decided to go out into the city to distract himself. Lost in his thoughts he found himself walking down Orphanage Lane, where there were two large orphanages on either side of the street: one for boys, the other for girls. He turned into the gate of the boy's orphanage and approached the door with indecision.

It had been several years since he had been there last. He had been stationed at the Summer Palace in the south as one of the Head Guardsman for almost three years now, but the new king had seen his potential and asked him to come to the main palace. Now that he had the time though, he found himself

back where he grew up.

The Boy's Orphanage of the King was a large brown stone building with several floors. Its main door was made of wood, and there were no glass windows at all, just open wind-ows with blankets covering most of them; to the right of the door hung the doorbell with a chain to pull on below it.

Steeling himself, Kavan pulled the chain and closed his eyes as the bell tolled three times.

He waited a few moments in silence. No one had come to answer the door yet so he turned away and took a step--and the door behind him opened.

A Quest for Her Roots

"Hello, did you want something?" a young voice said behind him.

He turned around and smiled at the young boy at the door. He could not have been more than ten, with a freckled face and brown curls on his head. The boy wore brown trousers that were a little too short for him, and his white tunic had food stains on it.

"Is Master Raymond available?" Kavan asked the boy.

"Who shall I say is calling?"

Kavan chuckled inwardly before saying, "Kavan."

"Just Kavan?" the boy asked, his eyes widened as he recognized what the single name meant. He nodded and started off down the hall.

Kavan took a step inside, looking around the hallways. Everything was just as he had remembered it; there were paintings of the kings along the main hallway, with a carpet runner of dark red on the floor. Oil lanterns lit the hall, and from the smell Kavan realized that they still used whale oil.

Hurried footsteps came down the hall and Kavan turned to see a man in his mid-sixties coming towards him with a large smile on his face.

"Kavan!" The man greeted him with an enthusiastic hug.

The young boy behind him stared at them in wonder as Master Raymond hugged Kavan. "Oh my boy, it is so good to see you again. I am glad to see that you survived the Pirate War, and the sickness."

Kavan winced as his former guardian brought up the wars, remembering laying in a cot with the wounds he had from one of the battles, semi-conscious and dreaming lucidly. He had turned eighteen that year, and was no longer a ward of the king, so he had joined the military. That was when the pirates, or the Tribes of the Archipelago, as they would rather be called, had waged a war against the people of the continent. The war had ended at a stalemate, which was another part of the reason no one tried to venture across the eastern ocean to the other continent. The war had lasted four years and ended just over three years ago.

Thankfully he had survived his wounds and had been sent to the Summer Palace. From there he had worked his way up in the ranks to become the Head Guardsman. An orphan as head guard of the Summer Palace--he was certainly proud of that endeavour.

Master Raymond waved his hand to dismiss his question and instead asked, "Come in for a drink with us and the other Masters? We can talk about it over a drink."

Kavan found himself reminiscing as they walked down the halls of the orphanage, spying his initials still carved into a door frame of a pantry.

"Masters Henry and John, look who it is," Master Raymond called out as he opened the door that led to the Study, which Kavan remembered being in only a handful of times. Each of the Masters had a desk there, and there were a few chairs in front of the hearth on the far wall.

The two Masters looked up from the papers on their desks and their faces brightened with large smiles as they saw him. Master Henry was Raymond's brother and they looked a lot alike, but Master John was a man with darker skin and hair and was a little bit younger. They wore the same style of clothes.

"Kavan!" The two Masters greeted him.

"It is very good to see you alive," Henry added as they both stood up and went to shake his hand. Master

Raymond went over to the hutch next to the hearth and grabbed a glass decanter and four glasses. He handed everyone a glass and poured everyone a drink.

"I survived the Pirate War," Kavan told them as he took a sip, savouring the taste of the old whiskey. "I was working in the Southern Palace after the war ended, and now I am the Arms Master for the Crown Prince and Princess."

Kavan finished his drink and accepted some more from Master Raymond.

"We are proud of you," Raymond told him and the other two nodded in agreement.

"Stay for supper?" Henry asked him, finishing his own drink. "We would love for you to meet the boys."

***

Later that night Kavan was returning to the palace, approaching the smaller west gate when he saw Roslyn walk out of the gate house and head down the street away from him. She was wearing breeches and a tunic with a sword at her waist, and a black hooded cloak with the hood drawn to cover her face-- but he knew from the way she walked that it was her. A princess leaving the palace at night with no guards?

He followed her at a distance; when he found himself in a lower level residential district he began wondering just what the hells she was doing down here where common workers lived. When she went into a small warehouse next to an apartment house he went down the side street of the warehouse and looked in through a window.

To his surprise he found a small training room where a group of young women were meeting with Roslyn. He saw her greet them all by name and they started arm strengthening exercises together. He stayed and watched as she started to show them self-defence methods, including how to use their hair pins as a weapon.

Impressed with the princess's knowledge of this kind of self-defence Kavan stayed to watch the whole session.

As they closed the warehouse up for the night Kavan came back around the front of the building and saw Roslyn waiting for him.

Chapter Six

Roslyn walked into the warehouse, knowing she was being followed. She knew it was just one person, so it did not overly concern her. She took off her cloak and hung it up by the door before heading down the hallway into a large open space that she had turned into a training room. There were weights along one wall, practice targets along another, and a large thick straw mat in the middle of the room.

Sitting on the floor were six women of varying ages, all of them dressed as she was.

"Hello ladies," she greeted them. "Mel, Ashley, Lisa, Lily, Fern and Suzie, how are you all tonight?"

Mel was the oldest of the group, in her late twenties. She owned the warehouse they trained in and had a clothing shop in the city. Roslyn had found her one night outside a tavern defending her younger brother against some drunks and Roslyn had stepped in to help. Mel was an eager learner in the ways of defence, and so they had struck up a friendship.

"I have been busy with work orders," Mel told her as she stood. She was a petite woman with fine brown hair she always kept up in a bun, and a slim figure. "It seems word has gotten out that I have been making dresses for the princesses."

"Ah someone probably saw my sister's maids coming to you and going back to the palace. I have tried to keep our friendship low key so as not to overwhelm you."

"It's alright, the influx of customers has added much to our business," Ashley told her. Ashley worked for Mel in her dress shop. She was a little younger than Mel and was much taller and fuller figured, but she usually wore loose clothing. Ashley kept her dark blonde hair cut short to her head because she hated having to deal with it.

Lisa and Lily were two dark haired sisters who lived nearby, and Fern, a full figured beauty, worked in one of the taverns. Suzie was a baker and already had the strong arms from kneading bread, but after having an issue with some drunks one night she wanted to learn how to throw a man as well as she could a bag of flour.

"Well come on now ladies, let's get started."

When they finished their session everyone helped to clean up and the girls started to leave. Roslyn and Mel were the last ones to leave, Mel locking things up behind them. Mel bade her goodnight and walked off down the street.

Roslyn turned around, arms crossed over her chest and she asked Kavan why he was following her.

"I was intrigued why you would go out of the palace unattended at night," Kavan told her.

"Well, now you know," she answered him as she started to walk down the street towards the palace district.

Kavan got into step with her and looked at her sideways. "How long have you been doing this?"

"Well, here I started soon after arriving. Back home I have been doing it for a few years."

"May I ask why?"

"Every woman deserves to know how to defend herself," she told him. "If I can help at least one woman from being beaten by a bad lover or an attacker on the street it is worth it."

"A noble quest," Kavan told her with a smile. "You keep surprising me."

"I try to keep everyone on their toes," she replied with a wicked smile.

They continued their walk in silence until they reached the west gatehouse.

"See you in the morning," she said as she headed up the stairs into the palace. Kavan's room was down the hall from the gatehouse so he stopped at the bottom of the stairs and wished her a good night.

***

The next morning Tiffany was waiting for Roslyn outside of her bedroom dressed in the training clothes Roslyn had lent her. They were joined by Edmond as they made their way down the hall.

When they got to the Training Yard Roslyn introduced her lady-in-waiting to Kavan who agreed to allow her in on the training, and so he started her on some of the simplest exercises with a wooden practice sword and a dummy. He focused on Edmond.

This time Edmond was able to hold his own again, having been rusty the day before. Kavan still managed to get through Edmond's defences a handful of times but when they were finished Kavan was satisfied with the difference.

While Kavan and Edmond had paired off, Roslyn watched Tiffany do her exercises. Roz gave suggestions here and there about how the older girl should be holding her sword and the proper stances she should be taking.

"You learn quickly," Roslyn remarked after a while. "I am impressed."

Tiffany's face blushed from the praise but she continued with the exercises until Kavan asked Roslyn to go over a few sword techniques with Tiffany. Roslyn was going over the three primary parries with Tiffany when someone knocked on the doorframe to the Training Yard. Roslyn turned to find an old friend standing there. He was wearing practice clothing like the rest of them, with a tall and lithe body frame. Curly dark hair adorned his tanned face, and he had a well-kept short beard.

"Rafi!" she cried out with delight as she dropped her practice sword and ran to hug the man in the doorway.

"Roz, darlin', you're beautiful as ever," Rafi replied as he hugged her back. "Your father told me I could find you here. Care for a bout, your highness?" He took a step back from her, a look of regret in his eyes as if he had wanted the embrace to go on longer. Kavan watched them with interest, Tiffany with slight confusion.

Roslyn smiled wickedly and said, "You bet I do."

Tiffany handed Roslyn her practice sword and Edmond tossed Rafi one of the extra ones. Roslyn and Rafi squared off in the middle of the Training Yard, their swords meeting in the titular salute before moving into on-guard. Roslyn smiled sweetly at Rafi now, and Kavan noticed the new man gulp uneasily.

Roslyn looked at Rafi, remembering the last time they had seen each other. They had once been lovers but she had broken things off with him because she felt they were not right for each other. He was not of the same opinion but had agreed to end it. Seeing him now she felt better about her decision--he no longer made her feel giddy just by the sight of him. Roz realized how much she had changed in the last year, and especially since coming to the capital.

Roslyn was the first to attack, leaving Rafi to defend himself. Rafi stepped back as she came forward, still smiling sweetly. Finally Rafi found his chance and changed the course of the swords so that he was the one attacking, but Roslyn managed to keep pushing him back towards the wall. She had not landed a hit yet, and neither had he.

Kavan thought the look in the princess' eyes reminded him of a cat playing with a mouse and he smiled as he watched the bout continue.

Roslyn finally saw her chance as Rafi blinked away the sweat that was getting in his eyes. She got past his defence, knocking his sword out of his grip and lightly tapped his throat with her wooden blade.

"You're dead," Roslyn whispered to him with a smile before straightening and turning to look at Kavan who started to clap.

"Well done, though I think if your merchant friend is coming with us he needs to brush up on his sword skills too," Kavan commented. "Master Rafi, I want you to report here every morning at the seventh bell as well."

Roslyn snorted a laugh and turned to look at Rafi again who at first looked taken aback by the order but was now amused. Tiffany was staring at Roslyn with wonder: no Lady would allow herself to snort-laugh like that in front of people--at least, none that Tiffany had known.

"I have missed your laugh," Rafi told Roslyn as he surrendered his wooden sword to her. "Would you like to have lunch in the city with me today?"

"Yes, I think I would. Tiffany, I want you to go to the Quartermaster and talk with Aidan about our supplies, see what he has been able to procure so far and if he needs help with anything else."

"Your highness, you will need a chaperone if you go out with a man," Tiffany spoke up, knowing that it was part of her job to protect her mistresses honour.

"This man is no stranger to me, and please I can protect my own honour as you have seen. I gave you a job and I expect it done Lady Tiffany."

Tiffany bowed to Roslyn and excused herself to go clean up.

"I need to go meet with your father again quickly," Rafi told Roslyn. "Oswick was supposed to be arriving soon and we were set to have a meeting together with your father. I'll meet you in the Main Hall at the eleventh hour?"

"Of course. Give Oswick my greetings, will you?"

Rafi nodded and bowed swiftly before handing over his practice sword to Edmond with a grin and walking out of the room.

"I think our time is done for the day," Kavan told Roslyn and Edmond. "Tomorrow should be interesting, with more people here. Mayhap we should get the young quarter-master up here as well, hm?"

"We could try," Roslyn said, amused at the thought of the robed apprentice learning to fight. "I will send him a message about it."

"Tomorrow I think we will go over some hand-to-hand combat," Kavan added as Edmond headed for the door and Roslyn went to help put away the dummy and practice swords.

"Ugh, more bruises await me tomorrow," Edmond said with a moan before he waved good-bye to his sister and left her there with Kavan.

Roslyn chuckled at her brother's comment and started to hang up the wooden swords. Kavan brought his sword over and stood beside her as he hung his up. He looked at her and could not help but say, "You are the strangest princess I have ever met."

"Well, how many have you known?"

"Not many. When I worked as Captain of the Guard at the Summer Palace I never really interacted with the royals."

"I see. Well for starters, I was not raised to be a princess. I am only here because my father lived so far north that the sickness did not affect us, leaving him the only one of royal blood left that was not questionable. I am used to doing things very differently."

"Like having merchants for friends?"

"Oswick's Head Guard for his merchant caravan was the one who taught me hand-to-hand combat," she told him. "Believe it or not, Rafi was the one who started me with the sword. He is actually better at archery. I can still beat both of them at cards though."

"Cards? As I said, the strangest princess I have known."

Roslyn chuckled at him and headed for the door. "Maybe I can show you sometime," she told him over her shoulder. "I've been wanting to try out one of the taverns in the city, I hear the ale there is really good."

She stopped in the doorway of the Training Yard to look at him staring at her with surprise. With a laugh she waved good-bye to him and went to clean up.

***

The bell hanging in the center of the city rang eleven times to indicate the hour of the morning. Roslyn met Rafi in the Main Hall of the palace, her hair in two fishtail braids and tied off with blue ribbons. She had chosen to wear light cotton leggings that were yellow and a simple blue tunic with a white sash around her hips. Her father's necklace hung over her tunic, and she fingered it as she walked up to Rafi. He wore fine black breeches made of velvet and a white cotton tunic that was embroidered with silk vines around the neck line and on the long sleeves. His hair was pulled back in a small queue at the back of his head, though one ringlet had escaped to curl down the side of his face; on the left side of his belt hung a sword in a simple black scabbard.

"It's so weird seeing you here," Rafi told her as she took his arm and followed him outside. The sun shone down on them from a clear blue sky, but from the humidity in the air and the smell of water Roslyn could tell it was going to rain later that day.

"When Oswick came to tell me about your father being crowned...I could not believe it. Our Roslyn, a princess! Though I am told you are not the heir?" Rafi led her to an open coach with an awning that was waiting for them, two roan mares at the fore to pull it. When they reached it he opened the door and motioned for her to get in first.

Roslyn looked around and saw her step-mother with her entourage of ladies sitting in a garden nearby. Some of the ladies were looking at her with scandalized expressions. Some of them started pointing at her, drawing her step-mother's attention.

Elle only smiled at Roslyn and waved, saying something to the ladies who were protesting what she was wearing. Roslyn wondered what her step-mother was saying but she could not hear anything that was being said. She returned her attention to Rafi.

"You heard true," she told him as she sat down, facing the horses. He sat beside her and nodded to the coachmen who sat at the front to get going. The man snapped the reins and the coach started moving. "I am grateful, really. Though my father promised me years ago I would never have to worry about an arranged marriage, if I were the Crown Princess I would have still had to marry for something beneficial to the realm, though I know he would not force a marriage on me. Edmond gets the fun of meeting eligible women of rank who he could fall in love with and marry."

"So how are you liking living at the palace?"

"Up until the other day I was ready to ask father if I could return home to run our family estates. I hated it here. That girl from this morning, Tiffany, she chose to stay when I told my ladies-in-waiting I did not want them there. If it were not for this quest, I would not have known her probably. I would have happily returned home to run things and be able to drink and play cards with you and Oswick as much as I wanted."

"But this way you can find out about your mother, hopefully, and her family."

"Yes, though I am sure if my cousin was alive he would have had my father go back."

"Did your father try to go back before?" Rafi asked her.

Roslyn shook her head and told him, "He said my mother was dead, and that there was nothing for him there.

He said that if I wanted to I could try finding a route, but he was not going to endanger anyone's lives by going through the pirates. Now that we have this route through the north...he knows how much it means to me. I want to go."

"It will be interesting to see where you come from, that is for sure."

Roslyn was silent for a time as she watched the buildings go by, and the people. Some of the passers-by stopped to look at who was in the fine coach and they smiled at her when they saw her.

"While we are out I need you to just call me Roz, okay?"

"I always do, do I not?"

"I just don't want to draw attention to myself."

"I think that has always been something you had no control over," Rafi told her, "You stand out whether you want to or not; but of course I will do as you ask, Roz. Ah, there is the place," he interrupted her to point out the fine inn and eatery called the Stag and Horn. The coach pulled up in front of it and came to a stop. Rafi got out of the coach first and offered her a hand in helping her down.

She looked at it with a raised eyebrow at first but took it with a smile. He looped her arm in his and led her inside while the coachman drove to the large stables nearby to await them.

Chapter Seven

Rafi returned Roslyn to the palace when the second bell of the afternoon rang. Elle and her ladies were no longer in the garden, much to Roslyn's relief. Rafi kissed her cheek with a 'see you later' and the coachmen whisked him away again. Roslyn shook her head and walked into the palace, aware of the guardsmen and a few nobles watching her. She held her head high and walked into the Main Hall where she found Tiffany, in a fine blue dress, sitting on one of the benches seemingly awaiting her return.

The lady-in-waiting fell in behind her quietly as Roslyn went straight to her rooms. It was only when they reached her door that Tiffany cleared her throat.

"Your highness, I still think you going out without a chaperone all alone with a man--"

Roslyn held up a hand to interrupt her and stated: "I think we need to have a talk. Come inside."

Roslyn opened her door and motioned for Tiffany to go inside. Tiffany did so, and Roslyn followed her in and closed the door. She went over to a device on the one wall that stuck out over a table. On the table was a cylinder with a latch on it, and some papers with a pencil. Roslyn quickly wrote something on the paper, folded it up and opened the latch on the cylinder. She placed the paper inside the cylinder, closed it up, and opened the device on the wall. She put the cylinder in and closed it, and there came a sound of air once the door was closed.

"I love these pneumatic tubes," she told Tiffany, "It is much faster than calling the servants." Roslyn motioned for her lady-in-waiting to sit down on one of the sofa's and she took her own seat, crossing her legs at her ankles and taking in Tiffany.

"There are a few things you need to know about me," Roslyn started to say when there came a knock on her door.

"Come in," she called out, and a servant girl entered the room with a trolley that held little cakes, cookies, and several bottles of wine with two wine glasses.

"Thank you, miss," Roslyn motioned for her to leave the trolley next to her seat. The servant curtsied and left the room without a word.

Roslyn opened one of the bottles of wine and filled the two glasses. She handed one to Tiffany.

"I think you need this," Roslyn told her. "Have a couple of sips and I will talk."

Tiffany did so, rather enjoying the taste of blueberries in the wine.

"Now, Tiffany...where do I start? Well, I guess I should start with this: my body is my own, and I will do what I want. No man or anyone else can tell me any different. When I came of age my father sat me down and told me that."

"Your own father told you that?" Tiffany seemed taken aback at that.

"Yes. My mother was her own woman, he said, and she had chosen him, had chosen to share her body with him. He told me that he wanted me to make my own decisions about love, sex, and marriage."

Tiffany took another long drink and reached for some of the cookies.

"I am not a virgin, Tiffany," Roslyn told her, and Tiffany nearly choked on the cookie she had just taken a bite out of.

"I gamble, I drink, and when I feel the need I have sex." Roslyn shrugged and leaned back against the back of her sofa and took a hearty drink of her wine. "I have a charm to keep me from getting pregnant as well."

Tiffany just took another long drink and did not say anything yet.

"Do you still want to stay with me?" Roslyn asked her. "My father has the same views for all of his daughters, and his sons follow them too. Father is preparing a change to the arranged marriages in our kingdom, and has had words with the priests of the Tri-Goddess to bring back the beliefs that a woman is her own again. Yes we have been able to help run our husband's or family's properties in their absence, but we cannot own our businesses and our bodies are never our own. We as women can look forward to a lot more freedoms."

Tiffany emptied her cup and motioned for Roslyn to fill it again. Roslyn did so with a chuckle.

"Careful, take this one slower. The first time I tried it I had the worst hangover ever the next morning," Roslyn advised her. "Are you going to say anything now?"

"I think...you are exactly who I was looking for," Tiffany said slowly. Roslyn raised an eyebrow at her and waited for an explanation.

"I don't like men," Tiffany said hesitantly again. "I don't like women either. I just want to be me and learn how to fight and..." she trailed off when she noticed Roslyn smiling.

"Yes, you would do perfectly with me. I can help you be your own woman and learn how to fight for sure. As long as you stop thinking I need to be chaperoned," Roslyn teased.

Tiffany raised her hands in a sign of defeat and said, "I assure you, it will not happen again."

Roslyn raised her glass in a toast and leaned forward so Tiffany could touch her glass to hers.

"To new friends, and understandings," Roslyn gave a toast. Tiffany smiled and repeated it before taking another sip.

"What are those cakes there?" Tiffany asked next.

***

Roslyn smiled at her step-mother as Elle walked into her solar. Elle was wearing a simple gown with a circlet on her brow, her hair down in an elegant braid that hung down her back. Roz was going over some paperwork, still wearing the clothing she had worn when she was out with Rafi earlier that day.

"What do I owe the pleasure of your visit, Mother Elle?" Roslyn inquired as Elle took a seat. "I hope your ladies did not cause too much of a fuss earlier."

"Nothing I could not handle. I wanted to apologize to you for their behaviour though. I made it known that we need to be more progressive with our thinking, especially when it comes to how we dress. I think it's time we shake things up here at court," Elle explained to her.

Roslyn leaned forward with her elbows on her desk, an amused expression on her face. "What did you have in mind?"

"Those outfits your seamstress friend made for you...do you think she would make me the same?"

***

Roslyn put her documents away in a drawer of her desk and locked it, putting the key away in her bag. She looked around her office, wondering what her cousin's solar had looked like before everything had been burned. She barely remembered her cousin Anna for it had been several years since the whole family had gotten together.

Roslyn shook her head to try to clear the thoughts forming in her mind and stood, gathering her bag and heading for the door. She closed the door behind her, locking it with a special spell that would make sure she was the only one that could enter, and turned to walk down the hallway.

"You, girl," one of the young pages must have mistook her for one of the king's messengers--she was wearing plain clothes, breeches and a loose tunic because she just wanted to be comfortable that afternoon. The younger page stopped her with his words and beckoned to her from down the hall.

"I beg your pardon?" Roslyn was trying to think of a polite way of getting out of the conversation.

"The king has messages for Captain Heath, and others in the city--I cannot get both done in a timely manner so would you deliver these messages out to the Guest Cottage--I will compensate you for the time," the red-headed freckled young man was saying to her as he handed her some envelopes.

Roslyn sighed inwardly but figured it would be a good time to go talk to Heath by herself. She held her hand out to accept the envelopes.

"What is your name, girl?" the page asked her as she took the envelopes from him.

"Princess Roslyn," she told him, a slight smile on her face as she watched his reaction when the name clicked into place.

"Princess...Your Highness, forgive me," he went down to his knee and declined his head, "I did not recognize you."

"I will forgive you this time," Roslyn told him as she tucked the messages away in her bag. "It gives me an excuse to go talk to the Captain. Just don't make a habit of it.; and please do not bow to me--just a few short months ago I was but a Lady."

The page cringed and straightened, taking her in now. "I'm not in trouble?"

"I know I have not socialized much with the rest of the nobles so it is no fault of yours. Though I do hope that you will pass the word around that I like to dress casually so no one else makes the same mistake," she told him. He must be sixteen, nearly a squire by the looks of him; he wore the colours of Lake Holyrood: brown, white and dark orange--for the fine clay that could be found in the region.

"I will, your highness," he assured her fervently before bowing quickly again and walking away.

Roslyn headed for the stairway that would take her out to the palace grounds. The guest cottage was a small house out in the Royal Forest next to the small King's Lake. She had not been able to spend much time out there in the forest yet, but she knew the general lay of it from maps. She followed one of the cobbled pathways that led to the lake, though there were little post signs showing directions. At a fork in the path she looked up to find two signs, one pointing either direction: Guest Cottage to the left, Training Grounds to the right. She went left, looking at the different trees and birds she could see. It was a pretty diverse forest, with some that flowered in the spring and others that flowered in the fall, to different shades of green or even red leaves. It was a spectacular sight to take in, even the songs of the different birds she could hear.

Finally she reached the cottage that was the guest house, meant especially for private guests. The grounds were highly guarded, and the cottage specially spelled for safety for important guests who wanted to remain beyond prying eyes.

One of the King's Guards saw her coming down the path in the dim light but he knew her by the colour of her hair. He saluted her by putting his clenched fist over his heart.

"I have messages for Captain Heath from my father," she told the guard.

He nodded and said, "You may go ahead. He is there, his Lieutenants are out."

Roslyn nodded in turn and continued past the guard, coming across two other guards who held their clenched fists over their hearts as well before reaching the cottage. It was a two-story stone cottage with a thatched roof and glass windows; smoke came out of the chimney above.

Roslyn knocked on the wooden door and stepped back, her hands held behind her back as she waited. The door opened, and Roslyn was greeted by the sound of a cat meowing. She looked down and smiled at the long-haired tortoiseshell cat who was now rubbing up against her legs.

"Well hello there sweet thing," Roslyn said as she knelt to pet the cat. "What is your name?"

"Selene," she recognized Heath's voice but did not look up from petting the cat. "Your highness, what do I owe the pleasure?"

Roslyn continued to scratch behind the cat's ears as she answered, "Messages from my father for you, Captain."

"Do come in, your highness," she heard him say and she looked up as he was about to bow to her.

"You do not need to bow to me," she told him, grabbing hold of his chest lightly to keep him from bowing. "It really unnerves me when people bow to me. A few months ago I was drinking in a bar, just the daughter of an Earl."

"No wonder Selene likes you," Heath said with a smile. "She does not like many people." He took in her clothing as she walked past him, taking in her simple scent of lavender and honey.

"A sea Captain with a pet cat?" she queried as she took in the cottage. It was rustic looking on the inside, with a lot of pelts and old sofas. The stone fireplace let off a blazing heat.

"She is my ship's cat," Heath told her. "They are important for keeping control of rats and mice."

"Except you are not on your ship, Captain," she pointed out, amused at the blush on his cheeks.

"She is my cat," he confessed to her. "It is hard for me to go anywhere without her."

"I understand that completely. I had a cat back home in Wardgrove that I had had since I was young and he was a kitten. When he died a few years ago I was devastated."

"A fellow cat lover I see," Heath smiled broadly at her and motioned for her to sit on one of the sofas. "What messages does your father have for me?"

Chapter Eight

Roslyn sat at the back of the tavern, her hair pulled back in a tight bun and covered by a red scarf. She wore simple brown breeches and a light blue tunic that was cinched at her waist by her sword belt. To all the other patrons of the tavern she looked like any other woman in the city, and only if they looked closer would they have noticed her unusual eyes.

She raised her hand to wave to Kavan as he entered the tavern. He nodded and went to the bar, joining her moments later with two large flasks of the tavern's finest ale.

"Did you want to order some food too?" Kavan asked her as he sat down beside her.

"Soon. Edmond, Heath and his lieutenants will be joining us too, if you do not mind. I wanted to have some time for everyone to get to know each other before we leave. What a better place than a tavern with some fine ale and food?"

"And here I thought it would just be you and I," Kavan teased her as he took a drink.

"We should have a few minutes; but I wanted to ask you something, if it is OK," Roslyn told him.

"Ask away," Kavan told her, before he remembered that she had seen his scars.

"Where were you stationed during the Pirate War?" Roslyn asked him.

"Ah." He grimaced, realising she knew part of his history. "The East Garrison."

"How did you survive the attack?" she inquired next.

"I almost didn't."

"Those scars I saw?" she asked him calmly. He saw no pity in her eyes as she looked at him.

He nodded slowly before telling her, "I was left for dead, one of few who actually survived the attack on the garrison."

"And you later became the Head Guardsman of the Summer Palace before my father asked you to come here?"

He felt his blood run cold for a moment, figuring she knew that he was an orphan and did not belong at the rank he had achieved.

"Your father the king saw my potential and asked me to come here to teach you and your brother—"

Roslyn held up a hand to stop him, recognizing the edge in his voice. "Kavan, I am not trying to insult you. I am trying to congratulate you."

He stopped short, and found himself asking, "Why?"

"Family and blood have nothing to do with what you can do," she told him. "You made your own path, despite what was behind you. You survived the Pirate War; you are strong. You made your way through the ranks; you have courage. You are here now because you are stubborn." She smiled and held up her hand to stop him from speaking, and he closed his mouth again. "I need to tell you, three of the people we are meeting tonight are from the Tribes of the Archipelago."

She saw him tense, and she held her hand up again.

"During the war Captain Heath and his lieutenants defected," she told him. "Before the attack on your garrison."

Kavan softened, understanding what she was trying to do.

"I like you, Kavan. I respect you for everything you have been through. I know that my father chose wisely. Now, can we be friends?"

After a moment he nodded, and she smiled.

"We will have several months on board a ship together to look forward to in the future. I'm bringing ale, don't you worry. We will drink and play cards the whole way there," she told him with a laugh.

"Ah, there is Edmond now," she interjected as she waved her brother over. He too was wearing discrete clothing, and he had left his guards at the palace. Roslyn refused to have guards, for as a mage and a skilled fighter she could protect herself.

Edmond joined them at their table and Roslyn motioned to the bartender for a drink for her brother. A serving wench brought the ale over to Edmond, who thanked her.

"This is a...quaint place," Edmond commented as he sipped the ale. "Oh, well, this is good," he added, talking about the ale.

"It lives up to its reputation for sure," Roslyn commented. "I am going to send a message to Aidan to buy several casks of this ale for our journey."

Just then Captain Heath and his two lieutenants, one a man and the other a woman, walked into the tavern. They were dressed as sailors, swords and pistols at their waists. Heath looked around the room and spotted her and Edmond; they headed their direction. Kavan tensed a little but Roslyn laid a hand on his arm and gave him a look before he calmed himself enough.

Roslyn caught the serving wench's attention and indicated their new companions. The woman nodded and went to go get some more ale for their table.

As Heath reached their table Roslyn stood to introduce her brother and Kavan to the sailors.

"These are my lieutenants, Jackson and Maeve,"

Heath introduced his companions before they took seats.

The serving wench returned with more drinks, and Roslyn asked her to bring another round as well for she was done with her pint.

"Done your drink already?" Heath asked her, appraising her anew. "How long have you been here?"

"Not very long," she answered him. "Are you hungry? We have not ordered yet. Food and drink are on me tonight."

When the serving wench brought them their second round they ordered food, and Roslyn proposed a toast, holding her pint up over the table.

"To our expedition, may we get there thawed out and in one piece," she said, causing a chuckle from her companions. They brought their pints up to meet hers and they all drank at the same time.

"Captain tells me you were born in Jay'Al," Maeve commented.

"Yes, my father was there as an ambassador when he met my mother. She died in childbirth and he brought me back with him."

"You certainly look like the natives there," Jackson said, "Though your eyes are very unusual."

"What clan was your mother from?" Maeve asked her, a strange expression on her face.

"The Wolf Clan," she told them.

Jackson and Maeve looked at each other, as if they knew something.

"When we arrived at the continent we were met by a woman in her early forties who had eyes like yours. She was of the Wolf Clan," Maeve explained.

"My father said I had an aunt who had the same coloured eyes as my mother," Roslyn told her. "It was probably her. Did she give you a name?"

"No, she just said to call her Shaman. We did not stay in her village for more than a few hours either," Jackson told her. "Though it was nice that they spoke our language; it appears your father had taught the whole clan our language during his time with them. Of course, with the Tribes of the Archipelago having a settlement in the south of Jay'Al now they would find that knowing the Common Tongue would be of great use to them all."

"My father lived there for almost two years, he knew their language well also; he taught me the language when I was old enough. It will be interesting to meet my mother's side of the family," Roslyn commented. "She had several brothers too. I probably have a lot of cousins."

"The land we bought for the king from the Clans is near the Wolf Clan territory," Heath told her. "I am sure you will have a lot of time to find your family and get to know them. You should also think of teaching your companions the native tongue before we go."

"The few members of the Wolf Clan we met told us about a war nineteen years ago," Jackson spoke up. "A quarter of the clan was wiped out before the clans involved came to a truce."

"My father never mentioned anything about a war while he was there," Roslyn said with a frown. "He said it was a thriving village. The Clan was a large one and well respected."

Jackson shrugged his shoulders, "I am just telling you what I was told."

"There was something I wanted to ask you,"

Roslyn spoke up after a few minutes of drinking in silence.

"Just how cold does it get on our route?"

"Everything will freeze," Heath told her. "I will not lie about how cold it will get. Beards will be frozen, sails will freeze. We had a handful of sailors lose fingers and toes from frostbite."

"And you expect us to take our soldiers through this route?" Kavan asked them.

"What if we had some protection?" Roslyn interrupted before Heath could answer. "I can make a charm for every soldier and sailor to keep them warm."

"Roslyn, that's a lot of people and a lot of magic," Edmond spoke up. "You will overwork yourself."

"It will be worth it, to keep our expedition safe, and all toes and fingers intact. I can even put a spell on the sails when it is time so they do not freeze."

"Mages," Maeve shook her head. "Could you not kill yourself using such magic?"

"No, the spells and sigils will hold their own powers," she told them. She looked at Maeve and wondered how such a beautiful woman, with her wavy golden brown hair and long eyelashes, her curvy figure and honey coloured eyes, could stand being a sailor. What was life like with all of those male sailors? What had her life been like as a pirate?

"That..." Jackson spoke up, "would make a huge difference, really."

Roslyn looked at the other sailor, seeing his young visage though his skin was weathered from the sun. His dark hair was pulled back in a queue and his skin was tanned like Heath's. Jackson was tall like Heath, as tall as Roslyn was but still a few inches shorter than Tiffany. Jackson's eyes were light brown and since she had met him she thought he looked amused at something.

"I will get started on it in the morning. I should have enough charms by the time we leave, and I can put sigils on the sails during the voyage," Roslyn told the sailors. "I know the soldiers would appreciate being warm during the voyage."

They spent the rest of the evening eating their dinner and drinking together, with Captain Heath telling stories from when he was a pirate. They stayed there late into the evening until finally Roslyn called it a night, though she wanted everyone to walk back to the palace together.

"We can stop by that one vendor that sells those sweet cinnamon buns for dessert," she told her companions.

"Wandering drunks up to the palace?" Edmond quipped, adding "What could go wrong?"

Roslyn thanked the gods that night that nothing did go wrong on their walk back to the palace. They got their hot cinnamon buns and ate them on the way to the palace, laughing and joking as they went. Heath and his lieutenants left them at the Servant's Gate to the palace, where the guards knew exactly who they were. Kavan supported Edmond to his room, and said goodnight to Roslyn there.

Roslyn watched him walk away, wishing he would stop and turn around to look at her. He did not, however, and so she closed her door slowly and went to bed.

***

The next morning Roslyn found her father alone in his study. He was still wearing his black night clothes, and he was reading a report so he did not notice her coming into the room at first. He finally happened to glance up and noticed her sitting quietly across from his desk in one of the chaises. He set the papers down and smiled at her.

"You've been taking lessons from my butler, hm?" he asked her with a laugh. "Did you have fun last night?"

"I did. It was good to get together with the heads of the expedition this way, get to know each other a little better." She paused and continued, "Heath's Lieutenant Jackson told me a story about a civil war among the Clans of Jay'Al."

"Ah," her father looked sad for a moment, looking down and closing his eyes. When he brought his eyes back up to meet hers he thought of just how much she looked like her mother, and he told her so.

"Father, what happened when you were in Jay'Al?"

"There were some Clans who were unhappy with us coming there, and they wanted us gone. The Wolf Clan had become our friends, our family, and other Clans sided with them. It was a small war, it did not last very long I believe."

"You told me mom died in childbirth," she whispered.

"She had gone into labour that morning," he told her. "The Clans against us had set fire to our houses. I left her with you and her family to go help put out fires, but it had spread too far too fast. I tried to get her out, but she was too weak and she ordered me to take you and go. Two of her brothers went in after her, but the building caved in." Tears were streaming down his face as he relived those memories. He wiped them away and could see the stricken look on his daughter's face. "My people left that night."

"So you never saw her body?"

He shook his head and spoke, "No, but there was no way she could have survived the building collapsing."

Roslyn was silent for a few moments, looking down at her clenched hands. "Well, it seems the Clans made peace after that."

"Yes, Captain Heath told me that the new Elders of the Clans think it would be beneficial to open themselves to trade now."

"It only took nineteen years and a handful of lives to change their minds," Roslyn added with slight disgust. "Thank you for telling me the truth, father."

"I never meant to keep it from you for so long; it still hurts to remember that day, but you would have found out once you got there," he told her. "Better it came from me first."

Chapter Nine

Tiffany was in her room lifting small weights one evening when a knock came at the door adjoining her room to Roslyn's. Tiffany put her weight down and went to answer it, finding Roslyn standing there in her training clothes and a cloak around her shoulders.

"What's this?" Tiffany asked her with a raised eyebrow.

"Get ready, I have something to show you," Roslyn told her with a serious expression on her face. "I will wait in the hall for you," she added before turning on her heels and heading to her door that led out into the hallway.

Tiffany quickly changed and grabbed her own cloak--if Roslyn felt it necessary for a cloak why could she not have one? She joined Roslyn out in the hall a moment later.

"Where are we going?" she asked Roslyn as the princess led her to the west gate house. There the guards let them through the gate with no questions asked, raising more questions in Tiffany's mind. Roslyn motioned for her to put her hood up and she complied. She remained silent though as Roslyn led her into the city.

Finally the two of them stopped in front of a warehouse in a lower level residential district. Tiffany was bursting with questions. When they entered the warehouse to find Kavan there with a group of young women in loose breeches and tunics, Tiffany found herself asking out loud, "Just what the hells is going on here?"

Tiffany found Kavan grinning widely at her and Roslyn smiling at her reaction.

"We've been teaching these women self-defence," Roslyn told her. "Kavan joined me not too long ago. This is Theophania everyone, or Tiffany is what she would rather be called." Tiffany found everyone greeting her shyly.

"I thought you could use some more training in hand-to-hand," Roslyn told her, "and we need an extra person to train with."

"I would gladly join you," Tiffany answered. "Who shall I partner with?"

Tiffany enjoyed the work out with the other young women, and could see the difference in their self-confidence by the end of the session. Roslyn had them go over several holds and twists if an attacker should come up behind them, making them do them until they were sore; but with each turn they became more confident and better at defending themselves.

"This is what I want to do," Tiffany told Roslyn as they were cleaning up after. "I want to help people protect themselves. I want to make a difference."

Roslyn looked at her thoughtfully before saying, "You are wasted as a Lady, Theophania. You were born to be a protector, a knight. I think that would suit you much better."

Tiffany blushed and waved her off before

Kavan spoke up from the doorway, "No, Roslyn is right. I know the King is trying to change things for women, maybe he can bring back women as knights too. I know these women who were here tonight would love something like that."

So Tiffany began to wonder if she could become a knight of some kind, but she thought of her family. "What would my family think of this? I was supposed to be here to become a proper lady."

Kavan laughed at that and said, "They don't know Roslyn at all." That earned a sharp elbow to the ribs from Roslyn but she started to laugh.

"I will write to your parents," Roslyn assured her. "I will champion your case, and get my father to help."

Humbled by Roslyn's assurances, all Tiffany could do was thank her. She had no idea what else Roslyn had in mind though.

***

Roslyn was in her solar going over some things when there came a knock at her door. Looking up at her open door--she kept it open these days because messengers were always coming and going with the planning of the expedition--she found a man in his late thirties dressed as a noble in fine velvet breeches and tunic, a fine leather coat over his tunic. Something about his red hair and facial features was familiar, and when he smiled she knew who he was.

"Ah, have you come in response to my letter about Theophania?" Roslyn asked him. "Please come in, Lord Hector."

"How did you know who I was?" Hector asked her as he took a seat in one of the chairs in front of her desk.

"Tiffany looks like you," she answered. "Though honestly I was only expecting a reply by letter, not in person."

"I felt it necessary to come in person, your High-ness," Hector told her with a decline of his head. "You honour our family in such a way it would not have been sufficient other-wise." He sighed heartily before continuing, "I know my parent's allowed her to stay away from court so long because she is the youngest, but since she is now in her early twenties I was unsure of what to do with her. She was always different; sure she enjoyed the dresses but her mind was sharper than anything. And no boy could ever hold her gaze. I am sorry that I ever dissuaded her from learning the sword."

"She came to me at the right time, it seems," Roslyn told him seriously. "I want you to know that I see her potential, and so does my Master at Arms. She has learned very quickly in the weeks she has been training and I am impressed, to say the least."

Hector smiled broadly and he nodded before telling her: "I breed horses, your highness, and I wish to give you a gift from my family for the honour you have given to us. I brought with me several of my finest horses, all broken in and trained, for you to choose from."

"I have heard of your stables, Lord Hector, and it would be my honour to accept one," she told him with a broad smile.

"I also come with a purse for my sister to cover any costs of armour or weapons," Hector told her, producing a large pouch from inside his coat pocket. He offered it to her and she accepted it with a smile.

"This will come in handy I am sure. In a few weeks I am heading an expedition to Jay'Al, and Tiffany will be coming with me," Roslyn told him.

Hector seemed surprised by that so Roslyn figured Tiffany had not written home about that yet. "I assure you, we will not be going anywhere near the Archipelago," Roslyn told him before he could say anything. "We will be heading north, through the Sea of Ice, instead of going near the pirates."

"Is that any safer?"

"I assure you your sister is safe with me, I am a mage after all. I also have plans in place to keep everyone warm during our journey."

"I defer to your knowledge and planning, your highness. Shall we go down to the stables so you can look at the horses?"

On their way down to the Royal Stables Roslyn sent a messenger to Tiffany to meet them there. They had just entered the Royal Stables from the enclosed breezeway that connected it to the palace when they heard someone calling to Roslyn from the other end. They both turned to find Tiffany coming towards them, but Tiffany stopped short when she realized that the person with Roslyn was her brother.

"Hector? What are you doing here?" Tiffany asked him with a frown.

"I have come to thank princess Roslyn for honouring our family by choosing you as her Royal Defender," Hector told her.

"Royal...Defender?" Tiffany looked between the two of them with confusion.

"I was going to tell you later, but now seems like a good enough time," Roslyn told her with a laugh. "It's kind of like a bodyguard and a knight, but you'll have more freedom to do things."

Tiffany hugged Roslyn before turning to her brother to hug him as well.

"I have a purse here for you from our family," Hector told her, motioning to Roslyn who produced the purse from her satchel. "To help you cover the costs of armour and weapons. I brought horses for the princess to choose from as a 'thank you' from our family, but I also brought a horse for you as well."

"Shall we?" Roslyn asked them, motioning to the stables before them. With a smile Tiffany linked arms with both of them and together they went into the stables.

Chapter Ten

King Lucius welcomed his nobles to the fencing tournament, everyone dressed in their best finery; young noblemen and noblewomen were also in attendance. Edmond sat to one side of Lucius and his queen on his other side. Below their dais sat their younger children and Tiffany, though Roslyn was not there. Elle looked at the empty seat that was supposed to be Roslyn's and at her husband with a raised eyebrow.

"Do not worry, she will be here somewhere," Lucius told her with a sly grin.

Elle was wearing a very different outfit for the occasion: it was a long tunic with slits down the side and leggings underneath. A fine belt was at her waist, and she had a decorative dagger at her waist. Her two daughters were wearing the same outfit. Elle looked out at the nobles and could tell that the women were talking about her outfit. She lifted her chin and returned her attention to the yard before her.

At that moment the contenders for the tournament entered the yard. All of them wore special padded clothing and special mesh headgear. Together the sixteen of them walked in a line into the yard and turned to face the king and his family, putting their fists over their hearts and bowing. Each contender had a number painted on the front of their padded tunic, and a thin bladed duelling sword at their waists.

Kavan walked into the yard and addressed the crowd, "I am Kavan, the King's Master of Arms and the judge of the tournament. The contenders will go up against each other and based on their points some of them will be eliminated in each round. All of the contenders are knights or nobles, and the names will only be announced at the end with the winner."

***

Edmond watched in half-boredom as the tournament commenced. Right away there were two contenders that stood out, numbers One and Sixteen: they were both taller than most of the other contenders, but he could not tell how well muscled either of them were through their padded outfits.

At the end of the first round two of the contenders were dismissed, numbers Three and Ten. Edmond now found himself wondering who the contenders were, though he did not know most of the knights or all of the noblemen. There was to be a feast after the tournament and all of the nobles would be introduced to the whole royal family; Edmond had to admit he would much rather be at the tournament than at the feast later.

Edmond found himself leaning forward to watch the next couple rounds as One and Sixteen kept advancing, using different techniques. The noblemen and noblewomen watching were cheering their favourites, and Kavan stood back against one of the walls watching intently, a calculating look on his face. Edmond wished he had had the courage to do the tournament but he was embarrassed by Kavan and his sister enough at their training sessions as it was. Tiffany was openly cheering for Sixteen.

Finally the second last round saw the third last, Fifteen, eliminated, leaving the final round to One and Sixteen. This last round lasted several more minutes than the other one did, Sixteen remained silent as they duelled against One. One, however, was a talker, and though he was not trying to goad Sixteen with insults it rather seemed that he was trying to bore Sixteen with facts about fencing. Edmond could only hear a little bit of what One was saying, but he had to roll his eyes at the man.

Finally Sixteen twisted their blade around One's and yanked, pulling the blade out of One's grip. The crowd cheered as Sixteen put their blade to One's throat, One put-ting his hands up in defeat. The crowd cheered and Kavan stepped forward, a smile on his face as he took hold of Sixteen's hand and raised it up, declaring them the winner. He motioned to the other contenders who were all sitting on a long bench on the other side of the room waiting for the tournament to be over.

"Line up in number order," Kavan told the contenders, "and take your helmets off and introduce yourselves to the room."

One took his helmet off and bowed to the king and queen, saying, "Sir Sullivan of Kintel." He was a good-looking man in his early twenties with curly blonde hair. Edmond thought he recognized the man from where he did not know.

Two took off his helmet and named himself, "Dominic of Yulton."

Three and Four were the brothers Klay and Kolby of the noble house of Gryshton. Five was the nobleman Aspen from some small estate in the south that Edmond had never heard of. From Six to Fifteen were more knights--Sirs Jerome, Kordell, Graeme, Emery, Kosey, Corbin, Holden, Douglas, Jaxon, and Edric.

As Sixteen pulled off their helmet Edmond's smile grew wide as he took in his sister who was smiling at him as she tucked her helmet under her arm. Edmond looked at his father who looked rather smug with himself.

"Princess Roslyn of Ellsgrove," she announced to the room. Kavan smiled at her and raised her hand up as the young noblewomen in the crowd began to whisper excitedly.

Sir Sullivan stared openly in surprise, as did Sir Graeme, while Roslyn tried her best to avoid their gaze. She recognized them from a few months ago in Ward-grove.

"The winner of this year's tournament, ladies and gentlemen, is Princess Roslyn," Kavan announced. King Lucius stood up and clapped, the queen and the rest of the royal family rising to their feet to clap at Roslyn's win. The rest of the noblemen and women joined in, some of the young noblewomen cheering.

***

Roslyn and Sir Sullivan sat together at the winners table with the king and queen. Kavan sat with Tiffany, Edmond and the rest of Roslyn's siblings, enduring their questions while he was trying to eat.

"It is good to see you again," Sullivan whispered to Roslyn. She remembered him quite clearly, and when he had announced himself she felt her cheeks warm at the thought of their former flirtations. She had asked her father about him once and he had told her that the knight had been assigned closer to his home. He must have returned to the capital just for the tournament.

"I was kind of hoping you would come calling before this," Roslyn told him. "We never got to finish our card game."

"Something I regret, though I could not go against my placement. I am only here because I was on the invite list to attend the tournament, which, by the way, you have impressed me," Sir Sullivan told Roslyn, louder this time. "I have never seen a woman fight with a sword before."

"Get used to it," Roslyn told him with a smile as she took a drink of her wine. "I imagine more young noblewomen will want to learn how to use a sword now."

"Surely it cannot be that simple," Sullivan told her, "after decades of men being the ones to wield swords and defend the realm."

"Us women live here too," Tiffany spoke up loudly, and many eyes turned in their direction, many of them young noblewomen. "Do we not have the right to help defend our realm, our families, against enemies? Do we not have the right to defend ourselves against unwanted advances?"

Several of the young noblewomen in the room began to clap, including several of the young men, even Tiffany's brother who had been in attendance for the tournament.

From somewhere in the room one of the noblemen spoke up, saying, "Only commoners and loose women wear breeches and fight."

Roslyn stood up and addressed the nobles herself, looking in the direction she thought she had heard the voice come from; from the look of several displeased young women glaring at their father she figured she was right.

"I'm sorry my lord, would you like to settle this on the floor with our swords? You have seen me defeat our realm's finest swordsmen already, so I think I could beat you," Roslyn criticized the man. That brought about some chuckles from several people in the room. Next Roslyn addressed the young women at the table where their father was turning a dark shade of red in the face.

"My ladies, you seem to think that men have the power over you; yet you are the ones that bear their children, you are the ones who manage their estates while they are out in their men's clubs. So tell me, my ladies, would you not rather have the power to do everything yourself?"

Sir Sullivan stood up and said, "I have two younger sisters. I would have loved for them to have someone like Roslyn to look up to. She is what our young women should be: they should be fearless, they should not have to hide, they should be able to protect themselves. I swear to the gods if anything ever happened to my younger sisters because I could not protect them, because I was not there...how would they know what to do? We need to teach them how to protect themselves--but how you would see it, you older noblemen would have seen it, to see a young noblewoman protect her own honour, would you have called her a whore? Hm? What say you, young ladies? You cannot win, can you?"

There was more whispering in the room, and finally she heard a young woman say: "I want to learn how to defend myself." Others spoke up as well, earning a satisfying smile from Roslyn and her father.

"Your King has heard your pleas," Lucius spoke, standing up to address the room. "I will do my best to change things so that you can do that."

King Lucius looked at the musicians in the corner and nodded for them to play something. They did so, picking up a lively tune that Roslyn hoped would help ease the mood. Sir Sullivan and Roslyn took their seats again as the attendees began to talk amongst themselves.

"Thank you," Roslyn whispered to Sir Sullivan. "May I ask why you did that?"

"I will tell you another time," he answered with a half-smile. "I believe we caused quite a stir tonight."

"How did you do it?" Edmond leaned over to talk to Roslyn. "Why did you not tell me you were joining the tournament?"

"I have been planning this for a while," his father leaned over to say to him. "It was my idea to be a part of the tournament, so the other nobles could see her fight without prejudice."

"And any young noblewoman can do it too," Roslyn said loudly as she looked out at the nobles sitting before her.

Some of the older gentlemen did not seem pleased, but to her delight many of the older women looked very happy and were nodding as many of the young noblewomen were talking about learning to fight. It made her extremely happy to know that she had made a difference, though the presence of Sir Sullivan made her heart beat fast. Would she get some more time with the knight?

Chapter Eleven

Several mornings after the tournament Roslyn was in her study going over some paperwork when there came a knock at her door. She looked up to find Sir Sullivan standing there in simple cotton breeches and a tunic, simple leather shoes on his feet.

"Oh, good morning Sir Sullivan," she said as she put down her pencil. "Please come in."

"I believe I told you before to call me Sully," he answered with a smile and he closed the door behind him.

Roslyn leaned back in her chair and crossed her legs, folding her hands in her lap. Roslyn was wearing an outfit like the one her step-mother had worn, a long blouse with splits in the side and leggings underneath. She had noticed on her walk around the palace that morning that several young noblewomen at court had already started changing their attire to dresses with split hems and leggings underneath in order to have more movement. Roslyn knew her mother would be proud of the progress they were making.

"To what do I owe the pleasure of this visit?" Roslyn asked him as he took a seat in one of the wicker chairs before her desk.

"My one younger sister was attacked last year," he got straight to the point. "Thank the gods I came upon it happening, but if I had not been there...If every Lord knew what it was like to find their daughter, or sister, being attacked--if they truly loved them--they would have no problem with their daughters learning to defend themselves. It was why I threw my lot in with you; you are what my sister needed. You could help so many others too."

"How old is your sister?"

"She just turned sixteen. Her name is Deirdre."

Roslyn leaned forward and rested her elbows on her desk, a serious expression on her face. "Would she come to the capitol to join my Honour

Guard?"

"Your what?" Sir Sullivan looked surprised at the name.

"My father thinks it would be a good idea to have a fully female--or almost fully female--Honour Guard for myself during my stay in Jay'Al. When one of our ships returns for supplies the women will come with them back to Jay'Al, having been training for several months before hand and during the voyage."

"Do you have someone to head this, someone who knows what they are doing?" Sully asked her after a moment.

"I have a few people in mind, but now I wonder...would you be the head teacher?" Roz inquired of him, a serious note in her voice.

Sully ducked his head and looked back up at her, his eyes shining with something she could not place right.

"It would be my honour, princess Roslyn, to do that for you."

***

Two days after the tournament Roslyn was heading for the Quartermaster's office when a group of young noblewomen stopped her. They were all wearing a version of Roslyn's new outfit, and one of them even had a splint on her arm.

"Your highness," one of the girl's spoke as the others bowed their heads lightly to her. "We wanted to thank you, princess Roslyn, for what you did the other night."

"We also wanted to let you know that we are going to fight for our right to learn how to protect ourselves," one of the others told her next.

"It looks like you already have been," Roslyn said, indicating the girl with the splinted arm.

The girl grinned and explained, "We were going over a couple of falls with an instructor when I landed weirdly. I have yet to see a healer, but the instructor put this on me until then."

Roslyn looked at the girls, her heart feeling warm that these young women were rising to the opportunity that was being given them. Two of them looked to be around fourteen, another maybe sixteen and the oldest looking one looked to be seventeen.

"Girls, this means a lot to me," she told them. "Keep up the good work. I hope to see you again someday."

"We heard you are going on an expedition to Jay'Al," the oldest girl spoke up. "How long will you be gone? We were hoping we could get to know you."

Roslyn felt tears coming to her eyes, happy tears that these young noblewomen actually wanted to know her. She regretted keeping to herself now the last few months.

"What are your names?" Roslyn asked them, fighting back the urge to cry.

"I am Rita," the oldest introduced herself, "of the noble house of Trunel. These are my sisters, Olivia, Aisley, Georgia, and my cousin Roberta."

"Well, Rita, Olivia, Aisley, Georgia and Roberta, I will expect progress reports from your instructor be sent to my father--I know he will be very happy to have you train to be knights of Ellsgrove."

It made her happy to see the girls' faces light up and they thanked her, excitement showing in their faces and their squeals.

"Be well, girls. I do not know when I will return but I know that if you put your minds to it you will reach your goals." Roslyn nodded her head and turned to continue on her way when she heard Rita say, "Be safe, princess Roslyn. You have given us hope that we can have a different future than what was expected of us before."

Roslyn ducked her head and left them, tears coming forth. She did not want anyone to see her cry and she made it to one of the servant's corridors that she was able to duck down as the tears flowed free. If only she had tried to meet the noblewomen before instead of moping about being there and not back in Wardgrove. She had isolated herself because she had felt sorry for herself, and now she knew that she had been very wrong. They were leaving soon for Jay'Al, which gave her no real time to get to know the girls.

Roslyn wiped her tears away and stood up straighter. She would learn from this, and hopefully open herself up some more for future girls who wanted what those girls did too.

Chapter Twelve

The morning of their departure finally arrived. Roslyn was awakened by Tiffany knocking on her door and telling her to hurry up for breakfast with the training group. Since it was their last day at the palace the group had chosen to take a break from their morning workouts and just have a casual breakfast in the kitchens. Roslyn had let the cooks know the night before what their plans were, and she knew that there would be a table set up in the kitchen for them with a good meal.

Wearing black breeches and a long flowing light blue tunic cinched at the waist by her sword belt, Roslyn joined Tiffany in the hallway. Her Royal Defender had taken to wearing breeches and long tunics as well, and Roslyn was amused to find that they matched that morning.

Edmond joined them when they reached the end of the hall, and together they made their way down to the kitchen. Rafi was already there, and Kavan joined them shortly after. Aidan, the last member of their training group, arrived last and out of breath.

At least he isn't wearing his robes anymore, Roslyn thought to herself as Aidan took a seat and accepted a plate from Tiffany; he wore simple breeches and a tunic. After his first meeting with them in the Training Yard, and an explanation of the dangers of Jay'Al, he had started to take it seriously. He was still learning, however. Kavan doubted the apprentice would be able to defend himself properly when the time came, but Roslyn was trying to encourage the young man to continue.

They ate sombrely in silence, the cooks bringing them fruit juice to drink but otherwise leaving them alone.

Roslyn cocked her head to the side as she listened to the sounds coming through the windows to her right. The clock in the middle of the city was ringing out the ninth hour of the morning already.

"Time to go, my friends," she told them. Aidan's face turned white but he stood as she did. The others did as well, and together they thanked the cooks for breakfast before leaving together.

Roslyn led the group to the Main Hall where her father, step-mother and younger siblings awaited them. The night before their luggage had been taken down to the ship, so all they had to do today was board.

"Roz," her step-mother spoke as she pulled her into a hug, "Be safe, and take care of yourself."

"I promise," Roslyn answered as they parted.

Roslyn hugged her younger siblings, Edmond holding her tightly. She kissed each of their foreheads and looked at them closely so she would re-member what they looked like. When she returned they would definitely be older.

Her sisters were openly crying, but Robert just looked sullen. Roslyn hugged him tightly last, and turned to her father.

"I love you," the king told her as he pulled her into an embrace. "Remem-ber, once you get there send me a message with your magic."

"I will not forget, father," she told him as they parted. "Be safe while I am gone."

Her father and Edmond smiled at her and assured her they would be fine.

"I wanted you to know before you go that the nobles have passed the bill to allow women to become knights," her father told her. "It seems your plan worked at the tournament and not only have the wives had a say but the young noblewomen have been pestering their families as well. They look up to you after you showed them what they could do. I will be recruiting teachers for the women who choose to join the knighthood."

"Might I suggest some of the commoner women I have been training?" she asked her father. "You know where my group meets."

"I will consider it," Lucius told her as he nodded. "I am proud of you."

With one last look at her family she and her comp-anions walked out the door and down the steps to their awaiting carriage, two horses on lead reins behind the carriage--the white mare with red patches was the one Roslyn had chosen, and the black gelding with white socks was the one Tiffany had cho-sen.

Guards saluted them at the gates, for they knew about the mission. Roslyn watched out the side of their carriage and at the gates to the city she saw a group of young women waiting there, and when they saw the carriage come close they stood at attention and saluted her. She leaned out the window and saluted them in turn, a tear rolling down her cheek. Tiffany squeezed her hand in comfort, knowing how much that group of young women meant to Roslyn. Kavan offered a supportive grip to Roslyn's shoulder, and Roslyn patted his hand in thanks before turning away from the city. She knew she was leaving them in good hands: one of the oldest of the group would continue to teach and train them and others who would join; and if her father had anything to say about it they might just help train the next female knights of the realm.

It would take them three hours to get to the port, and they would set sail immediately. The soldiers who would be accompanying them were already waiting for them at the port and should all be boarded by the time Roslyn and her group arrived there. Oswick, the second merchant, lived at the East Port and would be meeting them there.

The drive to the coastal port was mostly quiet. Roslyn got them to play a card game to pass the time. They passed through a few smaller towns and finally stopped for a break in the city of Eglan after two hours. They had stopped at a small inn where they relieved themselves and grabbed a small snack of pastries for the last leg of the journey.

Finally on the horizon the sky suddenly split into a darker blue: the ocean. They were finally nearing their first destination of the port. They topped a hill and Roslyn found herself holding her breath as she took in the port and the awaiting ships at the harbour.

"There it is," Roslyn spoke up, making everyone go quiet, and she continued to say, "the ocean."

The others joined her at the side of the carriage looking out the window. They were now descending the hill towards the city. Traffic during the middle of the afternoon was busy, holding them back on their schedule slightly, but Roslyn knew that Captain Heath would not leave without them.

As they approached the harbour, Roslyn hanging out the window of the carriage to be able to take everything in, she saw Oswick standing on some boxes facing the street and looking for them so she started waving. He spotted her and waved back, jumping down from the boxes and running to meet them.

Oswick's family had been from the southern tribes, so told by the skin that was as dark as Roslyn's. His hair, however, was black and cut short to his head. He sported a light beard, and his brown eyes shone with happiness as he ran towards them. Since his initial meeting with the King the day that Rafi had arrived he had not been able to meet with her for her father had sent him back to the port to start to help get things ready.

Roslyn told the carriage driver to stop and she got out of the carriage and ran to meet her friend. Oswick embraced her when they met, holding her only for a moment before letting her go and taking a step back.

"Your highness," he said with a bow. At first Roslyn thought he was joking, but she saw the look in his brown eyes and knew otherwise.

"No," she told him as she forced him to stand straight.

"No friend of mine will bow to me now."

A smile crossed his face and he said, "I am glad to see that living in the palace has not changed you too much."

Seeing that her friend was testing her she punched his shoulder, earning a satisfying groan from him. That was one thing she had worried about, how her friends from the lower class back home would think of her. Thankfully the new friends she made in the capitol had liked her, so maybe her old friends back home would not think differently of her either. Rafi had accepted her new position with grace, and it seemed like Oswick was fine with it as well. She had not seen him since that night in the tavern three months before. One of her worst fears was one of her friends thinking they could no longer be friends because of her new position, no matter that she herself had not changed.

"That is what you get for being a jerk," she told him before hugging him again. "I missed you at the palace, I could have used you there."

"What, with Rafi?" he whispered quietly as the carriage approached them. Rafi climbed out of the carriage and waved at Oswick.

Roslyn let Rafi do the introductions to the rest of the group because she saw Captain Heath coming towards them. Roslyn and Captain Heath greeted each other by clasping each other's forearms, and Heath inclined his head a bit. She had already made it known that she hated bowing, and he had become her friend during his time at the palace.

"Glad to see you arrived in one piece," Heath joked. "The city is very busy today."

"It's just the time of day," Oswick butted in, "The workers are heading home and the night market workers heading out. In a few minutes we will see the streets grow quiet until after sunset."

"But we will not be here after sunset," Tiffany retorted.

"You are right, Tiffany, I am just saying--"

Roslyn put a hand on Oswick's shoulder to stop him from going any further. "Shall we board the ship, my friends?" she asked them all.

"Oswick has been very helpful in getting everything ready for sailing," Heath commented as they made their way to the large gangplank that connected the ship to the harbour dock. "I do not think I have ever seen such an excursion start off so smoothly."

"Oswick is extremely good at preparing for the worst," Roslyn half joked. "I am glad my friend could be of help."

"Were you able to do those enchantments you were talking about?" Heath whispered to her as they stepped onto the deck of the great ship that would bear them north. One of his sailors had gathered up the horses reins and was leading the horses below deck to be with the other horses.

"I was," she answered. "We can hand them out to each ship when we get close enough to the north. I included a few extras for the horses as well--and your Selene."

Heath looked relieved and tried to change his expression to one of indifference but she saw it.

"Did you doubt what I could do?" she asked him.

"Yes, and no," he responded with a sly smile. "My men, and your soldiers, will be happy for this. I have heard grumbling from some of the soldiers about the cold. Selene will especially like it--last time she had to sleep in bed with me in order to keep warm."

"Well, I am glad to help in any way," she told him. "You can assure your lieutenants that I came through as I promised."

He bowed his head slightly in response and continued to usher the newcomers onto his ship. "Your quarters are this way," he said with a flourished bow. Tiffany giggled and Kavan rolled his eyes, but Aidan looked eager to find a bunk. Rafi was too busy conversing with Oswick to really pay attention though they remained with the group as Heath led them down a flight of stairs towards their rooms as arranged by Roslyn. Selene showed up out of nowhere, twining around Roslyn's legs until she picked the cat up, earning a very satisfying purr from the cat.

"All of your things are already on board, of course," Heath commented after he told them whose rooms belonged to whom. "Would you like to be on deck for when we embark?" he asked them.

"Yes, definitely," Roslyn answered, with a groan from Aidan. She looked at him and could already tell that he would get sea-sick. "Aidan, I have a charm I can give you for the sea-sickness."

His eyes lit up and he nodded, so she dug into her pack that she always had slung over her shoulder and pulled out a necklace with a charm on it; she offered it to him. She could see the green leave his face only moments after he put the charm around his neck. He smiled at her and motioned for her to lead the way back up to the deck, which she gladly did.

"We are sure everyone is here?" Roslyn asked Captain Heath before he could make the order to cast off.

"You were the last ones we were waiting for," Captain Heath told her. He took a whistle from his pocket and sounded off a quick sharp series of shrills through it, and the sailors started to scurry around the deck to prepare to cast off--even Selene took off from Roslyn's hold and went to stand by the helm. The gangplank was pulled in and the men on the wharf untied the ropes that kept the ship tied in place. Several tugboats started to pull each of the ships out into the harbour as the Captain and his lieutenants on the other two ships gave the order to unfurl the sails.

"We will travel along the coast to the north before entering the Sea of Ice," Heath commented, "You know the route from the briefings," he added as an aside. "Do you remember how long it will take?"

"Two weeks up the coast," she answered. "And if all goes well, three weeks through the Sea of Ice and another two to Jay'Al."

"I hope you do not bore easily," Heath commented.

"Nah, we will find things to do. I brought several thick books to read," she assured him.

Heath smiled at her and went to go check on something, leaving her at the bow of the ship to watch the coast go by.

***

It took a few days of getting used to the movements of the ship before they got into a routine. Every morning they would have their practice session, with Captain Heath joining in most days. Roslyn would teach them the native language of Jay'Al before lunch, taking their food from the galley and going up onto the deck to eat as a group. During the afternoon hours they would split off to do their own thing: Roslyn would curl up on her bunk and read while Tiffany did more muscle exercises on the other side of their shared room. Each afternoon Roslyn and Tiffany would go visit their horses, brushing them down and letting them know they were there.

For the evening meal they would eat together in the galley before breaking out a deck of cards and dice, and some of the ale from that tavern in the capital. The cat Selene would join them while they played cards, choosing one of their laps to curl up on. One by one the group would trickle off to bed, Roslyn usually being the last one. She enjoyed the time alone, where she would go up on deck and look at the stars for a bit before retiring to her bed.

One night after almost two weeks Roslyn found herself up on the deck under a full moon. The air had gotten much cooler, and that day they had seen some ice floats in the water. They were coming up to the Sea of Ice.

Roslyn pulled her coat closer around her as she stared up at the stars. She could make out several constellations she knew well from growing up in the north.

"The stars are lovely tonight," a familiar voice said from beside her. Roslyn turned to see Captain Heath standing next to her, dressed as he had been the day they had met except for a new heavy coat that matched his outfit--Selene was right behind him, ready to twine around Roslyn's ankles. "We should hand out those charms to our people tomorrow. It will only get colder from here."

"Share a drink with me, Captain?" Roslyn pulled a flask out from under her coat and offered it to him. Next she knelt down and put a small necklace around Selene's neck. "This will keep you warm," Roslyn' assured the cat, who at first was balking at the necklace but somehow understood. "Something a little stronger tonight," she added with a smile, indicating the flask.

"Call me Heath," he told her, "It's about time you did." He took the flask, opened it and took a drink. He gasped a little bit as he handed it back to her.

"I told you it was strong," she said with a laugh as she took a swig as well.

"What is that?" he inquired as she passed it back to him.

"It's made from potatoes, believe it or not," she told him. "Vodka."

"You really are quite a princess," Heath commented as he took another swig. "I have never heard of a princess who fights or drinks like you."

"Well, first time for everything, hm?" She smiled sweetly at him. "And call me Roz, all my friends do."

"Even though I used to be a pirate?" he teased her as she took another swig.

"That was your past," she answered, "You have proven yourself to me these last couple of months. I am happy to know you. Plus, the cat is an extra bonus."

"Well, goodnight Roz," Heath told her with a smile. "I look forward to the rest of our journey together."

Roslyn watched him walk back to his cabin, enjoying the way he walked with confidence even after a few swills of the liquor. Selene meowed at her before following Heath off. She took one last look up at the moon and the stars before she went to her room.

***

The next day Heath arranged for one of the other ships to be close enough for her to swing over on a rope, Heath accompanying her. She handed out the charms to all of the sailors and soldiers, and got to meet the three blacksmiths. They were young men just out of their apprenticeship: Colton was tall and brawny, dark skin and dark hair; Bryan was short and stocky, pale skinned and blonde hair; and Leon was a rather tall barrel-chested redhead with freckles all over, even his well-muscled arms. Roslyn appraised Leon well as she met him, enjoying how he blushed under her scrutiny.

Next they went to the third ship, and the rest of the soldiers were eager to be warm again. They all thanked Roslyn for the charms, for they felt the warmth as soon as they put the necklaces over their heads. Finally they made their way back to Captain Heath's ship in time for lunch.

Roslyn was sitting out on the deck of the ship reading a book when she heard Heath order his sailors to 'get the lanterns out.' She put her book down and observed as a group of sailors carried out a large oil lantern that they lugged to the prow of the ship. Heath came over to her as the sailors attached the lantern to the end of the prow so the light would cast out over the water.

"What is that for?" Roslyn inquired of Heath as the sailors lit the lantern. She could see the light reflecting off of nearby icebergs and she understood before he told her.

"So we can see icebergs before they can hit us," Heath told her, though he could tell by the look on her face that it had already dawned on her what the purpose of the lantern was. "There will be lookouts in the Nest all during the night, taking turns, so we can steer around them."

"How effective is it?" Roslyn asked him, seeing that the light cast by the lantern on this ship, and the ones being installed on the other ships as they spoke, only reached a good hundred yards or less from the prow of the ship.

"Effective enough, especially if we are fast enough at the helm," Heath assured her.

Roslyn was not reassured, so she went to her room that night and took several large crystals out of her packs and got to work. She did not even notice Tiffany coming to bed, and she fell asleep at the table she was working at.Tiffany shook her awake the next morning, and Roslyn groaned as her neck protested the position.

"What were you doing all night?" Tiffany asked her.

"You shall find out tonight," Roslyn told her. "I need to have a bath."

"I have water warming in the baths now for you," Tiffany told her. "And the brazier is heating the room nicely."

"Oh thank you Tiffany. What time is it?"

"I just came back from a bath after defence practice," came the reply as Tiffany walked over to her bunk. "I know you were up late so I let you sleep in."

"Ah shit. So you have all eaten breakfast?" Roslyn stood and started to massage her neck.

"Cook has food saved for you in the galley," Tiffany assured her. "Go have your bath and eat."

Roslyn nodded and gathered her bathing things before heading down the hall to one of two bathing rooms. The other one was down the other end of the hall and it had been agreed that the men would use that one; this one was just for her and Tiffany. She entered the warm room and locked the door behind her.

They tried not to have to bathe too often, only doing a quick sponge bath after their morning workouts so as to preserve the water for other times. The way Roslyn's neck felt, she definitely needed a full bath and she was very happy to see that Tiffany had enough water warming over the brazier for a full bath. She tipped the cauldron over and it spilled into the large wooden tub, steam rising from it. From a large bucket beside the tub she scooped cold water into the tub until it was just bearable before casting aside her clothes and climbing into the tub.

She laid back in the tub and closed her eyes, letting her mind wander. She thought about what would happen once she met her mother's family. Would they greet her warmly? Would they accept her? She was really nervous about meeting her family, though it was something she tried not to think about lately. She felt the nervousness as a sore stomach and tried to think of other things, like what the weather would be like there. It would most likely be winter, so she was glad that Captain Heath had left a group of cabins on the land that they had bought for the Crown. The warmth charms would definitely help them in their building efforts.

She found herself dozing off in the tub, but her neck finally felt better so she decided to finally get out. She wrapped herself in a towel and grabbed her clothes before peeking out the door. There was no one there, so she made for her room.

"Roslyn," she heard Rafi say from down the hall as she reached her door. She turned around to see him coming out of his room down the hall.

"Oh hey Rafi," she said nonchalantly.

"Missed you at practice this morning," he told her, taking a couple of steps forward.

"Don't Rafi," she told him quietly. "We agreed to end our relationship six months ago."

"And what if I regret it?" she heard him say quietly.

She looked warily at him for that and said, "Why now, Rafi? You had the whole time before we left to say something."

"I took you out, I spent time with you outside of weapons practice. I thought showing the interest would still be enough."

"I thought you were just trying to repair our friend-ship. We had not seen each other since that day we ended it."

"Is that all you want?" Rafi asked her, "Friendship?"

"I don't know what to tell you," Roslyn said, "We were great friends before we slept together, I was hoping we could go back to that. I just want to focus on this quest right now."

"Along with Captain Heath, hm?"

Roslyn stood up straighter and narrowed her eyes at him.

"Excuse me?" she said with venom in her voice. She saw him flinch and knew he regretted saying it. "Captain Heath and I are friends, nothing more. If I ever decide to share my body with him or anyone else, it will be none of your concern, do you understand?"

Rafi nodded sheepishly and said meekly, "I'm sorry," before going back into his room.

Shaking slightly with anger Roslyn turned and went into her own room.

***

It took her several hours of meditation, and a rant to Tiffany, before Roslyn was calm enough to join the group for supper. It was during the meal, Roslyn sitting as far away from Rafi as she could, that she mentioned to Heath that she had come up with something that would light their path ahead better than an oil lantern on the prow.

Oswick, who was sitting beside her, looked intrigued. "Like what?" he asked her.

"I will show you tonight once the sun is gone," she told them. "I just thought this would make the journey a little easier for all of us."

"I welcome anything that will ease the journey," Heath told her with a nod.
"Great, when darkness falls meet me on the deck,"
Roslyn told them. She had finished eating as much as she could, still a little angry at Rafi and unable to stomach much more. She pushed away from
the table and stood up, unable to look down the table. "I will see you."

As she walked away she missed the look that was exchanged between
Oswick and Rafi; Oswick had told Rafi not to say anything yet, but now he
knew from Roslyn's awkwardness that Rafi had gone against his advice. A
few minutes later Oswick excused himself and went to Roslyn in her room.

"I am really not in the mood to talk to anyone," came the response to his
knock.

"It's Oswick," he spoke up. A moment later the door opened and Roslyn
beckoned him inside.

"What is it Os?"

"Are you OK?" he asked her, a real look of concern on his face. "What did
Rafi say to you?"

"You knew about us?" she asked him.

"Of course I did," Oswick scoffed. "It was not completely obvious, so you
don't have to worry. I found out one night after one of our card games, when
Rafi offered to walk you home. I ended up leaving shortly after you, and I
came across the two of you kissing in an alley. I did not say anything, it was
none of my business; but now I am worried about you. You are my friend,
more like a sister really, and I would be as worried about my own sisters as I
am about you."

"Thank you, Os," she told him, truly grateful for his concern. "I am fine. It
really is none of his business who I have a relationship with now. He accused
me of being...I don't know, attracted?...to Heath. I got angry and made him
regret it."

"Are you attracted to Heath?" Oswick asked, crossing his arms in front of
his chest and regarding her as she had seen him regard his sister when he was
fact checking things.

"That is really irrelevant," she told him. "I am not going to compromise
this quest in any way. Believe me when I say that I will not make a move on
the Captain."

"You making a move is irrelevant," Oswick told her. "I can tell Heath is
attracted to you. So can Rafi, clearly. What if he makes the first move?"

"Honestly I don't know, Os. I don't know what to expect from Heath."

"And what about Kavan?"

"Now I wouldn't mind kissing him," she half-joked. She
certainly enjoyed watching him walk away. "But I think he is too proprie-
tary to do anything."

Oswick chuckled as he shook his head. "So would you make the first move on Kavan?"

Roslyn shook her head. "No, I would not. At least not if I can help it."

"Well, I know you can handle your liquor well enough, so I agree with you. However, circumstances can change. Just be careful, OK?"

Roslyn hugged him, thankful for his friendship. "Thank you Os," she told him. "What would I do without you?"

"Your life would be miserable," he said with all seriousness, earning a laugh from her. "And boring, really."

"Too true," she told him, and she kissed him on the cheek. "Now go, so I can prepare for tonight."

"Yes, your magic show for the Captain. Will you tell me what it is?"

"Nope," she replied with a smile. "You will just have to wait and see."

Oswick held his hands up in surrender and went to leave the room.

"Thank you, Os," she said again. "You are a true friend."

Oswick ducked his head in embarrassment and nodded before closing the door behind him.

Roslyn had to meditate some more before she was calm enough to go out on the deck once the sky was dark enough. Heath and the others were waiting for her on the deck. Without a word to anyone she threw the crystals up into the air where they levitated above the ship. With a flick of her wrist they spread out in front of the ship, the first one being two hundred yards ahead and the rest twenty-five yards behind the next in a triangular shape in front of the three ships; each crystal shone with immense light.

"That is spectacular," Heath commented, almost breath-less by the beauty of the light against the ice below. "This will help us immensely with avoiding icebergs," he said next. "Thank you, Roslyn."

Selene the cat looked up with wide eyes at the crystals in the sky, her pupils wide. She batted at the lights but could not reach them, meowing at them.

"You are my friends, and my people," she told him.

"Whatever I can do to ensure your safety I will. You know how much this mission means to me."

"I do," Heath nodded gravely. "I still thank you. My men will appreciate it."

It was then that Roslyn heard a few cheers from the other ships so she looked and saw the men in the Crow's Nests cheering for the light she had given them. She gave a flourished bow and said with a smile, "Who is in need of a drink right now?"

They went back down to the galley together and opened another cask of ale. Roslyn sat next to Oswick, with Kavan finding a seat on her other side. Thankfully Rafi remained far down the table as they started joking around and telling stories.

Kavan leaned over to talk to her, asking, "Is everything all right?"

Oswick heard and gave him an appraising glance before he took a drink and turned to talk to Captain Heath.

"What do you mean?" Roslyn asked Kavan.

"I was up the hallway earlier," he whispered to her. "If he bothers you again..."

She nearly spit out her drink, but she hid the motion with a laugh. "Oh gods," she said. "Do you not think I can take care of myself?"

"Oh, I know you can; but when it comes to you, I would not mind stepping in to protect you."

"My dear Master-at-Arms," she whispered back, "you surprise me. And I thank you."

"So tell me about Oswick some more," Kavan said a little louder. "How long have you known each other?"

Since Oswick had not been with them at the palace, and Kavan rarely had any interaction with the man outside of their weapons practice in the mornings, the Master of Arms had not had much time to get to know the merchant.

"I've known Roslyn since we were children," Oswick answered him, leaning around Roslyn to talk to Kavan. "She's like one of my own sisters."

"How many sisters do you have?"

"Three," Oswick told him. "One older, two younger. No brothers."

"Ah, I understand now," Kavan said as he took another drink. He found that his pint was empty and noticed the other two looking disappointedly at their own pints. "Shall I get us some more?"

Without saying anything they both handed him their pints, and they all started laughing as he tried to hold all three. "Cook!" Kavan yelled, putting the pints down on the table in front of them. "Another round!"

Chapter Thirteen

Roslyn got out of bed as there came a shout from above. She grabbed a coat and hurried up on deck. She met Captain Heath coming out of his own room and together they raced to the prow. Ahead of them lay a large sheet of ice that spanned quite a distance ahead and in either direction. Captain Heath used his whistle for a few trills and the sailors on all three ships started pulling in the sails so they would stop, and they lowered their anchors.

"I was afraid of this," Heath commented. "An ice sheet."

"Can we go around?" Roslyn asked him, but he shook his head in response.

"I can get us through," Heath told her. "It might take a few hours but going around would take several days."

Roslyn watched as a few of his sailors started to bring over a thick rope with a harness attached to it. Heath put the harness on and ordered them to lower him down into the water.

"Wait, what?!" Roslyn exclaimed as she grabbed hold of Heath's sleeve. Selene had arrived on the deck and was meowing her worry as her friend put the harness on.

"Not to worry, my magic works best when I am in the water. With your heat charm I should be better off than the last time I had to do this," Heath assured her.

Roslyn looked at one of the other sailors who told her, "He had hypothermia. Thankfully he pulled through."

"Gods, Heath, what if I could not have made those charms?" she wanted to know as he started over the railing.

"I would expect you to keep me warm after," Heath told her with a wink, earning a blush from her and a laugh from his men. "Lower me down now, men." He scratched Selene's head before he descended.

Roslyn watched him descend into the water until he was submerged up to his chest; the rope kept him aloft. Selene jumped up onto the rail and continued to meow her worry. Minutes went by until Roslyn noticed waves coming from behind them and pushing up against the ice sheet. The ship started rocking from the waves and Roslyn looked over the side to see Heath being pushed around a lot by the waves he was causing. She looked at the sailors and could tell they were straining, so she reached out with her magic and settled him in one spot with the waves stopping before they hit him.

Startled at the lack of movement Heath looked up to see Roslyn looking over the side, a look of concentration on her face. He nodded his thanks to her and refocused on the task at hand.

Minutes later the rest of Roslyn's group joined her at the prow, watching as the waves hit the ice sheet. The waves were growing stronger now and the ice sheet was starting to break apart. After several more minutes there was now a trench of sorts through the ice sheet. Heath used his whistle to trill off a command, and the sailors hurried about to unfurl the sails and raise the anchor. Selene was still meowing her concern, this time from the deck.

With a jolt their ship started forward again, and with them went the waves that continued to beat at the ice sheet and causing it to break apart more. Heath stayed in the water the whole time it took to get through the ice sheet, with Roslyn using her magic to hold him still. Finally their ships were clear of the ice sheet and the sailors hauled Heath back up.

"Thank you," Heath told Roslyn breathlessly as soon as one of his sailors brought him a towel. "You made it much easier to concentrate."

"I was worried you would bash your brains out on the side of your ship," she told him with a smile. "Couldn't have that, could we?"

Heath laughed and excused himself to change into dry clothes, Selene following after him.

***

They continued in their routine as their journey progressed, and finally they saw an end to the ice floes they had been traveling through, faster than what Heath had anticipated. He told Roslyn that her magical crystals and the heat charms were what made the journey faster, and Roslyn was happy to have made their journey that much easier.

***

One morning after they had cleared the last of the ice floats Roslyn came up onto the deck and found Aidan in the Crow's Nest. During the voyage he had asked the sailors to teach him the ways of the ship to keep him occupied. He was no longer pale but had some colour to him, and he looked like he had actually gained some weight during the voyage.

"Anything on the horizon?" Roslyn called up to him.

"Nothing!"

A Quest for Her Roots

Maybe she could help speed things up. With a spell she called the winds to their sails and with a jerk the ships started to go faster south.

Heath joined her, casting a glance at the sails. "Your work I presume?"

"Just a small spell, redirecting the wind," she told him. "Also, I've called in the crystals. No need to let every other sailor on these seas know where we are."

"A wise idea," he said as he inclined his head to her. "I wish you had been here on our first voyage."

She smiled widely at him and followed him over to the area where they did their weapons practice. Aidan came down from the Crow's Nest, replaced by another sailor, and Roslyn was surprised by Aidan's energy during the training. When it was over she congratulated Aidan on how well he did, and she and Tiffany went to go clean up before breakfast.

The next few days continued like that until one morning four days later, before their practice session, when Aidan called out, "Land!"

Everyone hurried to the bow of the ship trying to see what Aidan had. There on the horizon was a sliver of land.

Captain Heath appeared next to Roslyn and he said, "We should make landfall by this afternoon it would seem."

Heath noticed that Roslyn seemed agitated. "Is something wrong?"

"I cannot keep the wind up much longer," she told him. "It has really drained me."

"Then stop it. We are almost there, you do not need to continue this," he advised her, worry in his voice. "You have done more than enough."

With a nod the sails dropped some, but there was already a good breeze bringing them south without her help.

"Go get some rest," Heath told her. "Sleep the rest of the day, hm?"

She nodded again and went back to her room after a word with Tiffany.

It was almost nightfall when Tiffany awoke her.

"We just weighed anchor off of the coast," Tiffany told her. "The Captain wants to wait here until sunlight."

"I will defer to Heath's experience," Roslyn mumbled. "Goodnight," she managed to say before falling back asleep.

***

The next morning Roslyn was up before dawn standing at the bow of the ship looking at the continent in front of her. There was a cliff face, with a small beach and what looked like an old stone staircase leading to the top of the cliff. A light dusting of snow lay on the beach and the stairs.

"This is where we first landed," Heath told her. She flinched, for she had not realized he was there. "The land we bought for the King is over half a day's walk from here."

"Those stairs look like they could be slippery," Roslyn mentioned.

"What, you can't fix that?" he asked her in mock astonishment.

"What would you do if I was not here?" she asked him with a serious tone in her voice.

"Wait until spring?" he retorted with a smile. "We should not have been here for another week. There would have been more snow by then, Roz. This is good. We have more time to prepare the settlement before the deep cold settles in."

"All right, get me on the shore and I will thaw those steps," she told him.

"Are you good for it now? Yesterday you did not look well," he asked her, looking at her with worry in his green eyes. She kind of liked him worrying about her.

"With the wind spell gone and the sleep I have had, I am good," she assured him. "I would like to sleep on land tonight," she added.

"Very well," Heath said with a bow. "The first skiff is yours, Roslyn."

As they lowered the skiff down into the water, Roslyn had to try to talk herself into it. The water spraying over the side was cold and the wind was fierce, but she would do what she could to help their quest along. Kavan and Oswick went with her, along with a few of Heath's sailors to man the skiff. Once they were on the beach Roslyn headed for the stairs, reaching out with her magic to thaw the ice. They started unloading the rest of the ships, the soldiers joining her on the beach. Many of them thanked her for the warm and safe journey, but all she could do was smile and nod while melting the ice.

She was finally on the top of the cliff looking down at the ships, skeleton crews left on all three. Captain Heath–with Selene in hand--, Rafi, Oswick, Kavan, Tiffany and Aidan were the last ones up the stairs. All of their supplies had been loaded onto carts, and the few horses they had brought with them were eager to be on land again.

"By nightfall?" she asked Heath.

"We will be at our new home by nightfall," he assured her.

"What are we waiting for?" she asked them, looking out over the couple hundred people waiting for them ahead of her. "Captain Heath, you lead the way."

"It's a good thing the orc bands are all in the south by now," Heath commented. "Our group would be ripe for the picking for that lot since we are not of the Clans. We had to fend off a few small incursions while we were building the cabins."

"The palisade will definitely be the first thing we build," Roslyn told him. "I will put a protection barrier around the area until it is finished."

Roslyn chose to walk her horse, which she had named Sage, alongside her people. Tiffany followed suit. The rest of the horses were being used to pull the wagons of supplies so riding while the rest of the expedition walked was out of the question for Roslyn.

A Quest for Her Roots

The countryside was full of trees, but there were clear paths, or roads, worn into the landscape. Heath told Roslyn that the road heading inland to the south was heading in the direction they needed to go, so they followed them.

"We should send some scouts out, just in case," Heath told Roslyn. "Never hurts to be careful." Roslyn gave permission for scouts to go out and she watched as a couple of the soldiers rode off on a couple of the spare horses they had brought with them.

Since the sun set earlier in the winter they were not at the cabins Heath's people had left behind when the sun started to descend. Thanks to Roslyn's charms her people were comfort-able, but she still wanted to get to their new home that night; so they pressed on, using her magic crystals to light their path. She figured if anyone saw how big their party was they would not attack, and if they were friendly they would go to their clan and tell of their arrival.

Roslyn did not know what time it was when they came upon the cabins that marked their land. There were ten wood log cabins, each able to uncomfortably hold ten people. Several tents had to be erected, but with the charms Roslyn had made, the few who had to sleep in tents that night were not angry over it.

Roslyn, Tiffany, as well as Oswick, Kavan, Heath and his two Lieutenants, Rafi, and Aidan shared one cabin. As soon as Roslyn entered she used her magic to cleanse the cabin and helped get the fire in the hearth going. A watch was set up and finally Roslyn felt comfortable enough to sleep in her shared bed with Tiffany.

***

Kavan watched as Roslyn helped the soldiers and the sailors cut down trees. She got right in on the action, helping with the saws and holding the ropes as they directed the trees to fall. He knew that being a princess had been very different for her, but she had struggled against the restraints of the nobility and actually broke through to change people's opinions. He knew that by the time they had left the capital she was happier being there, more comfortable with who she was and with those around her. He could tell that she was enjoying herself getting her hands dirty by helping out, and it certainly helped the men like their princess more. She was not a stuck-up noble, she had gone to a university among other mage's from all walks of life, she enjoyed getting dirty and helping the soldiers with the building.

This was their new home for who knew how long. It meant a lot to the soldiers that their princess was helping them build their new home and Kavan had heard them talking about her. She was their princess, she cared about them--they would follow her anywhere.

Kavan smiled when Roslyn noticed him watching her, a noticeable blush on her cheeks. She had wood chips stuck in her hair and mud on her clothes, but she looked as beautiful as ever. "We are making good progress," Kavan told her. "This will be a real home before we know it."

"I hope so. I could use a nice bath," she commented with a laugh, adding, "I'm starting to smell like a pine tree."

Chapter Fourteen

Over the next fortnight they worked hard to build a palisade around the cabins. They felled a lot of trees, Heath and his sailors helping to carve the trunks into planks to be used. Thankfully the scouts that patrolled the area saw no orcs or anything else dangerous during the time it took to build the palisade, nor did they see any clansmen yet. During the time the palisade was being built they also worked to build a large communal building where the kitchens would be. A latrine was also built until they could get plumbing started in the spring, and Roslyn put warming charms around it to keep people warm while they relieved themselves. The blacksmiths were hard at work getting nails made, as well as hinges and locks for the new buildings.

Roslyn, Tiffany and Maeve were the only three females, so they were housed together. Oswick, and Rafi were in another cabin next to them; Heath, Jackson and Aidan were in the cabin on the other side. Barracks were erected after the palisade, and the soldiers happily moved into there after the first few weeks in either tents or the cabins. With the palisade up they could all sleep a little easier.

Several mornings after the palisade was completed Roslyn watched the sun rise on the walkway around the palisade. She had a thick cloak over her shoulders to ward off the cold for she had taken off her warmth charm that morning. Heath joined her there, a steaming cup of a special drink he drank in the mornings to help him wake up in his hands. Selene followed at his heels.

"I am sending Jackson with a group of soldiers back to where we left the ships so they can build a small outpost and a wharf where we can properly dock the ships," he told her as he tentatively sipped his drink.

"We should set up patrols between the outposts," she commented. "We will need more horses for that."

"I will take you to the Wolf Clan today," Heath told her. "I am surprised no one has come to visit us yet."

"They have been watching," she told him, pointing to the tree line. "Two men in furs have been there since I got up here."

Heath stiffened and squinted against the growing light but he did see two figures, about a hundred feet away from the wall at the tree line.

"Good eye," Heath commented, taking a larger sip of his drink. Selene jumped up onto the side of the palisade and started clawing up the wood. Roslyn and Heath watched her with smiles, chuckling together.

"I think we should start patrols around the compound today," Roslyn said with a sigh. "I will talk to Aidan about drawing up a schedule."

"After breakfast I will take you to the Wolf Clan," Heath reminded her. She nodded her head and went over to the stairway, heading for the Dining Hall for breakfast. She knew she would find Aidan there already for he was always an early riser.

They had chosen to wait until they were settled before having another practice session, but Roslyn thought they should build a place to do so if the weather got as cold as Heath said it would. She was not looking forward to the snow that threatened in the dark clouds above them.

She found that Kavan was already at breakfast as well, sitting with Aidan, so she told him about the men watching and how Heath wanted to take her to the Wolf Clan that day.

"We also should send back one of the ships for more supplies and workers if we are to build a trade city here," Kavan told her. "We should complete the compound before it gets any colder."

"The Hall is the only building we are missing," she told him, and on cue Aidan pulled the blueprints out of his bag and put them on the table in front of him.

"Thank you, Aidan," she told him with a smile. "The Hall is meant to be our house as well as our offices."

"We should have a barn somewhere too," Aidan mentioned. "We should be able to buy some livestock from the Clans. Once spring comes we will have fields to plough so we will need oxen for that."

"The Hall and a barn...we will put a building here next to the barracks for a barn, ok? It will have a paddock for the horses too." Her mind made up, she got up to go get a plate of food from the cooks. She returned to Kavan and Aidan to find that Oswick and Rafi had joined them.

"Good morning, Oswick, Rafi," she greeted them with a smile. "Would you like to join us on our excursion to the Wolf Clan today?"

Rafi, who had been rubbing the sleep out of his eyes, looked up at her with a sleepy smile and looked at Oswick. "What do you think?" he asked him.

Oswick shrugged and said, "Will we have to walk?"

"No, I think we can take a couple of the extra horses for this excursion," she told them with a chuckle. "We are hoping to be able to buy some horses today though."

"Might as well get to know the countryside," Heath commented as he sat down with them, his plate of steaming food set before him. "If we stay here it will be best to know the surrounding area."

"Each of us should spend time on patrol to get to know the area too," Roslyn added. "Aidan, we should get a map done of the villages as well."

Aidan sighed and said, "I wish I brought some scribes with me. I cannot do everything Roz."

Roslyn laughed at that, for she knew he was serious but she was glad that he was comfortable enough with her to tell her that.

"Tell you what, Maeve is going to be taking a ship back home for supplies and builders, how about you make a request for some scribes?" Roslyn asked him, slinging an arm around his shoulders and hugging him. "If I start to overwhelm you with requests, please tell me."

"I appreciate it. I will."

"Good. However, until you have scribes, you will still have to do it," she teased him. He stuck his tongue out at her and went back to writing his schedules.

"It will probably take Maeve longer to get there and back though," Heath commented. "Without you on board," he added.

"I will suggest we bring a few more mages. Her crew will still have the charms, and I can probably do a wind charm. She can take the light crystals too."

Heath nodded, accepting her options. "It might be fine."

"If one mage can do all that you can, imagine what having more than one would accomplish here," Oswick commented. "I wonder what the Clans Shaman's are like."

"Probably just like me, I would assume," Roslyn told him. "Magic should come from the same place no matter what continent, but again I do not know anything about the magic of the Shamans. I was born here but I learned how to use my magic back home. I wonder what I could learn here?"

"Maybe we could meet with the shaman today when we go visit the Wolf Clan," Heath commented. "She might be your aunt after all."

"Worth a try at least. I will go get ready. Has anyone seen Tiffany yet?" Roslyn inquired of the group.

"She was doing stretches in front of her cabin when we came here," Rafi told her. "Looked like she was going to go for a run around the compound."

"I will see if I can find her. We will meet at the South Gate in an hour."

She left the Dining Hall by the south entrance. In front of her was the empty area where The Hall would be built. To her left were the two rows of ten cabins, and the palisade wall beyond the cabins. To her right was the barracks, the soldiers only just coming awake and heading for the Dining Hall for their breakfast. After the weeks at sea on the different ships the soldiers were coming up with a camaraderie now between them, and Roslyn found that she liked it. As the soldiers saw her they declined their heads in greeting to her and continued on their way to the Dining Hall.

Roslyn found Tiffany jogging around the walkway of the palisade. She made up her mind that every morning she would try to accompany Tiffany on this jog for it would do her good to get out so early and physically exert herself. She laughed at that thought but knew it was true. At least until the snow came. Maybe she should have a special heated building just for exercising. She would talk to Aidan about it later.

"Sorry to interrupt your run," Roslyn said to Tiffany when she caught up with her. "A group of us are heading out to visit the Wolf Clan, I thought you might like to join us."

Tiffany nodded as she came to a stop at the south wall. "I will go get breakfast now."

"We will meet at the South Gate in an hour," Roslyn called after Tiffany as she jogged away.

As Roslyn headed back to their cabin she looked around and watched as the rest of the expedition were starting their day. The sailors who had joined them at the compound were helping carve wood to be used for building; all of them still wore their warmth charms so none of them wore any warm clothes still. The blacksmith's forge in front of the North Gate was fired up and smoking, the three blacksmiths starting their work for another day. Kavan was coming from his cabin too.

An hour later Tiffany joined her on the walk to the South Gate to meet the group. She had with her a pack of food for the journey.

"I thought a picnic might be nice today," Tiffany told her when Roslyn raised an eyebrow at her.

"If it doesn't snow first," Roslyn retorted, casting an uneasy look at the dark clouds above them. "We will be lucky if it doesn't."

"With our warmth charms we should be fine," Tiffany said. "Come on, Roslyn, you get to meet the rest of your family today! A little snow is not going to hamper this day."

Heath and Rafi were the only ones at the South Gate when they got there so they had to wait a few more minutes for the rest of the group to join them. Kavan approached with a few guards trailing behind him.

"Oh good, you thought to bring a guard," Roslyn told Kavan with a chuckle. "I was expecting our group would look fearsome enough."

"Kavan is right," Heath broke in before the Arms Master could answer. "The orc bands should be in the south with the winter but we can never be too careful; there are still wolves. Does everyone else have a weapon on them?"

It took a few more minutes of waiting while the group broke off to go grab their weapons. Roslyn already had her sword at her waist, and several daggers hidden on her person. Tiffany came back with her sword, which had been a gift from Roslyn. Rafi had a sword and his bow and arrows; Oswick had one of the new pistols that were starting to become popular with the army as well as his sword. Aidan, Heath and Kavan were already armed.

Finally they were all ready to go, so they all mounted their respective horses and Heath led the way through the South Gate. Soldiers closed it behind them.

The sailors had cleared a large area of forest when they had built the cabins a year ago. Most were deciduous trees with a handful of coniferous trees, but they were tall. The path Heath led them on went through the rest of the forest and brought them out to a flat plain on the other side with long grass. On the other side of the plain was a valley, Heath told them, and he smiled at Roslyn when he said, "And the Wolf Clan makes the valley their home."

With the clouds above them it was hard to tell what time of day it was when they reached the valley, but by the grumble of her stomach Roslyn figured it was probably late in the afternoon. They had already stopped to eat the food that Tiffany had brought with her, so they had nothing left to ease their stomach pangs. Thankfully it was an uneventful journey with only the landscape to distract them.

Heath halted at the top of the path that led down into the valley and dismounted before beckoning to Roslyn. The rest of the group dismounted and Roslyn went to stand next to Heath. She gasped as she saw the beauty of the valley below her. On the other side of the valley there were waterfalls coming down from a small mountain and into the valley below where the water made a large pool that turned into a river. The river in turn flowed out the other side of the valley. There was an abundance of trees, though most of them had lost their leaves for the winter; pine trees were still a stark green in the winter cold.

The village below was made up of wooden log cabins, smoke coming out of chimneys. There were a few farm buildings further down the valley where Roslyn could see animals milling about in fenced off areas.

"Thank you, Heath," Roslyn whispered to the sailor as Kavan started walking down the path into the valley. The rest followed, leading their horses.

"For what?" he looked at her with surprise.

"For fulfilling your mission," she told him. "And bring-ing us here."

"It was a pleasure to travel alongside you," he leaned in and whispered to her. "Come on, we're so close now."

Kavan waited for her a little down the path. He pulled her into a side hug as they walked. "How are you feeling?" he asked her.

"Anxious," she told him truthfully. "I wonder what they are like. Do you think they'll like me?"

"Who wouldn't like you?" Kavan told her. "You're a people's princess, Roslyn. You cared about your soldiers and sailors enough to make those charms, and those light crystals. They saw that, and let me tell you, all of the soldiers with us are loyal to you."

"Really?"

"I've heard them talking about you. They've seen how hard you have worked during the last few days, and they know the charms came from you. They like you."

"Well, I'm glad."

He squeezed her shoulder quickly before letting go. His gaze fell on Rafi who was walking just a little behind them. Kavan turned back to Roslyn and said, "I'm surprised you invited him along."

"It is time to get back to being friends," Roslyn told him. "He knows that he was wrong, and hopefully that will be the end of it."

"Wise and beautiful, you drink and swear...my kind of princess," Kavan said as he winked at her.

Roslyn playfully punched his shoulder and quickened her pace to walk next to Tiffany, trying to hide the blush on her cheeks.

They were coming to the bottom of the trail that ended at a tall wooden fence with a large two sided gate when the gate swung outwards and a group of people came out of the village to meet them. Heath was at the front now and he greeted them, clasping hands with one of the women who was dressed in colourful robes. Her hair was red like everyone else's, curly, her skin as dark as the rest of the village. It was only the colour of her eyes, one blue and one green, that told Roslyn who this woman was: the Clan's Shaman, who was most likely her aunt.

Heath was beckoning Roslyn to come forward now, and as she came near the people from the village grew quiet. The shaman's eyes widened with surprise at first but she smiled.

"You have returned, Roslyn."

"Are you my aunt?" Roslyn asked her.

The woman shook her head and pulled a necklace out from under her robes. Roslyn grabbed hold of her own necklace, her mind racing.

"My name is Amelia," the shaman told her. "I am your--"

"Mother," Roslyn interrupted her. "That can't...father said you could not have survived the fire."

Amelia smiled sadly, "I would not have if it were not for my brothers. My one brother has magic as I do, and he protected us from the flames all night. It was not until the fire was completely out two days later and my family had dug us out that I discovered my husband and my child had already left."

Kavan came over and held his friend's hand as this new revelation was sinking in.

"You should know," Amelia continued, "That three days after you were born I gave birth to your twin sister."

"My twin...just hold on a moment," Roslyn turned away from her mother and closed her eyes, rubbing her temples with her fingers as her mind and heart raced. She felt so many emotions all at once, anger and frustration at not being able to grow up with her mother, confusion at finding out that not only was her mother alive but she had a twin sister as well, and finally grief for the life that had been lost for both herself and her father.

Her friends gathered around her, Tiffany the first to reach out and put a comforting hand on her shoulder. Rafi followed next, until the whole group was lending her their strength by their touch. The three soldiers who were their guards stood back and out of the way.

"Her name is Cassidy," Amelia told her. "Your identical twin sister."

"Another Roslyn?" Kavan joked. "I am not sure I can handle another one like you."

Roslyn held back a laugh at that. She opened her eyes and looked at each of her friends before turning to look at her mother. She broke apart from their hold and went to hug her mother, who started to cry as she held her. Roslyn found herself crying as well.

An older man with grey in his red hair standing behind Amelia cleared his throat. Roslyn and Amelia looked at him and Amelia smiled.

"Roslyn, this is your grandfather, Chief Rotho," Amelia introduced them.

Chief Rotho held open his arms and Roslyn embraced him as well.

"Come, granddaughter, let us show you your clan," Chief Rotho said and he beckoned for the others to follow as he led them to the largest building in the village.

"This is the Chief's house," her grandfather told her as they approached the large double doors of the building. "You will be our guest here tonight?"

"Yes, I think I would definitely like to stay the night," Roslyn told him as she wiped away more tears.

"Best send a messenger back to the compound," Heath commented. "So no one worries. I will go." Roslyn nodded her head and watched as he mounted his horse and rode back up the path out of the valley. One of the other men with Rotho offered to take their horses to their stables.

Rotho led them into the Chief's House and bade them to sit in front of the hearth.

Roslyn's nose flared with the smell of incense, and the smell of the furs hanging on the walls. The floor was wood but there was a small fur rug in front of the hearth and a larger rug on the other side of the room that had pillows arranged in a circle as if it was a gathering place. To the right of the hearth was a large table where several people were sitting, gazing curiously at her and her companions. On the other side of the table was a door, and from the smells wafting out of there she figured it led to the kitchen.

"Cassidy is out on a hunt," Rotho told Roslyn when he saw her looking around at the people who were sitting at the table. "Let me introduce you to the rest of your family."

Rotho beckoned to the teenagers who sat at the table.

They were giving Roslyn a strange look, but once Rotho told them her name they relaxed.

"This is Roslyn, grandchildren," Rotho told them. "Cassidy's twin sister. She has come home finally."

Amelia joined them with a group of men who seemed to be in their early forties. One of them was holding her mother's hand.

"Roslyn, I would like you to meet your step-father," Amelia told her. "This is McKenna."

"I am honoured to meet you," McKenna said with a bowed head. "I had hoped this day would come in my lifetime." McKenna was taller than her mother, with his hair hanging to his shoulders. He was well muscled and from the look he gave her mother she knew that he loved her. His eyes were a dark blue and there seemed to be a hint of wit within them.

"Father remarried as well," Roslyn told her. "He is now king."

Amelia looked troubled by that, "What happened for your father to be made king? He was not even close to the throne."

"A great sickness went through the capital last year. Since we lived so far north we were not touched by it, but the king and his family died leaving my father the only one of royal blood able to take the throne."

Amelia shook her head in wonder and said, "Lucius would make a great king."

"These two youths here are your brothers," Amelia beckoned to two of the teenaged boys sitting at the table.

They stood up and came to her, shy smiles on their faces. They were almost as tall as Roslyn was with the same bright red curls as their mother's, but one of them had two blue eyes and the other's eyes were green.

"Quinn," the slender one of the two with the blue eyes nodded as Amelia said his name, "and Oko," that was the more barrel-chested green eyed youth.

"We have two daughters as well, but they are with Cassidy on the hunt," McKenna told her. "They should be back by nightfall."

"I have two younger sisters and two brothers," Roslyn told Amelia.

"I am glad that Lucius found happiness again. It took me two years of waiting until we learned that the pirates had taken control of the seas, effectively cutting off any hope of your father's return."

"He thought you were dead," Roslyn's words were no more than a whisper at first. She cleared her throat and repeated it, adding, "If he had known you were still alive, and that there was another child he would have done everything he could to get back to you.

Amelia squeezed her hand and said, "I know. We cannot change what happened. We can only move forward."

"These are your uncles," Amelia told her, indicating the other men with her. "Tanner, Martin, Joss and Grigori. My sister, Anna, is currently in another village helping with a birth."

"Some of these youngsters are mine," Tanner told her, indicating the other youths and maidens at the table. "A couple are Martin's. Joss and Grigori do not have families."

"Come," Rotho said. "I think it is time for some food, hm?"

Someone brought out more pillows for them to sit on in front of the hearth and then a steaming hot stew was brought out. There was a good amount of people sitting on the floor and conversing while eating that at first Roslyn was overwhelmed. She remembered that this was the way of the Clan, and she relaxed a bit. She was with family--she was with her mother!

A couple hours later Heath returned after relaying his message back to their compound that they were going to stay the night in the village--since it had just been him he had been able to make the journey in less than half the time it had taken them all to travel out there. Rotho greeted him with a hearty smile and ordered some more food be brought out for the sailor.

Heath managed to find a seat next to Roslyn and he asked her, "What did I miss?"

"Not a whole lot, really. I have two younger brothers AND two younger sisters. The girls are out on the hunt with Cassidy. Everyone here is related to me."

"Except us," Kavan told her with a wink. Oswick, Rafi and the rest of their friends raised their wooden mugs filled with cider in a toast to that.

Roslyn was thinking though of what she would be like if she had grown up there in Jay'Al. Jay'Al was a matriarchal society and women had a lot more freedom. There was no need for dresses or gowns here, all of the women she saw wore breeches or trousers. Roslyn thought of those girls, Rita and her sisters and cousin, and how they would have a better future now because of her. It was a confusing thing to think about, but she was glad that she did grow up in Ellsgrove and was able to make such a difference in the lives of the noblewomen there. She still felt like she was robbed of growing up with her birth mother and twin sister though, and it was not a nice feeling.

Later on Roslyn mentioned to her grandfather about how they had hoped to buy trained horses for their soldiers, and he smiled broadly at her.

"Our Clan boasts some of the best horses on the continent," he told her. "Your Uncle Grigori is the Horse Master. You can talk to him about it."

She approached her Uncle Grigori with a pitcher of cider and offered to fill his cup. His beard was neatly trimmed and his hair cut short, unlike most of the other men who liked to wear their hair longer. Both of his eyes were green.

"Thank you, Roslyn. It is good to finally have you home with us. I loved your father like a brother, and I miss him still," Grigori told her.

"Which of you went into the fire after my mother?" she asked him, curious to find which other family members had magic.

"That would be Tanner and myself," Grigori told her. "I am the uncle with magic. Both of my sisters--of course you know already that they both have magic."

She inclined her head and said that she did. "Thank you," she told him. "It would have taken a lot of bravery to go after her."

"She is my sister," Grigori told her. "Family needs to stick together in hard times."

They both took a drink from their mugs and Roslyn asked him about horses. Grigori smiled, showing a few missing teeth.

"Yes, I can help you with horses. My herds have become rather large. I was going to head to the Market with them in the spring."

"And they have training?"

"The majority of them my men have broken in and trained for riding," he assured her. "That is why they are well sought out in Jay'Al, we work hard with them."

"Would you be willing to sell me some?" she asked him.

"Aye, I think we could come to an agreement. Do you have coin or will there be some kind of trade?"

"Will you accept my coin?"

"Yes, we have started to use coin more in trading since your father was here. The pirates have an outpost on the southern coast, and through them we have a little bit of trade. They hold a monopoly though; since you have come we will have more options. I am looking forward to working with you."

"Thank you, Uncle."

"I will take you to my farm tomorrow morning, hm? You can pick out the horses that you like."

She thanked him again and he inclined his head before moving on to talk to his father.

"How are you doing?" Kavan asked her as he joined her, knocking his wooden cup against hers. "This is nice and cozy, isn't it?"

"Kavan, are you drunk?" she inquired of him, thinking that he could not have possibly drank that much already.

"Do you think this is hard cider?" he asked her. "I think this is hard cider. I'm no good with hard cider."

"Mother, is this hard cider?" she asked her mother. "I think my friend has had too much."

"Yes, it is; and I can see that. We have a cabin for guests next door, I can help you take him there," Amelia said to her, coming over and helping to hold Kavan up.

Roslyn shook her head and said, "Just point me in the right direction and I will get him to his bed."

Amelia pointed out the cabin which was only forty feet away from the front door of the Chief's House. Roslyn nodded and slung Kavan's arm over her shoulders to help keep him up. Her friends had not noticed them leaving. She helped Kavan over to the cabin and through its front door.

She placed him on the bed and went over to the hearth and put logs in it, using her magic to light them. She went back to him and started to get the blankets moved from under him to over him.

"Roslyn?" she heard him say.

"Yes Kavan I am here," she told him, but when she looked down see him sleepily looking up at her.

"You are quite the woman," he said before starting to snore.

"Goodnight Kavan," she whispered in his ear before tucking him in. He was snoring heavily by the time she reached the door.

It was dark out now, and the threatening snow had decided to give way. The Chief's House was still lit up, and she could tell that more people had gathered. She pulled her coat tighter against herself and headed back to her grandfather's house.

She entered the house and was welcomed again by her grandfather who pulled her into a group of people and started introducing her. She did not catch their names really but she shook their hands and said something about being happy to meet them before Amelia pulled her out of Rotho's reach and sat her down next to the hearth with a mug of cold water.

"Drink up," she told her daughter. "No more cider tonight I think."

"Usually I can handle my liqueur," Roslyn told her mother. "I guess I am just not used to hard cider."

"Probably not," her mother said with a smirk. "You got your friend to his bed all right?"

"Of course. I even lit the fire in the hearth so he would be warm."

"Good. Your friends can join him when they are done here."

"Thank you."

"More food will be served soon," Amelia told her. "And I am expecting Cassidy and your sisters to be home soon as well."

Roslyn downed the water and asked for some more. She wanted to be more sober when she met her sister.

Twin sister, she thought to herself. She had an identical twin sister. She wished her father was there. Roslyn had put off sending a magical message to her father until their settlement was more or less complete, but she thought that the next day would be a perfect time to do so.

Roslyn took another mug of water from her mother and went to sit down next to the hearth. Oswick joined her there with his own water. Slowly over the next few minutes the rest of her friends joined her, each with water.

"Where is Kavan?" Oswick asked as he looked around the Great Room. Slowly people had started to leave and it was now mostly only Amelia's family still there.

"He apparently cannot handle hard apple cider," Roslyn told them. "I took him to the Guest House a little while ago."

"Your mother said there would be more food soon,"

Oswick spoke up. "If it is anything like what we had earlier, I think I will enjoy it."

"I am sure it will be a good meal," Tiffany added.

Over the next few minutes the rest of the extended family left the Chief's House, leaving Rotho, Amelia, McKenna and their two sons sitting at the table next to the hearth.

"I fear if we wait for Cassidy, Leona and Sawyer to arrive before we have more food you will be more hungry. I will bring out something small for you to snack on," Amelia told them. "It should not be much longer though before they are home."

Amelia brought out a platter of cheese and smoked meat for them, and it was then that the door to the Chief's house opened. Three people entered, two of them carrying a gutted stag between them.

"Grandfather, mother! We brought a stag home for the village," the older of the three girls spoke up. She tossed her hood back and stopped short at the sight of Roslyn.

"Cassidy," Amelia stepped forward. "Cassidy, your sister has returned home."

The two younger women stopped short and cast their gaze on Roslyn. Her two younger sisters were a good three years younger, each with two multi-coloured eyes. Cassidy looked exactly like Roslyn, though as Roslyn looked at her twin sister she noticed that as her own right eye was blue, Cassidy's right eye was green. They were like a mirror image of each other.

Cassidy did not say a word, she just smiled weakly at her older sister before turning around and leaving her grandfather's house. Roslyn looked at her mother with questioning eyes before her two other younger sister's put the stag down and decided to step forward and offer their hands in greeting.

"I am Leona," the one sister told her. "Do not worry about Cassidy. She is just in shock at your sudden arrival. Give her time."

"I am Sawyer," the other sister spoke up. "Cassidy has always spoken of her wish to meet her twin sister, but I think this was a great surprise for her."

"You two are twins as well?" Roslyn asked them as they sat at the table together. McKenna came forward to take the stag elsewhere.

"No, we are a year apart although we do look very alike, it is only because we are sisters," Leona told her with a smile. "We all have the same eyes at least," she added with a laugh.

"Very true. Why is it that the boys don't have the same eyes?" Roslyn asked them, nodding at their teenage brothers.

"It's a girl thing apparently. None of our uncles have it, only the women," Sawyer told her.

"Do any of you have magic?" she asked them next.

Both of them shook their heads, and Leona said, "Cassidy does though. Do you?"

"I do."

"Interesting," Sawyer said as she glanced at their mother. "Mom would probably want to test you to see how powerful your magic is."

"Do you have a familiar?" Leona asked her.

"A familiar?" Roslyn was confused at the word.

"An animal that helps a magic user in various ways. It is a sort of an extra magical bond with the land."

"I do not have one, no," Roslyn told them.

"Strange. Mother's familiar is a cat. Uncle Grigori's familiar is a crow, and Aunt Anna's is a sparrow. Cassidy's is a pine marten," Leona told her.

"I wonder if you never felt the call of a familiar because you were not taught the ways of our shamans, or how to tap into the magic of Jay'Al," Sawyer reasoned. "Mother can help you with that."

"I would like to hear more about the shamans of our people," Roslyn told her mother as Amelia joined them at the table with bread and slices of smoked meat.

"I figured you would have magic like your sister," Amelia said with a smile. "I have a book that tells the history of the shamans of the Wolf Clan. You may look at it tomorrow."

"Why are we called the Wolf Clan?" Roslyn asked her next. "What are the other clans?"

"There are the Beaver Clan--they live in the marshes to the south-east of us; the Fox Clan, who live on the plains to our south-west; the Bear Clan, who live in the forests to our south-west; and the Hyena Clan in the deserts far to the south; there used to be another clan that lived on the plateau in the centre of Jay'Al but we have not heard from them in a very long time: they were the Dragon Clan. As to how we got our names, the legend tells of The First Six, who were the first Shamans. Each of them called on familiars, and they answered: The Wolf, the Beaver, the Fox, the Bear, the Hyena, and the

Dragon. So from there the people of Jay'Al fell under one of these Clans. Usually the Head Shaman is in the Chief's family."

"So are we descended from the first Shaman who had the wolf familiar?" Roslyn asked her.

"Yes, we are. Now enough of this history lesson for tonight, tell me about where you grew up."

***

Cassidy felt her heart tighten within her chest as she left her grandfather's house. She walked in a daze to the edge of the village where it opened up into the part of the forest that lay within the village walls. She had always known she had a twin out there somewhere, and had always wanted to know her--but to have her suddenly show up out of nowhere was quite a shock.

Her familiar Crick chirped at her from a low hanging branch nearby that was level with her face. Crick reminded her of how she had never felt complete before, and now was the time to figure out if it was because her other half was missing.

"She looks just how I imagined, not just her face but what she wears and styles her hair--could I have dreamt that? A vision of my sister?" she asked Crick as she bent over with her hands on her knees. She was finding it hard to catch her breath.

Crick ran back down the tree and climbed her way up Cassidy's pant leg to rest on her shoulder. She chittered at Cassidy for a moment and Cassidy sighed.

"You are right," Cassidy told her familiar as she straightened, taking a deep breath in and out again. "I will go to her soon."

Chapter Fifteen

Roslyn stared up at the slowly falling snow, the silence of the sleeping village calming. In her hands she held a steaming mug of hot cocoa, a delicacy that came from the Hyena Clan. Roslyn knew that Oswick would want to make a trade agreement with the growers of the cocoa, and he was already talking about a journey south with Rafi.

Her friends had all gone to bed in the guest cabin. Amelia had offered Roslyn the spare room on the main floor of the Chief's House; the Head Shaman usually lived with the Chief since they were always family, so the upstairs rooms were where her mother and siblings slept. Only Amelia, Sawyer and Leona were still awake in the kitchen. Roslyn had mentioned her need for some fresh air and Amelia had handed her the steaming mug and told her to take her time.

Cassidy had not returned yet.

Since Cassidy was of marrying age she had moved into her own house in the village somewhere. Amelia had told Roslyn that Cassidy still spent a lot of time at the Chief's house, so the fact that she had not returned for supper or family communion after had puzzled her. Sawyer and Leona both agreed that it was strange for Cassidy, but reminded them that it still was quite a shock to see Roslyn.

Roslyn sipped the hot cocoa, allowing the warmth and the velvety taste to cheer her up.

Just then a small creature appeared in the empty streets of the village ahead of her, its tiny eyes reflecting some of the lit torches from the Chief's House. Its body was at least fifteen inches long, with its tail adding another seven inches to it. It was too dark to properly see what its colour was.

Behind the creature Cassidy stepped out of the shadows. She drew back her hood so that Roslyn could see her, though Roslyn knew who she was just from her clothes. Her twin sister took a few tentative steps forward, and the creature went over to her and clawed its way up her pant leg to settle around her neck and stare inquisitively at Roslyn.

"Sister, I'm sorry," Cassidy began, "I was in shock at seeing you and needed to compose myself."

"I understand," Roslyn told her, amazed that they sounded so alike. TWINS! she shouted in her mind. "Father believed mother was dead. He had no idea..."

Cassidy closed the distance with outstretched arms and they met in a tight hug, Roslyn being careful not to douse her sister in hot cocoa. The creature around Cassidy's neck squeaked its displeasure but remained where it was.

"What is our father like?" she asked her. "Tell me about him?"

"Come inside and share some hot cocoa with me," Roslyn urged her. "We can talk next to the warm fire of our grandfather."

***

The next morning Roslyn awoke in front of the hearth on a bunch of pillows, her sister Cassidy asleep beside her. Two half-empty cold mugs of cocoa sat on the stones before the hearth. Cassidy's familiar, the creature known as a pine marten, slept curled up at Cassidy's head. In the light from the hearth and the candles their mother had lit for them Roslyn saw the pine marten was a brownish grey colour with a white patch on its chest. It was also a female and she was named Crick.

Sitting at the table on one of the benches was Kavan, who was looking between Roslyn and Cassidy with confusion. Cassidy had given her a pair of her night clothes to change into, a wool that came from something called an alpaca that was very soft; it seemed that Kavan could not tell which one was his friend while they were sleeping

"Good morning, Kavan," Roslyn said as she sat up and stretched. "How is your head feeling?"

"So this is your sister?" he asked her quietly.

"This is Cassidy, yes. You will meet Leona and Sawyer at breakfast probably," she told him.

"I think they are the ones in the kitchen with your mother," he told her. "When I came in I heard them so I just peeked in to see who was there before sitting down."

"Were you watching me sleep?" Roslyn asked him with a smile. He blushed and ducked his head.

"It was just strange to see two of you there," he told her. "I was only here but a few minutes before you awoke."

"Hm..." she stood up and went over to him, saying, "Come, let me introduce you to my other sisters." She grabbed his hand and led him into the kitchen.

Introductions over, Kavan helped them get breakfast ready. Cassidy awoke as the smells wafted out of the kitchen, and so she invited Roslyn to go to her house to find a fresh set of clothing. So they left together as Kavan went to wake up their friends for breakfast.

Cassidy's home was at the edge of the village against the side of the forest. It was a small two room cabin with a kitchen area just off of the great room.

"I haven't done much with the place, no furs or anything yet on the walls, but I plan to add a room for my herbs," Cassidy told her as they entered. "Come, let's find you something to wear."

The traditional clothing of the Wolf Clan in the winter were fur lined deer-skin clothing over linen under-clothes--so if one was inside and got too warm they could take off their lined shirt and have a linen tunic underneath. Most of the leather was the original brown colour but Cassidy had a few that had been dyed different colours. After putting on her linen clothing she donned a set of blue leather fur-lined pants and an over-shirt that was embroidered with white flowers. Cassidy chose a green pair that had brown leaves embroidered on it. Cassidy asked Roslyn if she could teach her how to braid her hair like Roslyn did her own.

By the time they returned to their grandfather's house the rest of Roslyn's companions were sitting around the hearth awaiting breakfast. Kavan was still in the kitchen with Roslyn's mother and other sisters, but as he heard Roslyn's greeting to their friends he came out into the Great Room.

Everyone was staring at them, Tiffany with a smile on her face and the other's with slight confusion.

"Which one is which?" she heard Oswick whisper to Heath.

"The one in blue is Roslyn," Kavan told them, "and the one in green is Cassidy."

"How do you know?" Rafi asked him.

"The eyes. Roslyn's left eye is green and right is blue. Cassidy is the opposite," Kavan responded with a smile to Roslyn. "I'm surprised you didn't see that, Rafi."

Roslyn inhaled slightly at the jab to Rafi. Thankfully Rafi shrugged it off and spoke instead of his desire to eat breakfast.

"Well it is a good thing it is ready," Amelia called from the kitchen. "Come get your plates and take what you want!"

They all sat down for a delightful breakfast feast where they told more of their travel to Jay'Al. As they were starting to clean up their plates Roslyn's uncle Grigori arrived.

"All of us do not need to go out to the farm," Roslyn thought aloud as she put her outer shirt back on--she had taken it off during breakfast because she was too warm. "Tiffany, Oswick and Kavan, would you all come with me to look at horses? The rest of you can stay here and relax."

"Sounds good to me," Heath commented, adding, "I know absolutely nothing about horses."

"Fine by me," Rafi commented as he reclined in front of the hearth.

"You will take the guards with you, right?" Aidan asked Roslyn. "They are waiting outside."

"Shoot, did they have food?"

"Sawyer took them out each a plate," Amelia assured her. "And they slept in the guest quarters last night as well, after I assured them that nothing would happen to you under my roof."

"They are only doing their job, mother," Roslyn said with a smile, glad that the soldiers were still looking out for her even though she was amongst family.

"I will go with you," Cassidy told her. "Uncle has a horse waiting for me," she told Roslyn.

Roslyn nodded with a smile and the group heading out to the horse farm followed Grigori out the door and into a light dusting of snow. The group got their horses and joined Grigori who was waiting with his own horse. Roslyn beckoned for Cassidy to ride behind her and helped her twin sister up. Once everyone was ready they headed out.

"Why could we not have been in the south," Roslyn heard Oswick complain, "I hate the snow, the cold..."

"You have my charm still, right?" she asked him.

"Oh, right, it's in my pocket." Oswick took the charm out of his pocket and put it over his head. He sighed with relief and thanked her for reminding him.

"What is it?" Cassidy inquired of the charm.

"It's a charm to keep the wearer warm," Roslyn told her.

"Indeed? Interesting. I would love to learn that," Cassidy commented.

"You don't have something like it here?" Roslyn was curious as to the differences in the magic.

"No, our use of magic is different, remember?" Cassidy reminded her.

"That is interesting," Tiffany commented. "You were taught how to use your magic so differently."

"Different lands, different uses for magic," Roslyn said with a shrug. "I can probably teach Cassidy a thing or two, and vice-versa."

"Mother mentioned something about taking you to the Clans Shrine later," Cassidy told her. "She can measure your powers there."

"I look forward to it," Roslyn said with a large smile. She turned towards her Uncle Grigori who was leading the group out of the village on a large stallion. "Uncle, what all can you do?"

"Just basic things, really. I got lucky when I saved your mother, honestly. I was able to draw on my brother's strength to help keep the fire off for so long. Any longer though, and none of us would have made it."

A chill ran down Roslyn's spine and she reached a hand back to hold her sister's hand. Cassidy took it and squeezed her hand tightly before her familiar Crick started chattering at something and ran off into the trees. Cassidy laughed and assured everyone that it was normal behaviour for the pine marten and they continued on.

"I had the magic, yes, but I was not interested in it as much as your mother or my other sister was. I had a knack for horses though, and that might be some form of magic but I don't rightly know. I only learned the basics, really, so I could control myself," Grigori told Roslyn as they walked past the last of the houses and followed one of the road paths to the west. "Your mother and aunt both went to learn how to use their magic from the High Shamans in the south."

The snow had covered the trees in glistening white, the sun reflecting off in little sparkles. Roslyn could hear the sound of snow falling from limbs in the forest, and the crispness of their footsteps in the snow. It was beautiful, but at the same time she still disliked the cold.

They rode for half an hour to the west of the village when they came across a wooden fence around a very large pasture filled with horses of all colours. Grigori dismounted and walked up to the fence as the whole herd came to greet him, their breath showing in the air.

Roslyn thought it was so beautiful, the reaction of the herd to Grigori. She watched as the horses tossed their heads and frolicked in the pasture before them.

"This is only part of my herd," Grigori told them. "The ones we have trained are in another pasture."

They all dismounted and continued to walk along the fence, the horses still frolicking along beside them. Finally in the distance they could see a grouping of barns and a house, and beyond that another paddock with more horses.

The house was a large ranch style log cabin, and the barns large bank style log barns. Oil lanterns hung around the paths from the house to the barns but they were not lit since it was daytime. There were several men hanging around the large double doors of the main barn, each dressed in leather fur-lined clothing for the cold.

"Those are my handlers," Grigori told Roslyn as he pointed out the men. They were standing there talking with mugs of hot cocoa in their hands. "It is break time again I see," he added with a laugh. "Come, let me show you the horses that will be yours."

He led them past the handlers and to the far barn that had a separate paddock beside it. There were at least two hundred horses in the large paddock, all of them shod with horseshoes.

"This is the stock you may pick from," Grigori told her. "How many will you need?"

As Roslyn talked to her uncle about how many horses they would need, Tiffany went over to the paddock to look at the horses. Kavan joined her, turning a keen eye to the horses.

"How do you think the rest of the Clans will handle Roz? She doesn't know their ways and they don't know her," Tiffany asked the Arms Master, worried about her friend.

"I am sure Amelia and Cassidy will have enough time to make sure Roslyn is informed before we head south," Kavan responded, not taking his eyes off the horses. "I have faith in her."

"The other Clans didn't like the idea of our two people having trade relations," Tiffany added. "I'm sure Cassidy is only accepted because she actually was raised here and looks like them."

"Things have changed here, you know that. With the pirates holding the western ocean routes and having a trade monopoly, the Clans will be looking for something better. What's better than someone who is half-Jay'Alian?"

Cassidy came over, she had gone to speak to the handlers while her uncle showed them the horses. "My uncle does amazing work with his horses, does he not?"

"Truly, these are magnificent horses," Kavan answered.

Grigori heard him and came over to them at the fence, Roslyn behind him. "I am glad you think so. You will be getting the best of them in this transaction, and I will allow you to pick out your personal ones to take with you today. The rest I will deliver in a few days."

"I like the sound of that," Oswick spoke up from further down the fence; a blue roan had caught his eye and he had been checking it out.

Grigori called over his handlers and the group picked out their horses, the handlers going out into the paddock to bring them to the main barn to be saddled; Roslyn chose a few extra horses for the companions who had chosen to stay in the village. Grigori then led them to the main barn where Cassidy's horse, a beautiful white mare, awaited them. She was already saddled and bridled, waiting for her new owner.

"She's beautiful uncle," Cassidy told her uncle when she saw the mare.

"From my finest stock, trained especially for you," Grigori told his niece. "I had hoped to give her to you for your birthday last year but the training took a little longer."

They stayed for lunch with Grigori and his handlers before riding back to the village on their new horses, the extras for the remainder of their group on a line behind Roslyn's horse. Kavan had chosen a pure black gelding, and Oswick the blue roan mare.

When they got back to the village Amelia was waiting for them with a saddled horse of her own at the edge of the village. A rather large fluffy cat sat at

Amelia's feet, its fur nearly the same colour as the snow. As Roslyn got closer she marvelled at how big the cat's paws were; it was almost the same size as some of her father's hunting dogs.

"That is the largest cat I have ever seen," Roslyn told Amelia.

"My familiar, Ecko," Amelia told her. Roslyn dis-mounted and let the cat sniff her fingers before it decided it liked her and started rubbing up against her legs.

"What is it like having a familiar?" Roslyn asked her mother and sister.

"Our connection with them makes them more intelligent," Amelia told her, looking down at Ecko with a loving smile. "You will be able to understand them and talk to them, and they can hold stores of your magic for you or help you channel your magic better."

"So your familiar will actually talk back to you?" Roslyn asked them. Both of them smiled at her and nodded.

"That would certainly be interesting," Roz commented, shaking her head in wonder. "We certainly have nothing like that back home, unless you want to compare the magical storage to certain precious stones."

"I would like you to come with me," Amelia told Roslyn. "Cassidy as well. I want to take you to our Shrine today."

"Good idea, we should head back to our encampment this afternoon," Roslyn commented. She handed the lead to the extra horses to Oswick and told her friends she would be back in a while.

Amelia mounted her red and white mare and led the two of them north of the village. They rode for several minutes before coming to a hill with a weeping willow at its top. There Amelia stopped and dismounted, her daughters following suit. There was a post near the tree that they secured the horses reins to and then Amelia led them down the hill. When they reached the bottom of the hill Roslyn gasped as she saw the entrance to a large cave under the hill, lit by glowing rocks and glowing lichen. In the center of the cave was the statue of a wolf, its facial features so precise that at first Roslyn had thought it was an actual live wolf. Around the statue in a semi-circle were tree stumps meant for sitting on; on the wall behind the statue hung a torch on the cave wall.

Amelia led them into the cave and beckoned for Roslyn to sit on the middle stump. Cassidy sat to her left, Amelia to her right. Her mother produced a small dagger and handed it to her.

"Just nick a finger, all you need is a drop of blood for this," Amelia told her.

Using the tip of the blade she pricked her left pointer finger at the tip and squeezed out a drop of blood.

"Touch it to the middle of the wolf's head," Amelia told her next. Roslyn did so, and watched in fascination as the blood was absorbed into the statue.

A moment later the ground began to move and rumble, and with surprise Roslyn noticed that an area of the wall near the torch had opened to reveal a passage.

Amelia smiled at her and said, "Your blood is true, you are of the Wolf Clan." Amelia stood, saying, "Cassidy, Crick, and Ecko, you wait out here. Roslyn, come with me."

Cassidy gave Roslyn an encouraging smile as Amelia led Roslyn into the passage. Ecko curled up on the ground next to Cassidy and decided to have a nap.

The smell of dirt reached her nostrils, as did other strong tangy smells she could not place. Amelia had grabbed the torch from the cave wall and used her magic to light it so it would help light their way in the passage. Roslyn followed a few steps behind her mother until they came out of the passage into a large cavern.

Amelia walked around the cavern and touched her torch to several more torches in the cavern so they had more light. In the centre of the cavern were dozens of roots twined around each other in a braid that came from the top of the cavern and went into the ground.

"These are the roots of the willow tree above,"

Amelia told her, beckoning her to approach the roots. "They are part of the land, part of Jay'Al, roots of our ancestors, and a part of the magic within our land. I want you to prick your finger again and let a few drops fall on the roots."

Roslyn did so, watching as a good ten drops fell on the roots and were absorbed. The roots before her started to pulse slowly before quickening the pace, only for it to stop suddenly. Roslyn looked at her mother and saw her nodding and smiling.

It was at that moment that she heard the whispers from around the cavern. They were quiet at first but then they intensified so that she could hear everything the disembodied voices were saying.

"*This is her*," said one voice, old and worn.

"*She has returned*," came another voice, younger than the first.

"*Can it be?*" another voice said, male and defiant.

"*We welcome you, sister*," said another female voice, wise and old. "*We have been waiting for your return home to us. Jay'Al is about to change, for better or worse we cannot tell, but we know that you are the one who will see us through it.*"

Roslyn looked to her mother and saw that Amelia had knelt on the floor with her head facing the ground, her eyes closed in reverence.

"*You must find the remnants of the Dragon Clan,*" came a younger male voice. "*There you will find your answers.*"

Then the voices were gone and Roslyn saw Amelia's head shoot up to look at her with awe.

"I have never seen such a communion with Jay'Al before," Amelia whispered. "Those were the ancient Shamans themselves." Amelia looked at her oldest daughter and saw the confusion in her eyes; and the fear.

Amelia went to Roslyn and embraced her, Roslyn hugging her tightly.

"Everything will be alright, my daughter. Cassidy and I will teach you the ways of our shamans so you are ready for when your familiar comes to you, and for whatever the ancient shamans have in store for you. The call has gone out now for a familiar for you: it took several days for mine to come to me, and over a fortnight for Cassidy's. The call will reach through the whole of Jay'Al and a creature will answer it, in time."

Roslyn felt different now, as if something had changed within herself. She looked inside herself at her magic and found a new source of magic that glowed like the magic she saw in the cavern. A small tendril of it came out of the ground and inside her, feeding her magic so it grew stronger.

"My magic is different now, and yet still the same," Roslyn told her mother. "I--I cannot explain it."

"I wondered how your magic would handle the connection, but it seems to have adapted, or rather evolved, to the circumstances it seems. You might just be the most powerful mage in Jay'Al now. I will have to test you to see."

"I thought that was what we were doing already," Roslyn said, shaking her head.

"No, that was to come after connecting you with the land," Amelia answered her with a smile. "Come, let us go back out to your sister where this last test will be done."

When they got back to where Cassidy was sitting patiently for them, Roslyn saw that Cassidy had a large wooden bowl set in front of her filled halfway with water. Roslyn was noticeably shaking when she sat down beside her sister, and Cassidy asked them what had happened.

"The ancient shamans have spoken to Roslyn, they want her to go find the Dragon Clan," Amelia told Cassidy.

Cassidy appraised her sister before shaking her head.

"Well then, things just keep changing don't they? I think we should hurry up with this last thing and get her back to your house, mother: the poor thing looks very shaken."

"Roslyn," Amelia spoke to her eldest softly, "Drink this potion and then I want you to think about your grandfather's house and your friends." Amelia handed her the vial and Roslyn took it, taking the cork stopper out and downing the liquid.

"Close your eyes and picture the house," Amelia continued.

Roslyn did so, and suddenly she found herself standing in front of the hearth at her grandfather's house. She looked down at her hands and saw that they were see-through. Heath, who stood nearby, jumped when he saw her there.

"Roslyn?" Heath asked, his brows knit together. "When did you get back? Wait, why do you look like that?"

"I think I am an astral projection," she said, and in the back of her mind she heard her mother affirm it. "Mother is just testing my magic."

In the back of her mind she heard her mother tell her to now think about her father's study at the palace. Her surroundings blurred and changed and she found herself standing in front of her father's desk in his study. He sat there going over some documents.

"Father?"

He looked up with a start and stood up, knocking his chair over.

"Roslyn? How are you here? What is going on?"

"I'm an astral projection, father. Not sure exactly how I can do it from all the way in Jay'Al, but…there is something you should know, father. Mother is alive."

Her father stared at her with his mouth hanging open for a moment before saying, "What?"

"Amelia is alive, and I have a twin sister," she told him.

Her father grabbed his desk to balance himself, and she knew his mind must be reeling with the news.

"I don't think I have time to explain it now," Roslyn said as she noticed that she was beginning to fade. "I will be sending a letter with Maeve when she brings the rest of our supplies."

Roslyn regretted telling her father like that, when she could not hold him for comfort as he began to cry.

Roslyn opened her eyes and found herself back with her mother and sister.

"That you were able to project yourself all the way around the world tells me you are now most likely the most powerful shaman in Jay'Al," Amelia told her. "I will show you how to make that potion when we get back to your grandfather's."

Chapter Sixteen

R oslyn and the others rode back to their encampment with the new horses, Cassidy letting Roslyn keep the clothing as a gift. When they got back Roslyn excused herself to her cabin after unsaddling Sage and brushing him down. Once in her room she took out some paper, ink and a quill to write out a letter to her father to send with Maeve. In it she told her father everything that had happened since they had left the palace. Getting to the part about her mother being alive made her cry, and she left the tear stains on the paper. After finishing the letter she was exhausted, so she threw herself on top of her bed and was asleep within moments.

***

The next morning Roslyn had a meeting with Heath and his lieutenants to go over things. Jackson was to finish building the harbour and outpost while Maeve headed back through the Sea of Ice for more supplies and builders. Heath would stay with Roslyn at the encampment and journey with her when she headed to each of the clans with the merchants.

"I am sending Selene with Maeve," Heath told the group as they were almost ready to pack things up. "Last time we were here we stayed in place; I will not endanger Selene on this journey south."

"I will take good care of her," Maeve assured Heath. "She has been through a lot with us."

"I know you will," Heath told her. "It will be hard traveling south without her but I will know she is safe with you."

"You do not have to come," Roslyn told Heath, "Not if you don't want to. I am sure your expertise would be valuable on the journey. What if she hits another ice shelf?"

"Maeve can make it without me: she has magic like mine but not as strong," Heath explained. "It's a guarded secret that there are two of us who can do it," he added. "You understand."

"I do. Very well--though I will miss Selene."

Roslyn left the sailors to go meet with Aidan and the soldiers in the barracks to assign the guarding details and horses. A group of twenty would patrol around their encampment and a group of ten would patrol between the encampment and harbour, changing guards every eight hours. Soldiers were then assigned to either the encampment or the harbour. Many of the sailors would go with Jackson to help them with the building of the harbour.

That meeting over, Roslyn and Aidan left the barracks for the Food Hall. The Main Hall was currently being erected, with the barn going up as well. Roslyn could not wait to have her own room and office, or plumbing for that matter. At least there was a river nearby that they could get water from, and she had plans to build an aqueduct to help bring the water right to them. That was next on her list.

Sitting down with a plate of steaming food, Roslyn rolled her shoulders and her neck, hearing a satisfying crack and felt some relief. With a sigh she started to eat, oblivious to everyone else around her while she satisfied her hunger.

When she looked up finally she found that Heath and Kavan had joined them at the table with their own plates of food.

"Look who came up for air," Kavan teased.

Roslyn stuck her tongue out at him and turned to Heath. "Maeve off well?"

"Yes, I just came back from seeing her and Selene leave.

She has the crystals and the warmth charms so they should do well."

"Good. We should still continue with the building, and especially the aqueduct, in the next couple of weeks before the deep cold settles in. Once Maeve returns we can start building the Trade City from the encampment."

"It'll be spring by the time she returns," Kavan reminded her.

"We should have plenty of animals in the barn by then anyways," Aidan interjected. "Did you ask your mother about animals?"

"No, I was a little distracted," she told him and he ducked his head. He could only imagine what it would be like finding out that the mother he thought dead all his life was actually alive and he had a twin--extremely overwhelmed came to mind.

Over the next two weeks they all focused on building the aqueduct to bring water to the encampment, Roslyn putting sigils along the side of it to keep the water from freezing. The reservoirs it emptied into were also spelled to keep the water from freezing as well as to keep out contaminants. Roslyn stood back from the reservoir as it started filling with water, hearing her people cheer around her. A large smile spread across her face and she felt relief. Satisfied with what she had finished she accepted a cold cup of water from a soldier and sipped it. It was starting to feel like home now.

***

138

A Quest for Her Roots

Roslyn watched in fascination as Amelia went through with a spell that brought forest birds to her palm. She watched as the birds, a couple blue jays and a cardinal regarded her mother with their dark beady eyes; they seemed to be communing. After a moment the birds flew off and Amelia looked at her eldest daughter with a spark in her eyes.

"See the things you can do?" Amelia asked her.

"Through your connection with the land you can call such creatures to you and ask them questions."

"And I will actually be able to understand?" Roslyn asked her, uncertain.

Amelia nodded. "Once you bond with your familiar you will see. Come, let me show you the texts so you can learn about some of our rituals."

They had been standing out in the forest for this latest example of spells and now headed back towards the village.

"How is your settlement coming along?" Amelia asked her as they walked towards the village through the layer of snow that had fallen over the last couple of weeks.

"The barn has been put up and is waiting to be filled," Roslyn told her, "which is another reason for my being here today, to buy some animals off of you, and feed. The Main Hall will be completed soon and I am very much looking forward to having a room all to myself again."

Amelia smiled at that and had her come with her into the Chief's house. She brought the tomes of their Clan out from her room so Roslyn could look through them.

"It's a good thing your father taught you to read Jay'Alian as well as speak it," Amelia commented as she watched Roslyn leaf through the tome. "It makes me very proud."

"He taught me a lot, and told me a lot about you and life here," Roslyn explained, looking up from the pages of vellum. "I was so happy to finally be able to come here and figure out where I came from."

"I am so proud of you, Roslyn," her mother said, cupping her face in her hands and kissing her brow. "It makes my heart sing to know you grew up so well."

They were going over different ways to do spells when Chief Rotho came into the house with a messenger bird on his shoulder, a rolled up piece of parchment in his hand.

"Father?" Amelia inquired of the Chief as he regarded them with slight amusement.

"It seems the other Clans know of Roslyn's arrival,"

Rotho told them, opening the message and looking at it again.

"Envoys from each of the Clans will be arriving at the encampment in the next couple of weeks."

"We should send an envoy as well," Amelia stated. "Cassidy should be the one to go."

Rotho nodded his agreement. "This sets a precedent, granddaughter," Rotho told Roslyn as he rolled the message back up. "We may have had a tentative peace these last eighteen years but we have not had people from each Clan under the same roof since then."

"What do you think I should expect?" Roslyn asked him, earning a shrug in return from her grandfather.

"I have no idea. If they sensed what happened when you joined with Jay'Al...well, I hope everything turns out good. None of them would dare oppose you with the Ancient Shaman's blessings."

Great, Roslyn thought as she closed the tome and handed it back to her mother. Now I am more nervous than ever.

***

Settling into her room in the Main Hall the evening after it was finished, Roslyn wondered what her siblings back home were doing. Feeling homesick, she lay down on her bed and started to cry. She missed her younger siblings, but at the same time her family had grown more; there were five more siblings here, including her twin sister. She had tried to spend as much time as she could with her new found siblings. Her life had certainly changed in the last couple of months.

Wiping her tears, she finished putting her clothes away in the dresser that Heath had built for her. She stoked the fire in the hearth in her room with some wood and was about to go draw herself a bath when a knock came at her door.

"Who is it?"

"Heath. Cassidy has arrived along with the rest of the envoys."

"That was quick," Roslyn said as she opened the door.

Heath took one look at her red puffy eyes and knew she had been crying.

"Are you alright Roz?" he asked her, concern showing in his green eyes. She shook her head and was about to answer when he pulled her into a tight hug. She could feel the warmth coming from his body and felt herself relax in his arms.

"Just homesick," she told him quietly from against his shoulder. She was at the right height to be able to lay her head comfortably there. She sighed and then pulled away, him letting her do so. "Thank you," she told him. "I needed that."

Heath blushed with a smile and ducked his head before reminding her that her sister and the rest of the envoys were waiting.

"Let me get changed and I will meet them down in the Meeting Hall," she told him. "Do you know where Aidan is?"

"In his office I think. I will let him know on my way back down."

Roslyn nodded her thanks before closing her door.

A Quest for Her Roots

***

Heath felt a tightness in his chest as he let Roslyn go from the hug. He had not wanted to let her go, but knew that if she had wanted to hug him longer she would not have pulled away. Feeling her body against him had given him feelings he had not felt in a long time. He was conflicted though, with his past and what he had hoped his future would be.

Heath met Kavan at the bottom of the stairs after topping at Aidan's office to let him know the envoys were there. He now told Kavan the same thing.

"Is Roslyn coming?" Kavan asked, changing direction to follow Heath to the main entrance of the Hall where everyone was waiting.

"Yes, she said she would meet them in the Meeting Hall. Help me usher them in?"

Chapter Seventeen

Kavan stood at the back of the Meeting Hall and watched the shaman envoys from the Clans settle into the wooden chairs. The five of them were talking amongst themselves, seemingly all with cheerful dispositions. All of them had their familiars with them. Kavan had been afraid that there would be some animosity still in some of the Clans that had opposed the arrival of the foreigners twenty years before. Thankfully everything seemed fine, though Kavan made note of the Beaver Clan shaman being a little stand-off-ish.

The double wooden door was opened by two guards who stepped back and lowered their heads for Roslyn to walk through.

Kavan caught his breath when he saw Roslyn. She was wearing a long sleeved light blue dress that had slits down the skirt to give her more freedom to move, with black tights underneath. Her red hair she had braided up around her head to look like a crown itself. Around her neck hung the wolf head necklace.

Roslyn walked down the middle of the room until she got to the chair meant for her. It was the same wooden chairs that everyone else was sitting in, on the same level as everyone else. She might be royalty, Roslyn had said when they planned the room, but she was not royalty to the people of Jay'Al and should not make the envoys look up at her.

"We welcome you all to our village," Roslyn spoke, trying not to be nervous but Kavan knew her tells by now. "I am Roslyn, the daughter of the shaman Amelia of the Wolf Clan and King Lucius of Ellsgrove."

Cassidy stood up with a smile, Crick in her arms, and said, "Welcome home, sister." Then she turned to address the rest of the envoys, "My clan has welcomed Roslyn and she has connected with Jay'Al."

Roslyn smiled at her sister as she sat down and looked at the other envoys. Each of them wore a necklace with the symbol of their clan on it, so at least it was easy to figure out who was from where. The Hyena Clan envoy looked like he might be cold in his clothing: he wore thin leather sandals and loose breeches that came to his knees, along with a thin linen tunic. He was young, probably not too much older than she was, and probably was trying to show how strong he was up here in the north. So with a flick of her wrist she lit the logs sitting in the hearth to the side of the room, watching as the envoys took in her use of magic.

The envoy from the Beaver Clan stood up, a woman in her early forties with high thin cheekbones and strong arms, who had her red hair cut short to her head. She wore sensibly warm clothing and smiled nicely at Roslyn. Just then Roslyn found it slightly amusing that Kavan and Heath were the only people of a different colour in the room. The familiar of the Beaver Clan shaman, a red cardinal, sat on her shoulder.

"We welcome you, Roslyn of the Wolf Clan and Ellsgrove. I am Willow, shaman of the Beaver Clan. We look forward to working with you and your people in the future."

"We look forward to working with the Beaver Clan," Roslyn answered with a smile and a nod.

The envoy from the Fox Clan, an older man in his early fifties with a lot of grey in his hair and heavier set then everyone else in the room, stood up. He too wore sensibly warm clothing, deer-hide and alpaca wool. His familiar, a white fox, sat at his feet.

"I am Daron, shaman of the Fox Clan. We also welcome you home. I knew your father, Lucius, during his time here, and was proud to call him a friend. I very much look forward to the trade you will bring to our clans."

"I thank you, Daron."

"I am Jerred, shaman of the Bear Clan," the next man stood up. He was very tall and had his hair in dreadlocks tied back behind his head with a leather thong. His chest was wide and his tunic looked like it could burst from his muscles; Roslyn was reminded of the first time she had met Heath and chuckled to herself. This man's familiar was a barred owl who was perched on his shoulder. "We welcome different trade options than that given us by the Tribes of the Archipelago, and we are honoured to welcome you back to Jay'Al."

Lastly the envoy from the Hyena Clan stood up, looking more comfortable now that the fire had heated up the room. Roslyn saw him taking her in, looking her up and down before speaking. He wore his hair just to his ears, and his beard was neatly trimmed. At his feet sat his familiar, a small fennec fox.

"I am Kai, second shaman of the Hyena Clan. My father is ill and could not make the journey himself. I welcome you on behalf of my clan back to Jay'Al, and we look forward to the trade you can bring us."

"Thank you all for coming. I look forward to talking to you all about what we can bring to you and what you could trade with us. My friend Kavan here..." she waved her arm at Kavan and watched him stand a little straighter at the door. "...will see you to your cabins. A feast will be prepared for tomorrow afternoon for us to enjoy together and we will start discussions afterwards."

She watched as the group stood up and she called Cassidy over before her sister could leave. "Would you like to stay in the Hall with us? There's an extra room on my floor for you if you want to."

She smiled but she shook her head, saying, "No, you cannot show any kind of favouritism now. I will be fine in one of your cabins."

"All right, I guess I will see you at the feast?"

"Yes; and sister? You did good this morning. Both Jerred and Kai are enamoured with you. They think you are a little more exotic than the rest of us women of Jay'Al," Cassidy told her with a chuckle. "They are both young, they do not know much."

"Just how old is Jerred?" Roslyn thought he must be at most thirty.

"He's only a few years older than us," Cassidy replied. "Kai will be twenty-one in the spring."

"How long do you think the envoys will stay?" Roslyn asked her, walking out of the Meeting Hall with her and Crick. "I will take you to your cabin, we can talk while we walk."

"We should probably be here for a week; I overheard that they all knew our birthdays were coming up and their Chieftains sent presents; shamans turning nineteen is an important time, though we are not their shamans I believe they wish to garner your favour by celebrating us."

"Great, I thought I would have left that all behind when I left the palace. I never wanted to be a princess, Cassidy. I liked my life before father was crowned."

"Well, it's a little too late for that," Cassidy teased her. "With what happened at the Shrine...all of the shamans felt your power. They will not know about the quest the ancient shamans have given you, but they know you are powerful. I overheard our Aunt talking to mother about different prophecies that could have been triggered, but mother did not seem to think they had any relevance. Though, I do find it interesting that the ancients spoke to you at your Joining and not to me."

"Do you hate me for it?" Roslyn found herself asking her twin sister.

Cassidy stopped in her tracks and appraised her slightly older sister. "No, no I could never hate you, especially not for that. I'm a little relieved that it's not me, to be honest, but I will stand by your side through it all. I just wondered, what made us so different? We are identical twins after all."

"Maybe because I was not raised here?" Roslyn asked her. They continued walking. "That I have two different magics?"

Cassidy shrugged her shoulders and looked down at Crick in her arms. "I wonder what your familiar will be," she said. "It will probably be something very rare and powerful," she teased.

Roslyn laughed at that and stopped in front of the cabin that was meant for Cassidy. A torch lit the doorway for it had grown dark. "Here it is," she told her sister. "Your things should have already been brought here," she added.

"I brought something for you from mother, for you to wear for your birthday celebration," Cassidy told her. She invited her sister inside, using a ball of magic in her hand to light the way inside until she saw candles around the room and lit them with her magic. She went over to the bed where her bags had been put. She grabbed one of the smaller bags and handed it to Roslyn. "Open it later OK?"

Roslyn thanked her sister and left her to get settled in the cabin.

Before heading back to the Hall she walked around the palisade and greeted soldiers on watch, each of them bowing their heads to her in greeting. When she reached the south gate she stopped there and looked out at the forest. Above her the moon was nearly full, and the stars were shining brightly.

The moon will be its fullest on my birthday, Roslyn thought to herself as she looked at it. Either something good is going to happen, or something bad.

"Here you are," a familiar voice from behind her.

It was Kavan, holding two steaming mugs of hot cocoa. "Care to share a cup with me?"

She smiled sweetly at him and took a mug, inhaling the delicious scent. He stood next to her on the walkway and looked around.

"You looked beautiful tonight," Kavan commented as he took a tentative sip of the cocoa.

"I was trying to make an impression on the envoys," she told him, looking at him sideways.

"Oh, you made an impression," he told her with a chuckle. "Jerred and Kai were nearly ready to fight over you on the way to their cabins."

"Tell me you're joking." She turned to face him and found him smiling widely. She punched him in the shoulder and got a satisfying groan from him.

"They almost were," she heard him mutter as he took another sip from his mug. "They really could not stop talking about you though. Kai said his father thinks you could unite the Clans and be their queen."

Roz was taking a drink when he said that, and she ended up inhaling it as she was taken aback by what he said. He thumped her on the back until she stopped coughing.

"Well, you are a princess in Ellsgrove, and since you are a chieftain's granddaughter you are technically a princess here too," Kavan told her. "I overheard Willow talking with Daron," he added when she looked at him with a raised eyebrow.

"Oh for goodness sake," she muttered as she took another drink. "I don't want to be a queen."

"Honestly, Roz, you would make an amazing queen. All of your soldiers here love you, and it would not take much to get the Clans to love you too."

"All my soldiers love me, hm?" she looked sideways at him with a mischievous smile.

It was Kavan's turn to choke on his hot cocoa, and he coughed as he blushed deeply. Roslyn snort-laughed as she thumped him on the back until he stopped coughing.

"That bad eh?" she asked him. "It's OK if you don't love me, Kavan," she added with a laugh. "I was just teasing you."

"You mean a lot to me, Roz, but you're a princess, and I'm an orphan...what hope would I have?"

"Women of my people give their hearts and bodies to whoever they deem worthy, and that's that. Whether you think you're worthy or not is not the question, it's whether I do. You might want to find out sooner rather than later before I meet any more handsome men," she told him and she turned and took the cup of cocoa with her on her way back to the Hall, leaving Kavan staring after her.

***

Tiffany yawned over her breakfast plate as Roslyn sat down beside her. The Meeting Hall was where their group gathered for breakfast in the morning, and so far they were the only two there. The double doors of the room were opened into the hallway and they could smell the food that the cooks were preparing for the feast that afternoon. Tomorrow would be another busy day for the cooks, since they were celebrating Roslyn's birthday the next evening. Roslyn would go with Cassidy back to the Wolf Clan village to celebrate Cassidy's birthday with her there. Cassidy told her that the rest of their immediate family would be joining them for Roslyn's birthday there in their encampment as well.

"We need to think of a name for this place," Roslyn told Tiffany as Tiffany slowly ate her bacon and eggs.

Footsteps on the stairs made Roslyn look up and she found Oswick and Rafi coming down the stairs together. They each waved at her and Tiffany before going into the kitchens to get their breakfast. The two of them joined them at the table in the Meeting Hall.

"I was just telling Tiffany that we need a name for our village," Roslyn told the two merchants. "We can't just call it our encampment, especially once we get more established."

"Well, you could style it after the names of the Wolf Clan villages in the area," Oswick commented.

A Quest for Her Roots

"Your mother's village is Bella Vale, and there are two other villages nearby: Breg and Myshk. Bella Vale means beautiful valley, Breg means knoll, and Myshk means moss."

"I get what you are saying," Roslyn told him, "I just don't know what to call it."

Just then Heath came down the stairs, carrying with him a bouquet of bright yellow flowers. Tiffany and the others glanced from him to Roslyn who raised her eyebrow at them.

"What? How should I know what he's doing with the flowers?" she asked them quietly. "Eat your breakfast before it gets cold."

Roslyn was dipping her buttered toast in her egg yolk when Heath entered the Meeting Hall with his plate of breakfast in one hand and the bouquet of flowers in the other. He set his plate down at the table and went over to Roslyn where he bowed low to her, taking off his hat, and offering her the bouquet of flowers with such a smile on his face that Roslyn felt her heart flutter a little bit.

"My dearest Roz, I saw these winter jasmine shining through the snow and they made me think of you, a shining light in the darkness of winter," he told her as she took the bouquet from him, her face red but with a wide smile. "Might I have the honour of sitting next to you for breakfast?"

"You never have to ask to sit next to me," Roslyn told him with a chuckle, for the seat on her other side was empty. Heath took the seat and Oswick passed his plate from down the table.

"These flowers are very beautiful," Roslyn commented as she looked at them before putting them down and continuing to eat. "However did you find these?"

"Cassidy knew where a bush grew," he confessed. "I went out first thing this morning to gather them."

"I see," she said, casting a glance at Tiffany who was trying hard not to laugh while she ate. "I appreciate the gesture," Roslyn told Heath.

"I was wondering if you would go for a ride with me after breakfast," Heath mentioned to her quietly as the others started to talk about names for their village.

"I would like that," Roslyn answered shyly and went back to eating her breakfast.

Next down the stairs came Aidan, who waved at them before going into the kitchen and coming back with plates of food.

"Good morning everyone," Aidan said as he sat down in-between Oswick and Heath. "Oh, who got you flowers Roz?"

"Heath did," Tiffany told him first.

"Oh, well then," Aidan looked down at his plate and tried not to look at Roslyn who was starting to blush.

Roslyn was the first to finish eating while the others still talked about what to name the village in-between eating their own food.

"How about: New Wardgrove?" Roslyn spoke up.

"Sounds good to me," Oswick commented, the others at the table nodding their agreement.

"I'll get the carpenters to make a sign," Aidan said.

"Great. I am going to go wash up," Roslyn said as she stood. "Heath, I'll see you in an hour at the stables?"

He nodded with a mouthful of food and watched as she picked up the flowers and took her plate to the kitchens to be washed.

Roslyn had just put her plate in the empty sink and turned around right into Kavan as he entered the kitchen.

"Roz, so sorry, are you--" he stopped short as he saw the flowers. "Oh, those are nice."

"Yeah...I'm done eating so I'm going back up to my room. Missed you at breakfast though." Roslyn moved around him to go out into the hall.

"I slept in," he told her. "Didn't sleep well."

"Well, I'll see you this afternoon at the feast, yeah?"

"Of course."

"Good," she said before she took off down the hall and up the stairs.

With a sigh she found something to use as a vase and put her flowers in it before trying to find something to wear for a ride in the countryside.

***

Kavan watched Roslyn go before walking into the Meeting Hall with his food. Everyone greeted him with a 'good morning' and continued to eat their food.

"Roslyn came up with a name for our little village," Tiffany told him as he sat down between Tiffany and Rafi. "New Wardgrove."

"Fitting," Kavan said before digging into his food. He leaned closer to Tiffany and whispered, "Who gave her the flowers?"

Tiffany nodded in Heath's direction without saying anything. When he sighed in resignation she looked at him sideways and smiled at him.

"You sleep in?" Heath asked him.

"Yeah, trouble sleeping." He had tossed and turned for hours thinking about what Roslyn had said. Had she told him that because she did like him? What was he supposed to do?

He could always ask Cassidy.

Quickly he finished his plate of food, watching as everyone else finished and left to go do their own things for the morning. They had decided to leave off with the training session until after the feasts and celebrations were done just so they all had time to get things together. He was still the last one done, but when he was he took his plate to the kitchen and thanked the cooks before heading to find Cassidy.

Chapter Eighteen

Rafi caught Roslyn on her way out of the Hall. She had her hair down in ringlets, two small braids starting from her temples and tied at the back of her head to hold the ringlets back out of her face. She was wearing the deer-skin outfit Cassidy had given her, the one that was dyed blue with the embroidery.

"Heath, eh?"

"Please, do not start with me now," she told him as she went to open the door.

"I'm sorry," he said as she yanked the door open. "He is a good man. So is Kavan."

"You are too," she told him. "And I know you will find someone who will actually bring you the happiness you deserve."

She walked away from him, heading for the stables. There she started to brush down Sage and get her ready for the ride, waiting for Heath to join her. He found her there only minutes later, with a picnic basket and a thick blanket which he had rolled up. He was wearing thick alpaca wool breeches and a long sleeved tunic with his heavy overcoat and his hat, along with a different pair of black boots that were made to be warm. He brushed down his own gelding and saddled him as she saddled Sage.

"Do you have a place to ride in mind?" Roslyn asked him, looking at the picnic basket he had attached to his saddle.

"I do. Is this OK?" he asked, worried that he might be going too far.

"Yes, yes this is nice," she assured him. "Shall we go?" she asked as she led her mare out of the stables and mounted. Heath followed suit and as they rode out of the north gate he led her west on the road.

It was a beautiful morning, the sun was shining and there were barely any clouds. The forest around them was awake with birds, and she could hear the odd wolf call or moose. Since there had been no sightings of orcs in the area at all since their arrival Roslyn was confident that they did not need any guards on their excursion.

"Tell me about where you grew up," Roslyn found herself asking Heath.

"The Isle of Coin, the capital of the Archipelago," he told her after a moment. "Our house was built on the side of a cliff with rope bridges connecting us to other homes built along the cliff or on the smaller rock islands."

"Did you leave family behind?" Roslyn asked him. She found herself wondering why she had not asked him these questions during their voyage to Jay'Al. Had she been waiting for him to tell him without asking? She shrugged inwardly and waited for his response.

"My parents, an older brother and a younger brother. So far as I know they all survived the War," he told her after a moment. It was hard to tell what he was thinking as he told her.

"You haven't had contact with them since you joined Ellsgrove?" Roz asked him, wondering what kind of family he had left behind.

Heath shook his head and told her, "It was difficult at first, but I knew I should not. They would have heavily disapproved of my decision."

"You were lucky to have Jackson and Maeve," Roz commented, thinking of the two lieutenants.

"Very lucky," Heath said, continuing after a moment, "They were like family to me before, more so now. We made a life for ourselves in Ellsgrove though, and the king was gracious enough to employ us after he learned of my magic. I suppose if it was not for your cousin you would not have been able to meet your family."

"I sometimes think that I would have tried to find a way, somehow, someday, to come here, but then I remember how hard it was for you to come here the first time, and it certainly was no walk in the park this time, so would I have made it all the way?" she voiced her worries to him. "We could have easily gotten stuck in an ice shelf if not for you."

"I thank you for your praise," he told her with a grin. "A lot has happened to bring us all here."

They were silent for the rest of the ride, which was only a few more minutes. There was a rock wall ahead of them with a narrow entrance that led...somewhere. Evergreen trees lined the path up to the rock wall. Heath dismounted there and tied the reins of his horse to one of the trees. Roslyn followed suit. He took the picnic basket and blanket off of his saddle and beckoned for her to follow him to the narrow entrance. There he turned sideways and started through the entrance, Roslyn following behind.

A few minutes later they emerged in an open area with pools of hot springs. The ground was bare of snow but rather a vibrant mossy layer. A birch tree stood nearby, still in full leaf because of the heat from the hot springs. Roslyn looked around in amazement at the flowers growing around the area still.

"How on earth did you find this place?" she asked him as he spread out the blanket on the moss and set the basket down.

"Cassidy," he answered with a grin and a laugh.

Out of the basket he produced a bottle of wine, two wooden wine cups, and a platter of smoked or cured meats and cheeses. "Shall I pour us some?" he asked her, going to open the bottle.

"Not too much, remember we still have the feast this afternoon."

"I promise. Just a couple."

Heath pulled the cork out with a special tool and poured them each a glass. Roslyn took a few pieces of meat and cheese to nibble on while she sipped the wine.

"What was it like growing up in Wardgrove?" Heath asked her.

"I was able to do my own thing, spend time with my friends--I could be friends with anyone, which was how I met Oswick and Rafi. I would go to the taverns with them and play card games and drink. I knew the whole of the estate like the back of my hand."

"A born adventurer, hm?" Heath said with a chuckle. Roslyn found that she liked his deep chuckle.

"How did you discover your magic?" she asked Heath. They were sitting in front of each other, their legs crossed, the platter of meats and cheese between them.

Heath closed his eyes, remembering how it had happened.

"My brothers and I were running along a path alongside a small cliff." He paused in his reminiscence before continuing, "I tripped and fell, and rolled over the side of the cliff."

Roslyn inhaled in shock and asked, "How old were you?"

"Seven. I knew how to swim, but there were rocks below. My magic saved me, the water coming up to catch me and taking me clear of the rocks."

"Do either of your brothers have the same magic?" she asked him.

"My younger brother, Everett, has the same magic," he responded, thinking of the brothers he left behind. She could see the sadness in his eyes as he talked about his brother.

"Do you wish you could go back home?" Roslyn asked him. She found herself getting warm so she took off her overcoat. The linen tunic underneath was a thin white one, not the one that came with the outfit. Heath took off his overcoat as well.

"Sometimes," he answered after taking a large gulp of the wine. He picked up a piece of cheese and took a bite out of it. "If I could go home to visit, I would; but I believe I would not be welcome home at all."

"Why not?" she asked him.

"They would have labelled me a traitor," he told her. "If they knew I was alive, that is. They probably believe I went down with my ship. If I went back now, they would know I had chosen to leave that life and I would be imprisoned. My father would be particularly angry with me."

"I'm sorry." Roslyn ducked her head and looked into her wooden cup. She downed the little bit of wine that was at the bottom.

"I have made peace with it," he told her, lifting up the wine bottle and refilling her cup. "I think I could have a good life here in New Wardgrove."

"What would your dream home be?"

"A place by the sea, where I could look over the water. Land where I could make something of myself. Or I could be a carpenter and build things after I retire."

"You don't want to be a captain till you're old and hurting from arthritis?" Roslyn feigned shock, earning a laugh from Heath.

"No, I would like to retire from the sea while I'm still young enough to enjoy myself on land. Settle down, eventually raise a family maybe."

"And what if the woman you want to settle down with has her own responsibilities?"

"She would come first, always," Heath told her. "I would be at home waiting for her."

"You paint a pretty picture, sir," she told him as she picked up another piece of meat.

"What about you?" Heath asked her.

"A house on a hill with a meadow around it," she told him. "A pasture for animals. A thatched roof and a warm hearth with a dog sitting by it."

"That sounds quaint and lovely," Heath whispered, watching her expression as she thought about her answer: she had looked pained as she said it.

"Do you not think you will get that?" He asked her, an eyebrow raised as he looked at her.

"I don't know. The ancient shamans seem to have a plan for me, the gods a destiny for me that I may not be able to control. I don't know what my future holds anymore," she explained, her expression one of confusion and sadness. "At least I found my mother and the rest of my family."

"Well, I know one thing: I will be with you every step of the way," Heath told her, reaching out to take her hand. He squeezed it gently and took another bite of cheese. "Care to put your feet in the hot spring with me?"

Roslyn smiled and took her boots and stockings off as he did so as well. Together they sat at the edge of the spring and dipped their feet into the water.

"This place is wonderful," Roslyn commented as the heat of the spring helped her relax. She had not realized how stressed out she had been until then, and she wondered at that. This mission turned from an easy outpost to so much more, and the ancient shaman's words made her uneasy. Just what did her future hold now?

"When we came here the first time it was spring, and the countryside was beautiful with the new flowers and the fresh grass," Heath reminisced as he took off his tunic, for he was getting too warm. Roslyn found herself looking at his chest, covered in a thin layer of dark hair. He was well tanned, and she already knew he had muscles but to see them bare...she swallowed as he turned to reach for the bottle of wine and she saw old scars on his back, as if he had been lashed.

Roslyn reached out and touched his back, earning a twitch from Heath but he sighed in resignation and let her feel along the marks that had been left.

Heath liked the warmth of her hand on his back, and felt himself warming at her touch. After a moment he turned back to her and handed her a cup before pouring more wine into it.

"Where did you get those from?" Roslyn asked him, her hand still on his back, tracing the lines. She sipped from her cup and watched his expression turn dark.

"My father was not a good man," he told her simply. "I do not even remember what it was that I had done wrong, but I received lashes for it. It made it so much easier to defect knowing how angry he would be at me, and that he would not have cared if I was dead."

Roslyn felt angry, that a father would do something like that to his own son.

"I was ten," he added quietly before taking a long drink from his cup. "I remember not being able to sleep on my back for quite some time."

Roslyn put her arm around his shoulders and pulled him close. "You survived, and you chose to get away from him, that life. And look at you now!" She laughed and waved a hand around. "You have your own ships, you work for my father, have a loyal crew…you are sitting here with me enjoying yourself."

Roslyn found his hand on her chin and she looked into his green eyes, now alight with emotion. She looked at his lips as he brought himself closer and when he met her lips with his she kissed him back.

A bird screeched nearby, causing them to pull apart and look around.

"We should head back soon," Roslyn said with resignation. "It's not really safe to stay out too long."

Heath nodded, sighing inwardly, and started packing up the picnic basket.

***

Roslyn and Heath returned to their compound sometime later and went about their business for the day. Roslyn watched the soldiers help rearrange the tables in the Meeting Hall for the feast that afternoon. Heath and the rest of the sailors that had stayed there were helping as well, Oswick and Rafi were putting up some wreaths and candles for decoration. On the ride back to New

Wardgrove the skies had grown dark and threatened a storm. The two hearths on either side of the Meeting Hall were stoked with wood and waiting to be lit soon in order to heat the whole Hall. With a smile Roslyn left the Meeting Hall and went upstairs to get ready.

Cassidy was waiting for her at the top of the stairs.

"I think we need to talk," Cassidy told her with a smile. "About two gentlemen--"

"Ah, not here," Roslyn interrupted. "Come into my room."

She followed her sister inside where with a flick of her wrist Roslyn lit the lanterns and candles around her room.

"You have been giving some advice I hear?" Roslyn asked her sister as she took a seat on her bed. Cassidy, standing in front of the now closed door, looked guilty.

"Well, first Heath asked me about a few things, and Kavan came to see me today to ask me what would get your attention," Cassidy told her.

"Oh for god's sake..." Roslyn put her head in her hands and laughed. "This is too much. Certainly Tiffany would be a better person for Kavan to ask, really."

A light knock came at the door and with a nod from Roslyn Cassidy opened it. Tiffany walked in and closed the door.

"Oh, he did come to me," Tiffany told her with a sly smile. "But if you want to know the land better, like places to take someone for a ride, Cassidy is the one to ask. Also, I think you need a thicker door."

"Well that hot spring was really nice," Roslyn commented, her cheeks warming as she thought of Heath's hands on her. "And I guess I'll talk quieter?"

Tiffany chuckled and took a seat next to Roslyn on the bed, beckoning Cassidy to join them.

"Well? Tell us everything!" Tiffany demanded.

Roslyn crossed her arms and looked at Tiffany with a frown. "Not before you tell me what you told Kavan."

"Nope, that was between him and I. You will just have to wait and see what he comes up with," Tiffany answered her, earning a nod of agreement from Cassidy.

"You pretty much told him you thought he was worthy," Tiffany added.

"Why the sudden interest from Heath though?" Cassidy asked her.

"He saw me crying yesterday before you arrived," Roslyn told them, "I was homesick. He comforted me...and it felt good." She blushed. "I think that might have given him the courage to bring me the flowers and take me to the hot spring."

"What will you do once Kavan does something?" Tiffany asked her.

"I have no clue," Roslyn said, putting her head in her hands again with a great sigh. "I did not think this could happen, and why is this happening now?!"

That earned some laughter from her sister and friend.

"Oh poor Roslyn," Cassidy teased her. "Two suitors and she doesn't know which one to pick."

"Do you have any advice for me, oh wise and powerful shaman?" Roslyn shot back at her sister.

"Nope, never had this happen to me either," Cassidy told her. "I had a fling last year with someone from the Beaver Clan at the spring market but it didn't last long. No one else has come to show any interest in me since."

"Oh. Sorry." Roslyn looked down at her hands.

"No, Roz, it's OK. I had fun, but I haven't been interested in anyone either. I figure the right man will come along, and when he does I will know."

"I wanted Kavan to do something first...but I am attracted to Heath too. I don't know what to do."

"Then maybe neither of them are the right man," her sister said. She laughed and added, "Oh boy, I sound just like mother."

Roslyn laughed at that and hugged her sister before hugging Tiffany.

"Thank you, you two. I am so glad to have you both in my life right now," she told them both.

"Okay, now that that's done, can you braid my hair like yours again? The crown? Maybe we could match today!" Cassidy said with a wide grin.

"Oh, would you do mine like that too?" Tiffany asked her.

"Anything for my Royal Defender," Roslyn told her. "Though I think something different would suit you tonight. I also have just the outfit for you both too."

Chapter Nineteen

Tiffany looked at herself in the mirror and could not believe it. The outfit Roslyn had for her was a dress much like the one Roslyn had worn to greet the envoys but the bodice was like the breastplates worn by knights, flat to protect her chest. There were no curves to show off the femininity of the wearer, just a normal breastplate. It was not very heavy at least, mostly just for show, but Roslyn assured her that it could stop an arrow or a sword blade.

"I cannot promise it would stop a mace though, at close range with something like that I doubt that bodice would hold up," Roslyn had joked.

The long sleeves of the dress were green and had a layer of light chainmail over them. The green skirt was slit down the sides to give her more movement, and she wore green leggings with more light chainmail overtop. Her boots were made of a thick leather that came up to her knees. Around her waist went the black leather belt with her sword attached to it. Roslyn had also done up her hair in a fishtail braid. Tiffany thought she looked startling, like something out of legend with her pale skin and her red hair, her hazel eyes startling against the green of the dress.

"Wow," Cassidy said from behind her. Roslyn had done their hair first before Tiffany went to her own room to get dressed, Cassidy getting dressed in Roslyn's bathroom while Roslyn got dressed in her own room. The twins had come to see how Tiffany was fairing with her dress.

"The perfect Royal Defender," Roslyn said with a smile.

Roslyn had done Cassidy's hair in a mermaid braid, not exactly what she had asked for but it was stunning nonetheless. Cassidy never did much with her hair, but seeing what Roslyn could do she rather enjoyed the different braids now.

The dress Roslyn gave to Cassidy was a match to Roslyn's with slits in the skirt, though today Roslyn wore a light burnt orange coloured dress and the one Cassidy had was a robin's egg blue. Roslyn's leggings were dark brown and Cassidy's white. Roslyn even gave Cassidy one of her extra pairs of knee high black leather boots to complete the outfit. Roslyn had done her own hair back up in the crown braid again.

"How many dresses did you bring with you?" Tiffany asked her.

"Only a few," Roslyn told her with a laugh. "The rest of my wardrobe are breeches and tunics and a couple coats. Plus the beautiful outfit that mother made me."

"Roslyn?" Aidan called from the hallway. "We cannot start the feast without you."

"In here," Roslyn answered and opened the door to Tiffany's room. Aidan stood in the hallway wearing his best blue velvet breeches and white tunic with silver embroidery along the neck, his leather boots shined. He had combed and oiled his hair just right too. Roslyn was satisfied with his appearance.

"Oh, wow, you three look amazing," Aidan told them. "Tiffany, that outfit suits you."

"Careful, she might beat you in practice next," Roslyn joked as they all left Tiffany's room. "Have you come to escort us to the Meeting Hall?"

"Yes, your highness," Aidan said with a bow, offering her his arm. He offered Cassidy his other arm and she took it. Tiffany followed behind them down the stairs where they met with the rest of their group on the main level.

Roslyn caught her breath as she saw her friends below. Oswick and Rafi wore clothes similar to Aidan's, brown velvet breeches and white linen tunics.

Heath had forsaken his hat for the feast, pulling his hair back in a queue. He wore a fine wine red velvet outfit, breeches and an overcoat over a white tunic with red embroidery around the neck. He wore his black sailor boots with the outfit still.

Kavan was dressed as a soldier in his finest garb, a blue gambeson with a high neck and the clasps on the right side, over black breeches with his black soldier's boots. He had his dark blonde hair slicked back and his icy-blue eyes stood out because of his blue gambeson. There was a sword at his waist.

"My Defender is supposed to be the only one with a weapon," Roslyn reminded Kavan when they reached the bottom of the stairs.

"I am your Master-at-Arms, I am also here to protect you so I will wear a sword," Kavan replied with a smile. "The majority of the soldiers are feasting in their barracks, besides the guards who will be at our feast, there should be no other weapons there that are not ceremonial."

Roslyn nodded in acceptance as Aidan steered her and Cassidy down the hall to the double doors of the Meeting Hall. Kavan and Heath opened both sides of the double door for them to go through, and their friends followed behind them.

The tables had been rearranged in a square formation, no one side being the head of the table. Each person had an assigned seat, their names written on place holders on top of their plates. The group each found their seats and stood behind their chairs waiting for the envoys to join them. With a nod from Roslyn one of the guards went out and opened the door to the Main Hall and invited the envoys in, and with them were Amelia and her husband along with Chief Rotho. They each came into the Meeting Hall and found their seats quickly.

"I welcome you all to our feast," Roslyn spoke with clarity from the middle of the top part of the square. "Please, be seated and we will start the first course."

Together everyone sat down and the chefs brought out the first course, a hot spinach dip with baked pita bread, a delicacy from the south of Ellsgrove. There were bottles of wine along each table and wooden cups for everyone so they poured at their own leisure. Both of the hearths were giving off heat from coals, and a servant was busy keeping the fires going enough to keep them all warm.

Roslyn sat next to Cassidy with Jerred on Roslyn's other side and Kai next to Cassidy. Tiffany sat at the corner by Jerred with Kavan next to her, Oswick, Rafi and Heath down the rest of that side. Aidan was at the bottom corner sitting next to Willow, with Daron sitting on Willow's other side. The far side was where Amelia, McKenna and Chief Rotho were sitting.

"Amelia, so good to see you again," Willow greeted the shaman of the Wolf Clan. "It has been too long since I had the pleasure to see you."

"It truly has been. How are your sons?" Amelia asked her after swallowing a bite of food. She turned to Roslyn and said, "This is delicious! What is it made from?"

"A plant called spinach, with cheeses and a few other things," Roslyn answered. "It's one of my favourite dishes."

Amelia turned her attention back to Willow.

"My sons are good, they have grown into strong young men," Willow replied to her question. "They oversee the mining of precious metals from the swamps, which is something we are open to trading with Ellsgrove."

"What kind of precious metals?" Roslyn asked.

"The frishna starmetal that is only found in Jay'Al, though mining it is difficult; gold and iron. The peat can be used to make coal, which would be a precious commodity I believe," Willow told them. "It's not all swamp either, we have hills and small mountains where we have found precious gems and a lot of material used by shamans. They might be of use to the magic users in Ellsgrove as well."

"I'm really interested in the cocoa," Oswick spoke up, directed at Kai since he was from the Hyena Clan. "I love the stuff, and I know it would make a huge profit back home."

They talked as they ate, and soon the second course was brought out: a roast pig with roasted potatoes and corn on the cob along with other roasted vegetables. By dessert, a pumpkin cake with frosting, they had gone through all of the things that the Clans had that they were willing to trade for either money or other goods that were only available in Ellsgrove.

Roslyn looked over at Aidan and saw him writing everything down on paper. At least he had eaten most of his food before writing, or had he been making notes the whole time? Roslyn had been engrossed with the conversations of trade that she had not noticed much else. The Clans had been hard pressed to trade anything with the Tribes of the Archipelago since they had cut off all other trade in the south. That Roslyn was half Jay'Alian meant more to them, and especially since she was such a powerful mage she had more influence. At least the Tribes no longer had a trade embargo in Jay'Al, though she bet they would not be happy once they learned about Ellsgrove's trading port in Jay'Al.

"Would we be able to buy more land around here?" Roslyn found herself asking. "We will be making New Wardgrove bigger in the future and will need more land, especially for farming, and maybe another quarry in the area?"

"Those hot springs, do they belong to any clan?"

Heath asked. "They would be a huge interest to people who would pay to use them."

"The Wolf Clan would be willing to sell you more land, yes; as for those hot springs...they do not belong to any clan, no, but to all. You would need permission from all of them to do anything with them like that," Amelia said.

"Maybe we, the Clans, could do something with them ourselves?" Cassidy spoke up. "The income would help us too."

"That is a good idea," Willow spoke up. "Heath, what did you have in mind?"

"Build something around it and over it, keep everything around it natural and maybe an inn overtop of it? You could charge people to use the springs and it would heat the whole inn too. There are not many hot springs in Ellsgrove, and certainly none as beautiful or energizing as these here."

They continued talking until Roslyn got an idea; she had them move the tables over into a corner and got blankets and pillows to put down in front of the hearths so they could converse like they were in one of the Clan villages. Willow seemed to appreciate the change of setting as they continued to talk through the afternoon. Roslyn ordered water be brought out and the wine was taken away. Everyone filled up their cups with cold water and they continued talking.

Roslyn was amused to find that Aidan took to one of the tables to continue to write, so she went over to him and bent down over his shoulder to see what he was doing.

"Do you mind, Roz?" Aidan asked her, slightly amused. "Your head is blocking my light."

Roslyn snort-laughed at that and moved out of his way. "Can you not do that later?" she asked him.

"No, I want to be rested for your birthday celebration tomorrow," he told her, not looking up from the paper. "Besides, if I get this done sooner rather than later we will have something good to tell your father and we can get things going more."

"Gods, I can't wait for those scribes to show up," Roslyn teased him. "You will be able to do more things with the rest of us."

Aidan looked up at her with a raised eyebrow. "On second thought, maybe scribes are not a good idea."

That brought a raucous laugh out of Roslyn and she had to put her hand over her mouth as others were starting to look, which just made Aidan laugh too.

"My friend, I thank you," Roslyn told him. "You are always honest with me. Continue, but I want your full participation at my birthday celebration tomorrow."

"You will have it, your highness," he answered with a grin. Roslyn stuck her tongue out at him and went to sit next to Kavan.

"Enjoying yourself?" Kavan asked her after she had plopped herself down on a pillow.

"I am. We have made good progress here, and I think a good impression," she answered as she took a drink from her cup.

"Jerred and Kai certainly liked your laugh," Tiffany leaned over to whisper to her.

"Oh please," Roslyn rolled her eyes. "I have known them for how many days?" she asked her friends. "No, I will be friends with them but I doubt there will ever be anything else."

Kavan found himself encouraged by that but did not say anything. He found Tiffany and Cassidy watching him closely as Roslyn talked with her mother.

"What?" he whispered to the two women.

Both of them looked at each other before breaking out in grins and moving away.

Chapter Twenty

Kavan left the feast shortly after, going for a walk to clear his head. He had been very uncertain at first about Roslyn's affections, and he still was confused. Tiffany assured him that all he had to do was show her he was interested by doing what Heath had done, but how could he top flowers and a day trip to a hot spring?

Cassidy had told him about a few groves in the area that were really pretty that time of year, and about a few other types of flowers that still bloomed in the winter like the jasmine Heath had gotten her, but he wanted to do something different. She was an adventurer at heart, he knew that, so where could he take her? Maybe Jackson, who had done more reconnaissance in the area, might know of something. That meant Kavan would have to go to the harbour to ask the lieutenant, so Kavan saddled up his horse and left New Wardgrove for the harbour.

***

Kavan knocked quietly on Roslyn's door, a lit lantern in his other hand. It was an hour from dawn and he had a surprise for her.

"Who is it?" he heard her mumble and he heard her coming towards the door.

"Kavan," he answered just loud enough for her to hear.

She unlocked her door and opened it; her hair was dishevelled from sleep and she wore just a long tunic to bed.

"Something wrong?" she asked him as she rubbed her eyes.

"I have something to show you. Quickly get dressed in something warm."

Her eyes widened with interest and she nodded and closed her door, coming out a minute later wearing the deerskin clothing Cassidy had given her, her hair brushed and quickly redone in a simple braid. Kavan offered her his arm and she took it, him leading her down the stairs and out the front door of the Main Hall where he already had their horses saddled. Roslyn mounted her horse and looked at Kavan expectantly once he was mounted as well.

"Follow me," he said with a grin, and he led her out the west gate, the guards opening it for them as they approached--Kavan had already talked to them before he had awakened Roslyn. The full moon above them lit the countryside though Kavan still had his lantern attached to his saddle.

He led her towards a small grouping of large hills to the west of New Wardgrove, large oak trees that had not completely lost their leaves dotting the sides of the hills. They rode the horses up the biggest hill and dismounted at the summit. Kavan tied the reins of his horse to one of the trees and Roslyn followed suit before he grabbed her hand and motioned for her to look to the west.

There the full moon was reflected against the many rivers in the countryside as it descended in the sky. Roslyn sighed at the beauty of it. Kavan turned her around and she saw the colours of the sky to the east changing as the sun was beginning to rise. They stood there watching the sun rise, Roslyn taking in the different hues of red that lit the sky. In the distance they could see New Wardgrove and the rest of the countryside as the sun rose higher.

"Happy birthday," Kavan said to her, squeezing her hand.

"This is beautiful," Roslyn told him, for indeed the skyline to the east was full of enchanting colours. To the west she could see that the full moon had turned an orange colour as it reflected the light from the sunrise. "Thank you, Kavan, for bringing me here."

"Oh, there's more," he told her, and indicated a campfire he had built the night before, wood at the ready to be lit. "I'm going to make you breakfast here," he told her as he led her over. "If you would do the honours of lighting the fire for us?" He turned to get the food and blankets out of his saddlebags and when he was back the fire was roaring and she was standing there watching the countryside and listening to the birds welcoming the sun.

Kavan put the blankets down and added some more wood to the fire from a small stash nearby. Then he took out a frying pan and a small metal grate with a stand to put over the fire. Roslyn sat down beside him and leaned into him as he put some sausages in the frying pan, so he put his arm around her and held her close as the food cooked. His heart was beating fast and he just knew she could feel it but he didn't care, it felt right holding her in his arms.

***

Roslyn handed the reins of Sage to Kavan so he could take both of their horses to the stables himself. She was more confused than ever, with the two different options presented to her.

The Meeting Hall was empty, for everyone else had already eaten. So Roslyn made her way up to Heath's bedroom and knocked on the door.

"Hey, where were you this morning?" Heath asked her when he saw her standing there.

"With Kavan," she told him honestly. "I like both of you, but I fear I do not know which to choose."

"Right now," he told her, a broad smile on his face. "We can both woo you," he reminded her. "We will respect whatever decision you have."

"Are you sure?" she asked him, sceptical about the whole thing.

"Trust me. Let me talk to Kavan. We will not fight over you, but we will try to win your heart," he told her.

"You promise?" she asked him, hesitant about the whole situation.

"Yes," he told her, a lopsided grin on his face. "You go get ready for your day. I will see you later today."

***

Heath went directly to Kavan's room. He knocked on his friend's door and waited.

Kavan answered, and when he saw Heath he frowned slightly.

Heath held up his hands and said, "She likes us both. I am not going to fight you for her, but I would rather win her heart by other means."

"I agree. We can remain friends while we pursue her?" Kavan asked him, a broad smile on his face

"I hope so," Heath said. "Your friendship means a lot to me."

"And yours means a lot to me as well," Kavan told him in turn. "I promise this will not come between us."

***

"Sounds like a great start to your birthday," Tiffany answered with a grin after Roslyn told her about where Kavan had taken her. "Aidan was looking for you so you could sign some things," she added. "He should be down in his office."

Roslyn nodded and turned to go back down the stairs.

Roslyn spent the rest of the morning and early afternoon in Aidan's office going over things and helping to re-write sections. When Roslyn's stomach started to growl Aidan went and got a platter of cheese and smoked meats for them to snack on while they continued to work.

Finally with an exhausted sigh Aidan handed over a reworked trade agreement for her to sign. Roslyn stood up and stretched, walking over to the window in Aidan's office and looking outside. The soldiers not on duty were starting to prepare for the evening's celebrations, building a large bonfire in the open square in front of the Main Hall. Metal braziers had been brought out and lit with coals to provide heat for the evening for those who did not have warmth charms. Snow had been removed and awnings put up, tables moved out of the Dining Hall. Thro-wing games had been arranged and set up, as was an archery contest. Aidan had told her at some point during the morning that McKenna was setting up a horse race, which was a popular event at birthday celebrations for the Wolf Clan. The horse race would be the first event of the evening, followed by the archery contest--and then the ale and other spirits would be brought out before the food was served.

Chief Rotho had gone out two nights before with Roslyn's younger brothers and brought down several deer and a wild boar to roast for the evening, and they had been busy since the night before preparing the meal. Roslyn's mouth watered as she thought about the food.

"Much better," Aidan said as he handed the document to Roslyn. She skimmed it quickly and agreed, handing it back.

"Great, tomorrow I will go over this with the envoys," Aidan said as he tucked the documents away. "You had better go get ready for the festivities."

Roslyn rushed up the stairs, for she badly needed to bathe and wash her hair.

***

Roslyn walked Sage over to the starting line. She was wearing riding breeches and a heavy tunic, her curly hair loose around her shoulders. Beside her were Tiffany, dressed as Roslyn was, already mounted on her horse, and Cassidy, in her deerskin clothing, already on hers. Her uncle Grigori stood to the side of the starting line with McKenna, with soldiers not on duty standing on either side of the well-marked race course. Jerred and Kai walked their horses over to join the women, and Oswick rode up on his.

"Is this everyone?" Grigori asked, and they all looked around to see if anyone else had horses they wanted to enter in the race. Kavan and Heath were walking up to the starting line to watch, talking and laughing as they came. Roslyn was relieved that the two could still be friends.

Roslyn nodded to her uncle and he bade the rest of them to mount. Amelia joined her husband at the sideline, her other daughters and sons joining the rest of the crowd to watch and cheer.

Grigori produced a white flag and raised it, and the racers got into positions. The flag was lowered and the horses took off down the race course, the people on the sidelines cheering. The race course went in a circle around the countryside and came back to the starting point, only taking a good ten minutes to go around. Roslyn was neck to neck with Cassidy for a while before Jerred pulled up; Tiffany and Kai were behind them. Roslyn willed her mare to go faster and Sage pulled ahead and crossed the finish line first.

Next everyone moved over to the archery range that had been set up. Roslyn would shoot against Cassidy, Jerred, Kai, Rafi, and her younger brother Quinn. They would each have three chances to hit the bull's-eye on their respective targets, and the two that had the most points would have one more chance to be named the victor. Rafi took the title in that event, earning a respectful bow from the two envoys who had come up second and third.

The guard shifts changed and soldiers withdrew from the celebration to be replaced by those coming off their shifts. Roslyn had assured them all that they would still be able to have some ale that night after their shift changed, and the soldiers left after saying 'Happy birthday' to her, putting their hands over their hearts and bowing to her. The night shift soldiers were already in their barracks away from the celebration, sleeping; Roslyn had already promised them that half of them could have the day off tomorrow and the other half the day off after that in order to get some ale and cake. New Wardgrove could not go undefended during the night just yet; Roslyn had plans to build a larger wall around where the new houses and warehouses would go in the spring. They had been able to buy more land and she could not wait to utilize it to make New Wardgrove grow.

The throwing events were bean bag toss, and horseshoes in which nearly all of Roslyn's friends participated. Some of the soldiers got in on it as well and Roslyn indicated to the cooks to bring out the ale. One of Roslyn's uncles had a penchant for ale and he had brought several of his own casks to the celebrations to add to Roslyn's. Wooden cups were passed around and the bonfire was lit, the group moving over to the bonfire area where Chief Rotho and his grandsons were getting ready to carve up the meat that had been cooking since the night before. There were roasted potatoes and other vegetables as well as hundreds of fresh buns that the cooks had been busy making.

Roslyn found herself seated in a large throne-like chair padded with pelts that Chief Rotho had brought all the way from their village for her to sit in. Her friends sat in normal chairs on either side of her, Kavan to her right and Heath to her left. Lots of people danced around the bonfire and some of the sailors and soldiers brought out instruments to play music.

Roslyn returned to her seat with a plate full of steaming food and a fresh bun, her cup full of ale, to find that Kai and Cassidy were talking about the Dragon Clan.

"My father would know where the old entrance to the plateau would be," Kai was telling Cassidy. "From what I remember though the tunnel had collapsed, and there is no other way up the plateau. It has been two hundred years anyways, there is probably no one left up there."

"My sister has been quested by the ancient shamans to find the Dragon Clan," Cassidy told him. "There must be a way."

Kai turned to appraise Roslyn as she took a hearty bite out

of the slice of venison on her plate. Cassidy covered her smile with a hand and laughed as her sister raised an eyebrow at Kai who was staring at her with his mouth hanging open.

"I'm hungry," Roslyn told him once she swallowed her food, chasing it with a long drink of ale. "Are there any tales about what happened to the Dragon Clan, besides the tunnel collapsing?" she asked him once she put her cup down.

"Rumours of magic gone wrong, others say they displeased the ancients," Kai said with a shrug. "Who knows for sure? You can come south with me and talk to my father, he will tell you where you need to go."

"Maybe the orcs got to them," Jerred added his opinion as he sat down next to Kai with his own plate of food. Heath had told them about the orcs, large creatures with thick skin and a penchant for raiding.

"Well, we seem to have a tentative agreement with the orc tribes, they stay away from us and we don't kill them," Jerred said. "Back a couple hundred years ago though there was no such agreement."

"When was the last time anyone saw a dragon?"

Roslyn spoke up. She had been busy eating while they had talked about orcs.

"My grandfather said he saw one when he was a boy, flying towards the plateau from the west," Jerred told her. "That was almost ninety years ago."

"You don't have dragons where you come from?"

Kai asked Roslyn and her friends. They all shook their heads, except for Heath.

"I've seen a water dragon, though they don't have wings that can fly," Heath spoke up. "That's what my people call them anyways."

"All right, looks like after Cassidy's birthday celebration we head south," Roslyn said next. "Oswick, you can get a good look at the cocoa plants while we're down there."

"What do orcs look like?" Oswick asked Kai. "We definitely don't have orcs back home."

"Over six feet tall, thick green skin and black hair, large teeth protruding from their mouths," Jerred described them. "Tribal creatures. My grandfather said that some of them were smart, but the consensus was they were mostly dumb brutes. However, they were said to have worshipped the dragons, something about their ancestors coming from dragons."

"Well, let's hope we don't run into any orcs," Roslyn said, raising her cup in a toast. "To birthdays, friends, quests and no orcs!"

With a laugh the rest of the group toasted her and drank heartily from their cups. The sun had set and above them the full moon shone brightly, casting a silver light on the festivities. The envoys excused themselves to go to their cabins quickly, coming back with their gifts for Roslyn. Each Clan had decided on their gifts before coming there, and now they hoped this foreign princess liked what was chosen--she was decidedly very different from what they had expected.

Willow presented her with a necklace of black onyx, which Roslyn recognized as a stone for protection. Daron gave her a dagger, its hilt made of some kind of bone, the blade a metal that Roslyn had not seen before. When she asked him what it was made from he smiled and told her, "The hilt is whale-bone, and the blade is made of frishna metal, which is a rare metal."

"I've heard of frishna," Heath leaned in to see the blade. "That is a fine gift indeed."

"If you were anything like your mother," Daron said, "I knew this would please you."

"It does, thank you Daron." She put the dagger in the sheath it came with and attached it to her sword belt.

Jerred had a fine bow with special arrows for her.

Roslyn tested the pull of the string and fitted an arrow, aiming at one of the leftover targets across the yard. She hit its center.

"It's beautiful," Roslyn told Jerred, unstringing the bow and putting it to lean against her seat. "I thank you."

Kai came forward next with a bronze bracelet decorated with desert ani-mals, which Roslyn gladly put on her wrist. She could feel the spells for pro-tection that had been woven into the making of the bracelet, and she thanked Kai for it.

Next the cooks brought out the mini cakes they had made and decorated, and everyone grabbed one as the cooks moved around the yard. Kavan and Heath had gone to go fill up their cups and Roslyn's as the crowd started to dwindle, soldiers and friends excusing themselves for the night. Rotho, Ame-lia, McKenna and their children remained as did Cassidy, Oswick, Aidan and Tiffany, as well as the envoys.

Kavan and Heath were returning with filled cups when Roslyn noticed the sky had grown darker. She looked up with a gasp, making everyone else look.

"A lunar eclipse," Willow whispered, looking at Roslyn. "The gods favour you with this."

Roslyn accepted her refilled cup, handed to her by both Kavan and Heath, as they all looked up at the eclipsing moon.

"Well then, that's a first," Roslyn said to her friends. "I've never seen a lu-nar eclipse before."

"Happy birthday!" Her friends said to her, raising their cups in celebration of her.

The group stayed out there until the eclipse was complete, Tiffany falling asleep in her chair. As the moon started to emerge from the darkness Roslyn announced it was time to go to bed and she went to pick Tiffany up in her arms.

"We would like to say good-night to you," Heath interrupted her, and Roslyn saw Kavan standing behind him.

"Guys," she told them, "I just want to get our friend to bed. You have both done very well today. We can continue your individual wooing tomorrow." She found it amusing to say it that way, so she chuckled.

A Quest for Her Roots

"Happy birthday, Roslyn," they both said to her then, grins on their faces, as they declined their heads and stepped out of her way. Roslyn picked Tiffany up in her arms and carried her friend up to her bedroom.

***

It was a crisp winter day when Roslyn and her friends rode into the village of Bella Vale, accompanied by Jerred and Kai. The other two envoys had left the day after Roslyn's birthday, though they had given gifts to Cassidy before doing so. Jerred and Kai wanted to travel with them; Jerred just as far as his home, Kai all the way south.

Amelia's familiar Ecko greeted them at the door to the Chief's house. Crick chattered at them from the hearth, Cassidy sitting cross-legged in front of the hearth drinking tea.

"Good morning," Cassidy greeted them with a smile. "Mother is in the kitchen with Leona and Sawyer preparing breakfast."

"Is Roslyn here?" came their mother's voice from the kitchen as the group came into the house.

"Yes," Roslyn answered her, joining Cassidy on the floor. The others followed suit. "McKenna saw our horses to the stables."

"Uncle Grigori was very impressed with that mare of yours," Cassidy told her. "He might ask you about breeding her with one of his prized stallions."

"She was a gift from Tiffany's brother," Roslyn told her sister. "As a thank you from the family after I named her my Royal Defender."

"There will be tournaments in the south by the time we get there," Kai spoke up. "I would love to see Tiffany join them and show some of our people the fighting styles of Ellsgrove."

"Oh, I think I would like to show off those styles myself," Roslyn said with a sly smile.

Tiffany smiled at her knowingly and added, "Yes, that would be fun."

"We have held off on our morning fighting sessions, waiting for celebrations to end," Roslyn explained to them, "So you would not have seen us fighting. Cassidy and the rest of my siblings here have been kind enough to show me some of their skills as well during the past few weeks so I might just surprise you."

"I look forward to seeing what you can do," Jerred answered, declining his head.

Amelia, Sawyer and Leona came out of the kitchen with platters full of food.

"Come, let us start our day off well," Cassidy imparted to the group. "This birthday has become even more special to me, for my twin sister is finally here to celebrate it with me."

Roslyn hugged her sister and accepted a plate of food from her mother.

***

Later that afternoon the horse races started. Roslyn rode Sage again, though there were more people of the village and from other villages of the Wolf Clan that attended. Roslyn came in third, Cassidy second, and a young man from the village of Breg came in first.

"Who is that guy?" Roslyn asked her sister after they had pulled to the side after the race.

"Guthrie," Cassidy told her with a sigh. "He is a few months younger than us, and has been a thorn in my side for a long time."

"Ah, meaning he has had a crush on you for a long time but you think he is too immature?" Roslyn asked her.

"Exactly," Cassidy replied with a lopsided smile. "If you had not won your race at your birthday, the winner would have been seated at your right side. As it goes, Guthrie will be my eating partner tonight."

Roslyn winced, feeling sympathetic for her sister. "And who will be at your left side?"

"You," Cassidy told her. "Maybe I can avoid talking to Guthrie with you and your friends on that side."

"Would that not be seen as an insult to him and his
family?" Roslyn asked her. They both dismounted and walked
their horses over to the stables attached to the Chief's house.

Cassidy sighed heavily and nodded. "I guess I will have to entertain him tonight."

"I will come to your rescue if I think he is being impertinent, ok?"

Cassidy laughed and they both got to work brushing down their horses.

***

Later that night Roslyn and Kavan walked back to Chief Rotho's house to-gether. Lanterns lit the streets, and snow fell from the darkened sky. Kavan held Roslyn's hand tightly as they walked, wishing that he could hold her longer. Behind them the great bonfire from the celebration still blazed, the people of the Wolf Clan still celebrating.

"Do you think you would be different, having been raised here?" Kavan asked her as they reached her grandfather's house.

"I don't know," she told him honestly. "I would like to think I would still be who I am now."

"I think you coming here now...you were meant to," Kavan told her. "You are of two worlds, two magics. You are different to these people because of it. I think that's why the ancient shamans chose you."

"So everything happens for a reason?" Roslyn asked him as she walked in-to her grandfather's house. One of the ground floor rooms was hers to use. Her friends would stay in the guest house, the two envoys who traveled with them sleeping in a separate guest house in the village.

"Yes, I believe so. If I had not been an orphan, joined the army...I would not be here today."

"Maybe. I guess we will see once we find the Dragon Clan." Roslyn stopped him, pulling him into a kiss. He tasted of ale and venison, and smelled of smoke from the bonfire.

Roslyn pulled away and smiled at him, taking a step back. "Goodnight, Kavan," she told him.

"Have you kissed Heath yet?" Kavan asked her, "You

know, just to make sure we are on even ground," he added with a lopsided grin.

"I don't think I can say," Roslyn told him with a mischievous smile as she entered her bedroom and closed the door behind herself.

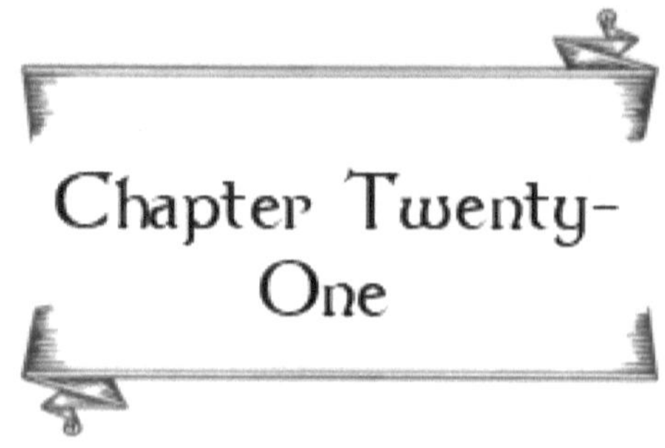

Chapter Twenty-One

Roslyn stared over the savannah, looking at the golden grass swaying in the wind. There was a large forest in the distance and a village up ahead. Above them the sun shone brightly, giving them a different warmth than they had a few days before. They were south-west of the Wolf Clan territory, going through the Fox Clan area on the way to the Bear Clan territory. The day before they had camped in a snowy glen, Roslyn using magic to protect their camp while they slept.

Daron greeted them at his village and they spent the day there eating and getting to know more of Daron's family. The clan was the same as the Wolf Clan, except they wore lighter clothing. Daron's youngest daughter, who was the same age as Roslyn and Cassidy, gifted them several outfits made of the hemp plant, which they grew. Roslyn found the clothing to be soft and very breathable, as well as comfortable. The next morning they headed south again, heading for Jerred's home territory.

"What's that?" Roslyn asked Kai suddenly as she saw something in the distance. She covered her eyes from the sun with a hand.

Kai smiled, knowing what she saw. "That is the plateau," he told her.

"It looks like a mountain with no end," Tiffany commented.

"The plateau is several days' ride wide," Jerred spoke up. "No one has ever been able to reach the top since the tunnel up to the surface collapsed."

They finally reached Jerred's village in a vast forest, the houses built in the trees and connected by rope bridges. Heath commented how it reminded him of the archipelago where he grew up, and the villagers liked how he handled the rope bridges. Jerred left them on their journey there, and they continued the next day with him waving goodbye from the edge of his village. He sent with them smoked meat and fresh baked bread.

***

Roslyn started awake the next morning, groggy and unsure why she had woken up. As Roslyn listened she heard the unsettled horses moving around at their lines. Quickly she got up and left the tent she shared with Tiffany and Cassidy to find Heath and Aidan standing outside of their own tents looking confused.

"It just started," Heath told her. "The animals just started acting weird."

By then the others had awakened, all of them sleepy-eyed and confused at the commotion going on.

Roslyn looked around them, at the forested part of the savannah where Jerred had said would be a good place to stop for the night. The savannah would give way to marshland in two weeks, and that would in turn become desert in another two weeks. The birds had taken flight, and other animals in the area were also giving off their frightened cries.

That was when the earth beneath them started to roll and heave, tossing Roslyn on her back. She heard Oswick yell out, "Earthquake!" as she hit her head and blacked out.

***

"Roslyn?" a familiar voice spoke her name.

"Huh?" she spoke, and found that her mouth was dry. She coughed and found that her head hurt as she did so.

"Roslyn?" This time it was Heath, both he and Kavan were holding her in a sitting position together.

"I'm awake," she heard herself say. "What happened?"

"There was an earthquake," she heard Oswick say.

"Never in my life have I ever witnessed something like that," she heard Kai telling the others. "I fear something bad is happening."

Roslyn looked from Kavan to Heath and up at the others. "What happened?" she asked them.

"The ground decided to teach you a lesson," Tiffany told her with a chuckle. "It didn't like the way you were sleeping on it."

Roslyn stuck her tongue out at her friend and looked around them. "Anything else?"

"The ground settled after a minute, nothing here but I heard something in the distance," Rafi told her. "Sounded like an avalanche."

"What's an avalanche?" Cassidy asked him.

"I was up in a mountain one time with my father's caravan, almost the dead of winter. The passes were still open and we were trying to be as quiet as we could; one of the horses balked and lost it, and cried out...we were lucky to miss the snow that fell off the side of the mountain at us, for we would have been dead if we were not close to the end of the pass."

Cassidy's face went white at the thought of so much snow careening towards her. She shivered and hugged herself closer.

"Has anyone made breakfast yet?" Roslyn asked them as Heath and Kavan helped her to stand.

That earned a laugh from her friends and they went about getting their breakfast together. It was almost midmorning when the group broke camp and started riding south again.

"What is that?" Roslyn asked one afternoon a week later as they were nearing the marshy part of the savannah. Kai covered his eyes from the sun and squinted.

"There should be a village up ahead," he said with concern. "I...that does not look right." Kai kicked his horse into a run and went ahead of the group, stopping a few minutes later and coming back to them.

"It's gone," he told them, "the village is gone; a giant chasm takes its place."

They rode with him to the edge of the chasm, each of them slowly approaching the edge to look over. The ground had been ripped far apart, and far below a river now ran though they could not hear it. The chasm ran in either direction as far as they could see.

"How many people lived in the village?" Roslyn asked Kai.

"A couple hundred," he told her grimly. "This is what we felt last week," he added.

"You said you have never felt an earthquake before?" Oswick asked the clansmen. Kai shook his head to answer.

"Back home in the south we had them," Oswick told them. "Though I have never felt something as strong as the one we did here."

"So this is abnormal?" Roslyn raised the question, adding, "What could cause this?"

"Orcs?" Tiffany suggested, earning a chuckle from Heath.

"Let's see how far this chasm goes. We might have to try to find a spot we can shoot a rope over and climb over," Roslyn said, though she was not happy about it. They rode west inland for several more days before they found the end of the chasm. There they found several clans people investigating the chasm--Kai went to go talk to them while the group went to set up camp.

Kai returned some time later as the other clansmen dispersed.

"They felt the same quake as we did," he informed them. "They were on their way to visit family in a village that is no longer there. That makes at least three villages lost, two of them Bear Clan and one of them Hyena."

"Anything else?"

"More orcs have been seen in areas they should not be. The orcs tribes were told they could only remain in certain areas of the south during the winter," Kai continued, "We are by no means close to those areas."

***

That night by the fire Kavan sat with Roslyn next to him, snuggled up against his side. He felt warm and safe with her there, like he had never been before. Growing up in the orphanage he had learned to not get attached to too many people; the Masters were the only ones he could depend upon. Several of his year mates had joined the mining crews in the south, a handful also went to the army. He had never heard from any of them again.

Kavan looked around the campfire, at Roslyn's twin sister flirting with Kai, to Tiffany playing with Crick, and Oswick and Rafi arguing over which of them would get the better half of the cocoa deal. Aidan sat in silence as he took in everything around him, smiling as he watched Tiffany and Crick. Kavan wondered what the life of a Quarter Master was like, and even if Aidan was just an apprentice it must still be boring--well, at least it had been before Roslyn broke him out of his shell. He seemed very different from the first day Kavan met him at the morning practice session; more alive. He certainly had filled out in the months since they had left. Kavan remembered how hard the sickness had hit; by the time it reached the far south though everyone was quarantined and only a handful of people died. Aidan had lived through that in the capital, and Kavan could only imagine how that was. Probably as bad as being one of the only survivors in an attack on a fortress.

"Aidan, where are you from?" Kavan found himself asking. "I am sorry it took so long to ask you that."

"I was born in the capital," Aidan answered him with a smile. "My parents are merchants. They sent me to apprentice at the palace when I was a youth."

"Any siblings?" Roslyn asked him.

"I had two," Aidan replied after a moment's hesitation. "They both died during the sickness."

Roslyn's head fell as she took in the information. "I am sorry to take you away from your family," she told him.

"No, Roz, no," he said as he sat up straighter. "This has been an adventure of a lifetime. I would not take it back for anything."

Kavan felt Roslyn lean into him again, seeking comfort from her own thoughts. He held her close, squeezing her hand in consolation. He knew he had doubted Aidan's abilities when they had first started out, but seeing him on the ship during the voyage showed him that Aidan had prospects. Every morning Aidan still held his own against his friends, but against a foe he did not know? Kavan was unsure how the young Quartermaster would fare. Kavan was resolved to ask Kai to practice with them in the morning, for they had let the envoys sleep through their morning practices before. If orcs were nearby they might need the advantage.

Katie M. Thornton

***

Roslyn arose one morning with the sun barely risen. Heath was already awake, sitting on a rock nearby watching the sunrise, still within the bounds of her protective circle. She was wearing just her tunic, her legs bare as she sat down next to Heath. The earth had become more sand like, streams scarce, and the days warmer. They were coming up to the desert part of Jay'Al, almost two months after leaving New Wardgrove.

"It's too quiet," Roslyn complained with a whisper to Heath as she got comfortable on the log next to him. "Where are the animals?"

Heath turned his head to listen.

"I think they're still sleeping," he whispered back.

Roslyn looked towards the east and covered her eyes, staring into the distance. "Something is out there," Roslyn told him. "I cannot tell what it is yet, but it looks like a large group of something."

"Should we wake everyone and break camp?" Heath asked her.

"It could be animals for all we know. We are safe within the confines of my circle, I have added spells for safety that make it so no one outside the circle can see or hear us, or come in without permission."

"Well that is handy," Heath said. "Shall we start breakfast for everyone ?"

***

Aidan awoke to the smell of food. He got dressed, washing his face quickly with a handful of water from his water skein. He left his tent and found Roslyn and Heath sitting around the fire working together to cook their breakfast.

"Ehhhh, you're the first one up," Roslyn welcomed him with enthusiasm. They heard someone in a nearby tent mutter something, which made the three of them laugh. After a short while the rest of the group joined them by the fire, drawn by the smell of food. Aidan loved this time of morning; back at the palace the apprentices always ate together in the morning. When he started with Roslyn and her friends he was worried about losing connection, but soon he had found that there was more connection in the new group of friends than he could ever dream. Roslyn was a young woman who could be queen, but because she had been born out of the laws of Ellsgrove she could not be. Kavan was an orphan and yet he had become basically the bodyguard of a princess and prince. Heath had once been a pirate, but now he was one of Roslyn's closest friends.

And Aidan, himself? Well, he had once been the youngest son of merchants who had become an apprentice to a quartermaster, and was now adventuring across the world. When Roslyn had asked him to join them in the mornings for their training sessions, at first he had been reluctant but she had made it fun. He saw how she treated Tiffany, and the friendship that grew between the two young women. During the voyage over, more things had changed for him: he had befriended the sailors and learned everything about sailing. Once they had built New Wardgrove he felt he grew even more. He was more than just a quartermaster; Roslyn was his friend and trusted him for advice that no one else could give. How many people could say they were such close friends to a princess? That did not even matter; he knew that if he had met her before the sickness that they would have been friends eventually. He would not change the last few months for anything.

"Woman, give me some sausages," Oswick said to Roz as he held out his plate for her to give him food. "Before you eat them all yourself."

Unsurprisingly, that morning Roslyn nearly decimated Oswick during practice. Kai was still no match for her, even with the differences in their fighting styles--Cassidy had shown Roslyn enough of the fighting styles of Jay'Al over the weeks that Roslyn knew them now. Aidan was still trying to learn, and Kai's way of the sword was different from the Wolf Clan even. Kavan assured Aidan that whatever they could learn could make the difference in their survival. Aidan had to wonder if orcs worked by the same fighting structure. He highly doubted it.

He would keep up though. Aidan wanted to see the look on Roslyn's face when he was able to keep up with her. He wanted to be able to share old stories with her children and grandchildren, and have Roslyn punch him in the shoulder for telling something wrong.

Aidan looked around the group as they broke camp, taking in the camaraderie and companionship, and feeling so at home there. He sighed heartily and mounted his horse, looking forward to the rest of their journey.

***

Roslyn stared at the desert behind them.

"How far away is your city?" she asked Kai. The capital of the Hyena Clan was a large city with thousands of people, with several outlying villages along rivers that connected each settlement together.

"Another week, if we were on the river," Kai replied, not holding back his disappointment. They were at the small harbour on the river Keenai, but there were no boats there waiting. Kai even suggested that the river looked shallower than it should be.

"It will take a little less than two weeks by horse, but we will have to ford the river at some point," Kai added.

"Could that earthquake affect the river here?" Roslyn asked Kai, earning a shrug from the clansman.

"Definitely," Oswick spoke up. "With that chasm, a whole lot of other things could have been compromised on this part of the continent."

"How far could the effects be?" Cassidy asked them, worried about her home.

"Not as far as home," Oswick told her. "The Wolf Clan is safe. I doubt they felt anything at all. I keep waiting for Jerred to show up with a small army because of the quake though."

"I want you to meet my father within the next week, so could we please ride with haste?" Kai spoke up, looking very impatient as he fidgeted in his saddle.

They had all changed their clothes a few days before to lighter layers, Roslyn and Tiffany wearing light brown cotton breeches and a white tunic, Cassidy the light linen underclothing that she had worn under her winter clothing, and the men each with breeches and loose tunics of varying colours. They switched out their heavy boots with lighter ones as well.

They rode south along the river for two days when they came across another small harbour that had a couple of river rafts at it. When Kai went to see what was going on in the Harbour Building, he came running back out with his face flushed.

"They're all dead," he told them. "Orcs by the look of it."

The group dismounted, Heath, Tiffany and Aidan staying with the horses. Roslyn, Kavan, Rafi and Oswick followed Kai into the stone building that was one big office space on the inside with desks and a small kitchen to the side. Four bodies were strewn around the room, all of them killed by some kind of slashing blade.

Kai directed them to look at something on the floor behind one of the desks, and Roslyn gasped as she realized what they were looking at.

"Is that truly an orc?" she asked Kai, who could only nod as his reply. The orc had been struck in the neck by an arrow and subsequently killed.

"So orcs attacked the harbour, that's why there were no river rafts up the river?" Rafi asked as Kavan knelt by one of the men's bodies to investigate.

"They've been dead at least a week," Kavan told them. "We shouldn't stay any longer, we need to get on one of those rafts and leave immediately."

"Agreed," Roslyn replied, looking grim.

They left the building and told the others what happened. Right away they got the horses onto two of the rafts and together with the large poles they pushed off from the harbour and started to float down the river.

"The river is very low," Kai said as he used one of the poles to direct their raft. He looked troubled as he looked at the pole, and Roslyn could see the watermark on the pole that was a good two to three feet higher than where the water was now.

"Water levels falling, orcs acting up...something is happening," Roslyn spoke up. "Will we be safe heading north again?"

"Let's get to the safety of my city first before we think about that," Kai told her. "Everyone keep an eye out on both sides of the river."

It was not a relaxing ride down the river; everyone was on high alert, and the horses could sense their anxiety.

Heath reached a hand into the water and after a couple of minutes he pulled it back out, a thoughtful expression on his face.

"What is it?" Roslyn asked him.

"Someone used magic similar to mine on the river," he told her. "Either the orcs have magic like mine, or someone from the Archipelago is responsible for this."

"How long have the Tribes of the Archipelago had a settlement to the south?" Roslyn asked the group. "Almost twenty years, right? How many people from the Clans could have had children with the Tribes since?"

"Well that doesn't help to narrow the culprits down," Oswick told her, "that's the exact opposite."

"I'm saying we cannot blame the Tribes for this yet until we have definitive proof. Ellsgrove has a tentative treaty with the Tribes, and the Clans are on good terms with them even if they haven't completed any kind of treaty yet. The last thing we need to do right now is cause any tension between us all by pointing fingers."

"Roz is right. Let's just get to where we are going and see if anyone there knows what the hells is going on," Oswick spoke up from the other raft. He looked worried as well.

***

They rode the raft in silence the rest of the journey, tying the two rafts together and two of them pairing off during the night to take watch. Three days later they reached Kai's city, coming up to a closed metal gate and the muzzles of pistols pointed at them over the wall.

"You can clearly see we are not orcs," Roslyn said, hands on her hips. "And I am sure you recognize Kai here."

The pistols were lowered and an older man with an apologetic expression appeared above them. "My apologies Princess Roslyn," the man said to her and motioned to someone nearby to open the gate on the river. "I see you are aware of the presence of orcs in the area."

"We found a body at the First Harbour," Kai told him before embracing the older man. "Uncle Erick, it is good to see you."

"We had hoped you would have been here sooner, like a couple of weeks ago," Erick replied as they parted.

"There was an earthquake that split the earth. There are three villages gone. We had to go around," Kai replied as Erick ushered their group forward. Erick's eyes widened in surprise and Roslyn noted the guards and other people nearby looking at each other with surprise and shock.

"One of my servants will see after your horses," Erick told them. "Please, come with me and we will have some refreshments while your rooms are being prepared."

Erick led them down open hallways of tiled floors, the open sky above them. Fountains ran in courtyards and people gathered around them, children playing and laughing. They came to buildings with actual roofs and Erick led them inside through large open doors.

There was a grouping of chaises in the middle of one large room, colourful murals taking up the walls. The floor itself was also a mural, and Roslyn found herself craning her neck to try to get a good look at it once she was seated. There were lizards and desert birds, but the rest of it she could not see completely.

A servant rolled in a cart with refreshments on it, several pitchers of water and juices along with cups.

"Nephew, tell me everything," Erick said to Kai.

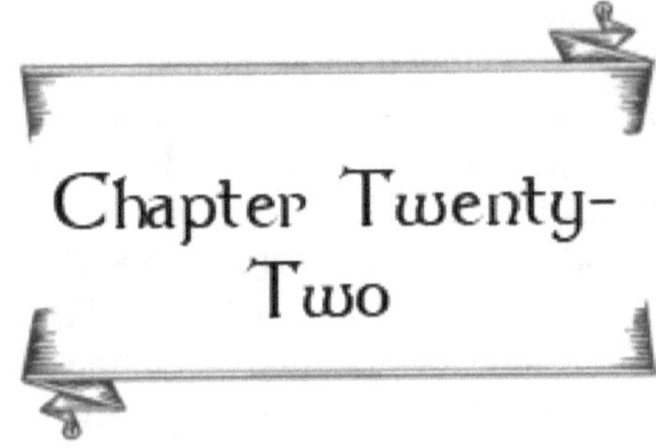

Chapter Twenty-Two

Karina stared out over the land far below her. She never could see much, just the landscape features and tall stationary objects that she figured were trees. Sometimes smaller dots could be animals, or maybe even humans.

"Oy, Karina!" came a shout from nearby.

Karina turned and smiled, her two top canines sticking out of her mouth slightly. Her own canines were nothing compared to those of the full orc that stood holding a large axe nearby with other orcs or half/part-orcs: his were a good few inches long.

"Your mother was looking for you," the orc told her. "She figured you might be out here staring down."

Karina stuck her tongue out at the man and sighed, knowing she had been out there too long, like always. The workers who were building the staircase down the side of the plateau were changing shifts now, so that must mean it was midday. She might as well wait for her father to come up and go home with him.

"Thank you, Ados, I will stay and wait for my father."

Ados shrugged and went along with the rest of the workers who were in charge of cutting the trees down to the sizes they needed. Others went over to the platform that hung over the side of the plateau. Karina herself was perched in a tree that hung slightly over the edge; it was the sturdiest of trees she could find. Her mother had warned her that if she fell she would be dead, but that had never deterred Karina. Sitting in the tree beside her was her familiar, a large feline that came up to her knees and took both arms to hold. There were several of his kind left on the plateau, and she had been very amused when he first came to her as her familiar a few years ago. Mister Scruffy was his name, and he indeed had long brownish coloured hair and spoofs of hair coming off of his big pointed ears.

The land below had always fascinated her. The whole eighteen years of her life had been spent on the plateau; what was it like down below?

Karina looked at the mountain in the center of the plateau; it reached high up into the clouds, two waterfalls coming down each side into two lakes. No one had traversed the mountain in a long time, or at least none who had lived to tell the tale. Karina wondered someday if she might try it, using her magic to help. Her mother had told her that the air got thinner up the mountain and that was what was so dangerous.

The rest of the plateau was made up of two valleys, one on each side of the mountain. There was an abundance of trees and meadows where the alpaca grazed. Deer had become scarce there long ago, but the rabbits, waterfowl, and fish in the lakes of each valley were abundant.

"Hey there, little one," a familiar voice called her attention back to the top platform of the staircase. Her father was coming towards her, looking worn out after his morning shift.

'Little' was a pet-name he liked to call her. She was as tall as he was, over six feet tall. Her father was a barrel-chested man who had canines the same size as hers, the same green-black skin and dark red hair that came with being part-orc. She got her green eyes from her father. His brown alpaca wool cloth-ing looked a little worn, as did the other workers' clothes. They had no way of dyeing the wool since the trade with the other clans had been cut off, so they had to go with the natural colours of the alpaca's wool. Karina wondered what dyes she would find if she was down below.

"You've been out here all morning?" her father asked her as she met him by the path that would lead back to their village.

She nodded and fell in beside him and the other workers, reaching out and taking his arm. Mister Scruffy walked alongside them.

"Ados said mother was looking for me, but I figured I would wait for your shift to be done and come back with you."

"You know she worries about you," her father scolded. "I know you can do much with your magic too, but if that maple tree you like to sit in ever broke, you may not have enough time to save yourself."

"That tree is as steadfast as you are, father," she teased him. "Come on, I wonder what mother has made for food?"

They entered the village under an old stone arch, the etchings on it mostly worn off. Chickens stalked around the paths of the village, eating grubs and other bugs as they went. Around the outside of the village were several farms that helped produce the wheat and barley for breads and ale, while the farms around the other village on the other side of the plateau planted corn, hay, potatoes, beans and peas. The two villages would come together come harvest and they would divvy things out to the makers: the bread maker got a portion of the wheat and barley, as did the ale maker; the corn, potatoes, beans and peas would be divided equally for each family, and the hay would go to the alpaca farmers. People traded other goods to the baker for bread, like eggs, honey, or crafts.

As the only shaman of the Dragon Clan Karina also traded spells or potions for things. Her mentor, the old shaman Krisis who had been her great-uncle, had died last year, but thankfully not before teaching her everything she needed to know. The Chief of the Clan was her father.

Since she was of marrying age Karina had her own house in the village, though since she was as of yet unmarried she still took food with her parents and younger siblings. They approached their mud brick house with its thatched roof and Karina could smell the cooking chicken from the front gate of their property.

More chickens wandered inside their short fence, as did a few smaller cats who scattered at the sight of Mister Scruffy.

"Darling Dacey, we are home!" her father called out as they reached the front door.

"We are in the kitchen in the back!" came the reply. "You are just in time for lunch."

They went through the front room of the house and down the hall to the back kitchen which had two wide doors that opened up onto a patio behind the house. The wooden table was set for the whole family, and already sitting around it waiting to be served were Karina's three younger siblings: Jaco, who at sixteen was the spitting image of his father and just as tall; Fadi, fourteen, who looked more like their mother with dark eyes and a heart shaped face; and Davin, the youngest at twelve who was a peculiar one--he had no long canines like the rest of them, and he was shorter and not as stocky as the rest of them. Every now and then the families who had orc-blood did find themselves with a more human child, but it was rare, and it only made Davin more special.

"There were a few people looking for you today," Dacey told her only daughter. "When I told them where you were they told me they would wait till this afternoon for you to return."

Both villages knew of her desire to go down from the plateau, and most of them could not fault her for it. They had lived their whole lives cut off from the Clans below and all of them wondered what the other Clans were like. Would the other Clans accept them now? They did still all have Clan blood, and were still connected to Jay'Al, but most of them had orc-blood and looked like orcs. Karina had to believe that they would still be accepted; the call she felt to go down there kept pulling at her.

"Lou darling, how goes the building of your stair?" Dacey asked her husband as she brought the roasting pan with the chicken in it over to the table. Lou and Karina had washed their hands and were sitting at the table with the others now. Mister Scruffy curled up on a floor cushion next to the table.

"It is slow going, but with the enchantments Karina made for us on the tools we have been able to anchor deep enough to steady it. It will take several more weeks though to reach the bottom."

"Well, let us hope there will be no more delays, for Karina's sake," her mother teased, knowing how antsy her daughter was about the build. Karina glared at her mother and reached over to cut off some of the chicken breast and grab some of the roasted potatoes.

A ringing sound came suddenly in her ears, and she blinked with uncertainty. The ringing in her ears usually meant a calling from the Shrine, but it had been years since she had last heard it. Dropping her utensils she excused herself, citing the call, and took off out the back doors heading for the Shrine, her familiar following in her wake.

She did not remember the journey there, though she vaguely recalled her best friend Cerise calling her name. Suddenly she found herself at the door of the Shrine that was built into the base of the mountain, a small Dragon statue, the serpentine creature on four legs with two wings protruding from its shoulders, sitting before it. She took a small dagger from her sleeve and cut a finger just slightly enough to put some blood on the statue and the hidden door opened as the blood was absorbed. Taking one of the torches from the outer wall she lit it and entered the tunnel down into the shrine.

A large grouping of roots, twined together very unnaturally, came from the ceiling of the main room and went down into the ground. Karina remembered the day she had joined with Jay'Al as a Shaman, when the roots pulsed and gave off light. This was much like it, but it was more an urgent pulsing. Karina reached out and touched the roots, and she felt her conscience pulled from her body and taken amongst the roots until she finally reached her destination.

She and several other shamans floated incorporeally around the chamber of a shrine looking down at two women. None of the other shamans looked at her or registered her presence, and Karina had to wonder if they could even see her at all. How could she see them? Was it her orc blood that made her magic stronger here?

"*This is her,*" she heard an ancient voice speaking to her. "*Karina of the Dragon Clan, you must find this young shaman and help her, to bring her up to the plateau where she will find what she needs.*"

"Who is she?" Karina asked the ancients as she peered closer at the young woman below her. The young woman was around the same age as Karina and had two separate coloured eyes, one green and one blue.

"*She will bring great change and unity to the Clans,*" the voice told her. "*To all of Jay'Al.*"

With a shock Karina found herself back in her own body, in her own Clans shrine. She was shaking as she made her way back out of the shrine and through the entrance, finding her friend Cerise waiting for her. Cerise was from one of the last remaining fully human families on the plateau, though her older sister had married a part-orc.

"What happened?" Cerise asked her, taking Karina in her arms and holding her as she shook.

"The ancient shamans spoke to me," she whispered to her friend. "They want me to leave the plateau and find someone to bring them up here for some reason. They said that she would change Jay'Al, change the Clans. Unify us." Her shaking had not stopped yet. Mister Scruffy twined around her ankles mewing in worry at his mistress.

"Let's get you back home now," Cerise told her as she slung her friend's arm around her shoulder. "Mister Scruffy, maybe you should go on ahead to get Lou and Jaco, she is heavier than she looks."

***

Karina stared at the fire in her own hearth. Several weeks had passed since the ancients had called to her, and in that time she had prepared to leave. The workers on the stairway had doubled their building efforts and the stairway was nearing completion, but it was still too high up for her to jump down from. She would have to wait for it to be complete before she could leave.

Voices outside in the village called her outside, and she found the whole village standing in the dark looking up at the sky. The moon was eclipsing.

"What do you think it means?" Cerise asked Karina as she joined her.

"Great change," Karina told her. "The woman the ancients showed me, I feel today is special to her. The gods, and the ancients, are showing her their favour, and announcing to the rest of us that something big is about to happen."

"Like what?" Cerise asked her. Karina shrugged and turned away, heading back to her own house.

"I will find out when I meet her," Karina told her friend. "Good night Cerise."

"You're not going to stay and finish watching the eclipse?"

"I feel very tired all of a sudden," Karina told her truthfully. "I will see you in the morning, hm?"

***

The day came for Karina to leave. Her brother Jaco was coming with her, as was one of the other part-orc young men who had been trained as a warrior, Jarrod.

"Remember, find your cousin Grau," Dacey told her from the top of the stairway. "He should be able to help you navigate the land."

Karina made a face. Her cousin Grau was the only other person with magic she had known besides Krisis. Grau had chosen to find his own way off of the plateau several years ago, digging a tunnel that had collapsed shortly after he had gone in.

"We do not even know if he is alive," Karina reminded her mother.

"Use your magic to find him," Dacey told her. "He will have to help you, you are kinsmen."

Her family and Cerise watched as Karina and her two guards made their way down the stairs and out of sight.

Chapter Twenty-Three

It was late in the evening when Roslyn and Kai were able to retire to their rooms. The rest of the group had asked to go to settle in for the night after they had eaten supper with Chief Erick. Since Roslyn was there as an ambassador she stayed up to talk with Chief Erick and some of the other elders over dessert and wine.

Kai led her to her room in the dimly lit house, yawning as he said good-night. With a flick of her wrist she lit the lanterns around the room. After a quick look around the room she found the private bathroom that thankfully had plumbing and drew herself a bath. She was weary after a long day and her neck hurt.

She had learned a lot from her meeting with the Chief: there had been sightings of orcs around villages down the rivers, and many villages had put up higher or new walls to protect them from the orcs. The pistols the Hyena Clan had traded with the Tribes of the Archipelago for were helpful in the defence of the city.

It seemed that they would either have to go by boat back up the coast to New Wardgrove or risk the road. Erick was amazed that they had not been attacked by orcs during their journey, and Roslyn had to wonder at that.

She had felt eyes watching from the dunes, but she had not seen anything. She wondered if some of them were indeed intelligent, or else why would they not have attacked their group? It was something to think about as she bathed, using some of the lovely smelling bath oils to help her relax. Finally she fell into bed naked under her covers.

***

Kavan entered the main hall of Chief Erick's house and looked around the room. Everyone but Roslyn was there. They were all sitting with Kai on pillows on the floor waiting for breakfast, so Kavan turned around and went to see if Roslyn was sleeping in.

He found her room easily enough, just down the hall from his own. He knocked and waited. A moment later Roslyn opened the door just enough to see out into the hall; she held a light blanket pulled around herself and he realized that she was naked underneath and that's why she did not open the door more.

"Ah, good morning Kavan," Roslyn welcomed him with a grin. "Come in while I get dressed?"

He felt his face flush but he nodded and she let him in, locking the door before going over to the changing screen.

Kavan and Roslyn had not had much time alone since they had left New Wardgrove. On their journey south they had no privacy, and so had barely any time to share affection with each other, especially around Heath. Now that he was alone with her again he felt nervous, like the time he had asked her to go for that early morning ride.

He saw her throw the blanket over the side of the screen and heard her ask him, "Am I the last one up?"

"Yes; I saw you were not waiting for breakfast with everyone else so I came to wake you," he told her as he looked around the room.

He heard her swear and she said, "Can you come here and help me do up my dress?"

He stood up and went over to the changing screen and she came around the side and turned around for him to see the strings at the back of the dress that she could not reach.

"I should have thought twice about this dress," she told him as he started to do up the dress. "Usually Tiffany is here to help me but this is the only dress that has the strings at the back."

Kavan's hand brushed the top of her back and he thought he felt her shiver at his touch. That only made him blush more.

When he was done doing up her dress she turned around and he took her in; the dress was a light pink colour with slits in the hem, black leggings underneath. The bodice had white embroidery along the top, drawing the eye to her bosom. Roslyn caught him looking at her and she took a step closer to him.

"Do you like what you see?" she asked him, reaching out to hold his hands.

He smiled and nodded, unsure he could trust his voice right. She pulled him close and kissed him softly at first, but when he responded the kissing grew more heated. His hands started to make their way up her back and he found himself about to untie her dress when a knock came at the door, startling them.

"Who is it?" Roz called out, annoyance clear in her tone.

"It's Aidan, just wanted to make sure you weren't sleeping in."

"Do you think Heath put him up to it?" Kavan whispered to her as she straightened her dress. She raised an eyebrow at him and scoffed before going for the door.

"Come on, we had best not keep everyone waiting," she told him with a sweet smile.

***

Cassidy put her cup of orange juice down and smiled across the table at her twin sister. Roslyn and Kavan had been the last to join them for breakfast, and Cassidy was pretty sure they had finally found some alone time during their journey to resume their romance. She looked at Heath, who sat on Roslyn's other side, and wondered what he thought of their lateness--Roslyn had told her that they were both wooing her, so was Heath jealous that he had not had more alone time with Roslyn? She could not tell.

Cassidy was happy for her sister. She was ecstatic she was able to be in her sister's life now.

Cassidy sighed, thinking of all the years they had gone not knowing each other. She now felt complete, for she had known something was missing in her life: her twin sister. Had it been the same for Roslyn? Had her sister felt something missing, not knowing that she had a twin sister out there across the world?

Cassidy had mused years before about trying to head to Ellsgrove to find her father and sister but she knew the journey would be dangerous if she tried to go through the Archipelago.

Now though she was very happy to have her sister here with her. She had been mildly surprised to learn that Roslyn could fight and knew how to hunt; once she learned her sister was a princess she thought she would be like some of the princesses in the books she had traded for from the Archipelago. Roslyn proved that idea all wrong. While they travelled through the villages, and through the clans territories, the people of Jay'Al had been able to see what kind of a princess she was: one with the same heart as any woman from Jay'Al. She was kind, she was strong, she showed courage and understanding, and she was not afraid to show who she was.

Cassidy was proud to have Roslyn as her twin sister and she knew their mother was proud of the way that their father raised her. He had respected the traditions and beliefs of Jay'Al, and Cassidy was surprised that it was not only with Roslyn that he had done so but he had adopted them for his own beliefs and raised the rest of his children that way too; not only that, but now that he was king he was reforming the way women were viewed in Ellsgrove too. Cassidy hoped that someday she could meet her father.

***

"We were going to go out to the market today," Roslyn spoke up, meaning she, Kavan and Heath. "Who would like to join us?"

"I will be your guide," Kai spoke first.

"I'd like to see what they have," Oswick spoke up next.

"Maybe there are craftspeople here who would be willing to trade with Ellsgrove."

"I will accompany you," Cassidy told her, with Tiffany chiming in as well.

"I just want to lay in bed all day," Rafi told them with a chuckle. "I just want to relax before we have to head home again. You all have fun."

"I wanted to talk to Chief Erick about how we should go home," Aidan told her. "We need to know what is going on in the area before we make a decision."

"Sounds like a plan. Let's meet at the front door in twenty minutes?"

***

The group left Chief Erick's house with Kai showing them the way down the streets. The city was built of mud bricks and stone and was the largest Clan settlement that Roslyn had seen yet. There were four waterways that came into the city and met in one small pool in the center of the city where the marketplace was held. As they walked over bridges heading further into the city Roslyn noticed the low water. She heard people whispering about orcs and what the low water could mean--they had never seen the water so low before.

The marketplace was dozens of wooden stalls with cloth overhangs, sellers declaring their wares from behind tables laden with goods. There were several food sellers and treat sellers as well, the smell of cooking food making Roslyn hungry even though they had just eaten breakfast.

There were sellers with clothing from all different clans, others with woven baskets, jewellery, boots; there was one older lady who was weaving a tapestry with alpaca wool.

They were taking their time going to each stall and looking over the wares when midday came along. They bought some lamb kebabs and fresh flat bread before getting some sweet fruit turnovers and some fruit juice. They sat down on the edge of the pool eating and watching children playing in the low water.

Once they were done eating they gathered up their newly bought items and started to make their way back out of the marketplace when Heath stopped in his tracks, staring wide-eyed across the marketplace. He ducked his head and quickly ducked behind the closest stall; his friends noticed his behaviour and went around the back of the next stall to see what he was doing.

"Everything OK?" Roslyn asked him as he peeked out from behind the stall he had hidden behind.

"My brother is here," Heath told her.

"Shit. Did he see you?" Roslyn asked him and was relieved as Heath shook his head. "Well, quickly let us leave before Heath is seen," Roslyn told the group. "Take off your top hat, Heath, and we will gather close around you to hide you."

The others were confused for they did not know what was truly going on though they still followed Roslyn's instructions. They quickly made their way back to Chief Erick's house and when the door closed behind them Heath let a sigh of relief out.

"Just what is going on?" Kai asked them.

"I left my Tribe," Heath told Kai. "My whole family thinks I died during the war but I actually went to Ellsgrove. If they found out I was alive and had gone over to the other side...I would be imprisoned and possibly killed as a traitor."

"I think you should stay here where it is safe until we are set to leave," Roslyn said as she crossed her arms in front of her. "We cannot risk them seeing you and taking you."

Heath nodded in agreement.

"So what are we going to do?" Tiffany asked her. "Do we risk heading north to the Beaver Clan on land, or do we go by boat?"

"I will have to talk to Aidan and Chief Erick about that," Roslyn answered after a moment. "Going by boat will be safer if there are rogue orcs, but if someone from the Water Tribe recognizes Heath..."

"I could disguise myself," Heath told her. "Though we were not attacked on our way down here, we might still be safe to go on land.

"Are you not heading to the plateau from here?" Kai asked Roslyn.

"I am unsure of what exactly to do," she told him. "We should head back to New Wardgrove first, I think. If it takes us two months to get back home, Maeve and the rest of the supplies should be there by the time we get back."

"I think we should head back to New Wardgrove...," Cassidy spoke up. "...by boat. We can stop at the capital of the Beaver Clan on our way up and continue by land from there."

"That sounds like a plan actually," Roslyn said as she smiled at her sister. She turned to Kai and asked him, "Where do you recommend we find a boat? Heath can captain it."

Erick and Aidan walked up to them, and Chief Erick overheard the conversation.

"I have a small ship you can take," Chief Erick told them. "It would probably be the wisest decision to go by sea up north. Kai could go with you and sail it back down."

"We stay a few more days. Kai, will you take me to your father this afternoon?" Roslyn asked the young shaman.

"I can take you to him now," Kai told her. "His living quarters are just across the courtyard."

The group dispersed back to their rooms with their goods from the marketplace and Kai took Roslyn across the stone courtyard to another wing of the house. Roslyn noticed that the Hyena Clan preferred one story houses and buildings as opposed to multi-story ones like the Wolf and Fox Clan. Her favourite had to be the Bear Clan's houses though; she knew she still needed to see how the Beaver Clan lived.

The double doors that led into the other wing of the house had glass panes to let in the sunlight. Kai opened the doors for Roslyn and she entered to find a room with a desk and a seating area, an older man in his mid-sixties sitting on a large cushion in the sunlight. Roslyn could see the resemblance between Kai and his father for they had the same hooked nose and slanted eyes.

"Father, I brought Princess Roslyn to talk to you," Kai said in introduction. When the older man looked up and around Roslyn realized that he was blind.

Roslyn went up to him and sat down beside him, reaching a hand out to hold his hand. "Hello, it is very nice to meet you, Shaman Layne."

The older man smiled in greeting, "I have heard a lot about you in the past few weeks, princess," he told her. "News has traveled far about your arrival and your joining with Jay'Al."

"Roslyn has come to ask you about the Dragon Clan," Kai told his father. "The ancient shamans have quested her to find them."

"Indeed?" Layne made a harrumph and answered,

"My grandfather told me a story about what happened, but I cannot say for sure if it is true or not. The tunnel entrance that ran up to the top of the plateau collapsed one day when my grandfather and his father were there visiting. They were on their way down the tunnel when they were told to run. They almost did not make it out alive."

"Where was the entrance to the tunnel?" Roslyn asked him.

"My grandfather said there was a large stone arch on the road leading up to the tunnel, and two willow trees on either side of the arch," Layne told them. "Whether the arch is still there, I could not say, but not a whole lot of people travel near the plateau anyways. It was always seen as a cursed place since the collapse you see, and there was no other way up."

"So we would have to travel around the whole plateau to find an arch and some willow trees," Roslyn said to Kai as they walked back across the courtyard. "If we take a ship north we will have to travel inland at some point to the plateau."

"Maybe travel north until you reach the one river that flows inland?" Kai asked her, leading her to his uncle's office where they had some maps. He pointed out the river he meant. "The orcs are down south, hopefully they have not made it up here near the Beaver Clan."

"Is there any way we can send word to the other Clans about the orcs?"

"Yes, we have messenger birds. I am sure my uncle thought of that already but I will go make sure. If he has not then we certainly shall do so."

A Quest for Her Roots

As it turned out Chief Erick had sent messenger birds out a few days before they had arrived and was still waiting for responses. It would take several days for the birds to reach their destinations and it would take time for the response to return as well. They would have to wait to see if any orcs were sighted elsewhere.

***

Kavan watched in amusement as their group of friends stretched before their morning practice. Kai was joining them, as were Chief Erick's two oldest sons, Gabe and Keaton. Kai's familiar, the fennec fox named Tej, sat off to the side of the training ground that was in the same compound as the Chief's house. A few other people from the Hyena Clan sat to watch as well, and Kavan had a feeling they were there to judge Roslyn.

Kavan watched Aidan as he stretched. He remembered the first time Aidan had joined their group: Edmond had had to go find him proper training clothes, and he had been much skinnier. Kavan had been very unsure at first how the apprentice would handle learning how to fight but the young man had done his best and had not given up. Now, the apprentice knew fighting forms from Jay'Al and was almost confident in his use of the sword. Too much confidence was a bad thing, so maybe Kavan had done well in teaching this young man how to fight. Well, it was not just him, but Roslyn as well.

Looking to where Roslyn was stretching next to her sister and Tiffany, Kavan felt his face go red as he remembered the other day. He could not wait for more time to spend with her alone, even if it was just a dinner. Maybe he could get Kai to help him plan something soon. He looked at Heath, his training partner for the day, and wondered if she and him had been intimate yet. He found himself jealous at the thought.

"Are you ready?" Kavan heard himself asking the group.

Roslyn paired off with Aidan, Tiffany with Cassidy, Kavan with Heath, Kai with Oswick, Rafi with Gabe and Keaton. They were just using normal swords but their blades were blunted with padding.

Kavan always found that he and Heath were equally capable with a sword, though he was pretty sure he was better with a bow than Heath was; though the former pirate was definitely better with a pistol than Kavan was. This morning was no different than any other morning practice against his new friend and rival.

Kavan did notice, however, that Aidan was doing very well holding his own against Roslyn this morning. He nodded in Roslyn and Aidan's direction and Heath looked over and nodded back, agreeing to stop so they could watch the other two spar. Tiffany and Cassidy noticed the two of them stop and they too stopped to watch.

***

Completely unaware of the audience, Aidan found himself enjoying the morning practice bout against Roslyn. She was smiling widely at him as they parried back and forth, each of them looking for an opening. He had hoped someday to be as good as Roslyn, though over the months since he had started training he never did feel quite good enough. Since coming to Jay'Al though Aidan felt very different, more himself again but yet different. He was no longer the shy apprentice who would rather be sitting amongst papers and helping the quartermaster. He was almost an adventurer.

* * *

Roslyn was still smiling as they danced around each other and she jumped over his blade as he swung low. She was impressed with how far he had come over the months, but she had been training for years. She waited for her moment, watching for any openings, fully aware that most of their friends had stopped to watch them. Finally she found her opening and went for it, drawing her blade point up short at his ribs just over his heart.

"And you're dead," Roslyn said with a huff, for she was a little out of breath. "I have to admit it was fun to keep up with you."

Aidan was about to reply when he realized the whole training yard was quiet. He looked around, startled, to find everyone else watching them.

"Well done," Roslyn told him, slapping a hand on his shoulder. "I think that is the longest you have held up against me. Now," she said as she turned to the others, "shall we continue?"

Chapter Twenty-Four

As they left the training yard a little later to go clean-up for breakfast Tiffany slapped Aidan on the shoulder and congratulated him on how far he had come.

"Care to be my partner tomorrow?" Tiffany asked him.

All Aidan could do was nod before ducking into his room.

Tiffany went to have a bath before breakfast, and she dressed in loose breeches and a tunic, her sword belt at her waist. She did her hair up in two fishtail braids as Roslyn had taught her. Satisfied with her appearance she went to go to the Eating Room for breakfast.

Kai was the first one there, wearing breeches that only came to his knees and a sleeveless tunic. He smiled at her in welcome and she returned the smile.

"You handle a sword well, Tiffany," Kai told her as she took a seat on one of the larger cushions in the room. "How well are you with a bow?"

She shrugged and told him, "Well enough, I suppose."

The rest of their group came in, including Gabe and Keaton. Chief Erick also joined them for breakfast that morning, and the talk in the room was non-stop while they ate their food.

"Gabe will go with you on my ship north," Erick told

Roslyn and her friends as the talk turned to returning north. "Kai needs to stay here in case the orcs do attack us."

"That sounds like a good plan," Roslyn answered with a nod to the Chief's son.

***

Kavan was about to get up from the table when a messenger entered the room at a run, out of breath and looking frightened.

"What is it?" Chief Erick asked the young boy, handing him a flask of water.

"Orcs, Chief," the boy spat out before taking a drink of water. "There are orcs around the city."

The group looked at each other and at the Chief, who looked stricken.

"Gather the warriors," Chief Erick told his son Keaton. "Meet me at the Front Gate."

"We will come with you," Aidan told Chief Erick. "Tiffany, go tell Roz. We will prepare the horses."

Tiffany nodded and went to do what he asked. Together the rest of the group hurried to the stables while some of the servants went to get their weapons. Kavan was saddling Roslyn's horse when Roslyn and Tiffany came into the stables both wearing their light armour with their swords at their waists; Roslyn also had with her the bow and arrows that Jerred had given her.

"I will finish, you get your armour and weapons," Roslyn told him and the others as she secured her quiver to Sage's saddle. "We will wait for you."

Kavan nodded and went to do that, coming back as quickly as he could along with the others. Chief Erick looked strained at waiting for the whole group and as soon as everyone was mounted the Chief led the way to the Front Gate, his son Gabe, and nephew Kai, riding beside him, all of them wearing light armour.

Once at the wall one of the warriors took their horses and Erick led them up a stair to the walkway around the wall. All of the guards on the walkway were looking out into the desert, and when Roslyn and her friends looked out they saw why: what looked like a couple hundred orcs all in full armour with weapons in hand were standing out there. These orcs were large, bigger than the one their group had come upon up river.

"Well then," Kavan heard Roslyn say. "I suppose we will not be leaving quite yet."

"Have they made any intentions clear?" Chief Erick was asking the guards on the wall. "They are very far from where they are supposed to be."

"I think them showing up here is a pretty loud intention in itself, father," Keaton told him. "All of the gates are barred?" he asked one of the guards next to him, getting a nod in return.

"Have the Tribes been made aware of the situation?" Chief Erick asked them.

"Yes, Chief, a messenger was sent to their compound near the harbour. No ships are to come in or go out yet, and we have warriors watching the land on either side of the harbour," one of the warriors informed him.

Kai turned to Roslyn and told her, "The Tribes built their own compound onto the city by the harbour, its walls as high as ours and just as thick. The orcs attacking our city will directly affect them. I suggest you hide your friend Heath in case anyone comes from the Tribes who could know him."

A Quest for Her Roots

"That is a good idea," Roslyn said. "We should have thought of it before we left."

"No," Heath spoke up. "I will not leave you to deal with this without me," he told her. "If the orcs attack we will need every warrior available."

"The orcs will not breach these walls," Erick told them. "They have lasted a long time."

"Gabe, will you see Heath back to your father's house?" Roslyn asked Erick's son. "Please?"

"I will make sure he is safe," Gabe assured her. "I promise."

"Thank you. Heath, please go. I need you to be safe, my friend."

With a resigned sigh he nodded and followed Gabe back down from the wall.

***

Roslyn was relieved when Heath did not fight her. She watched as he and Gabe rode off back into the city. A few minutes later more warriors of the Hyena Clan joined them along the wall, watching and waiting for the orcs to do something; so far they just seemed like they were waiting for something.

Some of the orcs moved out of the way for a large battering ram being carried by a dozen or so other orcs. Several more orcs with large shields came up beside them and together they walked towards the front gate of the city.

"We need archers on the wall!" Erick shouted out, and below them in the city warriors rushed forward with their bows and quivers of arrows to join them above the gate. As the orcs came within range though, the ones carrying the shields lifted the shields up over their heads and over the heads of those carrying the battering ram to protect them as they advanced.

Erick swore as the archers loosed a volley of arrows but none of them found their marks because of the shields. Roslyn looked at Kai and she took something out of her pack, a small glass ball that fit in the palm of her hand; inside the ball was a liquid.

"I thought I would show you guys some of my magic concoctions," Roslyn told Kai, and she tossed the ball over the wall where it struck a shield, exploding and throwing several of the orcs back, even killing some; it made room for the archers to kill several more of the orcs.

"Oh, I like that," Kai commented as she tossed another.

"You've been carrying those around in your pack?!" Aidan asked her, a slight look of mortification on his face.

"They are especially spelled to not break unless thrown," she assured him. "Thank you so much for your vote of confidence."

Below them the orcs had abandoned their battering ram and retreated back, leaving their dead on the ground before the gate.

"Well that did not last long," Kavan said with slight confusion. "What in the hells are they doing?"

They could not tell what the orcs were doing from a distance but a few other orcs started to pull something forward.

"Is that a catapult?" Tiffany asked.

Erick turned to one of his soldiers and ordered him to evacuate the part of the city behind them as fast as they could. Bells started ringing around the city and the people below dropped what they were doing and headed for the center of the city in some disarray. Roslyn could hear the cries of fear from the people evacuating.

Several more catapults were brought forward and loaded with large stones and together they were released, the stones hurtling through the air towards the gate. Roslyn, Cassidy and Kai all put their hands up and used their magic to create a shield before the city where the stones stopped short a good twenty feet in front of the gate, dropping to the ground with a heavy thud.

"Well they know we have mages now," Kai commented. "I wonder what they will do next?"

"How many more gates are there?" Roslyn asked Kai and his uncle.

"Five large gates, a few smaller ones," Erick responded.

"We will need more shamans," Kai spoke up as the orcs started to separate into groups and move towards the city, heading for other gates. "Roslyn, Cassidy and I cannot cover all of the gates."

"I will stay here," Cassidy told them. "You two go to the next gates while more shamans are summoned from the city."

"Best hurry," Kavan said as he nodded to the orcs; the three catapults were in different groups now and they were starting to aim.

Erick turned to Keaton, who had arrived with the rest of the warriors and thankfully a few more shamans. "Get the shamans to different gates, and reinforce the gates. Archers need to spread out on the walls as well."

"Right, let's split up and spread out," Roslyn said. "Oswick, you stay here with Cassidy. Rafi and Tiffany, spread out between here and the next gate with your bows. Aidan, come with me, and Kavan--"

"I'm with you," he interrupted her, crossing his arms over his chest.

"Sure," she did not want to argue. "Let's go."

The next gate to the left of the main one was a hundred feet away and it was where Roslyn stopped. Kai went to the next gate to the right of the main gate. As Roslyn put her bow and arrow down and started fishing through her bag the orcs who had stopped and aimed their catapult at the gate she was standing over let a stone loose. She put her hands up and reached out with her magic, stopping the stone from reaching the city. The other two catapults fired, Cassidy and Kai stopping the stones as Roslyn had.

"How long do you think they will keep this up?" Kavan asked Roslyn and Aidan.

"I guess we will have to wait and see," Roslyn answered as she blocked another stone.

"Do you need any help?" a man said nearby.

Roslyn turned to see a young man who was clearly a sailor, one of the Tribes of the Archipelago who had answered the Chief's call for help. Below there were more Tribesmen with pistols getting their weapons ready. There was something about the young man that looked familiar.

"And you are?" Roslyn asked him calmly.

"I am Captain Everett," the young man told her. Roslyn swore in her head, thinking it was a very good thing she had sent Heath away; no wonder the young man looked so familiar, he was Heath's goddamn brother. He had the same straight hair and eyes, even the dimples in his cheeks.

"And who exactly are you?" he asked her in turn.

"I am Roslyn," she told him. "I am sure Chief Erick would appreciate pistols on the wall in case the orcs come any closer."

Everett nodded and ordered his men to spread out along the wall.

"Your accent is very different," Everett commented as he stood beside Roslyn, his pistol in one hand. "It sounds more like an Ellsgrove accent than one from Jay'Al, yet you look like a native."

"I was born here," she told him, "but I was raised in Ellsgrove."

"So you would not happen to be princess Roslyn, would you?" Everett asked, looking sideways at her.

"Ah, so you have heard of me."

"Word of your exploits in the palace have reached us, yes. We were impressed by the stories, but now I see they were not exaggerated. So you have come to Jay'Al to open an outpost like we have, hm?"

"Could we talk about this later?" Roslyn asked him as she blocked another stone.

"Tell me, is it true your captain is from the Tribes?" Everett was not letting the conversation drop that easy.

"I am not sure where you heard that," Roslyn told him, feigning a confused look before turning her back on him and blocking another stone.

"They are loading the stones faster," Kavan commented. "Where are they getting all the stones from?"

"There is a quarry nearby," Everett told them. "I imagine that is where."

"Great, they have an endless supply of stones to throw at us. They are probably trying to tire the shamans out," Roslyn responded. "This is going to be a long day."

Several more times the orcs advanced with more crudely made battering rams, some of them protected by shields, some of them nearly breaking through gates before all of them in the group were killed. The sounds of pistols going off drowned out most of the noise the orcs made, and Roslyn found her ears ringing several times with Everett standing so close and firing his weapon.

Finally the catapults stopped slinging stones, and the orcs drew back.

Roslyn's stomach made a loud grumble, and Kavan chuckled.

"I think we can probably get some food," Kavan commented. He put his bow down and went to grab them all some food; thankfully one of the lamb kebab vendors from the market had come to bring the warriors food, though the smell of the cooking lamb had been driving Roslyn crazy for the last little while. Kavan handed out kebabs and flatbread to all of their friends and came back to Roslyn where she wolfed down the food.

Chief Erick came to them, and he looked as tired as Roslyn.

"We will replace the warriors on the wall with refreshed warriors to allow everyone time to rest and eat. I have more shamans coming in from across the city as well."

"My men will stay here a little while longer," Everett told Erick. "I do not have a reserve unfortunately."

"Your help is greatly appreciated," Chief Erick assured him. "As is yours, Roslyn. Now go and rest, please."

Roslyn nodded and motioned to Kavan and Aidan who gathered up their things and went to collect their friends as more warriors came to replace those who had been on the wall all morning.

As Roslyn rode back to the Chief's house she thought about Everett. Clearly the Tribes had spies in the capitol, so did that mean Everett already knew his brother was alive? Just how safe was Heath now?

"We might need to have Heath guarded," Roslyn told Kavan as they approached the Chief's house. "I did not like how Everett was asking those questions."

"It worries me as well," Kavan told her. "I will stay with Heath tomorrow and be his guard."

"I do not need a nursemaid," Heath told them when they explained their plan. "I should not hide, I should--"

"No," Roslyn interrupted him. "Out of the question. You are under my command, Captain Heath. I will not endanger my friend's life. You did what you had to do, I will not fault you for that. You have made a life for yourself and you have people here who care about you. We will not let you endanger your own life."

"How did I get so lucky to have friends like you, hm?" Heath teased her before sighing resignedly. "Very well, Roz, I will accept your order."

"Good. Now, what have you been doing all day? Did you make us lunch?"

***

Roslyn tossed and turned in her bed, the distant sounds of stones hitting magical barriers making it hard for her to sleep. Finally she got up, putting a robe around herself, and went to go for a walk around the open halls of the Chief's house. Roslyn had to admit she had grown to like the heat down here in the south of Jay'Al and the architecture of the houses, especially the open halls and courtyards.

Roslyn entered a dark courtyard and sat down on one of the benches, looking up at the stars. The constellations on this side of the world were so different, but they were still so beautiful. Cassidy had taught her a few of the northern constellations during their initial journey, but since Cassidy did not know the ones so far south they had ended there. The last couple weeks of their journey south had been busy, with the threat of the orcs looming, so she had not thought to ask Kai to teach her.

"Roslyn?" She started to hear her sister's voice. She turned to find Cassidy in her own robes standing under one of the arches of the hallway. "You could not sleep either?"

"No. Come sit with me?" Roz invited her sister over. Cassidy came over and sat with her on the bench and Roslyn put an arm around her sister to hold her close.

"Have you ever had to fight orcs before?" Roslyn asked her.

"Once, while out for a hunt. The Clans made an agreement with the orcs long ago: they stay in their territory and we stay in ours so there will be no bloodshed. I had been a hunter for a short while when I went too far into the mountains. I ran into an orc and had to defend myself. Thankfully I was a faster draw with my bow than it was."

"Gods," Roslyn said as she exhaled and she held her sister closer. "What did mother say about it?"

"I never told her," Cassidy whispered. "I was too afraid if something were to happen between my people and the orcs. I took my arrow out and made it look like a knife wound before throwing the body down a gully. I covered up the blood with snow as best I could and left."

"Ah, smart indeed," Roslyn told her. "I take it nothing happened after?"

Cassidy shook her head and buried her face in her sister's shoulder. "I never went into the mountains again after that though."

"I am glad you were safe," Roslyn whispered to her. "What do you think of the south?" Roslyn wanted to change the subject now.

"I prefer the cold," Cassidy told her, earning a laugh from Roslyn.

"I much rather prefer the warmth," Roslyn told her. "Back home I grew up in our north and had never been further south than the capital. I much rather enjoy not having to wear layers and worry about freezing to death."

Cassidy looked at her closely and asked her, "What happened?"

"I had snuck out to watch the sunset on my birthday when I turned sixteen," Roslyn told her. "There was a lot of snow but I was used to the snowshoes. It started snowing heavily while I was out there and I got disoriented and lost. I had to find shelter and used my magic for most of the night to keep myself warm, but I grew very weak...father found me the next morning. I had never seen him so angry or upset with me before. He cried."

Cassidy took her hand and squeezed it. "He sounds like a very good man, our father."

"He is," Roslyn found herself gasping as she started to cry. "I miss him so much."

Cassidy hugged her sister and let her cry, rubbing her back to comfort her. "I hope someday I can meet him."

Roslyn rubbed the tears away and looked at Cassidy. "Maybe you could go visit him when we get back to New Wardgrove. Maeve will have to make the journey back to Ellsgrove again."

"I will think on that," Cassidy told her seriously. "I will need to talk to mother about it."

"Hey girls," they both turned to find Heath standing under an archway in his breeches and a loose tunic.

Cassidy gave Roslyn a knowing look as Roslyn wiped the tears away with a sleeve, and said, "I think I will call it a night, I will leave the two of you alone."

Heath took Cassidy's seat and he pulled Roslyn close to him, letting her lean into him as he put his arm around her.

"Beautiful night, is it not?" Heath asked her as they looked up at the stars together. He raised an arm and pointed at a grouping of stars and told her, "That is the Great Ship. For my people there is a legend about the first ship that sailed around the archipelago, bringing our people together. That is it, up in the stars now."

"You know the constellations down here?" she inquired of him, and he nodded and told her a few more: The Spear, the Whale and the Mermaid.

"I sailed under these stars for many years," he explained to her, "before the Wars started. It has been many years though."

"What do you think of your brother being so close by?"

Roslyn found herself asking him as he twined his left hand with her right.

She watched as the expression on his face changed to one of contemplation. "Honestly," he began, "it's very weird. I had not seen him in so long but I find myself wanting to tell him about what I have been doing, about our journey, and most of all about you. The only problem, of course," he added with a dark laugh, "is that he would probably kill me if he found me."

"Then I will make sure he never finds you,"

Roslyn told him, squeezing his hand. "You mean a lot to me."

Heath looked at her, a very serious expression on his face. "I mean a lot to you? What about Kavan?"

"You both do. Which is why I still find it difficult to choose between you two," she responded sheepishly.

A Quest for Her Roots

She felt warmth inside as he took her chin in her hand and had her look at him, a warmth in his eyes that made her catch her breath. He leaned in and pressed his lips against hers, and she returned the kiss in kind. She felt a warmth spread over her whole body as they continued to kiss, his arms holding her close against his body. She sighed with relief as they slipped off of the bench together and onto the mossy ground, their hands making their way around each other's bodies.

Chapter Twenty-Five

The next morning Heath and Kavan watched their friends head back to the front gate with Chief Erick and the others. Roslyn had reminded Heath to stay in the Chief's house with Kavan, earning a wide grin and a 'Yes, mother' from Heath. Roslyn had stuck her tongue out at him before riding off.

"They are still out there," Kai told them when they reached the gate. He had been out there since before the sun rose. "They have withdrawn but they are still out there."

"Where are the Tribesmen?" Roslyn asked him, looking around.

"They went back to their compound just after I got here," Kai told her. "I was told that Everett went back to their compound last night though with a handful of his men."

"Should we send out scouts?" Roslyn asked. "They could be doing something out there."

"No, we cannot risk any lives doing that. We have been lucky so far, thanks to you and the Tribes," Erick responded. "We will wait and watch from the wall."

"Are we needed ?" Cassidy spoke up.

"I will stay with my warriors," Erick told them.

"You may return to my house unless you want to stay."

"I will stay for a few hours," Roslyn told him. She looked to her friends and saw how tired some of them were.

"Why do you not go back to the Chief's house and rest some more? Hopefully we can leave for home in a few days."

"I will stay with you," Cassidy told her. Rafi and Oswick looked at each other and shrugged before going back to their horses.

A Quest for Her Roots

Aidan and Tiffany chose to stay with them, but Kai chose to go back home.

"They are up to something," Roslyn said as she and her remaining friends looked out into the desert. "I bet anything they are up to something."

***

Kavan and Heath went to the training yard after Roslyn and the others left. They battered each other with covered blades for a time before choosing to just lay on the floor of the training yard and staring up at the blue sky.

"This is ridiculous," Heath said after a time. "I should not be hiding here."

"Yes, you should," Kavan told him. "I agree with Roslyn; you are too important to risk your life. It is also hard to find good friends."

"I appreciate that," Heath answered. "Does not mean I completely have to like it."

They were silent for a time before the sound of something shattering nearby disturbed them.

They both sat up, looking down the open hallways that connected to the yard they were in. Both of them took the padding off of their swords and Kavan nodded and motioned in the direction he thought he heard the sound come from. Together they walked back-to-back down the hallway.

They walked towards the front hall together, keeping their eyes open and their ears listening. A door shut hard somewhere nearby and they both started, before a voice called out:

"Hello, brother."

"Fuck," Heath said with feeling. "Everett, what the hells are you doing here?"

"Looking for you, dear brother," Everett growled as he stepped out of one of the rooms nearby. A few other sailors stepped out of other rooms. "It is surprising to find you alive."

"What can I say," Heath said with a shrug, "I find my freedom a whole lot better now that I am not under father's yoke."

"Damn you," Everett fumed, a sneer on his face. "Do you know how much I mourned for you?! Do you know what it did to our mother?"

Heath lowered his gaze, guilt showing on his features before he mumbled: "I did what I had to do."

Everett grabbed him and made him look at him. "You will pay for what you have done, brother."

Everett looked at Kavan and said to his men, "Bring them both, we might learn some more about the princess."

***

Roslyn was looking out over the desert with a looking-glass when she felt something tug at her breeches. She looked down to find Kai's familiar, Tej, tugging at her pants.

"Tej?" her voice made Cassidy and the others look.

"He would not be here if it was not serious," Cassidy told her, and Crick chirped to add her own thoughts.

"We need to get back to the Chief's house," Roslyn cautioned, and Erick overhead.

"What is it?" the Chief inquired of her.

"Tej came for me," Roslyn answered as they went for their horses. "Something is wrong."

Roslyn rode Sage harder than she wanted to; the horse was a great runner, but Roslyn was incredibly worried now. People moved out of their way as they came barrelling down the streets, finally coming to a stop in front of the Chief's house. Tej, who had been riding with Roslyn, jumped down and ran through the main gate of the house to where Kai and the others were waiting.

"What happened?" Roslyn demanded of Kai.

"Heath and Kavan are gone," Kai told her. "We found two dead servants in the house, their throats cut."

"Everett," Roslyn said it like a swear word. "He knew Heath was here, so he came for him."

"Heath's brother?" Tiffany asked. "That was who was on the wall with us yesterday?"

Roslyn nodded and threw her bag on the ground in frustration. Aidan came over to her and hugged her, Cassidy putting a hand on her shoulder.

"We need to go after them," Roslyn said. "Who knows what they are doing to our friends."

"I will talk to some of the Clansmen who work in the Tribe's compound," Kai told her. "We should be able to find a way in that way."

"Thank you, Kai," Roslyn told him heartily. "Once we know where they are being held we can plan how we will rescue them."

"How long do you think they will keep Heath alive?" Tiffany asked Aidan once Roslyn was out of hearing.

"Hopefully long enough for us to rescue them," Oswick answered through tight lips.

They were all feeling angry, for Kavan had started off as a teacher and become a friend, and Heath had started as just a captain but had become their friend as well. To Roslyn, however, they both meant so much more.

"We will do what we need to in order to get them both back," Oswick said, loud enough for all of them to hear. "Let's get to work."

***

Kavan growled at the man who pushed him into the cell after taking the cloth bag off of his head. Heath was thrown in after him. Both of their hands were bound in manacles, and Heath had a bruise across his face where his brother had struck him.

"Are you all right?" Kavan asked Heath as he knelt beside him and took the cloth bag off of Heath's head before helping him get up.

"Gods damn them all," Heath fumed as Kavan helped him up.

"Well, that was light," Kavan commented while Heath dusted himself off. "I would have a lot more to say about my brother for doing that, if I had a brother."

"Oh believe me, I would love to say more," Heath told him before he punched the bars in front of him, swearing some more. "This is very bad," he added.

Kavan looked down with a frown and shook his head. "Roslyn will come for us."

Heath chuckled and said, "I know she can do a lot of things, but with the orcs attacking the city she might not even know we are gone yet."

Kavan shook his head and looked around them at the wooden walls. "Where do you think we are?"

"We are on a ship in the harbour," Heath told him. "I can feel the ship rocking slightly in the water."

"Oh great," Kavan muttered with a sigh. "Damn it all."

"Hello, brother," they both turned to find Everett standing on the other side of the cell door.

"You are something, aren't you," Heath said to him. "Why could you not just leave me?"

"You are a traitor!" Everett yelled at him. "How could you defect to Ellsgrove when we needed you?"

"The war with the continent was absurd," Heath answered. "I did not want to fight; I wanted my own life. I found it in Ellsgrove, I found everything I wanted. I have my own ships, I have a great crew, I have a retirement plan! Even more so, I have found a new family!"

"Fuck you," Everett told him. "What do you think happened when we thought you were dead? What do you think happened when our spies told us you were alive?"

"You have never tasted freedom, brother," Heath rebuked his brother. "We were not meant to be beaten to submission by father, we were meant for more. So much more."

"You are not my brother," Everett seethed as he looked at Heath. "My brother is dead. You shall be soon as well." Everett turned to two of the men behind him and told them, "Grab the other man, bring him to my special room. We will see what he has to tell us about the princess."

***

Heath inhaled sharply as the door to the cell was opened, the metal grating against the side with a hideous sound. Kavan was tossed into the cell almost on top of Heath, who barely had time to help break his friend's fall.

Kavan coughed, the sound coming out roughly.

"What did they do to you?" Heath asked Kavan, holding him close. He took measure of his friend's appearance: Kavan had a black eye and bruising around his mouth--probably some loose teeth. A couple of his fingers were bruised and broken too.

"I told them nothing," Kavan told him through strained breaths. It seemed Kavan had a few broken ribs too.

"I know," Heath said to him, holding him close. "I am so sorry, Kavan. If you had not been with me--"

"No," Kavan stopped him. "We are family; brothers. This is not your fault."

"Is it not?"

Heath's head shot up at the sound of his brother's voice.

"He left his family, his Tribe, for your people," Everett told him. "This is all his fault."

"I am an orphan," Kavan said. "I fought in the Pirate Wars. I was one of a few survivors of the Outpost that was decimated."

Heath felt his face drain of blood; his family had been a part of that, even if Heath had not been--he had deserted before it.

"I knew Heath was of the Tribes when I met him," Kavan continued. "Roslyn helped me to see that Heath was not a part of what I had gone through. Heath became my friend, even though at first I did not want it. I know him to be an honourable man, and a good friend to both Roslyn and myself. He has shown me many things about life, and I will not desert him now."

Heath looked at Kavan and felt the water rise around the hull of the ship; the water was responding to him now that he had had time to connect with it.

"Hold me tightly," Heath whispered to Kavan, and Kavan grabbed hold of him as best as he could with his broken fingers. The water came crashing through the hull of the ship, washing the cell out of the ship, Everett along with it.

An air bubble surrounded Heath and Kavan, Kavan staring around them in wonder. Everett had been flung some distance by the water but he too had an air bubble surrounding him.

"We need to get up to the harbour," Heath told Kavan. "Can you swim?"

Kavan nodded, the pain of his broken fingers showing in his eyes.

"I will hold Everett off while you get to shore," Heath assured him. "Go!"

Kavan felt the pressure drop as the air bubble grew smaller and he started swimming up. Around him the water started to move but he ignored it and made for the wharf. Behind him he could hear the shout and cries from the sailors that had been on the ship as it sank in the harbour.

Kavan climbed a ladder up onto the dock and lay there for a moment as he tried to breathe. The sky was just breaking into dawn above him. Beside him something came shooting out of the water, and he turned in fright to find Heath beside him.

Heath grinned at him and helped him to stand up.

"Let's go find our family, shall we?" Heath asked him. At that moment Kavan heard a gunshot from nearby, and Heath's body jerked back from impact.

Heath looked down at his midsection as blood blossomed through his wet tunic. Kavan watched, immobilized by shock, as Heath fell back into the water they had just escaped from.

"Heath!" Kavan found himself screaming just before a shockwave threw him back against the buildings along the water. He heard shouting and swearing, and he looked out onto the harbour and saw something in the water. As his mind and vision cleared he saw what was out there: orcs were in the water, coming into the harbour on skiff's or by swimming.

As Kavan got up, still shouting Heath's name, Kai came running towards him and grabbed hold of him.

"Kavan," he said as he fell forward onto his friend. "Kavan, we need to go."

"Someone shot Heath!" Kavan shouted at him, pointing in the direction of the water. "We cannot leave him!"

"If we stay we die at the hands of the orcs," Kai told him, shaking him and pulling him along. "Do not have me tell Roslyn I lost both of you."

Kavan could not bring himself to say anything more, but as he willed his feet to move alongside Kai's he felt hot tears running down his face.

Chapter Twenty-Six

Roslyn stared into the fire, her knees up against her chest with her arms holding her legs tightly. She felt the fire reflecting what she felt in her eyes and she felt like screaming. A smashed mirror lay on the stone floor beside her; she had tried searching for her friends with magic only for something to break her mirror. Cassidy told her that that meant someone was warding them with magic. A mage or shaman was working with the Tribes.

Kai was still trying to find where their friends were being kept. He had returned once to the Chief's house to change his clothing before he left again, looking disappointed.

"Any sign of the orcs?" Cassidy asked Erick. The Chief had just returned from the wall. It was early morning, just before dawn, but the lot of them had barely slept.

Erick shook his head looking concerned. "I have doubled the watch along the wall and even have people watching the harbour," he told them. "I would think that they would not give up so easily."

"It is puzzling," Cassidy spoke up. "Their actions and this sudden attack. Why would they risk the wrath of the Clans to attack here, now?"

"Puzzling indeed," Erick nodded in agreement. "I know that every now and then there are intelligent orcs, maybe one has risen in the ranks and directs them," he said with a shrug. "We may never know."

Roslyn felt troubled by that. During their journey south she had felt something, a presence, in the distance. Could it have been the orcs? She had felt something watching them while they were on the river; could it have been them?

"What if they are after me?" she asked. Everyone stopped what they were doing and looked at her in shock.

"No, listen," she turned to her friends and put her hands up in the air. "Ever since that eclipse on my birthday, things have happened. The Clans thought it was a good omen; what if the orcs thought it was something bad?"

Erick looked to his sons and to Cassidy; Cassidy held his gaze steadily.

"It is true," Cassidy told him. "On Roslyn's nineteenth birthday there was a lunar eclipse. My fellow shamans and I took it as a good sign, a sign of positive change to our future."

"Maybe the orcs feel that our positive change means a negative change for them," Roslyn said. "Do orcs not have shamans; or hedgewitches? What if they interpreted the eclipse differently?"

Everyone looked troubled by that, but no one argued against it.

Roslyn stared into the fire again. "Something is happening," she said. "I can feel it; a shift. I am worried. Worried for all of my friends, my family...all of you. I do not want to bring something down on any of you."

Keaton reached out to her , putting a hand on her shoulder. "No," he told her. "I may not have known you long, but I know that you are special. Nothing you could do would harm us. We cannot account for those who take the truth the wrong way."

Cassidy took her hand, Tiffany her other hand. Rafi put a hand on her shoulder, as did Oswick. Aidan laid a hand on one of her knees. Gabe and Erick put their hands on Roslyn's back, giving their strength to her.

"We will find Kavan and Heath," Erick assured her.

"And we will not let the orcs into the city," Gabe added. "We are the Clans; we must protect each other."

Roslyn's head shot up as the sound of explosions reached them.

"That came from the area of the harbour," Erick told them, his brows knit together.

"That's it," she said. "We need to go to the harbour."

"Your horses are saddled and waiting," Erick told her. "Keaton, see them to the harbour."

Keaton nodded and motioned for Roslyn to lead. She nodded and headed for the stables. There Tiffany met her with her armour and helped her don it, Roslyn helping Tiffany in turn.

"I think we might need a page," Roslyn joked, "so we both have someone who can help us with our armour in times like these."

"With your Honour Guard coming I am sure we can find someone to do that," Tiffany reminded her. "If we live to see them arrive, that is."

"We will," Roslyn assured her. "I know we will."

"Then let's get going," Cassidy said nearby; she had on some frishna armour and her sword at her waist, her bow and quiver on her back.

"How do you do that by yourself?" Tiffany asked her.

"Frishna armour is lighter than your light armour," Cassidy told them with a grin. "I cannot wait to get you both equipped with frishna armour."

"Let us hope we see that day," Roslyn said. "Come, my sisters; let us show these orcs who they have messed with."

***

Roslyn rode Sage towards the harbour, her heart beating faster than normal. She was afraid of the events that were yet to come. She was uncertain of what would become of Kavan and Heath, and most of all she was unsure of facing the orcs.

People fled from the harbour area, and there was shouting and screaming as more explosions occurred. As they neared the harbour they saw orcs coming towards them.

Tiffany put an arrow to her bow and shot one of the orcs as Cassidy readied her own bow. Roslyn dismounted and drew her sword, letting Sage run off a distance.

Suddenly one of the larger orcs wearing black robes over armour saw Roslyn and pointed directly at her, saying something in his language; she watched with horror as all of the other orcs stopped to look at her before changing direction towards her.

"Shit," Roslyn breathed out and looked for Sage who had stopped just up the street.

"Roslyn!" Cassidy yelled to her from her own horse nearby, "I think they are after you! Come here!"

Roslyn took her sister's hand and got up behind her in the saddle, Tiffany shooting down several of the orcs that were coming their way. Keaton and Gabe rode up beside them and brandished their swords.

"There's too many of them!" Tiffany shouted as more orcs started coming down the street, the one in the robes staring at them but staying where he was.

Roslyn took one of her glass globes out of her purse and tossed it towards the orcs; when it broke it instantly froze all of the orcs within a ten foot diameter. She tossed more of the freezing orbs before Gabe told them they should fall back and regroup.

As Cassidy turned her horse around a power grab-bed hold of Roslyn and yanked her off of the back of the horse, sending her flying down the street. Orcs instantly closed in around her and her satchel was taken. Cassidy and Tiffany watched in horror as the orc in robes leaned forward and blew a powder into Roslyn's face, which seemingly made her pass out instantly. One of the other orcs quickly put her over his shoulder and the group of orcs turned together and headed to the nearest gate of the city.

"How the hell did that happen?!" Tiffany cried out as she turned her horse around and with the others took off after the orcs and Roslyn. The orc wearing robes threw something at the gate ahead and the wooden gate exploded outward, the guards at the gate being thrown several feet. Once the orcs were free of the city the robed orc threw something else into the empty gateway, causing a magical fire to break out, effectively blocking anyone from following them through the gate.

"This way," Gabe directed them to the next gate over, only to find another fire. They went to another smaller gate and found it completely blocked by stone from the walkway above.

"Damnit!" Keaton shouted. "They are getting away!"

The next gate was secure and the guards let them through, but the orcs were somehow already gone.

"They have magic," Cassidy said. "They probably used it to get away."

"Why not use their magic on the city to begin with?" Keaton asked, frustration an edge on his voice.

Cassidy shrugged and yelled, "Who cares why?! They just took my sister!"

"How can we find her?" Tiffany asked, the look on her face one of desperation.

"We will send scouts out, see if we can find a trail," Keaton told them. "We should return to the Chief's house and regroup. I am worried about Kai."

Tiffany swore as she looked out into the desert, trying to see where the orcs could have gone.

Cassidy reached out to Tiffany and squeezed her shoulder.

"They wanted her alive," Cassidy told her. "That is good. We can still find her."

Chapter Twenty-Seven

Roslyn awoke with a pounding headache. Her back was up against a thick tent pole, her hands bound behind her back by manacles. Someone had taken off her armour, leaving her in her normal clothes. She felt an emptiness inside of her and realized she could not access her magic. She looked around the tent and found that nothing else was in there with her. Two shadows on either side of the door flap told her that there were guards.

Roslyn swore and tried to turn herself so she could get a look at the manacles. In doing so she felt something in her back tighten and she bit her lip so as not to cry out at the cramping that she felt. She tried to stretch it out but could not, and she swore out loud because it was her own fault.

Footsteps approached the tent and Roslyn stiffened, looking at the flap.

In walked the orc with black robes. Roslyn had not had a good look at him before but now she did. He looked very unlike the dead orc she had seen; he looked more human. His head was not as wide as the other orc, it was more oval shaped. His two canine teeth that protruded from his mouth were much smaller than the dead orc's as well. If Roslyn did not know any better, she would bet that this orc was part human.

"Greetings," the orc said in the native tongue of the Clans. "I am Grau, Chief and Shaman of the North Snow Orc Clan."

"Greetings," Roslyn answered in the native tongue. "I am Roslyn, princess of the kingdom of Ellsgrove, daughter of the shaman of the Wolf Clan."

The orc looked pleased that she knew the language.

"I am sorry that we had to meet like this," Grau told her. "A couple of months ago we heard of your presence here in Jay'Al," he continued, "We felt your power even from our southern migration home. Then one of our sister's came looking for you, someone from an old place, and we knew you were important--and before that the lunar eclipse happened. To us, that means something dangerous. We knew we needed to find you so we could decide what it meant."

Roslyn raised an eyebrow at his explanation. "Could you not have come peacefully into the city? We could have had a very peaceful talk."

"We do not trust humans very much," Grau told her. "Yes, we made the agreement for safety, for us and for them, but beyond that we do not trust them."

"I see. Well, you have not harmed me, but I am a little tense over the fact that I cannot access my magic."

"You killed many of my men," he told her. "I am sorry we were trying to be cautious before we learned more about you."

"You were attacking the city," she told him. "How would you expect me to respond?"

He put his hands up in surrender and apologized. "The manacles are made special to keep you from using your magic. Until I am satisfied with your intentions they will remain on."

"I never wanted any of this," Roslyn told him. "I came to Jay'Al in search of answers. My father was in Jay'Al, working with the Wolf Clan and other Clans to try to make a treaty when a few Clans who disagreed attacked them. My father thought my mother was dead, so he took me, a newborn baby, back home with him. It was only when I returned that I learned my mother had survived the attack, and I have a twin sister. Then because I have magic, like my mother and my sister, I was joined with Jay'Al and something very different happened. My homecoming was a lot different than I expected it."

"I will take that into consideration," Grau said as he turned, his robes swishing around him.

"Are you half human?" she asked him as he was about to leave the tent.

Grau stopped and turned back to her. "Quarter orc," he told her. "My mother and father were both part-orc, born on the plateau."

"The plateau?" she asked him, not believing his words. "The Dragon Clan?"

"Indeed. I came down from the plateau a few years ago to find my own way, and I became Chief of this band of orcs. Half of the orc band that had been on the plateau were exiled a hundred years or so ago when one of the lesser orcs caused trouble. Most of the orcs down here are descended from them."

"You know the way up to the plateau?" she asked him. "I need to get there."

"If you prove trustworthy I might show you," he told her before turning and leaving the tent.

It was daylight out, she could tell that much for sure. How long had she been there? It had been early morning when the orcs had attacked the harbour city, and she felt that it was not late in the day but early; had she been asleep for a whole day?

Her mind reeled still. Grau had come from the plateau. There clearly was a way up to the plateau, so why had the Dragon Clan not been heard from?

A commotion outside of the tent made her head snap up and she tensed as two orcs, two very orc looking orcs, carried a young woman into the tent, bound in chains. There was a second tent pole a few feet away from Roslyn where the orcs moved her to and bound her hands behind the pole. They did not look at Roslyn as they left the tent.

"Are you all right?" Roslyn asked the young woman. She had dark skin with a greenish tinge, and dark red hair like no Clans-person Roslyn had ever seen; her clothing was rough-spun alpaca wool. When the young woman looked up Roslyn found herself gasping in surprise. The young woman had two canines sticking out of her mouth like the orcs; she was as tall as Roslyn was and had the same feminine figure, and if it had not been for the tinge of her skin or the canines Roslyn would have taken her for full human. Her eyes were both a startling shade of green.

"It's you!" the woman said in surprise, using the native language of the Clans.

"Who am I supposed to be?" Roslyn asked her, wondering just where this stranger could have seen her before.

"I saw you in the roots of Jay'Al," the woman told her. "The ancient shamans told me about you. They wanted me to find you in order to help you find the plateau and my people."

"Your people?"

"The Dragon Clan," the woman told her. "I am Karina, shaman of the Dragon Clan. I have come looking for you."

"Grau said he came from the plateau," Roslyn said as she leaned back against the tent pole.

"Indeed, he is my cousin," Karina told her. "His grandfather, on his father's side, was one of the orcs exiled from the plateau. Grau went in search of his grandfather several years ago. I had not known if he still lived when I came down from the plateau, but when I met him down here...he was different."

Roslyn cocked her head to the side and asked her, "How so?"

"Grau had been an intelligent person from the beginning. He was well respected in the community. We had feared what our existence to the rest of the Clans would mean--"

"What do you mean?" Roslyn interrupted her.

"Most of the Dragon Clan is part orc by now," she told her. "Only a handful of full humans remain. We had been completely cut off to the rest of Jay'Al when the tunnel collapsed. An orc band was up there with us. Some of the orcs started digging, trying to make their own tunnel. Other, more intelligent orcs, chose to make peace with our Clan and settled in. Finally some of the orcs made it out before their own tunnels collapsed, and apparently they made it to other orc bands down here. Grau himself nearly did not make it out of the plateau himself, for the tunnel he came out of collapsed when he went through."

"So you were afraid that since you had orc blood you would not be accepted?" Roslyn asked her.

Karina nodded, looking her straight in the eye.

"I am not full Jay'Al," Roslyn told her. "My father is white skinned, with light blue eyes and dark blonde hair; but he fell in love with my mother despite their differences. You and I are alike, Karina. I assure you, I would welcome you into my home."

Roslyn noticed a tear coming from Karina's green eyes. "We were so afraid," Karina said. "At first our people did not know if the crossing of species was even something that could happen, but then it did...and we were better for it. The half-orcs were more intelligent, stronger."

"Which is why now, under Grau's leadership, the orcs were able to attack the harbour city," Roslyn interjected. "We knew something was different, and now...now I know."

Karina nodded. "Grau told me of the treaties the orcs made with the Clans. I know it was a hard decision for him to break the treaties in order to figure out what you were, what you meant for the future of both the Clans and the orcs."

"But you are of both worlds, both of you," Roslyn told her. "How can I fault you for being of two worlds, like I am? You had no choice to be born into the circumstances you were born in. What do I have to do with it anyways?"

"The eclipse. To the orcs it means trouble. To the human shamans it meant great change. I do not think the orcs under-stand that the 'great change' could involve them in a positive way too," Karina explained to her.

"How can we show Grau that I do not mean them harm?" Roslyn asked her. "What do I need to do?"

"Unfortunately it is something very personal, that you might not agree to," Karina said slowly.

"Tell me?" Roslyn inquired.

"You must let him read your mind," Karina told her. "It is the only way he will fully trust you."

"I will think on it," Roslyn said slowly after a few minutes. "Thank you for your council, Karina. How did you come down from the plateau?"

"We built a stairway down the side of the plateau," Karina told her. "It took many years to complete but at least there were no cave-ins. We were able to anchor deep in the sides of the plateau, and with the help of magic, we stabilized the stairway. It does take a few days to climb it, but we made areas where people could rest. We completed it a month ago, and I finally was able to come seek you out."

"So a tunnel up into the plateau is completely out of the question?" Roslyn asked her, thinking of the stories Kai's grandfather had told her.

"The ground within the plateau was just too unstable," Karina told her as she shook her head. "After the last attempt of a tunnel collapsed we gave up for a while. My father came up with the idea of a stairway on the outside."

"Well, that will be an interesting journey," Roslyn commented. She sighed, thinking about what Karina had said about letting Grau read her mind. Could she actually trust Karina? Were they looking for something else?

At that moment Roslyn's stomach growled loudly and she started to laugh. "Gods be damned, I would kill for some scrambled eggs right now."

"They will feed us," Karina told her. "Grau is not cruel like that."

"I need to trust him too," Roslyn told Karina with a half-smile. "If he does not get me some sausages and eggs soon, I do not think I could trust him."

Karina ducked her head with a laugh, and she found herself liking this strange woman.

Chapter Twenty-Eight

Back at Chief Erick's home those who remained were happily surprised to find Kai waiting for them with Kavan. Kavan looked like he had had a healing, from the looks of the bruises on his face and hands that were already starting to fade. He also had red puffy eyes, as if he had been crying.

"Where is Heath?" Cassidy asked Kavan when she noticed that the sailor was not there.

"Gone," Kavan choked out. "He was shot while we were trying to escape, and he fell into the water." Kavan could not bear to look up at them, expecting a response from Roslyn. He heard Tiffany gasp.

"That was when I found Kavan and got him out of there before the orcs could get us," Kai interjected. Kavan looked up at the group when there was silence and noticed that it was actually Cassidy standing at the front of the group.

"Where is Roz?"

"The orcs took her," Cassidy told him. "We fought with them and we were falling back when someone with magic pulled her off of my saddle. We tried going after them but they had a magical escape."

"Shit. What are we going to do about Roslyn?" Kavan asked the group.

"We will send out scouts as soon as we can, hopefully find a trail," Cassidy told him. "They wanted her alive, so she should be safe for a while. We need to rest up and prepare."

"They were very organized," Keaton said. "I have never seen an orc band like that before."

"Yes, something is very different," Cassidy agreed. "I wonder what happened." She turned to Kavan and said, "Tell me what happened since you were taken."

***

Kavan awoke with a start and winced as his healing chest twinged. Kai had done a light healing on him because there were others who had a greater need of healing after the orc attack.

Feeling restless, feeling grief over the loss of Heath, and still worried about Roslyn, Kavan went in search of the kitchen. He found Oswick there sitting before the cooking fire. One of the older cooks stood at the baking table kneading bread that would be for breakfast; she nodded to him and continued kneading.

"Could not sleep either?" Kavan asked Oswick as he pulled up a chair beside him. Oswick had a flask in his hand and Kavan realized it was Roslyn's.

"No," Oswick whispered as he handed Kavan the flask. "Too much on my mind."

"What is it?" Kavan asked as he sniffed the liqueur. "Ah, vodka. She sure has good taste." He took a sip and handed it back.

"I am worried," Oswick said as he took another drink. "Roslyn always finds herself in some kind of trouble."

Kavan reached out and squeezed Oswick's shoulder in comfort. "We will find Roslyn," Kavan told him.

"Is this a party anyone can join?" Tiffany asked from the doorway. She had her cloak wrapped tightly over her bedclothes and looked as tired and worried as they did.

"Pull up a chair," Oswick said with a smile. "Have a drink?"

Tiffany grabbed a chair and put it beside Oswick before looking at the flask. "How did you get that?"

"She left it in her room," Oswick told them. "I know she would not begrudge us some of it now."

Tiffany took the flask and took a quick sip, wincing as the liqueur hit her. She coughed as she handed the flask back.

"How are you holding up?" Kavan asked her.

"I feel like a failure," Tiffany admitted. "Some Royal Defender I am."

"From what you said, the orc used magic to take her. You do not have magic. You were out matched," Oswick told her.

Tiffany thought about that for a moment. "Is there a way I can learn to null magic?"

"Kind of," Cassidy said from the door. The three of them turned to her, almost startled to hear her voice, which was so much like Roslyn's. Cassidy wore the same light linen clothing as the Hyena Clan. "Certain enchantments can be laid on your armour and weapons to protect you from certain magics. It can even encompass a certain area as well, so as to protect a group, especially if you are close together and holding onto each other."

"We should look into doing that before we go after Roslyn," Tiffany said. "We need every advantage we can get."

"I will let Kai know what I will need. Gather all of your armour together and bring them to the Shaman's Room," Cassidy told them.

"Can I help?" Aidan asked as he poked his head around Cassidy who was still standing in the doorway. Behind him stood Rafi, each of them looking as anxious as the rest of them.

"Looks like none of us could sleep," Kavan said, slightly amused.

"If you need help sleeping I can give you a sleeping potion," Cassidy told them all. "We need to be well rested before we go after Roslyn." She turned to Aidan and said, "Thank you Aidan, but I am unsure how you could help me with the enchanting."

"I could help gather up armour," he told her. "Or help Kai with the supplies you need."

"'Sure," Cassidy responded with a shrug.

"I could use a sleeping potion," Oswick spoke up. "What time do you think it is?"

"Just after midnight," Aidan told them as they all gathered together around the fire.

"Yes, I think we should all get some sleep and start in the morning," Cassidy recommended. "Let me go back to my room and get the potions, I will bring them to your rooms."

"One last thing," Kavan spoke as he held his hand up to stop them from dispersing. He grabbed the flask from Oswick and took down small wooden cups from a shelf nearby, handing out a cup to each of the group before filling it with vodka.

"To Heath," Kavan said as he raised his cup.

"May he find rest," Cassidy added as she and the others raised their own cups. Each of them downed their drink.

Slowly the group broke up and went to their rooms, waiting in their doorways as Cassidy went to get the potions. She handed a phial to each of them and went back to her own doorway down the hall. They looked at each other and raised the phials up together in a sort of toast before they each drank their potions down.

"We will find her," Cassidy told them. "Get some sleep."

They each nodded and went into their rooms, closing the doors behind them. All of them only just managed to make it to their beds before they fell asleep.

***

Roslyn awoke with a start as she heard shouting outside the tent she and Karina were in. Karina was awake and staring wide-eyed at the door flaps. The orcs were using their own language so Roslyn had no idea what they were saying.

"What is it?" Roslyn asked Karina.

"Someone is arguing with Grau over you," Karina explained. "They do not understand your importance and want to either enslave you or just kill you. Grau is trying to tell them how powerful you are and he needs to know more."

"Oh great. What if more of the orcs agree with the dissident?"

"I do not know," Karina said with a shrug. "Grau is connected to Jay'Al through his Clan blood, but the other orcs are not. He knows you are important, for some reason, to Jay'Al. I do not think he would allow harm to come to you."

"Oh well, great," Roslyn said with heavy sarcasm. "There is only one of him and how many of them? I do not like the odds, even if he does have magic."

Karina went quiet but the shouting had stopped and it was quiet outside the tent again.

"Tell me about the plateau?" Roslyn asked Karina. "What is it like up there?"

"Very different than down here," Karina answered with a half-smile. "We have a mountain that reaches high up into the clouds, a river and waterfall that comes down from the mountain and goes down through the plateau. We have the same trees and wildlife mostly, though I am sure a few species are now extinct up there but are still down here. At least we had several large herds of alpaca before the tunnel collapsed so we still have a large herd that feeds and clothes our Clan." Karina paused and asked, "Where did you grow up?"

"Ellsgrove is a kingdom across the ocean. Did you know that to the east of this continent the ocean has several hundred whirlpools that cannot be traversed?" Karina shook her head. "Beyond the whirlpools is just mist, no one knows what lies beyond. To the west of Jay'Al is the Archipelago, ruled by the Tribes who are basically pirates." She chuckled before adding, "One of my best friends used to be one."

"My father was a cousin to the king of Ellsgrove," Roslyn continued, "and we lived up north with our own city and land. My father taught me everything about Jay'Al because he had lived here for a couple of years. He taught me the language, he encouraged me to be my own woman, to learn how to hunt and fight. When my cousin died, along with everyone else between us and the throne during a sickness, my father was crowned king. My father learned of the expedition his cousin had sent out, through the northern Sea of Ice to Jay'Al instead of through the Archipelago, and here I am."

"You wanted to come here?" Karina inquired with a raised eyebrow.

"I wanted to know about my mother's family," Roslyn answered. "I needed to know more about Jay'Al."

"And now that you have come here? Seen it?"

"The Head Shamans I have met have been very welcoming, and I have made friends with most of them. I have yet to go visit the Beaver Clan, it was on our way back up the continent to our home, New Wardgrove. I named it after the city I grew up in. There is so much diversity here, with the different areas of the continent giving us different things. I liked the Fox Clan a lot, with their savannas and forests. I am very interested in seeing the plateau though. There was nothing like it in Ellsgrove."

"What about how different you are to the rest of Ellsgrove?"

"There are dark skinned people in the south of the continent, one of my friends is one. They have dark hair though. Still, I was not too exotic to people."

"What do you think they would make of me?" Karina asked her.

Roslyn looked at her closer before shrugging and saying, "You would be a curiosity at first since we do not have orcs in Ellsgrove. I think once they got to know you and understand that you are part human they would like you. Of course, I have only just met you so I cannot say for sure."

A look of guilt crossed Karina's face, and Roslyn narrowed her eyes at the young woman.

"Is there something you want to tell me?" Roslyn asked Karina.

"Grau has my brother," Karina told her after a moment. "Grau wants to try to control you and your powers so he can be the one to change things in Jay'Al."

Roslyn's gaze softened and she smiled slyly. "Thank you for telling me the truth, Karina." Roslyn brought her hands out from behind the tent pole, the manacles laying on the ground behind her, and she stood up. Karina stared at her with wide eyes.

"I know how to pick locks," Roslyn told her with a shrug before she went to do the same with Karina's manacles. "How about we find your brother and get out of here, hm?"

"I tried to help Grau trick you, but you would still do that?"

"You are not to blame for Grau's selfishness," Roslyn explained. "You could have led me right into his clutches, but instead you chose to tell me the truth. That shows me a lot about your character."

Roslyn offered her hand to Karina after she was done with the manacles. "Now, how do you suggest we disguise ourselves so we can get to your brother and get out safely?"

"Cloaks," Karina answered. "There were some hanging just behind the tent when he brought me in here. There is a tent behind us, though, that someone is staying in."

"Then we be very careful," Roslyn told her as she used her magic to quietly cut a slit in the back of the tent. There in a small alley between tents was a wooden rack with several cloaks hanging from it. Roslyn used her magic to float two cloaks across the short distance to her hands, and she handed the second one to Karina before donning the first one, making sure the hood hid her face well enough.

"What direction is your brother?" Roslyn asked Karina as they stepped out into the alley. Karina pointed to the east.

"He is being held in a sort of prison with a few other people," Karina told her. "They captured people from the city."

"Do you know where Grau took my bag?" Roslyn asked her. Karina shook her head. "Well it was worth a try. I'll have to just use a different spell to draw everyone's attention to the west."

"Like what?" Karina was curious.

"A fireball to make it seem like they are under attack," Roslyn answered. "I can disguise the direction it comes from so they cannot trace it back here," Roslyn assured Karina who was about to speak against it.

"Where did you learn such spells?" Karina asked her.

"Back in Ellsgrove we have different ways to use magic," Roslyn told her as she started to concentrate on her hands, and to Karina it looked like Roslyn was packing an invisible snowball. After a moment Roslyn smiled and threw the magic that was in her hand to the west, directing it to hit the very edge of the tent city. The ensuing explosion rocked the ground even where they stood and they ducked down as orcs started to make their way west, shouting and cursing. Finally Roslyn looked out around the tents and nodded to Karina, motioning for her to lead the way.

"Better throw another ball a little to the northwest now," Roslyn said as she worked with her hands. "Need to keep them busy."

"We are almost there," Karina told her. "Just around this corner."

Roslyn threw the ball and directed it with her magic before turning to see the large wooden cage before her. Several of the people inside looked like dock workers, two were part-orcs like Karina, and the last--

"Everett?!"

The young sailor looked up and cringed at the sight of her. His hands were bound in manacles just like the ones Grau had put on Roslyn and Karina.

"You know him?" Karina asked her as she went to the locked door of the cage. Karina used her magic to break the lock, and her brother embraced her as she opened the door.

"Unfortunately yes," Roslyn said as everyone left the cage.

"Where is Mister Scruffy?" Roslyn overheard Karina ask her brother.

"Grau has him," the brother replied. "Grau's familiar is a cat like Scruffy too."

At that moment they heard a loud meow from nearby and Roslyn turned to see a large cat the size of her mother's cat familiar running towards them.

"I contacted him through our magical connection,"

Karina told Roslyn, "I told him I was coming to free him and Jaco, and he told me he was not with them but he was able to get out of where he was from. Grau had assured him I was safe and no harm would come to Scruffy, but he does not like the man."

Mister Scruffy reached Karina and twined around her legs. "Good boy, Scruffy. Let us get out of here now, shall we?"

"What do you want to do with him?" one of the dock workers asked Roslyn, indicating Everett.

"You know who he is?" Roslyn asked the man in turn.

"Kai was looking for him before the orc's attacked.

The orcs fished him out of the water in the harbour before they left the city. Their leader, Grau, said his water magic might come in handy."

"Then we cannot leave him to Grau," Roslyn said with a resigned sigh. "Everett, tell me the truth, where are Kavan and Heath?"

Everett shrugged and said, "Cannot say for sure, for I think one of them got shot while they were trying to escape me. Which one, though, I have no idea."

Roslyn felt the blood drain from her face as his words set it. "No," was all she could manage to whisper. "No, you're wrong."

Everett shrugged. "Whether you believe me or not, when you get back you will find out for sure."

Roslyn gritted her teeth, a heavy feeling in her gut.

"The manacles stay on," she hissed at him.

Everett nodded solemnly and followed her as she led the group out the side of the tent city and into the desert.

"I can cover us with a spell to keep us from being seen," Roslyn told them. "Stay close to me and you will be safe." To add an extra distraction she quickly crafted two more fireballs and threw them across the tent city where the orcs were still looking for their attackers. With a flick of her wrist she covered the group with a spell to hide them as they made their way into the dunes.

Chapter Twenty-Nine

"It looks like someone attacked them," Kavan said as he and his friends sat on their horses on top of a dune, looking down at the orcs' tent city. The west side looked charred and had a few large holes in the ground as if a canon had fired on them.

Keaton squinted in the sunlight and shook his head, "The scouts said nothing about this when they found them this morning. It seems something happened between then and now."

"She is not here," Cassidy spoke up. "She was--I feel her magic in the destruction, but she is not here anymore."

"Can you tell where she is now?" Aidan asked her.

"I can sense some kind of magic to the east, like what she used to shield our camps at night."

"Then let us skirt around the orcs below and try to find Roslyn," Oswick spoke up. "I do not want to go up against that many orcs right now."

They urged their horses to go back down the side of the dune they had come up and Cassidy led them in the direction of where she felt the magic.

Kai pulled up beside Cassidy and said, "There are many hidden oases in this area, she may have discovered one of those."

"Wherever she is, I just hope she is safe," Cassidy replied. "I wish she had taught me that shielding spell, it would be handy right now.

"No one in that compound saw us," Kavan assured her. "They were too busy with something else."

"I hope you are right," Tiffany spoke up. She had Roslyn's horse Sage on a lead line tied to her saddle horn.

Cassidy led the way east first and then south a little bit more until they came to a stop at the top of a gully, a small stream flowing in it. The gully ended in a hole about four feet in diameter in the ground. Above the hole the ground rose up in a sort of dome like hill. Cassidy pulled her horse to a stop and stared at the opening in the ground.

"She's down there," Cassidy said as she pointed to the opening.

"That's a hole in the ground," Oswick started to say before Cassidy's pine marten and Kai's fennec fox jumped down from their seats on their respective master's horses and headed for the hole. A large cat, much like the one Amelia had, had emerged from the hole and was watching them with wide eyes, though it greeted the other familiars with sniffs and curiosity.

"Did she find a familiar, or is that another shaman's familiar?" Tiffany asked out loud as they all dismounted. By the time they had gotten down into the gully and were approaching the hole, Roslyn had poked her head up through the ground and greeted them with a smile.

"I thought I could sense your magic," she told her sister as she beckoned her friends to follow. "Let the horses have some water while I explain everything." She looked past Cassidy to see Kavan standing there and her face went white.

"Where is Heath?" Roslyn asked them, her voice coming out strained. "Is it true? Is he gone?"

"Roz…" Kavan dismounted from his horse and went to her. "I am so sorry." He jumped down the hole and she almost fell into his arms crying.

The others followed Kavan down the hole and each put a comforting hand on her shoulders as she cried. When she finally calmed down she turned to Cassidy who reached out her arms to her sister.

"How did you know?" Cassidy asked her sister as she held her. Roslyn sniffed, using her sleeve to wipe the tears away from her face.

"Everett told me," she said. "The orcs had him. Come, this way."

Roslyn led them down a tunnel that was smooth on all sides, beaten down by the water of the stream. The tunnel was tall enough that none of them had to stoop. She lit the way with a few floating balls of lights until they came out into a large chamber that had glowing stones around it embedded in the walls. There was a pool of water in the center of the chamber that had a small exit on the other side. There was a group of people sitting around the pool, the three familiars drinking the water. There were two small caves on either side of the chamber.

"What happened?" Kavan asked Roslyn when they came into the chamber and she stopped beside the pool.

"Do you have anything to eat?" she asked her friends. "I could use something to eat."

Tiffany produced some jerky from her bag and Roslyn accepted it with a smile.

"The orc who took me, Grau, is part-orc," Roslyn started to explain as she ate, still sniffling. "Which is why he has magic. Sure orcs have a sort of, what would we call it back home...hedgewitch type magic I guess; but Grau is part human, from the Dragon Clan, and he has the magic of Jay'Al as well."

"How did he get down here?" Kai asked her.

"He built a tunnel that collapsed after he went in.

No one else has come down from the plateau until now,"

Roslyn motioned to a young woman sitting by the pool and she came over, shyly ducking her head.

"Do not be shy, my dear Karina, let them see you."

The young woman lifted her face for everyone to see and Roslyn smiled as her friends only blinked before asking Karina how she had come down from the plateau. Karina explained to them about the staircase her people had built.

She hugged Kavan again, only for him to wince in pain.

"Are you all right? Were you hurt?" Roslyn asked him.

"Nothing one of Kai's healings could not fix," he assured her. "What about you?"

"Grau would not hurt me, though he did try to trick me into opening my mind to him so he could control me," Roslyn said as she nodded to Karina, "She warned me of his true purpose and helped me escape."

"So the ancient shamans sent her to help you?" Kavan asked her. She nodded and looked at her rather eclectic group with a broad smile.

"I do not yet want to leave," she spoke up. "I want to try to get my things back from Grau."

"Excuse me?" Tiffany had to ask. "You just escaped from him, why would you go back?"

"The things in my bag have value, sentimental and otherwise," Roslyn responded with a shrug. "Plus, some of them are dangerous."

"I will help you," Karina told her. "It is the least I can do."

"No, if your cousin captures you he would probably kill you this time," Roslyn told her. "I want to go in at night, sneak in and out hopefully without getting into trouble."

Tiffany smirked and leaned on Cassidy's shoulder, saying, "I think trouble finds you no matter what, my friend."

That brought a laugh from her friends, and Roslyn had to admit that it did seem that way.

"Nonetheless, I cannot let my things stay in Grau's possession," she continued.

"We wait till dark," Oswick said. "And you do what you need to do."

***

Roslyn went to one of the side caves where she had left Everett chained up. She glared at him, and she actually got the satisfaction of him recoiling in fear as a ball of fire floated above her hand.

"I take it it *was* my brother who got shot," Everett said, trying to avoid her unsettling gaze. "A pity, I would have loved to execute him myself."

"You bastard," Roslyn hissed through gritted teeth. "He missed you, he told me himself."

Was that a hint of regret in Everett's eyes? Roslyn was not sure.

"When we get back I will hand you over to Chief Erick and he will deal with you. I would be more than happy to kill you myself though if you give me trouble," she warned him before leaving him alone in the cave.

***

Roslyn held the stolen cloak close around herself as she moved slowly towards the campsite of the orcs. She was using her magic to make sure no one saw her approaching, and she tried to walk as carefully as she could in the sand. Above her a sliver of the moon barely lit the sand.

A nearby sentry turned in her direction, his gaze going over her and not seeing her. She continued her way into the camp, squeezing between two of the outer tents and into the walkways between tents. She would have to be more careful within the campsite for she could run into someone, get too close to someone, or accidentally knock something over. She had really not liked being a guest to Grau, and hoped not to experience it again.

Karina had told her that Grau's tent was in the center of the campsite so Roslyn headed in that direction. She tried her best to stay in shadowed areas away from torches just to help the effect her magic had on keeping her invisible.

She was almost to Grau's tent when she heard the sound of a cat growling nearby. She stopped in her tracks and looked around, her eyes setting on a large cat like Mister Scruffy and Ecko standing only a few feet away and looking straight at her. This cat was black and orange, with a white stripe on its chin and a devilish look in its eyes. Roslyn knew instantly that Grau would know she was there.

So close, she thought to herself as she skirted around the cat and up against the tent that was Grau's. *Do I risk it*? She asked herself, peeking through a section of the tent where the seams were joined together loosely. Grau was not in there, but she did spy her bag on the desk on the other side of the tent. Was it a trap? How much time did she have before he made his way back?

Roslyn cut open the seam of the tent and entered, torch light flickering around her. She left the seam open so she could leave through it again. She made her way quickly across the carpet on the sand towards the desk and reached for her bag.

"I had hoped you would return," a voice said from the entrance to the tent. She grabbed hold of her bag and turned to face Grau. As she repositioned her stance she put her hand in her bag, taking a quick inventory of what was in it. From what she could tell there was nothing missing.

"Where is Karina?" Grau asked her as he took a step into the tent. He did not look as menacing as he had before, and she thought he might actually be concerned for his cousin by the sound of his voice.

"Karina is perfectly fine," Roslyn told him. "As is her brother, and friend."

"Why would she follow you?" he wanted to know. "I am her family." He was getting upset now, Roslyn could tell.

"From the way you treated her, the things you wanted her to do, is that a real question?" Roslyn asked him. She slung her bag over her shoulder and let one of the knives up her sleeve loose in case he attacked her with the dagger at his waist.

Grau took a couple steps towards her, his hands getting closer to the dagger. "I would not have harmed her if she had failed," he told her, and Roslyn was very unsure if it was a lie or not.

"We grew up together; yes I left, but I never forgot her, nor did I stop looking for a way to get back to them up there," Grau explained. "I just got caught up in other things."

"Like trying to possess people with powers you know nothing about?" Roslyn asked him, watching his hands and muscles for any indication of movement. "Karina knew what you wanted to do was wrong and she picked a side."

Grau's face darkened and he lunged as he drew his dagger. Roslyn moved aside and with her dagger sliced a long cut down his left arm.

"I don't want to kill you if I don't have to," she told him as she moved towards the opening she had come in through.

Grau growled at her and advanced again, ignoring the cut down his arm. Roslyn pushed him back with her magic and he used his as well, resulting in his tent being blown apart, knocking him backwards against his desk and she out onto the walkway.

Orcs had definitely noticed the mess, for there was shouting and the sound of running feet coming towards them.

"This is not over!" Grau shouted at her as she struggled to stand, a piece of wood from a tent pole sticking out of her leg.

"Fuck you," she told him before she cast a spell that would transport her a short distance away. Several orcs had her in their sights and set loose their arrows, but she disappeared in time for the arrows to soar through the space she had been in and into the tent behind her.

***

Roslyn's teleportation spell knocked her against the wall of the underground cave she had discovered the day before. Tiffany and Cassidy were by her side in seconds, Tiffany pulling the piece of wood out of her leg and Cassidy healing the wound. Roslyn gasped as the wood was pulled from her leg, and two strong hands held her down so her sister could cast the healing spell.

Roslyn looked up at Kavan and Oswick, and cried out in pain until the healing spell swiftly took effect. She sobbed and threw her head back, staring at the ceiling of the cavern as she blacked out.

***

It took them several hours to reach the Hyena City for they had to keep stopping and hiding from orc patrols looking for them. Roslyn was awake again and kept using the wind to cover their tracks but she was always on the lookout and shielding them during the journey back. The constant magic use along with her healing was taking its toll on her by the time they reached the city, and she dropped the shielding just outside the front gate with a heavy sigh followed by a large yawn.

Chief Erick welcomed them with a huge smile, taking in Karina, Jaco and Jarrod with wide eyes.

"Chief Erick, may I introduce Shaman Karina of the Dragon Clan," Roslyn introduced her new friend to the Chief. "As well as her brother Jaco, and friend Jarrod."

"The Dragon Clan, you say?" Erick raised an eyebrow but said nothing of Karina's orc features. "It would be an honour to welcome you into my city," Erick said as he bowed his head to Karina. "Please come in."

As they made their way to the Chief's house people were stopping and staring at the group, some of them pointing. Roslyn was aware that Karina saw them because she felt her friend shrink closer to her as they rode together through the city.

"It's ok," Roslyn turned in her saddle to look at Karina, who was blushing deeply from the attention the people were giving her.

"Should we stop so you can appraise her more?" Roslyn asked the people in the streets. "You are acting like you've never seen someone from the Dragon Clan before."

That got people talking and the word spread ahead of them so that by the time they got to the Chief's house there were more people gathering to watch them.

"You should not have done that," Karina whispered in her ear.

"Nonsense, they will find out anyway," Roslyn told her.

"Do not be afraid of them, Karina." Roslyn turned to the crowd and pulled Sage to a stop just outside of the front gates to the Chief's house. She told Karina to dismount and Roslyn did so as well.

"People of the Hyena Clan," Roslyn addressed the crowd, "may I introduce the First Shaman of the Dragon Clan, Karina. I think you can look forward to seeing more of the Dragon Clan amongst us in the next year."

"Is she part orc?" she overheard someone say.

"Yes," Roslyn answered loudly. "When the plateau got cut off from the rest of us, there was a band of orcs living up there. In the two hundred years since they have intermingled, and most of the Dragon Clan have orc blood now; but they are still all a part of Jay'Al."

"Most of you by now know who I am," Roslyn continued. "My mother is the First Shaman of the Wolf Clan, but my father was from another place. The other Shamans of the Clans accepted me, because I look just like you. Karina only has a few differences, so I hope you can accept her as I was accepted. The rest of Dragon Clan will need our acceptance in order to be able to reintegrate with us. They will not need your prejudice."

Turning to Karina, Roslyn offered her her arm and Karina took it with a shy smile as Roslyn led her through the gates of the Chief's house, Kavan bringing her horse along with the rest of the group.

"Thank you," Karina told Roslyn as they walked into the Chief's house. "I wish I was as brave as you."

"Nonsense. You came down from the only home you ever knew to come look for me. You are already brave. We just needed to get past the prejudice people have against orcs; yes the ones down here have caused issues, but they are not all the same. You are not like Grau, for starters."

"You are not what I expected," Karina told her.

Roslyn laughed at that and said, "So many people have been saying that these past few months. I like to throw people off."

Karina laughed with her and accepted a cup of juice from Cassidy. It was weird to see two people who looked almost identical, but Karina realised their eyes were different and it was easier to tell the twins apart. Roslyn led their group into the dining hall where Chief Erick had some food waiting for them.

"So Cassidy grew up here?" Karina asked them.

"Yes," Cassidy answered. "I knew my sister was out there somewhere."

"But you had no idea, right?" Karina asked Roslyn.

"None at all. I always felt weird growing up, that something was not completely right," Roslyn told her.

Cassidy reached a hand out to her sister and took her hand, saying, "That was how I felt too."

"Do you have any other siblings besides Jaco?" Roslyn asked Karina. Jaco was sitting over by Tiffany, completely enraptured with the older woman and the sword she was showing him.

"Two more younger brothers," Karina told her. "And you, besides Cassidy?"

"I have two more sisters and two brothers on my father's side, two more sisters and two brothers on my mother's side."

"I hope I can meet my other half-siblings some day," Cassidy commented.

"I hope so too," Roslyn said, squeezing her sister's hand. "Karina, try some of the mutton; it is sheep meat, something I do not think you have had."

"Sheep?" Karina looked intrigued at the meat on the platter before her. "I am definitely willing to try."

A Quest for Her Roots

***

Roslyn stared at Heath's hat that he had left in his room.

They were getting ready to head north by boat and Roslyn was not going to leave Heath's belongings there. She dreaded telling Maeve and Jackson what had happened. Selene, his cat, would not be able to understand why her master would never return, and that made Roslyn's heart hurt more.

She finished packing up his things, trying not to cry anymore. He had been her friend, her confidante, and one of her sweethearts. Her choice had been taken from her; fate, it seemed, had chosen for her by taking him.

With a sigh she closed the door to the room he had been staying in, his belongings in a couple of bags she held in each hand. She handed the things off to Oswick who was gathering all of their things to be sent to the ship.

"I want to see where it happened," she told Kai, who was lounging against a doorframe nearby. He nodded.

"Meet me at the stables in a few minutes and I will take you to the harbour," he told her.

Together they rode out to the harbour, Roslyn taking in the damage to the city from the orc attack. They had already started rebuilding gates and buildings that had been most affected, though the smell of smoke from the fires still lingered.

The harbour had been the worst hit by an explosion caused by the orcs. The Tribes and clansmen were working together to rebuild it as Roslyn and Kai arrived. Some of them cast curious glances their way but they left them alone as the two of them dismounted and Kai led her to where he found Kavan.

"Was a body found?" Roslyn asked Kai as she stared into the water. Several yards away in the water were the remains of a ship sunken in the water, which she guessed to be Everett's ship.

"No, but there is an undercurrent here that takes things out to sea," Kai explained to her. "If the gunshot did not kill him…and he was unconscious and unable to use his magic, he would not have made it. Our fishermen have been keeping an eye out, but so far nothing."

"I see," Roslyn whispered, at a loss. "I still cannot believe this has happened."

"I am sorry, Roslyn," Kai told her, and not for the first time since they had found her.

"It's not your fault," she answered, finding the tears coming forth again. She wiped them with her sleeve. "This is all Everett's doing. At least he is in your Uncle's prison where he can do nothing more for the time being."

With one last look at the water she sighed heavily and headed back to her horse, Kai following behind her.

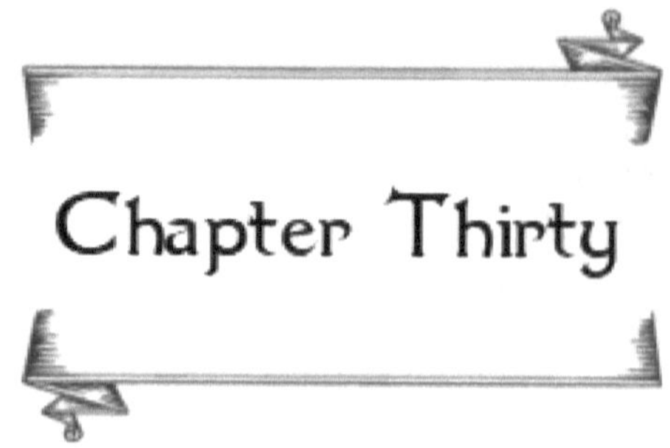

Chapter Thirty

Karina stared at the ship anchored in the water in front of her. She was shaking with fear, for she had never been on a boat larger than the fishing skiffs on the two lakes back up on the plateau.

"It will be OK," Roslyn told her. "If you get sea-sick I have a charm I can give you. It worked wonders on Aidan."

Aidan, who was standing nearby, was grasping the charm that hung around his neck as he looked at the boat. "I am ready," Aidan told them with a tight smile. "This is the fastest way to get back home."

"It took us two months to get down here," Roslyn said, "It should take us two weeks by boat to reach the Beaver Clan, and from there only another two weeks to reach New Wardgrove. We regroup there, and rest, before heading for the plateau."

"I am unsure," Karina said.

"It will be OK," Roslyn assured her. "We will be with you every step of the way."

Jaco and Jarrod, who stood on either side of Karina, nodded and told her that it was the best route. Going by water they would be safe from the orcs, and once they got into the realm of the Beaver Clan they would be even safer. Cassidy had told them about the fighting prowess of the Beaver Clan before, and now Roslyn hoped that it was true.

"I'm nervous," Karina reiterated.

"We know," Aidan told her, taking her hand. "Roslyn, give her the charm, and we can go."

Karina watched as Roslyn took a charm out of her bag. Roslyn handed Karina the charm, and Karina put it around her neck.

"Let's go," Roslyn urged her.

"All right," Karina said begrudgingly. She looked at the others and felt their strength as Roslyn helped her into the skiff that would take them out to the ship. Together they rowed out to the ship, with Roslyn at the head of the skiff.

Once she got on board the ship Karina knew that without the charm she would be throwing up over the side. She cast a look at Roslyn, but all Roslyn did was nod as she let the captain know they were ready to go. Karina watched as the Hyena City got farther away as the ship headed north along the side of the continent.

"You all right?" Aidan asked her as he leaned against the rail next to her; she was surprised to find that he knew the native tongue of the Clans.

"Yes, I think so."

"Good. Will you come down to the galley with me and the others, and see how we play cards and drink?"

Karina grinned widely and said, "Yes, I think I would like that."

***

Roslyn watched Hyena City disappear as they headed north on the water. The ship Chief Erick had provided them with was small and not big enough for their horses to come along. Chief Erick assured her that he would get his sons to bring their horses to the Spring Market where her Uncle Grigori could take charge of them and bring them home to Bella Vale with him. She knew that once they got to the Beaver Clan they would be able to borrow horses to get home, but she would miss Sage.

Turning to go below deck Roslyn thought she saw someone standing on the cliffs watching them, but after a second glance there was no one there. She took one last look at the cliffs along the shore before heading below deck, feeling slightly uneasy.

***

Kavan watched as his friends gathered in the galley, Roslyn pulling out her deck of cards. He watched as Aidan led Karina to the table, Jaco and Jarrod sitting in with them as well. It was different, that was for sure. However, it felt right still. Karina, her brother, and Jarrod only spoke the native Clan language, but since Roslyn had been teaching them the language for months now they all had a grasp of it.

"You have done a good thing," Kavan told Roslyn as they watched their friends eating together and drinking.

"Have I?" Roslyn asked him, smiling widely. "How so?"

"You have brought us all together," he told her. "You have befriended us, made us your family."

"Is there something wrong with that?" Roslyn asked him seriously. "Do we not deserve a family who understands us?"

"We do," Kavan told her. "I thank you." He hesitated, and she noticed.

"What?" She whispered to him.

"I am sorry I could not save him," Kavan told her. "If Kai had not found me I would have dove in after him."

"Please do not blame yourself," she told him. "It was Everett's fault. We can only blame him and his need for revenge."

***

Several mornings later Roslyn sat in the Crow's Nest next to Aidan, for she could not sleep. Aidan had welcomed her with enthusiasm, and she knew that he felt the most comfortable up there after everything. She was trying not to interfere in his space, but she needed to be away from everyone else for a little bit.

"How are you faring?" Aidan asked her. "You did not come here just for the scenery."

"I have had nightmares," Roslyn told him. "Of Grau. It is like he is haunting me."

"You said he has magic, could he be projecting himself?" Aidan asked her. "He could be trying to keep you off guard."

Roslyn thought about it for a moment and she half nodded, telling him, "He could be doing that, yes," she shook her head, "Or I could be losing my mind."

Aidan grabbed hold of her hand and squeezed it, saying, "In no way are you losing your mind Roslyn," he assured her. "I understand your frustration. You are stronger than you think you are."

"Thank you, Aidan," she whispered. "I needed that."

"Go back down and get breakfast with everyone," Aidan told her. "I will come down shortly."

"Thank you, Aidan," Roslyn whispered, before she swung herself over the side of the Crow's Nest and made her way back down to the ship.

"I'm always here for you," she heard him say as she descended.

***

Karina stared down at the water going around the ship. She was shaking as she looked out at the water. To the east, Roslyn had told her, were giant whirlpools that cut their continent off from the rest of the world. Now that they were going up the eastern side of the continent she felt a great unease. She was used to earth being beneath her, not water.

"You ok?" Karina looked up to find Kavan standing nearby, watching her. "Is Roslyn's charm working?" he asked her. She was relieved that he knew the native tongue of Jay'Al, for she did not know the Common Tongue the others spoke.

"I have not felt the need to be sick, so I believe so," Karina answered, trying to smile convincingly.

"The water is not for everyone. From what I understand, orcs are very much a being of the earth. It is perfectly fine for you not to like being out here."

"Why are you being so nice to me?" Karina asked him. "Roslyn I understand, but you and the others..."

"We are a family," Kavan told her. "You helped Roslyn, who I love dearly. If she trusts you, I trust you."

"And what I look like does not matter?"

"How would you like me to react?" Kavan asked her. "To me you look like a perfectly normal, rather intriguing Jay'Alian. Your tusks are a part of your heritage, if anyone found them wrong, well they themselves would be wrong."

Karina looked thoughtful at that and thanked him.

"For what?" he asked, cocking his head to the side like a cat, making her chuckle and think of Mister Scruffy, who was sitting nearby.

"For telling me the truth."

"I think we are about to eat supper, care to join us?" Kavan asked her as Roslyn's shout that the food was ready reached his ears.

Karina smiled widely and nodded, following him down to the galley.

"Come my lovelies, eat up my lovelies," Roslyn was beckoning her friends from the table using the native tongue of Jay'Al; the rest of their group had heard her call. There was a place set for each of them, and Roslyn motioned for Karina to sit across from her next to Cassidy, with Tiffany beside her; Kavan was on her left. Oswick sat next to Tiffany, with Rafi next to Cassidy, and Aidan next to Karina. Kai pulled up a chair at one end of the table.

Karina realized that the rest of the sailors were also eating on the other side of the galley, and that Jaco and Jarrod were over with the sailors eating with them. Kavan started to hand out filled pitchers of ale and large cups along the table while Roslyn served them all their food: roasted boar with roasted vegetables and a large bowl of gravy.

"This is what you were doing all day?" Kavan asked

Roslyn. He watched as she poured gravy over everything on her plate with a wide grin; Karina was looking at her in slight shock.

"What is the occasion?" Tiffany asked as Roslyn popped a large piece of gravy slathered meat into her mouth, earning a laugh from the rest of the group.

Cassidy answered, saying, "Roslyn wanted us to celebrate friendship and family. Especially the new members of our group: Kai and Karina. Kai, you have traveled with us almost three months and we have come to rely on and trust you. You will always have a place to stay in New Wardgrove should you ever come visiting again."

Kai bowed his head and thanked them before Roslyn lifted up her cup of ale, swallowing her food at the same time, and called for a toast.

"Lately we have been through a lot together," Roslyn said. "First the attack on Hyena City, to my own abduction by Grau… and losing Heath. It was then that I came upon Karina," Roslyn winked at the half-orc, "and found another dear person to bring into our fold. Karina trusted me with the truth, therefore earning my trust, and she helped us escape. I know that if we had not escaped, you, my lovelies, would have been there to rescue me too--I had no doubt about that. Thank you all, and know that I love you all. To family and friendship!"

The others lifted up their cups and echoed her last words before they each took a drink.

"So Kavan is your Master at Arms, Cassidy your sister, Tiffany your bodyguard, Oswick and Rafi are merchants--Aidan, what do you do?" Karina turned her head to ask her bench partner.

"Oh, well...I am the Quartermaster."

"What is a ...Quarter Master?"

"We help with the logistics of supplies, food, weapons and the like."

Karina looked puzzled, "What is a Quarter Master doing out here on this type of adventure?"

Roslyn almost choked on her roasted potato, Kavan thumping her on the back to help relieve her. Finally she waved him off and regarded Karina with an amused look.

"A few others were confused as well, though Aidan never complained," Roslyn told her honestly, earning a confused look from Aidan. She addressed Aidan next, "You see, when you started out you were so thin, and well you were not that great with a sword. After I saw how much you were progressing, coming out of your shell, I just could not leave you back at New Wardgrove. You are part of my retinue, Aidan, and would have been sorely missed during this journey."

Aidan looked embarrassed and lifted up his cup to take a hearty drink.

"What role could I play in your retinue?" Karina asked Roslyn.

"For now, a friend. You are the shaman of the Dragon Clan, your place is there. My sister Cassidy is our mother's second and will need to be available to her Clan in the future so I cannot give her a role either besides being my sister."

"Thank you," Karina said as she bowed her head, "You honour me."

Roslyn raised her glass in a silent toast to Karina and took a drink. "Eat up, my friends. Tonight, we celebrate!"

***

The next morning Roslyn awoke with a headache, groaning as she sat up. She, Tiffany, Cassidy and Karina shared a room, the bunks close enough together that they might as well have all been sleeping in the same bed. Cassidy stirred beside her but did not wake, Tiffany snored lightly, but Karina was awake and staring out the porthole.

"You all right?" Roslyn asked her.

"Just unnerved by the sea," Karina answered. "The waves have been restless most of the night."

It was at that moment that Roslyn noticed the rocking of the boat and she knew that it was not ordinary waves.

"I think we are heading into a storm," Roslyn told her.

"Stay down here, I will go check with Kai."

Kai and Kavan were captaining the boat together and were sharing the captain's quarters. Roslyn went above deck, noting the grey-green colour of the clouds and the very dark looking clouds coming off of the continent. Kavan and Kai were both standing at the helm, Kai holding onto the wheel.

"Ah, there you are!" Kavan had seen her out of the corner of his eye and turned to give her a grim look. "This storm has grown a lot in the last couple of hours and if it hits us it will push us into the way of the whirlpools."

"Well, shit," Roslyn said as she threw her hands up. "Should I go back to bed, since this is a nightmare waiting to happen?"

Kavan shook his head at her joke and motioned to the oncoming storm. "It is not natural."

Roslyn went cold, and she knew who would send a storm after her. "Could Grau have conjured up this storm?"

Kavan shrugged before telling her, "We keep trying to head for land to weigh anchor but the winds keep pushing us back out."

There was a crack of lightning followed by a very heavy rumble of thunder and the clouds above them opened up with a torrent of rain.

"By the gods!" Roslyn shouted as she used her magic to cover the deck of the ship with a shield to keep the water off; she was already soaked by the time she got it up though. "Captains, what do we need to do?"

"We have already brought in the sails--except for the storm jib, but we need to batten down the hatches and secure ourselves," Kavan told her. "It is all we have left to do."

"And if we hit the whirlpools?!" Roslyn asked him.

"Then we pray to the gods we survive," Kavan told her. "If Grau sent this storm he knows about the whirlpools and hopes to kill you with them."

Roslyn swore as Kavan and Kai ordered the sailors below deck. Kavan and Kai together went around the ship and secured the cargo hold roof before coming back to the door that Roslyn was waiting for them at.

"Is there nothing else to be done?" Roslyn asked them as they secured the door behind them.

"Someone needs to keep the ship pointed at the incoming waves," Kavan told her as he went back to the helm. "I will stay up here and do so, I have the experience."

"What happens if you do not?" Roslyn asked him.

"A large wave could hit the side of the ship and roll us over, and we would sink."

"I will help you with your life line," Kai told Kavan. Kai brought out a thick rope that he helped secure around Kavan's waist and shoulders, and the other end went around the helm and tied it with a very secure knot.

By then the waves had grown more and the thunder and lightning grew more frequent. Roslyn heard her name called from the door that led below deck and she found Karina there with Aidan.

"Go back below to your rooms, we need to secure ourselves!" Roslyn shouted to them over the thunder. A wave washed over her shield as they turned and went back down.

"You will not be able to maintain your shield, Roz," Kavan said to her from the helm. "You should go below and not waste your magic."

"We have four shamans on this ship," Roslyn told him. "If we cannot figure out a way to save the ship, what is the point of having all this magic?" She grinned at him and told him she would be back, lowering her shield to only cover Kavan, and going below deck with Kai.

"Could you extend your shield around the whole ship?" Kai asked her as they went to the room she shared with the other girls. Cassidy and Tiffany were sitting on their bunks and looking out the porthole with nervous expressions. Karina was pacing the small room but she stopped when Roslyn and Kai walked in.

"What is happening?" Karina asked her, shaking with anxiety. "I knew coming on this boat was a bad idea."

"Kavan says it is not a natural storm," Roslyn told her. "I believe Grau sent this after us in order to kill me since he cannot use me."

Karina threw up her hands and started pacing again.

"What do you want to do?" Cassidy asked her.

"We have four shamans, we should be able to do something," Roslyn told the group. "If we get pushed into the whirlpools we need a plan to keep the boat--and everyone inside it--safe so we can get back out."

"How would we get out?" Kai asked her. "We would be at the bottom of the ocean."

"I could put a protective shield around the whole ship," Roslyn explained to them, "but I will need our combined strength and power to do it."

"Well, it's something," Cassidy admitted. "Are you sure we can do this?"

Roslyn shrugged and smiled at her sister. "Only one way to find out, hm?"

Roslyn told everyone to stay in their rooms while she and the other shamans went back up on deck to the room Kavan and Kai shared. Roslyn left the door of the room open so she could see better and indicated to her sister, Karina, and Kai for them to sit on the floor. Roslyn also sat on the floor facing the door. Roslyn took a small knife out from under her sleeve and used it to cut a small line on her palm. She let a few drops fall onto the wood and she made another small cut on her other palm.

"I'm improvising here, using a spell I learned back home and the new knowledge of how my shaman side can access magic," Roslyn told them. "Please, each of you make a cut on each palm and allow some blood to soak into the wood, and we need to clasp hands, allowing our blood to mix and your magic to join with mine."

Karina was on Roslyn's left, with Cassidy to her right, and Kai sitting before the open door. The cuts done and the blood given, they each clasped hands. Roslyn closed her eyes and started her shield spell.

***

Kavan watched as the four of them came back up on the deck but they gave no reason for it--they went into the room he and Kai shared and sat down on the floor. He figured that Roslyn had some sort of plan, and he both watched and felt the magic that encompassed the whole ship a moment later.

The storm was over them now, the lightning and thunder coming more frequently. He was having a hard time keeping the bow straight into the waves that beat at them, and he knew they were being pushed further and further out to sea and closer to the whirlpools with each wave that hit them.

"Care to fill me in on the details?" Kavan shouted to Roslyn over the thunder.

"Just keep doing what you are doing, and let us do this," Roslyn answered him without opening her eyes.

Kavan rolled his eyes and said, "I would appreciate a little knowledge of what 'this' is."

"Trying to ensure we survive, Kavan. Now be quiet."

Kavan looked over his shoulder and could see the whirlpools in the water. "We are getting closer to the whirlpools!"

"Hold on tight as we go in!" Roslyn shouted. "We will hold the ship under this shield but you need to help direct it, Kavan! Pick a whirlpool and ease into it, we will try to ride it down."

"Are you crazy?!" Kavan shouted back at her. "We do not even know what is down there!"

"This is the only way!"

"Fucks sakes..." Kavan muttered. "All right!" he turned and looked for a whirlpool, reaching out with his magic to try to gauge which one was most likely to be the least deadly. "Ok, I think I found a good one. Hold on while I 'ease us in'!"

Kavan turned the wheel away from the waves and got into position, trying to time the entrance to the swirling water before him. The whirlpool he had picked was going clockwise and looked to be rather large, which would give them a lot of space on the way down. The ship entered the whirlpool and they started to descend, the shield Roslyn was holding around the ship keeping them safe. Above them cracked more thunder and the sky lit up with hundreds of bolts of lightning.

Kavan stared wide eyed at the abyss below them, terror keeping him from screaming. As they neared the bottom of the whirlpool Kavan vaguely re-called seeing something reach out and grab hold of the ship, or rather the shield surrounding the ship, and drag them down even further.

***

Kavan awoke with his face in the sand. He sputtered, sand and water leaving his mouth. He sat up and looked around him as the sounds of screams reached his ears. He turned in the direction of the screams to find one of the sailors fighting against a large reptilian monster. Blood sprayed everywhere as the monster ripped off one of the sailor's legs, and Kavan screamed.

Kavan drew the sword at his waist and stabbed at the reptile several times, trying to stay out of its reach as he tried to figure out where it was most vul-nerable. Finally he noticed that its stomach looked softer as it reared up on its hind legs, using its tail to balance it. Kavan stabbed its gut several times until it rolled over on its back dead. He was breathing intensely as he heard more shouting nearby.

"Is everyone all right?!" that was Roslyn, clear as day. "Kavan!"

"I am here!"

"Cassidy?!" Roslyn shouted.

A few heartbeats went by and they all heard the twin answer. Kavan felt relief that Cass was still alive.

"Aidan!"

Kavan held his breath as he looked down the beach and was relieved when Aidan answered his sister's call.

"Karina! Kai!"

Two voices called out at once.

"What the hells is that?!" he heard Aidan's voice nearby, and the sound of fighting. Kavan grabbed his sword and went towards the noise, finding Aidan defending himself from a large lizard creature like the one Kavan had killed. Kavan flanked the creature and together he and Aidan killed it.

"There must be more," Aidan said as he exhaled deeply. "We have to get to Roz."

"Roz!" They both shouted together.

"Over here!" They heard her voice and started toward her, only to be met by more of the lizard creatures.

Aidan and Kavan stood back to back as the creatures advanced on them, only for a flaming ball of fire to land on the two creatures. Aidan and Kavan covered their eyes from the fire, and when they could see again they found

Roslyn and the rest of their people standing around them.

"Are you alright?" Roslyn asked them.

"Lost a sailor," Kavan told her.

"A few sailors," Roslyn told him grimly. "These creatures are nasty, they went for the first ones on the beach."

"Where are we?" Kavan asked.

They were in a small lake in a gigantic cave, plants and trees growing on land nearby. There were also giant mushrooms of various colours. Very high above them was a giant gemstone looking object embedded in the ceiling of the cave that gave off a surprisingly bright light. Kavan could not see the far end of the cave.

"A subterranean cave," Kavan told her. "Heath told me legends about them, but no one ever came back from the whirlpools to confirm that this was where they led."

"Well, someone must have for there to be a legend about it," Roslyn said. She looked along the shore and saw what looked to be an old wreckage of a ship.

"How long could someone survive down here, do you think?" Tiffany asked as the group gathered together. She too had seen the wreckage on the shore.

"If there is good water to eat...and edible food? Maybe a while," Roslyn said with a shrug. "We need to find a way out of here."

One thing that was eerie about where they were: there was no wind. The gemstone above them gave off both light and heat, so it was a comfortable warmth down there.

They looked at the remains of the other ship on the beach, finding no bodies or bones to help indicate how long it had been there. One thing they did figure out: it had been a merchant ship for there were dozens of bolts of fine silk and other cloth.

"These bolts look too good to have been here too long," Oswick commented. "I would say not even a year."

Kavan scratched his head, thinking. "We all know that the whirlpools are dangerous; what mad merchant would even think to try this route?"

"I had heard word," Rafi started to say, "That one merchant wanted to try his luck, that he had spent years trying to map out the whirlpools so as to avoid the Archipelago."

"So you're saying this was him?" Roslyn asked him.

Rafi shrugged, and said, "Either him or one of his sons."

"Well, he never made it," Oswick said. "How are we supposed to get out of here too?"

"That is what we need to figure out," Roslyn said. "There has to be a way out of here."

The group looked at each other before looking back at Roslyn. No one wanted to say anything about them not being able to get out of there, but Roslyn knew their chances. If there had been legends amongst the Tribes, someone must have gotten out.

"Let's span out and look around. Groups of two, OK?" Roslyn said. "Cassidy and Karina with me, Kavan and Kai, Tiffany and Aidan, Oswick and Rafi."

"Stay sharp," Roslyn told them. "We know there are lizard things, there might be more dangers."

The others nodded and they split off into their groups, Cassidy drawing close to her.

"Let's look around, hm?" Roslyn said to her sister. She headed towards a grouping of trees in the distance, Cassidy and Crick following them.

They headed out, taking note of the different kinds of trees and the foliage. There was a stream that flowed down into the lake that they followed, filling their water skins once they found that it was freshwater.

"Where do you think the water comes from?" Cassidy asked her.

Roslyn shrugged and kept walking. They had just passed a grouping of large mushrooms when Roslyn stopped short. She turned and walked around the mushrooms, Cassidy following with raised eyebrows.

"Look at this," Roslyn said in a hushed voice, indicating a small hut-like structure hidden behind the mush-rooms. There were reed baskets and fish fillets hanging over some hot coals; someone was smoking the fish.

"Someone did survive," Cassidy commented. "Where do you think they are?"

Roslyn looked around them, very aware that someone was watching them.

"Oh, they are here somewhere," Roslyn told her. "They probably know the best places to hide here. Let's go see what is over there." She indicated the path they had been following.

"So what do you think we can expect?" Cassidy asked her as they walked away from the hut.

"Rafi mentioned a merchant with sons. Maybe someone from the crew, or one of the sons themselves survived. If they have been here by themselves for a couple of years though...who knows what their state of mind is."

They kept walking, noting more plants, but Cassidy commented on how quiet it was; there were no birds or any other animals besides the ones they brought with them: Mister Scruffy, Tej, and Crick.

"I think we should go back to the shore, regroup and try to find the survivor," Roslyn said, stopping in her tracks amongst the mushrooms. She could see another creature ahead, watching them. Since there were no other sounds she hoped everyone else was ok.

Cassidy nodded and turned to go back the way they came, Roslyn let out a shrill whistle that would let the others know to go back to the beach. When they reached the remains of their ship on the beach they found that everyone had gathered. Roslyn realized that none of the sailors had survived and she felt like she had let them down. At least all of her friends had survived. There were no bodies to bury though because the lizards had dragged their prey away.

"What is it?" Aidan asked her as she and Cassidy joined them.

"There is a survivor from the last shipwreck. How he survived with those lizards around...maybe he has figured out something that keeps him safe or something," Roslyn told them.

"Very smart," Oswick said. "So what happens when we find the creatures, or the survivor?"

"If we can find a way to leave again, the survivor can come with us," Roslyn said loudly.

Aidan was looking at her sharply, realizing why she was talking so loud.

"We should be looking for a way out instead of looking around the shore," Aidan said. "What do we hope to find down here?"

"There could be clues on the other side of this place on how to get out," Roslyn said. "We only see a part of the picture, not the whole thing. For all we know, there could be a way out on the other side."

There was a rustling noise in the bushes nearby and a man stepped out from them. He was scruffy looking, his ginger hair matted and his beard long. It was hard to tell his age under all of the hair, but Roslyn thought that he was still young under all of it. His clothes had holes in them and looked like they had not been washed in a long time.

Everyone else in the group brandished their weapons, but Roslyn told them to stop.

"Hello there," Roslyn said to the man. "I am Roslyn. Who are you?"

"Kasimir," came the reply after a moment. He seemed very unused to talking to anyone.

Roslyn grinned and motioned for everyone to sit down as she did; her friends did the same, with Kasimir copying them.

"You cannot go to the other side," Kasimir told them. "The creatures are there. There are dozens of them. They do not like the mushrooms, so I built my hut by them. They still roam around, eating smaller lizards or some of the plants. They ate the rest of my crew that survived."

"Are you Kasimir de Lauritia?" Oswick asked him.

Kasimir gasped and leaned back, asking, "How do you know my name?"

"We met when we were young," Oswick told him. "I am Leo Oswick."

"I remember you," Kasimir said.

"How did you come to be here?" Oswick asked him.

"My father thought he could get through the whirlpools," came the reply. "It turned out that we could not."

Roslyn looked at her friends, reading their expressions. "Do you know of any way out of here?"

Kasimir looked down into the water and pointed, "Down there is the only way," he said. "Passed the guardian in the water."

"Guardian?" Rafi asked.

"It's a creature, something like a squid. It pulled my ship down here."

"So there could be a way out?" Roslyn asked him.

Kasimir shrugged and replied, "If you could get through to the monster it might let us out."

"So what do we do in the meantime? We need a safe place to rest, and food," Rafi pointed out.

"I can put up a protective circle around us, and it looks like there are some of our provisions floating out there in barrels," Roslyn said as she pointed to the lake where there were indeed several barrels and chests floating in the water. "We can probably fish out things that sunk too."

"Like our armour?" Tiffany spoke up. "I would feel better against those lizards' teeth if I had my armour on."

"Exactly. Kai, do you think you could go fish our things out of the water with Kavan's help?" Roslyn asked as she got up and started making a protective shield. "Kasimir, is there anything else we should know?"

"Who are you people?" Kasimir asked her instead. "Roslyn is obviously a mage, but you talk of armour as well."

Cassidy smiled and told him, "Roslyn is princess of Ellsgrove, and I am her twin sister Cassidy."

"Technically you are a princess of Ellsgrove too," Roslyn told her.

"What? There is no princess Roslyn," Kasimir looked confused.

"How long have you been here?" Oswick asked Kasimir.

"I think almost a year."

"And you were able to survive that long down here?" Oswick asked him, impressed.

"If you call it surviving," Kasimir muttered. "I watched my brothers and the rest of the crew die. Somehow I made it."

"There was a sickness," Roslyn told him. "My father, Lucius, became king when his cousin and his heirs died."

"I missed a lot," Kasimir whispered. "I wonder if my mother and sisters are still alive."

"They are," Oswick assured him. "They will be extremely happy to see you, if we ever get out of here."

"Then I hope you can help me," Kasimir told him with feeling. "Can I go to my hut and gather my things?"

A Quest for Her Roots

"I will go with you," Cassidy voiced with a nod.

"Stay alert," Roslyn called after her sister as she and Kasimir stood, Roslyn letting them pass through the barrier she was putting up.

***

Kai waded out into the water with Kavan and together they gathered the barrels and chests that were floating around in the water. Thankfully their food stores were there, and a cask of ale. Their armour, however, had definitely sunk to the bottom--Kai could see the bags that held their armour on the sandy and rocky bottom, curious fish swimming around it. At least the water was warm.

Kai could feel a presence in the water, something ancient. Was he sensing the guardian that Kasimir had spoken of? In his mind it felt like music, a light tune in the back of his mind. Kavan had gathered some boards together to make a raft so they could take their armour back to shore, and he was waiting above, treading the water, as Kai retrieved their belongings.

Kai had grabbed the last bag of armour when he saw something out of the corner of his eye. He had to stop himself from freaking out at the sight of the very giant glowing eye in the distance, and the form of tentacles moving through the water. One of the tentacles reached out and gently wrapped itself around Kai's left wrist.

In his mind he saw an image of a stairway built into rock, and he felt compelled to find it.

"*This is the way out,*" he heard a voice in his head, one that reminded him of a sea storm.

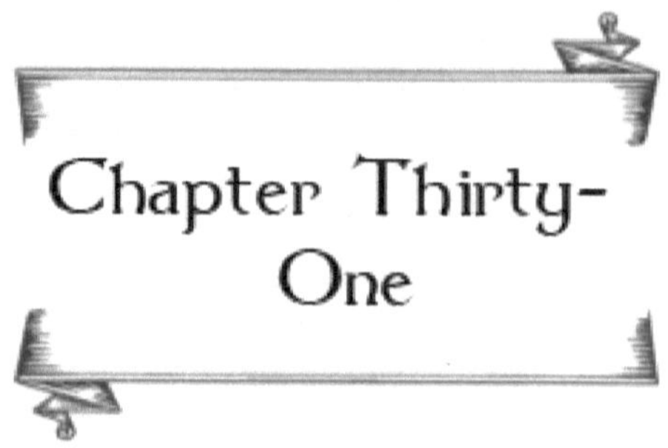

Chapter Thirty-One

Roslyn helped them lay out the armour to dry as Kai explained what had happened.

"Well, are we going for the stair?" Oswick asked. "Do we have any idea how to get through the lizards?"

"Kasimir said that the lizards do not like the mushrooms, so maybe we could use that to our advantage?" Cassidy spoke up. Kasimir, who was sitting nearby, nodded his head.

"But do we know where the stair leads to?" Rafi asked.

Kai shrugged and said, "Hopefully to the surface."

***

"How did you sleep down here, with the lizards out there?" Tiffany asked Kasimir as they started to get ready to go to bed that night. Roslyn had dried out their sleeping rolls, but they did not need a fire because it was certainly warm enough down there. Tiffany felt secure with Roslyn's protection shield around them, but Kasimir had not had that.

"I made a blanket out of mushrooms," Kasimir told her. "It will be refreshing to not have to worry about it tonight."

"That must have been uncomfortable," Tiffany commented as she stared up at the large gemstone in the top of the underground cave.

"I don't think I will be able to sleep if there is no darkness," Rafi said.

Roslyn lifted her hand up and waved it, and the area inside the protective shield darkened enough that they could get to sleep.

"Thank you," Roslyn heard Karina say before she drifted off to sleep.

***

Roslyn was the first one up and making breakfast using a small ball of light so as not to wake the others up. The smell of the cooking food awakened her companions eventually, and they gathered together to eat in silence. Finally it was time to get ready to search for the staircase.

The shield around them was growing lighter now, and as they gathered up their things it became completely opaque. Roslyn looked up from her pack and gasped, causing everyone else to look up as well: there on the other side of the shield were several of the large lizards sitting and waiting, their menacing fangs glinting in the light. Roslyn could see their scales, and the slits of their eyes, and she could tell that they were eager for more human flesh. A shiver ran up her spine and she felt goosebumps on her arms.

"Armour on, now," Roslyn told her friends, though she could see they were already moving to do so. Roslyn helped Tiffany secure her armour as Cassidy secured Roslyn's; Cass had quickly donned her own armour. Roz helped Kavan with his, and Kai helped Aidan while Oswick and Rafi prepared each other. Kai only had leather armour, and he voiced how jealous he was of Cass's frishna armour.

"Your clan should have invested in the frishna mines like ours did," Cass answered him with a broad smile. "This armour was passed down in my family though. Roslyn would have gotten it if she had been here."

"Someday maybe we could get all of us outfitted with it," Roslyn said casually as she readied her sword as well as her special globes.

"Back home lizards do not like the cold. Do you think these lizards are the same?" Roslyn asked her friends as she tossed one of her freezing globes up and down in her hand.

"Would not hurt to try," Oswick told her.

"Bringing down the shield in three," Roslyn told them, tossing the ball up and down three more times before she brought the shield down. She threw the ball at the closest lizard, it shattered against the lizard's side and froze the area around it. The lizard jerked as the ice took it over and it froze in place. The other lizards screeched and moved away from the coldness.

"Well, that's effective," Rafi commented as he drew his sword and struck the frozen lizard--it shattered before them, frostbitten bits of meat crashing to the ground.

"Who else wants some?" Roslyn asked the lizards, grabbing another globe from her bag and holding it up for them to see. One of the lizards hissed at her, its tongue flicking out of its mouth, and it started to advance. Roslyn tossed the globe at it, the globe shattering on the sand just in front of the lizard. The lizard froze in place as it tried to backtrack.

Another lizard hissed and charged, only to be met by Tiffany's blade. She struck at its eyes, piercing one of them--it batted her away with one of its claws, sparks flying as its claws met her armour. Tiffany brought her sword around in an arc and in one swift movement she beheaded the lizard. Blood spurted out on the ground and on Tiffany, where she started screaming in pain as it hit bare spots of her skin--her face and hands.

"The blood must have acidic properties," Roslyn shouted as she went to Tiffany's side, casting a healing spell on her friend. There were burn marks on Tiffany's face and hands, blistering wounds from the contact with the blood. Roslyn was able to halt the damage with her spell but in order to do more she would have to concentrate deeply, which was not something she could do at that moment.

Roslyn grabbed another one of her magic globes and threw it at the remaining lizards--half of them turned and ran before it shattered but two of them got caught in the proceeding freeze.

"We should make a run for the stairway," Roslyn told her friends as she watched the last of the lizards disappear from view. "Grab as many mushrooms as you can," she added after a moment.

They tried to go as fast as they could, but with Tiffany injured it held them back slightly. Roslyn was able to shield them as they went, but they had to remain close for it to work properly at the speed they were taking. Those who had familiars kept them close and quiet. Roslyn stopped them on the perimeter of the lizard's nests and made them wait for the lizards to move out; each nest had several eggs waiting to hatch. One lizard, presumably a female one, stayed with each nest.

"There it is," Roslyn said quietly, nodding towards the tunnel in the wall. "We need to get through this section and into the tunnel, and we will be home free since the lizards are too big to follow us."

The group closed in, Roslyn being in the centre so she could shield them properly. Those on the outside held the mushroom caps they had harvested like shields just in case the lizards could smell them. Roslyn breathed a sigh of relief as the first of the group reached the passage entrance and she stepped aside to let those behind her go up the passage. With one last look at the subterranean cave Roslyn followed her companions up the passage, dropping her shield as she went. Now she tossed her magic crystals into the passage ahead and that lit up the way.

"Just keep going," Roslyn told them. "All we need to do is keep going up."

"And you do not know how long it will take us?" Oswick asked.

"No idea. We have food with us, and our sleeping sacks if we need to rest," she reminded them.

***

Finally after some time they came across what looked like a stone doorway in the side of the tunnel. Roslyn halted in front of it and touched the door. Kavan raised an eyebrow at her and she nodded: together they pushed against the stone door and felt it budge. Oswick and Rafi added their strength as well and together they managed to get the door open several feet. Roslyn sent her crystals through the doorway and gasped at what she saw: racks of shining silver armour and weapons were arrayed around the room, along with dozens of chests. The room must have been twice as big as the Meeting Room back in New Wardgrove.

"That is frishna armour," Cassidy said with awe. "And those weapons are made from it as well!"

"Who could have left this here?" Oswick asked as they all entered the room and looked around. Roslyn saw some torches along the walls and lit them with her magic so they could see better.

There were a dozen suits of half plate armour made from frishna along with frishna chainmail on mannequins arranged on one side of the room, and numerous frishna weapons of various kinds on racks.

"These are old," Cassidy commented as she looked at the armour. "I would say several hundred years old because we have not needed such armour in a long time. My own set of frishna chainmail was handed down to me, but I have nothing like the rest of the armour."

"Well, you did say you wanted us to get our own frishna armour," Roslyn half joked. "Though I assumed you had a blacksmith in mind who specialized in it."

"I do, there is a woman named Jessamine in one of our villages who is a Master with frishna. Though, this is definitely a very inexpensive way of getting you all properly outfitted," Cassidy said with a laugh. "What are in these boxes?"

Cassidy knelt by one of the chests and opened the latch, finding it empty. "Well, if we are going to take some of the armour with us these are as good as anything to carry them in. Though they might be heavy."

Kasimir looked on with interest as Roslyn and her companions each grabbed an empty chest and picked a suit of armour. Roslyn did not want to leave the last two behind so she grabbed an extra chest and loaded the suits of half-plate armour and chainmail into it.

Next the companions picked out their weapons. Roslyn chose a bladed staff with a very large diamond in its top. Curious about the diamond she looked at the other weapons and found that almost all of them had gemstones in their hilts or handles.

"Why so many gemstones?" Roslyn asked Cassidy.

"That is some training we have not gotten to yet: they have magical powers," Cassidy explained to her. "That diamond in your staff is a magical catalyst: a shaman probably used it. This sword here, the ruby?--it is for protection against sorcery."

"So someone left these here, underground, with those lizards down there, for what reason?" Karina commented as she browsed the weapons.

"Times were different back then," Cassidy explained to her and the others.

"We had the orcs to contend with, as well as several other magical creatures that thankfully have not been around in a while. We could ask Willow if she knows anything about this place when we see her."

Kavan chose a two-handed sword with a ruby in its pommel. Karina chose a wooden staff that felt different, and upon further investigation she found that when she twisted the middle of the staff two frishna blades popped out of each end. Rafi chose a bow and a quiver full of arrows. Oswick chose a short sword and a dagger. Aidan chose a bastard sword. Tiffany, however, chose a long sword. Kai chose a bladed staff like Roslyn's, and in the end Cassidy chose a bladed staff as well.

"I think now would be the perfect time to eat something before we continue. And Tiffany let me see your wounds," Roslyn spoke up finally. Tiffany came over and Roslyn applied more healing to the burns as the others started to eat. When they were all rested and full they gathered up their things and headed back out into the tunnel.

***

They walked for what seemed like an eternity, a cool breeze coming down from above. When they finally emerged in a cliff side cave it was night out. They spread out their sleeping sacks after eating a quick meal and slept, the sounds of the waves crashing below lulling them all to sleep.

In the morning Cassidy climbed the cliff wall above with a rope and tied it around a nearby tree. One by one they climbed the rope, their belongings strung over their backs; the chests they tied to the ropes and brought up one at a time. Roslyn was the last one up, Cassidy waiting at the top to help pull her over the edge.

"Where to from here?" Kavan asked her.

Roslyn nodded in the direction of some smoke in the distance, "We find a village and find out exactly where we are. Then we meet with Willow before heading to New Wardgrove."

"Sounds like a plan," Cassidy said.

The group headed in the direction of the smoke which led them into a forest. They came across a group of shepherds herding alpacas and the shepherds directed them to their village; they graciously offered the travellers the use of their cart for their chests and belongings, telling them to leave it in the village for them. It took them the better part of the day to reach the village, and when they approached the gates to the village they were greeted by the warriors on the palisade, one of them heading to inform their chief of the arrival of travelers. The gates were opened for them and they were directed to the chief's house, several young children and warriors following them out of curiosity. Word had spread about Roslyn since Willow had returned to her Clan, and even though this was not Willow's home village they knew who Roslyn and her sister were. Their new companion, however, was even more of a curiosity than the twins were.

"My Clan must be the smallest of them all," Karina observed as they walked towards the Chief's house. "The Hyena Clan has its own city, and numerous shamans. Now the Beaver Clan is even more widespread with villages and shamans."

"The Dragon Clan will grow again," Roslyn assured her.

"Now that you have access to the ground."

"I hope so," Karina whispered to her. "I worry about my family now; I did not tell Grau how I got down from the plateau but what if he finds the stairs before we get there?"

Roslyn took her friend's hand and squeezed it, saying, "We have to have faith in the gods that that will not happen."

"Ah, welcome," the group stopped as they were met by a young woman not much older than Roslyn at the door to the Chief's home. She was shorter than Roslyn and curvaceous, keeping her hair cut short to her head. She wore simple linen clothing and a vest made from alpaca wool.

"I am Chief Ruby, and I welcome you to my village. My brother Shepherd," she indicated the young man beside her who looked a lot like her, "has already sent word to Willow of your presence here. I have lodgings for you, and we will prepare you a meal while you rest from your journey."

"We thank you, Chief Ruby," Roslyn told her with a slight inclination of her head. "We have had a hard journey and could use a respite."

"The last we had heard from Willow was that you were heading north by boat, not by land. I look forward to hearing your tale of how you came to be here."

"Willow knew of our plans?" Roslyn asked her.

"Chief Erick sent word when you left, along with warnings about the orcs. Willow urged us to keep an eye for your ship off the coast so we knew you were safe. When we did not see your ship we began to worry," Ruby told her.

"Well, it will definitely be an interesting tale to tell," Cassidy spoke up. "Where are these lodgings? I desperately need a bath."

***

Roslyn sank back into the tub of hot water, closing her eyes and trying not to think about the past couple of days. She had washed her hair already and now just wanted to let her muscles relax in the hot water.

The men had been seen to separate lodgings across the same path as the one the women were brought to. Cassidy told her that it would be easier for them all to bathe and recuperate from the journey without having the men watching over them. To Cassidy it meant being able to walk around the lodgings only wrapped in a towel, and Tiffany had become emboldened herself to do the same. Karina was still shy of the other women and had already dressed in clothing sent by Ruby for them all. Roslyn had been the last one in the bath.

Roslyn nearly fell asleep in the bath, jerking awake as she almost fell asleep. She managed to get herself out of the tub and wrapped in a towel before going out into the main area of the lodge. The other girls were already asleep in their beds, exhaustion having finally won. With a large yawn Roslyn climbed into her own bed and was asleep moments after her head hit the pillow.

***

Roslyn awoke during the night to find her sister and friends all still asleep. Roslyn put on some of the clothes Ruby provided for them. She had also managed to get a potion from the shaman, the one that would enable Roslyn to astral project. She had not had time to make her own during the journey south, for it took several days of brewing in certain conditions for it to work properly.

Roslyn downed the potion and sat down on the floor, her eyes closed. She felt the same sensation as the first time she had used the potion. Opening her inner eye she found herself floating in her grandfather's home before the hearth, her mother sitting at the table nearby.

"Roslyn!" Amelia breathed a sigh of relief when she saw her. "It is so good to see you! We were worried about you after you left Hyena City."

"We did have a couple of complications, but we are safely within Beaver Territory now."

"Chief Erick sent word that the orcs have started to head north," Amelia told her. "Willow sent word that they are mustering their warriors in case the orcs come within their territory."

"I am sure Ruby, the Chief of the village we are in, would have told me that in the morning," Roslyn commented to her mother. "We were herded away to separate gender lodgings for the night."

"I have heard of Ruby; her father was killed by rebel orcs last year which is how she became Chieftain of her village. She is wary of most strangers to her Clan."

"I will talk to her in the morning," Roslyn told her.

"Roslyn, I am sorry about Heath," her mother said to her, a look of compassion on her face. "How are you doing?"

"As well as can be expected under the circumstances," was all Roslyn could say. "I have not had much time to mourn."

"Oh, sweetie…"

"We will see you soon, mother. Take care," Roslyn told her, a slight stutter in her voice. Her mother nodded and watched as Roslyn's form began to fade.

Roslyn thought of her father now, and she felt her astral form whisked away from Jay'Al. She opened her eyes again and found herself in her father's study. She had not talked to him since she had revealed that her mother was alive, so she was a little apprehensive about seeing him again. She had sent a letter with Maeve for him, and he would have read it weeks before.

Her father sat at his desk going over papers, but he noticed Roslyn's astral form and stood up with a start.

"Roslyn!" he exclaimed, coming towards her before stopping, noticing that she appeared as she had the last time.

Roslyn wanted so badly to hug her father again.

"How are you, father?" she asked him, noticing that there were more greys in his hair.

"I am well, darling, but how are you? What have you been doing these past months?"

"We traveled south to the Hyena Clan, fought with some orcs and discovered some things about the Dragon Clan," Roslyn gave him a shortened version of events. "We lost Heath."

"I am sorry to hear that. How?"

"His brother interfered during the orc attack on Hyena City and he was shot," Roslyn answered. "It was a heavy loss for me, we had gotten close during the journey."

"I see," her father said. "Where are you now?"

"A village of the Beaver Clan, we are heading north again to regroup at New Wardgrove and wait for Maeve. I was tasked with finding the Dragon Clan, so we will head for the plateau after my Honor Guard has arrived."

"I wish you luck, Roz," he told her. "Do you have time to tell me about your mother, and your sister?

***

Cassidy woke Roslyn up in the morning with a slight shaking of her shoulders.

"Ruby is at the door inviting us all to have breakfast with her," Cassidy told her.

"Then let's," Roslyn said as she yawned, "go get breakfast."

The girls all got dressed and Roslyn braided their hair before they stepped foot outside of their lodgings. They were met by the men of their group, all of them looking refreshed. The only one who seemed a little off was Kasimir, who had no idea of the language of the Clans and had to rely on the others.

"Kasimir," Roslyn spoke his name in the Common Tongue and he looked at her with renewed hope. "Once we get back to New Wardgrove you can go back to Ellsgrove."

"I can?"

"We have a ship that is heading there once we get back to New Wardgrove," she assured him. "There is no need for you to stay here anymore."

"Thank you Roslyn, I will definitely take you up on that."

The group walked in silence till they came to the Chief's house where they found Ruby and her brother Shepherd managing a large fire pit with a spit over it; on the spit was what looked like a wild boar that had been roasting all night.

"Come my friends," Ruby greeted them. "There is plenty for everyone."

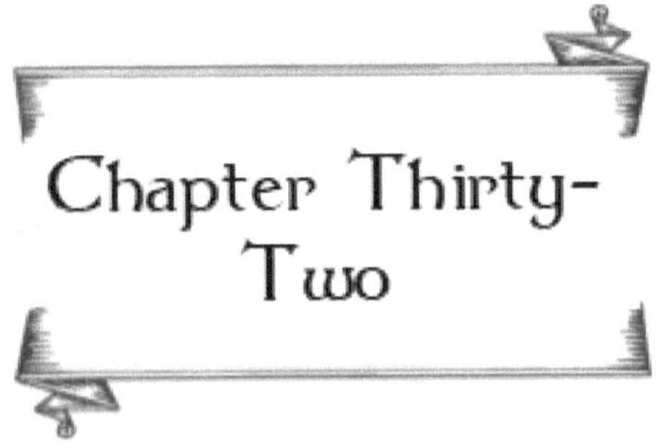

Chapter Thirty-Two

Roslyn looked back at the village of Amultree and hefted the pack she carried into a better position on her back. Ruby had given them horses to ride on and a wagon in order to reach their destination in better time; she had also sent with them the rest of the roasted boar along with plenty of smoked meat and bread.

Roslyn still shielded their group overnight, even though they were in friendly territory. It made her testy in the morning, enough that Cassidy knew to get her sister food first thing in the morning; the food definitely helped even out Roslyn's mood.

Everyone rode horses but Karina, her brother and guardian managed the wagon.

Ruby had directed them to the Beaver Clan's largest settlement where Willow resided so they headed there. There were paths marked out through the marshes by ropes and bridges, and after a two day journey they reached the settlement of Hollow. The whole place was built over part of a lake on stilts, a rope bridge providing access from land. Warriors guarded the marshes around the lake, the first group stopping them to ask who they were and why they were there. One of them recognized Cassidy and in turn knew of Roslyn so they offered to escort them to Hollow.

"This place is amazing," Roslyn commented as they walked over the bridge to the village. She was looking at the stilts holding the houses up and noticed people in canoes moving about the lake.

"It is one of our oldest settlements," one of the Beaver Clan warriors told her. "It has withstood many things."

Willow's house was in the center of the village and was only one story, though it had many rooms. Willow greeted them warmly and invited them into her home for food and rest.

"I got Chief Erick's message," Willow informed them. "I am glad you made it here safely."

"We did have a slight detour," Roslyn replied and told her about going down a whirlpool and coming out in a subterranean cave.

"You say the tunnel came out on the cliffs overlooking the ocean?" Willow asked as she led them to her dining hall. "I have heard old stories about some places underground where some of the ancient creatures had been imprisoned in; I wonder if this was such a place."

"Maybe if you had the right warriors and shamans to go down there and look around you could figure it out," Roslyn commented.

"An excursion might be just the thing once we have dealt with the orcs. Now, I bid you to stay here and rest for a few days. I can send a squad of my warriors along with you when you do depart for home."

"We appreciate that, Willow," Roslyn spoke up as a young woman brought out a platter of food for them to eat. "We will stay a few days before continuing."

***

Roslyn was standing out at the side of one of the 'streets' looking down into the clear water of the lake. Kavan came up behind her and wrapped his arms around her, kissing her on the cheek. The sky above them was an orange-peach shade as the sun was setting on the horizon.

"We will be safe here," Kavan commented. "And we do not need to be in different rooms here either."

They had not been able to spend much time alone together since Hyena City, though Roslyn had held back some since losing Heath out of respect.

"Not tonight, though I would like to spend the evening with you," she told him. "I hope you understand."

"I do," he assured her. "Let's find some ale and a fire to get cozy at, shall we?"

***

Cassidy sat with Crick by the hearth in Willow's home. Willow's familiar, a cardinal named Red, sat on Crick's shoulder and preened her fur. Willow sat on a cushion nearby, with Kai and Karina sitting beside Cassidy.

"Well, you are something different, are you not," Willow was saying to Karina. "The Dragon Clan had to survive some-how, I commend you for it. Orc blood will definitely make you stronger; I wonder how it affects your magic."

"Roz told me that her magic is strong, but I sense that it is not as strong as Roz's," Cassidy told Willow.

Karina shrugged, feeling uncomfortable under the older shaman's gaze. Willow was both the Head Chief of the Beaver Clan and the Head Shaman, an impressive feat. Karina felt slightly intimidated by her. Mister Scruffy sat beside her, swishing his tail back and forth.

A Quest for Her Roots

"You will be safe here," Willow assured Karina. "You are of the Dragon Clan after all, you are one of us. People might look at you with curiosity but none of them would harm you. Tell me, please, what is it like on the plateau?"

***

Tiffany was the first one up in the morning. The day before she had found the area where the warriors of the Clan practiced their weapons so she would know where to go in the morning. She started with her stretching exercises and her weight lifting as she waited for the others to join her. The night before she had told her friends where to go in the morning for their practice session.

Aidan was the first one to join her, doing his stretches before taking out his sword. He smiled at Tiffany who drew her own sword and squared off against him. They went through several different manoeuvres before picking up the pace. Neither of them noticed as the others started to trickle into the training area accompanied by a few of the Beaver Clan warriors. Only when the two of them found themselves at a draw and backed away from each other did they notice their companions had arrived.

"Well done," Roslyn told them as she clapped her hands. "You both have come a long way."

"We had good teachers," Tiffany told her with a smile. "Care to see for yourself?"

Roslyn smiled and drew her own sword while the others broke off into groups for practice.

***

They stayed in Hollow for a little over a week. Willow's warriors had all gathered and she sent them out to scout the edge of their lands and look for any signs of the orcs. With no orcs in the area Roslyn found it was time to continue on.

Finally they reached the edge of the marshes that were part of the Beaver territory. The weather had turned to freezing rain, leaving the path they fol- lowed all muddy. Roslyn had chosen not to accept a squad of warriors from Willow; they could travel faster with less people.

"I know where we are," Cassidy spoke up as they took in the countryside. "We are only a few days ride from Bella Vale."

Roslyn knew by now that the look on her sister's face also meant some- thing else. "And?"

"The North Snow Orc Clan's home is nearby as well."

Roslyn swore and looked around. She recognized the hills and small mountains, the same mountains where Cassidy had killed an orc.

"We know the orcs were heading north, so we should be careful," Kavan spoke up from behind them.

"We stick to the lower valleys, farthest away from the orc homeland," Roslyn said. "We go as fast as we can."

Cassidy nodded and together they led their group north, staying away from the area that the orcs claimed as their own. That night when they set up camp Roslyn set stronger wards around the area to ensure that they were all safe during the night. She made sure that everyone in the group knew where the edge of their camp was and that if they passed it they would no longer be safe. They reheated some of the boar meat over the fire and they all got into their sleeping sacks.

Roslyn awoke sometime during the night, a chill going down her spine. She sat up in her sleeping sack next to her sister, Kavan on her other side, and she looked around the area. Everyone seemed to be asleep still, except something did not seem right.

Getting out of her sleep sack she looked around the area outside of her protection, trying to find what felt wrong. She stopped in her tracks as she saw that only metres from the edge of her protection stood several large orcs. She knew that the orcs could not tell there was magic being used, and she also knew that her shield was capable of tricking outsiders into thinking there was nothing there at all. Was it just bad luck that they were right there, or had they been followed?

A hand touched her shoulder and she jumped a little, turning to find Karina crouched next to her.

"They are asking each other what they think of the area," Karina whispered to her, translating what the orcs were saying to each other. "They thought they saw tracks but now are not sure."

"That one is Grau's Second," Karina added, pointing to the bigger of the two orcs. "He will look around some more, but he should not find anything; though I know he might not give up so easily."

"What should we do?" Roslyn asked her.

"We'll wait them out," Karina told her. "And when we move again we remain shielded so they cannot follow us."

"How much longer till dawn?" Roslyn asked aloud as she looked up at the sky. "A couple more hours at the least."

"Do you want to wake the others?" Karina asked her. Roslyn shook her head.

"Let's wait out the orcs, see what they do."

Thankfully the orcs just looked around the area--not knowing what lay right in front of them--before turning away and heading north.

Roslyn let out a sigh of relief and turned to look at Karina who looked relieved as well. "Let's try to go back to sleep, shall we?" Roslyn asked her.

***

When the others woke up Roslyn told them what had happened. They packed up their camp and Roslyn continued to shield them as they maintained their journey.

A Quest for Her Roots

Above them the sky had turned dark, threatening more freezing rain. Her companions all still had their warmth charms at least, and at night it was easy to keep the heat from their fire within her wards.

They eventually found themselves on a well-used road that Cassidy said would take them straight to Bella Vale, and beyond that New Wardgrove.

"We should be with mother again in a few hours," Cassidy told Roslyn.

"Then let us pick up the pace, shall we?"

Roslyn got to thinking how long they had been gone as a group of Wolf Clan warriors approached them on horseback. It had taken them a little over two months to get to Hyena City. They had stayed there a couple weeks before heading north by boat. It had taken them another two weeks to get to Hollow, and they had stayed there for a week. They had been gone for just over three months now. Maeve might not even be back yet.

***

The Wolf Clan warriors escorted them to Bella Vale, leaving them at the front gates of the village before going back out on their route. The gates were opened for them and they entered the village to find Quinn and Oko racing to meet them. The rain had finally stopped and it had grown cold again so they could see their breath in the air.

"You are back!" the two brothers greeted their oldest sisters with hugs.

"Mother will be glad to know you have returned safely," Oko told them.

"We have been worried awaiting your return," Quinn added. "Come, let us get out of this cold and damp air and into grandfather's house."

"Mother told us what happened," Oko commented as they walked down the half frozen and half muddy streets of the village. "What an adventure you all have had!"

"We are glad you have made it home safely," Quinn interjected with a serious expression. "We have only just found you Roz, it would have been hard to not see you again."

Roslyn reached over and put an arm around her brother's shoulder and hugged him. "It was wholly a group effort to get back here," Roslyn told him. "Especially Karina's help had a part in my survival."

The two brothers took in the part-orc young woman and she watched as their eyes grew wide.

"Karina is the head shaman of the Dragon Clan," Roslyn informed them.

"The Dragon Clan?" Oko asked Karina. "From the plateau?!"

Roslyn chuckled as Karina answered the youth's questions one after the other. Finally they had to stop asking questions because they got to their grandfather's house.

Chief Rotho welcomed them with open arms and tight hugs before releasing them to Amelia who hugged them just as tightly. Leona and Sawyer ran from the kitchen into the main hall to hug them as well before heading back into the kitchen to finish cooking.

"You are just in time for supper," Amelia told them. "Why don't you all wash up and get ready in the guest house?"

"Actually, Roslyn, Tiffany, Karina, why don't you come to my home to wash and change?" Cassidy asked the women of the group. "After being on the road since Hollow I think we could all use a bath and clean clothes."

The rest of the group agreed and they split up at the door to the Chief's house.

"Oh, mother could you send a message to New Wardgrove to let them know we should be back tomorrow?" Roslyn asked Amelia before she left. Her mother nodded and turned to Oko and Quinn who ran off to get a messenger sent out.

Cassidy led the women to her house at the edge of the village. Roslyn was telling Karina how the walls encompassed all of the valley, including all of the farms, when they arrived at Cassidy's house. Cassidy ushered them inside and started preparing the bath while the girls relaxed and got out of their muddy clothes.

"Roz, I have been meaning to ask, what is that tattoo on your midsection?" Karina asked her as they started to strip down to their underclothes.

Roslyn looked down at the rune that was tattooed in white ink just a few inches below her bellybutton and smiled.

"It's my anti-pregnancy charm," she told Karina. "I got it a few years ago."

"There is such a thing?" Karina was interested. Cassidy poked her head out of the bathing room as well.

"That is a good idea," Cassidy commented. "We have herbal remedies that we use to keep us from getting pregnant, but a spell such as that would work a lot better."

"I can give you one if you would like," Roslyn told her sister. "Tattooing spells and charms like this was one of my favourite courses at the University. I had this one done by my professor, it cost a lot for the labour but it was well worth it."

"Interesting. I might just take you up on that," her sister said before going back into the bathing room. Karina looked thoughtful.

"I love that your father still raised you like you were in Jay'Al," Karina commented. "The notion that in other places women are not of equal status...it seems so alien to me."

"Oh believe me, I had to fight for a lot of it back home even with my father's blessing. The other nobles we knew were hard pressed to let their daughters spend time with me. I was allowed to wear breeches and I knew how to use a sword," Roslyn said with a shrug. "When I met Oswick and Rafi though...their sisters were so good to me. I have not seen them since before I moved to the capital."

"You told me about what happened after the fencing tournament," Cassidy spoke up from the bathing room. "Clearly some of the noblewomen thought what you were doing made sense since they went through so much trouble to get the new changes approved about them being able to fight or whatever."

"Yes, father told me things were approved, and I met a few young girls who were starting their training. I always felt so guilty that I never got the chance to know them before I left," Roz answered. She shrugged again. "Maybe if some of them are noble born they might be able to tell me what happened to get the approval of those starch old men."

"Did father tell you how many young women joined your Honour Guard?" Cassidy asked her as she came from the bathing room.

"No, I told him I did not want to know until they got here. I am sure Sir Sullivan and the women I recommended probably did not take all of them on anyway, and more would be let go if they could not keep up. So we will see once they get here. I think we are home too early. Maeve should not be back for another couple of weeks."

"If they were able to bring more mages with them, they might be early," Tiffany pointed out. "I guess we will see tomorrow."

"Water is hot," Cassidy called out; she had used her magic to warm the water. "Who wants to go first?"

***

Kavan led the men to the guest house, and Kai used his magic to warm the bath water while they put all of their muddy clothes in a pile.

"What is she like?" Kasimir asked the group.

"Who?" Rafi asked him in turn.

"Princess Roslyn. I met her cousins once, but since I was away during the last year it was a bit of a shock to find that the king had died and his cousin was crowned."

Kavan chuckled and said, "Have you not been able to tell for yourself? You have been travelling with us for a couple weeks now."

"She is not like her cousins," Kasimir commented. "Though I did not spend much time with the princesses before, Roslyn is very different."

"Oh, you have no idea," Oswick said with a hearty laugh. "Roslyn is so different from any noble woman you will ever meet. She is half Jay'Alian after all."

"So her father raised her as if she was still in Jay'Al?" Kasimir scratched his head.

"Her mother would have wanted that," Kavan told him. "Until we came here Roslyn believed her mother was dead. It turns out Amelia survived because of her brother's magic, and Roslyn had no idea of her twin sister until we came here either."

"Well, I look forward to going back to Ellsgrove under the rule of this new king," Kasimir said. "I know my sisters will feel more at ease."

"Roslyn has done a lot in her short time here," Kai spoke up. "Her magic is very powerful; the most powerful I have ever seen. I feel ashamed to be part of a heritage that took a part in what happened nineteen years ago."

Kavan looked at Kai sharply and Kai inhaled slowly. "My father," Kai began to explain, "was one of the shamans against the Ellsgrove people. It was because of his influence that the violence escalated. I remember the day I felt Cassidy join with Jay'Al...it was unique, and so different from our shamans; but when Roslyn joined with Jay'Al?" Kai shook his head. "I know my father felt so much shame and regret over what happened. Roslyn was a shock to us; that the spirit of the land wanted her to be the one to bring us all together spoke volumes. Cassidy has never left these lands; Roslyn was raised on another continent and taught to use her magic differently. With her connection to Jay'Al now she is the most powerful mage or shaman in these lands."

"Which makes her a target for Grau," Oswick said. "The half-orc does not understand what is going on. The orc superstitions hold precedence for him."

"What can we do to help her?" Kasimir asked.

Kavan shrugged, feeling very unprepared for that question. "We stand by her," he answered. "We support her. She is still vulnerable and we can help with that. Once her Honour Guard gets here she will be better protected, but until then her friends need to look out for her."

"And we will," Rafi told him, putting a hand on Kavan's shoulder. "You can count on us."

"Coming from you," Kavan said with a chuckle, "that means a lot. Thank you Rafi."

"You have grown on me, Arms Master," Rafi said with a laugh.

"I am glad to hear that," Kavan said, and he reached out his hand and was happy when Rafi grasped it back. "Thank you."

"You know she can take care of herself, right?" Oswick spoke up.

"Oh, we know," Kavan answered. "There are a lot of enemies out there who do not know that and will try to take advantage of what they think is a weakness," he went on. "Like Grau. She needs our support."

"Now that we have established that," Kai said as he came out of the bathing room, "Who wants to go first?"

***

The next morning Roslyn rode the horse that Ruby gave her back to New Wardgrove at the lead of her friends. Cassidy remained in Bella Vale, though she would be coming to New Wardgrove vafter a few days.

Roslyn walked up to her room with heavy steps, though she was grateful to be back. Karina was shown to Cassidy's cabin and Kasimir was given a cabin as well. Roslyn had the soldiers put Heath's belongings in his room, and it hurt to think about having to tell Jackson and Maeve what happened, but she was going to have to do it.

Sitting on the end of her bed, her door wide open still, she looked at her bags on the floor and thought about the last time she had been there. She thought of the time when she had been homesick and Heath had hugged her tightly when he saw she had been crying. Tears welled in her eyes as she remembered him taking her to the hot spring, and their first kiss.

"I heard you were back," she heard a voice call from the stairway and she recognized Jackson's voice. "How was the–Heath? Where are you?"

She imagined Jackson was standing in Heath's doorway, his belongings there but no Heath. That only made the tears come harder.

"Hey Tiffany, where is Heath?" she heard Jackson ask, his voice getting louder up the stairs.

"Jackson, I am so sorry," she heard Tiffany start to say. "He...he is gone."

"What? No! Roslyn?!"

She heard him come up the stairs and she was wiping her tears on her sleeve when he appeared in the doorway, a stricken look on his face.

"Tell me what happened," he said in a quiet voice, a hint of disbelief in it. He could see how upset she was.

"Everett was there at Hyena City," she started, trying hard not to cry more. "He took Heath and Kavan. They had escaped but Heath was shot."

"No," Jackson shook his head, "No, he can't be dead."

"He fell into the water," she continued. "His body was taken out to sea in the current."

Jackson leaned against the wall next to her door and sank to the floor, a sob escaping his lips.

"Everett is imprisoned in Hyena City for what he did," she told him as she went to sit beside him, tears running down her face again. She grabbed his hand and squeezed it as they cried together over the loss of their friend.

***

A few days passed after their return to New Wardgrove. Word spread between the outpost and the harbour that Heath was gone, and a celebration of life was planned for once Maeve got there. Jackson sent a message to Maeve to let her know what had happened to Heath to give her time to let it sink it.

In the meantime, Roslyn was trying to settle back into their former routine, and she also had a lot of paperwork to go through and sign. Trade agreements needed to be finalized, and more envoys from the Clans were expected sometime as well. Cassidy had arrived back at the New Wardgrove that morning.

"I want to go with you to the plateau," Cassidy told her when she arrived. "Father will still be in Ellsgrove after."

"Are you sure? We have no idea what dangers might lay ahead of us."

Roslyn had greeted her sister at the gates, who had arrived in a large covered wagon, and now the two of them walked around the palisade together.

Over the time they had been gone the last of the buildings went up and animals had been brought in, bought from the Wolf Clan.

"I cannot leave you now Roz, not when there is more adventure ahead."

"Well, if you are sure..."

"I am. Now, about those suits of armour we found: I want to do some enchanting on them so we can be better protected from enemy magic," Cassidy told her. "I brought everything I need to do it, as well as my friend Jessamine who can alter the armour for everyone." Cassidy beckoned to the tall, muscular older woman who stood nearby. Roslyn took her in, admiring the way she braided her hair tight against her head. The woman had a large cart behind her with a slew of equipment in it.

"By all means, we certainly have time to get it done while we wait for Maeve and the rest of our reinforcements to arrive. Welcome, Jessamine, to New Wardgrove."

***

During the two weeks it took for Maeve to arrive at New Wardgrove's Harbour Roslyn had everyone preparing. However, Aidan would not be coming with them this time because he would be needed to get the clerks settled in and Roslyn was not going to wait any longer than necessary. She would have to take a day to see how her Honour Guard were and get to know them before they would leave but no longer than that. There was also Heath to be remembered.

"I wonder if the women of your Honour Guard would like matching armour sets to yours, I should look into getting enough frishna. I am sure Jessamine would be up to the task," Cassidy commented.

"I would love to," Jessamine answered with a wide smile. "I do not get to work with it enough these days. I sell some of my goods at the Spring Market every year and have had a few good commissions, but it will cost a lot for both the material and the labour. Altering the armour was a pittance compared to creating new sets."

"That would be a good idea," Kavan said from beside Roslyn. "I cannot wait to see everyone in their full armour when we leave."

"Well, I would not be able to get the armour done for a few weeks anyways, which would give me time to get the measurements of the new ladies. I imagine they would be outfitted with some of the best armour from Ellsgrove," Jessamine said.

"Most likely," Roslyn said with a smile. "I think tonight I will ride out to the harbour and wait there for the ship. Anyone want to come with me?"

Kavan raised his hand and added, "With a full retinue of guards as well. We have been lucky so far that the orcs have not come into Wolf Clan territory to get to you. We cannot risk anything."

"I think I will stay," Cassidy said next. "I will meet them when you bring them here."

"Yeah, I'm going to sit this one out too," Oswick added, and Rafi nodded in agreement. No one else wanted to go it seemed.

"OK, just you and me Kavan...and a bunch of soldiers."

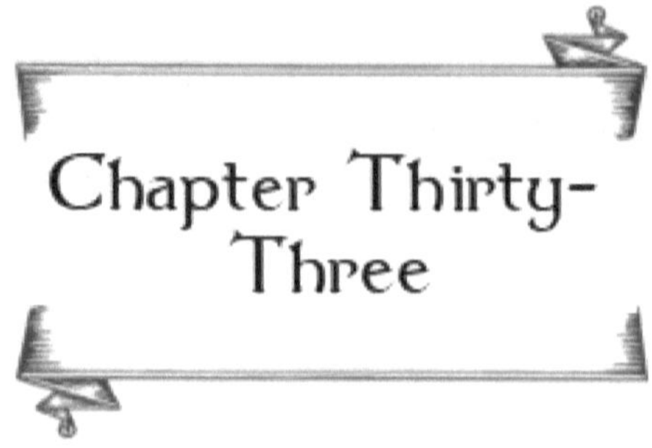

Chapter Thirty-Three

They left shortly after supper with a group of soldiers in tight formation around them. It had chosen to start raining on their way but Roslyn covered them with a shield to keep the rain off of them; it did not, however, keep the mud off of them. By the time they arrived at the harbour just after dark Roslyn was ready for a hot bath and dry clothes; it was a good thing she had brought another set of clothes along with her.

The Harbour had really grown since she had seen it last. The stairway down to the dock had been spelled by her to keep it from getting icy, and the large walls had been erected first thing when the building started. There were several large warehouses for incoming goods and more for outgoing goods. Roslyn was pleasantly surprised to find a few houses had been put up and a Jay'Alian merchant from the Fox Clan was staying in one of them: he had brought goods to trade with Ellsgrove which were in one of the warehouses.

Roslyn and Kavan were shown to one of the smaller houses, their guards joining the guards of the Harbour for the night. After brushing down their horses and making sure they were comfortable in the stables attached to the house, Roslyn and Kavan went inside the house to clean up.

Roslyn heated the water in the large wooden tub while Kavan tossed their clothes into a metal washing bin full of water so the mud could soak out. Together they climbed into the bathtub, washing each other with soap and a cloth. Kavan started washing her hair, massaging her scalp very nicely. She yawned and declared she needed to go to bed. Kavan rinsed her hair out and told her that he would wash his own hair before joining her.

Reaching the bed after draining the tub Kavan found Roslyn had already fallen asleep wearing only an undershirt. He smiled and pulled the blankets over her before climbing into bed with her and falling asleep as well.

****

A Quest for Her Roots

In the morning Roslyn awoke before dawn and got dressed, leaving Kavan asleep in bed as she went for a walk around the walls of the Harbour. She found herself staring out at the ocean to the north as the sun rose, when there on the horizon she saw a ship coming towards the harbour from the Sea of Ice. Roslyn stayed there as the ship came closer and closer until Kavan joined her.

"How long have you been out here?" Kavan asked her as he put his arm around her waist and held her close.

"Since before dawn," she told him. She nodded in the direction of the ship and said, "They are right on time."

"So it would seem," Kavan observed. "Where do you want to be when they dock?"

"Down on the docks," she told him. "They have come this far for me, I should wait for them there."

"Then let us make our way down there. Have you eaten?"

Roslyn shook her head and smiled as he produced a meat pie from his bag. "I stopped by the kitchens on my way here," he told her. "I knew you would be waiting for them."

"Just wait, I might switch things up on you for the fun of it," she told him with a laugh as she grabbed the meat pie and headed for the stairway down to the dock.

"I would not miss that for anything," he replied as he followed her, eating his own meat pie.

The hours passed as they sat on the bottom stair waiting for the ship to come in. When it finally docked and Roslyn heard Maeve's booming voice ordering the ropes tied she sprang forward and with deft proficiency tied the lines to the dock with Kavan's help. Heath had shown her the knots several times over their journey and now she felt that he would be proud of her skills. She felt a twinge in her heart as she realized how much she missed him.

"Ahoy Roslyn!" she heard Maeve call out as the gangplank was placed. Roslyn turned to see Maeve coming off the ship towards her and she ran to hug the woman. A tortoiseshell cat also came running towards Roslyn, twinning herself around their legs as they hugged.

"Welcome back!" Roslyn told her as she squeezed the woman in her arms. "I hope your journey was not too much."

"Very uneventful," Maeve answered her as they parted and Roslyn bent to pet Selene. "Though some of the women were seasick and could have used your charms, they did make it all the way here."

"Well they can rest easy now," Roslyn spoke up as she took in the young women on the deck. "We have housing ready for you and stable beds, as well as breakfast that is not seafood."

Most of the young women cheered at the knowledge of no more fish to eat, though some of them seemed more solemn than the rest.

"Bring your belongings and I will help get you set," Roslyn told them. As the young women walked off of the ship she counted them, and she was very surprised that there were more than ten women--there were fifteen. She was also surprised to see that all of them wore breeches and long tunics instead of dresses.

"So many," Roslyn whispered to Kavan.

"I recognize some of them," Kavan told her. "That day you were in the fencing tournament, they were in the crowd. Some of these women are noble born, Roz."

"Well then," Roslyn looked thoughtful. "I know my father said the nobles passed a few things but never had I thought that they would let their daughters come here."

"Only one way to find out, hm?" Kavan asked her as he saw Sir Sullivan at the top of the gangplank. "Don't look now, but a certain knight is looking your way."

Roslyn looked at Kavan with suspicion for she had not told him about her former occurrence with the knight.

"Do not play coy with me," Kavan whispered to her. "I was close enough at the dinner party to overhear that you two almost had something in Wardgrove. Do not worry, I am not jealous--I just worry that he might be."

"I do not think he is that kind of man," Roslyn told him. "I will not hide my relationship with you Kavan. Now come greet the nice knight with me, will you?"

Kavan groaned and nodded after a moment, linking arms with Roslyn as they walked towards Sir Sullivan. She watched as Sully took them in, and noticed the look of shock in his eyes. She felt her cheeks going red as she greeted him.

"I am so glad you made it here in one piece," Roslyn told Sully. "Maeve told me that the journey was uneventful; I hope that was so."

"With the help of your warmth and wind charms we were set," Sully told her. "Sir Graeme and I helped train your Honour Guard with the help of your friends."

"I am happy you had so much help. The soldiers will show you to where you will stay tonight. I will see you at dinner," Roslyn told him. She noticed Maeve was still standing nearby, Selene in her arms. Maeve was staring at the ship, a dejected look on her face.

"I am so sorry about Heath," Roslyn told her as she approached them.

"I know. Me too. He was one of my oldest friends," Maeve said, looking down at Selene. "Somehow I think she understood when I told her," she added, talking about Heath's cat.

"I wonder if she was kind of a familiar to him," Roslyn commented, reaching out to scratch the cat's chin.

"When will the celebration of life be?" Maeve asked her as she motioned for them to walk alongside her up to the harbour.

"Tomorrow night," Kavan answered. "We all miss him."

"Everett should pay for what he did," Maeve said through clenched teeth.

"He is in a prison in Hyena City," Roslyn assured her. "He will pay, trust me."

***

Roslyn helped serve her new Honour Guard breakfast in the Dining Hall of the Harbour. She got to know all of their names, and finally was able to put a face to Deirdre, Sullivan's sister. Deirdre was a lithe curly-blonde young woman who took her job very seriously now. She approached Roslyn with spunk, introducing herself and informing her of her progress in training. Roslyn was amazed by the young woman's skills and told her so, but also reminded her to not let it get to her head. The slightly younger woman took it with grace, vowing to become better.

"I like her," Roslyn told Kavan and Sully at breakfast. "I like all of them. They would not have made it this far without gumption."

"Do you know what happened in Ellsgrove after the fencing tournament?" Sully asked her. Roslyn shook her head.

"All of the noble women who were married went on strike," he told her. "None of them would give their husbands pleasure. Even the brothels shut down. They all demanded equal treatment. That is why the Noble Council agreed with your father. Though now there are more regulations and testing done but that is definitely for the best."

Roslyn snort-laughed, earning a surprised but relieved look from her Honour Guard.

"That is absolutely fantastic," Roslyn said. "That even the brothels got in on it...I am amazed." She left out the fact that she had helped several brothels in the capital out with special anti-pregnancy and disease charms when she moved into the palace. Women deserved to know that they could have multiple partners before settling down, and that sex was not some holy sacrament like some of the priests claimed. That she was able to set such things into motion made her extremely proud. Women could enjoy sex as much as the men did without being persecuted for it. Of course, in Jay'Al it was always like that. Roslyn was thankful that her father raised her as her mother would have wanted; and even more thankful that she got to meet her mother.

"Tell me what you have been doing here," Sullivan said as they continued eating.

"Well, we traveled down to the south and back again, going to each Clan Territory and meeting the Head Shamans and Chiefs. We ran into some orcs, I got kidnapped by orcs and escaped again..." By now all of the young women were listening intently. "...and on our way back up north by boat we ran into a huge storm that pushed us out to the ocean and we went down a whirlpool where this giant squid thing saved our lives and brought us to a subterranean cave that had man-eating giant lizards in it."

Roslyn looked at the women with amusement as they were all staring at her with wide eyes.

"How did you get out?" Sullivan prompted her to continue.

Roslyn smiled broadly and did so, "We found a staircase that led us out, and here we are now."

"I never expected so much," one of the women, Baylee, commented. "I mean, we knew about the orcs before but were told that they had a treaty with the Clans."

"They are after me because they do not understand the portents the gods showed us on my birthday: there was a lunar eclipse. Also, my mother performed a special ritual with me and the ancient shamans spoke to me and told me to find the lost Clan."

"Wait, what? What does that mean?" Sullivan asked her, putting his fork down.

"I will be heading to the plateau in a few days to find the Dragon Clan and bring the Clans back together. The orcs think it will cause issues or something and want to either stop me or control me and my magic. Personally I think bringing all the Clans together includes bringing the orcs in as well; the Dragon Clan is mostly half-orcs by now anyways."

"How do you know that if they are lost?" someone spoke up.

"Karina, the Head Shaman of the Dragon Clan, finally found a way down from the plateau and came to find me because the ancient shamans wanted her to help me: she is part orc. She had become one of my trusted friends."

"You trust a half-orc?" Deirdre asked her. "Even after you were kidnapped by orcs?"

"Karina saved my life," Roslyn told her and the others. "Her heritage is different, and so is mine. She is a person, a beautiful young woman who braved the unknown to come find me. I am sure that once you meet her you will agree with me."

"Why is Lady Theophania not with you today?" Lady Theodora asked Roslyn.

"She wanted some leisure time before we leave," Roslyn answered. "You will meet her later today."

The girls asked more questions and Roslyn answered them as best as she could during the rest of their breakfast. Finally the girls went to go gather up their belongings from the warehouse they had been put in after the ship had been unloaded. All of the women had their own horses that had been brought with them but their belongings would need to be carted back to New

A Quest for Her Roots

Wardgrove. Roslyn had already thought ahead and made sure she got a wagon ready.

Along with the women of her Honour Guard were several clerks who had been eating at another table in the Dining Hall; two male clerks and an older woman. They would ride at the front of the wagon together.

Roslyn was also surprised to find a stone mason had been sent along and he asked her about any nearby quarries. He was a tall muscular man in his late thirties with dark brown hair and white at his temples.

"A wooden palisade is flammable," he told her. "Your father sent me to get a stone wall built."

"We will have to ask my grandfather about any quarries, but I welcome the help. What do I call you?"

"Judd, your highness."

"None of that now, Judd--just call me Roslyn."

***

They arrived at New Wardgrove in time for lunch the next day, which Oswick and Rafi had been busy making all morning. When they served them the women voiced how good the food smelled and were amazed that the two merchants had cooked it.

"What, roasted lamb and all of the bread? You should taste my famous stew, it is to die for," Oswick answered, earning a laugh from the women.

"It's true, his stew is very good," Roslyn spoke up. Cassidy sat to her right with Karina beside Cassidy, and Kavan sat on Roslyn's left. Sir Sullivan sat beside Kavan.

Aidan was the only one of the group who was not joining them for lunch because he was seeing that the clerks were settling in.

"You have done a lot here in the short time you have been here," Sir Sullivan commented. "New Ward-grove is expanding already."

"The builders have worked hard to accomplish so much, that is their job; I had nothing to do with it," Roslyn told him. "We have, however, brokered trading agreements with the Clans for several items. I particularly think that alpaca wool will become popular."

"What's an alpaca?" one of the ladies asked, and Roslyn had to think of her name for a moment. This one had light brown hair with dark brown eyes and was stocky; she was also, if Roslyn remembered right, a mage.

"Well, Heather, they are animals a little smaller than a

horse with long necks that have a soft wool. You will see plenty here in Jay'Al."

"Lady Theophania, how have you found living here with this new life-style?" Lady Theodora asked Tiffany. Theodora was tall like Tiffany and was very curvy.

"Please call me Tiffany," she replied with a smile. "It has been quite an adventure but well worth the change."

"Then everyone should call me Teddy. What is your weapon of choice Tiffany?"

"Longsword," Tiffany answered. "Though Rafi tells me I am getting proficient with the bow as well."

"We should have a tournament to see how everyone fares with their weapons," one of the other ladies suggested. From this girl's lithe frame Roslyn bet that she used a bow for her weapon of choice.

"Good idea Dara, but it might have to wait until we are back from the plateau," Roslyn told her. "I am sorry to drag you guys out into an adventure so soon but it cannot be helped. I am sure during the journey we will all see how everyone fares with their weapons, especially during our morning practices."

"When do we leave?" another girl, Kris, asked.

"Tomorrow morning," Roslyn told them. "We pack light, full armour and weapons at the ready."

"How long will it take us to get to the plateau?" Teddy asked.

Roslyn looked at Karina who said, "A sennight at most."

The women looked at each other and back at Roslyn and they nodded in unison. "We will be ready at dawn," Teddy was the one to speak.

As the ladies left the Dining Hall for their assigned cabins, Cassidy announced that the armour was ready for their group to collect and told them to meet her in the Training Hall where she and Jessamine had already staged the armour. Rafi went to go get Aidan and together the group of Roslyn's friends headed for the Training Hall.

Jessamine was waiting for them there, all of the windows uncovered to let enough light in for everyone to see the changes to the armour. There were several different runes etched into the breastplates and hand guards. Cassidy bade them all to put their armour on so she could demonstrate a few things. Each set of armour had the chest they had been brought in laying before their mannequins, and Cassidy had added everyone's names to their chests.

"We talked about protection from attacking magic after you were taken, Roslyn," Cassidy told her as the group started to put on their armour. "The enchantments I put on the armour, and the chainmail, make it so you are protected from attacking magic and from the spell Grau used to pull you from the horse."

Roslyn nodded, impressed.

"Also, if you are in close together you can link hands and it will create a shield around you all like a dome," Cassidy continued. "I also included some healing runes."

"How are the alterations?" Jessamine asked once everyone was in their full armour. No one had any complaints so she was satisfied. "I will take my leave then, I need to be getting home."

"Thank you for coming Jessamine," Roslyn told her as the older woman turned to leave. "Sometime you will have to show me how to braid your hair so tightly."

Jessamine nodded to her with a smile before leaving the hall.

"Want to throw a couple balls of fire at me to show me how the enchantment works?" Roslyn asked her sister, earning a laugh from Kai and Rafi.

***

It was a new moon that night so torches were set up all around the main square of New Wardgrove in front of the hall. A bonfire had been built up and lit, kegs of ale brought out and food served to the sailors and soldiers.

Roslyn sat on a chair a few feet away from the fire with Jackson and Maeve sitting on either side of her. The sailors had sung songs to honour their captain before the food was brought out. All of the sailors were there, either sitting or standing around the fire, talking and reminiscing about their Captain.

"Where will Selene stay?" Roslyn asked Maeve as some of the sailors started dancing around the fire, a few of them playing a jig on lutes.

"The harbour needs a mouser," Jackson told her. "She will stay with me."

***

The next morning Roslyn awoke at dawn and gathered up her already packed saddlebags and headed out down the stairs, knocking on doors as she went. She got to the kitchens to find Sir Sullivan waiting for her.

"Good morning," Sully greeted her.

"Good morning, Sully. Is everyone ready for our departure?"

"Yes, they are waiting at the stables," he told her, motioning for her to go ahead of him out of the Hall and to the stables.

Roslyn quickly checked their packs to make sure they had packed light and was satisfied to find that they all had.

"What, you don't trust my training?" Sully asked from the doorway of the stables.

Roz stuck her tongue out at him and said, "I was just making sure."

The group met at the main gate which was opened for them. Everyone wore their armour and had their weapons with them. Roslyn was glad to see that her Honour Guard had all been outfitted with the best armour from Ellsgrove, though she had figured they would be.

Finally Roslyn gave the signal for everyone to head out, and she flicked the reins to get her horse going. She missed Sage, who had been trained as a warhorse and knew verbal commands well; she could not wait to get her horse back.

Jaco and Jarrod rode in a wagon with their rationings, happy to be heading home again.

The group numbered thirty-two people now, including Jaco and Jarrod. With all the others being warriors Roslyn had not felt the need to bring any soldiers with them for this. Hopefully they would get to the plateau before Grau and not have to fight any orcs at all. She would need to secure the plateau and whatever the ancient shamans wanted her to find up there; at least she figured there was more to it than just finding the lost clan. Roslyn supposed she would have to go to the Dragon Clan Shrine and ask them once she got there.

Karina led them south-east towards the plateau. The weather had remained dry so far with the days slightly growing warmer, and the land was starting to show signs of life again as it thawed out more.

Crick, Mister Scruffy and Tej all sat with their respective shamans on their horses for most of the journey. Now and then the three of them would run off into the forest together and return to them later that night.

"Do you not worry about your pets while they are gone?" one of the ladies, Isobel, asked Cassidy one night as they sat down to eat supper around the fire.

"They are not our pets," Cassidy explained to her, "they are familiars. We understand them and they understand us, and can even be our eyes and ears. We shamans get our familiars when we are joined with Jay'Al."

"How come Roslyn does not have one?" Isobel asked.

"Either it is making its way to her, or has not been born yet," Cassidy answered with a shrug. "A familiar answering the call takes time."

Roslyn set her magical guards around their campsite each night, raising them in the morning. Kavan and Rafi would scout ahead together while Sully was behind the group watching their rear. Thankfully no orc bands were seen and there were no traces of them anywhere in the valleys even though their homeland was only days away now. Roslyn was grateful for that.

Finally one afternoon after five days on the road Rafi and Kavan came back to the group after scouting ahead.

"It looks like your people have built a small settlement with a wall at the base of the staircase," Kavan told Karina. "That was a good idea, they can protect the plateau that way."

"My father had planned to do that, I am happy to see they got it done. They wanted to wait for my return before sending out envoys to the different Clans. Now they can do so and trade for different food and such." Karina seemed eager to get there now.

"Well what are we waiting for?" Roslyn asked them. "Let's make haste for this outpost to get Karina back with her family."

Karina rode at the front of the group, grateful for the riding lessons that Roslyn had given her when they got to New Wardgrove. As they approached the gate Karina smiled up at her father who stood waiting on the wall.

A Quest for Her Roots

"Father!" She shouted a greeting and waved at her father who waved back with a wide grin on his own face. Her father shouted at someone to open the gate and went out of view as the gate slowly opened. As the group rode through the gate and into the settlement Karina saw her father coming towards them and she dismounted, handing the reins to Roslyn.

Karina hugged her father tightly, Mister Scruffy rubbing against their legs. Jaco came over as well and his father brought him into the embrace.

"Welcome home, my daughter and son," Lou said as they parted. "It is good to have you home again. Which one is the one you sought?"

"Roslyn," Karina said, beckoning to her. Roslyn dismounted and came forward.

"Your daughter saved my life," Roslyn informed Lou.

Lou looked at his daughter with proud eyes and extended a hand to Roslyn.

"Welcome to our Base Town," he said to Roslyn as she clasped his hand. "Please come, rest and share our food."

***

It was after a quick bath and meal that Roslyn found herself staring up at the stairway that led up to the plateau. The stair zigzagged up the side of the plateau into the low clouds until she no longer could see it. Several platforms had been built along the way for rest, as Karina had told them before. Hearing about it and seeing it were two completely different things. Roslyn had never been that high up before and was very unsure about it.

"The stair is sound," Karina said from beside her.

"It's the height I am concerned about," Roslyn confessed. "I have never been so high up before."

"The great princess Roslyn is afraid of heights?" Karina feigned being shocked, earning a chuckle from Roslyn. "Your friends will be with you to help you."

"What was it like coming down the stair?" Roslyn asked her.

"I was scared," Karina told her. "I had watched from the top for so long that I was scared of actually seeing it in person, as if it would shatter my preconceptions of the down-land. I was used to the height, though. It was the down-land I was afraid of."

"You happy to be going home?" Roslyn asked her, sensing a hesitation.

"I have found so much down here," Karina told her. "I lived such a simple life up there."

"Sometimes simple is better than adventure," Roslyn said.

"I am glad to have met you," Karina said as she put a hand on Roslyn's shoulder.

"And I you," Roslyn reached up to squeeze her hand. "I guess we wait until dawn to go up?"

Karina nodded. "Come, let's go gather with our friends and relax together before our big climb tomorrow."

***

Karina was restless the next morning; she woke up before everyone else, or thought she had--when she went to the kitchen of the house they were staying in she found Roslyn sitting at the table with a steaming mug in hand.

"You could not sleep either?" Karina asked Roslyn as she sat down beside her.

Roslyn shook her head and sipped from her mug. "I feel something," Roslyn told her, "Something at the edge of my senses that I cannot place."

"I feel it too, but I know what it is," Karina told her grimly. "I sense Grau."

A shiver ran down Roslyn's spine and she hugged herself. "How far away do you think he is?"

"A few days, maybe more."

"What defences does Base Town have?"

"None so far as I know. The walls of the town are wood so they will not be able to withstand much of an attack."

"We should talk to your father about what can be done," Roslyn said. "You said it would take us a few days to reach the top of the stairs right? We should be up there before he gets here. We have quite a lead on him."

Karina led Roslyn to her father's room and they knocked, waking him up. Her mother and other siblings had stayed up on the plateau because it was safer, her father had chosen to wait down at Base Town for her to return.

"Grau is coming," Karina told him, and a troubled look came over him.

"You are right, we have no defenses," Lou admitted. "We had not gotten that far. None of our warriors even have good armour."

"Maybe we let them in and up?" Roslyn commented, thinking. "Everyone comes up with us, we leave traps along the way to hold them back more. It would also give you time to get everyone up on the plateau to a safe place."

"You have such traps?" Lou asked her.

Roslyn smiled broadly and nodded. "Oh you have no idea the magical traps I can lay in our wake. His band will be heavily depleted by the time he catches up to us."

"How come you are so powerful?" Lou wanted to know now.

Roslyn shrugged and said, "My mother explained it to me as my innate magic grew strong in other ways when I learned how to use it in Ellsgrove, away from Jay'Al. Normally a shaman is connected with Jay'Al when their powers emerge. I already had strong magic by the time I was connected, and Jay'Al amplified them even more."

"Your people in Ellsgrove use your magic differently than here?" Lou asked.

"Oh yes. I know spells that Cassidy and Karina do not, but they also know a lot that I do not know: like enchanting and gemstone magic."

"All right then, we go with your plan. I will go around and get everyone ready to evacuate. We will leave everything down here and only take what we need."

***

Roslyn and Karina went to wake their friends and the Honour Guard up, filling them in on the plan as they went from room to room. Shortly everyone was awake and they were sharing smoked meat sticks and cheese for breakfast as the people who had been in Base Town, only twenty or so people, gathered at the bottom of the stairs.

"What about our horses?" Oswick asked.

"I put a spell on the stable and paddock to hide them. They have plenty of food and water to last them," Roslyn assured him. "The gates will be left open and the path clear for Grau to follow us up."

Roslyn heard Lou give the order to head out. She watched him lead his people up the staircase. "We go now too, I take up the rear to put down traps," Roslyn told her group. "We do not stop until tonight when we reach the first platform."

"Wait, we will need to rest now and then," Rafi complained. "My poor knees will not take climbing those stairs so well."

"And what about bathroom breaks?" one of her Guards asked.

Karina chuckled and informed them that they did indeed put in small latrines along the way, thinking ahead for when more people would be coming up to the plateau. That eased their worries for a time, and Roslyn assured them that they would get small rest stops; though they would have to eat while they walked to make up time. She did not want to let Grau get closer while they rested.

Off they went up the stair, which was wide enough for at least five people to walk abreast on, Cassidy staying back with her sister. Right at the bottom of the stair Roslyn set a trap with her magic, one that would freeze whoever stepped on it. Every few turns on the stairs she laid another trap.

When they reached the latrines they each took a turn before continuing on. Finally the sun was setting as they reached the first platform, which was more than big enough for the whole group to spread out and sleep comfortably. Since sound travelled so well up and down the stairs they knew they would hear anyone coming so did not bother with lookouts during the night. Roslyn was pretty sure if anyone went through her traps she would hear them as well.

The next morning they ate more smoked meat sticks and cheese before continuing on their way. Roslyn was the last one up the stairs again with Cassidy as she laid more traps. They had another brief respite by a latrine and they continued on. During this time Roslyn had been taking small glances over the side of the high railings at the ground below, working on her slight fear of heights--it really was not that bad, but only if she did not look for too long. From way up here she could see Grau and his war party in the distance but she still could not make out how many there were.

Finally they reached the top of the stair and stepped foot on the plateau. The Honour Guard were grateful, though admittedly they complained a lot less about the climb than Roslyn expected them to.

Lou had sent a messenger ahead to the two villages, and now he and Karina waited for Roslyn and her group so they walked into their village together. Now they could have an actual hot meal and a good night's rest in Karina's village, which of course they were all looking forward to.

Karina led Roslyn and her group to an empty house near her parent's house, telling them that the couple who used to live there had moved in with their daughter and son-in-law in a bigger house in the other village to help with their children. Karina felt it would be best used by Roslyn now.

"Where is your Clan Shrine?" Roslyn asked her as her group started to settle in for the night. They could already smell the food cooking in the house next door; they were pretty sick of eating smoked food.

"Now is as good a time as any to take you I suppose," Karina answered with a sigh. "Follow me."

So Karina led her on the trail to the mountain, the light dimming in the sky as they went. They got to the door into the mountain and the Dragon Statue finally, and Roslyn pricked her finger on a knife, letting a few drops of blood fall on the statue. The statue absorbed the blood and a moment later the door swung inwards, revealing a passage down into the ground.

"Where is the tree?" Roslyn asked Karina. "The Wolf Clan tree was on a hill."

"It is up the mountain," Karina told her. "I have never seen it personally but was always told that it was there. It's an ancient red cedar tree I believe."

"Do you want me to come with you?" Karina asked Roslyn as she went to take a step across the threshold.

"Will you wait here?" Roslyn asked her, and Karina indicated she would with a nod.

Using her crystals to light the way Roslyn made her way down into the earth. As with the Wolf Clan Shrine the tunnel came out into a large cavern with a thick braid of tree roots coming from the ceiling and going into the ground. Roslyn approached the braided roots with slight hesitation, not knowing what to expect. Again she pricked another finger and let a few drops of blood fall on the roots. The roots started to pulse and give off light that only got brighter. Roslyn shielded her eyes and backed away from the roots.

"It's her!"

"She's come."

"About time."

A Quest for Her Roots

Roslyn recognized the voices from when she was joined with Jay'Al months ago. The light was still too bright for her to look around, but then there was another voice, a female one that told the others to hush and let her talk to Roslyn. The light now dimmed and Roslyn was able to open her eyes again.

Standing--or floating?--in front of her was what Roslyn could only describe as a ghost. The woman was in her late forties, her hair tied back in two plaits. She wore clothes much like the ritual clothes that Amelia wore, their colour faded as was her red hair. Her skin looked ashen in her corporeal form. Roslyn noticed the woman's eyes, which were two different colours: one blue and the other green.

"Welcome, Roslyn daughter of Amelia," the ghost spoke to Roslyn in her mind. *"I am Samira, the First Shaman of the Dragon Clan. We have been expecting you."*

"Your eyes..."

"It is a rare genetic condition that runs in my female line," Samira's voice rang within her head and the woman smiled.

"So does that mean I am descended from you? But I am of the Wolf Clan."

"My second daughter married the shaman of the Wolf Clan," Samira told her. *"The only one who married outside of the clan. That is how you are of my blood."*

"But I have a twin sister, could you not have called her?"

The ghost shook her head and Roslyn heard in her mind, *"You are special. More powerful. We knew the day you were born that you would be the one to bring peace to these lands."*

"How? Why?"

"We saw your future. Cassidy is quite something, but you are so much more, thanks to being raised across the ocean and learning your magic differently. Yes, when you joined with Jay'Al it amplified the magic you already had and gave you a deeper connection to the magic of Jay'Al. That is why you cannot have just any ordinary familiar."

"I do not like how ominous that sounds," Roslyn said as she put her hands on her hips.

She heard Samira chuckle in her mind before she said, *"Up in the mountain you will find that which you seek. It will help you bring peace to Jay'Al. All of Jay'Al: the orcs must be incorporated with us for there to be peace."*

"Some of them have been already," Roslyn pointed out. "Most of the Dragon Clan are now part orc."

"Grau and his band need to be brought in completely. They fear you because of your power."

"You know the only way I can really do that is to defeat Grau, right? I defeat him as the head Chief and Shaman, and his band becomes mine."

Katie M. Thornton

The ghost nodded, sadness coming over her. "*If he had not tried to possess you I would say you should try another way. He also already tried to kill you. Do what you must, Roslyn. We can only push you down the path, how you land is your own choice.*"

Roslyn scoffed at the ghosts' words and shook her head. "I will think on that," she answered Samira. "Where up the mountain do I have to go?"

"*Find the tree,*" came the reply as Samira's image began to fade. "*Nearby you will find it. I know you never wanted to be a princess,*" the ghost added, "*You were born to be our Queen.*"

"I hate vague ghosts," Roslyn huffed as she turned to go back out. "Not that I have known many," she added with a laugh, shaking her head as she ascended out of the earth.

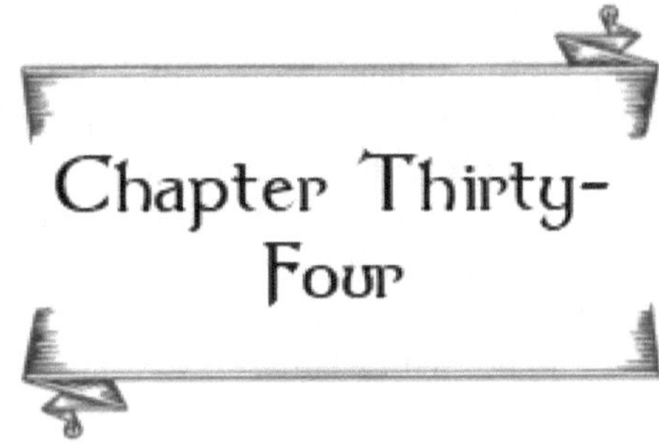

Chapter Thirty-Four

Roslyn told her companions what the ancient shaman had told her the next morning over breakfast. Karina looked troubled, for she did know what it would take to get the orcs under control. Roslyn knew that Grau was her cousin, but they were not close.

"Karina, I do not want to kill him," Roslyn told her friend. "If there was another way I would try it but honestly after he tried to get you to trick me into letting him control me I would not be able to trust him."

"I know, and I do not blame you Roz. You will do what needs to be done, and I will stand by you," Karina assured her, holding out her hand and squeezing Roslyn's shoulder.

Roslyn could feel her Honour Guard watching them closely. Over the last week they had been civil to Karina after what Roslyn said to them and she hoped that now the women would see what Roslyn saw: a trustworthy woman of equal heritage. They were both shamans, they were both of mixed blood; the only thing that made them look different was the green tinge in Karina's skin and her teeth.

One of Roslyn's Honour Guard was black skinned and from southern Ellsgrove like Oswick. Saffron was her name, and she had made a point to befriend Karina over the last week, something that made Roslyn very happy. The other women tended to stay closer to Tiffany as the oldest of the group. Sir Sullivan was there on the side listening and watching still. Roslyn had not had much time to talk to Sullivan since they left but she wanted to know what he thought of the young women who had become her Honour Guard.

The group broke up to gather their belongings. Now that Roslyn knew where they were going next they had to get the villages protected. Roslyn was sending Kai with Lou and the rest of their village to the other village on the other side of the lake. There, Kai would put a protective spell on the village once the orcs were up on the plateau. She would have sent Karina with them but Karina had always wanted to go up the mountain and see the tree.

Roslyn went to see Kai off with the villagers.

"Remember, you can draw on the strength of the villagers if they let you," Roslyn told him. "Or you can use those runes and place them around the village so you do not drain your magic too much."

"I know Roz," he told her with a half-smile. "You can count on me."

"Do you miss the south?" Roslyn asked him. "You could have gone home once we reached the Beaver Clan but instead you kept on with us."

Kai cast a shy glance at Cassidy, who was standing with Kavan and Tiffany nearby.

"OH," Roslyn said with a chuckle. "Good luck with that," she added, making him blush. "Be safe Kai."

"And you as well Roz."

Kai turned and followed Lou and the other villagers away. Cassidy joined her sister in watching the villagers leave.

"Kai will do well," Cassidy said. "He is a good shaman."

"And a good man I hope?" Roslyn asked her sister with a raised eyebrow. "You know he only continued with us because of you, right?"

Cassidy's eyes widened and she looked at the back of

Kai's head as he walked away. "No, I did not know that."

"Well now you do. Use that knowledge for good, dear sister," Roslyn told her. "I approve of him, he has been very good to us, and a good friend during the past few months."

Roslyn turned away from her sister and looked at her Honour Guard and her friends standing together waiting for her order.

"Let's head out," Roslyn said. "Karina, where is the path up the mountain?

***

Karina had been a young child when she had last played on the path of the mountain with Cerise. They had always been told not to go too far, and they were usually careful. The last time though, Karina's magic awakened. Karina always wondered if it was because of the mountain or if it was just her time, but now looking at the rough-hewn path up the side of the mountain she thought it silly that the mountain could have caused it.

She had seen Cerise off with her family earlier that morning. It was hard to come back and then see her off, but she knew that she would see her friend again once this was all over.

Two large boulders lay on either side of the path--once they had been carved into something but now they were unrecognizable as anything but rocks. Karina liked to imagine that they were made in the likeness of the first familiars, but she would never know.

A Quest for Her Roots

Mister Scruffy stalked beside her while Crick ran around the group and surveyed the area ahead. The mountain was mostly bare of snow down here, but up further there would be snow. The villagers were warned as children not to stray too far up the mountain because there were creatures up there, animals, that could hurt them. What they were none of the villagers could rightly say--it had just been passed down through the generations. Was there something up there? Hopefully they would never find out.

"This way," Karina told Roslyn, indicating the path. "It leads up into the mountain. Whether it leads straight where you need to go, I have no idea."

"Well, it is a start," Roslyn told her with a smile. "Let's get going"

***

Kavan checked his weapons, feeling a bit uneasy, but he continued walking behind Roslyn. There was something about the mountain that put him off. He was very sure that someone--or something was watching them.

"You all right?" Sir Sullivan asked; he had caught Kavan checking his weapons.

"I just don't feel right on the mountain," Kavan confessed. "I feel as if something is watching me."

Sullivan nodded and looked around them. "I feel it too," he told Kavan. "You are not being paranoid. Something is out there."

"Well just great," Kavan said under his breath. "Roz," he called out. "I think something is stalking us." Roslyn turned around and smiled ruefully at him. "I can feel it too," she told him. "There is something out there we cannot see."

"How do we fight something we cannot see?" one of the Honour Guards asked.

"You don't," Roslyn answered. "We are no threat to it, so do not act otherwise. If it attacks because it is territorial then we defend ourselves. We are merely passing through. For all we know it is just curious."

Kavan nodded and glanced around them again. He saw Crick and Mister Scruffy acting normal. Surely if there was anything out there that wanted to hurt them the familiars would be aware. He walked over to Cassidy and voiced his concerns to her.

"Crick has sensed something but it is not violent,"

Cassidy assured him. "I did not want to say anything after what Roslyn said. She is right, we are no harm to whatever is out there."

"And what if we get too close to its den?" Kavan asked her. "What if it has young ones to protect?"

"We will all keep an eye out, Kavan," Cassidy assured him. "I know that this is very different to you. Strange creatures are not your thing; but know that if Crick does not sense that whatever is out there could harm us, please believe me when I say that is true."

285

Katie M. Thornton

Kavan nodded solemnly. "I am sorry," he told her.

"I know. I am worried as well. I have never sensed this before. I know it is not evil, but it is different. Intelligent? Yes. It knows how to hide--but I still do not think it is a danger to us."

Kavan nodded again and fell back in with Sullivan. He relayed what Cassidy said to the knight.

"Then we keep going. The mages will let us know if there is trouble," Sullivan said.

***

Roslyn headed the way up the path. They had been walking for several hours when she decided that they should take a break. Her friends gathered around and they broke out some food as her Guards set up position around them. Roslyn told Sullivan to make sure that her Guards had a snack while they rested.

Above them the skies were calm, the clouds minimal in the blue sky. Roslyn appreciated the beauty of the mountain as they sat and relaxed for a time. What could be up there waiting for her? She had a vague idea. She would have to wait and see.

They rested an hour and were ready to head out again when Roslyn felt something at the edge of her magic.

"Grau is on the stair," she whispered. Karina and Cassidy heard her and they closed in on her.

"They are still three days away," Karina reminded her. "We have enough time to get up the mountain and back down before they are on the plateau."

"Let us make haste," Roslyn said, forging on.

Cassidy and Karina looked at each other with grim looks before following Roslyn up the path.

Kavan came up beside Roslyn and took her hand in his.

"What is going on?" he asked her.

"Something is stalking us, and Grau is on the stair," she told him. "We are in unknown territory here."

"The ancients wanted you here," Kavan reminded her. "Do you really think they would lay a trap for you?"

"No," Roslyn said as she shook her head. "What I sense, what Cassidy and Karina sense...it's different. Some kind of creature I cannot place. Karina has never been this far up the mountain but she told me about tales warning people off of the mountain. Someone is out there. Who they are, well, maybe we never find out. They are watching, weighing us. Should we be the ones up the mountain after centuries? We can only find out."

"How comforting," Kavan said. "I follow you wherever you go, Roz."

Roslyn took his hand and squeezed it. "I know. Thank you. Let's continue on, shall we?"

A Quest for Her Roots

Roslyn turned a corner in the path and halted as she saw up ahead a large stone arch built out of the mountain. Beyond the arch she thought she saw a large tree trunk. Her group had spread out along the path and Kavan and Sullivan had fallen behind and were walking along the edge of the path. Roslyn watched as Crick and Mister Scruffy raced ahead of them to the arch.

"Is this it?" Roslyn turned to ask Karina and stopped short as she felt the wind pick up. She looked at the clouds and discovered that they had suddenly turned black with storm rage. A bolt of lightning struck the side of the mountain nearby and the following roll of thunder was so loud that everyone had to cover their ears. When the rumble continued and only got louder instead of fading away Roslyn looked around at her companions in confusion.

Rafi's face had gone white as he remembered where he had heard the sound before but it was too late for him to warn everyone as a wall of snow came cascading down from the

cliff above them. The force of the snow barrelled into them.

Roslyn only had enough time to react to put up a small

shield around herself, Cassidy, Tiffany, Oswick, Rafi and Karina who were walking right next to her. She had to trust that Heather, the mage in her Honour Guard, would be able to do something to protect some of the others. The force of the avalanche was heavy and she had to put all of her concentration into holding the shield up.

***

Snow burst away from the ground as Roslyn used her magic to get out of the bubble she had made. Her sister and four friends climbed out after her and she was relieved to find Heather and the rest of her Honour Guard climbing out of their own air pocket nearby--all of the women were accounted for; but where were Sully and--

"Help!" She heard Sully yell from the edge of the cliff. Roslyn ran towards the edge and knelt down, leaning over to find Sully dangling from a ledge below.

"Hold on!" she yelled at him as someone produced a rope and handed it to her. She looped it around her waist and lowered the other end down to him where grabbed hold of it; together she and the others helped pull him up.

"Roz," Sully said as he breathed in and out deeply, shaking his head. "Kavan was walking behind. I don't think he made it."

He saw his words hit her like a stone and watched in equal sorrow as her face went white. She rushed over to the edge and looked down at the side of the mountain where the avalanche had chosen its path.

"Kavan!" Roslyn yelled out, hoping for some kind of answer. Cassidy was there beside her holding her as she went down on her knees, and held her still as she cried from both anguish and fury. Crick and Mister Scruffy, who had been under the arch during the avalanche, now came running back to their mistresses.

Another lightning strike nearby made them all flinch and look warily at the mountain above them, but thankfully no more snow came down. Rafi and Oswick were trying to get the Honour Guard to continue moving so as to give Roslyn a few moments to grieve.

Roslyn wiped her tears from her face and stood up, pushing her sister's hands away because she did not want the help. She was angry and she screamed her fury out into the mountainside.

"Grau will pay for this," she screamed at the storm. She turned to her sister and told her, "I know it was him who sent the storm to try to stop us, just as he did on the boat. He will pay for killing Kavan."

Another lightning bolt struck nearby and Cassidy urged Roslyn towards the arch where everyone else was waiting. Cassidy was telling her that all of the Honour Guard were there but she knew Roslyn was not listening as she ran along beside her.

Going through the arch they found a cone-like open corridor up into the top of the mountain, much like a volcano. The great red cedar tree grew up into the cone, its branches reaching up towards the sun. The trunk of the tree was the largest trunk any of them had ever seen and they all stared at it in wonder.

"Span out and look for anything," Cassidy was the one to tell their companions. Roslyn was in shock and had sat down against the trunk of the tree and was just staring out at the mountain path they had come from.

Tiffany went to sit beside Roslyn, reaching out and taking hold of her friend's hand.

"I am so sorry," Tiffany told Roslyn. "But you need to get up, Roslyn. The day is not over yet and Grau is still coming. You need to continue on."

Roslyn looked at Tiffany and saw the sadness in her friend's eyes. Kavan had been her friend as well, and she knew it took a lot for Tiffany to push Roslyn on. Roslyn nodded and Tiffany helped her up.

"We will make Grau pay," Tiffany assured her. "I swear it."

All Roslyn could do was nod as she turned to take in the tree and the surrounding area. The base of the cone was wide, widening even farther as it went up to the top of the mountain. The walls were marked with murals and runes up at least twenty feet.

"What do the runes say?" Roslyn asked Cassidy when she noticed her sister looking at a part of the wall that mostly runes.

Cassidy smiled a little to see her sister up and some-what back in action. Kavan had become her friend as well and she knew that he had cared for her sister greatly. "They are protection spells," Cassidy explained. "Others tell a story of the First Shamans and their familiars. See the murals? Each of them depicts the First Familiars."

Roslyn looked closer at the different murals and saw that she was right. What must it have been like to have a bear for a familiar?

The one in the mural looked rather small compared to the bears Roslyn knew of back home. Come to think of it, traveling through the Bear Clan territory they never did come across any bears; she remembered that bears hibernated in the winter and was glad for the distracting thoughts.

The mural of the dragon showed a great reptile looking creature with four legs and two wings coming out of its shoulders. Its eyes were mesmerizing and Roslyn found herself staring into them. Was this what waited for her up here?

"Karina, what do orcs think about dragons?" she asked her new friend who was standing next to the trunk with her hand on it.

"They revere them deeply," Karina told her without looking away from the tree. "I remember my grandfather telling me old stories passed down from his grandfather, how once the orcs had worshipped the dragons. Dragons have not been seen in a long time though."

Roslyn cast her gaze around the walls and looked up at the tree branches. Was there something up there maybe?

"I'm going to climb up and see if there is anything in the tree branches," Roslyn said, though she did not completely know how she was going to climb it when the nearest branch was at least a hundred feet away. "I would use my magic but it seems I cannot in here, for whatever reason."

"Probably the runes," Cassidy reminded her. "I cannot use my magic either." Karina echoed her words, as did Heather, confirming what they thought.

"We found nothing down here," Sullivan spoke up. "It's worth a shot. Why don't we shoot a rope up over the nearest branch and we haul you up there?"

"Do we have a rope long enough?" Roslyn asked them, only to find that all fifteen of the Honour Guard each had a length of rope in their packs.

"We should have enough if we tie them together," Deirdre said.

"I will tie them together; Heath showed me some good knots," Roslyn told them as she accepted the ropes. She got to work at tying the ropes together. When she was done she turned to the best archer she knew was in the group, Rafi. "Do you think you can do it?" she asked him.

"Yes," he told her without hesitation, and he got out his bowstring and readied his bow. He had seen the drop off the side of the path to the mountain side below: there was no way Kavan could have survived that fall even with the snow. In an instant he had vanished from their lives and Rafi felt a great sorrow over the loss of his friend. If Roslyn could carry on now, even with the pain he saw in her eyes, he could too; they all could. Once they were back at home, safe, they could grieve properly.

Roslyn handed Rafi the rope and he tied the one end to his belt and the other to an arrow before shooting the arrow up--they all watched in silence as it soared just above the lowest branch and dropped back down. Sully caught the arrow and Rafi untied the end that he had tied to his belt. Roslyn used that end to tie a harness for herself.

"Everyone is going to have to help pull me up," Roslyn said, looking at her Honour Guard. Sully nodded and took hold of the end that Rafi had untied from the arrow. Sully tied it around his waist and started to pull, and Rafi got in front and pulled more, lifting Roslyn off of the ground and making more room for the others to grab hold and pull.

Nearing the branch Roslyn reached out and grabbed hold, pulling herself up over the branch.

"All right, I am going up," she called down to them before going up to the next branch. "You can let go of the rope now."

"How will you get down?" Cassidy reminded her.

"I will throw it back to you when I come back down," she told them. Sully untied the rope and she pulled it up, looping it around her shoulder. She turned and started climbing up.

After going several branches she reached up to the next branch and felt something sharp against her hand--too late, it seemed, as she pulled her hand back and found a cut on her palm several inches long. Reaching up again, this time more careful to feel around, she got a better grip and pulled herself to look at what had cut her.

What looked like a large scale was embedded in the tree branch, as if it had fallen from higher up some time ago. She looked higher up in the branch-es and thought she saw something that looked oddly enough like a large nest. She grabbed a handkerchief out of her pocket and wrapped it around her hand to stem the bleeding before continuing on.

Reaching the bottom of the nest she looked for a way up its side. A large branch was sticking out of it so she tested it with her weight and found it sound so she used it to haul herself up over the side of the nest.

Plopping down into the nest she stopped short as she saw what lay in the nest: a large egg about four feet long and two feet wide lay in the centre of the nest. More scales littered the nest but there was nothing else there.

Roslyn looked up and saw that the opening of the mountain was not too far away, and it was definitely wide enough for a dragon to land there. Where was the mother? How long had this egg been here?

Tentatively Roslyn moved towards the egg. She reached out with her in-jured hand to touch it and could feel that it was warm. Taking her hand away she noticed she had left a bloody handprint on it; but before her eyes the blood was absorbed into the egg. Roslyn watched in fascination as the egg began to crack.

Chapter Thirty-Five

Cassidy sat down against the tree trunk to await the return of her sister, Crick climbing into her lap, Tiffany, Karina, Rafi and Oswick sitting in front of them. Sullivan and the Honour Guard took up watch along the breadth of the arch. Mister Scruffy decided to take that moment to sharpen his claws on the tree trunk, earning a scolding from Karina.

"Do you think he died quickly?" Cassidy asked Rafi, talking about Kavan. "You seem to have experience with avalanches."

Rafi shook his head and told her, "He might have been killed by the weight of the snow, or the impact against the face of the mountain. Or he would have suffocated. There was no way we could get down there to try to look for him, so he is definitely gone."

"I hope it was quick," Tiffany whispered, a tear running down her face. "He was the first man to say I was good with a sword."

"And he meant it," Rafi told her with a sad smile. "You will always remember him through your sword work."

"He could always tell Roz and I apart," Cassidy said,

"Though Roz told me the first time he saw us both sleeping that first morning he could not tell which was which. From then on though he knew the difference."

"Do we know if he left any family behind?" Rafi asked.

Tiffany shook her head and said, "No, Roslyn told me he was an orphan."

They all seemed contrite to know that he had no family back home.

"We were his family," Tiffany said. "And we will mourn him as if he was our blood brother. Just like Heath."

The others nodded in agreement.

Cassidy was about to say something when she saw something: the runes on the one wall were glowing. She pointed it out to the others and they all stood up as the glowing got brighter until it went out.

"I can feel my magic again," Cassidy said, and Karina nodded, meaning she could as well. "I wonder what made the magic stop?"

"Could Roslyn have had something to do with it?" Oswick asked, looking up at the tree. "She has been gone for a while. I wonder what she found."

"Roslyn?" Cassidy called up, using her magic to carry her voice up.

***

Roslyn stared in awe as the egg cracked more and more before her eyes. She heard a small chirp, and then another as a snout thrust its way through the shell. The dragonling pushed its head even further through the shell until it could see Roslyn sitting before it; Roslyn blinked as she noticed that the dragon had two different coloured eyes just like her: one blue and one green. It chirped again at her and started wiggling around inside its shell to try to get out more.

"Hello there little one," Roslyn greeted it as if it were a small kitten, slightly giddy and cautious. It cocked its head to the side and regarded her for another moment before its claws started tearing open the shell more.

Finally it had a big enough hole to get the rest of its body through. The immature wings growing out of its shoulders were small still and rested against its back. It was only the size of one of the hunting hounds her father had but it had more girth to it than the dogs did. At the end of its four legs were little claws that Roslyn imagined were quite sharp. The dragon's scales were a silver colour.

"Well, aren't you a pretty little thing," she said to it, and it took a step towards her. She held out her hand to it and after a moment's hesitation the dragonling came closer and rubbed its head against Roslyn's hand.

Roslyn's hand started to tingle, a sensation that spread to cover her whole body. She felt a magical connection with the dragon before her and realized that this was her familiar.

"Are you a boy or a girl?" Roslyn asked it, petting its chin as it hummed with pleasure at the attention. "I have no idea how to tell."

The dragon did not answer, but she felt something in her mind tell her that it was a girl.

"Cassidy said we could communicate psychically, so was that you telling me what you are?" Roslyn asked her. With a chirp she crawled up into her lap and snuggled up against her chest, curling her tail around Roslyn's arm.

Roslyn started crying, feeling guilty for feeling joy at finding her familiar so soon after Kavan's death. The dragon looked at her with those eyes and Roslyn could tell that she could feel her pain. The dragon began to hum again and Roslyn relaxed and let the tears flow.

"Roslyn?" she heard her sister's voice from below. Roslyn inhaled deeply as she wiped her eyes and realized that she could feel her magic again. It would be an easier descent from the tree with the use of her magic than the climb up had been.

"I am going to have to think of a name for you," Roslyn told her dragon. "Or do you already have a name?"

There was no answer so Roslyn shrugged and stood up with the dragon in her arms. She felt stronger than ever now with her connection to the dragon, and she remembered both Cassidy and Karina telling her about the innate magic of dragons. Would she be able to get Grau and the orcs to stand down and make a lasting peace now with her dragon by her side? She was unsure if she wanted Grau to live after what he had done--if he did not surrender she would have to kill him in order to take over and bring them under her rule.

As she used her magic to help herself descend from the tree, the dragon in her arms, she laughed at something: she had never wanted to be a princess, and now her ancient ancestors would make her queen here.

"Is she laughing?" she heard someone below say as she slowly floated down from the tree.

"Has she lost it?" she heard Rafi say next.

"I was laughing because I never wanted to be a princess, but the ancient shamans want me to be Queen of Jay'Al," she told them when they came into view.

Everyone stopped what they were doing and stared at her and what she was holding.

"What, you haven't seen a baby dragon before?" Roslyn teased them. The dragon was looking down at her friends with the same eyes as her, making them uneasy.

"You found your familiar!" Cassidy declared, and Crick made a few noises of welcome. Mister Scruffy was looking up at them with interest as Roslyn reached the ground.

"Have you a name for it yet?" Karina asked her.

"Her, and no," Roslyn told her as she shook her head. "I will have to think of something soon."

"Let's get back down the mountain," Sullivan suggested.

Roslyn looked out at the sky and saw that the storm Grau had conjured had dissipated.

"Yes, let's," she told them. "I want to be well rested to face Grau when he gets up to the plateau."

***

The sun was setting when they reached Karina's village; of course no one was still there for they were all in the other village across the lake. They went to the house Karina had showed them to and got the fire going.

"We need to send a message to Kai," Roslyn said, "Let him know we made it back before Grau got up here."

"I will go," Sullivan said. Roslyn nodded and watched him go.

"I think we should all get a good night's sleep,"
Roslyn said. With that her Honour Guard dispersed to their rooms and
Roslyn was left with Cassidy, Rafi, Oswick, Tiffany, Karina--and the dragon.

"Today was hard," Roslyn said, "By chance we only lost one person, and
the rest of us made it through the day."

"By the ancestors and the gods," Cassidy said, and Roslyn nodded solemnly.

"Are you all right with what our ancestors want of me?" Roslyn asked
Cassidy. "They want to make me queen of Jay'Al, but what about you?"

"To me you were dealt the wrong hand," Cassidy told her, using a phrase
that Roslyn had taught her while trying to teach her cards. "You were taken
from our mother, our people, and raised elsewhere. This is the gods' way of
making up for it."

"Thank you, sister," Roslyn said, holding tighter to her dragon that sat in
her lap.

Slowly the rest of their group dispersed, and Roslyn found herself alone
sitting in front of the fire. She felt a great loss still that Kavan was gone, just
like Heath. She had not even had a chance to choose between them, and now
fate had done that for her. Had she loved Kavan? What about Heath? Now she
would never know. She fell asleep in front of the fire that night with the dragonling in her arms.

***

Cassidy awoke her sister in the morning by gently shaking her shoulders. The
dragonling had left her arms and was curled up in front of the coals that were
still glowing in the hearth. Together they started to prepare breakfast, Tiffany
the first one awake at the smell of bacon. Sullivan and Kai had returned at
some point during the night and were the next one into the kitchens, following
the smell.

One by one the Honour Guard and the rest of Roslyn's friends came to eat
breakfast. Once they were done they got their things together and went to the
top of the stairs to wait for Grau.

Kai met them there with a few other people, including Karina's parents:
Lou and Dacey.

"This is fantastic," Lou commented when he saw the dragonling in Rosly-
n's arms. "The first dragon in generations. This is what the ancient shamans
foretold, a powerful shaman who would bring the whole continent together."

"Well," Roslyn said, "that remains to be seen really. I still have to confront
Grau and bring the rest of the orcs into our clan."

"What clan are you under now?" someone asked.

"Honestly, I cannot tell you, truly. My mother was of the Wolf Clan. One
of my ancestors revealed themselves recently: she was the one who bonded
with a dragon first, her daughter married the shaman of the Wolf Clan. If I

looked further through my lineage I am sure I would find that my great-great-grandfather was from the Bear Clan, and I had a Beaver Clan ancestor as well as a Fox and Hyena ancestor," she told them. "For some reason our ancestors chose me. Yes, at first I was against it. Back home I was suddenly made a princess, and now I am faced with this: our ancients would make me queen here. I am not comfortable with this at all. It has been cast on me, but I will not run from it anymore. This is what I was meant for, my destiny. You are my people, my family, my blood that I do actually choose. I don't know if facing Grau will come to anything but I will do it."

"Do you think the rest of the clans will fall in with us without any pressure?" Kai asked.

"The Wolf Clan and the Dragon Clan are already on her side," Cassidy said. "The Hyena Clan is as well, I presume?"

"Yes," Kai said without hesitation.

"I would say we can count on the Bear Clan, but we do not know how hard the orcs have been on them these last couple months," Cassidy said. "The Beaver Clan has a lot of different reasons for both siding with us and against us, but once they find out that your familiar is a dragon they should fall into line."

"We have been lucky," Roslyn said. "I survived the first attack by Grau, escaped even. We were even more lucky after that, surviving the whirlpools and the lizards. If I face Grau, what do you bet he will choose a battle of magic versus a battle of weapons?"

"He will underestimate you," Rafi said.

"Rafi is right," Karina added. "Grau is not used to your ways of sword skills. He will think that because you did not grow up here you cannot match him in either sword work or magic."

"You are his cousin, can you tell me anything about him?" Roslyn asked Karina.

Karina shook her head and told her, "He chose to leave the plateau before I came into my magic. He does know now that I am a shaman, though he does not know how powerful I am; nor really do I know how powerful he is."

"Well, we can assume he is as powerful as you are," Roslyn said before smirking and adding, "Though I had a teacher that told me that to assume anything would make 'an ass out of you and me.'"

Karina laughed, a full belly laugh that surprised the women of the Honour Guard.

"Good point," Karina said. "I think he does under-estimate you, so you should take that to your advantage."

"We will see," Roslyn said. "Let's go wait for Grau, shall we?"

Karina waited for everyone to leave the house before taking Roslyn aside. "What if you cannot beat him?"

Roslyn smiled and told her, "I do not expect to win. I am fighting not just for myself but for our friends and for you. I will win if the gods wish it."

"I will stand at your side," Karina assured her.

***

They set up tents around the area in front of the stairs and waited. Roslyn sat on a boulder with the dragonling curled up in her lap.

Sullivan was waiting down the stairs to keep a watch out for Grau--at this point Roslyn had disarmed the rest of the traps on the stair so Grau would get up there faster. The Honour Guard were practicing their sword skills with Karina in a nearby field. Cassidy, Oswick, and Rafi sat on the moss covered ground under a nearby tree.

The dragonling saw a leaf flying on the breeze and jumped down from Roslyn's lap to chase after it; the other familiars joined in on the chase as well, earning a laugh from the group.

"How about Leaf?" Roslyn voiced the name option to Oswick as he walked towards her.

"Sounds good to me," he told her. "She is an interesting creature, a lot like a cat but dragons are supposed to be intelligent like us right?"

"She is still young," Roslyn reminded him. "I have no idea how fast she will grow."

Sullivan came up the stairs and called out, "Grau is coming!"

Everyone gathered together and Roslyn told them to spread out in a semi-circle around the area. Roslyn gathered the dragonling up and handed her to Oswick before tightening her armour and grabbing her bladed staff. She took a few steps forward so she was in the middle of the semi-circle and would be the first one Grau would see when he came up to the top.

Grau emerged from the stair, a look of indifference on his face. His warriors fanned out behind him, mirroring Roslyn's group in a semi-circle. Grau moved forward and stopped a few feet away from Roslyn. He was wearing old armour and had a long-sword at his waist.

"I was surprised that you survived the storm I sent after you on the ocean," Grau commented. "I could feel your power still. How did you manage it?"

"I do not think you deserve an answer to that," Roslyn told him. "Not after you killed someone I deeply care about up on the mountain."

"You set traps for me on the stair," Grau reminded her. "You hinder me, I hinder you."

"Fair enough," Roslyn said with a shrug. "You did not stop us though, and I found what I was sent to look for." She indicated the dragon in Oswick's arms. Leaf was watching them intently.

Grau's face drained of all colour as he took in the young dragon. His warriors behind him began to whisper.

"You said she would destroy us all," one of his warriors said. "Her familiar is a dragon, that which we worship! Our ancestors' blood! Why are we fighting against the gods?"

"She did not have a dragon familiar when we captured her before," Grau answered. "This is new."

"Yes, our ancestors called me here to find this dragon," Roslyn spoke up, making sure all of the orcs could hear her. Some of them looked only part-orc and she wondered if they had come from the plateau as well. Would they listen to her? They were translating her words to the full orcs.

"The gods want me to bring peace to Jay'Al--not by destroying you though: I want to bring you into our Clan."

Grau scoffed saying, "Look how well that went before."

"My family live in peace here," Karina told them. "So can you all."

"We had peace," one of the orcs said, "Grau broke it to go after the princess."

"And how many of your brothers died under Grau's rule, hm?" Roslyn asked. "He has not been a very good leader, has he?"

Again the orc warriors whispered amongst themselves, moving closer to each other to talk it over.

"You need a new ruler," Roslyn said. "Grau, I challenge you for the rulership of the orcs."

"You are not even an orc!" Grau shouted at her. "What makes you think they would follow your rule?"

"I follow Roslyn," Karina said as she stepped forward, her parents joining her and echoing her words.

Roslyn smiled warmly at her friend and looked at the other orcs.

"You would be equal to us," she told them. "Protected, given land and homes, jobs. You would be able to trade anywhere, go anywhere--not just from your Winter Home to your Southern Home. Your children can go to school, learn about the world, travel the world if they wanted to! You can be so much more."

"Why would we want to be?" Grau asked her.

"Easy for you to say, Grau, you are a shaman. You are already educated. You took advantage of your brother orcs and look where it got them," Karina told him.

"How many of your band are dead because Grau broke the treaty?" Karina asked the other orcs, repeating Roslyn's earlier question.

"Too many," one of the part-orcs answered. The others grumbled agreement.

"You have a dragon as a familiar: you are favoured by the gods," another orc spoke up, talking to Roslyn. "The orcs that lived up here wanted to be close to where the dragons lived and now their descendants are part of the Clan, and are your friends. We would follow you."

Grau became angry and moved to strike the orc that had spoken. Roslyn lashed out with her magic, grabbing his arm and stopping him.

"Enough!" Roslyn said. "Either face me or face them."

Grau's answer was to turn around and lash out with magic, but it did not reach its target: the enchantments on Roslyn's armour shielded her from his magic. She smirked at him and twirled her bladed staff around her in hands as she moved forward. Grau drew his long-sword and advanced as well.

Roslyn caught his blade against her staff, using both her hands on the staff. She pushed his blade back and they circled each other. Grau growled at her and attacked, Roslyn blocking with her staff again--she was happy to see that the frishna bladed staff was holding very nicely against Grau's lesser made sword, and was not surprised at all to see a few chinks notched in Grau's blade where he had struck. She moved out of his range and kept her bladed staff at the ready.

Grau came with an overhead strike, Roslyn leaning back out of the way. She brought the blade of her staff up and positioned it so that as he moved closer with his attack the blade would stab him in his armpit. He did not see her movements at first but when he did it was too late for him to pull back. The blade of her staff entered his left armpit, cutting open his artery there; as she pulled the blade back out blood came spurting out, soaking the ground as Grau fell down. As Grau's life drained away his familiar let out a terrifying screech before it ran off.

"I admit, I am a little disappointed that it did not last longer," Roslyn said as she wiped her blade off. She took her eyes off of Grau's body and stepped away, feeling sick to her stomach.

"He was never very good with a sword," one of the orcs spoke up. "Magic was his weapon."

"Well, I guess we will never know if he could have beaten me with his magic," Roslyn said. She turned at the sound of her friends cheering and smiled at them before turning to look back at the orcs who were now on their knees, their weapons laying on the ground in front of them.

"We swear our fealty to you, Queen Roslyn," one of the part-orcs told her without looking up. "We will bring our tribe to you and we will live under your rule."

"There is no need to uproot yourselves from your homes," Roslyn told them. "Though you might find living here on the plateau will be a better idea."

"Or down in the new settlement?" Karina suggested. "We will need people down there."

Karina and her parents collected the orcs together to talk to them about where they could live while Kai used his magic to bury Grau off to the side of where they had fought. The others started to gather up their things so they could leave.

"Do you think this was the easy part?" Roslyn asked Cassidy as she joined her and their friends, taking hold of her dragon again.

"What do you mean?" Cassidy asked as she put her arm around her. "We did almost die, twice, in the last couple of months," she reminded her.

"If I am to be queen here, the next couple of months are going to be busy with bringing the Clans in and figuring out where I am going to live," Roslyn told him. "Should I live up here, on the plateau?"

"The Clans might have something to say about where you live," Cassidy told her. "We should have a capital city, and a palace for you."

"Well, not a palace," Roslyn said. "Maybe a big castle. I do not need anything so fancy as a palace."

Cassidy chuckled and looked at their friends. "Well, can we go home now?"

"Yes, I think that should definitely be our next move." Roslyn smiled as she looked down at the dragon in her arms. "Your name is Leaf," Roslyn told the dragon, and it began to hum. In her mind Roslyn knew that the dragon liked the name.

"Lead on, Queen Roslyn," Rafi joked. Their things had all been packed and they were ready to descend the stairs. Roslyn stuck her tongue out at her friend before turning and leading the way back down the stairs.

"I think we will need to figure out something else besides this giant staircase," she heard Oswick say as they went. "Maybe a lift, or a bridge?"

"What, tired of stairs already?" Roslyn half-joked. A different way up to the plateau would be welcome.

"I am sorry we could not bring Kavan back home to bury," Cassidy whispered to her as she hugged Roslyn closely.

"I don't know what to think anymore," Roslyn whispered back. "He was gone in an instant, I never got to say goodbye–to either of them. Am I cursed, Cassidy?"

"No, not cursed. I can say it will get easier, but I know it will take time," Cassidy told her as they parted. "Let us get home to New Wardgrove before we think about anything else."

Epilogue

Heath flowed through the current that took him out of the harbour of Hyena City into the ocean. He struggled with consciousness, and his magic, as he tried to bring oxygen to himself. The wound in his abdomen was bleeding, he could feel himself turn cold as he struggled. Then everything went black.

He knew nothing for a time. He had no idea how long it was when he felt hands grab him and he breathed in fresh air. His eyes opened and he blinked at the bright sunlight. It took time for his eyes to adjust but as he blinked them he saw a man kneeling beside him on a beach. After his eyes fully adjusted he saw that it was not just a man, but a merman–just below his navel his human body turned into a fish tail, green scales covering that part of his body. His human upper half was tanned looking, and the man had his dark brown hair in dreadlocks.

"Greetings, cousin," the merman said to him in the old language of the Tribes. "You are finally awake."

"Wh…where am I?" was all he could manage to say.

"The kingdom of the merfolk," came the answer. "Within the lands you know of as the whirlpools."

Heath sat up straight and looked around. They were on an island somewhere, and he could see half submerged buildings in the water around the beach he was laying on.

"You called me cousin?" Heath asked the merman next as he struggled to stand up.

"Where do you think your people got their water magic from?" the merman asked him as he slithered closer to the edge of the water. "The Tribes of the Archipelago are descended from merfolk who chose to stay human."

Heath stared at the merman in disbelief. "How long has it been since you found me?"

"Weeks," came the reply. "You were half dead, floating in the ocean when I found you."

Heath stumbled to his knees as that sank in. Roslyn probably thought he was dead. He put his head in his hands and muffled a scream.

***

Kavan hissed in pain as he came to after coming to a halt in the snow. The avalanche had barrelled him over and over down the mountainside until he had finally come to a halt; he had been knocked out at some point. The enchantments on his armour had created an air pocket around him, a good two feet in diameter. He had no idea if he was up or down so he spit, knowing that gravity would show him the way. The spit just went down his chin so he knew he was facing upwards.

He had no idea how long he had been out for. He started to dig, going upwards. It took hours, and he grew very tired. Finally he breached the surface, only because something else had been digging down.

The creature above him looked like a wolf, though it was the largest wolf he had ever seen. There was an intelligence in its eyes as it looked at him, and as he reached an arm out to pull himself out of the hole the wolf grabbed hold of his arm and started to pull him out. Kavan was thankful for the armour he wore, or else the wolf's teeth would have torn his arm apart.

"Thank you," Kavan whispered as he finally lay on top of the snow. The wolf had let go of him now and was regarding him with curiosity. The wolf snarled at him and attacked, biting his unguarded hand that he had reached out with. Kavan cried out in pain as the wolf suddenly let him go, and he saw regret in the wolf's eyes.

"Sleep," he heard a man say as he started to pass out. "I am sorry. It is my nature. You survived the avalanche, you will survive the change."

Book Two

A Weaving of the Roots

Prologue

Heath stared at the fire. Behind the pit he had dug he could see the merman resting nearby on the beach, the green scales of his tail shining in the sun. The merman's name was Nadim, and from what Heath understood they were distantly related. Heath had been dumbfounded at what Nadim had told him about the Tribes of the Archipelago, Heath's people: they were descended from merfolk who had chosen to stay human; that was how they had water magic.

Nadim and the other merfolk had the ability to change into human form when dry, and then once they were in the water again their tails returned. The ones who had chosen a full human form had lost that morphing ability completely.

On the island the merfolk partially lived on, they took turns farming both plants and animals: alpaca and sheep were the main ones, along with chickens. Some of them had mud huts built near the fields they worked, others chose to have their half-submerged houses along the bay. How they had gotten the animals onto the island was a mystery to Heath, though he imagined that maybe some
ships carrying them as cargo had probably been wrecked in the whirlpools that cut off the island from the rest of the
world, and the animals had been brought ashore by the
merfolk.

It was evening now, a few days after Nadim had found him. Heath had met Nadim's family, his wife and several children, all who chose to stay in the water unless they could not help it.

Nadim had offered to help Heath learn more about his magic, and the different things he should be able to do with it. Since the Tribes did not have any kind of Mage College, Heath only knew what had been taught to him by others of his people who also had the water magic.

"Have you thought about my offer?" Nadim asked Heath as he came closer to the fire, his dark brown dreadlocks pulled back from his face. "Once you have more understanding of your magic you will be able to return home."

Heath sighed and looked up from the fire. "Will I be able to use it to heal, like you healed me?" He put a hand to the spot on his abdomen where he had been shot, thinking of the look of shock on Kavan's face before he had fallen into the water. He should have died; he knew that everyone probably thought he was dead. He worried about Roslyn, but he hoped that she was able to carry on with her quest. What had become of his brother, Everett?

"Yes, you will," came Nadim's reply, his dark eyes serious.

"Then teach me about my magic."

***

Kavan awoke with a start, and he sat straight up on the pile of furs he had been lying on. He looked down at the hand that had been bitten, seeing that it had been wrapped with linen and was no longer bleeding. He looked around himself and discovered he was in a cave and there was another pile of furs that made up another bed a few feet away.

There was a fire pit nearby with burning coals in it. There were various jars of pickled food on shelves on the inside wall of the cave, and in the back of the cave was a female alpaca in a pen.

A shuffling sound from the mouth of the cave made him turn his head. It was daylight out, though all he could really see was blowing snow. Finally a silhouette of a man appeared in the snow coming towards the mouth of the cave. Kavan stayed still as the man approached and entered the cave.

"Good, you are awake," the man, who was wearing fur clothing with a large hood drawn over his face, said as he dropped a bag on the ground next to the fire.

Kavan turned himself slowly so his feet rested on the ground and he faced the entrance of the cave.

"Who are you?" Kavan demanded as he took stock of how his body felt.

"I am Alexander," the man answered as he came closer into the cave. "I saved your life."

"And you bit me as well," Kavan reminded him, remembering what had happened when the creature had dug him out of the snow. "Where are my friends?"

"I am sort of sorry I bit you," Alexander told him, putting down the bags he carried. "As for your friends… they grieved your loss in the snow."

"What?!" Kavan stood up, his head swimming.

"One young woman screamed after you, and had to be basically dragged away," Alexander said. "She found what she was looking for up the tree, a dragonling for her familiar."

A Weaving of the Roots

"Just who are you?" Kavan demanded.

The man threw back his hood and revealed red dreadlocks and dark skin. His eyes were both dark blue, his features striking with two tips of his teeth sticking out of his mouth like fangs, not so unlike the orcs.

"I am an ancient creature," Alexander answered. "Now you are one too."

"What does that even mean?!"

"I am a werewolf," the stranger told him. "Now, so are you. Where once there were few of us left, now there will be more, unfortunately. Something has been released, something long ago caged underground."

Kavan thought about the underground cavern that they had been in, and the connections fit.

"An earthquake hit the area just the other day," Alexander told him, seemingly reading his thoughts. "The stone that gave light to the underground cavern has been broken; it was also what was keeping the werewolves asleep."

"How do you know this?" Kavan asked, stepping back as the man came closer.

"I helped the Clans cage them there," was the answer. "And then I exiled myself up here."

"There were lizards–"

"And once that gemstone is broken the lizards will have little power over the rest of my kind," Alexander cut in. "From the looks of your weapon I know you were there; I recognize it. These weapons will be needed in the months to come. Tell me there are more above ground."

"The rest of my friends have them," Kavan told him, sinking back down to the furs that were his bed.

"That will give them a chance," Alexander commented. "Though if we want to give them more of a chance, you need to control your changing."

"How many of them are there?" Kavan wanted to know.

"More than a dozen, but if they reach the surface intact they will spread."

"What can we do?"

"I learned to control myself differently from the others," Alexander explained. "I was a mage first, a shape-shifter second. My traits pass to you now. I would not have done it if not for the others. We need to build an army of others like us."

Roslyn would not like this one bit, Kavan thought. Her people being turned into a shapeshifting wolf?

Then he had a thought–the Tribes would be a good source.

"What do you need me to do?" he asked Alexander.

"The full-moon is in a few days. It will last three days. During that time you will change, and you will feed. I will make sure everything goes well: most of the people on the plateau have gone down to the surface. There are just animals now."

"What will I change into?"

"A wolf," Alexander snarled. "One that can only be killed by the frishna metal, and if you do not die by it you will live forever."

Kavan sat back against the wall of the cave, hugging his legs. "What about Roslyn?"

"The woman who cried for you?" Alexander inquired, intrigued. Kavan nodded.

"She should forget you," was Alexander's advice.

"She will be Queen of Jay'Al," Kavan told him. "She is a powerful mage."

Alexander shrugged at his words and told him, "If you want to put her through the pain, go ahead and find her once we are done. Until you are ready for that, I sug-gest that if we are in her presence in the future you hide your face."

"I will never hide myself from Roslyn," Kavan insisted.

Alexander shrugged again, saying, "Just wait until your first change. You will see."

"How long have I been out?" Kavan thought to ask.

"A fortnight," came the unexpected answer.

Kavan closed his eyes and inhaled deeply–Roslyn would be all the way back in New Wardgrove by now.

Chapter One

Roslyn stared at the wall of the village of Bella Vale as they approached it on horseback. Sitting nestled in a ball in front of her on her saddle was Leaf, her dragonling familiar. Leaf's silver scales shone in the afternoon sun. The snow had started to melt, and the days had grown warmer by the end of their journey back to Bella Vale from the plateau. Cassidy had told her that an early spring was a good sign.

It hit Roslyn on the ride down the hill towards her mother's village: the first time she had been there both Heath and Kavan were with her. Now they were both gone. As she heaved a heavy sigh, Leaf reached out to her with both her front paw and her magic, a soothing touch that helped calm Roslyn down. She could feel the dragon's presence in her mind, and her connection to the land that had grown stronger since she had found her familiar.

Getting used to the familiar bond with the young dragon had been interesting over the last couple of weeks.

The mind of a dragon, even a young one, was very interesting, and Roslyn found that Leaf had a high intelligence and a knowledge passed down to her from her parents.

The gates to the village opened as they got closer and the Chief and his family, Roslyn's family, walked out towards them. The group looked somewhat wary at some of her companions: a few orcs from Grau's band had joined them. The rest of the orcs from Grau's band had gone to tell their Clans about what had happened and that they were going to be joining with the human Clans. Karina was also with them, but Roslyn's family had already met her. Roslyn knew it might take her family, and the rest of the Clans, time to get used to the new alliance with the orcs. At least with the part-orcs it would be a little easier.

"Roslyn!" her mother Amelia ran to her as she dismounted from her horse and took hold of Leaf.

Her mother stopped and gasped, "A dragon! A dragon is your familiar?" A huge smile broke out on her face and her mother laughed, adding, "Of course it is. Come here you, and Cassidy!" She waved Roslyn's twin sister over and the three of them hugged. Then her mother took another look at Roslyn's companions and noticed someone was missing. They had brought Kavan's horse back with them, led by Oswick on a line. Amelia looked back at Roslyn to see the sadness in her eyes.

"What happened?" Amelia whispered.

"Avalanche. He was swept down the side of the mountain," Cassidy told her after Roslyn closed her eyes and turned her head away.

Amelia reached out to squeeze her eldest daughter's hand, getting a tight squeeze back before Roslyn opened her eyes again.

"Let's get you inside and get you some hot cocoa," Amelia told them all. "I am sure you could all use a rest after your journey. You are all welcome."

Roslyn gave her mother a weak smile and let her lead her to her grandfather's house. The orcs who had accompanied them north went with Karina and Cassidy. One of Roslyn's uncles, Joss, collected the horses to take them to the stables. Roslyn's brothers closed in around them as they walked, each of them reaching out and squeezing her hands, until they were called off by their father McKenna who needed help with the wild hog he had just taken down. McKenna waved to Roslyn and she smiled back at him.

Roslyn's aunt Anna, Amelia's twin sister, was in the kitchen preparing food when they entered Chief Rotho's house. Roslyn sat down at the table and put her things down on the floor beside it. Her companions had gone to either the guest lodging or with Cassidy; only her Honour Guard went with her to the Chief's house–the Guard split up, some of them standing outside the Chief's house, whereas five went inside with Roslyn and her family.

Tiffany sat down beside Roslyn; Deirdre, Baylee and Harriet sat down by the hearth. Sir Sully chose to stand by the door. Leaf decided it was a good time to be curious, and she jumped down from Roslyn's grasp to run around the main floor of the Chief's lodging. This earned a few light chuckles from Roslyn's family as they went about serving the hot cocoa.

"Would you send a message to New Wardgrove to let them know we will be there by nightfall tomorrow?" Roslyn asked her grandfather, who nodded and went to go send a messenger.

"What is it like?" Leona, Roslyn's younger half-sister, asked her. "Having a dragon for a familiar?"

"She is far more intelligent than I thought she would be," Roslyn explained. "Dragons can pass down their knowledge to their young, so she has a lot of things in her mind that I was not expecting. For instance, she is descended from the first dragon that bonded with one of the first shamans."

"Are there more dragons around the world?" Amelia asked her.

"Yes, though they stay hidden and usually live up high mountains where they cannot be easily seen. They watch what they feed on, choosing to go after large fish in the ocean rather than the herded animals of humans," Roslyn answered as she watched Leaf approach the hearth with the hot coals in it. During their travels north Leaf had liked to sleep next to the fire. Now the young dragon curled up in a ball right in front of the hearth. Amelia's familiar, Ecko the large cat, approached the sleeping dragon cautiously before sniffing her. Ecko sneezed and then curled up beside the dragon.

"What have you been feeding her?" her grandfather Rotho was the next to inquire about the dragon.

"She will eat both raw and cooked meat. We shot down a few stags and a boar on our way north that she really enjoyed."

"Then she will enjoy the boar that McKenna brought down this morning," Amelia said with a smile. "I should go check on their progress in processing it. We will need to prepare a feast to welcome you home, and to celebrate your familiar."

***

Cassidy stood near the bonfire with Karina standing beside her. Oswick, Rafi, and Kai were standing on her other side. Cassidy had given Karina one of her deerskin outfits and had made a pair of boots for her which she now wore. The whole village was there at the celebration, and the orcs that had come with them were there as well. The four orcs, Alder, Cypress, Pine and Ash, were around the same age as Cassidy and Karina, and they got along well. The four were from the North Snow Orc Clan originally until Grau had convinced them to join with him; they had been some of the ones to immediately denounce Grau when they saw Roslyn with her familiar.

Cassidy saw a few of the young men of her own Clan watching the orcs who stood beside her. She knew her people would have a hard time accepting the orcs, so maybe she would have to remind them that it was the wish of their ancestors that the orcs be united with the Clans–it was what they had charged Roslyn with doing when she had first been connected with the lands of Jay'Al.

Amelia entered the area of the bonfire in her bright Shaman robes, bright painted lines on her face. She had in one hand a smudge bowl, the sage within burning as Amelia danced around the fire. She included the orcs in her dancing route, the smoke from the herb billowing around them. Next Amelia stopped in front of the fire and beckoned to Roslyn, who had been waiting just outside of the firelight. Standing guard around the village were Roslyn's Honour Guard, though they all knew that there was no longer any danger to Roslyn or the rest of the Clans.

Roslyn wore an elegant dress with lace around her neck, tight sleeves, and slits down the side of the skirts; she wore no leggings beneath, showing off her legs as she joined her mother in the dance around the fire. Then Anna,

Amelia's twin sister, came out with Leaf and handed her to Roslyn, who then danced around the fire again with the dragon to show her to the whole Clan. Roslyn then stopped at the four orcs, who all got down on their knees and bowed deeply to both Roslyn and Leaf.

"Today we mark the day that we bring our cousins, the orcs, into our Clan," Roslyn spoke up, using her magic to let her voice carry over the whole area. "We welcome our new brothers, Alder, Cypress, Pine, and Ash to our Clan. In the future there will be more of their people joining with ours, and they will be welcome, as our ancestors wanted."

Cassidy felt relief that she did not have to confront the young men about the subject.

"From this day forward we have an alliance with the Orc Clans that will be honoured by all of Jay'Al; if it is broken by anyone on either side they will be dealt with by the ancestors," Roslyn continued.

Amelia took her daughter's hand and addressed the village next, "In the next couple of days all of the Clan leaders will descend upon Bella Vale. A great change is coming to us."

"What is it?" someone asked.

"For the first time in our history, a Queen of Jay'Al will be crowned," Amelia answered, earning surprised murmurs from those of the clan who did not already know. "The most powerful Shaman of our time, my eldest daughter Roslyn: she will be our Queen, and we will all be One Clan."

Chapter Two

Aidan rushed towards the gates of New Wardgrove when he heard the horn call that announced Roslyn's arrival. The messenger had only told them the time of their arrival, not how many there would be or who all would be there. Aidan stood in wonder at the group, which had grown by several orcs, as they rode through the gates and into the Square.

"Aidan!" Roslyn called out a greeting to him when she spotted him. She dismounted and went to hug him. "It is good to see you."

Aidan hugged her back as he looked at the group of friends. Kai was still with them, as was Karina…

"Where is Kavan?" he found himself asking before he took in Cassidy's shake of her head.

"Kavan fell," Roslyn told him, her eyes growing a little dark as he looked at her. "We will mourn him together tomorrow night."

A chirp from within her cloak made Aidan step back, and Roslyn opened her cloak to reveal a silver dragon the size of a young hound dog.

"You did it," Aidan found himself saying in a whisper, still trying to get past the news of Kavan's death. "You found your familiar."

"And defeated Grau," Cassidy added, "and brought the orcs into our clans."

"Seems like I missed a lot by staying," Aidan muttered.

"You were safer here," Sir Sullivan told him.

"We will only be here for a few days before heading back to Bella Vale for the coronation," Cassidy informed Aidan as soldiers came forward to take the horses. "After that, we have no idea what we will be doing yet."

"The Tribes of the Archipelago need to be dealt with," Roslyn told them. "I think we should head south again to deal with Everett."

"In time," Cassidy told her, putting a hand on her shoulder. "The Chiefs will want to know where the capital will be, and where the orcs will live."

"Well we know where most of them will be living," Roslyn answered, looking at the four orcs that had come with them. "In the capital with me. Land will be given as well, for farms and such. Orcs are strong, they would make a lot of profit in wood work and stone masonry, as well as blacksmithing."

"I would like to learn to make weapons," Ash spoke up.

Roslyn grinned and nodded, liking that he was choosing the path he wanted.

"We will discuss this more later," Roslyn assured them. "Karina and Cassidy will show you to your lodgings and then bring you to supper in the Main Hall with us."

The four orcs bowed their heads to her and then followed the two young women.

Roslyn looked around at New Wardgrove and sighed deeply. It had only started to feel like home, and now she would have to make a new one, a capital. Well, she had always wanted to live further south where it was warmer. She would have to think about that. Where was there good land for growing crops? Where the orcs and the humans would have enough space to get along together for a while? She would need to ask the other Clan Chiefs about that when the time came. Gathering her bags and Leaf, she headed for the Main Hall and her rooms, looking forward to a soak in the tub and another hot meal.

***

Roslyn looked around the Dining Hall at everyone sitting there waiting. Cassidy and Karina sat on the right side of what was Roslyn's seat, with Tiffany sitting on the left side. Oswick and Rafi sat next to Tiffany, with Kai and the four orcs on Karina's other side. The four orcs had taken to wearing clothing like the Clans, provided by Roslyn's grandfather Rotho before they left earlier that day. The orcs were a bit taller and had broader chests than most Clansmen, but a few adjustments had been made to make sure the clothes fit right. They even had their dark hair pulled back and cleaned. Roslyn wondered if Karina had seen to their grooming.

"Good evening, everyone," Roslyn said as she entered the hall. Behind her came her Honour Guard who would be eating with them.

"Alder, do you know what you want to do in this new kingdom?" Roslyn asked the taller of the four orcs as she sat down in her seat.

"I want to farm," Alder told her. "We have never had the right resources to have good farms in the lands we were living in. Also, the ground was very rocky."

"Or too sandy," Cypress added.

"I want to make armor and weapons," Pine spoke up next. Roslyn looked at Pine, who was the second tallest of the group and had a more lithe frame than Alder. His orc features were strong, his tusks large. It was funny to think that he was just a little older than her.

Cypress was the shortest of the group, but he was still as barrel chested as Ash. Roslyn remembered seeing a few shorter ones like Cypress before they had split up, and even a few half-orcs who had been part of Grau's band that had gone with him from the plateau–those had remained at the outpost at the bottom of the plateau. Roslyn wondered how different the orc clans looked and if one could actually tell the difference. It was probably as simple as clothing style or jewelry that told the clans apart, much like the human Clans of Jay'Al.

Just then the cooks came in with roasted lamb and potatoes, and other roasted vegetables along with bottles of wine for the group. One of the cooks brought out a gravy boat just for Roslyn, and she chuckled when she saw the expressions on her Honour Guard's faces, along with the orcs.

"What? I like my gravy," she told them, drenching the meat and potatoes on her plate with the thick gravy. She passed the gravy boat down the table and then took a hearty bite of the steaming food. She groaned as the taste hit her palate and smiled broadly at the cooks to let them know it was delicious. Her friends laughed at her and started filling their own plates while one of the cooks came forward to pour glasses of wine for everyone.

***

Roslyn stared out at the land around New Wardgrove from the walkway along the wall as the sun rose the next morning. She pulled her cloak close around her for the mornings were still cool and she no longer wore her warmth charm. She had left Leaf in her room sleeping next to the fire.

The colours of the sunrise looked beautiful with its orange and pink shades. There was barely any snow left there, and the trees had started to show their new spring growth. Roslyn heard a wolf howl somewhere nearby and the hair on the back of her neck stood up, a shiver running down her spine.

The pitter-patter of little paws on wood made her turn to see Crick, Cassidy's pine marten familiar, coming towards her on the walkway, Cassidy not too far behind.

Roslyn's twin sister was three days younger than her, and was identical except for the eyes: their eyes, each with one blue and one green, were mirror opposites of each other. Cassidy wore a thick alpaca wool coat with the hood drawn up, along with leather boots.

"I thought I might find you here," Cassidy commented as she approached her sister. "How are you doing this morning?"

"Anxious. Sad. Nervous. Take a pick," Roslyn replied with a sigh. "I am not ready for tonight, though we have put it off long enough."

"Let his soul rest," Cassidy reminded her, putting her arm around her twin's shoulder in comfort. "You will never forget him. None of us will."

"I know…I just miss him. I miss them both."

Cassidy pulled her sister closer and let her cry into her shoulder as she rubbed her back. Finally Roslyn pulled back and wiped her face on her sleeve.

"I should go wash up before breakfast," Roslyn told her sister with a weak grin. "See you in a bit."

Chapter Three

Roslyn stared up at the full moon that lit the sky above them. She and her friends had gathered in the Square where a pile of wood awaited them. Roslyn used her magic to light it, and a few of the soldiers who had been friends with Kavan started playing music on their lutes. Each of the group had brought something that reminded them of Kavan, and they each took turns talking about him around the fire.

"The first time I met him," Roslyn started, "My father had wanted him to keep my training up. Kavan ambushed me in the halls of the palace and forced me to fight him. Of course, I kicked his butt."

The group chuckled softly before Roslyn continued. "Then we became friends…and more."

Roslyn took the wooden training sword she had in her hand and threw it in the fire. Tiffany, who stood next to her, reached out a hand to touch her friend's shoulder before looking down at the wooden training sword she too held.

"Roslyn had me come to their training sessions," Tiffany said. "He had not even balked at the prospect of training another woman–instead he saw my potential and went with it. Without him, and Roslyn, I would not be here today." Tiffany threw her item into the fire.

Rafi stepped closer to the fire, a small flask in his hand. "He became my friend even though he did not have to. I will miss drinking with you, Kavan," Rafi spoke before taking a sip from the flask and then throwing the flask into the fire.

"He became a friend, and a brother," Oswick said, holding a rolled up piece of paper in his hand. He unrolled it to show a sketch he had done of Kavan's face. He threw it into the fire.

Kai stepped forward next, a small wreath he had made in his hand. "Kavan taught me how to make something like this," Kai commented, looking down at the wreath. "This is for you, my friend."

Next each of the soldiers threw in some playing cards. The cooks brought out drinks for them as they stood and stared into the fire that took some of their pain with it.

***

Kavan gritted his teeth as the pain wracked his body. Alexander had brought him to a cave higher up the mountain that had an opening in the ceiling where the moonlight was coming through. Alexander had also brought another alpaca up the mountain, and had chained it inside the cave with him. This alpaca was a younger one with darker wool than the one in the back of the cave that they lived in.

Alexander had closed him into the cave with large boulders of ice earlier in the day. He knew that most of the people on the plateau had gone to the new settlement at the bottom, but there were some who had stayed up with the herds that could not be so easily taken down the stairs. He wanted to make sure that their existence was not found out before they were ready to reveal themselves.

Over the last couple of days Alexander had told Kavan his story. Several hundreds of years before the clans had fought supernatural beings, the very ones that Cassidy had talked about when they found the hidden cache of weapons on their way up from the underground cavern. Cassidy had thought the beings had been defeated, but Alexander told him a different ending.

The Clans had been able to keep people who had been bitten from changing by using a potion, and so the numbers dwindled until finally there were only a few dozen left. Alexander had been a shaman, but he thought it might be a good idea to infiltrate the werewolves by becoming one of them in order to finish them once and for all. The Clans had chosen mercy, however, so Alexander helped to trap the other werewolves in the very underground cavern that Kavan and his companions had found themselves in after they had survived the whirlpools. There the large crystal in the ceiling kept the werewolves asleep and provided light and warmth for the lizards that guarded them.

"Edwin was the leader of them," Alexander had told Kavan, "and he had become my friend. They wanted a piece of the land for themselves, but they were too violent about it in their nature. Once they discovered I could change and control myself better than they could they wanted me to show them; the thing was, it was my magic that had changed the shapeshifting curse."

Alexander had stood up and walked to the entrance of the cave at that point, looking out at the mountain before turning back to Kavan who was sitting by the fire.

"They had me bite someone to see if they would have the same abilities," Alexander continued, cringing as Kavan looked down at his bandaged hand. "It worked. They wanted me to be the one to bite more people, and it was then that I knew they could not be persuaded against it. I went to the Clans and told them everything, and my own Chief was able to confirm what I had done. So we came up with a plan to cage them."

Kavan thought about Alexander's story now as he was locked inside the cave, his body changing against his own will. The man had let himself be bitten only for them to try to use him as their own tool in furthering their shapeshifter population, and then he betrayed them so they would not be able to do it–but now he was willing to build his own army in order to make sure they do not take over.

Kavan had asked him, "How do I know you are telling the truth?"

Alexander had then shown him an image in the fire of a village that Kavan recognized: it was one of the Beaver Clan villages they had visited after getting out of the cave. There were large wolves, bigger ones than Kavan had ever seen, running around the village attacking the villagers. They were not killing, just biting and moving out of the way of weapons. Kavan saw them find the village shaman and bite him too before the image in the fire faded.

"This is what they will do," Alexander had told him. "This will happen tonight."

Kavan screamed as he felt bones break and be remade. He could hear the alpaca start to panic as he convulsed, and then the pain of the change became too much and he blacked out.

When Kavan came to, he was naked and covered in blood. He shivered in the cold of the cave as he struggled to sit up. His body ached, his bones…they felt like jelly. He stared at his hands that still had a slight layer of fur on them; he shook them and the fur fell off. He looked around and found the body of the alpaca that he had obviously fed on, which explained all of the blood. He saw his torn clothes strewn around the cave.

He gasped as he felt his body, felt his bones, crack back into place. Above him the sun was just starting to
shine through the hole in the ceiling of the cave. He had survived his first change. Now he had to take control of it.

Alexander wasted no time in releasing him from the cave. He had brought another pair of clothes for him to change into after using a small spell to clean the blood off of Kavan's body.

"I can use some magic still," Alexander told him. "The shapeshifting affected my use of it only a little. Best keep that between us, hm?"

Kavan followed him down to the cave they slept in, a little bewildered. Flashes came into his mind of what had happened after he blacked out, and he found himself throwing up. A cool hand rested on the back of his head and felt relief for his stomach.

"It will be difficult at first," Alexander explained. "You should be able to control yourself by the third night."

"I have to go through that two more times?!"

"Tonight you should be able to stay conscious, and tomorrow you should be able to change back before the sun rises," Alexander told him. "You have to break in order to mould yourself the right way."

***

Roslyn awoke with a start, the weight of Leaf on her chest a comfort from her dream. She had seen a wolf in her dreams, a very large wolf, but its eyes were grey and they seemed familiar somehow. She shook her head as she sat up, moving Leaf off of her chest first and onto the bed.

"Soon you will be too big to curl up on my chest," Roslyn told her familiar as she scratched the area between the dragon's ears, earning a sound that resembled a cat's purr.

She rubbed her eyes to get the sleep out of them before standing up and walking over to the window that looked out over New Wardgrove's square. She could see a little bit over the countryside as the sun rose but the trees blocked a lot of the view. Smoke billowing up from some-one's campfire somewhere in the distance caught her attention. The soldiers on duty around the outpost would most likely see the smoke and go to investigate so she need not worry about it. Thinking about what was needed for the journey south, Roslyn changed into clothes to work out in.

She was halfway around the palisade wall when Tiffany joined her. The air was cold enough that morning that they could see their breath as they jogged. Once they had finished their jog they went to their training building to do their morning exercises. There they were met silently by Rafi and Oswick, with the members of the Honour Guard joining them soon after. They had gotten into routine during the last two weeks north, and now they eased back into it that morning.

The group split up after they were done training to wash and change for breakfast. They were joined by Ash, Alder, Cypress, and Pine at the breakfast table.

Roslyn was just getting up with her dirty plates when one of her soldiers came running through the front door of the Hall.

"Princess Roslyn!" the soldier called out as he headed to the dining hall.

"What is it?" She dropped her plates and ran to the door where the soldier stopped short.

"A messenger from your mother just arrived, it is urgent," the soldier explained. He moved out of her way as she rushed out, followed by Sir Sullivan and the handful of her Honour Guard who had been at the table.

Sawyer stood by her horse at the gate, a frantic look on her face. She wore light armour and had her bright red hair pulled back in double braids, a bow hanging from her saddle and a full quiver on her back.

"Sister!" Sawyer yelled when she saw her coming.

A Weaving of the Roots

Roslyn hugged her younger half-sister before asking, "What is so urgent?"

"We got a bird from the Beaver Clan during the night," Sawyer started to explain. "There was an attack of some kind at one of the villages. Dozens of people are missing, including the shaman of the village."

Chapter Four

assidy rushed into the Meeting Room of the Hall with Karina close behind her. She saw her younger sister sitting by the hearth with a cup of hot cocoa in her hand, a blanket wrapped around her shoulders.

"I rode through the night to get here," Sawyer told her older sister when she saw her, getting up to hug her.

"The village, was it Ruby's?" Cassidy asked immediately as she pulled away from her sister's hold.

"How–how did you know?"

Cassidy looked sharply at Roslyn who was leaning against the wall next to the hearth. Roslyn's eyes widened as she realized what Cassidy was getting to.

"There is no way those lizards got up that stairway," Roslyn reasoned. "They were way too big."

"I think they were guarding something," Cassidy explained. "I asked Aunt Anna to look through our history for anything that would tell us about it, and Willow said she would do the same."

"Do you think this will delay Willow coming to the coronation?" Karina asked as Cassidy started pacing.

Sawyer sat back down in the wooden chair and sipped from her mug.

"She will have people all over it, she will not miss the events of the next couple of days." Cassidy told them.

"We should double our guards though, and inform Jackson at the Harbour that there has been trouble."

Roslyn turned to Sir Sullivan who stood in the doorway and he nodded before turning to go send a message to Jackson, who was one of Heath's Lieutenants and was in charge of the harbour they had built.

"Well, most everyone will have been warned except for Kai's uncle who is making his way up by ship, though he should be here soon anyways," Cassidy continued. "We should find out where he is planning on making landfall and send soldiers for added protection."

"Tiffany, go grab Kai for us please," Roslyn called out. Tiffany, who had been coming down the hallway towards the Meeting room, nodded and turned around, heading for the front door. It was still early so Kai would still be in his cabin; the cooks were still busy preparing breakfast and no one else had come into the Hall yet.

"There should be enough soldiers gathered at Bella Vale that we should not be worried, right?" Sawyer asked as she continued to sip from her mug.

"Us shamans will put up extra wards around the village as well," Roslyn told her. "I have a few tricks up my sleeve."

***

They rode out of New Wardgrove a few hours after Sawyer had arrived. Kai took a couple dozen soldiers with him to meet his uncle, whom he had been able to contact through magic to find out where he would be coming ashore. Luck would have it that Chief Erick had only just made landfall on the coast so Kai was going to go meet him and escort him to Bella Vale.

Roslyn watched Cassidy tell Kai to be careful before they split up, a large grin on Kai's face. Roslyn knew that Kai had only stayed with them so long because of Cassidy, but maybe now Cassidy might actually do something about it. At least one of them could find happiness in all of this.

They arrived at Bella Vale not harassed by anything, though they found that there were more lookouts and sentries along the way. It rained halfway there, but Roslyn used her magic to keep her people dry, though the mud was another problem. She remembered the last time she had rode through mud, with Kavan to the harbour, and she felt a melancholy wash over her. Leaf sensed her mood change and lifted her head to snuggle against Roslyn's chest.

Bella Vale was bustling with people: the Wolf Clan had all gathered in the village for the ceremony, and then the different Clan Chiefs with their shamans were also there. From the look of the banners displayed over the gate of the village, everyone but the Hyena Clan Chief was there.

"I wonder if Willow found anything in her records before she had to come here," Roslyn voiced her question aloud as the gates were opened to them and they rode through. "Or Aunt Anna."

"We might have that answer soon," Cassidy told her, nodding her head in the direction of both Willow and Anna who were walking towards them from the Chief's lodging. Anna wore similar shaman robes as their mother had.

"Good, you made it," Anna welcomed them, seeing Sawyer leading her horse to the stables. "We have more news than what Sawyer relayed."

"Anna and I went through our records and we found something," Willow told them.

Willow, a woman in her mid-forties, was both the Chief and Head Shaman of the Beaver Clan. She wore her bright red hair cut short to her head, and she wore light armour with a sword at her waist. Her familiar, a cardinal, sat on her shoulder.

"Hundreds of years ago there were shapeshifters: werewolves," Willow started to explain as Roslyn and her group dismounted. "They spread their ability to shapeshift through their bite, and they were trying to make more of themselves; the only thing that could kill them was the frishna metal."

"Our shamans came up with a way to stop the spread, a potion that needed to be given to the bitten before the full moon," Anna continued. "Then they found a way to capture them and keep them bound in that cave you found."

"There was an earthquake a few days ago in the very area, we assume it broke the crystal that was keeping them asleep," Willow added.

"What kind of ingredients do you need for it?" Cassidy asked her aunt. Their group dispersed, except for Roslyn's Honour Guard. Sir Sullivan went to talk to Chief Rotho about security.

"Some are rare herbs from the mountains, but we will find them and culti-vate more," Willow told them. "Unfortunately the full moon has already hap-pened, but we will be prepared for the next attack."

"Each Chief will take back with them the potion ingredients and disperse it to their people," Anna added. "We cannot allow this to spread."

"No, we cannot," Roslyn said. "We should send scouts out to see what can be found."

"We can discuss this further after the coronation," Anna said, steering her niece towards the river and the small lake that was fed from the mountains. "First we need to prepare you."

"What about the Hyena Clan?" Roslyn asked them.

"We will wait for Kai to return with his uncle to go into the Shrine," Anna assured her.

Amelia joined them on their way to the river, carrying a white robe and sticks of incense. At her feet was her rather large feline familiar Ecko, and close behind the cat was Karina's own familiar who was the same type of large breed. Karina's familiar, Mister Scruffy, had become fond of Ecko dur-ing their visits.

The river had grown from the snow melt, as had the small lake. The sham-ans had prepared an area next to the lake for the beginning of the ritual. Only the female shamans would perform it though, with Roslyn's female Honour Guard standing watch. Roslyn handed Leaf over to Tiffany who smiled at her with encouragement before stepping back with the young dragon in hand.

Roslyn shivered at the thought of the cold water; she would not be allowed to wear her warmth charm for the ritual. A large tub had been brought over to the lakeside and was being filled with hot water that was being heated over the fire next to it. Amelia helped her eldest daughter get out of the armour she had been wearing, the very set of armour they had found in the underground cave. Next Roslyn undressed, shivering as a breeze hit her bare skin.

Together Amelia and Cassidy drew runes with special white paint on Roslyn's face, stomach, and legs as they chanted. Anna walked around them with the burning incense chanting along with her sister and niece. When they were done painting runes, Amelia directed Roslyn into the water, going in with her. They went in until waist deep, Amelia's robes floating on top of the water. Amelia then helped Roslyn dip back into the water, submerging her whole body under the surface.

Her teeth chattering, Roslyn broke the surface after counting to ten, gasping from the cold. The paint had stayed on her body, the spell used making the runes look like tattoos. Her mother had explained that they were sacred runes that the first shamans had used, and it was these runes that the ancestors had told her to use.

From the freezing water to the warmer tub Roslyn went, but it was a short reprieve. Roslyn watched as the runes were absorbed into her skin. When she got out of the tub her mother helped put the white robe on her, cinching it at the waist with a white leather belt. White leather boots lined with wool went on her feet.

Walking back to the village Roslyn caught sight of Kai with his uncle. The streets of the village were lined with clans people watching solemnly as Roslyn and her group walked through the village heading for the shrine. The Chiefs all fell in with her group, as did her friends. All was silent except for the sound of their footsteps.

The hill above the shrine was covered in green moss, the willow tree above it sprouting fresh leaf buds. Roslyn approached the wolf statue and with a small blade handed to her from her aunt she pricked her finger, allowing a drop of her blood to fall on the statue. The blood was absorbed into the statue and the hidden door in the side of the cave behind the statue opened. Amelia went in first, followed by Roslyn and Cassidy, with the rest of the Chiefs coming last. Karina, who was there in place of her father, also accompanied the Chiefs down into the Shrine.

The group was silent as they descended into the earth. Finally they came to the open part of the Shrine where the roots of the willow tree above were twined together. Amelia had everyone stand in a circle around the roots and motioned for Roslyn to stand directly beside the column of roots that descended into the middle of the room. Amelia had a small wooden bowl in her hand that she passed around to all of the Chiefs, indicating to them to prick their fingers to add their blood to the bowl. Karina was the last to do so before Amelia took the bowl and poured it over the roots of the tree.

Roslyn shivered as she felt the ghostly presences of the ancestors, and she realized the others felt the same thing as the hairs on their arms stood up. She did as her mother told her now, going up to the roots. Several different types of roots were twined together, and Roslyn remembered her mother telling her how all of the shrines were connected through their roots. She thought of the cedar tree on the plateau she had found Leaf in and wondered at how those roots could reach this far north.

Using the same knife her aunt had given her she pricked a different finger, letting a few drops of blood fall onto the roots where her mother had poured out the blood from the bowl. The roots began to glow and thrum as they stood there watching. Whispers from the ancients filled the silence of the shrine as the thrumming grew louder as well. The glow of the roots intensified and Roslyn took a step back, shielding her eyes from the light. She found her mother beside her, holding her as the light finally dimmed. Amelia smiled encouragingly at her eldest daughter before turning to look at the roots.

"The ancestors have blessed Roslyn with their favour," Amelia said, her eyes wide with astonishment as she bent to pick up the device that had appeared beside the base of the entwined roots. She turned, picking bits of earth out from between parts of it. Using a spell she finished the cleaning, revealing to everyone in the room the device the ancients had given Roslyn: a diadem made of golden vines with a golden leaf from each of the Clan trees on it, with several gemstones embedded in the front.

Roslyn knelt before her mother then, head inclined down as Amelia placed the diadem on her head.

"Arise, Queen Roslyn of Jay'Al," Amelia said, and as Roslyn stood up, the Chiefs and everyone else knelt down. Amelia straightened and grabbed her eldest daughter's hand before leading her back up to the surface where everyone else was waiting.

With the diadem on her brow Roslyn stepped out from the doorway and immediately everyone who had been waiting there fell to their knees.

"Rise, my people," Roslyn shouted, excitement in her voice. "We are all now one clan, the United Clans of Jay'Al."

"Hurrah! Hurrah Queen Roslyn!" came a shout from the crowd, and as her people rose to their feet they began to cheer.

Chapter Five

Musicians played as her people danced around fires, the revelry of the day just getting started. Hunters had been bringing in boar and elk the past few days for the celebration, and Leona had made sure that her older sister knew that the biggest elk had been brought down by her. Her family sat beside her on a dais, though she wished her father could have been there.

Maeve had set sail again a few days before, with more letters from Roslyn for her father, and more trade agreements that had been signed. Kasimir had gone with her. Jay'Al and Ellsgrove were now allied completely, with King Lucius' oldest daughter on the throne of Jay'Al. She especially missed Edmond as she watched the dancers around the fires, knowing that he would have joined right in on the fun.

Thinking of missing people, she felt a melancholy wash over her as she thought of Heath and Kavan. Leaf, who was sitting curled up at her feet, reached out a paw to touch her.

"You will find love again," Roslyn heard a small voice in the back of her mind that reminded her of a thunderstorm. Roslyn looked down at Leaf to see the dragonling looking at her with her mismatched eyes that were so much like her own.

"Perhaps, but not yet," Roslyn said to her familiar before picking her up and placing her in her lap. The little dragon had grown in size again and there was barely enough room on her lap for her.

"During your journey back down south I want you to focus on healing your heart," Amelia told her.

"Yes, mother," Roslyn said quietly before Amelia reached out to squeeze her hand.

"You are strong, Roslyn. You will find that the days get easier."

"Was that how it was with father?" Roz wanted to know.

Her mother sighed and looked over at her second husband McKenna. "I knew in my heart that he thought I was dead, so he would not return. I could not go chasing after him, not with the routes closed by the Tribes and a newborn to look after. I accepted it, and I am glad I did. McKenna is a good man for me, and I have been very happy."

"I will try to use your wisdom, mother," Roz told her, glad that she had her mother now to give her such advice. Mother Elle had never lost anyone, so she was unsure what kind of advice her stepmother could have given.

"You will have your own wisdom soon enough," Amelia told her with a crooked smile, "Your Majesty."

Roslyn laughed at that and lifted up a hand to touch the diadem. "It seems so unreal," she commented, feeling the golden leaves and the gemstones with her fingers. "My father and brother would both find this really amusing, since I never wanted the crown of Ellsgrove."

"You were not born for Ellsgrove's crown," Amelia reminded her, "You were born for this one." She too touched the diadem. "I knew you would be special the moment I first held you."

Roz hugged her mother then before excusing herself to get another drink and some more dinner rolls.

Those she passed on the way to the food table tipped their heads to her or raised their cups; she had made it clear that she did not like bowing, but would accept these forms of respect from them. She smiled at them and made sure they were enjoying themselves as she filled up her tankard and grabbed more food.

Cassidy found her wandering amongst the clans people with her Honor Guard nearby as the sun was setting. She took Roz's arm in hers and led her away from the village and up a nearby hill so they could watch the sunset together.

"Well, how has your first day as Queen been?" Cassidy asked her as they took in the changing colours of the sky.

"A good beginning, I think," Roslyn told her with a smile.

***

Roslyn brushed Sage, her horse, down before they prepared to leave. Chief Erick had brought the mare north with him to reunite the two before the spring market. Roz was very happy to have the mare back, who had been a gift from Tiffany's brother; she had had to leave the mare down south when they had sailed north, which had been the right thing to do since they had ended up being pushed out to the whirlpools.

Footsteps coming up to the stable made her stop, and she looked out the narrow window to see who was out there so early. She saw Sully standing outside the stable door keeping guard.

"Is everyone getting ready, Sully?" she called out as she started to saddle Sage.

"Yes, majesty," came the reply. "We are all eager to see what full spring is like."

"It should be interesting with the dryads waking up here in the north," Roz told him.

"Dryads?"

"Tree spirits," she explained. "Like sprites or fairies."

"Truly? This land sure is magical."

"In the winter they hibernate, but they should be waking up now," she continued explaining as she led Sage out of the stable.

"Why did we not see any on our way up north?" Sully asked her as he walked beside her. "Or when we were down south?

"The way Cassidy explained it was that they like the wooded areas of the north the best though some have been known to go south. They *need* to hibernate though, and it works best to stay in the normal cycle of hibernating in winter when there is snow. Down south where there is no snow makes it difficult for them to hibernate properly."

"Were there any dryads or sprites in the trees we cut down?" Sully asked her after thinking about it for a minute.

"They hibernate in the ground," she reassured him. "They can attach to any tree they want to, so there should be no vengeful sprites or dryads after us."

"Well that is good," Sully said jokingly. "I will prepare the rest of the horses; see you at the gate in a bit."

Roslyn nodded her head and left Sully there, him going back to the stable and she to her grandfather's house to collect the rest of her things.

They were about to head to the North Snow Orc Clan before heading south, and they were going to take their time at each Clan capital. Roz was particularly looking forward to seeing the mines of the Beaver Clan.

Roz had said goodbye to New Wardgrove and the home they had built for themselves there, though she had made sure to cart along the dresser that Heath had built for her. She had wondered about making her capital the plateau, but she would need to make a few changes first.

Tensions were high amongst her people with the news of the werewolves. Amelia had left with McKenna, Cassidy, Sawyer, Kai and several of their warriors, including two of the orcs that had come with them, for the mountains to find the herbs that were needed for the potion. It felt strange to Roslyn to travel without her twin sister now, after having her company for the last several months. Hopefully once the potions were made they would rejoin the company again before long.

Roz watched as her people gathered at the gates: they were leaving a small contingent of soldiers at New Wardgrove and everyone else would be travelling with her. With the threat of the werewolves they would be traveling together with mages on high alert. Roslyn had already made several protective spells for the journey, ones she would put around the camp at night so no one goes in or out. Of course it would be slow going, though they had plenty of horses and wagons to help them along.

"There might be rain today," Roslyn mused to Sully as they rode through the gates a few hours later.

"Oh great, perfect start to our journey," Sully complained, looking up at the sky that clouded over some. "How long will it take us to get to the hills where the North Snow Clan lives?"

"We will not get to them tonight, most likely in the morning," was her reply. "I will keep you dry, sir knight," she added with a smile. She looked back at the column behind her, her Honour Guard headed by Tiffany, the soldiers on their horses and the clerks in the wagons driven by the blacksmiths. Aidan and the mason Judd were riding with the clerks, Aidan's horse on a lead behind his wagon. Karina and the two orcs Alder and Pine rode together behind the Honour Guard.

"It will be interesting, meeting with the orcs," Roslyn told Sully. "They should know I am coming by now—I will take a small group to meet with them though."

Sully nodded. "Sounds like a good plan."

"How is your sister settling in?" she asked him about Deirdre, looking back at her in the column. She remembered when he had come to her at the palace to give her his support and he told her about what had happened to his sister.

"She is doing well," he answered with a smile. "She is very stubborn, and I thought at first that she was pushing herself too hard but you have seen the results I believe."

"I have indeed," she told him. "You did a good job in teaching her."

***

Cassidy rode on the back of her white horse, the one her uncle had given her. She looked back at the group with her and smiled. Kai rode beside her, her mother and step-father on her other side, with Sawyer, Cypress and Ash behind her. The warriors were spread out ahead, behind and around them to watch out for any threats. They were coming up to the mountains now, snow still on the ground and on the peaks ahead of them.

"What are we looking for again?" she heard Cypress ask as they approached one of the trails that led into the mountains.

"Three different herbs: wolfsbane, vervain, and the plant called moonroot," Amelia explained. "Do you know what they look like?"

"Aye," Cypress answered. "Moonroot grows best in the gullies of the mountain."

Amelia cast an appreciative eye on the young orc. "That will be your task, if you know where to find them."

"My mother is the Clan healer," Cypress told her.

"I learned much from her. You may find that you have a lot in common when it comes to herbs, though she does not possess the magic you do."

"I look forward to meeting her someday," Amelia said to him, and Cassidy knew that she meant it. The future was looking very different for her people since her sister had returned, and Cassidy was enjoying the change.

Karina had become a good friend in the past couple of months, and she enjoyed the company of the orcs whom she travelled with. She probably would have never met Kai if it was not for her sister.

Cassidy thought about the kiss she had shared with Kai the night after the coronation and she felt her cheeks grow warm. She had not had time to tell Roslyn about it, or her other sisters, but she thought her mother might have some suspicions.

"Let us spread out," Cassidy told the group as she dismounted in a clearing. Ahead were gullies and trails up to caves in the mountains. Some of the deciduous trees were developing their spring buds, and as the day had warmed up there was a bit of fog hovering over the ground. She actually was not far from the place where she had been forced to kill an orc in self-defence years ago, which made her a little wary of being there. What if she came across the body? What if he was related to one of the orcs in the group? The only person she had told about it was Roslyn, and she was nowhere near to give her courage to keep going.

"Everything OK?" Kai asked her as they dismounted, tying their horses reins to low hanging tree branches.

"Yes, I just have never liked the mountains," she told him. "Let's get looking for those herbs, shall we?"

Cypress joined their group, making them four with Sawyer. Amelia was with McKenna and Ash, and the warriors spanned out to take watch while everyone else looked for the herbs.

"There is a gully over here that might have some good moonroot," Cypress told them as he indicated what direction they should go with a nod of his head.

Cassidy followed the orc, a little apprehensive but ready to gather the herbs. Crick bounded up a nearby tree to converse with another pine marten about the area while they searched. Ecko stayed close to Amelia, and Tej was playing around in the snow.

A low whistle split the air, and Cassidy halted in her tracks. Cypress was standing at attention, his mouth contorted in a half-snarl until he relaxed it a moment later when they heard another different whistle.

"What is it?" Cassidy asked him, moving towards him. The warriors had begun to move closer to her to protect her if there was something out there.

"Some of my people," Cypress told her with a half-smile. "They want to know what we are doing here."

"Would you go talk to them? And maybe introduce us?" Cassidy asked him as he nodded and headed in the direction of where the signal had come from. He came back moments later with two other orcs dressed in furs and carrying axes.

"This is Cassidy, the sister of Roslyn," Cypress introduced the two new orcs to her. "And this is Sawyer, Roslyn's sister. This is Terren and Louran, hunters from the North Snow clan."

"Well met," Cassidy greeted them with a smile. "My sister will be heading to meet with your people soon."

"So we have heard," came the gruff response from Louran in the language of Jay'Al. "Is it true she has a dragon with her?"

"Yes," Cypress responded before Cassidy could. "Leaf is a silver dragon, and she is Roslyn's familiar."

"So Roslyn is a shaman?" Terren asked. Cypress nodded. "How powerful is she?"

"What does her power have to do with anything?" Cassidy interjected, folding her arms over her chest.

"Weak shamans are useless to us," Terren explained. "I am sure she will be able to show you her strength when she meets your people, though I would think that the fact a dragon chose to be her familiar might say something about how powerful she is," Cassidy told him.

"That is true," Cypress commented.

"What are you doing in the mountains?" Louran asked them, eyeing the warriors that were watching them from a distance.

"Do you remember the old stories about shape-shifters? The wolves?" Cypress asked the two orcs who nodded. "They were not stories, and it seems they have returned. We are trying to gather herbs for a potion that will cure the bite."

"Truly?" Terren inquired with a raised eyebrow, a look of disbelief in his eyes as he looked at Louran who shrugged.

"There have been attacks, large wolf prints left behind and missing villagers," Cassidy told them. "We believe the earthquakes released the ones that were locked up by the Clans."

"Why were they not just killed outright instead of imprisoned? That seems like a dumb thing to do if there was any chance of them getting out," Louran commented, shaking his head with disdain.

"Pity, I assume, though really how could they have known there would be such earthquakes that would release them? At any rate, that is why we are here," Cypress told them. "Will you help us gather the herbs?"

Louran made a huffing noise but it was Terren who answered, "We can spare a little bit of time to help but then we have to check our traps and get back home."

"We appreciate the help," Cypress told him, adding, "We are looking for moonroot, vervain, and wolfsbane."

"We passed some moonroot and vervain on our way here, come let us show you," Terren told them, turning to head back the way he and Louran had come.

"I will go with them," Cypress said to Cassidy as he started to follow. "You stay here and look."

Cassidy nodded and looked at Kai, who was watching the orcs as they walked away.

"What is it?" she asked him.

"They had their own stories about the shapeshifters," Kai commented, "I wonder what an orc werewolf would look like."

"Do you think their shapeshifting appearance would differ from human to orc?" Cassidy asked him, intrigued at the idea.

Kai shrugged, saying, "It was just a thought."

Cassidy chuckled and moved ahead to search for the herbs, Kai and Sawyer following along behind. Sawyer had her woven basket in hand as she went around collecting sprigs of the vervain while Cassidy used a small trowel to dig up the moonroot. The ground was still slightly frozen so she had to use a bit of her magic to warm the ground enough to dig it.

They were catching up with Amelia and McKenna when Cassidy sensed something at the edge of her magic, something she had sensed before but she could not remember where. Then there came the howling.

"That sounded way too close for comfort," Amelia whispered as the warriors closed in around them.

"Has Cypress come back yet?" Cassidy asked her mother.

"Not that I have seen," was the answer.

They could hear barking now, coming closer from a trail in the opposite direction of where Cypress had gone. The group closed in together, weapons at the ready. A large wolf, bigger than any wolf any of them had ever seen before, bounded down the trail towards them, its mouth twisted in a snarl. Its fur was black with touches of gray in the mane, and its eyes were silver. Behind it came three more wolves the same size, two of them white with black paws and the third brown with the tip of its tail white. Each of them started growling at the group.

"It's not even a full moon," Amelia said as she reached out with her magic and called out a warning to Ecko who had gone up a tree with Crick and Tej.

"We do not want to fight you," Cassidy told the wolves. "Just leave us alone."

The black one snapped its jaws and growled at her before it leaped at them. Something large barrelled into the wolf before it could reach them, and it took Cassidy a moment to realize that it was Cypress. Louran and Terren were not far behind him; they threw their axes at the other wolves, killing one and maiming another. The third one advanced on the two orcs while Cypress wrestled with the black one.

Cassidy and Amelia looked at each other and joined hands, combining their magic to grab hold of the wolf that Cypress was wrestling with. Cypress looked up at them in surprise as the wolf was held down against the ground by invisible hands but he nodded his thanks and got up, backing away.

Louran had pulled a large dagger as the brown wolf advanced on them. As the wolf sprang at them he threw the dagger, hitting the wolf in the throat. It went down with a whine and a whimper, Terren going to it and using his own dagger to finish it off.

"You think these are those shapeshifters?" Cypress asked Cassidy as he eyed the black wolf that was snarling at them, fighting against the invisible bonds.

Cassidy looked at where the other wolves had fallen and gasped in shock, making everyone else look. Where the first two wolves had died were human bodies, two men.

The group turned to look at the brown wolf, where Louran was retrieving his knife, in time to see the wolf transform back into a human female.

"What are your blades made out of?" Cassidy asked the orcs.

"The frishna metal; we have a small mine near our village," Terren told her.

"Well I guess that settles it," Cypress commented, clutching his left arm. Blood ran down his arm and dropped into the snow. "The werewolves can only be killed by the frishna metal apparently."

"Show me the wound," Cassidy said to him as she stepped towards him. After a moment's hesitation he uncovered it, revealing that he had been bitten by the werewolf.

"How far is your village?" Cassidy turned to Terren and Louran.

"About an hour by foot, half that by horse," Terren responded.

Cassidy turned to her mother, "Mother, you and Cypress go with them and let them use my horse. You can make the potion with what we gathered today right?"

Amelia nodded. "What about this one?" She inclined her head at the wolf that they had captured as she bound Cypress's wound with cloth. The wolf strained against the magic that held it in place.

"Kai and I will find a way to bind him and bring him along," Cassidy told her. "You take half the warriors with you."

"What if there are more out there?" McKenna asked as the warriors went to gather the horses. Ecko, Crick and Tej joined them again.

A Weaving of the Roots

"The warriors that stay with us will look out, but I don't sense any more in the area," Cassidy assured them; it was then that she remembered where she had sensed a werewolf before; up in the mountain of the plateau, though the one up there had not been malevolent like the ones before her. "Cypress is the priority here."

Cypress smiled at her then as the other two orcs took in her words. "Thank you," he told Cassidy.

"I will stay with Cassidy," Terren said, "As more protection."

Cypress nodded his thanks to his fellow orc as three of the warriors came towards them with the horses that they had picketed nearby. Louran mounted the one whose reins McKenna handed him, and Cypress mounted his. Cassidy watched as they rode off at a fast gallop.

Terren retrieved his axe from the dead body and started cleaning it, watching as Cassidy and Kai talked about what to do with the remaining one.

"Well, we could try to get it to change back into its human form?" Kai commented, but as the last words came from his mouth the ground beneath them began to shake and Cassidy lost both her balance and her concentration. The werewolf, now released from its magic bonds, bounded away down the trail it had come from, Terren's thrown axe just missing it.

Kai helped Cassidy to her feet, shaking his head. "I guess we will have to keep a watch out for that one again," he told her. "Come on, let's catch up with the others."

"Have there been earthquakes like that around here before?" Cassidy asked Terren.

"We have had a few in the last couple of weeks," Terren told her, "Though I wonder at the timing of that one."

"I do as well," she agreed with him. "Very strange indeed." She turned to Kai, "Do you remember sensing a werewolf before?"

"It felt like whatever we sensed up the mountain on the plateau," Kai agreed with her. "But these were slightly different, these wanted to hurt us. The one up there was just watching."

"So what was a werewolf doing up on the plateau, and how long had it been there?" Cassidy said her question aloud, not expecting an answer. "Let's get going, we need to catch up with the others."

***

Roslyn looked around the camp that they had set up and then turned to look at the mountains. She knew Cassidy, Sawyer and their mother were there, but she was heading beyond there to where the North Snow Orc Clan lived. In the morning she and a small group would head to the main village to meet with them. One of the orcs who had been part of Grau's group, Ose, had met them as they were setting up camp.

"You will meet with our elders tomorrow," he had told her. "There are five of them, Avis, Malen, Bhag, Delon, and Leib. They will meet you at the edge of the village and then take you to our Sacred Grounds."

"What do I need to know about your rituals?" she had asked him.

"Drink the liquid offered to you or it will be a slight; answer honestly so they know you are true, and do not hold back with your magic when needed."

"My magic? Will they test me?"

"A weak shaman is useless," he had informed her. "They need to know you can protect them if it comes to it."

"I see. Well, I hope I do not disappoint."

Ose had smiled widely at her and looked at Leaf who was sitting at her feet; she had grown at least a foot again and was getting wider around the belly. "I do not think you could disappoint the elders," he had told her. "Your familiar is a god to us; you are special."

"Thank you, Ose," she had told him. "How is your family?"

"They were glad to see me home in one piece, thanks to you," he had replied.

Now Roslyn was anxious about the meeting, even after what Ose had told her. He had returned to his village after that, leaving them to finish setting up camp for the night.

"May I join you as you set up the wards around the camp?" Sully asked her as he walked up to her. Leaf was curled up at her feet, and she let out a chirp as Sully approached.

"Yes, you can," she answered. "I worry about my sisters and mother," she added.

"They will be safe," Sully assured her. "Kai is with them, and Cypress. You have nothing to worry about."

She sighed and looked at him, taking in his curly blonde hair that had been his main attraction for her when they had first met; he had been a handsome knight, a stranger, that first night they had met in Wardgrove. "Thank you, Sully."

"My pleasure"

Together they walked around the camp, Roslyn leaving small crystals at intervals around the camp. She had made sure that the latrine was dug in a secure spot within the camp, and that everyone knew the boundaries of the camp for the night. The spell to conceal and protect them started two feet away from the crystals and would last until she broke it herself, so no one would be able to leave the camp at all once she had it set up. Each crystal had runes etched in them, and once they were set down they started to glow slightly. As they got to the end of the circle around the camp the crystals flared with light and then dimmed again, signalling that the spell was in place.

"Now it is time to get some rest," Roslyn commented as she looked around the campsite that was settling down for the night. They were on a mission, and they knew there were threats out there so there was not much min-gling amongst the soldiers. There were a few lookouts stationed in certain areas to watch for the night–though Roslyn had said they would not be need-ed–it put the soldiers more at ease to have lookouts.

"Goodnight Roz," Sully said to her as he left her at her tent at the center of the camp. Tiffany's tent was right beside hers, with the rest of her Honour Guard two to a tent in a circle around Roslyn's tent, with Sully's tent all the way on the other side of that circle. Aidan had chosen to sleep in the same area as the clerks, and Karina was with the orcs nearby. Oswick and Rafi had their tents just on the other side of the Honour Guards' tents.

"There you are," Roslyn heard Tiffany say as her friend entered her large tent from the connected covered path between their tents. The female knight carried with her a tray of biscuits and a bottle of wine. "I brought us a snack."

"Ooooh biscuits. Thank you!" Roslyn smiled at her as she sat down at the small table to the side of her tent. Behind them was the dividing curtain that led to where her bed and changing area was. To the right of her table was what Sully called the War Table that had a rough drawn map of Jay'Al rolled out on it, held down by rocks and crystals. An armour rack stood next to the War Table with Roslyn's armour hanging on it, her sword and the staff she had found in the underground cavern hanging on a weapons rack next to the armour.

"Shall we invite the girls to join us?" Roslyn asked Tiffany as she pulled up a chair to sit with Roslyn, placing the platter of biscuits on the table.

"That sounds like an idea," Tiffany responded with a smile. "I shall go gather them."

"I'll grab more wine and cookies," Roslyn told her, getting up and going to the large chest in her room that she called her personal larder: it was spelled to keep food fresh and cool, like the food barrels on their journey had been. Inside she had several snacks and food items, including deliciously soft sugar cookies and several bottles of wine.

A few moments later the young women who made up her Honour Guard came into Roslyn's tent with Tiffany, each with a wooden cup and a chair. Sully's sister Deirdre, with her curly blonde hair, chose to sit next to Roslyn. They formed a circle of sorts around the table as well as they could with the seventeen of them. Cups were filled with wine, and food was passed around.

"Thank you for inviting us," Deirdre said to Roslyn. "We have not had much time to spend with you outside of training. Some of us have been want-ing to ask you some things."

"We will hopefully have more time on our journey south," Roslyn assured her. "Ask away though."

"Is it true you are not a virgin?" Teddy asked her first. Roslyn raised an eyebrow at her and then smiled broadly.

"That is true," she told her, and she noticed a few shocked expressions around the circle. "And if you want to have a physical relationship with any-one, you can. You are knights, and yes you are women, but your body is your own and no one can tell you any different here in Jay'Al. Just make sure you take precautions before you do."

"What precautions do you take?" Saffron asked her. Roslyn stood and lift-ed up her tunic to show them her tattoo.

"This protects me from getting pregnant," she explained to them. "If any of you want one I will happily give you one."

"Your father knew?" Heather spoke up now, a slight hint of incredulity in her voice.

"Of course he knew, he talked to me about protection when I got my first bleeding, and about everything else. He was proud that I made the decision to get this tattoo, and he knew I was being safe with my part-ners," she told them as she sipped her wine.

Some of the girls looked at each other; a few were smiling, a few looked confused.

"And you never had an arranged marriage set up for you, since you were close to the throne before the sickness?" Isobel asked her as she bit into a cookie.

"My father would have none of that for us," Roslyn explained, "We were all to find our own love our own way. Edmond has the choice to court whom-ever he wants to, though I know some nobles will not be happy with the range he will be allowed."

"When we joined your Honour Guard your father told us that the arranged marriages our fathers had planned for us were now void, and that we would have our own lands when we returned to Ellsgrove. A lot of us were joyous at the prospect," Deirdre told Roslyn. "Sully thankfully had not planned an ar-ranged marriage for me either."

"Is that why the brothels took your side?" Harriet asked Roslyn, "because you provided them with the tattoos to make sure none of them got pregnant?"

"I can assume so, though I also helped with other things. On our journey south to the capitol after my father was crowned I went to a lot of brothels to offer my assistance in that way free of charge. I even sent some mages I know to other brothels I could not get to yet, and they knew they were sent by me."

"And those women you were training in the capitol? Some of them be-came our instructors," Teddy told her.

Roslyn smiled and refilled her cup. "Mel and the girls were great," she said. "I am glad they were able to teach you."

"They were training other girls when we left," Deirdre informed her. "There were more girls, noble and civilians, who came out."

"That makes my heart happy," Roslyn told them.

A Weaving of the Roots

She popped another cookie into her mouth and closed her eyes for a moment. "So much has changed in the last year," she spoke after a moment. When she opened her eyes again she saw Tiffany refilling Teddy's cup and offering more wine to the others.

"Thank you, Roslyn," Teddy told her, "For the changes you made that allowed us to be who we are."

Roslyn blushed and waved a hand at her. "Nonsense, you ladies are strong willed, I have no doubt you would have made changes for yourself. Now, does anyone else have more questions?"

Chapter Six

Heath stared out over the ocean, anticipation making him shift from foot to foot as he waited. Nadim was testing his abilities today, and he was waiting for the signal. Nadim had been impressed with how quickly Heath learned things, and Heath himself had been very surprised at all he was even capable of doing. He had had no idea that the water magic his people had could do so much, and he could not wait to show Roslyn what he could do.

Thinking of Roslyn made him still for a moment. He wanted to get back to Jay'Al to help her with her quest; where was she at that moment? Was she with Kavan, in his arms? Had she found her familiar? What happened with the orcs? Where was Everett?

Nadim's tail broke the surface of the water, which was the signal. Heath ran towards the water, diving into the ocean. He used his magic to propel him through the water, and to bring himself oxygen. Nadim swam beside him, using his tail to keep up with him. Nadim led him out to the first whirlpool and then back, where they found a pod of dolphins. Heath found that he could understand what the dolphins were saying, and marvelled at their talk about which fish tasted the best to them.

Nadim led Heath back to land where he had set up targets on the shoreline. Treading the water Heath used his magic to hurl water in the shape of balls at the targets, hitting each one. Then he turned the balls into daggers of ice, striking the targets again with deadly accuracy, the daggers of ice puncturing the targets.

"Very good," Nadim voiced his approval. "Now comes the hardest one: I will teach you how to use astral projection with your magic."

"That is something I can do without a potion?" Heath asked Nadim, remembering that Roslyn was only able to astral project herself using the potion her mother had given her.

"We use the water, we have no need for a potion," Nadim informed him.

A Weaving of the Roots

"Come, let's go to land and I will instruct you."

Heath followed the merman to the beach where he watched him transform into his fully human form; Heath had a pair of leggings made from alpaca wool ready for his friend to put on. Nadim then led him up the small mountain on the island. There were alpaca's grazing on the path up, and a few merpeople in their human forms tending to them.

They reached a small cave which Nadim led him into. There were stools set in a circle around a small pool of water. Water dripped into the pool from above.

Nadim sat down on a stool and indicated for Heath to do so as well. Once Heath had sat down Nadim directed his attention to the pool between them.

"Using the water here, you can project yourself to another water source nearby. Your range will vary as your magical strength increases. Close your eyes."

Heath closed his eyes.

"In your mind, focus on the water. Let yourself flow into it," Nadim instructed him. "Then let it take you to a water source nearby."

It was a lot like other exercises Nadim had shown him at the beginning, and he eased his mind into the pool.

He could feel Nadim's presence nearby as he reached out with his mind to another water source: this was a cooking pot down at the village where one of the merpeople was cooking. He looked up through the pot at the person and watched them stir the pot.

"Good," he heard Nadim's voice in the back of his head. "Now try forming yourself with water droplets so you can stand beside the pot."

After a moment's concentration Heath found himself in a watery form standing next to the cooking pot. The merman who was cooking did not look in the least surprised to see him standing there in that form.

"You have come a long way," the merman told him. "We know you are eager to get home."

"Not that my time with you folk has not been interesting," Heath spoke, his words coming out a little louder than a whisper.

"Very good," he heard Nadim's voice again. "How far do you think you can go?"

Heath concentrated and sent his watery form out over the water, gliding with the wind towards the whirlpool he had swam to earlier that day. He was almost free of the whirlpools when his form began to slip apart. He let it, bringing his mind back into his body.

"Continue practicing and you will be able to go further," Nadim told him as he opened his eyes again. "That was very good for your first time."

"Will you take me back to Jay'Al soon?" Heath asked Nadim as they made their way back down the mountain.

"Our King would like to meet with you before you leave," Nadim told Heath. Heath stopped in his tracks.

"You have a King?" This was the first he had heard about it.

"There is a whole kingdom beneath the island," Nadim informed him. "You have only seen what we wanted you to see."

Heath continued walking beside him, saying, "Well okay then, when should I meet him?"

"Soon," was the reply he got. Shaking his head, Heath split off from walking with Nadim to go back to the hut that he had called home the last several weeks.

***

Kavan stood on the path that led down the mountain and towards Karina's village. He could hear the rabbits running around in the forest below, and hear the birds as if they were flying above him. Ever since his transformation he found that all of his senses had been heightened immensely. From their cave in the mountain he had heard the two villages on the plateau prepare to leave their homes; the people had even taken great pains to take all of the animals down the stairs to the village that had been built at the bottom of the plateau. Alexander had gone out to scout and scrounge up anything he could find that had been left behind.

Kavan wore alpaca wool leggings and a tunic, his frishna sword at his waist. He had leather gloves on his hands for he found that the metal burned his skin. He would not be able to wear his full armour again in case it touched his skin. For now the armour was in a bag that he carried over his shoulder.

Alexander appeared on the trail ahead of him, a couple of bags slung over his shoulder.

"Where are we heading to?" Kavan asked him when he got closer.

"We need to grow our ranks," Alexander told him.

"I think we should go to Roslyn and explain everything: we could get volunteers," Kavan told him. "It would be easier that way."

"Do you actually think so?" Alexander looked him in the eyes. "Do you think she would allow her people to be turned into what we are?"

"We can control it," Kavan reminded him. "I think that makes a difference. They will probably know about the werewolves by now too."

Alexander sighed. "I suppose it would be worth a try," he told Kavan. "Where should we go?"

"We head to New Wardgrove," Kavan suggested.

"Fine, let's head to New Wardgrove."

It took them only half a day to run down the stairs with their supernatural strength, something that Kavan marvelled at still after Alexander showed him; and they were out the gate of the new town at the base of the stairs before anyone even knew they were there. They headed north, only stopping to eat and sleep a handful of times, taking turns watching over each other as the other slept. Together they brought down deer to eat, and were able to reach New Wardgrove in a matter of days.

Kavan looked at the walls of New Wardgrove from a spot behind some bushes with both eagerness and trepidation. Roslyn most likely thought he was dead, so what would this reunion be like? He remembered the time he had brought out a cup of hot cocoa to share with her on the palisade; how her eyes had shone in the torchlight as she teased him. He was having trouble remembering the feel of her against him, and that just made him want to hold her again all the more.

"Well, are you going to approach the gate?" Alexander asked him.

"I just need a moment," he responded, feeling his heart quicken at the thought of holding Roslyn again. He could feel his body start to change and he had to focus to reel it back in.

"See, that is why it is dangerous for you to be around her quite yet, sometimes the emotions can turn you against your will," Alexander pointed out to him.

"I see what you mean, but I *can* control it."

"For both of your sakes I hope so," Alexander commented as Kavan left the bushes to approach the gates of New Wardgrove.

"Halt!" one of the guards shouted out to Kavan. "State your business!"

"It's me, Kavan," he shouted to the guard.

Silence. Then the small door of the gate opened and one of the soldiers walked out; it was Gideon, one of the soldiers Kavan played cards with.

"I thought you were dead," Gideon told him, "Roslyn thought you died in that avalanche."

"I almost did. By the time I managed to dig myself out she was long gone. I was wounded and needed time to heal as well." It was not exactly a lie.

"Welcome back then, my friend," Gideon said, extending his hand out to him; the two clasped each other's wrists in a soldier's greeting. "I know our Queen will be happy to see you alive again."

"The coronation has already happened?" Kavan asked as Gideon led him through the door of the gate and into New Wardgrove.

"A couple weeks after she returned with her familiar," came the reply.

"What is her familiar?"

"A silver dragon, she found the egg up the mountain and it hatched for her. It is quite the beautiful creature, and it is growing fast."

A *dragon*; now that was something. Alexander *had* told the truth.

"Tell me, what happened with Grau?"

"She killed him, and the orcs joined with her," Gideon told him; wait was that true? The orcs who had been hunting Roslyn now had joined with her?

"What? Why?"

"Something about Roslyn's ancestors wanting her to unite everyone on the continent, and the dragon being some sort of god to the orcs or something," came the uncertain reply. "That is where Roslyn is headed right now, to convene with the orcs."

Kavan stopped in his tracks; they had been heading towards the Hall. "She is not here?"

Gideon shook his head and told him, "They left several days ago. A small amount of us remained here to look after the place until she calls for us. Once they were done meeting with the orcs they were going to head south again. She needs to choose a place for her capital, and she wanted to deal with the Tribes of the Archipelago as well."

Kavan thought that quite a list of things to do.

"Do you know where Cassidy is then? Is she in Bella Vale?"

"Cassidy and a small group of her people went into the mountains to search for the herbs that will be a cure for the werewolves," Gideon told him. "You probably do not know about that at all, now that I think of it."

Kavan feigned surprise at the news. "No, I do not. Tell me what has happened?"

As Gideon explained about Sawyer bringing the message about a village being attacked Kavan remembered the vision that Alexander had shown him. They were already spreading. At least Roslyn knew of a cure.

"Something wrong?" Gideon asked him after he had been silent for too long. Kavan's expression had turned from determination to uneasiness.

"Any sightings around here yet?" Kavan asked him.

"None so far."

"I assume Jackson and Maeve are at the harbour?"

"Maeve left to go back to Ellsgrove," Gideon informed him. "That merchant Kasimir went with them."

"Do you think I can catch up to Roslyn up north?" Kavan asked Gideon after a moment.

"I do not know, depends how long she stays with the orcs."

Kavan thought for a moment. "Do you know where my things are?"

"Roslyn left your room exactly as you left it," Gideon responded. "Go ahead and take whatever you need. Will you need rations and a horse?"

"Rations, yes; horse, no. I have a travelling companion back at our camp with our wagon," he lied. "One of the Dragon Clan people came with me."

"I will inform the cooks and they will have things ready for you at the gate then," Gideon told him.

"Thank you."

Kavan headed to the Hall, finding it eerily empty. Aidan and the clerks were not in their office, the cooks were gone as well. Kavan headed to his room and quickly gathered his clothing up in a bag. He stopped at Roslyn's room, finding it empty. On the way back down he also stopped at Heath's room, it was left completely untouched as well. Heath's top hat was sitting at the end of the bed. In his mind he could see Heath being shot again and falling into the water, Kavan helpless to stop it. He closed his eyes and willed his heart to slow down before turning and walking down the stairs.

A bag of rations was left at the gate for him which he grabbed before saying farewell to Gideon again.

"Travel safely," Gideon told him. "Watch out for wolves."

Kavan nodded to him and walked through the gate.

Chapter Seven

Roslyn and Sully walked together with Ose towards the Orc village, Karina, Tiffany, Teddy and Harriet walking behind them with a horse and cart, the cart covered with burlap. The gates were being opened for them to enter, and there were orcs watching from the palisade that encircled the village. Roslyn wore no armour, just the deerskin clothing her sister had given her, though she did wear her diadem on her head. She had braided her hair in two fishtail braids that morning.

As the gate finished opening Roslyn was surprised to find Cassidy and her mother standing there waiting for them.

"What are you doing here?" Roslyn asked them as they walked towards each other.

"We were attacked by werewolves in the mountains," Cassidy explained. "Cypress was bitten, so we came here to get the potion made for him."

"Tell me what happened."

As Cassidy and Amelia explained about the attack, Kai, McKenna and Sawyer joined them. After Cassidy explained that she had sensed a werewolf before and where, Roslyn started to wonder about it.

"What was a werewolf doing up on the plateau?"

Roslyn asked the same question Cassidy had asked before.

"I guess we might find out if we go back up there. That is something for another time though; how is Cypress?"

"He is well, just resting with his family." Cassidy assured her. "After brewing the potion all night we gave it to him this morning, and healed the wound. I do not sense anything in him now; at first there was the slightest taint but now it is gone."

"Well, we know the potion works at least," Roslyn said with a half-smile. She turned to Ose who had walked off to talk to another orc nearby.

"The Elders are ready to see you now," Ose told her.

She nodded to him and smiled at her family before turning to follow him further into the village. He led her to a large log building with a rounded roof, a large bear skin covering the entrance. In the centre of the room was a fire pit with a small fire in it, the smoke rising up through a round hole in the ceiling. In a circle around the fire were tree stumps for seating, and the elders sat on most of them. One stump was empty.

"Greetings, Queen Roslyn," one of the female elders spoke first. Her hair was all grey and there were numerous wrinkles on her face. One of her tusks had been broken sometime in her life, and there were scars on her wrists. She wore deerskin hide as clothing, with a wolf pelt around her shoulders. "I am Avis, the oldest of us. These are my fellow elders, Malen, Bhag, Delon, and Leib." She introduced them around the circle clockwise; all of them looked almost as old as Avis, and Roslyn found it slightly amusing that Avis was the only one with a missing tusk and that many scars. "Please join us."

"Thank you for having me here," Roslyn said to them as she sat on the empty stump.

"You have come to ask us to join with your people," Malen spoke up. "Why should we?"

Roslyn turned to Sully who was standing just inside the door. He nodded and stepped outside, only to return a moment later with Leaf in his hands. The dragonling was almost too big for him to carry now, which was why she had been riding in the cart during the way there.

Roslyn heard the elders gasp as Sully put Leaf down and the dragonling came to Roslyn's outstretched arm, head-butting her hand. The dragon looked around the room at each of the elders, letting them take in her eyes, before she curled up on the ground beside Roslyn's stump.

"So it is true," Avis whispered. "Our people have worshipped dragons since the beginning, and you have one as a familiar."

"Where did you come across it?" Leib inquired of her. All of them were leaning forward trying to get a better look at the dragon.

"On the plateau," she told them. "High up in the branches of the Dragon Clan's sacred tree in the mountain."

"Did you meet any of our fellow orcs up there?" Delon inquired.

"I did, one of them is travelling with me currently, Karina: she is half-orc, and is the shaman of the Dragon Clan."

"Indeed? And what is her familiar?"

"One of those large forest cats, similar to the one my mother has," Roslyn told him.

"Pity she did not find the dragon up there, but then again it seems that was not her destiny but yours," Avis voiced her opinion next. "I have been told that there was a lunar eclipse on your birthday, is that correct?"

Roslyn nodded. "And you defeated Grau in fair combat?" She nodded again.

"What can you provide for our Clan?" Avis asked her, a serious tone in her voice.

"I can offer you acceptance and equality with the rest of Jay'Al. You will be given land in my capital and any jobs you want. You can farm, mine, build, or join the army; go to school, own businesses if you want you. There will be no more fighting because we will be one people," she explained to them, looking at each of them and taking in their expressions as she talked.

"What if we want to stay here?" Leib posed the question.

"The choice would be up to all of you. Everyone will be welcome to come with us, and together we can build the capital of our new nation."

"Would you bring Karina in so we can talk to her?" Avis asked Roslyn. "Privately."

Roslyn nodded and stood up, Leaf getting up as well. Together they walked out through the opening and Roslyn instructed Karina to go in. She watched Karina and Mister Fluffy go inside, and a few minutes later they re-emerged, Karina with a smile on her face.

Avis came out of the building using a walking staff and beckoned for Roslyn to follow her. "Just you and your dragon," she told Roslyn.

Roslyn followed the orc through the village, young orc children poking their heads out of log buildings and fur tents. Adult and orc youths looked on curiously as they passed by but did not say anything.

Avis led her to a small cave not far from the village, where on the walls were painted pictures of dragons and orcs, and some human men. In the middle of the cave was what looked like a large clay dragon's egg with dark orange handprints all over it.

"Give me your hand," Avis instructed Roslyn, and Roslyn extended her right hand to the elderly orc. Avis took out a small knife and made three deft cuts around the palm of Roslyn's hand, and then one up each of her fingers and thumb. Roslyn hissed as it stung but she did not pull her hand away.

"Add your handprint to our ancestors'," Avis told her, nodding to the clay dragon's egg. Roslyn stepped closer to the egg, trying to find the right spot to leave her mark as blood ran down her arm. Finally choosing, she extended her hand out and placed it against the egg.

Time seemed to slow as her blood touched the clay. She felt her hand warm up and there was a flash of light. Something not unlike a burning sensation went up her arm and she bit her lip to stop from crying out. She blinked and felt reality return, pulling her hand back slowly from the egg. She looked at her arm in wonder, for whatever magic she had just been part of had left its mark in the shape of a tattoo: a white vine now twined its way up her forearm ending at her elbow, its leaves giving off a silvery glow. All wounds on her hand were healed as well.

Avis let out a loud chuffing sound that made Roslyn startle and turn to look at the orc.

"They like you," Avis said with a chuckle. "They have marked you as one of their own, that is a traditional tattoo of my people. Our people will join together. We will hold a celebration tonight."

***

Roslyn found Cypress at his home, a large hut made of furs and leather canvas. He was sitting in a wooden chair by the entrance, his wound wrapped up. Beside him sat a younger orc, a youth by the looks of him, and a female orc, all dressed the same as the rest of the orcs in deerskin hide and furs. Sully, Tiffany, Teddy and Harriet followed behind at a distance.

"Here she is!" Cypress called out a greeting when he saw her walking towards him. "Our Queen!"

"I am glad to see you are well," she greeted him with a smile. "Is this your family?"

"My younger brother and my sister," he told her.

"Our parents are no longer with us. I see the Elders like you, as do our ancestors." He pointed to the fresh tattoo on her arm. "That is a rare thing indeed. They accepted you as not only one of us, but as our Queen."

"I think both of our ancestors might be working together," she told him jokingly. "They want us to unite the continent for some reason, and now I worry that some-thing big is coming."

"Werewolves aren't that much of a threat to you?" Cypress asked with a sarcastic smirk as he stood up to stand beside her. "I hate to think of what you deem an emergency."

Roslyn playfully hit his arm and sighed, saying, "Well ok, maybe it could be about the werewolves. I just hope everything works out."

"I will be fighting by your side, my Queen, of course everything will be alright," he told her with a laugh. "Have you eaten yet? My sister Anda has been preparing a boar stew."

"I would love to join you, thank you. And your brother is…?"

"Ulmer," Cypress told her, the youth not meeting her eyes. "He is shy still, and you probably intimidate him." Cypress let out a laugh as his younger brother huffed at him and stormed off into their hut.

"Do not tease him," Anda reprimanded her brother. "You were his age once, and she is very beautiful for a human, not to mention that she is now our Queen."

"You are right, of course, little sister," Cypress said, half teasing and half serious. "I will apologize to him."

"So what's this about a boar stew?" Roslyn interjected before Anda could smack her brother. "I am always up for good food."

Chapter Eight

Heath enjoyed wandering the island that had become a temporary home during sunset because it was the quietest time of the day. He had a walking stick with him as he explored, and always took some food in a basket for a snack. On this night, two days after Nadim told him about the king wanting to meet him, he was on the southernmost point of the island where there were tide pools and a sandbar that extended out into the waters some ways. He played with the water with his magic, creating shapes that he would dance along the beach. He had learned so much about his magic in the short time he had been there.

Nadim swam up to him from the ocean, the light of the day waning.

"It is time," was all Nadim said to him before he beckoned for Heath to follow him. Heath put his basket down and walking stick down and then dove in the water after Nadim. The merman led him down to what looked like an underwater cavern at first but it turned out to be a passage beneath the island.

Using his magic to draw oxygen to him Heath swam alongside Nadim. There were crystals that glowed, set at short intervals along the passage to light the way. Small fish swam through the passage as well, and they met a few other merpeople swimming up the passage who stared at Heath.

The end of the passage neared and it was lit with light. Heath swam out into a massive underground cavern that was filled with water, hundreds of stone houses arrayed like a city. In the middle was what Heath could only describe as a giant coral palace with doors and windows; merpeople swam in and out of the large open gates that were the main door to the palace. Above them in the ceiling of the cavern was a giant crystal that provided the light. Heath was reminded of the crystal in the underground cavern where they had found Kasimir and the large lizards.

"Oh wow," was all Heath could say, awestruck at the sight before him. "This has been here the whole time?"

Nadim smiled at him and nodded, beckoning Heath to follow him as he started to swim towards the palace. All of the merpeople they swam by stared openly at Heath, many of them curious, others shocked.

"How did my being here not get around?" Heath asked Nadim as they approached the palace.

"Only a handful of us work the surface, and the king swore us to secrecy," was the reply.

"Oh, well then. There is way more of you than I thought there was."

They entered the palace, the decorations exactly as Heath expected them to be: seashells and paintings of reefs and fish. The halls were wide enough for four merpeople to swim abreast, and there were crystals in sconces along the wall to add more light to the inside of the palace. The hues of colour of the coral changed as they made their way through the palace, Nadim leading him further into the building.

They came to large double doors cut out of the coral, two mermen with tridents floating on either side of the door. These mermen wore armour that looked strangely like the frishna armour that the Clans of Jay'Al had.

"Greetings, Nadim," one of the mermen spoke to them. A lot of the merfolk Heath had seen either had dreadlocks or had their long hair tied back in braids, but these two guarding the door had their dark hair cut short. "You and your guest are expected."

The other guard opened the door and ushered them through. The Throne Room of the merfolk's palace was grand, with a giant conch shell up on a dais on the other side where a merman sat on the shell like a throne. There were no other merfolk there, for it seemed like the king wanted to meet Heath in private. A chandelier hung from the ceiling with crystals in the sconces to light the room, and there were more crystals around the room. As Heath and Nadim swam towards the throne Heath noticed that the floor of the Throne Room was made of shells.

They stopped in front of the dais and Heath was able to see the king better: he looked to be not much older than Heath, and his hair was a lot lighter in colour than the rest of the merpeople. His eyes were green, and he had a scar that ran from the corner of his right eye over to his ear and down his jawline. On his head he wore a silver crown that had jewels in it. The scales of his tail were a brilliant green shimmer.

Heath bowed as best he could to the king, who looked slightly amused.

"You must be Heath," the king spoke to him. "I have heard much about your progress lately. I am King Ullas of Kyprago, the realm of the seafolk. Welcome to my home."

"Thank you for having me," Heath told him. "It is good to meet you."

"I must confess, when Nadim first brought you here I was wary; we had cut ourselves off from the outside world for a long time. Nadim has told me your tale, and of your people. I am interested in the goings on of Jay'Al, for they were once our friends long ago," Ullas told Heath.

"While I cannot say of the *current* events of Jay'Al, if my friend Roslyn completed the quest her ancestors gave her then she is now Queen of Jay'Al and is working to unite the clans," Heath explained.

"Truly? There has never been a ruler over all of Jay'Al before. Who is this Roslyn?"

"Do you know of the kingdom of Ellsgrove?" Heath asked the king first. The king nodded. "Roslyn was born in Jay'Al to a member of the Ellsgrove royal family and a Jay'Alian shaman. She was raised in Ellsgrove though, but her father taught her about Jay'Al and their ways. She is a powerful mage, a skilled fighter, and she is very intelligent; not to mention, beautiful. Roslyn went to Jay'Al to discover where her mother came from, and upon arriving her ancestors gave her that quest I was talking about."

"She is an honourable person?" Ullas inquired next.

"Very much so, Your Majesty."

"I would like to send you back to Jay'Al, with Nadim acting as ambassador between us. If she did succeed in her quest I would be interested in forming a new alliance with this Queen Roslyn, and maybe in turn with her father in Ellsgrove," Ullas informed them.

"Would we be able to sail through your seas to Ellsgrove?" Heath inquired of him. "The people known as the Tribes of the Archipelago hold the ocean on the other side; we traveled to Jay'Al through the Sea of Ice. It would make travelling to Ellsgrove a lot faster and safer if we could sail through your seas."

"That could definitely be arranged," Ullas assured him. "I can make arrangements for a route to be opened up for you."

"What would you want in return?" Heath had to ask.

"To broaden our scope, so to say; we could use different food and livestock, and I know there are a lot of my people who have grown bored with our secluded way of life, myself included," Ullas said with a shrug. "I think both of our people could stand to gain a lot from an alliance."

"Very well. When do we leave?" Heath was eager to get back to Jay'Al and discover what had become of Roslyn and her quest.

"You will leave in the morning. Go get some rest, if you can."

***

Kavan awoke with a start, Alexander sitting alert beside him. Alexander had shook Kavan lightly to wake him up.

"What is it?" Kavan whispered.

"We are being hunted," came the quiet reply.

"Who?"

"Two werewolves, they caught my scent it seems. We need to lead them away from where we are going, and try to hide our scent from now on."

"Why would some be this far north?" Kavan asked as they gathered their things and prepared to take off.

"A lot of the herbs for the potion to stop the change are in the mountains," Alexander told him. "Edwin would have found that out and sent scouts to make sure no herbs are gathered."

"Cassidy could be in danger," Kavan stopped what he was doing and looked in the direction of the mountains.

"If she is anything like her sister I am sure she is fine," Alexander commented. "We cannot head to Roslyn just yet, we need to lead these wolves away."

"How much longer do we have to do this?" Kavan asked Alexander as the older werewolf led him south, taking him further away from Roslyn yet again.

"Until these two wolves catch us and we kill them, or we successfully lose them," was the reply. Kavan sighed but he knew that Alexander was right; if they led the werewolves to Roslyn that would put everyone in unnecessary danger.

After a time Kavan realized they had reached the plains where Daron and the Fox Clan lived. Kavan mentioned to Alexander as they stopped for water about the Clan being nearby, and they agreed to evade them to make sure no more people were bitten.

"So are the two who are after us ones you bit?" Kavan asked Alexander as he closed his water skein. The river they found was overflowing from the spring melt and cold.

"Yes, there were several of them left at the end," Alexander answered after a moment. "Edwin was able to break the sire bond I held on them though, or else I would be able to command them to leave us alone."

"So I am sired to you?" Kavan turned to look at the man who had bitten him, who had passed on to him the unwanted change.

"Yes," Alexander told him honestly. "If I commanded you to leave Roslyn alone you would have no choice."

"How does the sire bond get broken?" Kavan knew he probably would not get an honest answer to that.

"You have to take full control, mentally and physically. Being able to turn at will means you have the ability to break the bond, you just need to know where to look for that thread to break."

"Are you telling me the truth?" Kavan stopped walking along the side of the river and crossed his arms over his chest.

"I have never lied to you, I would not start now."

Deep down Kavan knew that was the truth. Maybe when he had the chance he would look for the thread Alexander spoke of.

"Come on, let's cross the river here to get them to lose our scent for a while, and we can use the current to take us downstream into the woods.

There we can try to double back."

Kavan had caught the scent of their pursuers and he knew they were not far behind them. He jumped into the water after Alexander and let the current take him downstream; he barely felt the cold, and the armour in his bag did not weigh him down much, though the sword was a little awkward in the water. They came to a small bridge over the river and they decided to get out of the water there. From there they ran east, only stopping when they reached the coast.

"That should throw them off our trail for a while. Let's get some rest," Alexander told Kavan as he started to gather firewood. "Do you think you could catch some fish while I get a fire going?"

Kavan put his bag down and he nodded, though inwardly he just wanted to sit down for a minute. His stamina and strength were increased, yes, but they had run a long way. He could use something to eat though, so he waded out into the water to catch some fish. There were some interestingly coloured fish that he had never seen before but they were large and fat so he aimed for them. He had just caught a fish when he heard Alexander scream his name behind him on the beach.

Two werewolves, both of them black in colour, stalked towards Alexander from the dunes of the sand further down the beach. Alexander was in the process of changing as Kavan ran out of the water and towards his companion while the werewolves charged at them. Kavan drew his sword as one of them lunged at him, and he felt it connect. The werewolf fell away with a yelp, its side sliced open. The other werewolf was met by Alexander in wolf form, and they snarled and bit as they fought. Kavan watched for his chance to strike at the enemy but was wary of hitting Alexander.

Finally Alexander broke free of the other werewolf, clearly limping, and Kavan threw his sword at the enemy. The sword hit the werewolf in the chest, killing it instantly. Kavan turned to the first downed wolf and found a naked dead man in its place. He turned back to the other one and there was another naked dead man.

"Kavan," he heard Alexander whimper as he turned human again. Kavan turned to find Alexander cradling his left arm, blood running down it. "I need fresh blood to heal," Alexander whispered.

"I'll find you something," Kavan assured him, and he ran off to the grass before the beach, listening for any kind of rabbit or marmot. He was able to quickly catch a rabbit and he brought it to Alexander, looking away as he fed on it.

"How did they catch up to us so quickly?" Kavan had to ask.

"All I can think of is that they anticipated what I would do, or they still have some kind of link to me through what was our bond," Alexander told him as he wiped his mouth on his sleeve, leaving a bloody streak. Alexander looked at the two dead men and sighed. "They were Ryne and Merton."

"Do you think they sired any more werewolves during any attacks?" Kavan asked him as he watched Alexander's wound heal.

"Most likely," Alexander told him. "They would utilize the ones who had control."

"What do we do now?"

"Bury them, have some rest, and then do what we first headed out to do: plead our case with your Queen."

Chapter Nine

Roslyn helped Cypress and his siblings take down their hut to prepare to leave. They had wagons full of their scant belongings, and there were only a handful of huts like Cypress's; a lot of the other orc families had wooden homes which they were leaving behind. The Elders had talked to their people and told them of the homes they would have with Roslyn, large stone homes and fields of crops along with them. Many of the males were eager to be warriors, but some of them liked the idea of being builders or blacksmiths, even carpenters. Roslyn was glad that she could help them find their places in the new kingdom she was building.

The hides and everything rolled up and put in wagons, Roslyn went to go see how far along the dismantling of their encampment was going. Everything had been dismantled quickly, it seemed, and they were all ready to get under way.

"Have the Elders got all of their relics?" Roslyn asked Ose who had stayed close to her for most of the packing.

"Everything is packed up," Ose assured her. "Our ancestors were eager for this to happen, it seems: Avis barely had to do much to get everything uprooted."

Roslyn chuckled, "That sounds about right. They marked me quick enough." She showed him the tattoo, which she had covered for the better part of the day with her sleeve. "I just worry about those damned werewolves."

"You have frishna weapons, and we have frishna weapons; we can kill a lot if they come for us while we travel south."

"And how many people would be bitten in the meantime?" she asked him. "We need to send word out to everyone to protect their villages at all times. We cannot risk more attacks."

"We can send word out," Aidan spoke up behind her. He and the other clerks had been making sure everything was being packed up accordingly.

"We have messenger birds that will go to each Clan; just say the word and they will be sent."

"Do it. Have them put protective wards around their villages, and send a message to Willow stating we need as many frishna weapons as her people can provide us."

"We have some ore we can contribute as well," Avis told her as she approached them. "Enough to make armour and weapons for a couple dozen of our warriors."

"We unfortunately do not have time for them to be made as we head south," Roslyn told her. "And none of our blacksmiths know how to work the metal."

"We have a blacksmith who does," Avis assured her. "He can make weapons as we go, though the armour will be another matter."

"Weapons are the priority," Roslyn told her. "As long as it does not delay us. Our own blacksmiths can assist him as well."

"He can do it on the move, no problem. We will have more frishna weapons in a few days."

"We could get Jessamine to join us," Cassidy interjected as she joined them. "With two blacksmiths who can work with frishna it will get done faster."

"Alright, send her a message," Roslyn agreed.

"Let's get going."

"Where are you heading first?" Amelia wanted to know her plans since she, McKenna and Sawyer would be heading back to Bella Vale.

"The plateau will be our first destination," Roslyn informed her as she mounted her horse. "I have been thinking of making it my capital–with a few tweaks. There is a lot of land around it that can be utilized as well. I will send you a message when we arrive there."

"Safe travels, daughter," Amelia told her with a smile.

"You as well, mother," Roslyn replied as she reached down and clasped her mother's hand. With another look at everyone waiting to head out she nodded to Sully who put a horn to his lips. As the horn blared she ushered her horse into a gallop, her Honour Guard following behind her, with everyone else following after in a slow cantor on either horseback or riding in wagons.

✳✳✳

Cassidy rode just behind Roslyn, Kai on her other side. The days had turned from a nice thaw in the north to rain, and Roslyn could only hold off so much of it with such a big group. Leaf was enjoying the rain though, running alongside the column and jumping in the puddles. Cassidy marveled at how big the dragon had grown in the last couple of months; surely within the year the dragon would be able to fly. She was already testing her small wings out with Roslyn's help, getting them stronger.

Crick made a chirp from inside Cassidy's coat where the pine marten had chosen to stay dry. With the rain had come a cold dampness which had crept into their bones, making them all ache.

"We will stop for the night shortly," Cassidy assured her familiar. "We made a lot of headway today even with how long our train is."

The adult orcs could move fast and could go without their horses, while their young rode in wagons. The horses that pulled the wagons were bred to be strong enough to hold an orc so they were efficient in pulling the wagons. When Cassidy had first seen the horses she could not believe how tall they were, or how large their hooves were. Cypress told her that they used the horses most when they went south.

"When did your clan head back north?" Cassidy had asked him when they had first rode into their village after the werewolf attack.

"They would have gotten back just a week ago," he had told her.

They had uprooted again after just arriving back to their home, which had made Cassidy sad though she had not mentioned it to her sister. They needed to blend everyone together in the right way for everyone to get along; it might be hard for Cassidy's people after they were at odds for so long, but she knew her sister could do it. Was that why they were heading to the plateau first? The half-orcs of the plateau might be instrumental in helping the orcs fit in.

"There is an open plain not too far ahead," Roslyn called back, a scout having just brought back the information of the lay of the land ahead. "We will camp there tonight."

Aidan rode up beside Roslyn then with a messenger bird in his hand. He took the rolled up message he had in his other hand and handed it to her.

"There was another attack," Roslyn spoke after a moment of reading. "Another village of the Beaver Clan though this one was further south."

"It's still not a full moon," Kai pointed out.

"There must be some who are different, who can change without the full moon," Cassidy commented, "That's the only explanation we have for the ones who attacked us in the mountains and this new attack."

Cassidy watched as Roslyn looked up at the sky, seeing the moon start to rise as the sun had begun to set. "The full moon will be in a sennight or so," she heard Roslyn say. "More people will change." Roslyn turned to look at Cassidy and asked her, "Bring a handful of the herbs you have to me after we are set up, I have an idea."

When they got to the open plain the clerks and Aidan directed where the tents should be placed, and the cooks got started immediately on the evening meal which lately had just been smoked meat and fresh loaves of bread with cheese; Cassidy did not like what Roslyn called the 'Marching Fare', which was basically rations for a moving army. They had no time to cook real food and with such a big group it did not make sense to use up all of their rations for the journey. Roslyn promised that once they got to the plateau they would have a feast and Cassidy was going to hold her sister to that.

Letting the soldiers put her tent up, Cassidy grabbed the bundle of herbs and went to go meet Roslyn. Her sister's tent had been the first to be put up, and she had already put her bed and desk into place. Tiffany was standing watch outside the tent as Cassidy approached.

"Do you know what she is planning on doing?" Cassidy asked Tiffany when she got to the front of the tent. Tiffany just shrugged and led her inside the tent.

Roslyn had a few deep clay dishes on her desk filled with earth, and her hands were covered in a thin layer of dirt.

"What, did you dig with your hands?" Tiffany asked her with an amused expression.

"I slipped in some mud," came the reply as Roslyn stuck her tongue out at her friend. She turned to Cassidy, saying, "Let me have the herbs."

Cassidy handed the bundle over to her and watched as she took two of each herbs out, looking for seeds on them or a root that she could use. Finding what she needed she placed them in the dishes and covered them in the dirt. Closing her eyes she said a spell, light coming from her hands to envelop the dishes.

As Cassidy and Tiffany watched, tiny plants grew out of the soil within moments, and then in the blink of an eye they matured and spread even more until the dishes were overflowing with the herbs.

Roslyn opened her eyes with a happy sigh and yawned. "That should help make enough potions," she said. "Let me know if you need more."

"Will do," was all Cassidy could think to say. "Or you could teach me that spell."

"I can definitely do that, sister. Tomorrow when we stop for the night?"

Cassidy agreed and gathered up the herbs, ready to take them to her tent where she would start a new batch of potions.

"I'll go talk to the scouts and then get the barrier set up," Roslyn told Tiffany as Cassidy left the tent. "Then I'll meet you back here."

"I'll go grab our food from the cooks," Tiffany said as Roslyn gathered her bag of crystals. "Meet you back here soon."

Roslyn took her bag of crystals and went to go find the scouts who should be at the picket line where the horses were kept for the night. The orcs were seeing to their own large horses as her soldiers were doing the same.

"Scout Myles," she called to the Jay'Alian scout who was from Bella Vale. He looked up from brushing his horse down and waved to her.

"My Queen," he greeted her with a smile. He was a few years older than she and Cassidy and was a very good tracker and scout.

"Report," she told him as she walked towards him.

Other scouts were just coming in and they hurried up to join them, a few of them soldier's from Ellsgrove.

"We could meet you at your tent," one of her Ellsgrove soldiers, Finn, told her. She held up her still dirty hands to stop him and he smiled broadly. They liked seeing her get her hands dirty, it made her more like them.

"Nonsense, it saves us all time and I am sure you are hungry and ready to rest," she told him. "Scouts, report."

"No movement to the west," Finn told her.

"East is quiet as well," Myles spoke next, "though there were some frightened deer I came upon."

"Behind us to the north was quiet," the other scout, a female orc named Trys told her next. She was a short stocky orc who could throw an ax very well, and if Roslyn remembered correctly she was the orc Terren's sister.

"South is strange," the last scout, a Jay'Alian named Len, was the last to talk. "I do not know how to explain it, it's *too* quiet. There were fewer animal noises the further ahead I got, and they were all hiding it seemed."

"Now that tells me something," Roslyn commented. "I can sense something in that direction but it is being shielded somehow. What I sense to the east though is different, it's more like what I sensed up on the mountain on the plateau. I want more lookouts tonight."

"I will inform the soldiers," Finn told her.

"Good, thank you," she said as she spotted Sully coming towards them. He seemed to like walking around the perimeter of the camp with her every night, and she definitely enjoyed his company.

"Go wash up and get your food," she told the scouts. They nodded and went about their business as she joined Sully.

"What is the news?" Sully asked her as they made their way to the perimeter of the camp.

"There is something ahead of us that frightens the animals into silence and hiding," she informed him. "I can sense something, just not sure. I am putting more lookouts out tonight, and I will strengthen the barrier as well. There could also be something to the east, but it could just be whatever the animals ahead of us sense, could be sensed further away as well."

"I will take a partial watch tonight," Sully told her as she started placing the first of the crystals down. "Did you accomplish what you wanted to do with the herbs?"

"Yes, I grew more with a spell so we can make more potions," she told him.

"That will definitely help," Sully commented with his smile, showing his dimples. "I am worried about what we might get caught in here. We have no idea how many there are now, or how strong they are."

"I know we have no way of really knowing until they attack, but we have ways to protect ourselves," she assured him. "With the weapons we have already we can kill them."

"I know, it's just this is something completely new that I have no knowledge of dealing with; I feel like I can't protect you as well as I should be able to," Sully confessed. "I promised your father I would look out for you."

Roslyn chuckled at that, earning a slight frown from Sully. "My dear Sir Sullivan, *I* will protect *you*," she teased him. She looked around to see the camp starting to settle down, and she was almost done setting up the barrier.

Sully laughed, and she was happy to see a blush on his cheeks. "Queen Roslyn," he said with a flourished bow, "My hero."

That made her laugh out loud, and she had to turn away from him so he wouldn't see her blushing. The moment was interrupted by Leaf trotting up to them, a dried fish hanging from her mouth.

"Ah, cooks must have brought your dinner, hm?" Roslyn beckoned to her familiar who rushed over to twine around her legs like a large cat. "Sully, why don't you go ahead and get your food, I'll finish up here and retire for the night."

"As you wish, my Queen," he said to her again with less of a flourished bow this time, though he did wink at her before he straightened. She watched him walk away into the camp, admiring the view.

Leaf nudged her leg with her head, drawing her attention away, only for Leaf to gobble down the whole fish in one go. Roslyn put her hands on her hips and looked down at her familiar.

"Well aren't you proud of yourself," she teased the dragon. "Come on, girl, let's finish getting the barrier up."

***

Kavan sat by the fire Alexander had made; he was on first watch that night. They had taken down a small boar during their way west from the coast, and even though they had eaten part of it in their wolf forms they had saved half of it to cook up later, so the hind legs were roasting over the fire now.

It had been challenging at first to get used to his heightened senses, but now he felt like he was getting used to it. He could hear an owl as it flew through the night to catch a mouse, and if he really focused it was like he was right there with the owl. If he closed his eyes he could hear heartbeats of creatures nearby. It kind of soothed him now to hear the wings of a bat as it flew above him, and the snicker of squirrels in the trees.

At the edge of his senses he could feel werewolves again, the same kind of static on his mind as the two who had attacked them. He could tell they were further south; he was thinking that they could have stayed at the plateau and waited for her to come to them, but of course how could he have known she would head there after visiting the orcs.

He could sense something very different between himself and those other werewolves; it was a magical creature but how it felt to his mind was a combination of a thunderstorm and a wildfire. It was perplexing.

"It's a dragon you sense," Alexander spoke up from where he was supposed to be sleeping on the other side of the fire. "I can tell you are confused by its presence."

"So you are saying Roslyn is between us and the other werewolves?" Kavan inquired, worried that the werewolves might attack Roslyn and her people.

"Yes, though can you not sense the rest of the magic? Your Roslyn is powerful indeed, she put a whole protective barrier around their camp. They are very safe."

"Do you know how many werewolves there could be now?" Kavan asked him, trying to use his own senses to look that far but he could not.

"No idea. We will likely face some of them soon since we are getting closer and they should be able to sense us as well. We will need to be more on guard from here on."

"Oh great, less sleep," Kavan said with a heavy sigh.

"Devour more blood and you will be good," Alexander told him. He rolled over and looked at him sternly. "I can't sleep, you might as well get some shut eye while I watch."

Kavan sighed and agreed with him. He rolled out his bedroll and settled in. "Don't eat all of the food while I sleep."

He heard Alexander chuckle as he drifted off, and then he heard him say, "I'll try not to."

Chapter Ten

Roslyn awoke in the morning to Sully pacing outside her tent. She could just barely see him through the opening in her tent, but she knew it was him by the way he walked. The remnants of a dream where she saw the same wolf as other dreams, a wolf that had Kavan's eyes, was still playing in the back of her mind.

"Oh for goodness sake, Sully, just come in already," she called out as she rose from her bed. She grabbed her evening gown and threw it over herself, tying it. Leaf stretched by the coals of the makeshift hearth nearby, though the dragon was not ready to get up.

Sully entered her tent, slightly embarrassed by seeing her in basically her night gown.

"There were four werewolves seen through the night," he told her.

"Why was I not awakened?" she asked him as she went to sit at her desk with the war map displayed on it.

"They stayed at quite the distance, flitting in and out of the darkness beyond the barrier. I thought it was best to let you sleep since there was no immediate danger," came the response.

"And now that it is daytime?"

"Nothing; they seemed to have pulled back."

"So they are out there, somewhere, and we still have a few days to go to get to the Base Town of the plateau," she commented with a sigh. "I hope Karina's dad got our message about them and was able to put up some kind of fortification."

"You left behind a few frishna weapons, correct? Some of the extra weapons you found in that underground cavern you told us about," Sully asked her, trying to remember everything she had told him about that adventure.

"Yes," she answered, "But they did not have much fortification against Grau, I doubt they were able to put up something against werewolves."

"Well, you never know, especially with the orcs that are there; they are stronger than most humans, right?"

"Yes. I just did not want more of my people in danger if we can help it," Roslyn said.

"Roz, there is a lot you cannot control here," Sully reminded her. "You need to remember that."

She sighed heavily and put her head in her hands. "Don't you think I know that? Heath died when he should have been safe; Kavan died while on my quest!" She started to cry, overwhelmed with emotion. "Cypress was bitten while protecting my sister. How many more people I care about will be hurt?"

Before she knew it Sully had her in his arms, comforting her.

"You cannot blame yourself for their deaths," he whispered into her ear. "They would not want you to live like that."

She sobbed into his shoulder, knowing that what he said was true. She let him comfort her until she was done crying. She reluctantly pulled back from him and dried her eyes on her sleeping gown.

"Thank you, Sir Sullivan," she said to him, trying to pull herself together. There was so much she had to process still. "Please, tell Tiffany I am ready for breakfast." She could sense Tiffany standing outside of the tent at a re-spectful distance.

Sully stood awkwardly and slightly bowed to her before heading out of the tent. She heard him tell Tiffany what she said and then he walked away.

Tiffany entered the tent with a tray of their breakfast, one eyebrow raised when she saw Roslyn's expression.

"What just happened?" Tiffany asked her as she put the tray down on the desk. Roslyn reached out and grabbed one of the fresh buns and some jam.

Roslyn explained what had just transpired between herself and Sully as she ate. She looked over at Leaf who had barely moved since Sully had en-tered the tent.

"Oh, OK," Tiffany commented when she was done. "And what do you think of that?"

"Hell, Tiffany, I'm dreaming of wolves with Kavan's eyes, what do you think I think of Sully comforting me like that?!"

"There is a lot going on in your mind apparently," Tiffany said. "Why have you not said anything before?"

"There was so much going on," Roslyn told her. "Once we got home it was the ancestors and then the werewolves, and I still had to talk to the orcs."

"So you haven't talked to anyone, not even your sister Cassidy, about how you were feeling? Not even your mom?"

Roslyn shook her head as she took another bite of the bun with jam on it. Tiffany sighed and stood up, starting to pace around the tent.

"You know I am here for all of that, why did you not tell me?" Tiffany asked her.

"Like I said, there was so much happening there was not enough time."

"Sully is right, you should not blame yourself," Tiffany told her. "All of us are ready to put our lives on the line for you–and Roz, I know you would do the same."

"I would," Roslyn told her with a sob. "I just don't want to see any more of you die."

Tiffany ran to her and held her in her arms, Roslyn hugging her back. "It is good to get this out," Tiffany told her. "We know you care for us. We care for you too. So let us do our jobs. We are not just your friends; we are your protectors."

"Fine," Roslyn said in a whisper. "I will try."

"Good; because if we are to get through the werewolves in our way then we need you, our most powerful mage and shaman, to come up with something."

"Oh, no pressure then," Roslyn commented as she stood up and walked toward her armour stand. A thought crossed her mind. "Could we put enchantments on armour to repel shapeshifters?"

"Theoretically, yes," Cassidy said from the doorway to her tent. "I do not think Jessamine will get here in time though."

"Do you know the runes?" Roslyn asked her twin sister. Cassidy nodded.

"If the orc blacksmith can put the runes on pieces of metal on all of the wagons, and our horses, we can repel them long enough to get to the Base Town of the plateau."

"Do you really think it will work?" Tiffany asked Roslyn as Cassidy turned to leave.

"I have to hope it will," Roslyn answered, thinking about those she wanted to keep safe. "Get on it, please."

"I will, sister," Cassidy told her. "Give me an hour, do not break camp yet."

"Alright, do what you need to. Tiffany, go tell the guards: we are staying here longer than usual."

"On it," Tiffany responded, standing up and heading out of the tent. Cassidy smiled at her twin sister and then exited the tent as well.

Roslyn sat there for a moment, her eyes closed, and her senses reaching out. She could sense the exact same being she had sensed on the plateau, in the mountains; but now it was not alone; if she was right, they were werewolves, though slightly different from the ones to the south of them. What made them different?

Before she could go investigate she heard Cypress's voice calling from outside her tent.

"Just a moment," she answered, and she quickly got dressed. She emerged from her tent as she finished putting her shirt on. Leaf opened one eye slowly to look at her and then rolled over into a better position to sleep. Roslyn chuckled to herself and let her be.

"Good morning, Cypress," she said to him.

"Good morning, My Queen," he bowed slightly with a smile on his face, his tusks sticking out of his mouth slightly. "Would you care to break your nightly fast with my siblings and I this morning? We have honey cakes and fresh biscuits."

"I would love to, Cypress," she answered him with a wide smile.

"Please, call me Cyp," he told her. "What news is there today?"

As he led her to his and his siblings' tent she told him about the were-wolves that were seen during the night and her plan to keep them at bay long enough to reach Base Town.

"That is a good idea, I hope it works," Cyp told her as they neared the tents where she could see Anda and Ulmer sitting around a small fire. Anda smiled at her and offered her one of the sweet honey cakes.

Roslyn sat down beside Anda on the ground and accepted the honey cake with a 'thank you' and greeted Ulmer as well. Instead of being shy Ulmer greeted her in return.

"I am sorry I have not been by since we headed out," Roslyn told them.

"We have seen you, at the head of the column," Anda told her. "And you have kept us safe every night."

"You are my people now," Roslyn told her, reaching out a hand to hold hers; Anda took it in hers. "I will do whatever is in my power to keep you all safe."

After she had finished eating with them Cypress offered to walk her back to her tent.

"I heard you talking to Sir Sullivan earlier," Cypress confessed as they walked. "Thank you for caring about me. I know you are friends with Karina, but she is only half-orc. It is good to see that you care about full orcs as well."

"I am only half Jay'Alian," she reminded him. "Karina and I were never that different; stuck between two worlds. Now though, I feel like I am whole. I know I belong here."

"Then you have to let us be your protectors," Cypress reminded her, echoing Tiffany's words. "My fellow warriors and I want to be there with you at the front."

Roslyn sighed and nodded in agreement. "When we get moving again, you and your warriors can be beside me at the front of the column."

Cypress bowed to her as they reached her tent. "Thank you, Your Majesty," he said to her before giving her a wide grin and turning to walk off.

Roslyn sighed and entered her tent, finding Cassidy and Tiffany waiting for her there.

"Tell me it's good news," Roslyn spoke to them as she took a seat.

"The rune might not be as strong as we hoped, but we can keep marching without any interference from any kind of shapeshifter within fifty feet of us," Cassidy told her. "We think. It might vary."

"Well I guess we will find out," Roslyn answered. "How long?"

"We should be able to move again by noon," Cassidy told her.

"Get it done," Roslyn told her. "Please and thank you, my sister."

Cassidy smiled widely at her before exiting the tent. Roslyn turned to find Tiffany looking at her with a raised eyebrow.

"What?" Roslyn asked her.

"Where did you have breakfast this morning?" Tiffany asked her.

"With Cypress and his siblings," she answered. "He asked me to let his warriors help protect me."

"And will you?"

"Yes," she told her.

"Good. They need to know they are equal to the rest of us; though honestly they are probably much stronger, but I digress. Hopefully everything works out."

"Between the frishna weapons and the repelling runes, it freaking better," Roslyn commented.

"You found your familiar and beat Grau," Tiffany reminded her, pointing to the still sleeping dragonling by the coals. "Have a little faith in yourself."

Roslyn sighed and leaned back in her chair. "Thank you, Tiffany," she said sincerely, reaching out her hand to grasp Tiffany's. Tiffany squeezed her hand back in return.

"Let's go do drills with your Honour Guard, and then we can start getting packed up," Tiffany told her as she stood up. "I know Karina is looking forward to seeing her family again."

"I know," Roslyn commented. "I worry that I tore her from her home needlessly."

"Never say that," Tiffany told her, crossing her arms over her chest. "You know Karina is very happy being here with us."

"Still," Roslyn said with a shrug. "She would be in less danger."

"Do you really think so? Do you not think the werewolves would have found a way up the plateau? If what Cassidy said was true, there was already one up there! Please, do not belittle our choices."

"That was never my intention," Roslyn told her, standing up as well. "You know why."

"Then accept it," Tiffany reminded her. "Because it is not going to change."

"Fine," Roslyn told her with a deep sigh. By the coals Leaf stirred finally, and she stretched like a large cat.

"Good. Now let's go, I know Deirdre is waiting to show you how good she has gotten with the bow and arrow."

"Yes, let us go," Roslyn said to both Tiffany and Leaf. "I could use some more fresh air."

***

Kavan watched the column march by, saw the orc warriors both male and female that surrounded Roslyn in a defensive march along with the human soldiers and knights.

"Looks like your Queen brought the orcs under her banner," Alexander commented to him. "That is impressive. She also managed to keep any shapeshifters from getting more than oh….about fifty feet close to the edge of the column."

Kavan could not help but smile at Roslyn's ingenuity, though it meant they would have to wait to get in contact with her since they themselves were repelled from the column. Kavan was starting to get a little impatient: he was so close but she was still out of reach.

"We need to keep an eye out," Alexander reminded him. They had been waiting hours for them to break camp, wondering why they had waited so late in the day. They had their answer now. "The other werewolves will be able to sense us, they might come for us."

Kavan and Alexander stayed a distance off from the column and they could sense the few other werewolves that stayed to the south. None of them seemed to care that they were there though.

"Maybe they think we are with them," Kavan commented after a while. "What do you think?"

"They should be curious though, we should be slightly strange to them," Alexander told him. "Maybe they were instructed to leave us alone, since the other two did not make it back."

It had started getting warmer the further south they went, and the trees were starting to grow their new leaves. Flowers were starting to sprout out of the ground as well. Kavan breathed in the fresh spring air and caught himself smelling a whole lot of things he had never smelled before. He looked around in wonder, smelling something sweet nearby.

"What is that?" Kavan asked Alexander. Alexander sniffed the air and smiled.

"Honey," he answered. "There is a beehive close by, and with the new spring flowers the bees are busy making fresh honey."

At that moment Kavan's stomach rumbled, and he felt his mouth start to water at the thought of fresh honeycombs. "Do you think…?"

Alexander laughed and nodded in the direction of a large oak tree where he could see bees buzzing around an opening in the trunk. "Yes, the bee's stingers will not hurt us, and we will not take much."

Chapter Eleven

Heath stood at the bow of a large galleon, its sails full of wind and moving fast towards Jay'Al. King Ullas had surprised him with the ship, telling him they had repaired it by using several sunken ships. Heath recognized the figurehead as one the Tribe of the Archipelago's ships, and he mentioned that to Nadim.

"Most of the ships that have sunk in the whirlpools were of your people," Nadim told him. "They have not tried to sail our oceans in several years now though."

Nadim was ordering some of the merfolk-turned-sailors around; apparently the group of them had practiced sailing the ship around their island home by the order of their king, who had hoped someday to send an ambassador out to either of the continents. Heath had to applaud the king's foresight, though he had to wonder who had taught the merfolk in the art of sailing to begin with.

He had asked Nadim, but Nadim just smiled and told him not to worry about it. Heath had started to trust the merpeople after his time with them, but why could they not tell him who taught them to sail? He had to wonder about that.

The whirlpools that had been between Kyprago and Jay'Al had disappeared as they approached them, allowing them through the ocean, and then they appeared again as soon as they were through the area. Heath watched each time, thinking that the whirlpools were probably the best form of defense a water creature like the merfolk could have.

Some of the merpeople who had gone with him were wearing armour like the two king's guards had, the metal looking like frishna metal, the weapons made of the same material. They were meant to be his and Nadim's guards, though Heath was not sure how well they would do fighting, though he had to admit he definitely did not know the full capabilities of the merfolk.

They had been sailing for four days when Heath saw the sliver of land on the horizon. He had told Nadim that the best place to start was the capital of the Hyena Clan which was on the southern tip of Jay'Al. From there they would be able to find out what had happened since he was last there, and where Roslyn was most likely to be now.

As the day progressed he could see the city walls of Hyena City, and the harbour that had been rebuilt since the orc attack on the city. The Tribes of the Archipelago were still in their compound, though by the looks of it the compound was heavily guarded by Jay'Alian soldiers. Heath wondered again what had happened to his brother Everett when the city had been attacked.

"The guards of the city will be surprised to see a ship coming from the direction of the whirlpools," Heath commented as he watched the walls of the city as they drew closer to the harbour. He could see people on the wall pointing out to the sea. He looked up at the flag they were flying, a fishtail twined around a trident, and he wondered if there was anyone alive in Jay'Al who could possibly know that standard.

"Well, I am sure there will be some sort of welcome party waiting for us," Nadim commented as he signalled his sailors towards the wharf, the sailors bringing in the sails. Two smaller boats came out from the wharf to help direct them over, and finally they laid anchor. As a gangplank was put down a group of soldiers with guns at their waists led by Keaton, Kai's cousin, were coming down the wharf to greet them. When Keaton saw Heath walking down the gangplank he stopped short for a moment before turning to a soldier behind him, saying something to him that made the soldier turn and run down the wharf.

"Heath, is that really you?" Keaton called as they drew closer to each other. "By the ancestors, it is you!" He reached out to grip Heath's forearm and Heath returned the gesture. "We all thought you were dead, Kavan saw you get shot."

"I washed out to the ocean on the current, where I was discovered by the merfolk of Kyprago," Heath told him, gesturing to the men behind him, and the standard flying on the ship. "They healed me, and now they have come with an ambassador to do dealings with Jay'Al."

"The merfolk…my people have heard stories passed down of the water kingdom of Kyprago, but never in my lifetime would I have thought to meet one. Do they truly turn into half-fish people in the water?" Keaton inquired, looking at the men who stood behind Heath.

"Indeed, we do," Nadim told him, stepping forward to stand next to Heath. "I am Nadim, King Ullas' ambassador."

"Welcome, Nadim, to Jay'Al. Please, come with me to my father's house. There we can converse better," Keaton said to him. "How many of your people will be accompanying you?"

"Just myself and my guard," Nadim told him, gesturing to the few soldiers in armour who had tridents in their hands. "The rest will remain here on the ship."

Keaton nodded and turned to lead them off the wharf and through the rest of the harbour. They walked through the city, the people of Hyena City marvelling at the new-comers who wore alpaca clothing and armour that resembled the frishna armour. Whispers spread through the crowd about the insignia Nadim wore, which was the same as the flag they had flown on the ship. They passed open courtyards attached to open houses, cool gardens and awnings providing people of the city with some relief from the heat.

Heath recognized Chief Erick's home as they approached it, remembering the last time he was there: when his brother Everett had taken him and Kavan hostage while the orcs attacked the city.

"Keaton, what happened to my brother?" Heath asked Kai's cousin as they neared the gates of the Chief's house.

"He was captured and imprisoned," Keaton told him. "He is still in my father's dungeon awaiting trial for what he did."

Heath stopped short just before entering the Chiefs main house. "Who captured him?"

"Roslyn did," Keaton answered as he ushered Heath and his entourage inside. Heath started moving again after a second.

"Do you know what happened with her quest?" was Heath's next question, but Keaton held up his hand to stop him as Chief Erick came down the hallway to greet them.

"Heath! It is good to see you alive, I know a certain Queen who would be extremely happy to see you again," Erick reached out to grasp Heath's forearm. The

Chief of the Hyena Clan was a barrel-chested man in his sixties, his hair mostly gray with the slightest bit of red left in it. Erick's brother Layne was Kai's father, and was also a shaman.

"Tell me of Roslyn," Heath implored as Erick led him into the meeting room. There was food and drink already waiting on the low table, and there were enough cushions for everyone. Erick bade everyone to sit and refresh themselves before he would answer. The floor of the room was a mural depicting desert plant life and animals.

"First, do you care to introduce me to the ambassador that comes with you?" Erick asked him.

"My apologies, this is Nadim," Heath told him with a sigh. "Nadim is here on behalf of King Ullas of Kyprago."

"By the ancestors, truly? Kyprago? I thought that realm was a myth," Erick looked at Nadim with wide eyes. "Welcome, Nadim of Kyprago, to Jay'Al."

"Thank you for the welcome, but I believe my friend here wanted an answer," Nadim nodded to Heath, earning a slight chuckle from Erick.

"Roslyn found a dragon on the mountain of the plateau," Erick told Heath, his companions listening beside him. "She defeated Grau on the plateau, and is currently working to bring the rest of the orcs under her banner as Queen of Jay'Al. I was there when the ancestors gave her her crown, I witnessed her become our Queen. She will be needed in the times coming."

"What do you mean?" Heath asked, noticing the dark look in Erick's eyes.

"Have you heard of shapeshifters, werewolves?" Erick asked him and Nadim.

"I have," Nadim told him. "My ancestors knew of a struggle between your people and the werewolves a long time ago."

"Well, they have returned," Erick informed them.

"Wait, what? Werewolves?" Heath could not believe what he was hearing.

"Truly," Erick assured him. "Several villages have been attacked, and werewolves have been sighted in several regions."

"Do you know where Roslyn would be now?" Heath asked the Chief. He noticed that Nadim and his guards had taken glasses of orange juice and were tasting the pastries on the table.

"If everything went well with the orcs, she should be heading to the plateau," Erick told him. "After the plateau she was planning on coming here to deal with your brother and the rest of the Tribes."

"And the rest of my friends? Do you know how they are?" This question made a shadow go over Erick's eyes and Erick looked down and away from him.

"I am sorry to be the one to tell you, but while Roslyn and your people were on the mountain of the plateau there was an avalanche, and Kavan was swept away by the snow. He did not make it."

Heath could feel blood rushing to his head, and he heard a ringing in his ears as he bent over, head in his hands. He felt a cool hand on his shoulder, Nadim's, and he breathed a little easier.

"I know you were great friends with him," Erick told him quietly. "I am sorry."

Heath felt tears in his eyes and he looked up at Nadim who squeezed his shoulder.

"I am sorry," Nadim spoke in a calming tone, using his magic to help Heath calm down. "You spoke very fondly of him."

Heath wiped the tears that were running down his face and a memory of himself with Kavan practicing with swords came to mind. He wanted to remember his friend's determination, not the look of shock that had been on his face when he saw Heath get shot.

"Do you want a message sent to Roslyn?" Erick asked after he had dried his tears and calmed down.

"Yes," was all he could say.

"Keaton will show you to your guest rooms, and we will celebrate Kyprago's ambassador tonight with a fine dinner," Erick said as he stood up, nodding to Keaton who had been standing in the doorway. "Do you want new clothes brought to you?"

"We would appreciate it," Nadim answered. "I know Heath would like to wear something different after his time with us."

"It will be done," Erick told him. "Please, make yourselves at home here."

***

Heath sat in the open courtyard after changing his clothes, remembering the last time he and Roslyn had been in the exact same place. It had been nighttime, the first night after the orcs had started attacking the city. He could remember kissing her, holding her, her touch against his skin. He could not wait to get back to her, to show her what he had discovered about himself since he had been separated from her.

He mourned Kavan, taking a shot of liquor in his honour. Who was with Roslyn now, protecting her? What were the others doing?

Nadim walked up to him, aware of his mood.

"Are you all right?" Nadim asked him, taking a seat next to Heath.

"Just letting everything sink in," Heath commented, putting the small wooden cup and the bottle of liquor down on the tiles beneath the seat. "She found a *dragon* as her familiar," he told Nadim.

"She must be very powerful, your Roslyn," Nadim observed. "In our history dragons have been a sign of great change. My King will find that very interesting indeed."

Heath narrowed his eyes at Nadim. "Please tell me he does not want a marriage alliance with her."

"No," Nadim assured him, "Nothing like that. He has been looking for signs to justify bringing our people back out into the world, although I am not sure what he would think of the werewolves coming back now too."

"Will that hinder negotiations?" Heath wondered aloud.

"Well, that depends on the outcome," Nadim told him. "Why don't you practice with your magic, see how far you can astral project yourself on land?"

Heath nodded with a sigh and closed his eyes, focusing on his inner self and the water around him. He felt his magical form separate from his solid form, and he found himself soaring over the city on the clouds. He let the clouds take him north along the river that had brought him and the others south to begin with; the First Harbour where they had found the dead orc, and then the giant chasm in the ground that they had come upon. He willed himself to head towards the plateau where he saw a giant staircase down the side of the plateau, a large settlement sitting at its base. In the distance, a good few days' ride northeast, he could see smoke columns from several camps. Could that be Roslyn's camp?

"Excuse me," Heath was disturbed from his trance by Erick talking. Heath opened his eyes with a sigh and looked first at Nadim and then Erick.

"I could see the plateau; there is a compound at its base," Heath informed Nadim.

"The Dragon Clan who used to live on the plateau built the compound," Erick told him, looking at him with raised eyebrows. "You saw this?"

Heath nodded and explained how his magic worked.

"I think the fires I saw were from Roslyn's group," Heath explained. "They are close to the plateau."

"I am sorry to have interrupted you reconnaissance, but I thought you might like to see your brother," Erick told him. "He is in the dungeon below." "Yes, I think I would like to have some words with him, thank you." Heath stood up and nodded to Nadim who nodded in return. "Please, show me the way."

Erick led him to a doorway down the hall that was locked; he unlocked it with a key that he carried around his neck.

Down the stone staircase they went, lit by sconces of burning candles as they descended. At the base of the stairs was another door which Erick opened for him; one guard sat at a table doing paperwork, and there was a weapons stand on the other side of the room. The guard greeted Erick with a nod before going back to his work.

Between the table and the weapons stand was another door that Erick opened that led to a hallway lit with more candles, three more metal doors on each side of the hallway. Erick led him to one of the doors in the middle where he opened a small window into the room behind the door.

"I will be in the guard room," Erick told him. The Chief turned and walked away, closing the door to the guard room behind him.

Heath peered through the window, seeing a room lit by crystals not unlike the ones Roslyn had made. There was a cot at the end of the room, and a bucket for the use of relieving oneself. Sitting on the cot wearing ragged clothes, his hair matted slightly, was Heath's younger brother Everett.

"Hello, brother," Heath said, enjoying seeing the blood drain from his brother's face as if a ghost stood there; well, for all Everett knew, Heath *was* dead and it was a ghost that came to haunt him.

"Who is there?" he heard Everett call out, a slight tremble in his voice.

"Oh come now, brother, it's me."

"It cannot be, you were shot," Everett argued, pulling his knees up in front of his chest and hugging his legs.

Using his magic, Heath unlocked the door, letting it swing open. Everett started as the door clanged against the wall, and he stared with wide eyes as

Heath walked into the cell.

"Do I look like a ghost to you?" Heath asked him, taking a few steps forward. He pulled together some water into a ball in his right hand and played with it, tossing it between hands, as Everett continued to stare wide-eyed at him.

"No words for your older brother, hm?"

"Heath could never use magic like that," Everett spoke finally, letting go of his legs. "You cannot be him."

"The current took me out to the ocean, and I floated in the water, bleeding from the gunshot wound; my magic protected me from drowning. I was found by merfolk, Everett. They healed me and taught me how to use my magic," Heath explained it to him.

"Merfolk?" Everett whispered.

"Did you know that we are descendants of merfolk? Ones who chose to become human on the islands we call our home?" Heath asked him. "That is where our magic comes from, Everett, our ancestors."

Everett sat up now, looking at Heath with clearer eyes. "I remember mother telling us stories when we were children, but I never thought them to be true."

"They are all true," Heath assured him.

"What do you want with me then?" Everett asked him finally.

"I just wanted to show you what I can do," Heath answered him, turning the ball of water into ice. "I will let Roslyn decide your fate when she returns though."

"You would let me live still?" Everett was unsure of what he was hearing.

"You are still my brother," Heath told him as he dropped the ball of ice on the stone floor, shattering it into pieces. "I have thought about this moment, after what you did…I forgive you. Do better next time, hm?"

Heath closed the door, locking it with his magic, and walked down to the guard room.

Chapter Twelve

Roslyn looked up at the moonlight; the moon was full and shining brightly down on the plain, illuminating places that would normally be dark beyond the camp. They were only a day away from the Base Town now, but the werewolves had stayed with them just beyond their barrier. There were only three, watching them and waiting. Now that there was an actual full moon though she wondered if more would be coming.

She was putting up the night time barrier by herself tonight; she had sent Sullivan to make sure every-one's weapons were sharpened and that their horses were ready for the morning. They would travel faster in the morning, trying to cut short the distance between them-
selves and Base Town. She had sent a message ahead to Lou, Karina's father, and a message had been received in return: they had fought off a couple werewolves already, there were no injuries, and they were awaiting Roslyn's arrival now. Roslyn had sent several orcs ahead with frishna weapons, with the special runes that Cassidy had found to repel shapeshifters on their ar-mour. They could run faster ahead of them and prepare Base Town for their arrival, as well as help defend Base Town if more werewolves attacked under the full moon.

Leaf walked along beside her, flapping her wings a bit as she hopped along beside Roslyn. The dragonling's stomach was full of smoked fish again, as well as a small boar that the dragonling had taken down earlier. Roslyn wondered if her familiar was going to go through a growth spurt soon with how much she was eating.

A howl split the silence of the plain, making her skin crawl. She shivered, pulling her cloak closer around herself. She quickly finished up the barrier and watched as the magic enclosed their encampment. Roslyn headed back along the barrier to the eastern side, and she stopped to watch as two large wolves emerged from the grass of the plains. She had seen them the night before; when she had described them to Cassidy her sister had confirmed that they were werewolves. One was almost completely black except for its right ear, which was white, and its left paw, which was also white; its eyes were a bright blue colour. The other werewolf was a light chocolate brown colour with lighter streaks in its fur, its eyes a gray colour that seemed familiar to Roslyn. In the darkness right now all she could see was their fur colour, but she knew it was the same two. They stayed away from the other werewolves who haunted their south, making Roslyn wonder why these two were so different.

Sully approached her, two cups of hot cocoa in his hands. He handed one to her, and she accepted it with a smile. He was wearing just his gambeson and trousers, his bracers still on his wrists. His leather boots came up just to his calves. At his waist was a frishna sword that Roslyn had given him from the stash they had found in the underground cavern.

"Those the same werewolves you saw yesterday?" he asked her as he noticed the very large wolves to the east.

"Yes," she responded as she sipped from the cup.
She turned to keep walking along the barrier, Sully following along beside, and Leaf still bouncing about.

"How do you think Cypress and the other orcs you sent ahead are faring?" he asked her.

"I know they made it to Base Town," she told him. "Everything will be set up for our arrival tomorrow."

"What will we do once we are there?" Sully asked her as he sipped his drink.

"Well, we might need to parley with the werewolves to figure out what they want," she told him. They were walking amongst the tents now, heading for the center of where her tent was. "And I am going to do something about the plateau."

Sully raised his eyebrows at her and inquired, "What does that mean?"

"That stair takes too long," was all she would tell him, giving him a sly smile. "Thank you for bringing me the drink."

"My pleasure," he replied as they reached her tent. Her Honour Guard were all sitting outside of Tiffany's tent looking after their gear. "Goodnight."

He left her there, heading for his own tent, saying goodnight to his sister as he passed by her. A few of the young women watched him walk by, and Deirdre chuckled.

"Don't even think about it," Roslyn heard Deirdre say as she entered her tent. She stood just inside to listen to their banter.

"We can look, we just won't touch," Harriet responded with a laugh.

"I was not even looking at him," Teddy told her. "He is really not my type at all."

"What is your type then?" Baylee asked.

"Maeve is my type," Teddy responded as she put her sword away, having finished caring for it.

Roslyn smiled to hear them opening up to each other now that they were freer to be themselves here. She was happy to hear none of the other girls gasp with shock, but just words of encouragement and compliments about how pretty Maeve was. Back home in Ellsgrove it would have been quite the scandal, but here nobody cared about things like that and that was how it should be.

Roslyn took off her sword belt, placing her frishna sword on the stand next to the bladed staff. She started taking off her half plate armour and then the chainmail, hanging them up on the rack next to the armour stand. She slipped off the cotton tunic she was wearing and tossed it on her bed before putting on her night shift. She was ready to get to Base Town and sleep better, but more specifically to find out what the werewolves wanted.

She slipped into bed and settled onto the pillow, Leaf jumping up beside her to curl up next to her feet. Roslyn chuckled at the dragonling and closed her eyes. She drifted off to sleep listening to her Honour Guards talking outside.

Roslyn dreamed, though this particular dream was different, feeling more like an astral projection than a normal dream. She found that odd, because she did not have any potions.

She was back home in Ellsgrove, standing by the desk in her father's study in the palace. Her father sat at the desk, writing something, and both Maeve and Kasimir sat on the other side of the king's desk. Guards stood just outside the door, and the king's butler stood in one of the corners of the study.

Kasimir, the merchant they had found marooned in the underground cavern, had his red hair cut short and cleaned, a slight bit of beard on his jaw. He was dressed in fine merchant clothing and looked to be in good health.

Maeve was wearing her sailors outfit, her hair held back in a plait. Her boots had been shined, as were buttons on her coat. She was giving King Lucius her report and informing him about where Kasimir had been when he was found.

"It pains me that she lost both of them," Roslyn heard her father say. She waved her hand in front of his face but he did not see her. Definitely not an astral projection. "You say she found a dragon that became her familiar?"

"Indeed. She will have been crowned Queen by now, too," Maeve continued, "And her next plan was to go visit the orcs before heading south again."

King Lucius chuckled. "I bet that was something she had to think about," he said. "She never wanted that life."

Maeve smiled, knowing exactly what he meant.

"These orcs that joined the group, are you sure they are to be trusted?" Lucius asked Maeve next.

"Roslyn vouched for them," she answered. "Once she killed Grau they swore themselves to her."

King Lucius looked down at what he was writing, notes on the mission report.

"Well, looks like we need to send an ambassador to Jay'Al," he said with a chuckle. "I will have to look into that soon. Does she need anything from us?"

"Not at this time, Your Majesty," Maeve told him. "They have everything they need to deal with the werewolf threat there. I think an envoy to the Tribes of the Archipelago could be sent though, to see about a proper peace treaty."

"Yes, I was thinking that as well," Lucius responded with a smile. "Clearly I cannot send you, since you would be in trouble for changing sides, but do you have anyone in mind?"

"I might know a few people who would be up for it," Maeve told him.

"May I be of assistance in any way?" Kasimir spoke up.

"From what I understand you need to head home to your family," King Lucius told him. "Your father's company passed to your mother, but I know she will be extremely happy to have you back, alive. I will send you in one of my coaches so make it there faster. Get settled in and figure things out first. If I have need of you I will let you know."

Kasimir ducked his head and said, "Thank you, Your Majesty."

"Go have some rest and food now," Lucius told them. "Maeve, I'll expect your recommendation by tomorrow morning."

"Of course," she told him as both she and Kasimir stood and bowed to him.

Roslyn watched as the two left the king's study. Her father turned to talk to his butler, Roland.

"I do hope she is all right," he spoke, worry in his voice.

"Having known Roslyn her whole life, sir, I am adamant that she is," Roland responded. "You really need to worry about the rumours our spies have heard about the possibility of an assassination attempt."

A chill went down Roslyn's spine at the butler's words. An assassination attempt on her father?

"I know the conservatives were angry with some of the changes I made, but it is hard to believe that they would go this far," her father responded as he stood and started to pace the room.

"You stirred the pot, sir," Roland told him. "Something was bound to spill."

"Have our people look into it further," Lucius told him. "Make sure the palace is secure against any and all threats."

"It will be done," Roland was saying as the room began to blur in Roslyn's eyes. She jolted awake in her bed back in Jay'Al.

"What the heck was that," she said to herself as she sat up in her bed. She could hear shouting from outside the tent, and as she got out from under her blanket Tiffany ran into the tent.

"What is going on?" Roslyn asked her.

"Those two werewolves that were following behind us are fighting with the other ones," Tiffany told her.

Roslyn grabbed her coat and the bladed staff from its stand and followed Tiffany out of the tent. Tiffany led her to the east side of the camp where a group of guards and Sully watched the werewolves who were not yet in a physical fight but were snapping and growling at each other.

"What do you think this is about?" Sully asked her when he saw her, though he had to do a double take because she was only wearing a coat over her nightshirt. She could feel the cool air on her bare legs.

"They do not seem to be friends," Roslyn commented, watching the exchange in the distance.

"Two factions of werewolves?" Tiffany wondered. Sully raised an eyebrow at her and she shrugged. "What? Stranger things have happened lately."

Sully shrugged too and looked back out at the werewolves.

Roslyn wanted to get out there to intervene, to see if someone would talk to her. Clearly some of them had the ability to change without a full moon, and it seemed like all five of them had that ability. Roslyn went to the nearest crystal and tapped it, opening up a small doorway that she could go through.

"What do you think you are doing?" Sully and Tiffany were right behind her, weapons drawn.

"Something either really stupid or really brave," she replied as she aimed her bladed staff at the three werewolves that had been hounding them from the south.

Roslyn had discovered not long after finding the ancient weapons that the bladed staff could be used as a conduit for her own magic, and now she used it with a spell to hurl balls of ice at the three werewolves.

The first one that was hit stopped growling at the other two and shook itself before turning to find Roslyn coming towards them, Tiffany and Sully right behind her.

"If you want to live another day I suggest you leave now," Roslyn told the werewolves as she gripped her bladed staff in order to use it as a weapon. "We all have frishna weapons and can kill you."

The three werewolves looked at each other, and then as one gave a final snap and growl towards the other two werewolves the group of three bounded off into the grass.

Roslyn turned to look at the other two werewolves; the black and white one was looking at her with its head cocked to the side as if it was curious. The brown one whined at her and its tail wagged as if it was happy to see her.

"Well, can you two change back?" Roslyn asked them as she leaned on her staff. The black and white one seemed to nod. "Go change back and get clothes on, I'll wait here."

Sully was looking at her in exasperation now, which made Tiffany chuckle.

"She wanted to talk to one of them," Tiffany reminded him. "This is as good a chance as any."

The two wolves had run off to a grouping of bushes not too far away, and after a few minutes two men came out from behind them. Both were wearing alpaca clothing a lot like the Dragon Clan wore, with one of them wearing a hooded cloak, the hood drawn to hide his face.

She could see that the man's hands were light skinned though, whereas his companion had the dark skin of a Jay'Alian as well as the red hair. The one with the hood carried a bag over his shoulder, as well as a sword at his waist.

"Greetings, Queen Roslyn," the dark skinned man said to her. "It is good to finally meet you."

"How do you know who I am?" she asked him. "Who are you?"

"I am Alexander," he told her. "I was the one who helped the Clans trap the other werewolves in the underground cavern, the very one you got your bladed staff from." He pointed at her weapon. "I exiled myself to the plateau after."

"You were what we sensed on the mountain," Tiffany commented.

"Yes."

"And your companion?" Sully was the one to ask.

Alexander looked at the man beside him and nodded. The hooded man reached up and drew back the hood.

In the moonlight Roslyn took in Kavan, who at first she thought must be a ghost. She heard Tiffany gasp behind her so at least she knew they were seeing the same person.

"Hello, Roslyn," Kavan spoke, and she knew in her heart that he was indeed alive standing before her. "We have been trying to catch up with you for days."

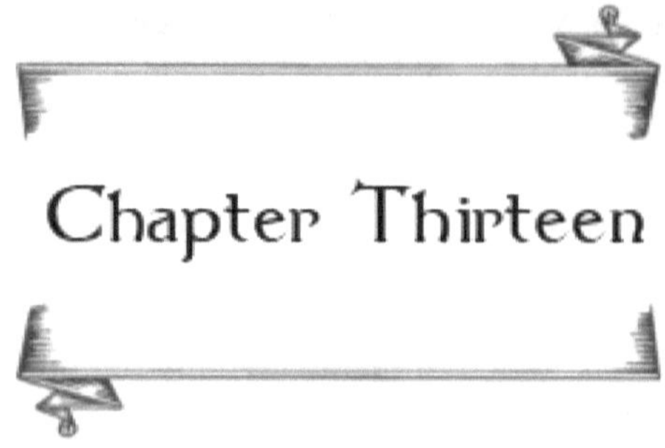

Chapter Thirteen

Roslyn stared into her cup of the wake up drink that Heath had liked so much–it was not quite dawn yet. Across the table sat Alexander and Kavan, with Cassidy, Tiffany and Sully sitting on either side of her. They were in the cook's tent. Kavan had told her what had happened since they last saw each other, from Alexander digging him out of the snow and biting him, to their journey to find her.

"We needed to tell you about them," Kavan told her. "The other werewolves. We had to make sure you were not attacked."

"So this Edwin is the leader of the werewolves who are attacking villages?" Roslyn asked them. Alexander nodded.

"How many can turn at will?" she asked next.

"No idea," Alexander answered her. "There were a handful left of my line, but if they bit another shaman then there could be more."

"So it has to do with magic?" Cassidy asked them.

Alexander nodded. "My magic changed the curse somehow; I was able to change whenever I wanted to."

Roslyn exhaled slowly, though she knew he had changed back to his human form earlier it was good to hear that it was actually true. She had Kavan back, that was all that mattered. The only problem was that he was acting distant since their reunion not too long ago.

"Why did you bite Kavan?" Roslyn demanded next.

Alexander shrugged and told her, "It was my nature, no matter how much I tried to fight it. I knew there were more out there, so I had to try to even the lines. Kavan lectured me on that however, so for now there are just the two of us until we can get some volunteers to join our cause."

"Volunteers?" Sully scoffed. "You have got to be kidding."

"No, Sir Sullivan, we are quite serious," Kavan answered him.

"We have frishna weapons," Cassidy told them. "We have the repelling charms. We can defeat them."

Alexander was about to argue when Roslyn held up a hand to stop him. "What if we can reverse it?"

"Impossible," Alexander told her. "Your ancestors tried to before."

"How?" Roslyn wanted to know. Alexander seemed to be at a loss for words now.

"Can I try with either of you?" Roslyn asked them next. "I can see what I can do."

"I might work best," Alexander told her. "Kavan would do anything to make you happy."

Kavan shot him a dark look, which told Roslyn that Alexander knew about their relationship.

"It would seem to be that way," Roslyn answered.

At that moment, Leaf, who had still been asleep when Roslyn had left her tent earlier, pounced into the tent looking for Roslyn. Both Alexander and Kavan startled a little, but when Kavan saw the dragonling he smiled.

"So it is true," Kavan commented as Leaf went to rub up against Roslyn's legs. "You found a dragon up in the mountain."

"Yes," Roslyn whispered. "Her name is Leaf."

Kavan seemed at a loss for words. Alexander sighed and looked at Roslyn, saying, "I was worried about this, his reaction to you. Either it would be too much for him to handle and it would cause him to change or he would try to block it so much that he would act like this."

Kavan looked at him sharply. "How am I acting?"

"Like an awkward idiot," Alexander answered. "You told me about her, how you felt. Since you can control the change, *control it*. Stop acting distant."

"Stop pressuring him," Roslyn spoke up. "A lot has happened. I know some things can be overwhelming."

Alexander looked at her now with respect. "Good, you understand," he said to her. "In the morning you can test me."

"No, as soon as we break camp we are heading straight for Base Town," Roslyn told him. "Once we are there we can experiment."

"Can you feel the runes still?" Cassidy asked him.

"No, you have moved them far enough away that they do not affect us now, though they will keep the others away still," he told her.

"We will take you to one of the covered wagons," Sully spoke up. "You will be guarded."

"I would not have expected anything else, Sir Sullivan," Kavan told him. He looked at Roslyn again and could see that she was hurting. "May I have a moment alone with Roslyn?"

Roslyn looked at her sister, and then Tiffany and Sully. Cassidy nodded and grabbed the other two by their arms. Alexander stood up and followed the three of them out of the tent.

"I would have come back to you sooner, but he bit me," Kavan explained, feeling torn. "I was unconscious for a while and then it was the full moon."

"You do not have to explain anything," she assured him. "None of this was your fault. I am just glad to have you back in one piece." She stood up and went to him, him standing to embrace her hug. She pulled away a little bit just to look at him quickly and then she leaned in to kiss him. For a moment he let her press her lips against his but he felt that it might not be safe so he pulled away.

"I'm sorry," he told her, breathing hard. "I don't want anything to happen to you."

"We have the cure." Roslyn told him. "We have the herbs to make the cure. As long as we get it into the person bit before the next full moon, it works."

"You are sure?" Kavan asked her, reaching out to hold her hands. She took them in hers and nodded.

"Cypress, one of the orcs who joined us, was bitten while he was with Cassidy in the mountains, looking for the herbs. He was treated with the potion and it cured him," Roslyn told him. She looked him straight in his gray eyes.

"I've been dreaming about a large wolf with your colour of eyes," she told him. "I wonder if I was dreaming about you."

He pulled her close and kissed her again, this time not pulling away. After a few moments Roslyn pulled back, a large smile on her face.

"It is good to have you back," she told him. "I'll walk you to the wagon."

They came out from the tent to find Rafi, Aidan, Kai and Karina standing there waiting.

"Tiffany told us you were back," Aidan spoke first, taking in the sight of his friend. "It is good to see you alive and well, my friend."

Kavan smiled at him and went to shake his hand, gripping the younger man's forearm. "It is good to see you guys too."

Rafi and Kai greeted him the same way and Karina hugged him.

"You are not afraid of me?" Kavan asked as Karina let him go.

"You are still you," Karina told him, Aidan and Rafi nodded in agreement. "Just a little different now."

Kavan's smile broadened at that and he turned to look at Roslyn who was smiling as well.

"Come on," Roslyn told him. "There will be more time to catch up once we are at Base Town."

Kavan shrugged to his friends and followed Roslyn towards where the wagons were kept.

"What is it like?" Roslyn asked him after a moment of awkward silence.

He knew she meant what it was like to be a werewolf now.

"Everything is heightened," he told her. "I can hear people across the camp talking, the horses shifting at their lines. My strength is way better, and I can run very fast."

"How did you know where to find us?" Roslyn asked him next. They had reached the wagons.

"We went to New Wardgrove first," he told her. "They told me where you were heading."

"It's good to have you back," Roslyn said again as Sully opened the canvas cover of the wagon to let Kavan go in. "We will talk more once we are in Base Town."

***

Roslyn had to put special protections on the wagon that Kavan and Alexander rode in, to keep the repelling runes from hurting them. Once they broke camp they rode hard and fast for Base Town, the other werewolves keeping their distance still.

It was just after noon when they arrived at Base Town, Lou opening the gates up for them. Cypress and the other orcs greeted them, while Karina was relieved to be with her family again. They were short on space, however, with all the people Roslyn had with her, but they all crammed into the Base Town.

"Uhm," Tiffany spoke up when she saw how much room they had left. "We might have a problem."

"I know," Roslyn told her. "If it were not for the werewolves we could have camps outside, but it would be safer to have everyone within the walls now."

Roslyn and Tiffany stood on the palisade of Base Town looking out over the land beyond. More werewolves had joined the three that Roslyn had chased off the night before, making it ten werewolves sitting just beyond the reach of the repelling runes.

"I need to talk to Alexander more," Roslyn told Tiffany as she yawned. She knew she did not sleep as much as she needed to the night before, and the emotional toll of finding Kavan alive definitely did not help.

"Do you need more of that drink?" Tiffany asked her, meaning the wake up drink.

"No, if I have more I will not sleep at all later," Roslyn told her. "I can make it through the rest of the day."

"If you are sure," Tiffany answered with a sigh. "Come with me, we have them both still in the wagon at the back of the town."

Roslyn followed her down the stairs and through the small town, weaving through the people. The horses at least had their own paddock, and there was plenty of room since the Dragon Clan had no horses of their own, just a few dozen alpacas.

Roslyn saw Cypress and the rest of the orcs who had gone ahead and he waved to her, she waving back with a smile. She had known they had made it but seeing them just set her more at ease. She saw Karina with her family and smiled, happy to see them back together even though it made her a little homesick for her own family.

She thought about the dream she had the night before and wondered if it was actually true. Was her father really in danger? What about the rest of her family back in Ellsgrove?

They reached the covered wagon and Roslyn climbed up the back, moving the canvas out of the way so she could get into the back. She saw Kavan and Alexander lounging on the benches, an empty bowl of soup beside both of them.

"Good, you have eaten," she commented. "Now, tell me more about Edwin and what he wants now."

"All I can think is that he still wants a home for the werewolves," Alexander told her. "Though there might be a bit of revenge in there as well, for what I and your ancestors did to trap them."

"Should we capture one of them and find out?" Roslyn asked him next. "That was a long time ago."

"Not to them," Kavan reminded her. "It would have been mere moments between when they fell asleep and woke up again. So much has changed up here."

"And Alexander has spent all that time trying to get past it," Roslyn looked at Alexander, feeling his gaze on her. "I am sorry you had to deal with that."

Alexander shrugged and said, "I did what I had to do to save my people."

"That is what we have in common," Roslyn told him. "They are my people to protect now."

"What does your connection with Jay'Al tell you?" Alexander asked her. "Can you tell how many werewolves are out there?"

"What do I look for?" she asked him.

"A taint," he responded. "They'll appear like blobs of taint in your vision."

Roslyn closed her eyes and reached out, feeling the land beneath her. She had not tried that connection since she was crowned Queen, but now it was interesting to explore. She could see the ten werewolves outside of Base Town but she moved beyond them. She found more of the taint on the western coast close to where they had emerged from the passage on the cliffside after coming out of the underground cavern. There were dozens of them. Pulling back in she noticed that the two blobs that were Alexander and Kavan looked different than the others.

Roslyn opened her eyes again, a troubled look in her eyes. "Why do you look different from them?"

A Weaving of the Roots

"Probably because we are at peace with what we have become," Alexander told her with a shrug. "I had no idea we would look any different in your sight."

"I think we need to send a message to Edwin," Roslyn told them next. "We need to figure this out without more people being turned."

"By all means, send a message," Alexander told her. "I have no idea what he will do."

"It is worth a try," Roslyn answered as she yawned. Kavan looked at her with concern.

"Are you okay?" Kavan asked her.

"My sleep was interrupted last night," she told him. "I will probably have an early night tonight so I am all good for tomorrow."

"So what will you do?" Alexander asked her as she turned to leave the wagon.

"I will toss them a message to take to Edwin," she told him. "Then all we can do is wait."

Kavan nodded to her as Alexander sighed. "Get some rest," Kavan told her. She smiled at him and jumped down from the wagon. Next she went to find Aidan so he could write out the message she wanted to send to Edwin.

"You really want to meet with this guy?" Aidan asked her as he finished the letter, using her seal–dragon wings over crossed blades–at the end.

"We need to get this figured out," she told him. "The only way we can do that is talk to the leader."

Aidan shrugged and handed her the letter. She rolled it up and used a leather thong to tie it shut. She left Aidan's tent and went to find Rafi, who was the best marksman with a bow and arrow that she knew. She handed the letter to him and told him what she needed him to do.

"Fine, but I want it noted that I am not happy about it," Rafi told her as he grabbed his bow and arrows, following her to the palisade. Once there he put the letter on one of his arrows and aimed at an area near the werewolves but far enough that it should not hit any of them. He let loose, and when it landed one of the werewolves grabbed the letter off of the arrow and ran off with it.

"Now we wait," Roslyn told him, putting a hand on her friend's shoulder and yawning at the same time. "I think I will go take a nap," she said. "I'll see you later."

Rafi smiled at her and watched her head to her tent.

Chapter Fourteen

Alexander looked at Kavan as Roslyn left the wagon. "She is everything you said she was," he commented. "I am impressed by everything she has accomplished."

"She is something special, hm?" Kavan said with a chuckle. "Sometimes I wonder what she sees in me."

"You are a good man," Alexander told him. "Do not question yourself. She thinks you are worthy, that is all that matters."

"You sound just like her," Kavan replied with a laugh.

"Your friends accept you?" Alexander asked him next.

"Yes, they were not even afraid."

"I wish mine had been like that," Alexander told him. "After I had helped trap Edwin and the others below ground, my people turned on me. It was best for me to leave."

"You never mentioned that before."

"It can be a painful memory, but I am glad you do not have to go through that," Alexander said, putting a hand on Kavan's arm. "You are not me, and these are very different times."

"What if Roslyn can find a way to reverse the curse?" Kavan asked him. "Would Edwin take it?"

Alexander shrugged and told him, "I have no idea, though it is hard to imagine that Edwin would give up the abilities that come with being a werewolf."

"Hopefully she can come up with something," Kavan mused. He looked down at the empty bowl of soup, still feeling a bit hungry.

"Hey Sully," he called out, "Any chance I could get seconds?"

A Weaving of the Roots

***

Cassidy sat down with Tiffany and her sister's Honour Guard outside of Roslyn's tent. She had gone in to have a nap not too long before, and the young women were looking after their weapons and armour. There was not much room to put up everyone's tents, but they knew Roslyn would get something figured out once she was awake.

Leaf curled up next to Cassidy with a large smoked fish in her mouth. Crick chirped at the dragon from her spot on Cassidy's shoulder, earning a chirp in return from the dragon.

"Is it true?" Deirdre asked Tiffany and Cassidy. "That Kavan is back and he is a werewolf?"

"Yes," Cassidy answered. "The creature we felt on the mountain turned out to be a werewolf, and he dug Kavan out of the snow before biting him."

"How awful," Baylee commented, "What does Roslyn think about that?"

"She is just happy he is alive," Tiffany responded. "He is in control of his changing abilities so he is of no harm to any of us."

"Are we sure?" Teddy asked them. "He is a werewolf after all."

"He is different from the ones that have hounded us, Roslyn and I can both feel that," Cassidy told them.

They seemed satisfied by that answer.

"Do you know why we are here to begin with, in Base Town?" Harriet asked.

"Roslyn wants to make it her capital," Tiffany told her.

"How? It's a plateau and there's all of this open plain," Deirdre commented. "And that was *a lot* of stairs."

Cassidy shrugged and told them, "I have no idea what she plans from here on out. I just know that she knows what she is doing."

Isobel groaned and said, "I *really* do not want to go up those stairs again."

"Just have faith that she knows what she is doing," Tiffany interjected. "I do."

Isobel nodded and went to go figure out their sleeping arrangements with the clerks who were still talking with Lou.

"She got a message sent to the werewolves' leader?" Deirdre asked Tiffany and Cassidy. Tiffany nodded.

"How soon do you think we will have a reply?" Baylee asked them. Both of them shrugged.

"Hopefully not too soon, so Roslyn can sleep. Speaking of which, let's leave her tent alone," Tiffany told them.

"No, it's ok," Cassidy told her, "She put a dampening spell on her tent to keep noises out, I can feel it."

"Well that must come in handy," Tiffany commented. "All right, well I am going to wander around because I am bored, anyone care to join me?"

*****

Roslyn awoke feeling finally refreshed. She sat up in bed and looked around her tent, seeing some sunlight still outside. She lowered the dampening spell on her tent, relieved to hear the normal sounds of their camp outside.

She could hear Tiffany talking outside to someone, from the accent she figured it was Lou, Karina's father.

"The message was delivered not too long ago," Lou was saying. "Do you think she will wake up soon?"

"Most likely. With everything that happened in the last day I am sure she is both emotionally and physically exhausted," Tiffany answered. "I am sure she will be up soon."

"I am awake," Roslyn called out, rubbing her eyes. "Tiffany, bring the message to me please."

Tiffany entered the tent and handed her the rolled up parchment. The binding that held it was some kind of hair braided into a string. Roslyn took the message and undid the string, opening it up to read it.

"*Greetings, Queen Roslyn,*" she read aloud. "*I am Edwin, leader of the Wolves. You have the traitor, Alexander with you. Is he your captive or your ally? If you want to meet and discuss peace, he is to be handed over to me.*"

"I think we might have a problem," Roslyn stopped reading and looked up at Tiffany.

"Maybe you should figure out if you can reverse the curse sooner than later," Tiffany suggested.

"Well, we can take him with us, just not hand him over," Roslyn told her. "I mean, that's *one* idea, anyways."

Roslyn looked back at the message, "*We have heard about your potential, and look forward to being able to try to come to some kind of truce.*"

"Oh for goodness sake…" Roslyn put the message down. "This an…thinks very highly of himself."

"Well, what do you want to do?" Tiffany asked her.

"I need to talk to Cassidy, Alexander and Kavan," Roslyn told her. "Maybe even the Ancestors and the Elders."

"Well, one step at a time, hm?" Tiffany looked concerned.

"I will start with what I had planned to begin with," Roslyn told her. "I think it would be best to start it now so our people have protection."

"What are you planning?" Tiffany asked her.

"Ah, you will just have to wait to see," Roslyn replied with a sly smile. "I will need to be left alone for a bit. No matter what happens, ground shakes or whatever, I need to be left alone."

Tiffany looked at her with raised eyebrows and then nodded.

"I will be at the bottom of the stair, but everyone should keep back," she told Tiffany as she started to get dressed. "Let Cassidy know that I am going ahead with my plan."

Tiffany nodded and left the tent, going to spread the word. Roslyn finished getting dressed and then went to the chest that was at the end of her bed, opening it and taking out a small willow sapling in a ceramic bowl. She took it with her as she headed for the bottom of the staircase that led up the side of the plateau. When she reached the area she dug a shallow hole with her hands, placing the willow sapling in the hole. She sat down on the ground a few feet away from the sapling, crossing her legs and resting her hands on her knees. She closed her eyes and focused.

Roslyn tapped into the magic of the land and her ancestors, and using that she urged the willow tree to grow, using its roots in her plan. Along with the willow's roots she called on roots of trees on the plateau to help her with what she envisioned. The ground beneath her started to shake, and rocks started falling out of the side of the plateau several feet in front of her. She could hear shouts from behind her, and Tiffany's voice telling everyone to stay calm, that it was Roslyn causing the disturbance.

After several minutes the shaking subsided and the sounds of worry and fright from Base Town stopped.

Roslyn opened her eyes again and exhaled deeply when she saw the result of her work. She smiled, happy with what she saw. She heard footsteps behind her and turned to find Karina and her father along with Cassidy, Tiffany and Sully.

"What did you do?" she heard Karina say, awe in her voice. Roslyn looked up to see Karina taking in the newly grown willow tree that was towering over them now.

"I made a tunnel with roots up to the top of the plateau," Roslyn answered. "It should take you only a couple of hours to traverse it. I'm going to put the repelling runes around the entrance to keep the werewolves away."

"Will the tunnel not be dark?" Tiffany asked her as she approached the opening of the tunnel to peer inside. She could see shafts of light coming from somewhere. Tiffany looked up the side of the plateau where the staircase had been–it was gone now. Had Roslyn absorbed it into the plateau?

"I made tunnels for light during the day, on our way up I will put crystals along the way to light the path at night," Roslyn explained, standing up. "I want everyone packed up and on the move up to the plateau within the hour. We will rest a few days before we give Edwin any kind of response, and enjoy some proper food as well."

"Oh thank the ancestors," Cassidy commented, "I am so ready for a hot meal."

Roslyn chuckled at her sister. "Me as well, dear sister. Let us get a move on, shall we?"

***

Cassidy stared in wonder at the woven roots that made up the tunnel. She rode her horse at a canter at the head of the column with Kai riding beside her. Roslyn was just in front of them, Leaf draped over the front of the saddle, Sully and Tiffany on either side. Behind Cassidy rode the Honour Guard and then the orc warriors led by Cypress, followed by Rafi, Oswick, the people of the Dragon Clan and the clerks in their wagons; this included the covered wagon with Alexander and Kavan on board. The Ellsgrove soldiers brought up the last of the column.

"This is amazing," Kai whispered as he looked at the roots as well. He peered down and noticed that there was a layer of dirt on the ground. "The ground is even."

"Magic and a bit of imagination," Roslyn called back to them. She was using her magic to attach crystals to the ceiling of the tunnel as they rode. "No need to worry about cave-ins either."

"I wonder what else you can do now," Cassidy commented.

"Some more experiments might be needed," Roslyn told her. "I look forward to it."

"What do you think about Edwin's message?" Tiffany asked Roslyn.

"Well, I know we cannot give in to him," Roslyn responded. "I wonder if I could make some sort of talisman that can make sure the wearer cannot shapeshift?

"Would the ancestors not have thought of something like that?" Cassidy inquired.

Roslyn shrugged, "We have no idea, unless Aunt Anna and Willow found something in the histories that they did not tell us, which I doubt."

Cassidy knew that their aunt would have told them if there had been any attempts. With what Roslyn was capable of doing now could it not be possible?

"I will work on a few things once we settle," Roslyn assured her. "I have a few ideas in mind."

Cassidy noticed then that Roslyn was holding a string of braided hair in her hand. Tiffany had told her that the return message from Edwin had been tied with a string of braided hair; just whose hair was it?

Chapter Fifteen

Kavan looked out at the plateau as they rode towards the villages. His life had changed up there during his first journey up the plateau, and now he was returning a little bit sooner than he would have liked. He was glad to be back with Roslyn though, and hopefully he could have some more time alone with her soon.

Alexander watched Kavan with a relaxed expression; Kavan could never tell what the older man was thinking. He had been alive for so long that Kavan was sure that Alexander had mastered hiding his emotions a long time ago. What was going through his head?

"What do you think Roslyn will do with me?" Alexander asked him. "If I know Edwin he will demand I be handed over to him."

"I do not think she will do that," Kavan assured him.

"She might not have any other choice," Alexander responded.

Kavan looked troubled at that. Even though he knew he was sire bonded to Alexander he still had formed a connection with the man as a friend in the weeks since they had first met; even though Alexander had turned him into a werewolf when they first met.

The wagon rolled to a stop and Roslyn appeared at the end of the wagon.

"Come on out, stretch your legs and let's get you to a house," she said to them, beckoning them to follow her.

"That was quite the feat," Alexander told her as he jumped down from the wagon. "The tunnel you made."

"I've learned a few things," Roslyn responded. Kavan recognized the house they were going to as the empty one they had stayed in when they had first arrived on the plateau a couple months ago.

"You will stay here for now," Roslyn told them as they entered the house. "Kai, Rafi and Oswick will stay here with you as well."

"Where will you be?" Kavan asked her.

"In my tent not too far away," she assured him. "All of Karina's people are going back to their homes, and the orcs are being brought into some of the homes as well."

"So you plan to farm the area around the plateau?" Alexander asked her. She nodded.

"With the tunnel people can be down in a few hours to take care of the crops and everything," she told him as she turned to leave. "We will build my palace up here and then have the rest of the city down there."

"Why would you build your palace here?" Alexander asked her.

"The plateau is in the middle of the continent, for one," she answered. "It is also a highly defensible position."

"Fair enough," Alexander said. "I chose it for exile because it was the farthest I could get from Edwin without crossing an ocean." Alexander sniffed the air. "What…what is that?"

"What is what?" Roslyn asked him, puzzled as he started coming closer towards her, still sniffing.

"I smell Edwin," Alexander told her. "You have something of his on you?"

Roslyn reached into her bag and pulled out the braided hair that had been wrapped around the message. Alexander grabbed it from her and brought it towards his nose.

"He used his own wolf fur," Alexander commented. "Interesting."

"This is Edwin's hair?" Roslyn looked at it with interest as Alexander handed it back. "This could actually be incredibly useful."

Roslyn left them then with a wave, promising to come back later to eat with them. The sun had begun its descent in the sky already and there was a lot to be done before there was no longer any sun at all.

"You could have traveled," Kavan commented to Alexander as he showed Alexander around the house, noting where the privy and water well were.

"And risk spreading my curse more?" Alexander said with a shake of his head. "No, I think not."

"And yet you bit me," Kavan reminded him.

"I was desperate," Alexander told him. "If I could have seen the future, that there might be another way to defeat Edwin, I would not have."

"Mh-mmm," Kavan said with a slight shake of his head. "Pick a room and I'll get a fire going. It's still a bit chilly in here."

***

Roslyn unloaded all of her mage instruments from where they had been stored in special boxes. She had barely used them since coming to Jay'Al, having used her mother's tools instead. Now though what she needed was those instruments in order to find a way to cure the werewolves.

Since she had Edwin's fur she could use that as a place to start, and hope

394

fully she would not need his blood as well. As she arranged her alchemy table Cassidy watched, fascinated by the devices. Roslyn had explained to her some of the differences in how mages did some of their work as opposed to the shamans of Jay'Al, but seeing it was something else. Shamans could make potions with certain herbs, like the one they had to stop the werewolf curse from taking over, but nothing like what Roslyn could do with her devices.

Roslyn used what she told Cassidy was a tincture and dropped a few drops of it on some of the wolf hair that was in a ceramic bowl. It fizzled a bit and then became a liquid that she then put in a flask with a spout at its top. Roslyn placed the flask over a lit candle and added a few more drops of something else before putting a lid on and connecting another flask to it by way of the spout.

"The vapours will get caught in the spout and fall into the other flask," Roslyn explained to Cassidy. "With that mixture I can use a few different spells to hopefully figure out the curse."

"Amazing," Cassidy told her. "If only our people had the means to do this the first time the werewolves were a problem. How long will it take?"

"I will check on it in the morning," Roslyn answered. "Have you had a chance to eat anything tonight?" Her sister shook her head. "Let's go see if the cooks brought anything to our friends, shall we?"

Together they left Roslyn's tent, Roslyn telling her Honour Guard to guard her tent. "I want four people guarding this tent, one on each side. No one who is not me is to get near it," she instructed them. "I will be eating with my friends."

The lady knights nodded and four were chosen to guard her tent, the rest following after Roslyn. Roslyn felt a little more relaxed, though she hoped nothing would interfere with the process that was going on within her tent. She had not known a werewolf had been on the plateau the first time, so there was no harm in taking precautions.

The sun had set a little while ago, and the paths around the village were lit with torches. The people of the Dragon Clan were happy to be home for now, and safe again. Roslyn hoped not to displace them when her palace was built, but she still had to talk to Judd, the mason that her father had sent with Maeve, about plans for a modest palace. She already knew that she would build the city in a half circle around the base of the plateau, with farms outside the city walls. It would bring a lot of commerce to the country, and once she had dealt with the Tribes of the Archipelago it would bring more trade from around the world. She was planning on building a great library as well as a Mage University that she hoped to combine both ways of magic from her two countries to be taught.

The two sisters entered the house their male friends were staying in, inhaling the scent of hot food. The Honour Guard remained outside where they would be served their own meals. The cooks had cut up a boar and had roasted the chops for them, adding roasted vegetables and buns to their meal as well. One of the cooks was still there with a cart on wheels, more food waiting for Roslyn and Cassidy since she had sent word that she would eat there. Tiffany and Karina came in just after them.

The men were all sitting at one end of the table, which was really two tables put together in the dining room to make enough for everyone. There was an empty seat next to Kavan that Roslyn took, and Cassidy sat next to Kai. Aidan handed her a wooden cup and poured some wine into it.

"So how is everyone tonight?" Roslyn asked everyone as the cook brought her a plate of food. She got mumbled responses as her friends were busying eating, making her smile.

"Sorry, Roslyn, no gravy tonight," the cook told her with a smile.

"It is fine, I know once you have more time to prepare meals in the coming days there will be some," she responded with a chuckle. "Thank you for this delicious looking meal," she added.

Alexander swallowed his bite of food and asked her, "What can we expect from Edwin?"

"Well, he wants you handed over," Roslyn told him. "If we want to do peace talks, that is."

"I figured he would," Alexander responded. "What do you plan on doing?"

"Nothing yet," she said before she took a bite.

"I told you she would not hand you over to him," Kavan told Alexander.

Roslyn swallowed her food and took a sip of wine. "Definitely not," Roslyn assured him. "I am working on something."

"Kavan has told me to trust you," Alexander told her. "I am trying to. Your acceptance of him has been astonishing to see, since my own people cast me out at the end."

"You have seen my group of friends, right?" she asked him. "I have been different my whole life. It would not do for me to hate someone else just because they are different as well."

"Here-here," Cassidy said, raising her own cup of wine. Everyone else at the table copied her, and the chorus went around the group, making Roslyn smile. Alexander looked slightly perplexed.

"We are a new generation," Roslyn told him. "We are the ones who will change the world."

Just then a messenger came into the house, with one of Aidan's messenger birds in his hands. He went straight to Aidan who took the small message satchel off of the bird's legs. He noticed the sigil and looked up at Roslyn.

"It is from Chief Erick," he told her as he handed the message to her.

Roslyn opened the message and started reading, only for her eyes to widen in surprise at the words in the brief message.

"What is it?" Cassidy asked her. Roslyn looked up at her and then at Kavan.

"A ship came from the direction of the whirlpools," she told them. "The water kingdom of Kyprago wishes to make an alliance with me."

"Kyprago?" Alexander asked her. "Are you sure?"

"Who are they?" Roslyn asked him.

"Merfolk," was the answer. "Though they have not been seen since my early time."

"Does it say anything else?" Cassidy inquired as she popped a bite of roasted potato in her mouth.

Roslyn looked back down at the message and continued reading, only to gasp as she read a certain name.

"Heath," she stuttered. "Heath was on the ship with the Kypragons. He's alive."

Chapter Sixteen

Heath accepted the cup of wine from Keaton and sat down at the table with Chief Erick, his sons, and Nadim. They were sitting down for the evening meal after a day of planning: Heath and the Kypragons were going to be heading inland to meet Roslyn at the plateau. Supplies, wagons and horses had to be gathered for the journey, so they had been busy most of the day and Heath found that he was very hungry.

"Your kingdom sounds fascinating," Erick was telling Nadim. Nadim had spent the last few minutes describing the underwater kingdom of Kyprago to him. "Though how would normal humans be able to visit it?"

"My king said he would figure that out when the time came," Nadim answered him, amused at what his king had told him when he had voiced the same question before he had left Kyprago. "I have no idea right now about whatever it could be."

"The island above is large and quite nice," Heath told them. "An outpost could definitely be built, along with a harbour for trade. There were many exotic fruits growing there."

"That does sound lovely," Keaton commented. "I cannot wait to travel the world someday soon."

"If Jay'Al and Kyprago can form an alliance, you might just be able to without having to go through the Sea of Ice," Heath told him. A servant brought in a platter of food just then, and Heath could smell the braised lamb and roasted vegetables. His mouth started watering and his stomach made a gurgling sound.

"Go ahead, young man," Erick told him with a chuckle. "Fill your plate and start eating."

Heath did so, eating as the others talked about different things. Nadim really liked the architecture of Hyena City, with their columns, open courtyards and waterways. He particularly liked all of the open gardens.

"I love to tend the earth," Nadim told their hosts. "It is very soothing."

"Interesting, a merman who loves to garden," Erick commented. "There is much you could learn from our gardeners here, I think."

"I look forward to it," Nadim told him with a smile. "Thank you."

"I have noticed that your soldiers have frishna metal weapons," Keaton mentioned as they ate. "Where did you get it from?"

"We mine it as well," Nadim informed him. "Just from under the continent along the ocean."

"Interesting. Do you have more than one mine?" Erick asked him.

"Just the one. We have not needed to make more weapons in a long time since we isolated ourselves."

"I see. Do you have blacksmiths who know how to use it?" Heath asked him. "I saw nothing that looked like a forge."

Nadim shook his head and answered, "Like I said, we have not needed to make new weapons in a long time."

"We have a few blacksmiths here who are capable of working with the metal," Erick told him. "If things go wrong with the werewolves we may need to make more weapons."

"Where are your frishna mines?" Nadim asked them.

"To the north, where the werewolves first attacked," Gabe informed him. "We may need another source of the metal."

"That could be arranged," Nadim mused. "I would have to talk to my king first if it was needed."

"Hopefully things do not get out of control," Nadim told them after he had taken a sip of his wine. "The werewolves could wreak havoc across your country if they wanted to."

"Well, let us hope that Roslyn can figure out how to deal with them, hm?" Heath spoke up. He was taking another bite of food when a messenger came through the door, handing Chief Erick a small rolled up message.

Erick opened it and started reading, telling them, "It is from Roslyn."

Heath leaned forward on the table, eager for the news. Erick glanced up at him once while he read the message, a slightly perplexed look on his face. Finally he put the message down and took a hearty drink from his cup.

"What is it father?" Keaton asked him with a raised eyebrow.

"Roslyn says they are safe atop the plateau but the werewolves are nearby. She is beyond happy that you, Heath, are alive, and as much as she wants to see you for herself she wants us to stay here. She also informs us that Kavan survived the avalanche on the mountain and is with them now. There is more she has to tell us but cannot just yet."

"By the ancestors," Keaton exclaimed as Heath struggled to process what Erick just told him.

"Wow," Heath said finally. "Kavan is alive!" He was honestly relieved to hear that his friend, and rival for Roslyn's affections, was alive. The werewolves being there was a definite problem.

"How does she expect us not to do anything about the werewolves that are there?" Gabe spoke up finally. "Should we not do something?"

"She must have some kind of plan," Heath assured them. "I know she does."

Keaton nodded and added, "I agree. We should prepare our defenses in case the werewolves come this way."

"Someone needs to talk to the Tribes," Gabe commented. "They need to be informed about what is going on."

"I will send a messenger in the morning," Erick told them. "Their ambassador arrived a few days ago to discuss Everett's incarceration, so we will have a lot to talk about since I have been putting him off."

Heath chuckled at that and asked, "Who did they send?"

"A man named Jonah," Erick told him.

"Short and stocky, silver-blond hair?" Heath inquired, thinking it might be someone he had known.

"Yes, that would definitely describe him," Keaton answered for his father. "You know him?"

"We were friends once," he replied.

"Well he had been very insistent on meeting with me, but as I said I have been putting him off," Erick informed Heath. "I guess I will have to meet with him soon though."

"Let me know when you go, I would like to be there, discreetly," Heath told him.

Erick nodded, one eyebrow raised. "I will let you know."

"Thank you," Heath said to him. "It will be interesting to hear any news from home."

***

Heath watched through the screen as Erick met with Jonah in the room on the other side of the hollow wall. He had not aged much in the last few years it seemed, but he had chosen to cut his hair short after wearing it long like Heath remembered. The slightly older man was wearing the traditional sailor outfit much like the one Heath had worn when he first met Roslyn. Now Heath felt more comfortable in the alpaca wool leggings and tunic that Nadim's wife had made for him.

They were in the meeting room of Erick's home, sitting now at the table.

"Thank you for meeting with me," Jonah was telling Erick, though from the hint in his voice Heath knew that in his mind his old friend was thinking 'Finally' as well.

"I wanted to inform you of the change of power amongst the Tribes of the Archipelago," Jonah continued. "After much infighting these last months, several leaders are out of the picture. We have a new leader, our Commandant

Mortimer."

Heath knew that name well, a rival of his father's, though he had been several years younger. What did that mean for his father? Was his father even still alive? What did that mean for the rest of Heath's family back home?

"I see, and what does that mean exactly?" Erick asked him.

"Our Commandant wants to make treaties with Jay'Al *and* Ellsgrove," Jonah explained. "He also has pardoned Captain Heath and his crew, who we have been told are working with Princess Roslyn."

"Queen Roslyn," Erick corrected him.

"Oh? I was not aware that her father had died–"

"She is Queen of Jay'Al," Erick interjected.

"Oh…I see," Jonah took a moment to try to figure out what to say. "Do you know where Captain Heath and his crew are now? Or are they to be assumed as still traveling with your queen?"

Erick glanced at the screen that Heath was standing behind in the hollow part of the wall and nodded. Inhaling deeply, Heath lifted the latch that closed the hidden door and walked out into the meeting room. Jonah turned in surprise and then his expression changed to one of delight.

"Heath!" his old friend exclaimed in greeting as he took a few steps towards him. Heath met him half way and embraced his old friend. "It is very good to see you."

"You as well," Heath told him. "Tell me, what has happened to my father?"

The smile was wiped instantly from Jonah's face. "Heath…your father is dead. So is your older brother. They were killed in the power struggle."

Heath took a step back. "I cannot say I am sad to hear of my father's passing, but my brother Graydon deserved better."

"It may comfort you then to hear that Graydon had switched sides before the end," Jonah explained. "He was trying to negotiate terms with your father and a few others when the worst of the fighting broke out."

"And my mother?"

He saw Jonah's expression change again and knew that it was not good news either. "She took her own life after their deaths."

Heath stumbled back, tears welling in his eyes.

"You are now the head of your family," he heard Jonah tell him. "Commandant Mortimer would like to see you come home."

Chapter Seventeen

Roslyn paced around her tent. She had slept terribly the night before after receiving the message from Chief Erick. She had sent a message back right away, but the thought that Heath was alive still had been what kept her awake. Also, *merfolk*?! There were too many thoughts going through her head.

She stopped to look at her alchemy table and saw the liquid in the second flask. It had turned a dark blue colour, which was promising. Now she just had to do a few more tests, but right now her mind was still reeling.

"Calm down, Roslyn," she said aloud to herself as she forced herself to sit down on the end of her bed. "Focus."

Leaf nudged her foot as she curled up next to her. The dragon had been watching her from the doorway of the tent, but now she used her own magic to calm Roslyn down.

"Thank you," Roslyn whispered to Leaf as the dragon put her head on her lap, a vibrating sound emanating from her that was not that far off from a cat's purr. Roslyn felt her body relax and her mind calm so she breathed in deeply and then out again.

"Okay, let us focus on what comes first," Roslyn said to Leaf as she stood up and went over to her alchemy table.

Roslyn reached for the dried herbs that were used for the potion that would stop the werewolf curse before the full moon. She needed to test their properties now against the liquid in the flask, but first she needed to do the same to them as she had to the fur, though it would take way less time to get a final result. She got to work, Leaf jumping up on Roslyn's bed and curling up in the middle of it. Roslyn glanced at her familiar and chuckled upon seeing that she now took up most of the bed.

First Roslyn took a bit of the dried moonroot and crushed it up, placing it in a flask and adding a tincture to it. She did the same with the other two herbs, placing them over heat and putting the spouted top on them, each with a different connected flask. She was so busy with what she was doing that she did not notice Kavan standing in the doorway.

Kavan cleared his throat, making her startle. She whirled around to see who it was, stopping herself when she recognized who it was.

"Sorry," he mumbled an apology. "Just wanted to see if you were coming to join us for breakfast."

"Is it that time already?" she walked towards the opening and squinted at the sunlight. "Seems past breakfast now," she added with disappointment, her stomach starting to rumble.

Kavan smiled at her and produced some fruit pastries from his bag for her. "I figured you would miss breakfast," he explained. "The cooks made these special for you."

"You know me too well," she joked as he handed them to her. She bit into one of the pastries to find sweetened blueberries within. She groaned as the taste hit her palate and she closed her eyes, enjoying the flavour and earning a chuckle from Kavan.

"That good, hm?" He teased her.

"I was very hungry, OK," she replied as she opened her eyes, taking another bite. "Could you bring Alexander here? I think I need something from him."

Kavan nodded and turned to leave the tent, crossing paths with Tiffany as he did so.

"Good, he brought you something to eat," Tiffany commented when she saw Roslyn eating. "I was worried about you."

"I am going to need some of that wake up drink," Roslyn told her. "I slept horribly."

"I can imagine," Tiffany responded as she turned to the opening of the tent. "She needs the drink!" Tiffany shouted out the opening. Roslyn heard Sully reply and a moment later Sully was there with a cup of the wake up drink.

"Sweetened as you like it," Sully told her as he handed it to her. "Do you need anything else?"

"Thank you, Sully. Nothing for now, though I might need a reminder for lunch," she told him.

Alexander entered the tent as Roslyn started sipping from her cup, and Roslyn indicated for him to sit.

"How are you this morning?" Roslyn asked him. "You settling in nicely? Kavan told me you had been living in a cave, so this must be quite the change."

"I slept pretty well last night," he answered. "Yes, quite the change. Kavan said you needed something from me."

"I need your blood," she told him without further preamble. "I might also need some of Edwin's blood but how we can get that right now, I have no idea."

"I see. Well, I can definitely give you mine, though…would it have to be fresh blood of Edwin's?"
Alexander asked her.

"I mean, preferably, but if you have some old blood available I could try it out," she told him.

"I might have something," Alexander responded. "Let me give you my blood first and then I will go get it."

Roslyn took a syringe from her table and placed a new needle on it, and instructed Alexander to give her his arm. She drew blood from a vein in the inside of his elbow. When she was done she took the syringe over to her table, emptying a bit of it into another clean flask.

"I will be back in a few moments," Alexander told her has he stood up. "I left it hidden up the mountain."

She blinked and he was gone in a blur. Could Kavan run that fast? Of course he could, she chided herself. Kavan was a werewolf too.

Focusing on the flask with the blood, she marked it with her magic, placing an 'A' on the side of the flask. She added a tincture to it and did the same as the other flasks. Alexander returned as she was placing the flask on a flame. He had in his hands what looked like a wolf's canine with a lot of blood clotted inside of it. It was remarkably well reserved, as if by magic.

"This was Edwin's," Alexander explained as he handed it to her. "During our last battle it got embedded in my shield, and I…uh…pulled it out."

"This might just work," she told him and she offered him a clay bowl to place the tooth into. "Thank you for this."

"Whatever I can do to help," he responded. "If you need anything else, you know where I will be."

Roslyn watched him leave, relieved that he had turned out to be on their side. She wondered how life in Jay'Al had been in his time; they had the frishna armour and weapons, so what had the society been like? Alex-ander had even known about the merfolk. It would be fascinating to learn more about that part of her peoples' history. Roslyn thought that some archaeologi-cal expeditions would be one of the first things she would fund after building a university there. She definitely knew a few archaeologists from her time at the Mage University who would love to do just that.

Roslyn got to work, at first splitting the tooth in half. She was not going to use all of it at once; she had a teacher once who made sure that they never used all of their special ingredients for one experiment. Next she ground the part of tooth and blood up using her mortar and pestle. By the time she had this last piece of her experiment over the heat, the flasks with the herbs were done. She was transferring the herbal concoctions into three new flasks when

Cassidy brought her some food to eat.

"Thank you," Roslyn said to her sister as she accepted the bowl with steaming meat dumplings and rice in it. She inhaled the spices and popped one of the dumplings in her mouth, inhaling a bit because of how hot the dumpling was.

"How are things going?" Cassidy asked her, looking at the mess of Roslyn's alchemy table.

"Honestly, it has been amazing," Roslyn told her once she finished chewing. "I think we might just have something here."

"Truly?" Cassidy tried not to be sceptical, but if their ancestors could not find a complete cure before then why could Roslyn find one now?

Roslyn heard the tone in her sister's voice and frowned. "Cassidy, the Mage University has been doing research and experiments on different things for a long time. I do not know what equipment our ancestors had the first time around but I doubt it was any of this," she waved a hand towards her alchemy table. "I was taught to do this kind of thing, and honestly it hurts that you think I should not be able to do it."

"I am sorry, sister," Cassidy pulled her into a hug. "I did not mean to hurt you, I just…I don't know…feel at a loss to help."

"We will need a delivery system that encompasses a large area," Roslyn told her. "Maybe you could come up with something?"

"How do you make those special freeze bombs?" Cassidy asked her. "I think a few of those things might do the trick."

Chapter Eighteen

Nadim was meditating in one of the shallow pools that Erick had in one of his open garden courtyards when Heath found him, still fully in human form. Nadim opened one of his eyes to see who it was who was about to interrupt him before he closed it again with a light sigh.

"You seem shaken," Nadim commented without opening his eyes. "How was the meeting with the ambassador?"

"My parents and older brother are dead," Heath sputtered out the words. Nadim opened his eyes wide to look at his friend. "There was a power struggle, a new leader…he wants me to go home, he pardoned me."

"That is a lot to digest," Nadim spoke as he stood up, using his magic to draw the water out of his trousers. "Have you told Everett yet?"

Heath shook his head.

"I see. Will you tell him?"

"Of course I am going to tell him…I just…need it to process more for myself."

Nadim nodded in understanding. "Come meditate with me then," he told Heath as he sat back down in the water. "It might help you process. I am sorry for your losses."

Heath sighed and walked over to the pool, taking off his shoes and socks first before sitting down opposite of Nadim, legs crossed and hands resting on his knees. He closed his eyes, trying to let his mind go blank. After a few moments he felt himself floating, his astral form taking shape against his will. He found himself drifting away from his body, and he decided to let it happen to see where his subconscious mind wanted him to go, though from the general direction he knew that his mind just wanted to see Roslyn.

Across the desert his astral form went, using the rivers to maintain his form. There was plenty of moisture in the plains between the desert and the plateau as well to sustain him. Finally he got to what he assumed was Base Town, only to find it empty and a good handful of large wolves sitting waiting just beyond the gate. He went into the town, heading for the stair that Erick had told him about. Though he did not find a stair, he found a large tunnel made out of woven roots that must lead up to the top of the plateau. Feeling Roslyn's magic in it he knew that she had created it; just how powerful was she now?

He followed the tunnel up, marveling at how the roots were used to reinforce the tunnels. There were shafts of light here and there that let the daylight in, but around the rest of the tunnel were the crystals that Roslyn had created to expel light. Heath thought it was a really good idea to create a tunnel like that, and from the feel of the magic he had felt at the entrance to the tunnel, it was protected from the werewolves. The top of the plateau would definitely be a good defensible position.

Heath made it through to the plateau within minutes. He followed the wagon wheel tracks to a village near a lake, where there were a few large tents set up around the village. He could see the Ellsgrovian soldiers standing guard in a perimeter around the village and tents.

So far he kept himself hidden from them as he tried to find Roslyn's tent.

He recognized her tent and moved towards it, stopping as he saw her come out through the opening, a silver dragon the size of a large hunting dog following behind her. He admired the dragon from afar, watching the both of them as they headed for the village. He was floating there when the dragon stopped in its tracks and turned to look at him, cocking its head to one side as if curious. Wait, could the dragon see him? As the dragon started to move towards him Heath opened his eyes in his physical form and pondered about the dragon being able to see him.

"Feeling better now?" Nadim asked him as he stood up again and dried his trousers for the second time.

"A little bit," he replied, standing up as well and drying his own trousers. "I need to go talk to Everett now."

He headed for Chief Erick's study, finding him there at his desk.

"Sir," Heath said as he knocked on the doorframe. "I need to see my brother, please."

"Of course," Erick responded, knowing exactly what Heath needed to tell his brother. "I will get Keaton to take you down there."

Moments later Keaton was leading him back down to the dungeon. Keaton left him at the guard room, letting him go to his brother's cell by himself. Steeling himself, Heath approached the door and opened the small window.

"Brother," he called out. "I have news from home."

"Oh, do tell me brother."

"Do you remember Mortimer?" Heath inquired of his brother.

"Of course," Everett responded. "He was the leader of the southern isles."

"He is now leader of the whole of the Archipelago," Heath explained.

"Father is dead, I presume, if Mortimer is the Commandant of the Tribes," Everett said after a moment of silence.

"Along with Graydon…and mother," Heath told him. "Commandant Mortimer wants me to come home to take control of our family."

"I…see," came the response, sadness evident in the words.

"I have chosen to head to the archipelago," Heath told him. "I want you to come with me."

Silence.

"You would leave your precious Roslyn?" Everett asked him after several moments.

"I know she will understand."

"How did mother die?" Everett asked him.

Heath closed his eyes, trying not to imagine what Jonah had told him. "She took her own life."

Everett swore, and Heath thought he heard the sound of a fist hitting the wall.

"I will go with you," Everett told him.

"I will talk to Erick and hopefully we will be sailing soon," Heath told him. "Until then, brother."

***

Roslyn noticed Leaf's strange behaviour instantly, feeling through their connection that Leaf saw something that was not supposed to be there. An image flashed in Roslyn's mind, a person standing there that Roslyn herself could not see; it looked like Heath, though slightly transparent. It looked like an astral projection to Roslyn. The image faded and Leaf stopped in her tracks, confused at the sudden disappearance of the man only she could see.

"I do not know how he did it," Roslyn told Leaf as the dragon rejoined her in walking towards the village. "It looked like Heath was astral projecting himself here."

"*Checking in on you maybe?*" Leaf's voice echoed in the back of her mind. Roslyn shrugged but could not help but smile: both Heath and Kavan were alive! She hoped she would be able to see Heath in person soon.

Roslyn walked into the house her friends were staying in and was greeted by Rafi and Oswick who were sitting in front of the fire with cups of hot cocoa.

"How goes whatever it is you have been doing?" Rafi asked her, making her chuckle.

"Surprisingly well," Roslyn told him. "I will have to test it though."

"Who will you test it on?" Kavan asked as he came into the room from the kitchen, holding his own steaming cup. "Myself, or Alexander?"

"Neither," Roslyn answered him. "I want to catch one of the werewolves from below and test it on them."

"Well that sounds like *so* much fun," Oswick quipped. "I think I will stay here by the fire."

"I was not going to ask you to help anyways," Roslyn retorted. "I will need Kavan and Alexander, Cassidy, Karina, and Kai."

"I can go get your sister and Kai," Rafi told her. "They went for a walk a little while ago."

"Thank you," Roslyn told him. Rafi got up from his seat and Roslyn took his place. "Is there anymore hot cocoa?" she asked her friends. "I could use a cup right now."

Kavan smiled at her and turned to head back to the kitchen, saying, "Of course there is some for you." He returned within moments with a steaming cup for her. She accepted it with a smile and a 'thank you'.

"How do you plan on trapping one?" Kavan asked her as he leaned against the wall next to the fireplace. Leaf was already curled up next to the coals.

"Going to use you and Alexander as bait," she answered as she tentatively sipped the hot cocoa.

"I am betting they will want to capture Alexander. Lure a few out, hit 'em with my cure, and haul them away fast."

"Definitely staying here," Oswick mumbled into his cup, earning a chuckle from his friends.

"Should be entertaining at least," Alexander spoke up from where he had been standing in the doorway to the kitchen. "Hopefully it works." He smiled broadly. "When do we leave?"

***

Kavan helped Roslyn load the round containers that had what looked like blue smoke inside into a wagon. There were only a handful of them, but it was all they needed for this part of the experiment. He had seen her alchemy table, the contents of the flasks still bubbling away as more of the cure was being made.

Karina sat at the front of the wagon, ready to take it down the tunnel. Cassidy had readied their horses with Kai's help, and Alexander was waiting nearby as he scratched Leaf's head. Cypress had joined them once he heard of Roslyn's plan, and he was waiting nearby.

Kavan was nervous. If Roslyn's cure worked then he could go back to being fully human again; but would he miss the perks that came with being a werewolf? His speed, his hearing…he was unsure of what he wanted to do. Was there a way he could keep those aspects, but not be able to physically turn into his werewolf form? He would have to ask Roslyn when he had a chance.

Roslyn mounted her horse, the one that Tiffany's brother had gifted her. Tiffany and the Honour Guard were not pleased that they were not included in Roslyn's plans, but Roslyn assured them that she would not be in any danger.

"I will not be even remotely close to the werewolves," she had told them. "Trust me."

Kavan mounted his horse as well, and everyone else followed suit. Karina urged the horse pulling the wagon to get moving and they headed towards the tunnel. It took less time for them to descend the plateau through the tunnel than the first time they had used it since they were a much smaller party this time.

"Where are the other orc clans located?" Karina asked Cypress. "You are the North Snow Clan, what are the others?"

"There are two smaller ones," Cypress explained, "The Desert Clan, where most of my Clan heads during the winter, and the Hill Clan to the east. Messengers were sent to them, so they will send envoys to meet with Roslyn soon probably. Or they are waiting for the werewolf issue to be dealt with."

"Probably a wise decision," Roslyn spoke up. "Though hopefully we can resolve it soon."

"So how are you going to use us as bait?" Alexander asked Roslyn as they approached the end of the tunnel. Roslyn would need to remove the runes that repelled the shapeshifters so Alexander and Kavan would be able to go through, which she was about to do now.

"You two will turn into your wolf forms and go out, mock them a bit, and then lure them back into one of the buildings where we will be waiting with my potion," Roslyn told him as she dismounted and went to the opening of the tunnel so she could remove the runes. Once they were outside she would put the runes back up, so she ushered them through and did that.

"Really?" Alexander asked her.

"What, you think we can jump them out there on the plain? 'Here doggy, let me throw this at you, just standing still'? In an enclosed room we can hit them better. I think I have the perfect building in mind, the Dining Hall where there is a balcony. There are also two doors, so you lure them in through the one side and then go out the other side."

"You do make a good point," Alexander told her with a sigh. "Fine. Show us where the building is."

Roslyn and most of the group had been to the Dining Hall already during their first time at Base Town. The Dining Hall was a log building with two stories, two gallery balconies on either side of the hall with stairs up to each side. The tables had already been taken down and pushed to the sides of the hall, the stools piled in one corner. A thin layer of dust had already settled on the building even though it had not been abandoned long.

Kavan watched Alexander as he assessed the Hall. Kavan knew there was no other building that would work for the ambush Roslyn had planned. Kavan nodded to Roslyn and went through the door on the other side of the Hall that led to the kitchen so he could shapeshift in privacy. Alexander followed him after a moment.

Roslyn had the group split up, sending Cypress, Kai and Karina over to the one balcony with Roslyn and Cassidy taking the other side. They each had one of the glass balls with the smoke in it, and would have to aim them carefully.

Kavan and Alexander came out of the kitchen area in their wolf forms and after a quick glance at Roslyn they headed out in search of any of the other werewolves to lure into their trap.

"What if something goes wrong?" Cassidy asked Roslyn as they waited. Roslyn was using her magic to hide them from sight and smell so the werewolves would not detect them before the trap was sprung.

Roslyn shrugged and told her, "We can only control so many things. We will deal with anything that happens when it happens." She leaned against the railing of the balcony while she waited.

It did not take long before they heard the sounds of wolves howling and barking nearby. Everyone was attentive as the sounds grew closer until Alexander burst through the one door of the Hall followed by Kavan. They headed straight for the other door on the other side which had been left partially open for them. Two of the werewolves who had harassed them before came through the door next, sniffing for their prey. Roslyn used her magic to pull the door closed as the two werewolves got to the middle of the room. Both of the werewolves jumped and turned in circles looking up at them on the balconies. Roslyn took the chance to throw her potion down as did the others; the glass broke open and the smoke seemed to cling to the werewolves as they howled with rage.

The two werewolves collapsed on the dirt floor as their bodies started to change back to their human forms. The smoke had been absorbed into their bodies and now the potion was doing what it was supposed to. Roslyn and her friends watched the painful change back to human form, Roslyn wondering if Kavan went through that each time he changed.

Finally the change was over, some leftover wolf hair falling off of the bodies of the two now naked men who were unconscious. Cypress covered them with a piece of canvas and appraised Roslyn with new respect.

"What?" she asked him, hands on her hips. "Did you think it would not work?"

Cypress smiled and shrugged, telling her, "I am not sure of what I expected. Maybe them melting or blowing up?" That earned a laugh from Kai and Karina. "Good job, my Queen."

Alexander and Kavan came through the door that led to the kitchen, fully dressed. Alexander looked at the men on the floor and appraised Roslyn the same way that Cypress had.

"You can dress them," Roslyn told him as she turned towards the stairs.

"I'm going to check the perimeter." She glanced at Cassidy and then Karina, both who started to follow her out of the Hall.

Chapter Nineteen

Heath looked out over the ocean as Jonah's ship cut through the waves. He had left Nadim in Jay'Al so the ambassador could meet with Roslyn. Everett stood beside him, his wrists held together in manacles that would keep him from using his magic. Everett had questioned him about the need for them but Heath told him he either wears the manacles and can be on deck with him, or he can stay in a cell below.

They had set sail from Jay'Al three days before and now they were just coming up to the outer islands that made up the archipelago that Heath had called home for the first part of his life. Jonah joined them, having left a second ambassador in Jay'Al. Jonah had explained to Heath that his main mission was to find Heath if he was alive and make sure he got the pardon, then bring him home. Now his old friend was making sure that Heath made it home.

"What do you think Mortimer will do with me?" Everett asked his brother.

"Do you think you can live under his banner?" Heath asked back. "You could swear fealty to him as our Commandant."

"You think he will accept that?" Everett inquired. "You knew him before, what kind of man is he?"

"I was young when I met him," Heath told his brother. "I barely remember the man. If Jonah trusts him though, then I do too."

"Did Commandant Mortimer pardon Maeve and Jackson as well?" Everett asked him next.

"Yes."

"That was nice of him," Everett commented. "So he wants to form alliances with the rest of the world, hm?"

"That is what Jonah says."

"What about your merfolk friends?" Everett asked him. Everett still found it hard to believe that their ancestors had been merfolk who had chosen to stay human.

"Nadim said King Ullas would send an ambassador to the Archipelago as well, they should arrive around the same time as us."

Everett remained quiet for a time, leaving Heath to think about certain things. He had not been home in several years, since he had defected during the Wars. He had left behind several friends, including Jonah, and now he wondered if all of them were still alive. *I guess I will find out*, he thought to himself. *I miss Selene.* He thought of his cat, and he had no idea where she was at that point. Had she stayed with Maeve on her ship, or had Jackson taken her in?

Finally on the horizon he could see the island of Coin where he had grown up. He swallowed hard, knowing he would never see his mother again. That was the hardest part of going home: graves awaited him. He sighed heavily, earning a look from his brother.

"Can we go see her first?" Everett asked him, guessing about the sigh.

"Yes," was all he could say. He tried to remember the last time he had seen her: she had been making bread, kneading the dough with her fists. He would miss those loaves of bread.

Jonah walked up to them, and Heath turned to tell him that he wanted to visit his mother's grave first.

"Of course," Jonah answered. "Commandant Mortimer will understand. We will drop you off at your town and then go ahead to the Isle of Mast and wait for you outside the Commandant's House."

Jonah directed the captain to head to the south of the island where they docked at a small wharf. Heath remembered his last time there, with Jackson and Maeve and the ship that had been theirs. That ship had been broken apart on the shores of Ellsgrove during the Wars. That seemed like a lifetime ago.

Heath walked down the gangplank with Everett close behind him. They knew where the cemetery was and they headed there. The path had been worn down a lot, and Heath remembered it as being slightly overgrown the last time he had been there when his grandfather had died. The cemetery was on a cliff above the town where Heath grew up, overlooking the ocean. There were three fairly fresh graves with headstones that Heath headed for.

He saw their names etched into the headstones and he fell to his knees, Everett beside him doing the same.

"Do you think if we had been here, she would not have done it?" Everett asked him. "If she had known that you were alive?"

"You never told her?" Heath stared at his brother.

"No," came the whispered reply. "Father told us that until we knew for sure, until we *saw* you, we were not to tell her."

"Then is it not on me," Heath said, looking at the headstones. "He made the choice."

A Weaving of the Roots

Everett looked at Heath and then at the headstones again before sighing. "You are right. We knew you were alive, we should have told her."

"What is done is done," Heath told him. "Will you stand with me now?"

Everett nodded as Heath pulled him up to his feet. "Yes, brother. I am with you."

Heath reached out and unlocked the manacles, letting them fall at his brother's feet.

"Good," Heath said. "Let's go meet with Commandant Mortimer."

The smaller islands were connected with some of the close-by larger islands with rope bridges. The two brothers used one of those bridges now, passing other people as they went. The bridges were wide enough for four to walk abreast and had been sturdily built so as to withstand high winds. Support columns had even been built up out of the water below for some of the bridges that spanned slightly further distances. The original builders had even used some of the natural rock formations between islands as supports so some of the bridges were built in zig-zag formations because of this. Of course, the bridges were maintained monthly because of their importance for traversing the archipelago.

The main island of Mast was the largest of the archipelago and had hundreds of cedar trees growing around its shores. The houses were made of stone, whereas the businesses were built of wood. The Commandant's House was the largest building in the centre of the island, several stories tall and built of both stone and wood. The top of the building was shaped like a ship, and there was a lookout at the top of it.

Heath and Everett passed by the Gunsmith shop, where some of the best guns were made. Heath had left his gun back in Hyena City and thought about getting a new one, but that would have to wait. He could smell the forges from the street outside.

There were hundreds of people going about their day as the two brothers headed for the Commandant's House. A cart rolled by pulled by a miniature horse, the cart laden with fruits from one of the other islands. Jonah and his men were waiting for them at the steps of the building, and as the two brothers reached them Jonah nodded to them and headed up the steps ahead of them.

The main door to the Commandant's House were large double doors, inlaid with mother-of-pearl designs of ships on the sea. As Heath looked at it he thought he noticed something he had not seen before: what looked like a merfolk tail splashing out of the water, just at where the two doors met. Jonah opened the doors so Heath could not look at it further at that moment. How had he not noticed that before? Part of their history had displayed there his whole life and he had never noticed it.

It had been a long time since he had been in the Commandant's house.

Much of the inside was decorated with the theme of ships and the open sea, a lot of blues and sand colours, seashell designs and water fountains that looked like coral reefs. The sconces on the walls were shaped like whales, the windows shaped like the windows in the hull of a ship.

Jonah led them to the Commandant's office where two men stood guard on either side of the door, both with a gun at their left hip, a short sword at their right hip. When they saw Jonah they nodded, and one of them reached out and opened the door for them. Jonah ushered Heath and Everett through the door and then the guard closed it behind them.

"Greetings," the man sitting at the desk at the other side of the room spoke as he stood up. He wore a sailor's hat with a large feather sticking out of it, and wore a much nicer looking version of sailor's garb than Heath had ever seen: fine silks and velvet instead of just cotton and leather. His boots were almost knee high and made of very fine leather. His silky gold hair he had held back in a queue with a leather thong. His face was slightly weathered and tanned for a middle-aged man.

"Heath, it is good to see you again," the man spoke to Heath. "I am glad to see you alive and well."

"Commandant Mortimer," Heath greeted him with a slight bow. "Thank you, sir."

"And you brought your brother Everett with you I see," Mortimer commented. "Do you trust him, Heath?"

"Yes, sir."

"I see. Everett, will you swear yourself to me as your Commandant?" Mortimer asked Heath's brother.

Everett got down on one knee and bowed his head, saying, "I swear my fealty to you, Commandant Mortimer. I will serve you."

Mortimer let out a sigh of relief. "Thank you, Everett. You may stand." He looked at Jonah and then Heath. "Jonah sent word about the merfolk. The ancient kingdom of Kyprago still stands, it seems. You have been there, Heath?"

"I have. An ambassador should be arriving shortly to talk with you."

"What did you learn while you were there?" Mortimer asked him next. "Tell me about our distant cousins."

"You know that we are descended from them?" Heath inquired, surprised.

"When I became Commandant I was allowed to read some of our ancient texts," Mortimer informed him. "Where our people came from was included in them."

"Amazing," Jonah commented. "What can you tell us, Heath?"

"Nadim, the merman that saved my life, taught me how to unlock more of my magic," Heath told them. "It was very interesting learning how to do more."

"Can you show us?" Jonah asked him.

Heath called on his magic and made a ball of frozen ice appear in his hand. "I can shoot daggers of ice too," he told them. "Take water out of things to dry them."

"That is very useful," Mortimer commented. "If we gathered up everyone who has the water magic, could you teach them as well?"

"Perhaps," Heath responded. "Though there is a chance not everyone will have the same innate abilities that I do."

"I see," Mortimer went over to his desk and leaned on it. "Are the whirlpools their way of protecting themselves from the outside world?" He asked Heath.

"Yes."

"If they form an alliance with us, will they get rid of the whirlpools?" Mortimer asked him next.

"I believe so, yes."

"That sounds promising then. It will be interesting to finally have peace with the mainlands, and renewed relations with our cousins," Mortimer commented. "I have sent an ambassador to Ellsgrove as well. He informs me that Maeve was there, and he gave her her pardon. She will be arriving here soon, I believe, before heading back to Jay'Al."

Heath smiled at the news. "It will be good to see her again."

"You will stay here as my honoured guests as long as you need to before you have to head back to Jay'Al," Mortimer told them as he sat down at his desk now. "Think about what I said about teaching others what you have learned, hm?"

"I will, sir," Heath replied. "Thank you sir."

"Also," Mortimer paused. "We have had reports of earthquakes around the northern islands."

Heath looked slightly surprised at first but then he told Mortimer, "Jay'Al has been experiencing earthquakes as well. They lost a few villages."

"Should we investigate, Commandant?" Jonah asked Mortimer.

"I think it would be an idea," Heath commented. "Might I be of assistance in this?"

"Perhaps. For now though Jonah will show you to your suite," Mortimer told him. "I will see you at suppertime."

Chapter Twenty

Roslyn approached the tents where the captured were-wolves had been taken. The guards had informed her after breakfast that the two captives were awake now, so she brought with her some food for them to eat. As she walked from the village to where the tents were, Leaf walked beside her with a large piece of boar meat in her mouth.

The tents had a spell around it to keep anyone from leaving it, only Roslyn could go in. Alexander and Kavan had put trousers on the two men and placed them in the tent with blankets over them.

Both men were standing talking to each other as she entered the tent. They were young men not much older than herself, with the same dark skin and red hair. Each of them had deep blue eyes. Roslyn remembered their wolf colours, dark black with a bluish tinge to the fur.

"How did you do this?" one of them asked her in amazement when he saw her coming. "I can no longer feel the wolf inside me."

"Magic," she told them as she offered them the fruit pastries. Each of them took one.

"Are you otherwise all right?" Roslyn asked them. "Are you angry that you are human again?"

"Angry?" they both scoffed at the same time.

The one on the left told her, "We are from the Beaver Clan; you have saved us! As werewolves we were sired to Edwin, but I feel no such connection now."

"Well I am very happy to hear that–"

"Edwin will not be," the other one told her. "He will think we are dead, but when he finds out what you are capable of doing he will be furious. You can take away his whole army: he will want you dead."

"It's not just what *I* am capable of doing," Roslyn told them. "*Any* mage who knows how to can make the cure. Our ancestors did not have the means to, but I am here now and I can do it."

"He will still be angry," the one man reiterated. "That just puts you in more danger."

"I cannot let him keep attacking my people," Roslyn told him. "I will offer him a compromise: give me my people back and he can go."

"You really think he will just give up his army?" the other man asked her. "If you let him go, he will just start all over again somewhere else."

Roslyn knew that he was right; yes she had a cure if given before the full moon changes someone who has been bitten, and now a cure for after, but he could spread it far and wide and she might not be able to do anything about it. Either she cured them all or more people would be in danger. She could not let that happen.

"What are your names?" she asked them.

"Glendon," said the one on the left.

"Mack," the other one told her.

"Nice to meet you both. Now, how many more werewolves does Edwin have now?" she asked them. "Where is he hiding?"

***

Roslyn looked down at the map on her war table. Outside her tent the light was dimming, the sun setting for the day. She had placed markers over where Glendon and Mack had told her Edwin had made his camp: the area near the cliffside entrance to the underground cavern where the werewolves had initially been held prisoner. For some reason that did not really surprise her, for the underground cavern would be a well defensible position since you had to go down the side of the cliff to get to the entrance, and then the stairway.

She put her hands on her hips and started thinking about how to confront Edwin. Confront a werewolf. *Confront a WEREWOLF?!* Thinking that inside her head seemed ridiculous. She had confronted Grau, what was a werewolf versus an orc?

"Well for one, Roslyn, a werewolf can bite you and turn you into one of them," she said aloud to herself. "Grau was overconfident. Edwin is hundreds of years old and has a lot more experience."

"He *is* dangerous," someone said behind her, and she turned to see Alexander and Kavan standing there. "Will you try to use your cure on him?"

"I am not sure yet," she answered Alexander. "I want to make sure there are no side effects that cannot be seen yet: like if the next full moon comes and they just straight up die or maybe revert back."

"That is wise," Alexander told her. "Though it is unfortunate that we have to wait a whole month almost for the next full moon."

"Well, until then we can send one of them as a messenger to tell Edwin that we have a cure," Roslyn told them. "That he needs to back off and stop attacking my people."

"Are you sure whoever you send will be safe?" Kavan asked her. "From what Alexander has told me about Edwin he is just as likely to kill whomever we send in a fit of rage."

"We can tell him that the messenger needs to come back alive for there to be any kind of truce," Roslyn said as she started pacing. She sighed heavily. "I cannot wait for this to be over."

Kavan looked at Alexander who nodded and left them alone. Kavan turned to look at Roslyn, taking in her braided hair that was coming loose and her creased clothing. Had she slept in her clothes?

"What do you need?" Kavan asked her, stepping towards her and taking hold of her arms to make her stop pacing. "Tell me what I can do."

He saw a slight change of expression as she bit her lip while looking at him but then she looked away.

Roslyn hugged herself as she thought about all the ways that he could relieve her of stress, but she could not give in right now. In the blink of an eye though he had her in his arms, kissing her. She felt her hands make their way around his back and down as his stayed steady around her waist. Suddenly he pulled away, his breathing hard. She looked at him and saw that his eyes had changed to his werewolf eyes, and that his hands had started to change. He turned away from her and breathed deeply, willing himself to take control and remain in his human form.

"I am sorry," he whispered. "I thought I could control it better, like when we kissed before. I wanted to do more…maybe that is why. I still do not want to risk hurting you during the change."

"I understand," she told him, reaching out to put a hand on his shoulder. "Companionship and some ale," she told him. "Some cuddles by the fire maybe?"

He turned and smiled at her before telling her, "Well, you get a fire going and I will gather our friends and round up some ale."

She smiled back and he turned and started walking away. Roslyn followed him out of the tent and went to gather up what they would need for the fire. The village Karina had grown up in had a large communal fire pit in its town square so Roslyn started bringing wood there. As she brought chairs out Kavan and the rest of her friends joined her, a couple casks of ale carried by Cypress and Karina. One of the chefs even brought out a platter of smoked sausages and cheese for them before retiring for the evening.

Roslyn got the fire going with her magic, watching as the flames grew taller. As she looked into the flames she remembered mourning both Kavan and Heath; now both men were still alive, though only one was with her that night. She had started falling for them both, the two very different men: Kavan the orphan, who had made a name for himself in the king's army; Heath, the sailor, who had betrayed his own people to defect to Ellsgrove for a better life. Heath who had water magic, Kavan just his skills with a sword.

A Weaving of the Roots

"Here sister," Cassidy shoved the cup of ale in her sister's face, noticing the look of melancholy that had become a common occurrence in the past few months. Leaf chittered nearby, enjoying the growing heat from the fire pit.

"Thank you," Roslyn told her, accepting the cup. She took a swig of it, letting the flavour hit her palate.

The sky had started growing darker and it had become chilly, but the fire she had built let off just enough heat to make it cozy. Roslyn sat down in the high backed chair she had brought out of her tent, Kavan moving his chair to sit next to her. Cassidy moved a chair to sit on her sister's other side, and Tiffany moved one to sit next to Cassidy. Karina sat on Kavan's other side, angling around the fire pit, with Cypress next to her. Aidan sat next to Tiffany, with Rafi and Oswick next to him. Kai came up to them, paused as he saw how they were seated around the fire, shrugged and went to sit on the ground in front of Cassidy who offered him a drink.

Roslyn finally felt relaxed, sitting there with her friends and family. She felt her shoulders loosen and she sighed, grateful for those around her. She missed Heath though, and she found herself wondering where he was and what he was doing. She was dying to hear his story, and to learn about the merfolk.

Mermaids, she thought to herself. *Werewolves.* There was so much to take in still. Then she remembered the vision she had of home, her father talking about an assassination attempt. She should be home to protect her father. If she could not be, what could she do?

Roslyn turned to her twin sister and told her, "I want you to go to Ellsgrove, I fear father is in danger."

Cassidy halted putting her cup to her mouth and her eyes darted to Roslyn and then down to Kai who was leaning against her legs, now looking up at both of them.

"With the merfolk possibly letting us across the ocean, and the Tribes looking for peace," Cassidy brought up the latest message from Chief Erick, telling them about Heath leaving for home because of a leadership change, "I could be there in a week."

"We could be there in a week," Kai spoke up. "I will go with you."

"I want half of my Honour Guard to go with you as well," Roslyn told her sister. "You are a princess of Ellsgrove as well. You will be in a place you know very little about. I know Sully will keep you safe."

"You would send Sir Sullivan back to Ellsgrove now?" Cassidy asked her sister, eyebrow raised.

"I would only be sending half of the Honour Guard," Roslyn reminded her. "I also have Cypress and his orcs to protect me."

"If you are sure," Cassidy said, "I will gladly go."

"Thank you. I fear there is something brewing in Ellsgrove that could be dangerous," Roslyn told her. "I would feel better knowing you were there to protect our father."

Cassidy bowed her head and told her, "It would be my honour to do this." She smiled and added, "It will be nice to meet our father and my other siblings."

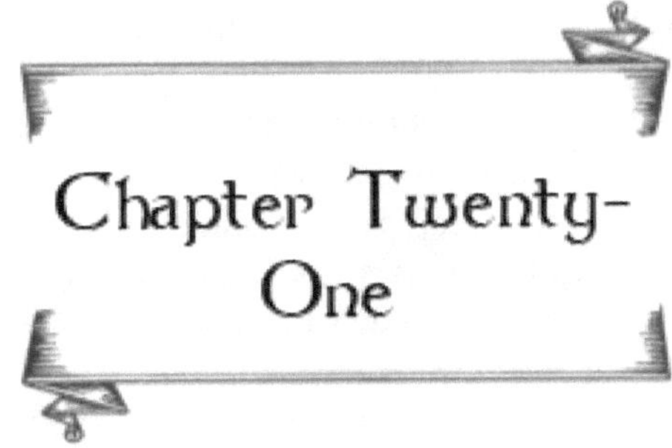

Chapter Twenty-One

Edmond looked up from the papers he was reading to see Rupert, his valet, coming into his study with a tray of baked goods and a pitcher of water. It had grown hot in the Capital now that it was getting into spring, and he had found that the palace could get rather warm. He was still not used to the warmer weather down south, having preferred the coolness of Wardgrove up north. It was only morning still, and he knew it did not help that his study faced east, for rather large windows that let the sun in.

"Thank you, Rupert," Edmond told his valet as he placed the tray down on his desk and started pouring the water into a cup for him. "What is on my schedule today?"

"The King would like you to accompany him to the meeting with the Ambassador from the Tribes of the Archipelago," Rupert told him. "The man arrived yesterday."

Edmond raised an eyebrow at the news. "Well that is intriguing."

"Indeed, sir. It seems there has been a change in leadership of the Tribes, and there might be some great changes ahead."

"Anything else after that?"

"You are to meet with the ambassadors from the Under Kingdoms," Rupert informed him. "The princesses have arrived with them."

Edmond nearly groaned out loud. He would not have an arranged marriage; Lucius had told him that he hoped his son would find someone to fall in love with, so it was up to Edmond to make the choice. It was something he had been dreading, and he had really wished that Roslyn was still there to offer advice. He was only seventeen, soon to be eighteen, but still…the conservatives were still pushing for an heir, and with everything going on with the backlash of the new decrees that gave women more freedoms, it would be best not to stir the pot more.

"Do you have their profiles for me, like I asked?" Edmond asked Rupert next. The valet handed him a folder that he opened: not just portraits of the young women, but Rupert had gone to the King's Spies to help get information for his charge.

"I love how absolutely thorough you are, Rupert," he told the man. "Have I ever told you how much I appreciate you?"

"A few times, your highness," Rupert told him with a grin. "You are like a nephew to me, and I know how nervous you are about this next step."

Edmond smiled and put the folder down. "When is the meeting with the Tribes' Ambassador?"

"In an hour in your father's study," Rupert informed him. "Your meetings are not till this afternoon."

"Thank you, Rupert. Could you bring me some tea at the meeting? I need a little extra energy."

"Yes, your highness," Rupert said with a bow, leaving him in his study.

Edmond ran his fingers through his blonde hair and stood up, walking over to his window to look outside.

Down below was a courtyard that had a walkway that led out to the Royal Forest and the Guest Cottage that Maeve was currently staying in. The news she had brought back from Jay'Al had been both interesting and shocking.

Roslyn had been made Queen of Jay'Al, and she had been tasked with uniting the people of Jay'Al, including the orcs that lived there; and now, perhaps, did that mean the werewolves that had surfaced? Edmond was dying to learn more.

The sun was just starting to light up the courtyard, and he could see the fountain at its centre. A young woman was sitting on the edge of the fountain, dressed in the traditional clothes of one of the Under Kingdoms with a long light blue jacket that fit at the waist and flared down for a long skirt. Sequins sparkled in the light. She wore a matching scarf around her head covering her hair. Edmond could not see much of her face from the distance, and she was not really facing him; but he could see that she was putting her hand in the water and playing with some of the fish that were in the fountain.

The young woman could only be one of his potential brides, for there were not many nobles from that specific Under Kingdom in the Capital of Ellsgrove. What was she doing out so early by herself? It would be inappropriate for him to go out to see her while not being chaperoned, so he turned back to his desk and the folder. He flipped through the profiles and found the one of the young woman below: her name was Alara, from the Under Kingdom called Raistminestine that was wealthy for its silk worms. The Kingdom was just to the direct south-east of Ellsgrove, and besides its silk it was well known for its mages. As Edmond read the profile on the young princess he realized that she had some sort of water magic, so that was probably why she was out at the fountain. Edmond found himself intrigued.

The city clock rang the hour and Edmond left his study for his father's down the hall. Maeve met him at the door. She bowed slightly to him and he greeted her with a smile.

"I did not know you would be here, Maeve," he commented as a guard opened the door to the king's study.

"Your father summoned me this morning, he thought I would like to be here for the meeting," Maeve explained. "The news of home is quite interesting, though a little sad."

"Oh?" Edmond raised an eyebrow and looked at his father who was sitting at his desk. The Ambassador was not yet there.

"There was a coup," Lucius explained. "They have a new Commandant, a man named Mortimer. From what our spies have told me Heath's family were killed in the fight, except for his brother Everett who is in Jay'Al."

Edmond looked to Maeve who had tears in her eyes. "Sofia was a wonderful woman, she did not deserve that fate."

"Sofia was Heath's mother?" Edmond asked her. She nodded as she wiped her tears away.

"His brother Graydon was fighting on Mortimer's side at the end," Lucius informed Maeve. "Their father Matteo apparently died at his hands."

"That redeems him in my eyes then," Maeve said, standing up a little straighter. "I wonder if Everett has heard the news."

"From what this ambassador has told me another one was sent to Jay'Al, so if he has not heard the news yet he soon will," Lucius told them.

"Who is the ambassador?" Maeve asked him, finally taking a seat. Edmond sat down in the cushioned chair beside her.

"A man named Lorenzo," Lucius told her, only for Maeve to start smiling broadly. "You know him?"

"He is my brother!" Maeve told them. "My younger brother. Oh it will be good to see him again."

"You seem to have had a very different home life than Heath," Edmond commented as there was a knock at the door.

"We had complete opposite home lives," Maeve explained as Roland opened the door and announced the arrival of the ambassador. He had the same curly hair and eyes as Maeve, and dressed much the same as Heath had the first time Edmond had met him. When the ambassador saw Maeve his expression turned into a broad smile.

"Sister!" he exclaimed as she got up from her chair and went to hug him. They embraced, Lorenzo commenting on how much she had changed since they had last seen each other.

"You as well, brother. Come, you have met King Lucius already but this is Prince Edmond," she introduced her brother to Edmond. The two shook hands and the three of them sat down at the king's desk.

"I requested this mission in hopes you would be here," Lorenzo explained.

"Mortimer has sent a pardon for you. You will be able to come home to visit now."

"I was hoping to hear such news," Maeve told him as she grabbed his hand. "It will be good to be able to go home again."

Lorenzo turned to Lucius and told him, "Mortimer would like to have peace with Ellsgrove, and offers you an alliance. You will have access to sailing routes again."

"I am pleased to hear this," Lucius responded. "I assume the same olive branch has been extended to the rest of the continent and to Jay'Al as well?"

"Correct, your majesty."

"Very good. He will have his alliance, it will be nice to finally have peace again," Lucius told him. "Maeve will no longer have to sail north to get to Jay'Al then, it will take them only a week to reach the shores now. Trade will pick up a lot faster now."

"That is Commandant Mortimer's hope," Lorenzo told him. "The Archipelago has their gunsmiths, which we are offering their patents and knowledge in making the weapons. You have a lot of produce and meat animals that we would like to trade for."

"That can definitely be arranged," Lucius said to him. "Maeve, would you like to be the first of our trade ships in the Archipelago? You can stop there on the way back to Jay'Al."

"I think Kasimir's family should head that expedition," Maeve answered him, thinking of the young merchant who had to bring his family business back from basic ruins.

"That is a good idea," Lucius conceded. "I will send word of this opportunity to him and see what he says. You can still stop at home on your way back to Jay'Al."

"Of course, your majesty. Was there anything else?" she asked Lorenzo, who looked like he was dying to tell them something else.

"I got a message from Commandant Mortimer this morning," he told them. "Heath is alive, and he brought merfolk back with him."

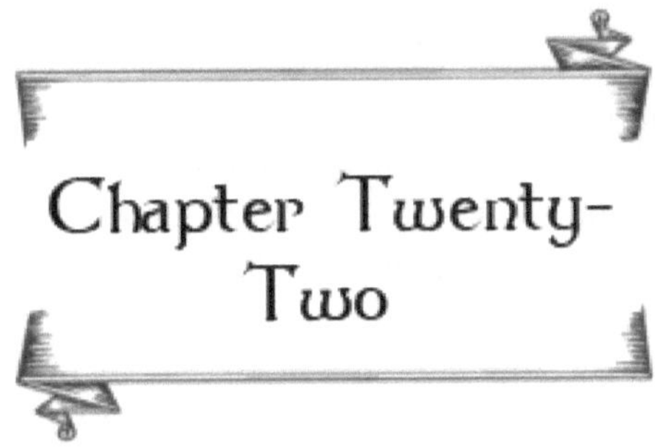

Chapter Twenty-Two

Edmond could not believe what he was hearing. First werewolves, now merfolk?

"What next?" Edmond asked aloud. "Redcaps, dwarves, and dark elves?"

"To be fair, my prince," Maeve addressed him, "There is historical documentation in your Mage University of those creatures you just named. Some disappeared centuries ago, though I know that the dark elves were banished underground. I even remember my mother telling me stories of gryphons flying around the archipelago that had been passed down through our family."

"Yes, well from what Mortimer told me, it seems that the Tribes of the Archipelago are descended from merfolk who chose to stay human," Lorenzo explained further. "That is where our water magic comes from. It seems that Heath's body washed out to sea where a merman found him and healed him, and he had been on their island of Kyprago since then. He just returned to the Archipelago."

Maeve looked like she was going to cry again, though Edmond knew that it was from happiness. She and Heath had been very close. "That news makes me incredibly happy," Maeve spoke up. "Does Roslyn know he is alive?"

"I am unsure," her brother responded. "That was all the message said."

Maeve shook her head. "I hope he sent word to her at least."

"Knowing their connection," Lucius commented, "I know he would have."

"So should we be expecting an ambassador from Kyprago as well?" Edmond asked. "If they have revealed themselves after all this time then they must have a plan."

"Hopefully a peaceful one," Lucius said. He shrugged. "We will have to wait to find out."

Lucius looked at Maeve next and told her, "I want you *and* Kasimir to go to the Archipelago, and then from there I want you to go to Jay'Al and find out what is going on. Have Roslyn use one of her special potions to contact me."

"Yes, your majesty."

"Lorenzo, I assume your Commandant brought documents for this proposed alliance?" Lucius asked Maeve's brother next.

"Of course, your majesty," Lorenzo told him as he reached into the satchel that was slung over his shoulder. He handed the documents to Lucius.

"Thank you," Lucius told him. "I will go over them today. Edmond, I believe you have some important meetings this afternoon that you still need to prepare for."

Edmond groaned out loud this time, earning a chuckle from Maeve who had heard the rumours of eligible princesses from the Under Kingdoms arriving in the Capital.

"Yes, father," Edmond told him as he stood up. "Right away, father."

Edmond left his father's study and headed back to his own where he found Rupert with the tea he had asked for, along with a platter of food.

"Sorry it is late," Rupert told him. "Your mother wanted me to make sure you had lunch before your meetings this afternoon."

"She would," Edmond chuckled, thinking about the time his stomach had rumbled extremely loudly and embarrassingly during an important meeting with the guild leaders. "Thank you, Rupert."

Rupert nodded and left the prince alone in his study. Edmond sighed and reached out for one of the bacon and cheese scones, biting into it. The butteryness of the scone was delicious, and he found it very satisfying. He took a sip of the tea that Rupert had brought him and got back to reading about his potential royal brides.

Including Alara there were five in total, one from each of the Under Kingdoms. There was a page of eligible noblewomen from Ellsgrove as well should he find none of the princesses acceptable.

The Under Kingdoms were made up of the five kingdoms: Raistminestine, Emberstine, Tellemeracus, Andromustine, and Cassandtine. After Alara there was Harita, Makani, Kyara, and Vanna. All of them were either seventeen or eighteen, and were all rather pretty. They were, of course, all well-educated, and each of them brought vastly different marriage alliance rewards. Silkworms, saltpeter mines, diamonds, armies…

Edmond thought of his father's cousin, the king who had died in the sickness. He had married a noblewoman from Ellsgrove, one of the old families of Ellsgrove. However, with how weak most of the continent got from the sickness, which had not reached the furthest most southern kingdom of Cassandtine, a marriage alliance would greatly help.

They were at peace now though with the Archipelago, so they would not need armies. Diamonds were well enough to make the treasury grow, which would help with a lot of the changes his father was making. The saltpeter would be beneficial with the new access to guns that the Archipelago was giving them. Silkworms were rare and highly valued, which would most likely cause a boom in the fashion industry of Ellsgrove.

Edmond leaned back in his chair and downed the rest of his tea. He popped a piece of cheese into his mouth and stood up, going over to the window and looking out into the courtyard again. The courtyard was empty but for gardeners tending the flowerbeds. He sighed and went over to the doorway, opening it to find Rupert on the other side about to knock.

"Just here to remind you of your meeting soon," Rupert told him with a smile. "You have eaten?"

"Yes," Edmond told him. "I just want to go back to my rooms to freshen up before the meeting," he added. "Maybe change my clothes."

"Of course, your highness," Rupert said as he bowed out of the way. The guards standing on either side of the door followed him after he had closed and locked his study, then headed for his suite of rooms across the palace. Once there the guards waited outside his suite while Rupert helped him pick out a different outfit.

"I wish Roslyn was here," Edmond told Rupert.

"I know, your highness," Rupert said in return. "I miss her as well."

Edmond laughed and said, "Really? You were always so annoyed with her antics."

"Not so, your highness," Rupert told him with a lopsided grin. "She kept me on my toes. You are too easy to deal with compared to having her around."

Edmond could not help but laugh at that. "I am not sure if that was a compliment or not," he told Rupert as he brushed his hair. He sighed as he looked at himself in the mirror.

"Tell me the truth, Rupert: How do I look?"

"Like a prince, your highness," Rupert told him with a broad smile. "I am proud of you. I would never have imagined I would be helping the Heir of the Ellsgrovian Crown pick out his outfits or his future bride when I first started working for your father."

"Me neither," Edmond responded with a slightly lopsided grin. "And thank you, Rupert."

"Come now, your highness," Rupert said as he went to the door and opened it. "You cannot procrastinate any longer."

Edmond chuckled and allowed Rupert to usher him through the door. He had to make haste to the meeting, which was to be in the Throne Room. His father was already there, having made his own wardrobe change, as was Edmond's mother Queen Elle; both of them sat on their thrones, their crowns adorning their brows. His mother Elle was wearing an outfit that was very similar to one of Roslyn's, with leggings and a long skirt slit down the sides, a finely embroidered tunic that was cinched at the waist by a dagger belt. His father was wearing fine dark green velvet breeches with a simple white tunic that was embroidered with dark stitching of vines along the sleeves.

The Throne Room had been decorated lightly, fresh banners of the family's colours of dark blue, white, and dark green were put up. The chandelier had been polished and the carpets cleaned.

"Finally," Lucius greeted him with a grin. "We will usher in the court and then the ambassadors and the princesses will be shown in," he added as Rupert directed Edmond to sit down on his own throne on the dais.

Edmond hurried up and as his butt hit the seat of his throne his father told the herald waiting at the end of the room to let the court in. The nobles of Ellsgrove had seemingly been eagerly waiting for this day, for it looked like all of them had chosen to be there: there were hundreds of them.

Edmond recognized a lot of the younger crowd from the fencing tournament, but there were a lot of the older nobles he did not know. Edmond was very pleased to see that most of the younger women were wearing dresses similar to his mother's.

The nobles of Ellsgrove took their seats and started to quiet as Lucius raised his hand. Next the herald moved to a different door where the ambassadors and princesses would enter through.

The herald opened the door and they came through two at a time as the herald announced them.

"Duke Gabor and Her Royal Highness, Princess Alara," the herald called out as the young woman Edmond had seen that morning walked into the room with a middle aged man who looked like he was her uncle. Duke Gabor wore dark blue wide legged breeches with simple dark brown flat shoes, a dark blue silk jacket with a matching vest were worn over a white tunic. He wore a light blue scarf around his head. Princess Alara wore something very similar to what she had been wearing that morning when he saw her in the courtyard, but this time her colour theme was robin's egg blue coloured silk and light brown velvet. He could see that her hair colour was light brown, her complexion slightly tanned looking, and her eyes slightly slanted. As she got closer he could see that her eyes were green and she wore makeup that accentuated her eyes. Her lips were plump and the colour of rose pink.

He barely heard the herald introduce the other four princesses and the ambassadors. Alara's eyes were mesmerizing and she had locked eyes with his, her eyes somewhat questioning and yet there was a smile there as well.

"Welcome, my cousins, to Ellsgrove," Edmond heard his father greet the ambassadors and princesses with the vernacular kings used with fellow royals. "It is a great pleasure to have you here with us–"

A Weaving of the Roots

"Heretic!" Edmond heard someone shout, and there was the sound of a flintlock gun being fired. Edmond instinctively pushed his father down out of his throne, putting himself between any bullet coming towards them, but felt no impact as they landed. He looked up in surprise to find a wall of water between the dais and the bullet, and he turned to see Princess Alara concentrating on stopping the bullet with her magic. Beyond the water barrier soldiers had descended upon the would-be assassin as nobles scrambled to get out of the way.

"Well," he heard his father say as his mother knelt down beside them both. "It looks like our information was correct."

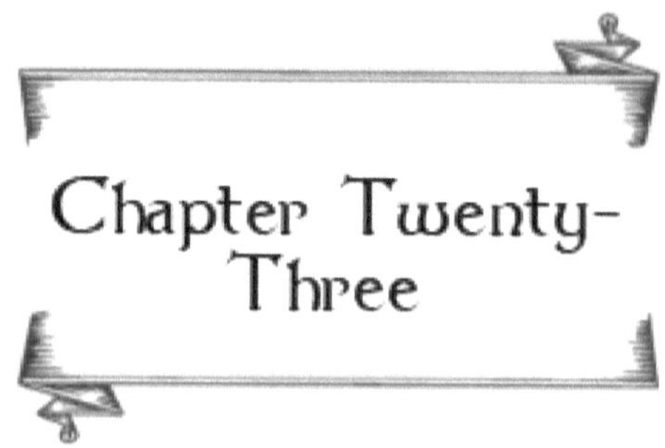

Chapter Twenty-Three

Edmond remembered the people screaming as the assassin tried to get off another shot before the soldiers had him in hand, but thankfully they were quick enough. Edmond had stood and nodded to Princess Alara, she in turn dropping her shield of water: both the water and the bullet hit the floor. As the soldiers dragged the man out of the Throne Room, Edmond had been shocked to find that he recognized the old man: Count Vernon, a wealthy conservative noble.

Edmond's father had quieted the crowd, who had all migrated to the opposite side of the gallery of the Thro-ne Room, some of the women hiding behind the columns. Edmond did not know what else happened immediately after that for Rupert and his guards had whisked him away while more soldiers came into the Throne Room to search the remaining nobles.

"How had Count Vernon smuggled that gun in?" he had heard his father ask Roland. "Find out who was supposed to be searching them before they came in."

Someone had either not been thorough when checking people in, or someone had been paid off. Either way, Edmond knew, Roland would find out who was responsible. As his father had said, they knew now that the rumours were true, and there would most likely be another attempt.

"I suppose we will have to have private meetings with the ambassadors and princesses," Rupert mused as they headed for Edmond's suite. "That should be a little less daunting then meeting them in front of the whole court."

"Where are my Eliza, Poppy and Robert?" Edmond inquired after his siblings, who he had not seen in the Throne Room.

"They were in one of the private galleries to the side," Rupert assured him. "I saw them being taken out just as I was bringing you out."

Edmond sighed with relief, glad to hear that his family was safe. Two of his guards entered his suite of rooms first and checked it over before allowing him to go inside. Rupert ushered him in as more soldiers ran down the hall heading for the Throne Room.

"Thank goodness Princess Alara used her magic to stop the bullet," Rupert commented as Edmond sat down on a sofa. "That one has a cool head on her."

"And very entrancing eyes," Edmond commented, remembering her green eyes.

Edmond did not see, but Rupert smirked and had to look away, nearly chuckling out loud. Rupert had definitely seen how Edmond was looking at that particular princess, and he wondered what was going through the young man's head. After the princess had saved Edmond's and his father's life, she was now on the top of the list for possible brides it seemed. Rupert had to admit, she might be a good fit with the family.

There came a knock on the door a few minutes later and Rupert answered it, opening the door only a few inches so he could hear what the guard on the other side of the door had to say.

"All clear," Rupert told him as he shut the door. "Your father is asking for you to go to his study."

Edmond followed Rupert out of the room, two guards walking ahead and two behind. They arrived at the king's study to find several guards outside of the room, including the guards of Raistminestine. One of the king's guards opened the doors for them and Edmond went in, the door being closed shut behind him.

Inside the study were both his parents, his younger siblings, and princess Alara along with Duke Gabor. When Eliza and Poppy saw him they ran to hug him, forgetting the other royal presences in the room.

"I am all right," Edmond assured his younger sisters. "I am very glad to see you too, girls." He looked over at Robert who was smiling faintly; he knew his younger brother would have been the most scared to wit-ness the assassination attempt. When his sisters let go of him he went over and put a hand on Robert's shoulder, squeezing it ever so slightly. Robert looked up at him and Edmond could see his lips tremble, so he took his brother into his arms. Looking up, he saw Alara watching them with compassion in her eyes, and something else he could not place.

"Come here, Robert," Elle said as she came up beside them. Edmond transferred his brother's embrace to her, and Elle picked her youngest son up and carried him out of the study.

"Son," Lucius called Edmond's attention from Alara at that moment. Lucius came over to him and embraced him. "Thank you for what you did, even though it was rash," Lucius told him.

"You have more heirs after me," Edmond whispered. "You are important to this kingdom."

"Tut-tut," Lucius stopped him. "Brave, and rash, but still brave. Your life is worth just as much, and I will not hear that nonsense. Now," he turned to the princess, "This is Alara, princess of Raistminestine."

"Greetings, your highness," Alara had stood and was now curtsying; her voice was light, musical, and almost as mesmerizing as her eyes. "What you did was very brave."

"Thank you, princess, for what you did," Edmond told her. "You saved my life today."

Alara blushed and looked down, but then she looked back up at him and said, "I could not have my future husband die before our wedding."

Edmond found his own face growing hot, and he glanced at Rupert who was trying to suppress a laugh.

"Oh really now?" Edmond said, crossing his arms, one eyebrow raised. "I have yet to even meet the rest of the princesses," he reminded her. "I have time to make a decision."

"With the assassination attempt, you would do better to choose quickly in order to solidify your claim to the throne," Alara explained to him. "Though the malcontents might think you would be easier to control than your father, they would be sorely mistaken. You need to build a strong foundation and root out those who seek to tear you down. My people and I can help you do that."

It was Lucius' turn to speak up, though he had been listening with amusement until now. "How?"

"Our agents have magic like mine," she told them. "Though mine is a little different. I can measure truths and white within a person."

"What is this 'white'?" Edmond asked her.

"You could call it the goodness within a person," she responded. "I could sense it this morning in the courtyard, but it was not until I saw you in the Throne Room that I knew it was coming from you. You are the heir to a great king, you have learned much from him, and you yourself will be even greater; especially with me as your queen."

Edmond looked at his father who only shrugged.

"Let me talk to the assassin," Alara implored them. "I will get the truth out of him, and find out if there will be others."

Lucius looked at Duke Gabor who looked conflicted. "My dear duke, what do you think of this?"

Alara looked at her uncle expectedly and he sighed. "She was not supposed to reveal her powers so readily," Gabor explained. "We were not yet sure about your family."

"What do you mean?" Lucius asked him, leaning back against his desk and folding his arms over his chest.

"Raistminestine is a very different culture than Ellsgrove, more progressive. We had heard rumours about changes here in the past several months but our spies had been unable to fully infiltrate your palace," Gabor told them with a crooked grin. "Alara's older sister will be queen once their father is dead. She told her father that she wanted to be the one to come here and find out; and it seems she has made a wise decision again."

Lucius chuckled and told him, "My oldest daughter Roslyn placed special runes around the palace to keep spies out."

"Where is Roslyn now?" Alara asked them. "Why is she not the heir?"

"I would have made her my heir if the nobles had allowed it," Lucius responded. "She has found her own throne in Jay'Al, where she was born."

"Truly? Jay'Al has a Queen now?" Gabor looked thoughtful.

"With the coming peace treaty with the Tribes of the Archipelago it will open trade up once more with Jay'Al," Lucius told them. "If you join houses with us we can make quite the powerful trading empire."

"Let me talk to the assassin," Alara reiterated. "I want to protect my new home."

Chapter Twenty-Four

Roslyn awoke to find Cypress waiting for her outside her tent. "Yes?" she called out as she got dressed.

"The werewolves are burning Base Town," Cypress informed her, still standing with his back to the opening of her tent. "I think Edwin wants to talk with you."

"How long has it been now since we cured Mack and Glendon?" she asked him. Her days had started blurring together since the night of their campfire. She had not spent much time alone with Kavan since then.

"Two weeks."

Cassidy had left two days after that campfire, taking with her Kai, Sully, Rafi and half of the Honour Guard. She had sent word a week later that they had reached Hyena City unhindered and they were awaiting a ship to be prepared for the voyage.

"Only another two weeks to go until the full moon," Roslyn commented as she walked out of her tent.

She adjusted the shoulders of her tunic and started to do up her sword belt.

"What are you going to tell Edwin?" Alexander asked her as he and Kavan walked towards them from the town.

"That he better leave us the hell alone or else I will take away his army," she answered as she went back into her tent to grab the mages staff that she had found on the way up from the underground cavern. "Think that will work?"

Alexander shrugged, saying, "I have no idea if that will work. He might get really angry with you, like Mack and Glendon said."

"Well, go get the two of them, we will ride down and meet with Edwin," Roslyn told them. "I will be preparing the horses."

She turned to Leaf, who was looking at her curiously from her spot on

Roslyn's bed. "I want you to stay here, please," she told her familiar. The dragon let out a sound that was like a whine but then she curled back up into a ball.

The two former werewolves were wearing alpaca wool clothing and looked slightly scared when Cypress brought them to Roslyn. Alexander and Kavan joined them again, this time with weapons. Tiffany had joined her already in full armour, sword at her waist.

"Do we have to go down there?" Mack asked her. "What if he tries to kill us?"

"He has to see that you are alive, and that the reason he cannot sense you is that I cured you," Roslyn reminded them. They had talked about the possibility of this meeting before. "He cannot get up the plateau, you will be safe."

The two men begrudgingly mounted the horses she had prepared, and she did as well. Kavan, Alexander and Cypress would run alongside them down the tunnel.

They did so in silence, taking only an hour or so with their small group to reach the bottom. Before the entrance of the tunnel they dismounted, Roslyn motioning for them to wait. She approached the entrance, seeing the buildings in the distance on fire and smelling the smoke that now wafted around her.

"OK, everyone but Cypress and Tiffany stay here," Roslyn reminded them.

"Will you not remove your wards in case we need to come out?" Kavan asked her. "What if he attacks you?"

"We will not be far from the entrance," Roslyn assured him. "If something happens I will not have far to go."

Kavan frowned at her words as he crossed his arms over his chest but he did not say anything more. Alexander nodded to her to let her know that he would do as she said. Tiffany had dismounted and joined Roslyn and Cypress at the opening of the tunnel. Together the three of them walked out towards the burning buildings.

Roslyn could sense at least four werewolves, and as they walked forward more she could see human silhouettes through the smoke. Four people walked forward out of the smoke to meet them, leaving several feet between them. One of them stepped forward, a man who looked to be in his late twenties, with the same dark skin as Roslyn and red hair that had become dreadlocks that hung down his back. He wore simple breeches and a tunic that looked like they were made out of alpaca wool. Roslyn thought that if his hair was better kept he might be attractive, but it looked like he had not had proper grooming in a while.

"You must be Edwin," Roslyn greeted him. "It is good to finally put a face to the name."

"Queen Roslyn," Edwin greeted her with a slight bow. "You have killed two of my people, it seems. I thought we were going to try to negotiate?" His green eyes were accusing, his mouth a slight snarl.

"Oh, they are not dead," Roslyn told him, glad to get right to it.

His eyes narrowed. "Their connection to me was cut two weeks ago," he told her.

"I cured them," she told him. "See for yourself."

She waved her hand towards the entrance of the tunnel and both Glendon and Mack moved into view. "They are very happy to be free of your curse."

Edwin stepped back in shock, his three companions whispering to each other. "It must be some magic trick," Edwin hissed. "Your ancestors tried before, all they could do was cure it before the first full moon could change them."

"I was taught magic in a very different way in Ellsgrove than the shamans of Jay'Al were," she told him. "I was able to do it. This is no trickery."

"So we are at a stalemate," Edwin barked out. "Can I bargain?"

"No," she told him. "You are to grow your army no further. You will be banished to the south where I will place markers that will keep you there. If anyone wants to be turned back you *will* allow them the choice."

"I could just kill you right now," Edwin said, looking at his hands that were starting to turn into claws.

"I am not the only one who would be able to make the cure," Roslyn told him as Tiffany and Cypress prepared to pull their weapons. "Any mage from Ellsgrove could do it."

"Or you could be lying to save your skin," he said through gritted teeth.

"Are you willing to risk that?" she asked him. "I could cure you right now." She pulled a glass orb with blue smoke inside it out of her satchel. "I could end this right now, but I want to give you the choice even though you did not give any of the people you turned a choice."

Edwin retracted his claws and looked at the men with him, all who were looking at him expectantly. "Do you want to go back to being normal?" he asked them.

"They are sired to you, do they even have the choice to answer truthfully?" Roslyn asked him.

"No, we do not have the choice," one of them told her, but she could tell that it hurt the man to speak against his sire.

"So what will it be, Edwin?" Roslyn asked him. "Can you release them from your control?"

"Why would I do that? They are my army," Edwin explained to her. "We will go north, for now, and I will not turn any more people. I swear it on our ancestors."

"I will make sure you pay for it if you go against your word," Roslyn told him.

A Weaving of the Roots

"I have no doubt about that, Queen Roslyn," Edwin said. "Where would you have us go exactly?"

"Gather everyone here just after the next full moon and I will travel with you south," Roslyn told him. "You will allow those who want to be turned back to do so at that time."

"Very well," Edwin responded, but she could tell he was not happy about it. "I will return with my people after the full moon."

Roslyn looked at the men who had come with him and spoke to them, "You will make sure he upholds his end, if you can. I believe you can fight the hold he has on you, you have already done a bit today."

Using her magic she put out the fires Edwin had started, letting him see how powerful she was. "Do not disappoint me," she told him as they turned to leave.

Chapter Twenty-Five

Cassidy watched from the bow of the ship as the islands that made up the Archipelago came into view. They had only been sailing for a couple of days, and Cassidy had to think about the alternate route that Roslyn had taken to get to Jay'Al: through the Sea of Ice to the North, which had taken weeks to traverse. Now they would be able to travel back and forth in two weeks. Then if the merfolk opened up their oceans they would have another path as well.

Cassidy worried about Roslyn. She had not liked leaving Roslyn to deal with the werewolves, but she knew that she had the others to protect her. Cassidy was nervous, too, about going to Ellsgrove. She had never travelled so far from home before, and it would be very different there. Thankfully she had Sully and her own Honour Guard to help her navigate the palace and the nobles.

Kai joined her at the bow and put his arm around her waist, pulling her closer. She sighed and kissed his cheek, saying, "This is quite the adventure, hm?"

"It will be interesting meeting the rest of your family," Kai commented. "And seeing a new land for the first time."

"The Archipelago will be something different too," Cassidy responded. "Heath should be here. It will be good to actually see him alive rather than a message."

"Yes, and to hear his story. Merfolk!" Kai had talked to his father about it while they were in Hyena City and they had dug out some of their old historical records that had mentions of the kingdom of Kyprago. "I wish we could see some in their water form."

They had met Nadim in his fully human form while they were in Hyena City, but had not had the opportunity to see him in the water.

"I wish we could go to Kyprago," Kai commented.

"Maybe on our way back to Jay'Al," Cassidy told him. "We have a lot to do in the coming weeks."

They stayed on the deck as the ship pulled into the wharf and docked on the main island called Mast. Cassidy covered her eyes from the midday sun as she looked at the wharf and she smiled suddenly.

"Heath!" she exclaimed as she ran over to where the gangplank was being put down. Sailors got out of her way and she bounded down the plank to where Heath was waiting. She embraced him, Kai coming up behind them and hugging them both. Their familiars, Crick and Tej, followed along behind them.

"Cassidy!" Heath welcomed her. "It is good to see you."

"How did you know we were coming?" Kai asked him as the three of them pulled apart.

"We got a message about a ship from Jay'Al arriving, so of course I had to come see. I used my magic to check who it was and I saw you," Heath explained. He smoothed down his leather vest and adjusted his hat as he took them in. "It is very good to see you both. How is everyone? I was very relieved to hear that Kavan was alive after learning of what happened on the plateau."

Cassidy and Kai looked at each other and Heath could tell there was more to the story.

"What is it?"

"You heard about the werewolves, right?" Kai asked him. Heath nodded.

"Well, while he was on the plateau the thing that saved him was a werewolf," Kai told him. "It bit him."

Heath's eyes widened and he stared at them with disbelief. "Kavan is a werewolf?"

"Yes," Cassidy responded. "Roslyn was able to make a cure though, so he should be fine."

Cassidy knew he could tell there was a little more to it than. "What is being done about the rest of the were-wolves then? Is Roslyn going to cure them all?"

"Last I knew she was going to give the leader of the werewolves a choice," Cassidy told him.

"Of course she would," Heath muttered, shaking his head. He sighed and told them, "Well, come along my friends, you can rest and have a good meal with me before you head on the rest of your journey. I assume you are heading to Ellsgrove now that the way is open?"

They followed him as he led them into the city. "You are correct," Cassidy told him. "Roslyn thinks our father might be in danger, so she sent us." She motioned back to the ship where Sully, Rafi and part of the Honour Guard had gathered on the deck and were preparing to disembark.

"Ah, good to see you Sir Sullivan!" Heath called out in greeting to the knight. "You made it to Jay'Al after all."

"Indeed," Sully responded with a smile. "I hope you have some ale, I think we could all use a drink tonight."

"Well come along then, we shall have a feast tonight now that we are reunited," Heath called to him.

"Welcome to the Archipelago, my friends!"

***

Heath watched as Kai and Cassidy sat down next to each other at the table and Kai put his arm around her. It made him miss Roslyn even more, seeing her twin sister with her lover. He wanted to go back to Jay'Al but he had important things to do here too.

"I will be heading north in a couple of days," Heath told the group as he poured them each a drink. "There have been earthquakes around here as well, and I am going to investigate."

"That should be something done back home too," Kai commented. "That chasm that opened up should be looked at. We avoided that area on our trip south to Hyena City because we knew it was there. I wonder if there have been any more earthquakes since we left Jay'Al."

"Don't say that," Cassidy chided him. "We do not want any more, who knows what other damage it will cause to the land."

"Well, maybe Roslyn will do something," Heath suggested. "Where was she when you left?"

"The plateau," Cassidy told him. "I believe she planned on travelling south in a few weeks. They were going to start building her palace as soon as there was peace between the werewolves. The orcs are excited to help use their skills to build their new home as well."

"How are the orcs integrating into the Clans?" Heath asked her. He had missed a lot since he had been shot and washed out to sea.

"Oh they love Roslyn," Kai told him. "Karina, she is a part orc from the plateau who had joined our group. She was very helpful when it came to talking to the orcs because Roslyn saw her as an equal. Cypress, he used to be part of Grau's group, and the rest of the orcs who joined us after she defeated Grau, were very helpful when it came to going to talk to the orc Elders."

"Yes, the Elders were very impressed with Roslyn, I guess their ancestors really liked her too because they marked her with a special clan tattoo," Cassidy added.

"She never had trouble making friends, eh?" Heath chuckled. "Good for her."

"Yes, well, the werewolves might be a different matter. I wish I could have stayed to see how that was going to go," Cassidy told him. "But Roslyn wanted me to go protect our father."

"Hopefully there will not be any trouble for King Lucius," Sully spoke up from where he had sat down at the end of the table. The seven young women of the Honour guard sat on either side of him, all of them looking at Heath with curiosity. "We will guard him as best we can, and root out any possible threats."

"Well, I wish you luck with that," Heath told them.

"What was it like being with the merfolk?" Cassidy asked him as a servant brought them a platter of cooked fish and other seafood. "We briefly met Nadim while we were in Hyena City, so we did not have the time to ask him about his home."

"The island was nice and balmy, but I did not see the underwater part until just before I left," Heath explained. "I had no idea it was even there until Nadim took me down to meet King Ullas. It was magnificent though. I can see now where my people got a lot of their designs from."

"What did you do the whole time you were there?" Sully asked him.

"Nadim showed me how to tap into the rest of my magic," Heath answered, holding his right hand up and creating a ball of water in his hand that he turned to ice. "I can make ice daggers too."

"Impressive," Cassidy commented. "You have come a long way."

"I also hiked around the island and napped in the afternoon," Heath added, earning a chuckle from his companions. "Once they open the island up it will most likely change. Nadim spoke of them building on the surface to welcome merchants and travellers. I hope they do not take away the beauty of the is-land."

"We were thinking about going that way on our way back to Jay'Al," Cassidy told him. "It would be interesting to see in person."

They stopped talking for a time as they ate, the seafood something differ-ent for them to eat. Cassidy made a passing comment about being tired of al-paca meat and that the seafood was a welcome change.

Heath looked up as his brother entered the room they were in, and Cassidy noticed him as well.

"What is he doing here?" she asked Heath.

"We have made our peace," Heath told her, gesturing to his brother to come join them. "He will be travel-ling north with me to investigate the earthquakes."

"Greetings," Everett said to them as he took a seat next to his brother. "Thank you for keeping my brother out of trouble," he added jokingly.

"Well if Heath trusts you," Cassidy commented, "even though I am sure Roslyn would have a thing or two to say about it, it is good to see that you have made peace."

"She must be quite a woman," Everett said as he filled his plate. "I did not think Jay'Al would ever unite the clans under a single ruler, let alone include the orcs."

"The ancestors chose her," Cassidy told him with a shrug. "She has proven her worth to Jay'Al."

"I miss her," Heath told Cassidy. "I hope I can finish up my business here quick and return to Jay'Al."

"She is not going anywhere," Cassidy assured him. "You have important things to do here, she knows that."

Heath looked at his brother who was taking in the young women of the Honour Guard. "Brother, do you have everything ready for us to leave?

"Our sailors are preparing the ship," Everett told him. "Provisions are being loaded as we speak. We should be ready to leave in the morning."

"We will probably be heading out at the same time," Cassidy commented.

"It is good to have you here," Heath told her. "To have friends around again."

Cassidy smiled at him and raised her cup to toast him, saying, "To being alive and with friends."

Heath laughed and raised his own cup, the others following suit. "To being alive and with friends," they chorused around the table.

Cassidy leaned closer to him and whispered to him, "I have something for you from Roslyn. I also need to meet with your new Commandant."

"I will take you to him after this," Heath told her.

***

Cassidy followed Heath to the Commandant's dwelling, a large building shaped like a ship. She was impressed by the size and decorations, noting the extensive use of sea-shells and fishtails. She carried with her a special covered basket.

"This way," Heath said as he led her into the house after a servant opened the front door. He took her to what she assumed was the Commandant's study from the bookshelves and the desk. A middle-aged man with silky gold hair hanging down passed his shoulders sat at the desk looking at maps. He was dressed in casual evening clothes, a loose tunic and breeches, his feet bare.

"Commandant Mortimer," Heath greeted the man. "This is Cassidy, Queen Roslyn's twin sister."

"So that makes you both a Princess of Ellsgrove and a Duchess of Jay'Al," Mortimer commented as he stood to greet her. "Well met, Cassidy."

"I have a gift for the Tribes from my sister," Cassidy told them as she handed Heath the basket. "Roslyn wants Heath to plant it though."

With a raised eyebrow Heath opened the basket to reveal a blue spruce sapling that was only half a foot tall, settled nicely in a ceramic bowl.

"Roslyn is eager to form an alliance with the Tribes
of the Archipelago," Cassidy continued. "This tree represents our connection to each other, for it will grow and weave into our own roots, joining our two people together."

A Weaving of the Roots

"I know just the spot," Mortimer told her. "Come with me."

He showed them through a door on the other side of his study that led out to an expansive flower garden. Mortimer waved his hand over an empty plot in the gar-den, telling them, "I had not decided what to put here yet, but I think this would be the right spot for the tree."

Cassidy handed a trowel to Heath who took it and started digging in the plot, carefully extracting the blue spruce sapling from the ceramic bowl and placing it in the hole. One of the roots poked out of the soil and seemed to be expecting something.

"Give me your hand," Cassidy told Heath, and as he handed it to her she used a small knife to prick one of his fingers. He hissed at the sudden pain but understood what she was doing. He allowed the blood to fall on the root where he and Mortimer watched it absorb instantly.

"Now it is your turn, Commandant," Cassidy turned to the older man.

"What will this do exactly?" he asked as he held out his hand to her.

"View this as a blood signing for the alliance," Heath told him. "Signing papers is a formality, this is binding."

"Very well then," Mortimer said, and Cassidy pricked one of his fingers as well. He let the blood drip onto the root where it was absorbed as well. The root, satisfied with the offering, sank itself down into the dirt.

***

Heath awoke at dawn the next morning feeling slightly different. He got dressed for the day in his sailor's outfit, brushing his hair back into a queue and tying it with a leather thong. He put on his leather boots and grabbed his new gun belt, the bullet pouch dangling from it and the pistol in the holder. He straightened his vest and went to go meet with the others for breakfast.

Cassidy greeted him with a tired smile from the table. Crick sat on her lap, eating some of Cassidy's food. The cooks had made eggs and sausage for breakfast, as well as fresh buns for them to eat. They had even prepared bas-kets of food for each of their respective journeys they were about to embark on. Heath saw the baskets were waiting by the door.

"I am nervous about meeting my father and half-siblings," Cassidy told Heath. "Do you think they will find it strange that I look like Roslyn?"

"They will get used to it, like I did," Heath assured her. "I know your fa-ther will be eager to meet you–"

"Heath!" Jonah called from the door to the house. "Two ships flying Ellsgrove's flag are sailing for Mast!"

Heath and Cassidy hurried to the door together where Jonah was waiting.

"You are sure?" Heath asked him.

"Yes. One is flying a merchant flag, the other one is flying a second flag that looks identical to yours," Jonah told him.

"Maeve," Heath said, grinning widely, "It must be her."

"They should be here within the hour," Jonah told him. "What do you want to do?"

"We will greet them at the docks," Heath said. "It will be good to see her. I wonder if Selene is with her?"

"Selene is with Jackson at the Harbour," Cassidy informed him. "Sorry."

"Ah well, at least I know where my cat is. Thank you. Still, seeing Maeve will be very good."

As they headed out of the house Heath caught sight of something behind the Commandant's house: a full grown blue spruce was towering over the city now. He grinned, knowing it was part of Roslyn's magic, and felt better to have the connection with her once again.

Chapter Twenty-Six

Roslyn looked up from her desk to find Cypress carrying a tray of food to her. He was outfitted with frishna armour that the blacksmiths had recently made, and she had given him one of the two-handed frishna swords they had found in the underground cavern.

"You did not have to bring me food," she told him as he placed the tray down on her desk. "But thank you," she added.

"I've got your wake-up drink as well," he told her, pointing to the steaming cup on the tray. "Tiffany made it how you like it."

"Where is she anyway?" Roslyn asked him.

"Training with the new orc recruits," Cypress told her. "Karina is there as well."

"Ah well then. How do they seem to be doing so far?"

"There are several who show great potential," Cypress informed her. "Especially some of the part orcs, Karina's brothers included."

"Good."

"Your stone mason, Judd, is eager to get started on building your palace," Cypress told her. "The orcs are also eager to stake claim on the land below, and build your new city."

"Does he have some blueprints for me to look at and approve?" she asked him as she bit into one of the fruit turnovers on the tray.

"He does, and Aidan has a city plan drafted as well."

"Bring them both here so I can look at things," she told him. "Thanks again for bringing me breakfast."

"My queen," he responded, putting his hand over his heart and bowing to her. Before she could say anything about not wanting him to bow to her he had left her tent.

A few minutes later both Judd and Aidan were in her tent, showing her the blueprints and plans that they had drafted. She had finished her wake-up drink and eaten so-me more food while she waited for them to join her.

"I am impressed," Roslyn told them both as she looked at both blueprints. "I like that you have my rooms attached to a greenhouse," she said to Judd. "And my personal library looks amazing."

"And the city with the outlying farms looks very good. I like where you placed the university and library," she told Aidan. "I had no idea you knew how to draft a city plan."

"Part of my training," he told her with a shrug.

"Well, I guess I approve," she told them. "You may start the process."

"We are including the small lake in the palace grounds," Judd informed her, pointing out on the plans where the lake was. "Does that please you?"

"Yes, we can stock it with different fish to supply the palace and the city, it is a good idea," she told him. Judd looked pleased. "Thank you."

"Aidan, let me know how many men you will need to outline the city and its walls," Roslyn told him.

"Most of Base Town suffered fire damage and should be torn down as well."

"Cypress has sent word to the other orc clans," Aidan informed her. "They will be arriving in the next couple of weeks, and bringing with them lumber. There is a quarry within a day's ride of the plateau as well, so we can start bringing stone from there."

"Do it," Roslyn told him with a grin. "I am eager to establish my capital."

"What will you call it?" Judd asked her. "Your capital?"

"Unsure as of yet, but I will think about it," she answered. "Would you send my mother a message to let her know that they can start planning their move down here?"

"Are you sure you should not wait for after you escort Edwin and the werewolves to their new home?" Aidan asked her. "What if he betrays you?"

"They have the runes and frishna weapons, they will be protected," Roslyn told him, though she did have doubts about Edwin in the back of her mind. She was not completely sure she could trust him, and Alexander had even voiced that concern after they had met with Edwin.

"I will send the message then," Aidan told her. "Do you need anything else?"

"No, I do not think so right now. Thank you for your work," she told them both. "I cannot wait to see the finished product."

They bowed slightly to her and left her alone in her tent. Leaf, who had left before Cypress had come, returned now with a large piece of smoked meat in her mouth. She had grown yet again, now being a little larger than a pony, and had started experimenting with her wings.

"That looks delicious," Roslyn commented to her familiar as the dragon curled up and started eating her food. "The cooks love to feed you it seems."

"What do you think?" Roslyn asked Leaf after a moment. "Do you think

Edwin will keep his word?"

"*If I had been allowed to go with you I would have a better sense of him,*" came Leaf's voice in the back of her mind. "*I cannot say for sure, but I think he will.*"

"You can meet him when he comes back," Roslyn told her, chuckling. "I just felt that you were not needed that day."

"*A familiar is always needed,*" Leaf reminded her. "*It is who we are.*"

"Okay, okay, I will not leave you behind again," Roslyn assured her. "Sorry."

Leaf looked at her and nodded before going back to devouring her meal.

"What do you think I should call my capital?" Roslyn asked Leaf.

"*You cannot think of anything?*" Leaf asked her. "*You have plenty of time*".

"Well fine then, be of no help," Roslyn teased. She sighed. "I wonder where Cassidy is right now."

"Probably half-way to Ellsgrove," she heard Kavan say from the door to her tent. "I see you have eaten breakfast already."

Roslyn turned to find him holding a basket with a cloth over it. "Yes, Cypress brought it to me."

Kavan looked down at the basket in his hand with disappointment. "I had hoped to take you for a picnic," he told her.

"That sounds lovely. Could we do it for lunch maybe?" They had not spent much time alone since the last time they had kissed.

"Of course. Hey, Roz…I was wondering…could you make an amulet that would keep me from changing? I would have the strength and everything still but just not be able to change?"

"You do not want to be cured?" she asked him, surprised.

"I like the abilities," he told her. "Just not the shapeshifting and the passing it on part."

"I might be able to," she answered after a moment of thought. "I'll need a bit of your hair, in both forms, and some of your blood, and possibly some of Alexander's blood."

"I can have that all to you within the hour," he told her.

"Very well, I will prepare my alchemy table. I should be done by noon and we can go for that picnic," she assured him. He smiled at her and left with the basket. She turned to Leaf, who was looking at her curiously.

"What do you make of his question?" Roslyn asked Leaf.

It would be interesting if you could do what he asked, Leaf told her. I understand the thought of losing the powers he just got used to. He might think that having the powers still would be a good idea, you know, to protect you better.

"He knows I do not need him to protect me," Roslyn commented as she went to her alchemy table and started to bring out new beakers and flasks from the boxes beneath it. "Though I get what you mean about losing what he just got used to."

She got to work, preparing the tinctures she would need. There were a few different ways she could go about making the charm, so she was going to try each of them just in case. Half an hour later Kavan returned to her with the items she had asked for and she got started.

"I will need to be left alone for a while," she told Tiffany who had just come to check on her. "I am attempting to make a charm to keep a werewolf from shape-shifting."

"Really? Why would you do that?"

"Kavan asked me if I could make it for him."

"Oh. I will let the others know to leave you be then, and I will set a guard to make sure you are not disturbed," Tiffany told her. Roslyn thanked her as she turned to walk away.

As Roslyn worked she thought about what to make the pendant out of. Frishna would burn his skin, so that was no good. Was there any other kind of metal or gemstone she could use? Then it struck her: a sunstone would be perfect to include in such a pendant and spell. She did not have any though.

Roslyn went to the door of her tent and found Deirdre and Teddy both standing guard. "I need Karina," she told them. "Would one of you get her for me?"

The two looked at each other and Teddy nodded before going to find Karina. A few minutes later she returned with the part orc.

"What do you need?" Karina asked her as she stepped into her tent, her familiar Mister Scruffy following behind her.

"I need a sunstone, do you know where I can find one up here?" Roslyn asked her.

"The shrine probably," Karina told her. "You should theoretically be able to use your connection with Jay'Al to call some sunstones to you from there."

"Oh, ok then I did not know that," Roslyn commented. "I guess I will go there then."

"Do you want me to go with you?" Karina asked her.

"Sure, come along," Roslyn told her with a smile. "How is it being back home?"

Together they walked out of the tent and headed towards the shrine, Leaf at Roslyn's heel just as Karina's familiar was at hers. Teddy went with them, Deirdre staying to guard the tent to make sure no one tampered with what Roslyn was doing. The day, which had started out sunny, and turned to clouds that threatened rain.

"It is very nice to be home, though I am eager to see how the palace and the city will look. It will be a great change, but it will make our people a lot better to be united like this. And the trade that will come!" Karina bounced a little as she walked. "What do you think of all of this? This is the exact opposite of what you wanted."

Roslyn shrugged and answered, "I feel at home here, truly, for the first time in a long time. I belong here, whether as the Queen of Jay'Al or not…this is apparently my destiny."

"I am glad you have accepted that," Karina told her with a smile.

They arrived at the shrine, the dragon statue standing as it had been the first time Roslyn had gone there. As Leaf admired the statue, Roslyn nicked a finger and allowed a drop of blood to drop on it, watching as it was absorbed into the stone. A part of the wall behind the statue opened and Roslyn turned to Teddy.

"You can stay here," she told the young woman. "We will be safe down there."

Teddy nodded and turned around to stand guard next to the dragon statue. Leaf bounded down the stairs ahead of them with Mister Scruffy, Roslyn and Karina following them down the tunnel into the shrine. The green moss along the wall lit their way.

The path opened up into a large open cave, large tendrils of roots from the great cedar tree that was up in the caldera on the mountain twined together from the ceiling to the ground of the cave. Roslyn walked up to the roots and placed her hand on it, letting her magic and mind flow into it. She voiced what she needed inside her mind, letting her magic relay it to the land.

A few moments later the ground behind the roots began to move and a grouping of roots emerged like a hand. Leaf and Mister Scruffy sniffed it for a moment, interested in what it was. Tendrils opened like fingers to reveal dozens of sunstones of various sizes, none bigger than an eyeball though.

"Oh wow," Roslyn said as she scooped up the sunstones and watched as the roots and tendrils descended back into the earth. "That was incredibly interesting and yet freaky at the same time."

Karina looked at her with wide eyes. "That is putting it lightly," Karina told her. "You have quite the connection with the land now. I wonder what all you could do."

"Well we can do some testing later on," Roslyn told her as they made their way back out of the shrine. She placed a hand on the roots again and sent her thanks through her magic. "I would definitely be interested in knowing what my limitations would be."

Karina stopped in her tracks, feeling a slight vibration in the ground. "Do you feel that?" she asked Roslyn. "What is that?"

Roslyn's eyes widened and she barely had time to answer, "Earthquake!" and throw up a protective shield around them as the ground gave way beneath them and they tumbled down into the earth.

Chapter Twenty-Seven

Alexander and Kavan were standing talking to Oswick and Tiffany when they felt the ground roll beneath them. The houses nearby shook, items falling off of shelves and tables to smash on the floor. Horses and alpacas spooked.

"What was that?" Alexander asked as the group picked themselves up from the ground.

"Earthquake," both Oswick and Kavan said in unison.

"Where is Roslyn?" Alexander asked them.

"She was in her tent doing an experiment earlier," Kavan told him. Together the group headed for Roslyn's tent which they discovered had fallen down. Deirdre was there with a group of soldiers trying to put the tent back up.

"Where is Roslyn?" Kavan asked the young lady knight.

"She and Karina went to the shrine, something about finding a sunstone," Deirdre told them.

The group looked at each other in panic and ran to where the shrine was. They all stopped suddenly though as they realized there was a giant sinkhole where the shrine had been. What was left of the braided roots of the cedar tree dangled out of the opposite side of the hole.

"Roslyn!" Kavan shouted.

"Help!" came a cry from somewhere below them.

"I've landed on an outcropping!"

"Who is that?" Kavan turned to ask Tiffany.

"Sounds like Teddy, she was the other knight guarding Roslyn's tent," Tiffany told him.

"Let's get some rope and haul her up," Alexander told them. Oswick nodded and went to go get some rope.

"Teddy!" Tiffany yelled as she got down on her stomach and inched towards the edge.

A Weaving of the Roots

She could see the young woman on a small outcropping of rocks in the side of the sinkhole. "Where is Roslyn?"

"She was inside the shrine!" Teddy answered. "She and Karina were inside the shrine."

Tiffany looked up at Kavan and saw the panic on his face.

"We need to try to find a way down there," Kavan said as he started pacing. "Start digging."

"First let us get Teddy up to safety," Tiffany told him. "Alexander, go gather up a group of soldiers and orcs, tell them what has happened. We will need more rope, lumber and shovels."

Alexander nodded and went to go do that, meeting Oswick who was coming back with some rope to get Teddy.

"I cannot believe this has happened," Kavan said as he stopped pacing and bent over, hands on his knees. He started breathing heavier and Tiffany was worried that his emotions would trigger him to change into his wolf form. Tiffany reached out and grabbed his chin, forcing him to look at her.

"She would not appreciate a freak out right now," Tiffany told him. "Keep it together Kavan!"

Kavan nodded, swallowing hard as he stood up straight again. Oswick arrived with the rope and together they pulled Teddy up.

"Was that an earthquake?" Teddy asked Tiffany as she lay on the ground after being hauled up.

"Yes," Tiffany told her. "Are you hurt?"

Teddy shook her head. "A little bruised but I will be fine."

"Good," Tiffany said as she helped the young knight up. She turned to find Alexander with a cluster of soldiers and orcs coming towards them with the tools they would need.

"Now, we are going to make a way down there and start digging," Tiffany told them as Alexander and Cypress stopped in front of them. "Roslyn and Karina are somewhere under this," she told the group.

"How are we sure they are even alive?" Cypress asked them, though there was hope in his eyes.

"I am sure she found a way to protect them as it happened," Tiffany told him. "Like when we were caught in the avalanche up on the mountain, she put a shield around us. I am sure she would have done that again."

Cypress nodded and started to direct the people. Karina's father Lou came running towards them now and Tiffany went to meet him.

"Where is my daughter?" Lou asked her. "Tell me it is not true, tell me she isn't under there."

"She was in the shrine with Roslyn," Tiffany told him. "I am sure Roslyn protected them both when it happened. Please calm down."

Lou looked taken aback by her words at first but then he took a step back and nodded. "What do you need me to do?"

"Help with the digging when we get down there," Tiffany told him. "Find more shovels so we have enough."

Lou nodded and took off at a run for the village.

Tiffany turned back to find that Cypress had built a rope pulley and had started lowering people with shovels down.

"Quick thinking," Tiffany told him. "Where did you learn how to make a pulley?"

"We have them in our mines," the orc explained. "I have had to fix many of them."

"Well, good work Cyp," she told him. "We shall have them out of there in no time."

***

Roslyn awoke to the feel of a rough tongue against her cheek. There was darkness, but her hands told her that the thing licking her cheek was Leaf. She called light to her hand and illuminated the air bubble they were in, revealing Karina lying unconscious not too far away, with Mister Scruffy trying to wake her up.

Roslyn stood up and went to Karina, checking to make sure the younger woman was alive. Finding a pulse she looked at Mister Scruffy and smiled, telling him, "She is all right. Let me try to wake her up."

Mister Scruffy meowed at her and watched patiently as Roslyn shook Karina by the shoulders.

"Come on Karina, wake up," Roslyn said to her.

Karina groaned and opened one of her eyes to look up at Roslyn. "What happened?" she asked her as she sat up and opened her other eye to look around. "Where are we?"

"There was an earthquake. I think we are within the plateau," Roslyn explained.

As Roslyn helped Karina stand up there was another rumble and the ground gave way beneath them again. This time they dropped into a slide-like tunnel that took them even further within the earth. Mister Scruffy meowed his concern as Karina grabbed hold of him, and

Leaf let out a distressed noise as she slid along beside Roslyn. Roslyn lit the way with her magic, and after what seemed like hours she could finally see the bottom. The tunnel spit them out into a cavern, and they tumbled a few times before coming to a halt.

"Ouch," Roslyn said as she rubbed her behind after standing up. She used her magic light to light up the cavern, seeing crystals around it. She put her magic into the crystals and the cavern lit up, revealing paintings on the walls of the cavern.

"What is that?" Karina asked her, seeing the paintings. Roslyn helped her to stand up as Mister Scruffy and Leaf started sniffing around. They approached the wall closest to them to look at the paintings better. There were images of creatures Roslyn had never seen before, creatures with wings like a birds but the body of a feline, its head a strange mixture of the two with a beak and feline ears at the top of the head.

"I think…" Roslyn touched the wall as she looked at the rest of the paintings, images of humans riding on the backs of the winged creatures. "I remember reading ancient lore about gryphons," Roslyn told her. "I think these are them."

"Well how does that explain why there are these paintings here?" Karina asked her. "Are we still under the plateau?"

"We fell quite a ways," Roslyn told her. "I have no idea."

"How are we going to get back up?" Karina asked her, hugging herself as she realized they might be stuck down there.

"I can probably make a tunnel with roots like I did with the plateau," Roslyn told her. "I think we should look around here a little bit first. There looks to be some kind of doorway over there." Roslyn pointed to the other side of the cavern where there was indeed a hole in the wall that led to what looked like a corridor.

"I think I should try to contact our people though, let them know we are still alive and everything," Roslyn said. "Leaf!" she called after her familiar who had started moving towards that door. "Stay with me for now."

The dragon looked at Roslyn and then back at the door before turning around and coming back, Mister Scruffy beside her. Roslyn closed her eyes and astral projected herself up to the surface, finding a large group of soldiers and orcs digging inside a sinkhole where the shrine had been. She found Kavan, Tiffany, and the rest of the Honour Guard amongst the diggers.

Kavan stopped what he was doing and looked up, having sensed her magical presence there.

"Roslyn!" he exclaimed as he stopped digging. Tiffany looked up and saw Roslyn's astral form floating there in front of them.

"I take it you are alive," Tiffany commented as she stopped digging as well.

"Yes, Karina and I are somewhere beneath the plateau in a cavern. I have no idea how far down we are but we are alive and safe. We found something that I want to explore further, evidence of gryphons and some kind of ancient civilization," Roslyn told them. "It is very strange."

"Gryphons?" Kavan asked with raised eyebrows. "Those are old wives tales."

"I would not be so sure," Roslyn answered. "After all, you are a werewolf. Why would Gryphons be any different?"

"What do you want us to do in the meantime?" Tiffany asked her.

"Heather should be able to complete what I was doing for Kavan, creating a magical pendant with a sunstone to keep him from changing form," Roslyn told her.

"There are a few sunstones right here," Roslyn pointed to the gemstones at their feet. "Looks like more were called up than I thought. Also, stop digging. I should be able to get us back up when we are done exploring down here."

"All right, will do." Tiffany went to go tell Cypress to get everyone to stop and go back to what they were doing before.

Kavan looked at Roslyn and crossed his arms over his chest. "Are you sure it is wise to go exploring down there right now? What if another earthquake happens?"

"I will deal with that when it happens," she responded as she started to fade. "I will be careful, promise."

Roslyn opened her eyes again and saw Karina looking at her.

"What?" she asked her friend as they started to move towards the door, their familiars at their ankles.

"Do we need to do this now?" Karina questioned her. "It isn't going anywhere."

"But what if there is another earthquake that closes this passage?" Roslyn asked her.

"And what if that happens while we are down here?" Karina retorted. "What if you are not fast enough to save us next time?"

"Do you want to go back up to the surface?" Roslyn stopped in her tracks and turned to face Karina. "I will make a passage for you to go up if you want to, you really do not need to come with me."

Karina glared at her and she made a chuffing noise, telling her, "Kavan and Tiffany would never forgive me for leaving you alone."

"You have a choice though," Roslyn reminded her. "I will respect your choice."

"No, I am staying," Karina told her. "Are we going to explore or what?"

They came to the doorway which Roslyn could tell was not made naturally. A slight breeze came down the passageway. The doorway connected the cavern to a corridor that had been reinforced with wooden beams. As they walked down the corridor Roslyn noticed that the beams were still structurally sound and showed no signs of rot either. Touching one of the beams she could feel that some kind of magic protected the beams.

"Someone with magic helped build this," Roslyn told Karina.

"Where do you think we are? Like how far under-ground and in which direction?" Karina asked her as they walked. The corridor led in only one direction, and some-thing told Roslyn that they were heading east and she told Karina that.

"I also think we are very deep underground," Roslyn told her. "I wonder how old this place is."

There were a few more markings on the walls as they came to a section that opened up into a separate corridor.

"What do you think they mean?" Roslyn asked Karina. One of the images on the side of the doorway for the new corridor looked like a large egg; there was an image of wings over it as well.

"Maybe a hatchery," Karina told her with a shrug. "Which way should we go?"

"The images on the main corridor tell me there might be people ahead," Roslyn said. "We should go that way. Also, the breeze is getting stronger."

Karina nodded and they continued down the first corridor.

"How long do you think we have been down here?" Karina asked her after a time.

"Maybe a few hours?"

"I'm getting hungry," Karina told her with a sigh.

"If we do not find someone soon I will make a passage to the surface," she assured her friend. "Wait, what is that up ahead?"

In the distance there was a lot of natural light coming into the tunnel, and the breeze had picked up. There was some debris on the corridor as they came up to the opening, peering over the edge to see raging water below.

Looking up they could see the sky, and across they could make out an opening on the other side.

"I know where this is," Roslyn told Karina. "There was a chasm caused by an earthquake that destroyed three villages. We are south-east of the plateau."

"Well there is no way across," Karina commented. "Shall we go back to that other corridor?"

Roslyn nodded and they turned around, picking up the pace this time in their backtracking. They reached the second corridor and went down it, this time feeling a definite incline as they walked it.

"Well this is interesting," Roslyn commented as they came upon an opening into an underground cave that was very much like the one they had found after being shipwrecked by the whirlpools, except there were no mushrooms, lizards, or a giant crystal providing warmth. There were, however, green moss that lit the cave up and large stone towers that had what looked like nests on top of them.

"I'm going to climb up there and see if there is anything up there," Roslyn told Karina, motioning to the closest tower that must have been at least thirty feet tall.

"Maybe I should be the one to do it?" Karina told her, but Roslyn was already starting to climb it, Leaf watching from the base.

Karina looked at Leaf and Mister Scruffy, both who looked at her now as if to say, 'You know how stubborn she is, right?'

Roslyn reached the top of the tower and found it empty, though there were what looked like eggshells for a rather large egg and a lot of very large feathers of varying colours. She looked around at the other nests and found them all empty.

"Nothing," she called down to Karina before she started her climb back down.

"Can we go back up to the surface now?" Karina asked her.

"Yes, yes we can. Though I really want to find out what is on the other side of that chasm."

Chapter Twenty-Eight

Heath looked over at Maeve who was watching Everett with suspicion. Everett stood leaning against the side of the ship watching the water go by. Heath was manning the helm, and Maeve was sitting on some barrels nearby. They were heading north to investigate if there was any damage on any of the islands due to the earthquakes that had been occurring.

"I do not trust him still," Maeve told him when she saw him looking at her.

"I know," he responded. "He promised me over mother's grave though."

"And that ever stopped anyone from betraying another?" Maeve asked him. "I am honestly surprised you do not have him chained up."

"Maeve," Heath turned to her. "What he did is in the past. Leave it there."

"He kidnapped you, tortured you and Kavan, and you nearly died!" Maeve stood up, fists clenched. "I mourned you Heath! We all did!"

Heath remembered seeing the look on her face when she saw him waiting for her on the dock, as if she was seeing a ghost. Her brother had told her Heath was alive but she was not going to believe it completely until she saw him. They had not had much time to talk about it since they set sail shortly after she arrived.

"I know," Heath whispered, stepping away from the helm and reaching out to pull her into a hug. "I thought I was dead. I remember drifting in and out of conscious-ness while I floated, unable to do anything."

"How did you survive?" Maeve asked him as one of the sailors with them took over the helm.

"Nadim, a merman, pulled me from the water. He showed me how to tap into my magic more. You should see what I can do now Maeve."

"You will have to show me when we get to our destination," she responded. "I look forward to seeing what our people can do."

Everett came over to them, looking at Maeve timidly. He had avoided her at first, knowing how angry she must have been at him. Heath watched his brother approach with slight trepidation.

"Good to see you–" Everett started to say, but the rest of his words were stopped when Maeve punched him in the face. He started swearing, holding his nose, as Maeve smirked while shaking her hand.

"That is for what you did to Heath," Maeve told him. "Try anything and you will see what I can do," she threatened before walking off.

Heath was trying really hard not to laugh though he knew Everett could probably see it on his face.

"She was always a lively one," Everett commented through the pain.

"Here," Heath beckoned his brother, reaching out to touch his broken nose. A spark of his magic was all he needed to heal his brother's nose, Everett flinching when the cartilage moved back into place.

"Nice trick," Everett commented as he wiped the tears from his eyes.

"I can teach you how to heal," Heath told him.

"You really think I can unlock the rest of my magic like you did?"

"I do not see why not," Heath told him. "We have the same magic running through us."

"You could always wield it better than I," Everett responded with a sigh. "As soon as you touched it you could use it. It took me a long time to get it right, remember?"

Heath did remember. Their father had been angry that Everett could not use his magic as effectively as Heath. It was another reason Heath had hated their father, pitting brother against brother, making Everett feel like he was not good enough. Graydon, the eldest brother, had not had the magic but he was skilled at other things that their father valued. Heath had always felt sorry for Everett and had wished he could have helped Everett escape when he had left. It was one of his deepest regrets.

"We are in a better place now," Heath told his brother. "We are free from the restraints we had over the years. We can be anyone we want to be now. I believe in you."

"That actually means something, coming from you," Everett whispered. He looked away for a moment and then back at his older brother. "I am sorry, Heath. I allowed my anger to get the better of me before."

"I know. I have already forgiven you."

"I think we are here," they heard Maeve call over from the bow of the ship. Heath looked up at the island they were coming to and frowned.

"Yes there is definite damage to this island," he commented as he took in the freshly broken cliffside and the ruined rope bridge that had once hung there.

"I wonder how long ago this happened," Everett commented. "Surely the residents of the island would have sent word that their bridge was out."

"Let's get in the dinghy and row to shore to find out," Heath answered him.

The three of them got into the dinghy with two other sailors who manned the oars. The island was the northernmost island of the archipelago and was almost the size of the island of Mast. There were several dozen families on the island. A handful of trees grew on the island, most of the plant life being bushes or flowers. They left the dinghy on the beach with the sailors and headed for the path near the cliffside. They followed the path inland, finding abandoned houses as they went further in. Chickens wandered around outside their coops, unbothered by any natural predators it seemed, as they hunted for bugs and worms.

They checked each empty home they found to make sure it was indeed empty. In most of the houses it looked like they had sat down to eat when their meals were interrupted.

"Food is cold," Maeve called out from one of the houses. The two brothers were checking out two other houses nearby.

"Same here," Everett responded.

"Likewise," Heath called out as well.

"Where do you think everyone is?" Maeve asked as they joined back together on the path.

"There is a Hall further inland if I remember correctly," Heath told her. "They may have gone there."

They kept on the path, finding more abandoned homes, and more unattended animals. A few goats wandered by them, and a cow watched them from her pen as she chewed her food. Heath saw that her food was getting low so he went over to give her more when he saw something he did not like.

"Guys," he called over his companions.

"Is that blood?" Maeve asked as she knelt down to touch it. She sniffed it and then wiped her hand on some grass. "Yes, it is."

"So we have only one sign of something bad amongst abandoned homes and missing people," Heath commented. "I do not like this."

A twig snapped nearby and all three of their heads shot up. They looked around as they each drew their weapons.

Heath saw a child's head duck behind a bush as he scanned the area.

"Put your weapons away," he whispered to his companions. "There is a child."

They each put away their weapons as Heath approached the bush the child was hiding behind.

"Hey there," he called out. "My name is Heath. We were sent by Commandant Mortimer to check out the island. Are you okay?"

A little blonde head rose up from behind the bush. The boy could not be much over ten years old. His clothes were rumpled and dirty, as if he had slept in them some-where that was not his bed. The boy shook his head, clearly scared about something.

"Where is everyone?" Maeve asked the boy. "Where are your parents?"

"Taken," the boy croaked out from a dry mouth. Heath handed him his water flask and watched as the boy took a long drink.

"Taken where?" Heath asked him.

"The creatures," the boy said. "They came up from the hole, and took them back down."

Heath looked at Everett and Maeve. Just what was going on there?

"Can you show us the hole?" Heath asked the boy. The boy's face turned white and he shook his head vehemently.

"Which direction is it?" Heath asked him next.

The boy pointed in the direction of the Hall.

"Maeve, take the boy to the ship," Heath told his friend. "Just get the sailors to take him over and then come right back," he added when he saw her starting to object.

"What is your name?" Heath asked the boy.

"Garret."

"Garret, this is Maeve. Go with her, you are safe ow," Heath told him. He and Everett watched the boy take Maeve's hand and she led him back down the path they had come up, moving a lot faster this time.

"We will continue on to the Hall," Heath called after her. "We will meet you there."

"I will make all haste," Maeve called back.

"What do you think it is?" Everett asked his brother as they started walking in the direction Garret had directed them. Everett drew his sword just as Heath drew his pistol. Heath checked to make sure that his barrel was fully loaded and found that it was.

"I have no idea," Heath answered. "He looked really scared though."

"Should we not send for more men?" Everett asked, clearly not liking the idea of going any further.

"We will check it out and see before we send for more soldiers," Heath told him.

Everett sighed and followed his brother down the path. The trees thinned out as they went, and there were more signs of distress: more blood, torn clothes, and drag marks.

"I do not like this," Everett whispered as they approached the Hall. The building was made out of the hull of an old ship, taken apart on the shore and brought inland, much like the Commandant's home. There looked to be bullet holes on the side of the building, and there were large scratch marks and broken windows.

"Why does it look like the windows were broken from the inside?" Heath questioned aloud as they surveyed the area before them without getting closer.

"Could the creatures have come from inside the Hall?" Everett asked him. Footsteps behind them made them turn, only to find Maeve and a few other sailors with pistols in their hands.

"What are we thinking?" Maeve asked them.

"Something came from inside the Hall it seems," Heath explained. "We were just about to take a peak."

"After you, Captain," Everett told him with a nudge and a slight smirk.

Heath stuck his tongue out at his brother and started towards the building. Heath headed up the rough-hewn staircase towards the building, the front doors busted open from the inside and half hanging on their hinges. Where there had once been benches and tables for eating communal meals together there was now a large hole in the ground, as if the ground had sunken in. An obvious tunnel could be seen at the bottom of the sinkhole, as were the remains of the tables and benches. There were signs that several things were dragged back down into the tunnel as well.

"Please tell me we are not going there," Everett said to his older brother, his eyes scared and pleading. "We have no idea what could be down there."

"Everett, you can stay up here if you want to," Maeve told him as she followed Heath towards the sink-hole. The sailors who had come with her squared their shoulders and advanced along with her, pistols at the ready.

"Fine, I'm coming," Everett said through clenched teeth as he stepped forward. He was right behind Heath now as his brother got close to the edge. One side had an incline of earth and rocks that was clearly how the creatures had made their way up from below. There was a rumble and Everett saw Heath start to lose his balance. He reached out and grabbed hold of his brother's arm and pulled him back as the edge where Heath had just been standing crumbled away.

"I've got you," Everett said to his brother, but before Heath could say anything in return the ground rolled beneath them and the sinkhole opened up even wider, like a gaping maw swallowing them whole.

Chapter Twenty-Nine

Roslyn entered her tent to find Heather, the lady knight who was also a mage, attending to the alchemy table. The tent had clearly been knocked down by the last earthquake but by the looks of it the alchemy table had been spared for she saw no broken glass.

"How goes it?" she asked Heather.

"I followed your notes," Heather told her. "I was able to use what you prepared to make the pendant."

Roslyn turned to look at Kavan and Alexander who had followed her into the tent. "Care to try it?" she asked Kavan.

Kavan nodded and accepted the pendant from Heather. The sunstone was the size of his thumb and had silver wire wrapped around it, a silver string attached to make it a necklace. He put it over his head and let it rest against his chest.

Alexander tilted his head a little bit, a slight smile on his face. "I cannot sense him," Alexander told her.

"Try to shapeshift," Roslyn told Kavan. He shrugged and concentrated, but nothing happened.

"I still feel the same," he told her.

"Keep that on and you should be good to go," Roslyn told him with a wide grin. She was thinking about being able to kiss him again without worrying about him turning into a werewolf.

"It should work with the full moon too, right?" Alexander asked her. "For those who do not have the control we do."

"Yes, it should. It should also, theoretically, stop the curse from spreading," Roslyn told them.

"We can offer this to Edwin," Kavan spoke up, knowing exactly what Alexander was thinking.

"That is one idea, yes," Roslyn told them. "Though we would have to personalize every single pendant."

"It would be worth it though," Kavan commented. "It gives them another choice."

"And it would probably sever the bond between Edwin and those he sired," Alexander spoke up.

"We can offer it to them, yes," Roslyn told them. "We will have to talk to them about it first."

"Well, what are we waiting for?" Alexander asked her. "This is a break-through of a lifetime! This changes everything for the werewolves."

"Okay, we can take a party out to them and tell them what we were able to do," Roslyn told him. "Heather, we will need the alchemy table and everything with it loaded into a wagon."

"Right away," Heather responded as she started to clean things up.

"Tiffany," Roslyn turned to find her friend waiting just outside the door of her tent. "Gather Cypress and his guard, we are going to parley with the werewolves again."

***

Tiffany watched as the group assembled at the opening of the tunnel Roslyn had made to get up the plateau. A year ago she would never have imagined something like it happening, let alone even being there to begin with. She was very different from the woman she had been a year before; before she had met Roslyn.

"What are you thinking?" Roslyn asked her, noticing the faraway look in her friend's eyes.

"You know it has been a year since you first taught me to use the sword?" Tiffany asked her.

Roslyn thought about it for a moment, not realizing how long ago that was. "Wow, you are right." Roslyn smiled though, remembering when her father had told her about the expedition. So much had changed for Roslyn in the last year as well.

"That can't be right," Kavan commented.

"It was spring when my father told me about the expedition. Six weeks later we left, and it was early winter here in northern Jay'Al by the time we arrived. We have gone through winter here and now early spring. Yes, it has been a year," Roslyn told him.

Kavan looked slightly taken aback by that, then he shook his head as if realizing she was right. "How has a whole year gone by already?"

"We did do a lot of travelling," Roslyn reminded him. "I guess sometimes the days just blur together, do they not?"

"Indeed," Kavan responded with a sigh.

Tiffany chuckled, looking back at the group. Cypress was wearing new frishna armour, as were the other orcs in his group. The remnants of the Honour Guard, including Teddy, Heather, and Deirdre, were also wearing frishna armour. Cypress had a large axe strapped to his back, as did Terren and Louen. Roslyn had both her frishna sword at her waist and was carrying her bladed mages staff.

Tiffany thought again about how eclectic their group was now. They had orcs, part orcs, werewolves, Jay'Alians, and Ellsgrovians. Well, technically, were the remaining Honour Guard still of Ellsgrove? They had sworn their swords to Roslyn, who was now the Queen of Jay'Al. That was something to think about, no longer being of Ellsgrove. This was a new home, a new start for a lot of them.

"Let's head out," Roslyn said once everyone was ready. Karina had already mounted her horse next to Tiffany, but now Tiffany mounted her own horse. The rest of the Honour Guard followed suit, and the orcs lined up behind them. Leaf trotted along beside them, and Mister Scruffy lounged on the front of Karina's saddle.

Roslyn led the way down the tunnel and they stopped at the bottom so she could remove the runes in order for Alexander and Kavan to pass through. She replaced them after they were all through, just in case.

"Do we know where to find them?" Karina spoke up as Roslyn remounted her horse.

Roslyn looked at Alexander, who pointed to the east.

"That way, presumably," Roslyn commented with a chuckle. "Any say on how far?"

"Not too far," Alexander told her.

So they headed east, with Heather directing the wagon that the alchemy table was in. They rode for several hours, Alexander giving some minor adjustments in where they were heading now and then. They stopped at sundown to make camp somewhere near the plains, not too far from the chasm.

Roslyn put up the wards around the camp as Karina handed out the food for supper: smoked meat and cheese, with buns that had been freshly made that morning.

Alexander was about to take a bite of his smoked meat when he sensed something coming close. He stood up quickly, looking east with his enhanced vision, and he swore.

"Edwin is coming," he shouted to Roslyn, who was just about to finish the wards. "With the rest of the werewolves. Something is wrong though, it looks like they are running from something."

Kavan stood to look where Alexander was pointing as the rest of the group gathered to look as well.

"What is that behind them?" Kavan asked Alexander.

"What is it?" Roslyn asked them both.

"Some kind of…massive creatures," Alexander said. "I have no idea what it is, but if the werewolves are afraid of them then maybe we should be too."

A Weaving of the Roots

Roslyn took out her looking glass and swore as she took in the were-wolves, some in their wolf forms and most in their human forms, running from several creatures that looked like something out of a nightmare. They were scaly creatures, bigger than a horse, with large glowing red eyes in the front of their heads. Their snouts were pointed, and Roslyn could see razor sharp teeth the size of daggers in their mouths.

"We have to do something," Roslyn said as she mounted her horse and took her bladed staff out from where she attached it to her saddle. "Karina, I want you to open the wards up in this section and get ready to close them again. Leaf, you stay here!"

Neither Tiffany nor Kavan had time to argue with her as she urged Sage into a run. Alexander had turned into his werewolf form and was running along beside her as she went to intercept Edwin and his group.

"Edwin!" Roslyn called out. "This way!"

The werewolves changed direction and she shouted for them to head past them towards the camp. The werewolves ran by her and Alexander as she raised her mage's staff and started casting spells of ice at the creatures coming towards them. One of them was hit with an ice spear that took it down, another evaded the raining shards of ice.

There were five of them now advancing on Roslyn and Alexander. She called to her connection with Jay'Al and felt the ground beneath her start to shake as tendrils of roots shot out of the ground to stab and grab at the creatures, halting them in their advancement. They let out a shrill cry as they were squeezed by the roots, thrashing around and trying to gnaw at the roots.

"What the hell are they?" she heard Alexander ask as he turned back into his human from, covering himself with his hands. Kavan was coming up behind him with his cloak now, eyes wide at the creatures she had caught. Edwin had left the rest of his pack at the camp and was now standing beside Roslyn as well.

"Thank you," Edwin told Roslyn, looking her in the eyes. "You could have let them kill us, but you did not; you saved us."

"You are my people too," Roslyn told him. "Tell me what happened."

"We had camped in the plains not too far from a chasm," Edwin told her. "They came from a sinkhole that developed right next to the chasm as the sun started setting, and they attacked us. We lost several who tried to fight them, ripped to shreds right there. I had to get my people out of there so we ran."

"Roslyn," Karina spoke up as she joined them. "Roslyn, we were down there!"

"And we did not see anything," Roslyn reminded her. "They must have come from the other side of the chasm or something."

"Where were you?" Edwin turned from looking at the now dead creatures to look at Roslyn.

"A sinkhole opened up on the plateau and took us down beneath the surface," she explained. "Karina and I found a cave with paintings, and a corridor that led to where the chasm had split it off from wherever the rest of the corridor led. There was also an aerie of some kind, we saw eggshells and feathers, but nothing else, and certainly no creatures like this."

"What if our people are being attacked right now?" Karina asked her, panic in her voice.

"I sealed up both paths," Roslyn assured her. "I also put some wards to stop any more sinkholes from forming. If you want I could astral project myself up to the plateau to make sure."

Karina nodded and Roslyn closed her eyes for a moment, doing what she told Karina she would do. She opened them up again and told her friend, "Everything is fine on the plateau."

"Interesting," Edwin commented as he looked at the creatures again. "What were you doing out this way, anyways?"

"Looking for you," Roslyn told him. "We made a pendant that can stop someone from shapeshifting, and from passing the curse on. We wanted to tell you there was another option than the first one we gave you."

"Well that was very good timing. I thank you. Like I said, you could have let them kill us."

"And like I said, you are my people too."

Edwin sighed and looked at her, and she could tell that he was using all of his senses to judge her, to figure her out.

"I had a lot to think about since you told us about the cure," Edwin told her. "For so long I thought I would never be able to go back to how I used to be. Centuries I was imprisoned." Edwin looked at Alexander. "I did a lot of things wrong. If there had been a cure when I was first turned…I would have taken it. I could have been a different man."

"You still have time," Roslyn told him. "You can make the right choice now, Edwin."

"My Queen," Cypress got Roslyn's attention as he and the others approached the creatures. "What should we do with the creatures' bodies?"

"Burn all but one, I want to study it," Roslyn told him. "We need to figure out where these things came from."

Roslyn turned away from her companions and felt a trickle of heat come from her nose. She reached up and wiped blood away, staring in shock at her red tipped fingers. No one else saw the blood trickling from her nose.

Leaf nudged her leg, sensing what was happening. "*Your body is not used to this level of magic use,*" her familiar told her. "*You might want to ease into the magic a little more; I cannot tell what might happen otherwise.*"

A Weaving of the Roots

"Great, one more thing for me to worry about," Roslyn half-joked; though now she was worried about what she could do. "Come on, let's rejoin the others."

Chapter Thirty

Heath felt something digging into his back. He groaned as he tried to move, finding dirt and gravel on his legs. He turned and found Everett behind him: it was his brother's knee digging in his back. Everett was unconscious and a little scraped up but Heath could tell he was breathing. Coughing from nearby made him look around to find Maeve and the other sailors mixed in with the debris like he was.

"You okay?" Heath asked Maeve as she tried to free herself from the ground. One of the sailors was above the dirt and started to help dig her out.

"I think so," Maeve responded.

Heath looked up and found that the hole they had fallen into had gotten both deeper and wider, taking with it what was left of the building above.

"I am not sure how we are supposed to get out of here now," Heath commented as he removed himself from the debris and started to drag his brother out as well.

"Does everyone still have their weapons?" Maeve asked as she struggled to stand. Her pistol was lying nearby and she grabbed it. The sailors each showed that their pistols were still with them as well. After a little digging, Heath found his pistol.

"If I had to replace another pistol…" Heath commented as he checked it to make sure it was not damaged.

Maeve chuckled at him. "Come now, you get yours free. Do you know how much I spent on mine?"

"I can use my connections for you," Heath told her with a wink. He looked down at his brother and started to shake him lightly to get him to wake up.

"Ugh," Everett said as he woke up. "What happened?"

"The rest of the ground gave out from under us," he told him. "Thank you for trying to save me though."

"Lot of good it did," Everett chuckled as he stood up. "All of us ended up down here."

470

A Weaving of the Roots

"I think we were going to have to come down here anyways," Heath told him. "We need to figure out what happened."

"And there is no way of going back now," Maeve spoke up. "Unless you can make us a frozen staircase to get out of here."

"I have not done anything like that yet, so I doubt it," Heath retorted. "Onwards it is, I suppose."

"Do we have any supplies?" Everett brought up the question. "How are we going to survive down here for more than a day?"

Heath smiled at his brother and told them to wait a moment. He closed his eyes and focused, projecting his astral form up and out of the whole and towards the ship. A moment later he opened his eyes again.

"The sailors are bringing rope and supplies," he told them.

"Could you not have used your astral projection to check what was down the tunnel to begin with?" Everett asked him, hands on his hips.

"If anyone was alive down there we would have to go get them anyways," Maeve told him. "At least now we will have the supplies we need to do this properly."

"Exactly," Heath said with a wider grin.

"Are you going to teach me that trick too?" Everett asked him while they waited for the sailors to get there.

"Perhaps," Heath teased his brother. "Let's just take this one problem at a time shall we."

They did not have long to wait for the other sailors to get there. They lowered the supplies down, which included food, water, more guns and ammunition as well as torches and bedding.

"If anyone does not want to come, you can go back with the others," Heath said to the sailors who had fallen down the sinkhole with them. None of them chose to go back.

"Can you do protective shielding like Roslyn?" Maeve asked Heath as they were preparing to head down the tunnel.

"Yes," Heath responded. "We can sleep under protection."

"Good, because if you had said no I would not be going with you," she told him.

"I would just *hate* not to have you along," he told her as he led the way, using his magic to light the tunnel.

Maeve picked up a clump of dirt and threw it at Heath, hitting him in the back of the head.

"Ouch!" Everett heard his brother exclaim, making him laugh. "Maeve, I know that was you!"

"That *totally* fell from the ceiling," she retorted as she and the sailors followed after Heath, guns at the ready.

"Guys," Everett called as he trotted after them. "Guys, wait up!"

Katie M. Thornton

***

Heath used his magic to light part of the passage, the sailors behind him using their torches. It was quiet, for the most part, though Heath thought it was eerily too quiet.

"This passageway looks like it was partially dug," Maeve commented as they ventured further down into the earth. "Not too long ago it looked just like the sinkhole though. Do you think someone caused the earthquake to clear the rest of the earth?"

Heath shrugged, saying, "Honestly, at this point, anything is possible."

"Yes, we have werewolves and merfolk, what else could we possibly run into," Everett commented.

Maeve gave him a look. "You have just jinxed it," she told him, turning to Heath and pointing at Everett. "You hear him?!"

"Come now Maeve, what could possibly be down here?" Everett asked her.

Heath, who was up ahead, turned a corner in the tunnel. He quickly came back around the corner and lessened the extent of light that was in his hand.

"How about dark elves," Heath whispered.

"Those are legends," Maeve retorted, though it was just a whisper as well.

Heath indicated the corner and so Maeve moved to look around it. Ahead there was a sudden drop, and what looked like a ladder descending into a cavern ahead. Maeve inched forward and looked down. The cavern was lit by odd crystals embedded in the walls and ceiling, along with a few dozen torches down below.

Below were dozens of figures that looked like men, though they were more lithe and stocky than most men. They had dark black skin and striking white hair, with pointed ears that stuck out slightly. These dark elves were wearing armour that was made out of dark scales, which Maeve guessed probably came from the serpentine looking creatures that the dark elves used as mounts. Beyond the group of dark elves was what looked like a paddock, in which there were a dozen or so humans being held prisoner. They had found their missing people.

Maeve turned to look at Everett who was also peering over the edge to look down at the cavern.

"You just had to jinx it," she told him in a whisper. "I hate you."

"What do we do now?" one of the sailors asked Heath. "There are more of them than there are of us."

"We have the advantage of surprise though," Heath told them. "Are any of you a good shot?"

A couple of them nodded. "Okay, good. Aim for the mounts' heads, preferably their eyes. Maeve and Everett, shoot the ones that fall off the mounts. I will use my magic to strike others down."

472

A Weaving of the Roots

There was just enough room for them all to either kneel or lay down to shoot. Heath gave a low whistle and the shooting started. There were cries of anger and pain mixed with confusion as Heath unleashed his magic on the dark elves without mounts. Thankfully the sailors were actually good marksmen and had been able to shoot the creatures in the eyes, and Maeve and Everett were able to shoot the riders as they fell. Heath got most of his targets, though one of the last ones had hid behind the paddock with the humans in it.

"Careful," Heath told his companions as he started to go down the ladder. "Keep an eye out, I might have missed one."

The others followed him down the ladder one at a time, each of them watching to make sure that no one would pop out of a nook and cause issues. Heath looked at the people in the paddock: men, women and children, all who looked scared, still with their arms and legs tied up. He could tell that they knew they were saved, but they were still worried for their lives down there beneath the earth.

"Commandant Mortimer sent us," Heath told the hostages. "I am Heath. Let us get you back up to the surface."

"There is one hidden," one of the men whispered to Heath as he cut the man's bonds. "Behind us."

Heath nodded his understanding and let the man go with the others. There were some crates behind the paddock, perfect for hiding behind. Heath slowly made his way over, making sure his pistol was still fully loaded; he took a few bullets out of his belt and added them to the barrel of his gun. He rounded the corner, aiming it at the dark elf that hid behind the crates.

"Mercy," the dark elf told him, holding up his hands in surrender. Heath had to think about the words the dark elf said, for it was a slightly different language than the common and almost a mix of the Jay'Alian and ancient Tribes, but he understood somehow.

"What were you doing with them?" Heath asked the dark elf. "Why did you attack us?"

"Earthquakes broke the earth," the dark elf said. "We see what is above. We learn."

"You kidnapped people," Heath answered. "You killed people."

"More of us go to the surface, where other earth-quakes happen," the dark elf continued. "The big land, full of magic. It interests our king."

"The big land?" Heath whispered, thinking of Jay'Al. Could the dark elves be attacking Jay'Al at the same time?

"Tell me what you know," Heath told the dark elf. "I have people I care about there, do you understand me? Do you know what I would do to protect them?"

The dark elf nodded, fear evident in his wide dark eyes.

"They are looking for the power," he told Heath. "The power that makes up the land. I know nothing else."

Heath turned to look at Maeve, who was staring at them with her mouth partially open.

"What?" he asked her.

"They are going after Roslyn," Maeve told him. "She is the Queen of Jay'Al. She *is* the power."

Heath swore. "We need to get back as fast as we can," he told them. "We have to send a messenger to her."

"Brother," Everett called his attention. "Use your damn astral projection."

"I can only reach so far," Heath told his brother. "I suppose I can try but if I cannot then we have to do it the old fashioned way."

Heath closed his eyes, and Everett could feel a change come over his brother, like earlier when he was reaching out to the soldiers. After a few minutes Heath opened his eyes again, shaking his head.

"I cannot reach her," Heath told him. "We need to get back to the surface and send a message from there."

"Heath, look at this," he heard Maeve's voice from somewhere nearby. When had she wandered off? He followed her voice to what looked like a nest. Inside it was one large egg that was the size of his forearm.

"What do you think it is?" Maeve asked him. "More of the scaled mounts that the dark elves had?"

"No," Heath told her, sensing something within. "No, this is something different."

"How can you tell?" Maeve asked him as he reached his hand out to touch the egg. Mere moments after he touched the egg fractures appeared on the outside. He stepped back as the egg cracked more. A beak bit through the shell, devouring as it went. The creature within was not a scaly creature like the ones they had just killed, but had the head of an eagle and the front paws of a feline, its back paws those of a bird of prey. It was rather bigger than most newborn kittens, and as it stepped out of its shell it became evident to Heath that this creature had wings springing from its shoulders. Its head was featherless but for its cat-like ears, and the rest of its body had fur including its long cat-like tail.

"My gods," Heath said aloud as he took in the creature.

"Is that?" Maeve asked him.

"A gryphon?" Everett completed the sentence.

The gryphon kitten ate away at the eggshell for a few more moments before it cocked its head sideways at Heath, looking at him with slit eyes like a cat, blinking its double lids. It took a couple tentative steps out of the remains of its shell and rubbed its head up against Heath's leg. Heath himself felt different as the gryphon touched him, like there was a surge of energy between them.

A Weaving of the Roots

"What just happened?" Maeve asked him as he scratched the gryphon's head.

"I…think I found a familiar," Heath told her. "When Roz gave us that tree, and I added my blood to it…I think I was connected with Jay'Al, the magic of the land. This gryphon is now my familiar. I can sense her."

"Well Roslyn has a little explaining to do I think," Maeve commented. "How come you get a familiar and I don't?"

"Add your blood to the tree on Mast," Heath told her. "That might do it."

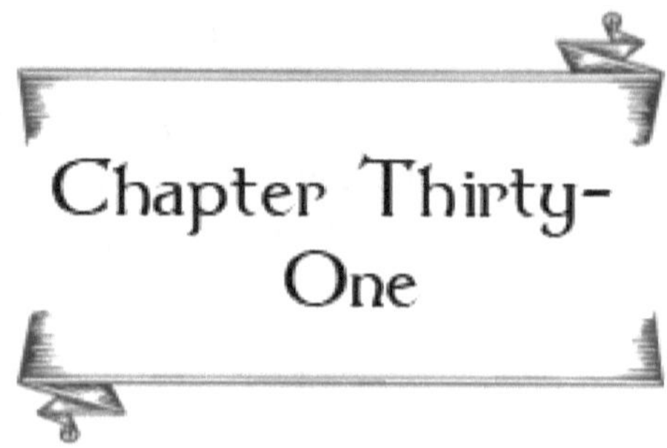

Chapter Thirty-One

Roslyn looked at the dead creature that Cypress had brought back. He had had to cut the roots out of its body to get it out so it was slightly mangled. A lot of the orcs had looked at her with what looked like fear, but Cypress told her that it was respect and awe.

"You called on the land," Cypress told her. "You are the Queen of Jay'Al, you are connected to the land. We are glad we are on your side."

Alexander and Kavan were with the werewolves at the base of the plateau now. Roslyn was not quite sure she could trust Edwin yet so they were guarded by her magic. She was going to talk to them after she had taken a closer look at the creature.

"You asked for me?" she heard Aidan as he walk-ed towards her. They were just at the top of the tunnel off to the side. Roslyn was still wearing her armour, her Mage staff attached to Sage's saddle who was grazing nearby.

"Dear gods, what is that thing?" he asked as took in the creature.

"That is what I am going to find out," Roslyn told him. "I will dictate what I find to you, if you would be so helpful as to write it down for me."

"Of course, your majesty," Aidan responded with a grin as he sat down, taking his writing implements out of the satchel he carried with him always. Roslyn stuck her tongue out at him and he did the same in return.

"How was it killed?" Aidan asked her as she prepared her frishna dagger to cut into the creature.

"I called up roots from the ground and speared it. There were more of them, I just asked Cypress to bring one back so we could study it."

Aidan looked at her with wide eyes as she checked the creature's eyes.

"Nocturnal eyes, by the looks of it," she told him. "Or rather they are used to being underground in the dark."

"Do we know where they came from?" Aidan asked her as he wrote down what she said.

"Edwin said they came from that giant chasm to the east," she told him.

A Weaving of the Roots

"Karina and I were on the other end of those tunnels, but we saw no sign of those creatures."

"So they came from underground, and they look to be predators from where their eyes are set," Aidan said as he wrote that down.

"And their rather sharp, large teeth," Roslyn commented as she opened the creature's mouth.

Roslyn looked up to see Karina and Heather coming towards her. "What is it?" she asked them, stepping away from the corpse.

"I can dissect the creature," Heather told her. "I was top of my class in biology at the Mage University. You have more important things to do."

"Oh, well then," Roslyn said as she put her dagger down. "Thank you, Heather. Do you still want Aidan to take notes for you?"

"His help would be appreciated," Heather looked at him and smiled, Aidan smiling back at her.

"I guess I should head back down to what is left of Base Town to talk to Edwin," Roslyn said as she headed over to Sage. "Karina, would you get Tiffany and the three of us can go down?"

Karina nodded and ran to go get Tiffany. The two of them returned a few minutes later on their horses, both of them wearing their armour. Together the three of them rode down the tunnel.

They found Alexander, Kavan, and Edwin sitting around the tree that she had grown next to the opening of the tunnel. All of the men and women who had been turned by Edwin were all in their human forms nearby, dressed in alpaca wool breeches and loose tunics. They watched Roslyn apprehensively, and she knew they were waiting to hear about the cure.

"I wanted to thank you again," Edwin spoke first as she approached them. "You could have let us all die."

"Like I said, you are my people too. I hope you have been getting along," Roslyn said as she looked at Cypress and the other orcs who had been guarding them. Cypress nodded to her, indicating that they were all getting along.

"Tell us about the pendants," Edwin said to her. "Kavan here told me that it keeps him from changing but he still has his abilities. You can make one for all of us?"

"I should be able to, yes," Roslyn answered him. She leaned against the tree and looked at Edwin. "Will you make peace with us?"

"Yes," he told her without hesitation. "I want peace. I want to be able to live my life again."

"Good," Roslyn told him, reaching out to take his hand. He gripped her hand in return. "I will get what I need and we can start on making the pendants for every-one. For now, I want to invite you all up to the plateau. We have no idea where those creatures came from, or if there are more of them out there, so to be safe we should all be together."

Katie M. Thornton

"I will definitely feel safer with our Queen to protect us," Edwin told her. "What you did was spectacular. I have never seen anything like it."

Roslyn smiled at him and looked at the others. "You will be home with your people soon," she promised them. "I know your families have been waiting to hear news."

***

Roslyn was petting Leaf as they sat next to the fire in the town square when the hairs on the back of her neck stood up. Leaf cocked her head to the side as a shape formed in front of them.

"Heath!" Roslyn said as she recognized who the astral projection was.

"I do not have much time," he told her. "Do you remember anything about the dark elves in Ellsgroves legends?"

"Yes, they were banished like a thousand years ago…why do you ask?"

Heath's expression was grim. "They were banished *underground*, Roslyn. We came across some dark elves while checking on earthquake damages. They had these large lizard-like creatures with them, they were using them as mounts."

"Fangs as big as daggers?" Roslyn asked him.

"Yes. Were you attacked?" He seemed really worried.

"The werewolves were attacked by a group of them," she told him. "We did not see any dark elves though."

"It could have been a scouting party. I was able to interrogate one of the dark elves: their king is interested in the magic of Jay'Al. *Your* magic, Roslyn. I think they are coming after you."

"You have got to be joking," Roslyn said. "First Grau, now some dark elf from the bowels of the earth?"

"Your connection to Jay'Al has changed you," he told her. "You are more powerful now as the Queen of Jay'Al because you are connected to it. Certain entities will seek out that power to try to possess it, to use it for themselves. It is what they do."

"Where are you now?" Roslyn asked him.

"Still in the archipelago at the moment," he told her. "Once I get back to Mast I'm coming back to you, and I'm bringing friends."

"What do you mean?"

"Maeve came to the Archipelago, sent by your father," he explained. "Also, whatever you did with that tree you gave us…I found a gryphon egg and when it hatched the kit imprinted on me like a familiar."

"I had no idea that would happen, but that is very interesting," Roslyn told him. "Karina and I found an underground cavern below the plateau that had drawings of gryphons in them, along with nests full of broken eggshells."

"You will have to tell me more about that when I get there. You also might want to contact your father soon," he told her as his image started to fade. "I miss you."

Before she could say anything else his form was gone.

Roslyn looked at Leaf, who was peering up at her now. "You will finally be able to meet him," Roslyn told Leaf. Leaf started to make a sound like a cat purring and she flapped her wings slightly with excitement.

"Come on, Leaf," Roslyn said to her familiar as she stood up, "We have a job to do."

She had only been taking a break from working on the pendants; now she needed to get back to it. With Heather dissecting the creature she was the only other mage with the knowledge to do it. There was no more time to waste. She had more than enough sunstones to use, and all of her ingredients were brewing and waiting.

"I wonder where Cassidy is right now," Roslyn mused aloud as she walked back into her tent, Leaf at her heels. Thinking about what Heath had said about contacting Cassidy she would have to start making the potion that would help her astral project herself far enough to reach Ellsgrove and Cassidy; since it took a few days to brew she would have to get started that day.

***

Cassidy walked down the gangplank onto the dock, with Kai right behind her. Sully and the Honour Guard were right behind, and they fanned out around her as she walked down the dock, Sully getting in front in order to lead her. Rafi came off the ship last though he caught up with them quickly enough.

"It is a day's ride to the Capital," Sully told Cassidy as they reached the streets of the harbour city. "I will get us horses."

"Very well," Cassidy responded, very aware of the people who were staring at her. She was dressed in her deerskin hide clothing, her hair braided back as Roslyn had taught her. At her waist was her frishna sword. Crick sat on her shoulder, taking in the new city with chirps.

"Wait here," Sully told her, looking at the lady knights who made up her Honour Guard. They nodded to him and closed in on Cassidy and Kai, hands on the hilts of their weapons. They moved over to the front of a small bakery, Cassidy taking in the smells of the baked goods.

"Are those cinnamon rolls?" Cassidy asked, looking at one of the buns with white frosting. "Roslyn described them to me once."

"I'll get you one," Rafi told her, entering the bakery and coming back out a moment later with two rolls, one for her and one for Kai. "Here you go."

Cassidy thanked him and took a bite, enjoying the savoury taste of the cinnamon and gooey sugar.

"Mhhmmm, this is exactly how Roslyn described it," Cassidy commented as she licked her fingers clean, having devoured her treat already.

Sully came back to them then with horses for everyone. They mounted the horses and followed Sully out of the city, heading inland to where the Capital was. They stopped a few times to rest the horses, relieve themselves, and eat, but they were on a mission and stayed on time. They reached the Capital by sundown.

"I really would rather meet my father in the morning," Cassidy told Sully as she stared at the palace in the distance in the waning light. "Can we go to an inn for the night?"

"Yes, I suppose we could," Sully answered her.

"Thank you. I really need to bathe and find appropriate clothing," Cassidy commented as he steered them in the direction of a reputable inn.

"I think I can help with the clothing," Rafi told her as they reached an inn. "The seamstress who made Roslyn's clothing would be delighted to provide you with something nice to wear."

"Could you go find her and bring her to me?" Cassidy asked him. He nodded and veered his horse down another street as the others dismounted. A few stable boys came out to take their horses and Sully led the way into the inn. Within minutes they had rooms and Cassidy was soaking in a tub of hot water with a lot of bubbles.

Baylee and Kallista guarded the bathing room while she was in there, and walked her back to her room after she was done. There Cassidy found a woman in her late twenties, a petite woman with fine brown hair, stand-ing in her room with a satchel of clothing.

"Whoa," the woman said when she saw her.

"When Rafi told me you looked like Roslyn he really meant it. Hello, I am Mel. I was told you need some clothing fit for a princess."

Cassidy grinned. "Roslyn told me a lot about you, Mel. Thank you for coming at this late hour."

"How is Roslyn doing? It has been quite a while since she left," Mel commented as she arrayed some articles of clothing over the bed.

"She is the queen of Jay'Al," Cassidy told her. "Her familiar is a dragon, and she has grown in power since her joining."

Mel stared at her for a moment while the news settled in. "Roslyn, a queen?" Then she broke out in a smile. "Oh that is grand!" Mel laughed. "So not only are you a princess of Ellsgrove, as the queen of Jay'Al's sister you are a duchess of Jay'Al."

"So I have been told," Cassidy said with a chuck-le. "Show me what you have, Mel. I know from the outfits Roslyn wore that I will definitely like whatever you have for me."

***

Edmond sat down next to his father in the Throne Room for the morning meeting with some of the nobles. His mother and princess Alara sat just be-hind them so they could participate if needed. Edmond felt his ears turn a little red at the thought of Alara. He had not seen her much over the last couple sennights, but he had heard about her from his father. She had interrogated the would-be assassin and found out quite a few things. They were coming up with a plan to draw out any more nobles who were against the new changes, but it took time to put things into place.

As some of the last nobles trickled into the Throne Room, Edmond saw the herald talking to a knight with curly hair. He leaned forward, trying to get a better look, but then the herald blew his horn and knocked his cane on the floor for attention. Edmond looked at his father with a raised eyebrow as everyone turned to look at the herald standing in the doorway.

"The Grand Duchess of Jay'Al, Cassidy Amelie," the herald announced, and Edmond watched as a young woman who looked identical to Roslyn walked into the room with Sir Sullivan right behind her, along with half of the Honour Guard that had been sent to Roslyn. Edmond also noticed that Rafi was at the back of the group of lady knights, along with another man from Jay'Al who had a small fox-like creature following at his heels. Cassidy was dressed in an outfit much like the last one he saw Roslyn wear, leggings with a long tunic that had slits down the side. A weasel-like creature was perched on her shoulder.

Lucius stood up and went to meet Cassidy, saying, "Welcome Cassidy Amelie, second born daughter of Ellsgrove." There were already murmurs going through the crowd of nobles, now they got even louder. "It is good to finally meet you."

"Well met, father," Cassidy told him with a grin as she embraced him. She turned to look at Edmond, and he could see that her eyes were the opposite colour of what Roslyn's were. "You must be Edmond," she said to him. "Roslyn has told me a lot about you."

"What a lovely surprise," Edmond managed to say before she hugged him. He felt the weasel's fur against his nose and stifled a sneeze. "Why have you left Roslyn's side at this time?"

"She sent me," Cassidy explained. "Roslyn sent me here to protect our father."

"How could she possibly know there was trouble here?" Edmond asked her, but she just raised an eyebrow at him much like Roslyn would have.

"My Queen has her ways," Cassidy told him. "It is good to be here, despite the circumstances. My orders are to help root out the conspiracists and protect the king."

"Your help will be greatly appreciated," Princess Alara spoke up as she and Elle stood and approached her.

"Cassidy, this is Princess Alara from Raistminestine," Edmond introduced them. "She is my betrothed. Also, Elle, my mother."

Cassidy curtsied slightly and smiled warmly at Elle. "May I call you

Mother Elle, as Roslyn does?" she asked. "I have been looking forward to meeting you. Thank you for accepting my sister into your family and raising her as you did."

Elle smiled and pulled Cassidy into a hug. "Of course," she responded, slightly teary-eyed. "It is so good to finally meet you, Cassidy."

Edmond looked around and noticed that the nobles had been trickling out of the meeting, seemingly having been dismissed for the morning. He looked at the herald who was ushering people out, and earned a wink from the man.

"What is the creature on your shoulder?" Alara asked Cassidy.

"My familiar, Crick. She is a pine marten. Kai," she nodded to the other Jay'Alian man in her group, "is also a shaman like I am, a kind of mage. His familiar there is a fennec fox, Tej."

"What do the familiars do?" Alara asked, intrigued.

"They connect us more to the land, and we can hear their thoughts. They can help us store magic as well as control our magic better," Cassidy explained. "Roslyn's familiar is a dragon."

"How does one get a familiar?" Alara asked her next. "Is it only for those of Jay'Al?"

"I am unsure," Cassidy responded with a shrug. "It could be possible."

"Let us retire for the morning," Lucius interrupted them. "We can have some tea and talk in more privacy."

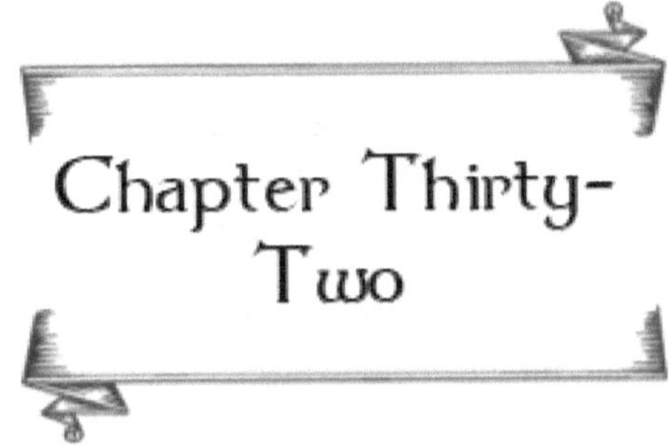

Chapter Thirty-Two

Heath watched as the island of Mast came into view. They had loaded up all of the people who had lived there onto their ship, along with their animals and what belongings they could carry. The dark elf they had chained up in the brig, but the gryphon stuck by Heath's side. At that moment it was devouring a fish that Maeve had caught for it to eat.

He had contacted Roslyn as they had left the northern island and he felt better now that he had talked to her. The last time he had talked to her they had been in Hyena City when the orcs were attacking the city. Something about her was different now though and he could not quite place it. Was it her connection to Jay'Al that he felt, or the connection with her familiar? He guessed he would figure it out once he got back to her.

Everett approached him, leaning against the side of the ship beside the gryphon sitting on the railing.

"Well this is interesting," Everett commented. "I remember hearing the stories of gryphons, but seeing one…do you think it will grow feathers on its head?"

"I would imagine so, as with its wings," he replied. Without any feathers the gryphon looked kind of funny, as did most newly hatched birds. The fur on its body had dried, revealing calico colourings.

"I want to come with you to Jay'Al," Everett told him. "I have some apologizing to do to your queen."

"I need you to stay in the Isles," Heath told him as he turned to look him in the eyes. "You will represent our family on the council."

"You trust me to do that?"

"You pulled me back when I almost fell," Heath told him. "You could have let me fall."

"You are my brother," Everett whispered, and then he cleared his throat and said, "Thank you. I will not let you down."

"I know you will not," Heath reached out a hand and squeezed his brother's shoulder. "What do you think I should name her?"

"You are sure it is a female?"

"Very sure. I can sense it," Heath responded.

"I have no idea," Everett told him with a chuckle. "I am sure you will come up with something. She is *your* familiar after all."

Heath sighed and looked at the gryphon again, who was now peering up at him with her yellow eyes. She started to stretch, reaching out her front paws to touch his arm as she did.

"Solana," Heath thought aloud. The gryphon started to purr her pleasure as she came forward to butt her head against his arm.

"I think she likes that," Everett commented.

"Solana it is then," Heath smiled as he petted her. "I wonder what Roslyn's dragon will think of you."

"I wonder what Selene will think of Solana," Maeve commented as she joined them, chuckling. "You and cats."

"Hey, cats love me," Heath told her as Solana rubbed up against his chest, purring even harder now.

Maeve laughed and shook her head. "This is wonderful," she said. "Though if we found dark elves and gryphons, what else could be down there?"

***

Roslyn handed out the pendants to the werewolves, all of whom were still in their human forms. They were down in what remained of Base Town, though she was going to get them to come up to the plateau with her after the pendants were all handed out. Edwin received his last, watching as the rest of his werewolves placed the necklaces over their heads and let it rest on their chests. He could no longer sense any of them. Now he put his on, shivering slightly as a sensation covered his body.

Roslyn had suspected that Edwin's change of heart might not be real, but watching him accept the pendant and actually putting it on solidified that it was real. From what she had gathered from watching Edwin and Alexander, they had been lovers before Alexander had betrayed him to the Clans. That was why Edwin had been so vengeful at first, and Roslyn definitely understood where that rage came from: pain and heartbreak. Now though as she watched Edwin put the pendant on and look at Alexander who was also watching him, she could feel that the connection they had once had was still there. This was the life Edwin wanted to live, with Alexander.

"You still have the option of a complete cure," she reminded Edwin. The full moon had come the day before and the two werewolves she had cured had remained in good health.

"Thank you," Edwin told her. "We will keep that in mind if needed."

"Do you have a plan on where you will go?" Roslyn asked him.

A Weaving of the Roots

"I was thinking about sticking around to help you, actually," Edwin responded. "If there are dark elves coming here, you will need more help."

"We will stay with you as well," another of the werewolves spoke up. From what Roslyn had been told, four of the werewolves that remained were some of Edwin's original pack from the beginning. All of them were men who looked to be in their late-twenties, each of them Jay'Alian. "We will serve our Queen."

"These are Ari, Nav, Selig, and Waylon," Edwin introduced her to the men.

"It will be our honour, Queen Roslyn, to fight alongside you to protect our home," the one named Waylon told her.

"Thank you," Roslyn told them. "I accept your swords. Now, until we know where those creatures came from and what they are doing, let us all go up to the plateau together."

The group grabbed their respective things and headed for the tunnel, Karina and Tiffany standing on either side of the tunnel. Kavan had been standing with Alexander and had already headed up the tunnel. Tiffany was not watching the people as they went by her though, for she was looking at something in the distance behind Roslyn. Roslyn noticed this and turned to see dust in the distance.

Roslyn took her spyglass out of her satchel and used it to look into the distance, smiling as she recognized those were travelling in their direction.

"It is the people of the Wolf Clan," she told Tiffany and Karina. "I see my mother and grandfather Rotho at the head of the group."

"We should go greet them," Roslyn added as she turned and started walking to where Sage and her friends' horses were picketed nearby. The two women joined her, mounting their own horses and riding out to meet with Amelia and her people. There were several dozen wagons with people in them, the warriors of the Clan riding on horses around them.

"Mother!" Roslyn greeted Amelia as she rode up to her in her wagon. Rotho rode a horse beside Amelia's wagon.

"We have come to join you," Amelia told her. "As we had planned."

"I see you did not get our message in time," Roslyn told her, though she had known that would probably happen. "Please tell me you have not seen any large lizard-like creatures on your travels."

"I cannot say that we have, though that is oddly specific," Amelia responded, earning an explanation from Roslyn.

As Rotho listened his eyes grew wide. When Roslyn finished he spoke, "Dark elves? Here? This does not bode well."

"What do you know, grandfather?"

"Not much, just old stories, much like the werewolves. There were a few skirmishes with creatures described as dark elves in our histories, but nothing came of it. If they have found a way to get to the surface again though…"

"Well the werewolves have been dealt with," Roslyn told him. "They have surrendered to us and accepted peace. They have joined our side."

"That is wonderful to hear," Amelia told her. "Though if there is danger we should keep going to the plateau."

Roslyn nodded and the travelers continued ahead, Roslyn, Karina and Tiffany staying behind them with a few of the Clan's warriors. McKenna rode his horse over to talk to Roslyn.

"We used the runes you provided to mask our camps at night," McKenna assured her. "I saw some strange tracks near the swamps before the plains but nothing like you described."

"Good," Roslyn responded, feeling a little more at ease. "What did the tracks look like though?"

"Footprints, though they were smaller than any man's," he told her. "It was strange."

"Anything like a sinkhole nearby?"

"Yes, actually, we found a small one near the swamp, right where those footprints were," he said, now thinking there might just be a relation to everything else going on.

"Interesting. That might be something to look into then," Roslyn said. "Come on, let's get going. We are having venison stew for dinner and I am really looking forward to it."

"Have you heard from Cassidy?" McKenna asked her as they rode along beside each other.

"No, but Heath is alive," she told him, earning a surprised glance. "He found merfolk, they saved him. He is currently in the Archipelago, though he will be on his way back soon."

"So both Kavan and Heath have returned to you," McKenna commented. "You are lucky to get a second chance."

"Yes, well...what do you think made those foot-prints?" she asked, trying to change the subject.

McKenna smirked, understanding what she was doing. "Like I said, I had no clue," he reminded her. "There used to be a lot of different creatures hundreds of years ago that disappeared. What if they just went underground somewhere, and with the earthquakes they are now being forced above ground?"

Roslyn thought that was definitely something to think about.

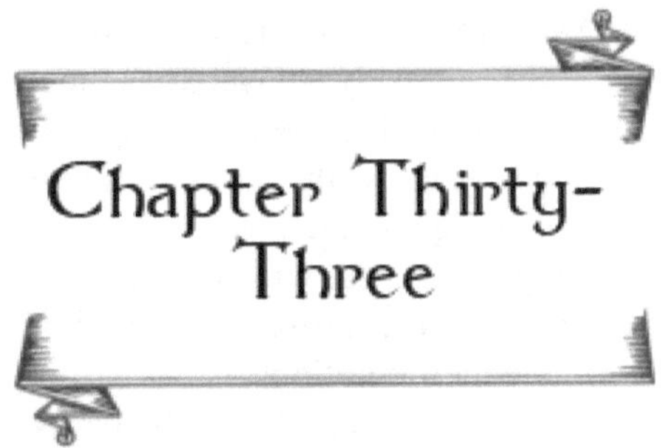

Chapter Thirty-Three

assidy stepped out onto the balcony to watch the sun rise, feeling the cool late-spring air. She could hear the birds of the Royal Forest awaken with the sun. Crick leapt up onto the railing and sat there listening with her. It was all so very strange to be in Ellsgrove finally. The birds even sounded slightly different.

Cassidy turned to look at her satchel that was sitting on one of the small tables in Roslyn's suite. Inside it was a sapling that Roslyn had grown specifically for Ellsgrove, just like the one that Cassidy had given to Heath. She was supposed to present it to their father during the treaty signings; Roslyn had said for him to plant it in the Royal Gardens and have him do the same as Heath had done. Cassidy had felt the magic of the tree on Mast as it had grown so she knew the same would happen with this one. Roslyn was using the roots to weave the nations together. It was an interesting idea.

There was a knock at the door. Cassidy went to answer it, finding Sully standing there.

"I am to escort you to breakfast," he told her.

"Alright, let me get changed and I will be right out," she answered, thinking about what to wear. She ended up choosing her normal alpaca wool clothing, and she quickly brushed her hair out before tying it back in a braid. She joined Sully in the hallway a moment later, Crick at her heels. He led her across the palace, as she took in the paintings on the walls of her ancestors, all of whom looked like her father or brother.

"Have you heard anything from Roslyn?" Sully asked her as they approached the doors to the king's suite. Guards on either side of the door were looking at Cassidy with slight confusion but then they still put their fists over their hearts to salute her.

"No," she told him. "It will take Maeve more time to get to her, the plateau is quite a ways inland, you know that."

"I just wasn't sure if maybe she could have sent a message ahead or something," Sully replied. "Anything is possible with those mages these days."

"I suppose you are right," Cassidy answered as they went through the doors and into the suite of rooms that were the king's–her fathers. Lucius met them at the door, greeting Cassidy with a hug. Behind him was Elle and Edmond, as well as two younger girls and a boy who would be Eliza, Poppy, and Robert. Robert was staring at her with wide confused eyes, his hands behind his back. Eliza and Poppy looked confused as well, though they were a little older and more able to hide their emotions.

"You remember me telling you that Roslyn had a twin sister," Lucius told his younger children. "This is your second oldest sister Cassidy."

"Hello," Cassidy greeted them, bowing her head slightly. "Hello Eliza," she spoke to the fifteen year old girl with the long blonde hair. "Hello Poppy," she said to the thirteen year old with the shorter blonde hair. "And hello," she turned to say to the youngest. "Roslyn has told me so much about you. I hope I do not confuse you, but if you look at my eyes you will see the difference: they are the opposite colour as Roslyn's were. You see?" She scrunched up her nose as they peered at her eyes, making them giggle.

"What is that?" Poppy asked, pointing to Crick who was peering up at them from behind Cassidy's pant leg.

"This is Crick, she is my familiar," Cassidy explained. "Did you know that Roslyn has her own familiar now too?"

"Is it really a dragon, like father told us?" Eliza asked, excited now.

"Truly it is. Leaf is a beautiful silver dragon," Cassidy told them.

"Can she fly yet?" Robert inquired, and Cassidy noticed that they were loosening up.

"Not yet, her wings are not strong enough. She is growing in size though. She used to be the size of my mother's cat but now she is as big as one of our largest hunting dogs."

"How is your mother?" Cassidy looked up to find Elle asking. "And your stepfather, McKenna?"

Roslyn must have told them a lot in her letter, she thought to herself. "They are both well," she answered. "They should be joining Roslyn soon at the plateau along with the rest of our village."

"Good," Lucius responded. "Please join us for breakfast," he waved a hand at the table nearby that had plates and cups waiting. "We would love to have you this morning."

"Of course," Cassidy told him. "I would love that."

***

Cassidy walked into the library, thinking how awkward breakfast had started out being but then they all relaxed and it had gotten a lot better as they sat down to talk. Edmond had recommended to her to see the Royal Library, and had hinted to her that Princess Alara would be there. Cassidy had become curious of the young woman who was her brother's betrothed, finding it interesting that her father would arrange a marriage. Edmond had asked to walk her to the library though, and he explained on the way.

"Alara saved father's life," he had told her. "She was one of several possibilities before that happened. She is a lot like Roslyn, but she is a little more confident in what she can do."

"Brother, if you saw Roslyn today I am sure you would find her much changed," Cassidy told him. "Especially since she joined with her familiar."

"I will have to take your word on that," Edmond replied meekly. "I'm sorry, Roslyn spoke a lot about you in her letters that Maeve brought, I guess I felt comfortable telling you that."

"I understand, Edmond, but…it's just, Roz has gone through a lot to get where she is today. How much do you know about Alara?"

"She has magic, and she is very good at interrogating someone," he replied, earning a laugh from Cassidy. "We have not had much of a chance to spend time together."

"And yet she is your betrothed?"

"I would like you to meet with her," he had told her. "I can tell you have the same intuition as Roslyn. Then after, maybe the three of us could have lunch together out in the Royal Forest?"

Alara was sitting at one of the tables, a large book open in front of her that she was slowly leafing through. There was no one else in the library except for one of princess Alara's guards who stood just a foot or so behind her. Cassidy saw that Alara had her light brown hair tied back and a dark blue scarf over her head. Her complexion looked naturally tanned, and her eyes were slanted slightly. Alara looked up at Cassidy with green eyes as she entered the library; her guard started to draw his sword but Alara shook her head and stood up.

"Grand Duchess Cassidy Amelie," Alara greeted her with a wide smile. "Princess of Ellsgrove. I only knew of your existence a few days before you arrived, but to actually meet you now!" Alara moved away from her table and went to embrace Cassidy. Cassidy allowed Alara to hug her lightly, returning the light hug. "Welcome to Ellsgrove. It is very good to have you here."

"Thank you," Cassidy replied as they separated. "I confess I do not know as much about the Under Kingdoms as I should."

Alara waved a hand to dismiss her thought and offered her a seat at her table. "I know basically nothing about Jay'Al," Alara confessed. "Your father has been the only one from this continent to go to Jay'Al in the last few decades. Before that most of the histories we had of Jay'Al were lost in the Great Fires, which happened several centuries ago."

"What are you reading?" Cassidy asked next. The book Alara had looked old and very thick.

"It is from around five hundred years ago," Alara told her. "The Ellsgrove Royal Library is sadly more extensive than ours, but thankfully it had what we needed."

Cassidy raised an eyebrow and asked, "And that is?"

"A history lesson," Alara told her. "We have forgotten a lot, but thankfully it was written down."

"Like what?"

"This morning I received information from our spies in the Archipelago," Alara told her. "It seems that Heath came across some dark elves where he went. Now, I know you are going to ask, 'what are dark elves', which is precisely why I am reading this; though apparently I have been told that your Mage University teaches this part of your history; sadly I did not have that same learning since all our knowledge of it was lost."

"Alright, I will bite. What are dark elves?"

"They are lithe creatures, barely over five feet tall. They have ink black skin and stark white hair, their eyes dark. They were creatures of the night, creatures that wreaked havoc on several continents until they were banished below ground."

"That is what Heath found?"

"That and some sort of large scaly monster that the dark elves use as mounts," Alara told her. "Oh, and apparently Heath found a gryphon that he claims is now his familiar."

Cassidy's eyes widened at that news. The tree that had grown on Mast must have done something, but Cassidy was unsure exactly what. She had never heard of any-one outside of Jay'Al having a familiar.

"I take it you had no idea that could happen outside of Jay'Al," Alara commented, seeing her expression. "What changed recently for that to occur?"

"I am not sure," Cassidy lied. She was not positive she should tell Alara the truth, even though Alara was revealing a lot to her right now. After all, Cassidy had no way of confirming that the tree Heath planted on Mast had caused any kind of change since she was not there after.

"I can tell you are unsure that you even know," Alara commented. "That is good, because you cannot lie to me."

Cassidy stood up, unsure of what to think. "Who are you?!"

"I am Alara. My magic can tell me if you are withholding the truth from me. I can also manipulate water. And no, I am not related to the merfolk like Heath, my magic comes from somewhere else entirely. You have been as honest with me as you could be. Now, would you like to learn about the other beings that disappeared around the same time as the dark elves?"

"Let me guess, redcaps, dwarves, and gryphons?"

"How did you–?"

"We have our own historical records in Jay'Al," Cassidy responded, crossing her arms over her chest. "Do you know the difference between a redcap and a dwarf?"

Alara shook her head.

"A redcap has a ninety-nine percent more chance they will kill you over a dwarf," Cassidy explained. "They may look a lot alike, but oh boy, are they different."

"How do you know?" Alara asked, almost demanding.

"They are in my history books," Cassidy told her. "The dwarves dug deep. Our people thought they were lost centuries ago. The redcaps…around the same time they disappeared as well. Now, is there anything else you have to tell me?"

"The group of people going after your father are all old conservatives who somehow managed to survive the sickness," Alara told her. "They were all conveniently far to the south when the outbreak happened."

"If they were targeting everyone with close ties to the throne then how come Lucius and Roslyn are still alive?" Cassidy asked her.

"I had my spies go to Wardgrove," Alara told her. "Mage spies. Your sister had the whole city under her protection. There were a handful of cases of sick people going into Wardgrove but it never spread; that was Roslyn's doing. She protected her home. Rightly so, since someone was targeting the throne."

"After Lucius and his family, who benefits to gain the throne?" Cassidy asked her.

"No one," Alara told her. "Seemingly that was the whole point. They wanted to have a new royal family, or to get rid of the royal house completely."

Cassidy smirked and said, "I bet they never planned on Lucius and his reforms. He has changed a lot for women. Though now, if something happened to him there would be a huge backlash: the women will not so easily give up their new freedoms."

"Exactly," Alara told her. "If these people were in my country, they would be rooted out and…well…dealt with," she continued. "We are heavily progressive."

"Thank you," Cassidy told her. "You saved my father."

"I was actually aiming to save Edmond," Alara responded with a sideways smile. "He had thrown himself in the way of the bullet meant for your father. Yes there are more heirs after him, but Edmond is different: he is not that much younger than Roslyn and he understood the importance of allowing women their autonomy. Edmond is a lot like your father, which is really no surprise with how Lucius raised him. We have your mother to accredit for that, I think."

"Thank you," Cassidy repeated herself. "For saving Edmond *and* my father."

"My pleasure," Alara responded. "What should we do about the rest?"

"We hunt down the old bastards who thought they could kill my family and replace them," Cassidy told her. "Will you help me?"

"By the gods, yes," Alara responded, giving Cassidy her forearm to grab. Cassidy reached for it and they shook hands in the warrior style. "I definitely think I would like Roslyn too."

Cassidy laughed at that, telling her, "Oh you have no idea. I am pretty sure Roslyn would ask you to spar with her and nonchalantly put you on your ass."

Alara grinned widely and said, "I look forward to that day. Now, can we go have lunch with Edmond?"

Someone cleared their throat from the direction of the door, and Cassidy turned to find Edmond standing there with a picnic basket in hand. He had gone to the kitchens to get their lunch while the two women had talked.

"Yes," Cassidy told Alara. "Let's go eat. Do you have a place in mind?"

"The Royal Forest, by the lake," Edmond chimed in. "It is a really nice day for a picnic."

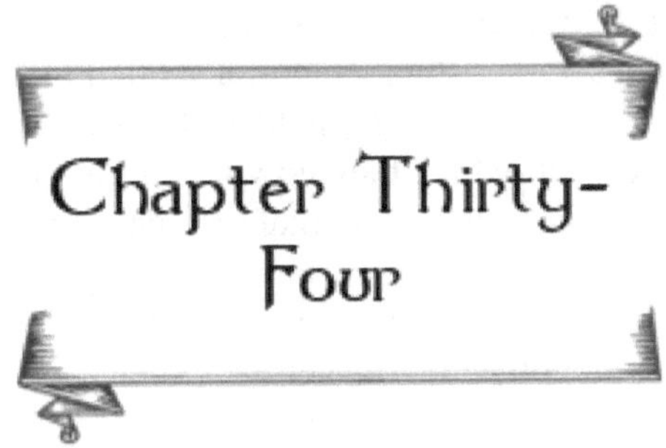

Chapter Thirty-Four

oslyn watched Edwin's reaction to the sight of the sinkhole in the swamp. His eyes widened in surprise, taking in the footprints that were coming out of it.

"This looks a lot like the one the creatures came out of," Edwin told her. "Though these tracks are definitely not from the same creatures."

"Our theory is that the earthquakes might be making the creatures come to the surface," Roslyn told him. "And that there are more than one type of creature below. The dark elves Heath told me about are the masters of the creatures that attacked you. These might be some-thing like a dwarf or a redcap."

"Redcaps were nasty little buggers," Edwin commented. "My grandmother told me of a time when her grandfather got attacked by one. He lost an eye."

McKenna chuckled from behind them. "Their calmer counterparts, dwarfs, were miners and inventors," McKenna chimed in. "How do you think the people of Jay'Al found the frishna metal to begin with? The dwarfs found it for us a long time ago."

"Interesting," Roslyn said as she surveyed the footprints that looked like they were heading east. "Let's take a look around here and see if we can find any clues about what came out here."

McKenna nodded and dismounted from his horse, tying its lead to a tree branch. Her stepfather was one of the Clan's best trackers, and the werewolves had their heightened senses so they should be able to find *some-thing*. Alexander yawned before he started to sniff the air, and Kavan winked at Roslyn as he started to follow the footprints.

Kavan was wearing his old armour, having traded it back from the frishna armour he could no longer wear. Roslyn had hoped that the pendant might allow him to wear the special armour without burning him but unfortunately it did not work that way. He had his old sword back as well, which Roslyn had kept with her things along with the rest of the armour and weapons they had found in the secret room above the underground cavern.

McKenna wore a set of frishna armour, a set that had been passed down in his family just like the one that Cassidy had. Roslyn had found normal armour for Edwin and Alexander, which they now wore. The orcs had also given the two of them weapons, large hammers that they carried as if they weighed nothing.

The swamp had been quiet since they had arrived, which Roslyn thought was odd. Leaf walked alongside her, her eyes keen as she looked around, her nose sniffing the air for any strange scents.

"The earth smells strange here," Roslyn could hear Leaf say in her mind.

"It's the swamp," she explained. "The decay of the wood and the water of the swamp make it smell different."

"There is something else," Leaf commented as she sniffed the air. Roslyn saw Kavan, Alexander and Edwin stop in their tracks, their hackles rising.

"We have something," Edwin said as the three of them headed in the direction of the smell, McKenna, Roslyn and Leaf following behind them.

"Does it smell familiar at all?" Roslyn asked Leaf. "Do you have any memory of it at all?"

"It does smell familiar," Leaf told her. *"A memory passed down to me of the smell, I just…watch out!"*

Roslyn grabbed hold of McKenna as a spear arched through the air towards him, pulling him back for it to whiz by him and impale a tree. Things began to move in the brush as a war cry reached Roslyn's ears. Beings only four feet tall emerged out of the brush, stocky legs and arms, their teeth sharp. They wore ragged clothing, nearly all seven of them with a spear in hand. Their hair was unruly, and they all looked scared and angry.

"We mean you no harm!" Roslyn told them, holding her hands up in front of her. She had pushed McKenna behind her, and now the three werewolves were watching angrily from nearby, Kavan holding onto Edwin's and Alexander's arms to keep them from attacking.

"Redcaps," Leaf said to Roslyn.

"Damn it," Roslyn said under her breath. "They are redcaps."

Kavan, Edwin, and Alexander heard her with their heightened senses, now more on guard.

"Why are you above ground?" Roslyn asked the group of redcaps. "Where have you been living all these centuries?"

"The dark elves invaded at first," one of the redcaps spoke up in broken common. "Then there was something else, whatever drove the dark elves from their home deeper in the earth. We had nowhere else to go but up."

Roslyn looked at Kavan, who was watching her now.

"How many of you are there?" Roslyn asked the redcaps.

"A few dozen, maybe, if we are lucky. We got separated," the first redcap who had spoken told her.

"From our histories we know that redcaps are violent, dangerous even. Is that true?" Roslyn asked them.

The group shrugged in unison. "True enough, I suppose. What is it to you?"

"Well, you nearly killed my friend here," Roslyn answered. "Unprovoked."

"You were following our trail!"

"We were interested in the tracks. Some friends of ours were attacked by large scaly creatures a little while ago; they came from a sinkhole as well."

Each of the redcaps' eyes widened. "That means the dark elves are coming to the surface as well," one of the other redcaps spoke up.

"What could drive dark elves from their homes?" Edwin raised the question they were all thinking. "What else could be down there that could be a threat to the dark elves?"

"Where do we go where the dark elves cannot find us?" another of the redcaps asked, clearly afraid.

"As long as you do not attack the people of Jay'Al, my people, you can stay in the north," Roslyn told them.

"Who are you then?" another one of them spoke up.

"She is Queen Roslyn, the Queen of the lands that you stand on," McKenna told him.

"Well, Queen Roslyn, you would suffer redcaps on your land?" the first redcap asked her in disbelief.

"You are refugees, are you not?" Roslyn asked them. Slowly they nodded their heads. "I offer the redcaps asylum in Jay'Al, and any of the other creatures seeking refuge, but only if you remain peaceful with the rest of the denizens of Jay'Al."

"Aye, I think we could do that," the first redcap spoke after looking at his companions. "Where should we go though?"

"McKenna, do you have a map to show him to Bella Vale? The buildings that were left behind could be put to use by them," Roslyn asked her stepfather.

"What about others that come to the surface?" one of the redcaps asked. "How will they know where to go?"

"The tunnel you came up, there are other tunnels that connect and that is how you all got separated?" Roslyn asked them as she started to sit down on the ground, allowing her palms to rest on the mossy ground.

"Yes."

Roslyn winked at the redcaps and closed her eyes, focusing as a couple tendrils of roots looped around her fingers. She could feel the silky surface of the moss on the palms of her hands, and then she felt the tingling sensation as her senses followed the roots into the ground. Leaf sat down beside her, earning wide eyed glances from the redcaps who had only ever heard stories of dragons but never seen one. The dragon familiar leaned against Roslyn slightly to help provide more strength, control, and magic to what Roslyn was trying to do.

Roslyn felt her consciousness in the earth and the roots as she descended. She found the tunnels the redcaps had told her about, finding many that had small cave-ins that had caused groups to split up and find another way. She found several groups of redcaps not far away, but there were more on the other side of a cave-in that had not been able to find a way around yet. Looking further she found beings that looked a lot like redcaps but were wearing better clothing and had wagons and carts with them that they pulled along behind them with their belongings, and though they looked slightly scraggly from their journey Roslyn knew that these were dwarfs. She started to do what she had planned, connecting the tunnels slowly so that they all converged and came to one place: the sinkhole in the swamp. She saw many hesitate, so she gave herself a slightly corporeal form for them to see.

"There is safety on the surface," she spoke through the roots into her form. "I am Queen Roslyn of Jay'Al, and I welcome you."

Roslyn pulled back into herself, satisfied that those below were moving again. She smiled at the redcaps as she pulled her hands away from the moss, the tendrils of roots letting go of her fingers.

"They are on their way," Roslyn told them as McKenna produced a roll of paper and began drawing them a map. "There are dwarfs coming as well. Will you welcome them?"

The redcaps nodded after a moment.

"Thank you. Now, what are your names?"

"I am Darton, if it pleases you my lady," the first one spoke. His hair might be dark blond under all that dirt, and he had a scar on his upper lip.

"Fiske," said the second. He was wearing an eye-patch over his right eye.

"Inek, Kanu, and Mahir," there were three of them that looked like they might be brothers, the one named Inek introducing them.

"Ogo," was the sixth, who looked like he was missing an ear.

The last one, who looked a little younger than the rest, piped up after, "Ravi."

"Nice to meet you all," Roslyn said to them. She looked at McKenna who was just finishing up the map for them. "You should not have long to wait here for the others. There are maybe a hundred or so redcaps and dwarfs coming. You could stay the night here, and I can offer you protection for the night with my magic and then continue in the morning, or travel through the night."

"What protection do you have for us?" Darton asked her.

Roslyn held up a handful of crystals and told him, "Place these around your camp, say a few special words, and you will have a protective spell until you lift one of the crystals in the morning. No one can go in or out, and no one outside will be able to see you."

"Well ain't that nifty," Fiske commented. "I think it would be safer to wait till morning, if the dark elves' creatures are up here."

"Those creatures, do you have a name for them?" Roslyn asked them.

"Dekellians," Kanu told her. "The dark elves use them for hunting and as mounts."

"Good to know." Roslyn turned to look at McKenna who handed the map to Darton. "I think we need to go see the sinkhole the dekellians came out of."

"Do we really?" Edwin asked her. "They tore apart several of my were-wolves."

"I will be there this time," Roslyn reminded him with a slight smirk. She handed the crystals over to Darton and whispered the phrase to him. "You can remember that?"

"Aye," he answered, and repeated it to her in a whisper. She nodded, satisfied.

"Good. I will check on you in Bella Vale in a few days," she told them. "Though please leave the farms outside of the village alone."

"We will, and…thank you, your majesty," Darton said to her, kneeling. "You could have easily banished us back below ground again, but you have welcomed us."

Roslyn smiled at him and nodded before turning to mount her horse again. "Until next time, Darton and crew," she told them.

Chapter Thirty-Five

Cassidy liked the Royal Forest. There were dozens of beautiful birds that she had never seen before, and Crick enjoyed running up and down trees. It was peaceful. The paths were well taken care of, and along the paths were little lanterns on each side that would be lit at night, but only in certain spots. The flower gardens were blooming with the spring flowers, adding a sweet smell to the air.

Edmond led them to a small gazebo overlooking the lake that had a low picnic table. The breeze coming off the lake was cool, and Cassidy breathed in the spring air. Edmond started to unload the picnic basket as Cassidy looked around the gazebo, finding a mural painted on the ceiling of forest life. Alara sat on the bench and watched Edmond as he placed the plates on the picnic table and started to divide the meal between the three of them.

"So Alara, what was it like growing up in Raistministene?" Cassidy asked the princess as Edmond started to divide the cheese up.

"I spent my childhood learning many different things that would help me rule if I ever ruled," Alara told her. "My sisters learned alongside me as well. We learned self-defence at the same time as reading and writing. We also had to help take care of the silk worms that the palace grows."

"That sounds interesting, the silk worms," Cassidy commented. Alara wrinkled her nose.

"They smelled," Alara whispered, smiling. "The silk they produce is expensive, so we had to tolerate the smell."

Cassidy chuckled at that.

"What about you, Cassidy? What was life like in Jay'Al?"

"Well I wish I could say it was the same, though centuries ago life would have been a lot like yours. We had large cities, the chieftains had bigger homes, and we had large schools. Then the conflicts between the Clans got worse, and the orcs did not help matters at all. I think Hyena City is the only city left that is hundreds of years old," Cassidy told them, and she stopped to think about it for a minute. "I think the frishna mines are the only other thing that remains that is as old as Hyena City."

"How depressing," Edmond commented.

Cassidy smiled at him and told him, "We live a simple life, though we remember our pasts very well. We have farms but we also hunt a lot; it is a tradition to hunt. The shamans–mages–learn from their village shamans, they do not go away to school. Each Clan lives differently, though I know now things will be very different. Roslyn has a lot of plans now to bring the clans together, which is what our ancestors wanted."

"Do you not like the changes she wants to make?" Alara asked her.

Cassidy shrugged and told her, "We have known this way of life for so long. However, bringing back the glory of Jay'Al…I know Roslyn can do that."

"Were there things handed down through your family?" Alara asked her.

"Yes, especially with shaman families, and those who fought against the werewolves. We had a set of frishna armour passed down through several generations that is now mine."

"I would love to see the frishna armour," Edmond commented. "Roslyn has mentioned them in her letters."

"I will wear it for the beginning of the ball tomorrow so you can see it," Cassidy told him. "Then I will change outfits before the dancing begins."

Edmond smiled at that and popped a grape into his mouth. "Oh those old conservatives are going to love th–"

The sound of a gunshot cut off Edmond's words, but Alara was as fast with her magic this time as when she stopped the assassination of the king: she stopped the bullet with her magic, though this time it was definitely not Edmond who was the target, but Alara herself.

Cassidy stood up and looked around, finding the shooter trying to reload behind a bush next to the water. She started towards him when Alara told her to stop. Cassidy looked at Alara who was now smiling grimly.

"I have this one," Alara told her, and as Cassidy watched a giant hand made of water erupted from the lake and grabbed hold of the assassin, pulling him down into the water. There was a shout as their guards, who they had left at the entrance of the forest, came running.

"The royal forest was supposed to be safe," Edmond said through gritted teeth. Cassidy could tell that he was angry. "Guards, find out how that man got into the grounds!"

"All of the entrances are supposed to be guarded, and only people with royal permission are allowed thro-ugh," Edmond explained to Cassidy. "There are only three entrances, the one we came through, the one to the ballroom, and the one in our father's greenhouse."

"Why were they targeting Alara though?" Cassidy asked the real question as Crick ran to her from where she had been playing in a tree.

"Because they do not want a progressive queen on the throne," Alara piped up. "They wanted Edmond with a meek queen that they could control."

"These idiots need to be dealt with very soon," Cassidy said as the guards swarmed around them, half of them going over to where the gunman had been. His bag and gun had fallen when Alara's magical hand had grab-bed him, and his body now floated in the water. "Can we not get a moment's peace here?"

***

"Are you three all right?" Lucius asked them as they joined him in his study. There were soldiers all over the palace trying to find out how the assassin had gotten into the Roy-al Forest, even going along the stone wall that surrounded it to see if someone could have climbed over. There were enchantments on the top of the wall to keep people from climbing over as an added protection. The assassin had managed to get into the Royal Forest somehow, and King Lucius wanted it found out right away.

"Yes, we are fine," Edmond assured him. "Our lunch was interrupted, but we managed to finish it."

"They are getting very brave," Lucius commented as Cassidy sat down. Alara and Edmond took the other two seats in front of the king's desk. "I can-not fathom what could possibly be going through their minds right now."

"They are getting anxious," Cassidy informed him. "They see their chanc-es slipping through their fingers, like sand. I do not think my being here helps either."

"Why do you say that?" Alara asked her.

"Everything Roslyn stood for is everything they hate," Cassidy reminded her, "and I look just like Roslyn. With you and I here, Alara, I am sure they are feeling very threatened."

"Now that we know who is responsible though we need to stop them," Lu-cius told them. "We have to catch them all, however, or risk further attempts."

"Well, can we first shock them at the ball?" Cassidy asked him, telling him her plan.

"We have to get through the signing of the alliance papers in the morning first," Lucius reminded her. "The alliance with Jay'Al is a very big deal, as is the alliance with the Archipelago. They may want to put a stop to that before there is any ink on the papers."

"Triple the security, bring in Roslyn's mage friends for more magical pro-tection," Edmond suggested. "I am sure we can prevent anything from hap-pening in the morning."

"Let us do that then," Lucius told them. "Alara, will you add your guard to our security?"

A Weaving of the Roots

"Of course. I have several mages in my guard as well. It will take any assassin quite the gall to try to attempt anything with so much security," Alara told him.

Lucius smiled grimly at her, saying, "I am afraid they might try even harder, but nevertheless we need to try to stop them." He turned to his butler Roland who was standing by the door. "Get all of Roslyn's mage friends here tonight so we can strategize," he told Roland. "Include the mages from Alara's guard as well."

Roland nodded curtly and bowed before leaving the room.

"I have a special gift for you from Roslyn," Cassidy told her father. "It is a sapling that Roslyn grew specifically as an alliance gift. She wanted me to give it to you after the papers are signed but I think it might be a better idea to give it to you now."

"If you think so, then of course," Lucius responded with a smile. "I assume it is in your quarters?"

Cassidy nodded and got up, leaving the study to find Sully waiting for her.

"What were you thinking, going out into the Royal Forest without a guard?" Sully asked her as he walked with her.

"We were thinking that it should have been safe," she told him.

"You got lucky," he retorted.

"Yes, well, it happened so let it go," she replied.

"Cassidy, do not be like that. Roz sent me with you to help protect you as well as the king," he reminded her. "Where was Kai?"

"He had gone to the training court," Cassidy told him. "He is probably still–oh never mind there he is now."

"Cassidy!" Kai called from down the hall, still in his practice clothing that was wet with sweat. He had been on his way to her rooms by the looks of it. "I heard what happened, is everyone alright?"

"Yes, we are all fine."

"Why did you not come get me?" Kai asked her. Cassidy rolled her eyes.

"You were busy, and like I told Sully, the Royal Forest was supposed to be safe."

"You will have a guard with you at all times now," Sully told her. "Kai?"

"Of course," Kai responded with a broad smile. "It would be my pleasure."

"Of course it would," Cassidy commented as she reached the door to Roslyn's room. "While you get changed, Kai, Sully will escort me around. Sully, you can come in while I grab the sapling for the king."

Kai nodded and went to go get cleaned up while Sully opened the door for her. He did a quick security check of her rooms, hand on his sword hilt the whole time. He turned to her and nodded, and she quickly went in to grab the tree sapling. With it in hand the two of them returned to her father.

"You are to plant this in the Royal Forest, and let a few drops of your blood fall on the roots," Cassidy told

Lucius as she plopped the ceramic bowl down on his desk.

"Then shall we do that?" Lucius said, standing and picking up the ceramic bowl with the maple sapling in it.

Alara and Edmond stood and followed them out to the Royal Forest with Sully in tow as well as the king's own guards. Kai joined them along the way, wearing clean clothes, a small trowel in his hand to help with digging.

The king's guards fanned out when Lucius agreed on a place, and Cassidy held the ceramic bowl and Lucius dug a hole in the ground. Once the hole was done Cassidy helped him pull the sapling carefully out of the ceramic bowl and place it in the hole. As they watched, a couple of roots came out of the earth.

Lucius looked at Cassidy and she nodded, handing him one of the small knives she had on her belt. He used it to nick one of his fingers and allowed the blood to fall on one of the roots. As the blood was absorbed, the other roots stretched out to Alara expectantly. Alara looked at Cassidy with a raised eyebrow.

"Might as well solidify the alliance with your kingdom too," Cassidy told her as Lucius handed the princess the knife. She too nicked a finger and allowed the blood to fall on the second root. The root pulsed as it absorbed her blood and then descended back into the ground.

The hairs on the back of Cassidy's neck stood up as she could feel the ground beneath her feet vibrate slightly. Crick and Tej both looked at the ground with heads cocked to the side, and Cassidy was pretty sure both Kai and Alara felt the same thing from how they looked at the ground.

They all stood there for a moment as the sapling started to pulse slightly but then stopped after a moment. Lucius looked at Cassidy with a raised eyebrow.

"You will see in the morning," she assured him. "Come on, let's start preparing for tomorrow."

***

Edmond stood in his office watching the sun rise over the Royal Forest when he noticed a tree that had not been there the day before: the sapling Roslyn had given them had grown overnight to be over fifty feet tall, its leaves reaching for the new sun. Edmond wondered just exactly what the tree was meant for, and what it would change for them. His world had changed so much in the last year, and old kingdoms bringing forth alliances, what else could possibly change?

A knock at the door had him turn to find Sully and Cassidy, both of whom were outfitted in their armour with their swords at their waists. The frishna armour that Cassidy wore looked almost brand new compared to how he thought it would look after being handed down through the generations. He supposed that was the thing about the armour, it did not degrade or get rusty, and it was impenetrable.

"You are up early," Edmond commented as he sat at his desk.

"So are you," Cassidy replied as the two of them joined him in his study. "I hope you got some sleep."

"A bit. Is everything in place?"

"We just came from meeting with the mages, they are all in place." Cassidy assured him. "All of the guards have been double vetted and put into place as well."

"The guard on my mother and siblings?" Edmond asked.

"Both mages and normal guards," Sully told him. "They will be well looked after during the ceremony and the ball."

Edmond nodded and looked down at the papers on his desk before sighing. "Why did they think they could get away with this?" he asked them. "These assassination attempts."

"A lot of the progressive nobles are condemning the attacks," Sully informed him. "I have spoken with a lot of my noble counterparts and they are on our side. A lot of them will be here today."

"That is good news," Edmond commented. "At least the whole of our nobles are not against us."

"What will happen to the nobles who are part of the conspiracy?" Cassidy asked her brother.

"If they are caught, they will be executed," Edmond told her. "If they flee, their estates will be taken for the crown."

"Just the ringleaders executed, or their whole families?" Cassidy asked.

"Just the ringleaders. The rest of their families might be arrested, or just heavily taxed," Edmond told her. Cassidy nodded, liking that answer.

"Let's go have breakfast before the ceremony," Sully spoke up after a moment of silence. "We need to all be at our top form for today I think."

After grabbing a breakfast to go from the kitchens that consisted of fruit turnovers and buttered bread, they went to the Throne Room where the servants were almost done setting things up for the day. Cassidy peaked into the Ballroom that connected to the Throne Room, marvelling at the decorations. Maybe a few hundred years ago they had celebrations like it in Jay'Al, but she had never seen such finery before. With what Roslyn hoped to build in Jay'Al, could she expect more of this in the future?

"Here you all are," Lucius said as he entered the Throne Room to find Edmond and Sully talking with the guards and mages while Cassidy observed off to the side. Alara was behind Lucius, wearing her royal garments, and Elle was beside her wearing clothing that was a mix of the two kingdoms. Lucius was wearing fine purple velvet breeches with a white tunic that was tucked in, fine embroidery along the edges of his tunic that matched the embroidery on Elle's top as well.

"Good morning," Cassidy greeted her father as he approached her with open arms. "All ready for the day?"

Lucius embraced her with a smile, though he shrugged. "About as ready as I can be when there is a target on my family."

"Hopefully we catch them today," Sully commented. "They cannot allow these treaties to be signed if they want you out of the picture."

"At least we have a contingency in place," Lucius responded quietly with a wink. "Shall we prepare? The ceremony will start in a little over an hour."

***

Cassidy waited in the side room off of the Throne Room with Kai, who was also dressed in his armour, the ambassador from the Archipelago, Lorenzo, and Princess Alara along with her uncle Duke Gabor. Sully stood by the door that led into the Throne Room, and a redheaded mage named Jessica along with Sir Graeme stood guard at the other entrance into the room. Cassidy knew there were more soldiers on the other side of the door that led into the palace, so she felt at ease as they waited. Crick and Tej were both curled up by the fireplace in the corner of the room even though there was no fire going.

Sully peaked through the door as the various nob-les from around Ellsgrove filled the Throne Room. A lot of them were talking about the trea-ties that were to be signed, but Sully heard some conversations about the as-sassination attempts, with many of the nobles noting the increased security. There had been several checkpoints set up around the palace for the noble guests to be checked for weapons, especially guns. Several checkpoints had mages at them who used their magic to find traces of gunpowder and the like; Sully would not know until the ceremony was over if anyone was caught.

Cassidy walked over to Sully and peered through the slight opening of the door that he was looking through.

He moved over for her to do so.

"That is quite the crowd," Cassidy commented.

She could see her father and brother sitting on their thrones, Elle with them. Her younger half-siblings sat on a slightly lower dais, her sisters dressed in the same style as their mother with their hair braided back. Robert was dressed like his father was, his hair slicked back. There was a table in front of the dais with a couple of chairs, documents laying on the top with writing utensils waiting to be used to sign the treaties.

Cassidy wished Roslyn was there, and that made her wonder what was happening back in Jay'Al. A wave of homesickness washed over her so she looked at Kai who moved to be beside her and took hold of her hand.

"It will be alright," he assured her.

A Weaving of the Roots

"It's not this," she told him, "I miss home."

"I know," Kai told her with a smile. "I do as well."

"What do you think our families are doing back home?" she asked him, squeezing his hand for comfort.

"Knowing Roslyn?" Kai chuckled, making Cassidy chuckle too. "Who knows? But I think they are alright."

"I hope so," Cassidy muttered as her attention was brought back to the Throne Room. There were no longer people coming into the room, and the herald was making his way to the door she was looking through with his horn. "I suppose it's time."

Sully nodded and waited for the herald to blow his horn before opening the door. As the herald announced their names they each left the room and headed down the aisle towards the table as the nobles watched in silence. Crick and Tej walked with them, Cassidy and Kai at the front followed by Sully and then Lorenzo, with Alara and her uncle behind them, Sir Graeme and Jessica bringing up the rear.

As they approached the table and the dais behind it, King Lucius stood and addressed the nobles that had gathered.

"My people," he started to say, "Welcome to this momentous occasion. Today we sign several treaties of alliance that will make our kingdom stronger. Today we join hands with not only Jay'Al, but the Archipelago *and* Raistminestine. Please, join me in welcoming Duchess Cassidy Amelie from Jay'Al, Ambassador Lorenzo from the Archipelago, Princess Alara from Raistminestine." He started to clap and the nobles joined him. After a moment he put up his hands to signal quiet again. "Now we will sign the treaties." He motioned to Cassidy to come for-ward and offered her a writing utensil. She accepted it as he moved the paper she was to sign to be in front of her. She signed her name and handed the utensil back to her father before moving out of the way for Lorenzo. Crick rubbed up against her ankle as she stood at attention, peering out over the crowd to make sure another attack would not happen yet. Kai stood beside her, with Sully just behind them.

Finally Alara stepped up to the table and took the utensil from Lucius. Edmond smiled at her as she started to sign the papers that would solidify their marriage agreement and the alliance between the two kingdoms.

Cassidy felt herself holding her breath as Alara signed the papers, watching the crowd for any signs of sudden movement. Alara straightened and moved away from the table as her uncle added his signature to one of the papers.

The crowd had remained still, as if they too were holding their breath. Finally the Duke stepped away from the table and bowed to King Lucius.

"It is an honour," Gabor said to Lucius. "Thank you for accepting the marriage alliance between our two kingdoms. I look forward to working with you in the future."

Cassidy exhaled finally as Alara went to sit in a new throne next to Edmond that had just been brought up to the dais by servants. The nobles in the crowd began to clap and cheer as Alara sat down, and Cassidy found herself clapping as well.

Lucius held up his hand to quiet the crowd. "Now let us move to the banquet hall for a small luncheon before the ball begins, shall we?"

Chapter Thirty-Six

Roslyn wondered about the redcaps and dwarfs the whole way back to the plateau. Where had they lived underground all those decades? What had it been like to live underground? What other creatures were below the sur-face?

Tiffany and the rest of her Honour Guard awaited her on the plateau. They were supposed to be preparing to leave for the chasm and the other sinkhole, which thank-fully they had completed that task while Roslyn had been gone. A wagon was laden with supplies and weapons, and their horses were all ready. Karina was coming towards the wagon as Roslyn and her group emerged from the tunnel onto the top of the plateau.

"What did you find?" Karina asked her as the short distance between them grew smaller.

"Redcaps, and dwarfs," Roslyn replied. "Thank-fully we managed to come to terms with the redcaps and I offered them a safe place to live above ground."

"Well then," Tiffany said, "that will be interesting to see a redcap. Where did you send them?"

"Bella Vale," Roslyn told her. "They swore they would remain peaceful in exchange for safety."

"Are you ready to head to the chasm?" Karina inquired as she climbed up into the front seat of the wagon.

"Yes," Roslyn replied. "Where are Cypress and his warriors?"

"They will be here shortly," Tiffany assured her.

It was only a few minutes of waiting before Cypress and the rest of the orcs joined them, all of them out-fitted in their armour, their great war hammers in their hands.

The group now complete, Roslyn started back down the tunnel as the word spread from her Honour Guard to the orcs about what they had found. As they talked amongst themselves Roslyn found her mind wandering to Leaf, who was walking alongside her horse. The familiar was thinking about other magical creatures that she knew about, and Roslyn was fascinated. There were more than Roslyn knew of, including drakes of different kinds, wyverns, ogres, fauns, and centaurs. Flashes of images of what each of them looked like crossed Roslyn's mind, and she wondered if they all still existed somewhere below Jay'Al.

"If the redcaps and dwarfs survived this long, it may be safe to assume most of the others did as well," Leaf told her.

"How come you never told me about the merfolk?" Roz asked her familiar.

Leaf looked at her, and Roslyn could have sworn that the dragon smirked at her as she heard in her mind, *"You never asked."*

"Well aren't you cheeky," Roslyn told her with a chuckle. "What can you tell me about them?"

"It is interesting that they have revealed themselves to you after all this time," Leaf told her. *"I am eager to see what the king of the merfolk does next."*

Roslyn felt the same way.

It would take them a couple of days to reach the chasm and the sinkhole, so at the beginning of sundown they made camp. Kavan, Alexander and Edwin had brought down a fair sized boar during the day that was now cooking on a spit over a large bed of coals. The Hon-our Guard set up their tents and a small one for Roslyn, while the orcs wiped down the horses and made sure they were secure for the night after feeding them. Roslyn and Leaf walked around their campsite as Roslyn used her crystals to set up their protection for the night.

It was dark by the time the boar was done roasting, and as Roslyn started to carve the meat up for her companions she noticed Cypress start to cook some flatbread over the coals.

"What's this?" she asked him as she handed him a wooden plate with the steaming meat on it.

"One of our main food staples," Cypress told her, "for when we are travelling. It's simple ingredients with a bit of spices, but it goes a long way when the only thing is some meat."

Roslyn shrugged and accepted a fresh flatbread from Cypress on her own plate, loading the meat onto it and folding it up as Cypress was doing to eat it. It tasted a little bit like coal and smoked wood, but with the seasonings it actually accentuated the boar meat.

"Mhmmmm," Roslyn said as she ate. She swallowed and took a drink of water. "Thank you for making that, Cypress."

"My pleasure," Cypress answered. "I am glad you liked it."

A Weaving of the Roots

Roslyn looked up at the stars, remembering the last time she had been out on the plain. They had been only a group of eleven heading south, now they were twice that. Now, however, the dangers had increased, and Roslyn was unsure of what was out there waiting for them.

At least Aidan was safe back on the plateau, and Cassidy…well she should be safe with Kai, Sully and half of the Honour Guard. And Heath? As far as she knew he was still safe, on his way back to Jay'Al.

Thinking of having them both back, Roslyn thought of the first time she and Heath kissed, in the hot springs, versus the last time, in Hyena City; and the first time she and Kavan had kissed, the night of Cassidy's birthday, and the last time they had kissed when he had nearly lost control. What if they were all so different now? She worried about that the most.

"What is on your mind?" Tiffany asked her as she joined her by the fire.

"Worrying myself silly," she responded truthfully. "About Kavan and Heath, and how different we might all be now."

"Ah," Tiffany said quietly as she accepted a flatbread with meat on top from Cypress. "I wish I had some advice for you."

"I will figure it out," Roslyn told her. "Eventually."

"Do you still feel the same for Kavan?" Tiffany asked her before she took a bite of her food.

"When we kissed last I still felt the same as before," she replied. "Now Heath is on his way back and I can tell he still feels the same way about me too, but what if his experiences changed him? *I* feel changed myself, after becoming the Queen and joining with Jay'Al."

"I see," Tiffany responded after she swallowed. "Well hopefully things clear up for you after Heath is back."

Roslyn snorted and shook her head. "Thanks."

"I know, I know," Tiffany told her. "Maybe you'll meet someone completely different?"

"Now why go adding someone else to the mix?" Roslyn demanded. "That would be even worse."

"If you are unsure of both of them, why not?" Tiffany chuckled. "Makes life interesting apparently."

"No thank you," Roslyn replied as she shook her head. "I think I will go to bed now."

"Goodnight, Your Majesty," Tiffany teased as she continued to eat.

"Try not to stay up too late," Roslyn told her, "I need my Lady Knight at her best in the morning, just in case."

Tiffany stuck her tongue out at her and Roslyn laughed before turning around and heading for her tent.

"You two get along really well," Cypress commented as the rest of their party came to get food.

"She understands me," Tiffany told him. "It was refreshing to find someone like her."

"That is good. We like to see her interacting with her companions: she does not behave like she is above everyone else," Cypress commented. "Most people who are given such powers do not always act like this."

"Roslyn is smart," Tiffany told him. "She never wanted to be queen, but she has embraced it finally. The powers that came with it? I think she was as surprised as the rest of us."

"She changes things," Alexander interrupted. "She is a force to be reckoned with."

"Yes, she is," Kavan spoke up from where he was sitting and eating. He smiled broadly, thinking how he was lucky enough to have kissed Roslyn and have her affection in return, even though he knew she had not made up her mind between him and Heath.

McKenna smiled at Kavan, thinking of his stepdaughter and the two men who sought after her heart. He had known Heath before Kavan, and he thought Kavan had his work cut out for him, but he liked the young soldier. It would be interesting to see which one Roslyn did end up choosing.

"Finish eating and then head to bed," McKenna suggested to everyone. "As Roslyn mentioned, we should all be at our best for tomorrow, just in case."

"Yes, sir," Cypress and his orcs echoed. Edwin and Alexander nodded, and Kavan watched them all go to their respective tents. Cypress quickly carved up the rest of the meat to put in the special preserving chest Roslyn had with her before going to his tent. Kavan sat there alone next to the fire for a little bit, staring into the flames until he nodded off there.

***

"Kavan," Roslyn said as she shook him awake in the morning. He opened one eye to look at her before yawning and stretching.

"Did you mean to fall asleep out here?" she asked him.

"Kind of," he replied. "I was thinking of some things and then the fire kind of entranced me to sleep."

"Well there is a stream nearby, you should freshen up with the rest of them," she told him. "I moved the barrier to go around the stream."

Kavan nodded and went to go do that as she stoked the fire for breakfast. She started reheating the leftover meat from the night before, and started making scrambled eggs in a pan. One by one the men came back from the stream, their hair wet, and she spooned the scrambled eggs and reheated meat onto their plates.

"What is our Queen doing serving breakfast?" Cypress asked as he returned from the stream.

"Oh hush you," Roslyn told him. "Take your food and eat up, I want to get going soon.”

Cypress smiled at her and handed her his plate.

“The women are washing up now,” he told her. “You should go to the stream as well. I will take this over.”

She smiled and nodded, standing up and heading back to her tent for her towel. Leaf, who had been sleeping next to her bedroll still, awakened and joined her in going to the stream. Tiffany and the rest of the Honour Guard were at the stream, having stripped down to their under-things and starting to wash themselves down. Leaf jumped into the water, splashing Tiffany and causing a round of laughter from the rest of the young women. Roslyn put her towel down on the bank and started to undress as she tried not to laugh at Leaf who was now paddling around in the deeper parts of the stream and trying to catch fish.

Roslyn entered the water, shivering at first because it was rather icy, but after a moment her body got used to it. She splashed her face with the water, feeling more awake after. She glanced at Leaf, but something in the corner of her eyes caught her attention: standing just on the other side of the barrier were two dekellians, both with crude saddles on their backs that were occupied by two black skinned beings with stark white hair, their eyes wide and dark as they watched them. The dark elves wore crude armour, but the swords in their hands were sharp looking.

“Girls,” Roslyn hissed to her companions, indicating with her hand that they had company.

One of the dark elves cocked its head to the side with interest as each of the lady knights grabbed for their swords that they had left on the streambank. Leaf paddled over to Roslyn who was preparing to use her magic.

“What do you want?” Roslyn called out to the dark elves. “What are you doing here?”

“Are you the one who killed our dekellians?” the dark elf asked her, its voice low and raspy.

“What are dekellians?” Roslyn feigned ignorance.

“Our mounts,” the dark elf told her, indicating the creature beneath it with a flourish of its hand.

“What, those ugly lizard things you ride? I cannot say I have seen them before.”

“She lies,” the second dark elf hissed. “I can sense her magic, it is the same magic we found with the bodies.”

“What of it?” Roslyn asked them, putting her hands on her hips. “They were attacking my people.”

“*Your* people?” the first dark elf narrowed its eyes at her, taking in Leaf at the same time. “Where did you find that dragonling?”

“None of your business,” she responded, folding her arms over her chest.

"Now if you do not mind, my companions and I were trying to wash ourselves in privacy, a privacy in which you have invaded." She flicked her wrist and roots started coming out of the ground slowly to wrap around the one dekellian's front paw. The dark elf hacked the root away and the two of them urged their mounts backwards.

"Careful, human," the second dark elf hissed at her.

"No, dark elf, *you* be careful. I am Queen Roslyn of Jay'Al, ruler and protector of these lands that you trespass on. I will not suffer you to pass. Be gone to wherever you have come from!" More roots started to come out of the ground as the ground below the dark elves started to move. The dark elves hissed at her as they turned their mounts around and urged them into a run as the roots went after them.

"Everything alright here?" Roslyn heard Kavan's voice from nearby. She turned to find him covering his eyes, sword in hand.

"Nothing I could not handle. I think we can safely say that the dark elves came from the chasm, so we do not need to go there now," Roslyn told him.

"What do you want to do now?" Kavan asked as he turned around so he was no longer facing them.

"We should go meet Heath in Hyena City," she told him. "Let's get everything packed up, we need to ride with haste."

"What about the dark elves?" Tiffany asked her. "They were obviously scouts sent ahead to find you."

"The roots will follow them to where they came from, and they will close in the hole," Roslyn explained. "That will keep them busy for a while."

Chapter Thirty-Seven

Cassidy changed from her armour into the ball gown that Mel had made for her. It was an elegant gown, with a well-made corset that was slightly on the modest side–at least it did not plunge very deep. The sides of the corset were not too tight, allowing her more movement in case she needed it. The skirt of the gown was made up of a few different panels so it looked like a full ball gown but if she needed to fight in it she would have full movement.

Cassidy hoped there would be nothing like that to interrupt the ball, but she had a feeling that something was going to happen. Why would the men behind the assassination attempts allow the signing of the treaties to happen? The luncheon had been thankfully uneventful, but there was still a chance they could kill Alara at the ball if they did not want her to marry Edmond, but that would spark a war. Is that what they wanted? Gods she hoped not.

She brushed out her hair and started braiding it, using one of her favourite styles that Roslyn had taught her, the crown. She left a few strands of hair on either side of her face and then used a little bit of makeup to accentuate her eyes. Satisfied with how she looked she went to go meet with Kai, finding Sully and Jessica waiting for her outside of her rooms. Crick, who had been washed and groomed, walked along beside her, a nice bow that matched Cassidy's green gown around her neck.

"All quiet still?" she asked them as they walked towards Kai's room down the hall.

"A few people were taken aside," Sully informed her. "Before the treaty ceremony. They each had different pieces of a gun in their possession, all of them together would make a complete one. They were all nobles from the south who heavily disagreed with your father's changes."

"So we caught them?" Cassidy asked.

"Part of the group," Sully told her. "We will interrogate them to find out who the ringleader is, and if there are any more of them."

Cassidy knocked on Kai's door and he opened it, greeting her with a smile. Kai was wearing clothing similar to Edmond, his red hair pulled back in a queue. Tej, who had also been bathed and groomed, was admiring Crick's bow.

"You look amazing," Kai told her as he joined them in the hall. "Any word?"

Sully told him the same information he had just told Cassidy as they headed for the ballroom. Jessica left them at the door to the ballroom so she could go meet with the other mages who were there and find her new post.

"She's Tiffany's cousin," Cassidy mentioned to Kai as the mage excused herself. "She told me she attended the Mage University with Roslyn."

"Roz has a lot of friends willing to help," Sully told her.

The ballroom was filling up with nobles as they entered from their separate door that led them straight to the dais. There was seating there for Cassidy next to Alara, who sat beside Edmond's throne. Lucius and Elle sat in their thrones behind them. Edmond's younger siblings were not in attendance at the ball; Lucius had felt it would be safer for them to not be there in case something happened. Eliza, Poppy and Robert were well guarded in a separate area of the palace.

Musicians played a lively tune as the nobles started to socialize. There were drinks handed out, and mini-cakes on tables for them to pick over. Cassidy found it loud in the ballroom but she was able to tune some of the sounds out. Some of the nobles started dancing while the rest continued to socialize and watch the dancers.

"You look lovely," Elle told Cassidy as she sat down next to Alara. Kai had a chair beside her. Sully stood behind them off to the side. "That colour always looked good on Roslyn as well."

Cassidy smiled her thanks as Kai leaned forward to pick Tej up. Cassidy looked down to see Crick sniffing around the dais.

"Smell is strange," she heard Crick say.

"Sully, did anyone check the dais for tampering?" Cassidy asked as she stood up, turning to look at the knight. "Crick smells something strange."

"Everyone get onto the dance floor," Lucius whispered to them before they hurriedly left the dais, the nobles parting to make room for them. "Get a mage in here to check it out," Lucius said to Sully as he helped Elle down from the dais.

Sully nodded and waved Jessica over, but as Elle stepped down from the dais the platform behind her erupted in an explosion that threw them back. Cassidy was close enough to her father that she grabbed hold of him, pulling him away from the explosion and shielding him with her magic. She watched in panic and horror as Elle was struck by debris and flames before she could reach her with the shield.

Screams erupted around them as the nobles fled the ballroom. Alara used her magic to put the fire out as Lucius and Edmond ran to Elle's side.

"Elle!" Lucius cried out as he held his wife in his arms. Cassidy rushed over, taking in the look of horror on Edmond's face. She knelt next to them and saw that Elle was not breathing. Blood pooled on the floor beneath Elle, and Cassidy could see the splinter of wood sticking out of the side of her head. Elle stared blankly up at her husband who started sobbing as the realization hit him: Elle was dead. The Queen of Ellsgrove was dead.

"I want the palace locked down!" Sully yelled to the guards. "Nobody leaves until we find out who did this!"

Edmond looked up at Cassidy, his eyes pleading. "Can you do anything?"

Cassidy shook her head as she felt tears well in her eyes. "I'm sorry," she told Edmond. "I'm so sorry."

***

The next few hours were a blur for Edmond. His father had gone with his mother's body, leaving Edmond with Cassidy, Sully, and Kai. Somehow he found himself back in his room, Crick and Tej cuddled up against him on a chaise. Crick's fur was slightly singed, her bow blackened. Kai and Cassidy were both standing in the doorway to the hall, talking with Sully. Had he been dreaming? Was his mother really dead?

"Cassidy?" he heard his voice crack. He cleared his throat and looked to find her coming towards him. Her dress was singed and torn slightly, her hair slightly a mess. Her eyes were as red as he imagined his to be.

"I am here," Cassidy told him as she took his hand.

"Where is father?"

"With the death priests," she whispered.

"Have they found who did this?"

"We have a few people in custody," Sully spoke up from the doorway. "Alara is with them now, interrogating them."

"Was anyone else hurt?" Edmond asked.

"Lady Jessica, the mage, has a broken arm, and a few nobles who were standing near the dais were injured as well," Cassidy told him.

"Crick smelled the gunpowder they used in the explosive?" Edmond asked as Crick nuzzled against him. He put a hand on her head and started petting her. "If not for her we would all be…" Edmond choked on his words as he saw in his mind his mother's lifeless gaze. Tears welled in his eyes again.

Cassidy sat down next to him on the chaise and hugged him tightly. "We will find those who did this, and they will pay," she told him. "They will pay with their lives."

***

Cassidy joined Alara in the dungeons below the palace. She had left Edmond with Sully after giving him a sleeping potion, and had changed back into her armour. The ladies of the Honour Guard went with her, all of whom were slightly shaken by the attack still. They had been on the other side of the ballroom when it happened, and a lot of them felt like they had failed to protect the queen. Cassidy felt the guilt weighing heavily on her as well, though she knew that since Elle was so close to the dais still that she could not have done anything else. She dreaded telling Roslyn, and seeing her younger half-sibling's faces when they found out that their mother was gone.

"What news do you have?" Cassidy asked Alara as the princess came out of one of the rooms in the dungeon, wiping her hands on a towel.

"I have a name," Alara told her. "Does anyone know Count Gresham?"

"I do," Nadia spoke up. "He has a large estate in the south, very conservative."

"Was he here today? Do you know what he looks like?" Cassidy asked the knight.

"Yes, I remember seeing his name on the list of attendees this morning," one of the other knights, Perdita, spoke up.

"I know what he looks like," Nadia told them.

"Well let's go find him then, shall we?" Alara asked them.

Together they headed back up into the palace and to the Throne Room where the nobles were being kept while the soldiers checked the grounds and the mages investigated the explosion. There were a handful of mages in the room healing the people who had been too close to the dais, and there were soldiers guarding every entrance to make sure no one left.

"We are looking for Count Gresham," Cassidy said to one of the soldiers guarding the door.

"There he is," Nadia said, inclining her head in the direction of a man in his late fifties dressed very well who was sitting on a bench against the far wall. He was busy talking to other nobles his age and seemed not to notice the newcomers to the room.

"Come at him from all sides, slowly," Alara told them, so the group split up, surrounding him from all sides as they moved their way through the crowded room. The nobles they waded through grew quiet, however, as they noticed that something was happening. Count Gresham looked around as Cassidy stopped in front of him, the others giving no room for him to even attempt an escape.

"Count Gresham, you are under arrest for treason and the death of our Queen," Nadia told the nobleman. "Guards, also take these men into custody," she added, meaning the other men Gresham had been talking to.

"We did not do anything!" one of the noblemen protested, only to be silenced by a look from Alara.

"Then you can prove that later," Cassidy told him.

She looked at Count Gresham who almost looked a little smug. "Knock that look off your face or I will do it for you," she told him. "For your crimes against Ellsgrove your estates will be seized and you will go to the executioner's block," Cassidy informed him. "Or did you forget that was the fine for treason?"

She found satisfaction as his face turned white. Cassidy turned to the guards and told them, "Get him out of here before I kill him myself. Take him to the dungeons."

"How did he think he would not get caught?" Nadia asked Cassidy as they watched the guards lead the noblemen away.

"They were not expecting our Princess' skills," Cassidy smirked and looked at Alara. "If it had not been for her, he would have gotten away with it."

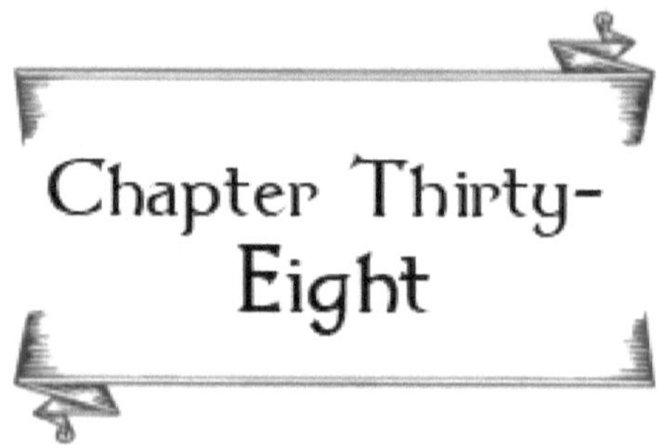

Chapter Thirty-Eight

Roslyn watched in her astral form as the dark elves retreated back to the hole in the ground they had come out of and the roots did their job, filling in the hole to trap them. She smiled with satisfaction as she opened her eyes, looking at her companions who were all watching her.

"What?" she asked as she stood up, dusting her behind off. She had wanted to make sure the dark elves were heading back to where they had emerged from, so she had stopped them where the desert started.

"Well?" Tiffany asked her in return.

"They went back underground and my roots are holding them," she responded. "Let's keep going."

"Will everyone on the plateau still be safe?" Karina asked her, worried about her family.

"Karina, I wove dozens of protective spells in the plateau after our mishap with the sinkhole. Everyone is safe," she assured her as she mounted her horse. "Let's try and ride as far as we can today, shall we?"

"You are the one who stopped," Kavan reminded her. She stuck her tongue out at him and urged her horse into a run. The rest of them hurried after her, Cypress letting out a holler as he ran to catch up with her, a large smile on his face. Kavan shook his head with a chuckle and looked at Alexander who was also shaking his head.

"Come on, Alexander, let's show them how fast we are," Kavan said to his friend who was not on a horse.

The three werewolves did not need horses. Alexander grinned at him and together they urged ahead with Edwin just behind them, to catch up with Roslyn and Cypress.

***

Heath helped the gryphon kit groom itself, marveling at the colour of the feathers that had come in over the last few days. The feathers were a dark blue, shimmering slightly in the daylight. Solana played with his hand, wrapping her tail around his wrist and nibbling at his fingers. Her breath smelled of fish, for she ate dozens of fish a day and had grown larger quite fast. She had already started strengthening her wings.

"I'll be damned," a voice said from the gangplank. "Am I hallucinating?"

Heath looked up to see Mortimer standing there, his eyes wide. They had just docked back at the isle of Mast to drop Everett off and Mortimer had been waiting for them.

"No, you are not hallucinating," Heath told him. "Though you might think you are dreaming when I show you the dark elf we have in our hold."

Mortimer's expression changed from disbelief to alarm. "You found dark elves?"

"Yes. We rescued the people who were living on the island from them. We brought them with us. There was a sinkhole that led to an underground tunnel where they had been taken, and we found an egg that hatched into this beauty," Heath explained. "This is Solana, my familiar."

"Your familiar…? I thought the shamans of Jay'Al were the only ones who had familiars," Mortimer commented.

"I think whatever Roslyn did with that tree changed something," Heath told him. "We might soon find that more mages will find familiars."

"Note taken," Mortimer told him.

"Now, I am just leaving Everett with you, I need to get back to Jay'Al," Heath explained to Mortimer. "The dark elves are after Roslyn."

"You are sure?" Mortimer asked him with surprise.

Heath nodded and told him, "The dark elf in the hold told me they were seeking the power of Jay'Al, and that is Roslyn."

"I will send guns and ammunition with you to help," Mortimer told him. "Give me a few hours to get everything to your ship."

"I would appreciate that," Heath told him. "Thank you."

Mortimer left him then, hurrying off to get everything done. Maeve and Everett joined Heath on the deck, Maeve sitting down on a barrel beside him and Everett standing in front of him.

"Are you sure you do not need me?" Everett asked his older brother.

"I need you here," Heath assured him. "I do not think Roz will be particularly happy to see you either."

Everett grimaced, thinking of the last time he had seen Roslyn when she had locked him in a prison cell in Hyena City. "Yeah, better I stay here I think. I guess I will see you whenever you get back."

"Take care, brother," Heath told him as he shook his hand, pulling him into a hug.

"You as well," Everett replied as he hugged him back before turning and walking off the ship.

"Mortimer is getting us some weapons," Heath explained to Maeve. "We will leave after everything is loaded."

Maeve smiled with excitement. "Can I have some shore leave?"

Heath laughed, knowing that she was probably going to go to the tree that Roslyn had him plant on the island. "Yes, just be back in two hours."

Maeve let out a hoot and ran off the ship, heading for Commandant Mortimer's house. Heath looked at the sailors who had all stopped to watch Maeve run off, earning chuckles from all of them.

"She's a lively one, eh?" Heath commented, making the sailors laugh as they returned to their duties. Heath wondered just what kind of familiar would answer Maeve's call, thinking about any other magical creatures that could possibly be out there. Of course it did not have to be a magical creature, for the other familiars he had met were normal creatures. Maybe she would get stuck with a rat as a familiar; thinking that made him laugh out loud, making Solana tilt her head at him.

"Admit it, it would be really funny," Heath told her as he preened her feathers with his fingers. She started to purr and in the back of his mind he felt her laugh as well.

***

Roslyn sighed with relief when she saw the walls of Hyena City in the distance. The river that led into the city was larger than it had been the first time she had been there, which was good to see. They had also done repairs to the city walls after the orc attack several months ago. Roslyn had plans to put protective spells along the walls of the city in case the dark elves came with their dekellians, or if anyone else decided to attack the city.

"I am looking forward to a hot bath," Roslyn commented as they grew closer to the city.

As they approached the gates the guards opened them and Chief Erick came out to greet them.

"Your Majesty!" He greeted Roslyn with a flourished bow. "It is good to see you again. We will host a feast in your honour!"

"Thank you, Chief Erick. I bring grave news," she told him. "Dark elves have re-emerged, and they seem to be after me for whatever reason."

Chief Erick's eyes widened and he looked at her companions, taking in the orcs and the men working together.

"You are sure?"

"Saw them with my own eyes," she replied. "Heath got a message to me several days ago: he encountered dark elves in the archipelago as well."

"This is troubling indeed," Erick said.

"There are also redcaps and dwarves that have co-me to the surface," Roslyn continued. "I directed them north for their safety."

A Weaving of the Roots

"Indeed? Indeed. Well then…" Erick seemed to be processing everything. "By the ancients, these are some interesting times. Please, Your Majesty, come into my city and relax. I am sure you did not just come here to warn me about the dark elves."

"Quite right. Heath is coming here," Roslyn told him as they started walking into the city. "I wanted to be here when he got here, and to meet the Kypragon ambassador Nadim."

"Very well, Your Majesty," Erick responded. "It will be good to have you all here again. Even your new companions."

"This is Cypress," Roslyn introduced him to the orc warrior. "He is one of my trusted warriors."

"Pleasure to meet you," Erick said with a nod to the large orc. He spotted Karina and smiled.

"Karina! It is good to see you again," Erick told her. "My son Keaton has been eager to learn more about your people from the plateau."

"I look forward to telling him whatever he wants to know," Karina responded with a smile, glad to be accepted.

Roslyn smiled at their interaction, remembering the first time Karina had set foot in Hyena City. They had all come a long way since then.

The city was much as she remembered it being, with open courtyards and gardens, large fountains flowing in most courtyards. Most people in the streets stopped to watch them, noting the orcs with their war hammers.

"Is that her?" Roslyn heard someone say. "Is that Queen Roslyn?"

Though Roslyn did not want to cause a scene she smiled and waved at the people of Hyena City as word spread that their new queen was there. Roslyn's face turned red as more people came out into the street cheering.

"We will have a feast tonight in the Square!" Erick announced. "In honour of our Queen!"

"Oh, no, it is quite alright Erick–"

"Roz," Tiffany cut her off. "You are going to have to get used to this treatment. You are not just their queen, you defeated the leader of the orcs that had attacked this city, and you brought the orcs under your banner. Your people have a right to show you their love and appreciation."

Knowing that Tiffany was right she shut her mouth and nodded, trying her best to smile genuinely.

"Thank you, everyone," she said to the crowd. "We can celebrate more tonight, hm?"

Finally they made it to Chief Erick's estate and were within the gates. Roslyn dismounted, handing Sage's reins to a stable boy. She exhaled, feeling a little over-whelmed.

"Tiffany is right," Kavan commented to her as he came up beside her. "You are going to have to get used to that."

"I know," Roslyn responded. "We haven't been around such a large group of people since my coronation so I was just thrown off a little."

"Understandable," Kavan commented. "Man, the last time I was here was…when Everett took us."

Roslyn put a hand on Kavan's shoulder and squeezed it. "Heath is alive," Roslyn reminded him. "And he will be back here soon."

"I know," he said quietly. "And we will go back to wooing you until you decide."

"What, you cannot handle the competition again?" she teased him.

"I am glad he is alive, but I was enjoying having you to myself, even if it was not much with everything going on."

"You only say that because he is alive," Roslyn reminded him. "I know you mourned him when we all thought he was dead."

"Yes, which is why I can say it and not have you thinking I am cold hearted," he replied with a grin. "I will still greet him like a brother when I see him next."

"I know," Roslyn told him with a broad smile. "It will be good to have you both at my side again."

"I know you must want to bathe," Erick said as they headed for the main door to his estate. "My servants will lead you to your rooms so you can do so."

Roslyn smiled at Kai's uncle and grabbed her bags, Leaf hopping along beside her as a servant led her to a room very similar to the one she had been in the last time she had been there. She put her bags on the bed and headed for the attached bathing room.

Chapter Thirty-Nine

Roslyn sat at a large table with Tiffany beside her, Kavan on her other side, with the rest of her companions spread around the table amongst some of the richer people of Hyena City who would be on par with noblemen. They were at the feast that Erick had promised, and the musicians were playing while the richest families socialized and ate the meal that Chief Erick had provided. Nadim sat on Erick's other side, though he had to lean around the Chief to talk to Roslyn. Their conversations kept getting interrupted, however, so they agreed to meet the next day at noon.

Since their arrival in Hyena City the cooks of Chief Erick's house had been preparing the meal for the evening feast: boar, beef and alpaca had been roasted during the day, and some of the favourite street vendors had been hired to cook for the feast as well.

Lanterns lit the streets as the sun set, and the people of Hyena City just seemed to get louder. Roslyn ate and drank with them, though thankfully the majority of the people did not come straight up to her. She managed to sneak back to her room after she could not stop yawning.

There was a light knock at her door as she started to change into her bedclothes. With a sigh she went to the door, opening it to find Kavan on the other side. She opened the door up enough for him to come through the threshold.

"You snuck out," he said as he took her in.

"I was getting tired," she told him, well aware of the closeness between them. It had been some time since he had last kissed her.

Kavan tipped her chin up and kissed her, she nearly melting at his touch.

"Kavan," she said his name as she pulled back slightly, yawning. "I have a lot of emotions for you, but right now all I can take is your skin against mine."

He grinned at her and kissed her again, his hands reaching for the edge of her tunic.

***

Roslyn awoke in the early morning with only her tunic off. She remembered that she had been so tired that Kavan had agreed to just kissing and then falling asleep along with her. Kavan lay asleep next to her, his chest bare. She looked at the scars on his chest, from wounds that almost took his life in the Pirate Wars. From an orphan to a soldier, to working for the king of Ellsgrove as Arms Master and now one of her most trusted companions; he had come a long way.

Roslyn got up and went to wash herself, changing into a different set of clothes. Kavan remained asleep as she did so. She looked at him sleeping peacefully and then left her room quietly. Leaf, who had come into her room at some point after she had fallen asleep and had curled up at the end of the bed, joined her.

Roslyn headed for the harbour, thinking that if Heath was on his way she might meet him there. The sun had barely risen as she traversed the harbour, pacing back and forth as Leaf pounced around her feet between eating fish she had just caught. Slowly the city woke up, and the harbour became alive with the dockworkers. Most of them gave her curious glances, others inclined their heads in greeting.

"Thought I would find you here."

Roslyn turned to find Tiffany coming towards her, her arms crossed over her chest. She was wearing simple leggings and a tunic, a leather bag slung over her shoulder.

"You should still have a guard inside the city, you never know if there are any assassins here," Tiffany reminded her. "Have you eaten?"

Roslyn shook her head but smiled as Tiffany produced some warm fruit scones wrapped in a cloth from her bag.

"Thank you," Roslyn told her as she took a scone.

"Think they will be here today?" Tiffany asked her.

"Hoping," she replied as they walked together to-wards the lookout tower that was part of the outer harbour. They climbed some stairs to a platform where they could see out to the ocean. There were a few benches up there for people to sit and watch, so the two of them sat down. Leaf had a fish in her mouth as she joined them a few moments later.

Roslyn took a bite of the scone, enjoying the buttery flavour mixed with the blueberries that were in it. Tiffany smiled at Roslyn as she ate her own scone.

"One thing I like about Hyena City," Tiffany told her, "is the street vendors and their morning baking."

"My new capital will have street vendors," Roslyn assured her. "All kinds, for every part of the day."

Tiffany chuckled, thinking she would definitely like that. "I don't know, I think after a while I will need my armour adjusted, or you might have to roll me places."

Roslyn laughed, finding that image amusing.

"Nah, I will just keep you exercising every day running up and down the tunnel, that will keep you in shape."

Tiffany groaned, shaking her head. "You wouldn't do that to me," she teased. "I'll be fine, I will be keeping the other knights active with morning practices anyways."

"Yes, you most likely will," Roslyn responded with a wink.

Tiffany looked at Leaf who was almost done eating the fish she had caught. "Do you think Heath's gryphon and Leaf will get along?"

"I don't see why not, Crick and Tej got along fine," Roslyn commented. "It will be interesting to see a gryphon though."

"I wonder if those nests you found underground were gryphon nests," Tiffany said as she finished up her scone. "If so, where did they all go?"

"I have been wondering that as well," Roslyn told her. "Did the dark elves kill them? Capture them? Why was there a gryphon egg with the dark elves that Heath encountered, and how did it get there? Could it have been from that place? Too many questions and not enough answers yet."

Tiffany sighed, knowing what Roslyn wanted to do. "You want to go underground and find out what is going on, don't you."

Roslyn grinned at her, saying, "You know me too well."

Tiffany groaned. "But Roslyn, something is forcing those creatures to come back up. Like something bad; and you want to go find it?"

"Yes."

"You're the Queen of Jay'Al now though, is it wise to go on such a dangerous mission?"

Roslyn looked at Tiffany sideways. "How could I send anyone I care about down there without me, just because I am Queen?"

"You are too stubborn for your own good," Tiffany told her.

"I will have people I can trust handling things up here," Roslyn assured her. "I will have to appoint some people to my council, though I have a few people in mind."

"Fine," was all Tiffany could say, though she was still not completely happy with Roslyn's decision.

"Something has to be done," Roslyn told her. "I know you do not like it, but I would never forgive myself if something happened to the people I send down there when I could have been there."

"And what if you get injured or worse," Tiffany retorted.

"That is not going to happen."

"You cannot say that for sure," Tiffany told her.

"You do not have to like it," Roslyn responded. "It is my plan going forward from here."

"Well I will be filing a formal complaint with Aidan when we get back," Tiffany joked, making Roslyn laugh.

Roslyn looked out to the ocean and narrowed her eyes. "Is that a ship coming in?"

Tiffany stood up and walked over to the railing of the lookout, shielding her eyes from the sun. "Looks like it."

"Is there a looking glass somewhere?" Roslyn looked around the platform and found a sailor standing there with a looking glass for her.

"Your Majesty, please use mine," the sailor told her. "I am on duty for watch, but if you need it you may certainly use it."

"Thank you," she told him as she accepted it. She looked through it towards the ship and smiled as she recognized the flag. "It's Heath!"

"Let's go wait for him," Tiffany told her, heading for the stairs. Roslyn handed the looking glass back to the sailor with a nod and a smile before following Tiffany, Leaf at her heels.

Together the three of them watched from the pier as the sailors on Heath's ship brought the sails in and a smaller ship attached a lead line to bring it in to dock.

Sailors threw several ropes towards the dock that dock workers grabbed to tie down, and the anchor dropped to keep them in place. Finally the ship stopped swaying enough for the sailors to drop the gangplank, and Heath appeared at the top of it, a large grin on his face. He was wearing a sailor's outfit with a green vest over a cream coloured tunic, his thigh high leather boots shined. He had let his hair loose, the waves of his hair coming down just to his shoulders. At his waist was his gun belt on his right side, a short sword on his left.

"Roz!" he shouted his greeting as he came down the plank to them. He pulled her into a large hug, lifting her up off of the ground and swinging her around. "Oh, you are a sight for sore eyes!"

As he put her down he kissed her, and she felt her stomach do a flip-flop. She could feel his strong arms around her as she kissed him back.

Tiffany cleared her throat, and Roslyn pulled back to look at Heath who was grinning.

"I have waited a long time to kiss you again," Heath told her. "It was just as I remembered."

Roslyn felt her face turn red as she looked at Heath and then Maeve who was standing on the gangplank with her hands on her hips, an amused expression on her face. Standing at the top of the gangplank was Heath's gryphon, looking at her curiously.

"Oh, what a beauty you are!" Roslyn said to the gryphon as she moved around Heath and towards the gangplank. "Hello there."

A Weaving of the Roots

The gryphon started towards her, purring as it moved around Maeve and started to rub against Roslyn's ankles.

"This is Solana," Heath told her as he watched his familiar sniff Roslyn's fingers.

"I can sense the magic in her," Roslyn told him.

"It's a mix of you and the magic of Jay'Al. Interesting. I wonder how this happened."

"I think you did it," Heath told her. "With that tree you had me plant on Mast."

"I will have to investigate that," Roslyn commented. "I did not foresee that happening, only that it was a way to connect our peoples like the Jay'Alians are connected."

"I'm not complaining," Heath told her as he saw Leaf, who had been off catching another fish when he had arrived. "By the ancestors, that's a *dragon*. Look at you! You must be Leaf," he greeted Roslyn's familiar who was proudly walking over to them with a large fish in her mouth. They watched as Leaf approached Solana and placed the fish down in front of the gryphon. Solana blinked slowly at Leaf and then started eating the fish, purring loudly as she did so.

"I thought they would get along," Roslyn said as she watched the two familiars interact. Solana bit the fish in half and offered a piece to Leaf who took it, chewing it happily.

"How have you been? Have you contacted your father yet?" Heath asked her as the sailors started unload-ding the ship under Maeve's supervision.

"We are good, and no I have not yet. I was waiting for the potion to finish, and then a lot of stuff happened to distract me. I brewed enough for a few doses as well. I will probably do it today, after I meet with Nadim; we did not have much time to talk last night during the feast Erick had in my honour," Roslyn told him. Roslyn noticed the large crates that the sailors were unloading, seeing the gunsmith emblem on the side. "Are those guns?"

"Yes," Heath affirmed. "Commandant Mortimer thought you could use them against the dark elves."

"I will have to send him a 'thank you' basket," Roslyn said with a raised eyebrow, noting how many crates there were. She turned to Heath and asked, "Where is the dark elf?"

"In the hold," he told her. "You want to see it now?"

"Yes, please," she replied, and he sighed.

"Ok, fine, let's go visit the dark elf now," Heath said as he directed her to follow him onto the ship.

"What, can I not want to talk to it now? We encountered a couple on our way here, though I did not have much time to talk to them since I was forcing them back where they came from," Roslyn informed him. "Can I not want to see if I can get some more information out of it?"

"You have valid points," Heath told her. "My apologies." He squinted at her arm, seeing the tattoo that the orc ancestors had given her. "Where did you get that from?"

Roslyn looked at her arm and shrugged, "From the orcs. Their ancestors marked me as one of them."

Roslyn followed Heath down into the hold, remembering their first voyage together and the time they had spent getting to know each other as friends. How had a year gone by already? Roslyn then found herself thinking of his kiss, and was glad that her body had still responded to his touch after the time apart.

They arrived at the brig, and Roslyn found herself looking at a dark elf that looked exactly like the other ones she had encountered. It looked like a male, though it had long stark white hair that was pulled back with a leather thong. He was wearing what she imagined was the under padding that went under armour; Heath would have taken his armour when he captured him.

"Hello," Roslyn greeted the dark elf. "Can you tell me why all of the creatures are coming back to the surface? What is chasing you out from beneath the earth?"

The dark elf said nothing, though he narrowed his eyes at her as she spoke.

"I met some redcaps," Roslyn informed the dark elf. "They were fleeing from the dark elves, but the dark elves were also fleeing something. What is it? What has the dark elves running away?"

Still the dark elf remained quiet.

Roslyn sighed. "Should we keep it here, or should we move it to Erick's dungeon?" she asked Heath.

"I think Erick's dungeon would be best, we can keep a better eye on him there," Heath responded. "It would be best to have a covered wagon, so as not to scare the people."

"Alright, that will be the first thing we do when we get to Erick's," Roslyn said as she turned away from the dark elf in the cell. She stopped as the dark elf reached out and grabbed her arm.

"Oy, no touching!" Heath yelled at the dark elf, but Roslyn held up her hand to stop him; the dark elf was not gripping her too tightly, and was looking at her with a curious expression.

"You are her," the dark elf said, his voice deep.

"And who would that be?" Roslyn asked him.

"The Queen of these lands, the power behind it."

"Why do you think that?"

"I can sense it," the dark elf told her with a shrug. "I am…sensitive to magic."

"What are the dark elves running from?" Roslyn asked him again as he let

her go.
    "We call them Behemoths," the dark elf told her.

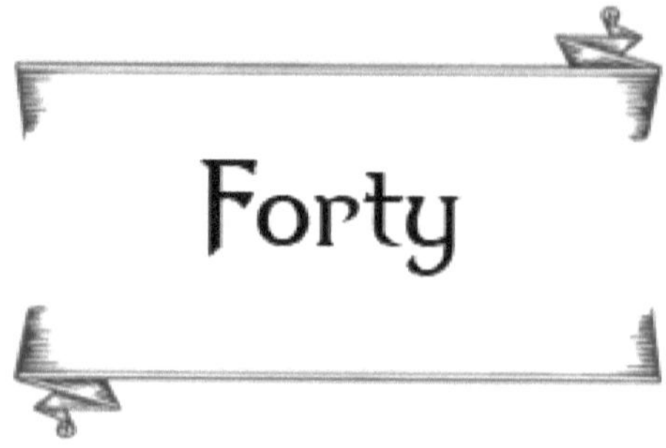

Forty

Roslyn watched as Kavan came out into the courtyard and saw Heath sitting there. She was leaning against one of the pillars, Leaf playing nearby with Solana. Tiffany had gone to get them some refreshments and talk to Erick about moving the dark elf off of Heath's ship and into his dungeon.

"Heath!" Kavan exclaimed as he saw his friend, and Heath jumped up from his seat and ran to him, pulling him into a bear hug.

"It is good to see you," Heath told him as they hugged each other. They let each other go and then sized each other up. "You are stronger than I remember. A werewolf now, I am told?"

"I have this trusty pendant Roz made me so I can stop the shapeshifting but I still have all of my powers," Kavan explained, showing him the crystal.

"Sure has been an interesting few months," Heath commented as he noticed Nadim walking down the hall-way towards the courtyard. The merman was wearing alpaca wool breeches and a simple cotton tunic that had been dyed a light pink colour, his dreadlocks dangling around his shoulders.

"Nadim, my friend, come join us!" Heath called out.

"I had heard you were back," Nadim said with a smile as he entered the courtyard. "How was going home?"

"It was very interesting," Heath told him, nodding to the gryphon kit sitting on the floor.

"Is that…" Nadim started to say, his eyes wide. "Is that truly a gryphon I see before me?"

"It is," Heath told him, excitement in his voice. "Her name is Solana, and she is my familiar."

"How did that happen? I thought the shamans of Jay'Al were the only ones who had familiars," Nadim commented.

"I believe I am to blame," Roslyn cut in. "I sent a tree as an alliance gift, and I added a bit of my magic to it. I think I somehow wove the magic together between the two places and people."

"Powerful indeed," Nadim commented. "You will be a good ally to Kyprago."

"I did not even *mean* to do it," Roslyn told him. "Somehow it just happened from what I did."

"All the same," Nadim said with a shrug.

"Well," Heath said as he sat down, "Where is everyone else? Besides Cassidy and Kai."

"Aidan and Oswick are back on the plateau," Roslyn told him. "We have Karina, a half-orc shaman from the plateau in our group, as well as some orc warriors from the North Snow Clan."

"It will be interesting having some orc warriors with us," Heath said as Kavan sat down next to him.

"We also have a group of werewolves," Kavan chimed in.

"We will need all the help we can get, I think, if I am going underground to investigate," Roslyn spoke up. "I talked with the dark elf that Heath has in custody, and he told me what they are all running from: some creatures they call the Behemoths."

"What is it?" Kavan asked her.

"From what I can gather, it is some kind of dinosaur," Roslyn explained. "Someone dug too deep and unleashed them from wherever they were below the sur-face. It seems there was what I would describe as a 'hollow earth', much like the large cavern we found Kasimir in, only bigger, where the majority of the creatures we are seeing emerging had lived, with the dark elves in a similar area not far from the first. The Behemoths came from somewhere below, probably from another 'hollow earth' area."

"You are really going down there?" Heath asked her. "The dark elves fled them. What good do you think we can do?"

"What if the Behemoths get to the surface?" Roslyn asked him. "All hells would break loose."

"Would it not be easier to fight them above ground?" Nadim asked her.

"Why don't you do what you did with the redcaps, and make a path for the Behemoths to come up to a designated spot," Tiffany spoke up. "And we have an army waiting for them."

"I will have to do some recon first," Roslyn suggested. "Figure out where they are and how many of them there are in order to plan better."

"That sounds like a better plan," Kavan told her. Heath and Tiffany both nodded in agreement.

"Whatever you plan, know that King Ullas and Kyprago will help you with the battle," Nadim informed Roslyn.

"And the Archipelago as well," Heath told her. "I am sure your father could even send an army as well."

"Right, I need to contact him," Roslyn commented. She stood up straight and stretched. "I should go do that now. I will meet you all for lunch?"

***

Cassidy sat with Edmond, Alara, and Lucius in the king's study. Lucius looked pale, dark circles under his eyes, his fine clothes rumpled from having been slept in. Cassidy knew her father had not slept much since Elle was killed, first spending time mourning her as the death surgeons prepared her for burial, and then explaining to his younger children what had happened to their mother; Edmond at least had been there to help with that. Cassidy had felt too guilty about Elle dying to face them just yet.

She looked up at Kai who was standing behind her, his hand on her shoulder to give her strength. He had been sleeping in her room with her to help with the nightmares, and it was comforting to have him there now.

"Do we have an idea of who all was in on it?" Lucius asked them. Edmond looked to Alara, her expression soft.

"The man we arrested was the one to plant the explosive device," Alara told him. "We have figured out where he got his orders from and have the names of everyone involved."

"I want to see the list–Roslyn?!" Lucius stopped as he noticed Roslyn's astral form materialize next to Cassidy's chair.

"Sorry I did not contact you sooner, I–Father, are you ill?" Roslyn inquired as she took in her father's dishevelled look and the dark circles under his eyes.

"No," Lucius said softly.

"Roz," Edmond turned to her, and she saw the dark circles under his eyes as well. "Something happened."

"What do you mean? What happened?"

Cassidy inhaled sharply as she felt tears about to surface. "There was an assassination attempt," Cassidy told her. "Elle was caught in an explosion and killed."

Roslyn stared at her sister blankly for a moment before looking at her father and brother. "What?" she whispered. "No, no that cannot be!"

Cassidy went to reach for her hand but remembered that it was just her sister's astral form.

"I'm sorry," Cassidy told her. "I failed to protect her."

Roslyn struggled with the tears that were threatening to come. "Do you know who is responsible?"

Lucius nodded.

"Then you find them, and put their heads on the city walls," Roslyn told them. "I...I will be back." Her form faded away.

Cassidy put her head in her hands and started sobbing, Kai still holding her shoulder. Lucius got up and went to her, kneeling before her and placing his hands on her knees.

"This is *not* your fault," Lucius told her. "It is the Count's fault, and those he answered to. We will do what Roslyn said: we will find them and put their heads on the city walls."

***

Roslyn sunk against the wall in her room and cried, Leaf wrapping around her legs to comfort her. Mother Elle was gone, killed by men who were after her father. Elle had raised her, seen her first steps, her first bruises, had comforted her during nightmares. She had been proud of her skills with a sword, and even more so her hunting skills. When Roslyn had left for the Mage University, Elle had cried because she was going to miss her. Roslyn remembered how tightly Elle had hugged her before she had left on the expedition, and tried to remember that feeling now as she cried.

Leaf left at some point and returned with Heath and Solana in tow. Heath took one look at her and in an instant he had her in his arms.

"What happened?" he asked her in a whisper.

Through her sobs she told him, and he held her closer. He kissed the top of her head and she looked up at him. He used his sleeve to wipe the tears on her face, and then produced a handkerchief for her to blow her nose.

"They will catch whoever is responsible," Heath assured her as he held her again, this time as she just sniff-led. The death of his own mother still near, he let loose a few tears of his own. He had met with Queen Elle several times during the planning of the voyage and thought she was a wonderful woman; she had helped raise Roslyn after all.

She nodded, unable to speak anymore because the crying had her exhausted. She buried her face into his shoulder.

There was a knock at the door.

"Who is it?" Heath asked.

"Heath? It's Tiffany."

"Come in."

Tiffany opened the door as Heath stood up, leaving Roslyn on the floor leaning against the wall. He took Tiffany aside, her eyes wide at seeing Roslyn in that state, and Heath explained what had happened.

"Go tell the others, will you?" Heath asked her. Tiffany nodded, taking in his red eyes, and left again.

Heath turned to look at Roslyn and went and scooped her up in his arms and carried her to her bed. He arranged her pillows and blankets to caress her and she gave him a weak smile before closing her eyes and falling into the abyss of exhausted sleep with Leaf resting against her legs.

***

The sun was just rising as Heath and Solana found Kavan in the kitchen, sitting at one of the small tables with a steaming cup in his hands. Kavan looked up at him, a sad look in his eyes.

"How is she?" Kavan asked him.

"Tiffany just checked on her, she is awake," Heath told him. "She slept all day and through the night."

"Understandably," Kavan commented, Heath nodding in agreement. "Do you want a cup?" Kavan asked him. "I brewed enough for a few people." Kavan indicated the pot sitting on the kitchen counter next to the hearth.

"I think I am going to need it today," Heath told him as he grabbed a mug from a shelf and poured himself a drink, adding some sugar and milk to it. He took a tentative sip and then another.

"We mourned you in this kitchen," Kavan told him as he continued to look into his cup. "Roslyn had been taken by Grau, and you were gone. We all gathered in here and had a drink to honour you."

"I appreciate that," Heath told him as he sat down beside him. "I am very happy to be alive, and back here with you all."

"I am glad as well," Kavan said as he looked up. He smiled and continued, "Though I did enjoy having Roslyn all to myself for a while."

"Well you will just have to get used to me being back," Heath teased him. "I have been waiting to continue our dance with her."

Heath yawned and then took a longer drink. He looked to the doorway to find Maeve standing there, Solana curled up in her arms.

"Here you are," Maeve said as she came towards them. "She was sleeping in the strangest place, on top of your wardrobe."

"Just like a cat," Heath mused as she put Solana down by his feet. He reached down and scratched her head, running his hand down her back and scratching her rump. "What a beautiful, good girl you are, Solana."

"How is Roslyn?" Maeve asked them as she poured herself a cup and joined them.

"She is bathing and will be joining us soon for breakfast," Tiffany said from the doorway to the kitchen.

The three of them turned to look at her. Tiffany looked a little disheveled, for she had not slept very well: she was worried about what was happening back in Ellsgrove.

"I will inform the cooks," Maeve said, who got up and left with her mug.

"Where are Karina, Cypress, and the rest of the orc warriors?" Kavan asked her.

"They are doing a ritual for Roslyn's stepmother," Tiffany told him. "To help her soul find peace."

Kavan looked down, thinking about Roslyn's step-mother. He had only met her a few times after he had first arrived at the palace, but she had been a good woman. He could only imagine what Roslyn's younger siblings were going through. Kavan did not remember his parents; all of his earliest memories were of the orphanage.

Heath put a hand on Kavan's shoulder. "Come on, let's get out of the kitchen so the cooks can make break-fast," Heath told him, nodding at the cooks in the doorway. "We will take our breakfast with Roslyn in the dining room."

"I think it is time for you to meet the rest of our party," Kavan commented. "I believe Karina will have planned the ritual in the practice yard."

"Alright, seems like a good time," Heath answered, standing and grabbing his mug.

Kavan led the way to the practice yard with Heath, Maeve and Tiffany behind him. The orcs had just finished up their ritual and were cleaning up the ashes from their fire.

"Karina, it is about time you meet Heath," Tiffany said as Karina noticed them. "There is also Cypress, Louran, Terren, Karina's brother Jaco, Tirren, Loua, and Resba."

Karina smiled warmly at Heath and told him, "I have heard a lot about you. It is good to finally meet you."

"Nice to meet you as well," Heath responded. "Thank you all for standing with Roslyn."

"How is she?" the orc Cypress asked, his brow furrowed.

"She is awake and coming for breakfast soon," Tiffany assured him. "We just thought Heath should meet you all."

"Does Roslyn have a plan to deal with the dark elves?" Louran asked them.

"I do."

They all turned to the doorway to find Roslyn standing there, Leaf at her feet. She was wearing a simple loose cotton gown that was dyed blue, a dark green shawl wrapped around her shoulders. She had her hair up in two braids.

"Will you all have breakfast with me?" Roslyn asked them. "I could use the company this morning."

Epilogue

The cooks outdid themselves that morning, Roslyn thought. She was sure they had heard the news and were being extra careful, making all of her favourites they had learned the last time she was there. She was comforted by the scones with jam and the scrambled eggs, and there was fresh wake-up brew.

Heath sat on her left, Kavan on her right. Tiffany sat beside Heath, with Karina on Kavan's other side, the rest of them arrayed around the table. Roslyn felt at ease with her friends–her family. She was still very upset after learning of Mother Elle's death, but it was better having those she loved around her.

"After breakfast I am going to check where the Behemoths are underground," Roslyn told everyone as they ate. "If they are close to the surface I am hoping we have time to gather an army to deal with them."

"And if we do not have time?" Cypress asked at the same time Louran asked, "What if they are further down?"

"Well, I hope we have time," Roslyn joked in a low voice. "If they are further down, then I am going to go after them."

"Down within the earth?" Jaco, Karina's brother, spoke up.

"Yes."

"Is that not more dangerous?" Terren asked.

"If that is the case, them being further down bel-ow, I really do not know what else to do," Roslyn told them. "They have pushed all of the other creatures that had been underground back up to the surface. We do not know if they will all be as easily swayed as the redcaps, though I know they were only afraid that is why they agreed to the peace terms so easily."

"How can you trust them?" Karina asked her.

A Weaving of the Roots

"I don't completely, but I want to give them the chance," Roz told Karina. "Just like I gave you the chance."

Karina's face softened and she looked down. "True."

"Who would you take below ground with you?" Cypress asked her.

"All of you," Roslyn told them. "I will need every-one who will come with me."

"Alright, go check after you eat," Tiffany spoke up softly. "Then let us know what the next step will be."

"I will," Roslyn answered her, giving her an appreciative smile. Roz looked down at her plate, realizing she only touched half it. "I think I will go do that now."

"Do you want company?" Heath asked her.

"No," she told him. "I think I can do this myself, for now."

He nodded and watched as she got up and walked out to the courtyard. She sat down on the ground, her legs crossed, and called on the earth beneath her. Small tendrils of roots reached up and wrapped themselves around her feet and her hands that were resting on her knees.

"Do you think she is OK?" Kavan asked Heath.

"No," Heath responded. "There is still a lot of pain and guilt within her. I know how she feels."

Kavan looked down, well aware of the fact that Heath only recently lost his own mother and older brother.

"Where is your brother Everett?" Kavan asked him.

"He is on Mast, with Commandant Mortimer," Heath informed him. "I needed him there."

"So you two separated on good terms?" Kavan asked him, slightly surprised at that.

"Maeve got to punch him first," Heath told him. "And do not forget, I had him in the dungeons below before we went home. He saved my life when we were investigating the earthquakes on the northern islands. He has proven himself to me."

"He tortured us and was the reason you got shot," Kavan said, his voice heated.

"Kavan, at one point in time you and I were enemies," Heath reminded him. "I remember Roslyn had a talk with you before introducing us."

Kavan ducked his head, remembering that night in the inn that Heath was referring to.

"True," Kavan said softly. "I am sorry."

"It was hard, hating my brother," Heath told him. "It was hard trusting him, believing in him again; but I did. He proved himself to me during our journey home. I hope you can take my word on it."

"I will try to," Kavan responded with a weak smile.

Roslyn stood up, and they watched her brush herself off and come back to them. She walked towards them, concern on her face.

"The Behemoths are nowhere near the surface," Roslyn told them. "They are somewhere further down."

"So the plan of bringing them to the surface?" Tiffany asked.

"If I cannot push them forward, I do not think they will," Roslyn told her. "We will have to go below."

Tiffany sighed, as did Karina.

"Well, we will stand by your side," Tiffany told her.

"We will," Karina echoed. The other orcs nodded their heads in unison.

"Thank you," Roslyn told them. "I appreciate you helping me."

"We will always be here for you," Kavan spoke up.

"We will," Heath agreed. Tiffany, Karina, and the others all nodded their heads.

"Thank you," Roslyn told them again. "I need to talk to my father again. I made more than one potion so I had them in case I needed them."

"Go ahead, we will still be here when you get back," Kavan told her.

Roslyn smiled weakly at them and went back to her room to get the potion that she kept there. Once there, with Leaf sitting at her feet, Roslyn took the cork stopper out of the vial with the potion in it and drank it.

She felt the energy rush through her as her astral form moved across the world to Ellsgrove and the palace where her father and half-siblings were.

She found her father in his study alone, looking at papers on his desk. His clothes looked better than they had the day before, and the dark circles under his eyes were gone.

"Dad," she announced her arrival. He looked up and smiled at seeing her astral form there.

"Roslyn," he greeted her as he stood up.

"How are you faring?" Roslyn asked him.

"Your friend Jessica gave me a sleeping potion," Lucius told her. "I believe you know the one."

"I will let Tiffany know her cousin has been a great help to you," Roslyn commented. "How are Edmond, Eliza, Poppy and Robert doing?"

"Robert does not fully understand yet," Lucius told her. "Edmond has been a great help with his sisters in dealing with all of this."

"I am glad to hear that. Do you know who was responsible?"

"We have names," Lucius assured her. "We are planning their capture now."

"Good," Roslyn said with steel in her voice. "I hope you get all of their heads."

There was a knock on the door of Lucius's study and he called out for them to enter. Sully entered the room, a slight look of surprise on his face as he saw Roslyn's astral form there.

"How are you doing?" Sully asked her, concern in his voice.

"I am ok," she told him.

"Sir Sullivan," Lucius brought the knight's attention to him. "What do you have for me?"

"Your Majesty," Sir Sullivan went to his knees. "I have no idea how it happened, but the Count is missing from the dungeons."

"Excuse me?" Roslyn heard her father ask.

"The Count is missing," Sullivan repeated. "None of the other men who were arrested with him are missing."

"What does that mean?" Roslyn asked her father as Roland, the king's butler, entered the room. The Count would have gone missing from within the palace dung-eons, which meant there was a mole in the palace.

"Your Majesties," Roland said when he saw Roslyn there, and he bowed to both of them. "King Lucius, I bring news from the south."

"What is it, Roland?"

"Several mercenary groups have crossed the southern borders," Roland said. "They seem to be camped at the Count's estates."

Lucius swore and looked up at his daughter.

"Dad, is this man about to start a civil war in Ellsgrove?" Roslyn asked him.

Lucius frowned and looked down at the papers Roland just handed him. "Where did they get the money for the mercenaries?"

"It may be that they were withholding taxes," Roland told him, "Or they came across some funds from a joint venture in order to pay for them."

Lucius waved those words aside. "I knew I would come across some big-ots," he said. "There are more misogynist men in this kingdom than I had hoped."

"To be fair, father, that was how they were raised," Roslyn spoke up. "We are a rock dropping violently into their pond."

"They need to get used to the waves," Lucius responded. "Lest they drown."

Roslyn ducked her head and smiled, appreciating what he was saying.

"Do you know where Cassidy is?" She asked him.

"In the Royal Forest with Edmond, Alara, and Kai," Lucius told her. "They have a lot of guards."

"I will go talk to them," Roslyn told him. "Dad, I love you."

"I love you too, Roslyn," he told her before her astral form disintegrated. She reformed in the Royal Forest where Cassidy, Edmond, and Alara were having a picnic by the lake on a blanket.

"Roslyn!" Edmond exclaimed when he saw her. He looked a lot better than he had before.

"How are you?" Roslyn asked him.

"Dealing," he told her. "Alara has been a major help in dealing with…"

"I am but a crutch," Alara broke in. "The loss of a mother is devastating."

Edmond looked at the ground and Roslyn saw tears forming in his eyes.

"I wish I was here for you," Roslyn told him, and he looked up at her astral form.

"I wish you were here as well," he responded. "Maybe those assholes would not have gotten away with it."

"They were cunning," Roslyn reminded him. "They probably would have caused some damage before we got to them." And she told them of the news that Sully and Roland had just told her father.

"What do we do now?" Cassidy asked her.

"I will be going below ground to find what caused the creatures to come to the surface," Roslyn told them. "After that, I have no idea."

"Just be safe," Edmond told her. "I need you."

"I will be back," she promised her brother. "I love you."

Before Edmond could reply her astral form was gone.

Cassidy looked to Alara and Edmond, her face troubled.

"What is it?" Alara asked her.

"I fear Roslyn is running into danger," Cassidy explained. "I am worried for her."

Edmond closed his eyes and pinched his nose, thinking of the advice his older sister had given him over the years.

"Roslyn will be OK," he said after a minute. "I know she will."

Cassidy raised an eyebrow at him but said no more. She wished she was back in Jay'Al with her twin sister and their friends.

Kai put a hand on her shoulder and brought her back to reality.

"What do you want to do?" Kai asked her.

"I want to go back home to help her," she told him truthfully. "But I think we would be better here rooting out the traitors."

"I agree," Kai told her.

"What should we do next?" Cassidy asked Edmond.

"We now know of the mercenaries," Edmond commented. "We need a way of breaking their contract."

Cassidy smiled, a few ideas floating through her mind.

"Leave that to Kai and I," she told him. "Those responsible for Elle's death will meet a worse fate.

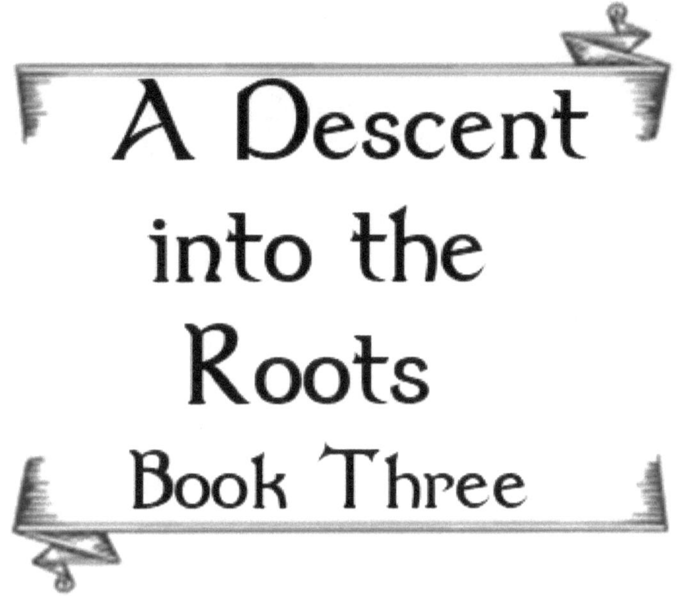

A Descent into the Roots

Book Three

542

Katie M. Thornton

Prologue

oslyn packed her bags, getting ready to head out of Hyena City for the plateau again. She had decided that she needed to regroup there before they embarked on their quest to find out what the behemoths wanted. She had a feeling that the rest of the magical creatures who had been living underground would be coming to the surface sooner rather than later, and she wanted her people to be prepared for that.

Roslyn thought about what her ancestors had told her when she had visited the Hyena Clan shrine the night before: she had asked them about her nosebleed when she had killed the dekellians.

"Your body is not used to this amount of magic. You need to use your familiar to help channel the magic from the land," they told her. *"You also have friends who we know will be more than happy to help you. We know you are afraid of your*
friends getting hurt. They know the risks. You need to let them help you."

They were right, and she knew it.

Leaf sat at the foot of her bed, taking up the whole space now that she had had another growth spurt. The dragonling stretched her wings out and tried flapping them, causing a gust of wind to blow into Roslyn. Roslyn grabbed hold of her bags so they would not blow off of the table and turned to look at Leaf who was looking sheepish.

"Gee girl, practice outside please," Roslyn told her. "Or at least wait until there is nothing to break or make a mess of."

Leaf made a noise that sounded like a laugh and the dragon jumped off of the bed and headed for the door. Using her front paw she opened the door and walked out of the room, meeting Heath and Solana as she went.

"Oy, watch it," Heath said to Leaf as he moved out of her way. Solana, who was on Heath's shoulder, chittered at the dragon as she went by, earning a look from Leaf. Solana jumped down from Heath's shoulder and followed the dragon out to the courtyard. The gryphon's front paws were cat paws, her hind legs those of an eagle; her talons clicked on the floor as she followed the dragon. Her dark blue feathers shimmered in the lantern light.

"What's her problem?" Heath asked Roslyn as he entered her room.

"She wants to exercise her wings," Roslyn told him. "Looks like Solana might want to do that as well."

"I see," Heath responded, looking back at the opening of the courtyard. "I know Solana has been strengthening her wings, but I am not sure I am ready for Solana to fly. It seems too early."

"Gryphons grow quickly I believe," Roslyn told him as she closed her traveler's chest and went to her armour stand to take it down. "Just like cats and certain birds. Solana will probably go through a growth spurt soon where she will be too big to be on your shoulder."

Heath looked saddened at the thought but then he smiled at her, the dimples in his cheeks showing. "How are you, my sweet?" he asked her as he took her into his arms and hugged her.

"I am well, darling," she told him as she looked up at him, taking in the sparkle of his green eyes as he looked at her. Next thing she knew his mouth was on hers and she felt her stomach flip, her knees growing weak as she answered his kiss in kind.

Heath pulled away reluctantly, his hands still on her waist. Roslyn had to catch her breath, and she felt her face turning red. "Everyone is ready to go," he told her, smiling at her. "Erick gave us some wagons to make it easier with all of our supplies."

"Sounds good. I just need to put my armour and weapons in their trunk and I will meet you all out there," she told him as she turned to her armour and weapons stand in the corner of the room.

"All right," he said, sliding his hands off of her hips and turning to walk out the door of her room. "Are you hungry? The cooks made some delicious scones this morning."

"I will never pass up one of their scones," she replied as she opened the trunk she kept most of her weapons in.

"I will save some for you then," Heath promised her as he left her room. She called her thanks after him, seeing that he was headed for the courtyard after leaving her door wide open. She could hear him call for Solana and the sound of claws on tiles. Moments later Leaf returned to her, excited to be heading out again.

"What, you like adventuring?" Roslyn asked her familiar. The dragonling wagged her tail and behind in excitement, and Roz could hear her response in the back of her mind.

"Yes, and more opportunity to spend with Solana," Leaf told her. *"I like the gryphon, and her mage."*

"Me too, Leaf, me too."

As she put away her armour and weapons, Roslyn thought about home. They would have laid Elle to rest by now in the Royal Catacombs, and Cassidy, her twin sister, would be working hard to ferret out the men responsible for the attack that had killed their stepmother. Her father would be worrying about the chances of a civil war brewing as well. She wished she could be back in Ellsgrove to help them, but what was happening beneath Jay'Al could not be ignored.

Finished putting away her armour and weapons, Roslyn put her sword belt on and sheathed her sword. She smiled at Leaf and told her, "Come on let's get going, they are all waiting for us."

***

Cassidy looked out of Edmond's study window at the tree that towered above all of the others in the Royal Forest. The sapling Roslyn had given Ellsgrove to seal their alliance had grown quite quickly and was now the tallest tree out there. She had heard servants remark about the new tree, and even some of the nobles who remained in the palace had noticed it as well.

After the assassination attempt that had claimed the Queen's life, most of the nobles who were staying in the palace had left for their city homes in order to be safe. Cassidy could not really blame them, but Edmond called them cowards just the same.

Cassidy looked at Edmond, her younger half-brother, and sighed inwardly. Her familiar Crick, the pine marten, was snuggling up against the young man to provide comfort. Tej, Kai's fennec fox familiar, was also there offering his own comfort. Kai, Cassidy's travelling companion and lover, was sitting on a chaise in the corner of the room looking over maps of Ellsgrove. Princess Alara was sitting at a small desk in the opposite corner of the room looking over communications from her network of spies that had just been delivered.

"What is the news?" Cassidy asked the princess of Raistminestine. The young woman had only recently been betrothed to Edmond after she had saved the king's life in the first assassination attempt. Cassidy remembered Edmond telling her how he had fallen in love with the princess that day, and she had to admit that the princess was more than she seemed. Not only was she a mage, she was in control of her kingdom's spy network and was a skilled interrogator.

Alara looked over at her with a weary smile. Her light brown hair was held back in several small braids, and her green eyes looked tired. The last few days had been extremely tiring for all of them, with the funeral and all of the information that had needed to be gathered.

"The mercenaries are still in the same place," Alara told her. "They seemingly have no plans to move as of yet."

"Do we know for sure that Count Gresham has left the capitol?" Cassidy asked her. Alara shrugged.

"My spies have not seen him at his estate yet," Alara informed her. "It does take time to travel there so he should not be there yet. Whether he could still be in the city?" Alara shrugged again. "He could still be biding his time to leave."

"We need to find out where he is then," Edmond commented. "We need to search the city."

"We have to be discreet though," Alara reminded him. "We cannot just go door to door and search all of the houses."

"We talk to the servants," Cassidy spoke up. "The shopkeepers will know which servants are buying more food than normal, or could have heard about someone secret staying in their house."

"I was going to suggest that. Maybe I am rubbing off on you," Alara told her with a grin and a wink. "I will get my people on that. Anywhere else we should look?"

Cassidy thought about it for a moment and then smiled, remembering something Roslyn had told her. "The brothels," she recommended. "Let the women know you are friends with Roslyn and they will help you."

"Why would Roslyn know anyone in a brothel?" Edmond inquired, looking up at her.

"Roslyn helped them with anti-pregnancy tattoos," Cassidy informed him. "They also had a huge hand in the Council siding with your father's changes last year."

"I heard about that," Alara commented. "Very well, we will add the brothels as a place to check. I know they usually have information to sell, so it will be a good place to start."

Chapter One

Roslyn shaded her eyes as they rode over a sand dune, the savannah coming into view. They had left Hyena City eight days before. Karina directed the wagon that was laden with the supplies the Archipelago had sent along with Heath, her horse on a lead off of the wagon. Cypress directed the second wagon that had all of their trunks and chests in it, along with their food supplies. The rest of the orc warriors ran alongside the wagons, and the lady knights rode behind them.

"Do you see that?" Roslyn asked Kavan. Kavan was riding to her left, with Heath on her right. Heath took out his spyglass and pointed it in the direction that she indicated, a little ways off where the savannah and desert met.

"Looks like someone on a horse…" Heath started to say. "No, not on a horse…" He handed the spyglass to Roslyn who gasped.

"They are centaurs!" she exclaimed with excitement.

She looked to Leaf, who was running along beside them.

"Leaf showed me all of the old magical creatures that were most likely living underground and one of them was a centaur: half human and half horse."

"Are they peaceful though?" Kavan asked her.

"I think we are about to find out," Heath commented as he noted that they had been seen, and the group of five centaurs were now coming towards them.

"Weapons down," Roslyn told her companions. "We will not greet them with hostility."

"What if they greet *us* with hostility?" she heard Cypress ask quietly. She gave him a look and he grinned at her, winking.

The five centaurs coming towards them were unarmed, the two females of the group wearing worn cloth over their chests. The two females looked like they could be sisters, with their horse parts a blue roan colour and their hair blonde. The three males had their dark hair cut short, and they had scars on their hands and backs as if they had been lashed. All of them were very pale, and they looked like they were having trouble seeing in the sunlight.

"Greetings," one of the male centaurs stopped a stone's throw away from Roslyn and her companions. "We seem to be lost."

"I'm telling you, we cannot trust the above-grounders," Roslyn heard one of the other male centaurs speak to the females. These four were behind the one that spoke to them.

Roslyn dismounted from her horse and walked up to the centaur who had greeted them.

"Lost is an understatement," she told him. "Your eyes must be hurting from all of this natural sunlight. May I try to help you?"

The centaur, whose human half looked to be early-twenties, looked at her with blue eyes that strained. After a moment he nodded and bent down for her to put her hand over his eyes, using her magic to help heal them. She took her hand away and he blinked at her in surprise, taking her and her companions in.

"You have magic?" one of the other male centaurs asked her. She nodded.

"Thank you," the first one addressed her again. "My name is Malvin. My family and I have been traveling for some time and we have no idea where we are."

"How long have you been on the surface?" Roslyn asked him.

"How do you know we are not from up here?" the male centaur who had spoken about not trusting them asked.

"Hush Samman, she clearly knows about where we come from," Malvin told his companion. "What is your name?" he asked Roslyn.

"You are talking to Queen Roslyn of Jay'Al," Cypress interrupted. "The Queen who has brought together not only the tribes of Jay'Al but the orcs of Jay'Al under her banner."

Roslyn held up a hand to stop Cypress. "Thank you, Cyp." She turned back to Malvin who was looking at her with a perplexed expression.

"As Cypress said, I am Queen Roslyn of Jay'Al," she told them. "I have met redcaps who came from beneath the ground, and stood my ground against dark elves."

"Indeed? Luck would have us find you now then. We have fled our dark elf captors to the surface ahead of them, and we seek refuge amongst your people," Malvin told her. "We have been slaves to the dark elves for dec-ades."

"Your people would be most welcome amongst us," Roslyn told them. "Are you hungry? We have food to spare."

"Thank you, your highness," Malvin told her. "This is my wife, Bei, and her sister, Dorrit, and Dorrit's husband Luc. This is my brother,

Samman."

It was Malvin's brother Samman who had spoken about not trusting them. Dorrit's husband was a dark skinned centaur with black hair, his eyes dark.

"Would you heal my family's eyes as well?" Malvin asked her after the introductions were out of the way. "I cannot believe how bright the sun is up here."

"I can. Come, let's make camp for the evening and share food, and I will heal their eyes as I have healed yours."

***

Roslyn watched the centaurs talk among themselves after she had healed their eyes and given them food. Her companions were all gathered around the fire for the evening, each of them watching the centaurs as well; they were all curious about the centaurs and everything they had endured to get to the surface. None of them had dared to broach the subject yet since the newcomers were still getting used to being on the surface and being able to see better after Roslyn's healing.

"Do you think they can be trusted?" Heath asked her, nodding in the direction of the centaurs. He was sitting beside her, Kavan on her other side with Tiffany next to Kavan. Karina sat on Heath's other side.

"They certainly look malnourished and those scars are evidence of mistreatment," Roslyn commented. "Malvin seemed genuine in asking for help. Samman is most likely a suspicious type after all that they have endured."

"So does this change anything?" Tiffany asked her.

"Well actually, I have been thinking," Roslyn told them. "The dark elves' dekellians were able to tear apart a couple werewolves, correct?" She aimed that question at Edwin who was sitting on the other side of the fire.

"Yes. Though if the dekellians had not ripped them to pieces too fast they would have healed. They are fast and vicious. Otherwise, it is only the frishna metal that can kill a werewolf," Edwin responded.

"So what do we do with the werewolves in our group? How do we protect them from the dekellians that we might encounter under the surface?"

"I do not like where this is going," Kavan huffed. "I am going with you."

"No," Roslyn told him. "All of the werewolves should stay on the surface."

"What if they break through again?" Edwin asked her.

"I will use my magic to keep them underground," she explained. "I will also feel much better knowing that my people up here will be safe with werewolves to watch over them."

"You trust Edwin to do this?" Cypress asked her, slightly incredulous. "Just a few weeks ago they were trying to turn your people."

"I trust *Kavan* to do this," she replied. "And Alexander to keep Edwin in place if it came to it."

"You will have no issues from me," Edwin told her. "I promise. I will follow Kavan's lead."

Kavan sighed heavily, shaking his head. "I do not like it," he told her. "But I will do as I am ordered."

"Thank you," Roslyn said, sighing inwardly with relief. She was not sure he would follow this particular order. "That will help me worry less about the people I leave behind when I go below ground."

"It won't help *me* worry less about *you*," he commented, looking at her with those eyes of his.

"She has me," Heath spoke up with a lopsided grin, knowing that he would not like that response since they were each attempting to woo Roslyn.

Roslyn had to duck her head as she smiled, hearing Kavan give a 'harrumph' and then announce he was going to check the perimeter before they camped for the night.

"He will be ok," she heard Heath say. "He had his time alone with you over the last while, now it's my turn."

"Oh really?" she asked him, teasing. "I never thought of that," she added, feigning ignorance. She had to admit that she had thought about that part, though the circumstances were not the best.

She saw Heath look at her sideways and he grinned.

"Let's set up camp, shall we?" Roslyn asked her people. "I will set up the protective shield."

As her travelling companions started to set up tents she went over to the centaurs.

"You can rest easy tonight," she told them. "Nothing can get through my protective shield. Do you need blankets? How do you sleep?"

"We sleep lying down," Malvin informed her with a light smile. "And blankets would be most welcome."

"All right then. Feel free to make a fire for yourselves as well, we will have a few around the campsite," she told them. "I will set up my shield now. Cypress is digging the latrine and he will be by shortly to show you where."

"Thank you," Malvin said as she turned to walk away. "For everything."

"I can see a future for you in my kingdom," Roslyn informed them. "You can rest easy now, Malvin and family. You are under my protection."

***

Alexander found Kavan walking around the perimeter of the camp. Edwin was waiting for him by the fire, but Alexander had something he needed to discuss with his protégé.

"Hey," Alexander greeted Kavan quietly. "Can we talk?"

Kavan nodded and walked over to him. "Of course. What is it?"

"You have the chance to take the cure," Alexander said to him. "Why do you not take it?"

A Descent into the Roots

"I like having these abilities," Kavan explained to him. "My garrison was attacked during the war, and almost all of my friends died. All I could do was ring a damn bell to warn the other soldiers outside the wall of the attack. I can use these new powers to protect my friends now."

"You know that you will not age, right?" Alexander inquired of him. "Is it fair of you to continue to woo Roslyn when she will grow old and you will not?"

Alexander watched Kavan's expression fall, and he knew that the young man had not thought about that part of it.

"The pendant we wear keeps us from changing, but we are still cursed with immortality," Alexander explained. "The cure is the only other way."

"I do not think I can give up these new powers," Kavan told him quietly.

"Then you need to let Roslyn go now, before it becomes too hard."

Kavan sighed. "I will need to think about it more," he promised Alexander. "Thank you for the insights."

Alexander put a hand on Kavan's shoulder and squeezed it lightly. "You are a good man, Kavan. Strong, as well. You will make the right decision, I know you will."

Chapter Two

Cassidy tucked a stray strand of hair under her bonnet and adjusted her skirts. She felt very out of sorts in her disguise, dressed up as a laundress. She had volunteered to go to a few shops to ask some questions, but so far all she had was a better understanding of how the common people of Ellsgrove washed their clothes, and that there was a need for really good hand lotion in the city. As it was, she was waiting at the last shop of the day for one of Alara's agents to pick her up in their wagon.

The whole day she had been aware of her silent protectors, more of Alara's agents who were watching her from afar to make sure she did not get into trouble. She did not know what they looked like but she could tell they were there, which had reassured her during the day.

It was the first time she had ever done anything like it so she had been nervous, but she had fought an orc before and survived, so what was a little espionage compared to that?

"Mistress Rebekah?" a man in a cart that had just rolled to a stop addressed her. Since that was her code name she looked up. The young man was not much older than her, with tanned skin and dark brown hair, his dark eyes slightly amused at something.

"Fine day for a cinnamon bun," Cassidy said to the man.

"They are freshest in the morning," came the coded reply.

Cassidy accepted the man's hand in helping her up into the cart. "Thank you," she told him. "I am ready to go home."

"Of course, mistress," the man responded as he flicked the reins, his horse starting forward again. "What did you find out today?"

"That I should invest in making potions for laundress' hands," she told him, earning a laugh. "No, seriously, their hands are so dry and cracked. A lot of the shopkeepers did not believe I was a laundress until I told them I had just started working and was looking for supplies."

"Quick thinking," the man responded. "You will learn as you go."

"I thought it would be interesting learning about what you do, but it was rather boring today," Cassidy told him. "Alara seems to have the patience for this, but I do not."

The man shrugged and told her, "There will be other uses for you, do not worry. Once we find the right clues we will need people to carry out arrests."

"True," she said with a smile. "Where are we going now?"

"Warehouse district," he replied. "Alara is meeting with all of her people in her warehouse so they can quickly go over notes."

Cassidy listened as she looked around the streets of the Capital, wondering at the size of the city. Jay'Al had once had such grand cities before the clans had fought amongst themselves, and the aftermath of the Werewolf War; she had read about her people's history in the texts that had been passed down through her family. Hyena City was the only large city that remained, and now she wondered at what Roslyn would build. It would definitely encourage the other clans to build larger cities, and with the seas opened up again for trade and travel they would probably see their populations grow. Cassidy thought for a moment that she had not even accounted for the creatures that were coming up from beneath the ground. Roslyn had sent them a message several days ago about the redcaps and dwarves; what else was down there? Would they integrate into the Jay'Alian society?

The cart came to a stop in front of a warehouse that looked the same as all the other warehouses. Her driver gave her a smile as he helped her down from the cart.

"Pleasure doing business with you," he told her with a wink before he got back into his cart. "Stay safe."

She thanked him with a smile and went to the door to the warehouse where a guard was standing watch. He nodded to her and opened the door up for her so she could enter. Inside the warehouse there were crates piled up in sections, barrels stacked in another corner, and a table in the middle that a group of people were standing around. There were mage lights floating along the walkway to lead her to the table, the rest of the warehouse lit by oil lamps.

Kai was one of the people standing around the table. Tej and Crick played nearby; Crick sensed her coming and broke off playing to come to her. Cassidy had left Crick with Kai because her familiar would have raised too many questions while she was pretending to be a laundress. Crick now climbed up her skirts to rest on her shoulder and started sniffing her bonnet.

"Hello, Crick," Cassidy greeted her familiar with a chin scratch. She looked at Kai who was watching her with a smile.

Alara stood next to him, and she recognized a few of the other people around the table as some of Alara's best spies. "How are things?" she asked Alara as she joined them at the table. Cassidy handed Alara her notes so she could browse them quickly.

"We have a few clues," Alara told her without looking up from the paper in her hand. "Servants from a household with familial ties to Count Gresham have become extremely secretive. From what your information tells me about how much extra washing is being done in their household they have several more people staying with them than have been seen coming and going from their estate. My other spies have confirmed that the amount of food being delivered also suggests that there are several more people there than there should be. Soldiers of the crown will investigate the estate as soon as I give the order."

"Really? We got all of that information from this morning's activities?" Cassidy asked her, looking down at the map of the Capital on the table. There were little markers over a part of the city where Cassidy knew was where the noblemen from the countryside had estates.

"We have been gathering information for a couple days," Alara informed her. "Today's information just solidified our target's location."

Cassidy made a face as if to say that she should have realized that before asking, and Kai chuckled as he put an arm around her. "You will get used to the intrigue," Kai whispered in her ear.

"I think you have adapted faster than I have," she responded in a whisper.

"You are used to action, not espionage," Alara reminded her with a comforting hand on her shoulder and a smile. "There is nothing wrong with that."

"So when will you give the order?" Cassidy asked Alara. "If we wait too long, will that not give him time to escape?"

"As soon as we are done here," Alara told her with a smile. "Do you want to come with us for the arrest?"

"Yes!"

"Then let's get going."

***

The estate house was made of brick with a slate roof, a three story building with an extensive garden behind it that was surrounded by a stone wall. Smoke trailed out of one of the chimneys, most likely from the kitchen since it had been a warm day. A few servants could be seen working around the outside of the house, but no one else was visible. There were clear lights in several of the upstairs rooms. The street lamps were being lit as the sun was fading in the sky.

Cassidy stood with Alara and Kai just outside the main gate that led up to the house. Sir Sullivan and a group of soldiers had just arrived with a wagon and were about to knock on the door of the cousin of Count Gresham.

A Descent into the Roots

Cassidy could hear Sullivan talking to someone at the door, and then she saw them enter the house in order to search it. The servants were brought out of the house and lined up in a row beside the walkway, with the family members gathering in a group on the other side of the walkway. There were two young children in the family, with the adults looking like they were in their early thirties. There were six family members in total standing outside, which was the correct amount that was supposed to be there. If the Count was hiding in his cousin's house, the soldiers and Sully should be able to find him.

Crick peeked out from her perch on Cassidy's shoulder, mostly covered by her red hair. She chittered, nervous. Cassidy could sense that something was not quite right so she looked at Alara who must have sensed it as well. Together the two took off towards the house, Kai and Tej behind them.

"Sully!" Cassidy called out as she entered the main foyer of the house. There was no response, so the three of them moved through the house together. Descending a staircase into the basement they found a strange sight: Sullivan and the soldiers stood still, as if time had frozen. Sully looked like he was in a position to open a door, though the door in front of him was open. The soldiers all had their hands on their sword hilts, as if they were about to draw them.

"Someone hit them with a powerful spell," Alara observed as she stepped in front of Sully, noting that he was looking straight at her though he could not say anything.

"I think I should go to your Mage's University, I could learn some new tricks," Cassidy commented as Alara produced a flask out of her belt pouch. She threw the flask on the floor and when it broke out came a white smoke that flowed around each of the men frozen in time. Cassidy watched as Sully and the soldiers began to move again, if slowly at first. Finally Sullivan blinked and turned to look at them.

"Bastards had a mage with them," Sully told them. "They escaped while we were frozen."

"Damn it," Alara hissed. "I should have been in here with you, I could have prevented this."

"We had no way of knowing they had a mage," Sully told her. "We will be better prepared next time."

"There probably will not be a 'next time'," Cassidy spoke up. "He would be stupid to stay in the city any longer. He is probably on his way out of the city as we speak."

"We could close the gates of the city," Sully suggested.

"We will not be able to get the word out on time," Alara told him. "There are too many gates to the city. However, my spies at the gates will inform me when he leaves and we can try to follow him and catch him on the road."

"Well I hope that us flushing him out of his hidey-hole helps us catch him," Cassidy commented. "We cannot let him get home to his army of mercenaries."

Chapter Three

Roslyn looked behind her as she rode into the entrance of the tunnel that led up to the top of the plateau. Malvin and his family stood there watching her group go into the tunnel. The centaurs had chosen to stay below and stay in one of the remaining buildings because they did not want to go through the tunnel.

"We have been underground for so long," Malvin confessed their fears. "I know you said it is only a couple hours but we would rather stay here for now. We just cannot do it, not yet."

Roslyn had Karina put up a protective barrier for them before they parted ways for the time being. Roslyn thought that she might need to bring up the building of the lower part of her capital city to Aidan so everyone would have a proper home. A centaur home would need to be built specifically for their rather different needs, which might prove a challenge for her friend.

"Are you sure we can trust them?" Cypress asked her as they rode up the tunnel.

"Unsure," she answered honestly. "They have been through a lot, but whether they are telling the truth? I did not sense a lie, though there was hesitation. If they were slaves to the dark elves then they might be worried about becoming slaves again to someone else."

"They will learn, in time, just what kind of Queen you are," Cypress commented. "Though I think you might be trusting too easily."

"I will take your words into consideration," Roslyn told him.

Their group rode onto the plateau where they were greeted by soldiers on guard. Roslyn explained to them about the centaurs before heading to Karina's village where her mother and their family were. Heath took her horse's reins from her when she dismounted so she could go talk to her mother in stead of brushing down her horse. The rest of the group dispersed with their horses.

Roslyn thanked Heath before turning towards the house where her mother, step-father, and younger siblings had taken up residence since arriving there from the north. Amelia met her at the door with a hug and ushered her into the main room where Leona and Sawyer were sitting at a table drinking hot cocoa. Leaf and Amelia's large feline familiar, Ecko, started to bathe each other by the fire.

"Where are McKenna and the boys?" Roslyn asked her mother as she accepted a cup of hot cocoa from Leona.

"They are with Judd working on the construction of your palace," Amelia told her with a smile. "I did not think you would be back so soon," she added. "Where is Heath?"

"With the horses," she answered. "He has a gryphon for a familiar!"

"How did that come about?" Amelia asked her, intrigued.

"Whatever I did with that tree sapling must have done something, I really have no idea," Roslyn told her mother. "We also found a group of centaurs who are now camping in what is left of Base Town."

Her mother halted as she was about to take a sip of her own hot cocoa and stared at her with wide eyes.

"What?" Sawyer asked her. "Centaurs? Wow, I…really?"

"Makes sense, first the redcaps and dwarves emerge, now centaurs," Leona commented. "And of course, the dark elves," she added as she sipped her hot cocoa. "What are you planning to do?"

"Heath had captured a dark elf in the Isles, and I was able to talk to him in Hyena City. There are creatures called 'behemoths' that are pushing all of the other creatures above ground again. I am going below ground to find the behemoths," Roslyn told them, earning wide eyed concerned looks from her family. "We came back here to regroup and make sure we have the right supplies before we go."

"Are you sure about this?" Amelia asked her. "These behemoths sound very dangerous if they are causing the dark elves to flee."

"Something needs to be done. I would rather face them down there than up here on the surface," Roslyn explained.

"But you cannot know what you are walking into," Leona told her. "They know the area, it's their home."

"I know there are risks," Roslyn assured them. "What I cannot risk though are these behemoths coming to the surface and wreaking havoc up here also."

"Can you not send a small party of warriors down to do reconnaissance?" Amelia asked her. "Surely you would rather have an army to fight these creatures and not just your group."

"*Let your people fight with you,*" she heard Leaf say in the back of her mind, reminding her of what the ancestors had told her in Hyena City. *"You are not alone."*

"Okay," Roslyn told them. "A small group will go do reconnaissance, though I will lead it. We will not engage the behemoths below if we can help it. I can probably lure them to the surface at a certain spot where an army would be waiting."

"That is a better plan," Amelia said with a sigh. "I will get Aidan to send out the call to muster. Where do you want them to gather?"

"Base Town seems as good a place as any," Roslyn answered with a sigh. "The chasm will probably be where we will aim to resurface. We also brought guns with us, courtesy of Commandant Mortimer. I will have people start training on how to use them in the next few days."

"Guns will definitely be of use," Amelia commented as she got up. "Should I have your people gather so you can talk with them about your change of plans?"

"I assume you are going out to tell Aidan to send the call to muster now?" Roslyn asked her mother, getting a nod as a reply. "Then yes, I guess now would be the time to tell my friends about the change of plans."

***

Roslyn filled up her friends' cups with wine as they sat together on pillows around a low table. Aidan sat at the table itself with papers in front of him, a writing utensil in hand. He barely glanced up at his cup as she filled it, but he gave her a smile as she moved around him.

Smells of food cooking wafted out of the kitchen nearby where the cooks were preparing them a meal. Roslyn figured that they could all use a hot meal right now as they were about to talk about the change in her plans.

"My mother has talked some sense into me," Roslyn announced to her friends. Oswick raised an eyebrow at her, and Cypress gave her a sideways smile. Heath smiled and took a drink from his cup as Kavan looked at her with interest. Karina and the women of the Honour Guard were watching her with attention. Aidan halted in his writing and looked up at her.

"A small party of people will be going underground to determine where the behemoths are and assess what to do," Roslyn explained. "I will lead it, with Heath, Karina, Heather and Cypress going with me. During that time, Kavan and Oswick will train the army on the use of the guns that were given to us by Commandant Mortimer."

"What about us?" Teddy spoke up, meaning the Honour Guard that had remained with her when Cassidy had left for Ellsgrove.

"You will learn how to use guns," Roslyn informed them. "Aidan, after you have sent out the call to muster I want the lower city to start construction. We need fields outlined as well so we can start growing crops."

"Yes, ma'am," Aidan answered without looking up, though she could see a slight smile on his face. "I have already been in contact with Maeve who is still in Hyena City and she has seeds for us, compliments of your father."

"Thank you, Aidan," Roslyn said to him as she put a hand on his shoulder and squeezed it lightly. She looked up to find her mother in the doorway to the kitchen, carrying a platter of steaming food. "There is also something I need to tell those of you who were not with me in Hyena City…There was an assassination attempt on my father's life. He is fine, however…" she felt the tears coming to her eyes again and Heath reached out to hold her hand and give her the strength to say it. "Queen Elle is dead."

Oswick gasped in shock, and Aidan frowned deeply, with Roslyn's mother Amelia halting in her tracks.

Oswick had known Elle for years and had been invited to dinner dozens of times as Roslyn's friend. He could only imagine the pain Roslyn had gone through when she found out. Why had she not said anything sooner to him? He frowned, but realized that Heath holding her hand like that meant that he had been there for her; as long as she had someone who loved her to help her through it he was okay with that.

Aidan had not known Elle at all, just as his queen. He had heard how fondly Roslyn spoke of her though, so he knew it was a devastating outcome. What was going on back in Ellsgrove? What else was she not telling them?

"Have they found those responsible?" Amelia voiced Aidan's question before he could ask it. It was a quiet question, for it pained her to think about him losing another wife. It made Roslyn think about learning that her mother had survived the burning building, and that her father had thought Amelia dead for eighteen years.

"The men responsible escaped, and they apparently have an army of mercenaries awaiting further instructions," Roslyn answered. "Civil War is brewing in Ellsgrove."

That last bit she had been waiting to tell everyone since they had left Hyena City. "Cassidy is working with Princess Alara, Edmond's betrothed from Raistminestine, to find the men responsible and stop any war before it starts, hopefully."

"Well shit, Roz," Oswick commented. "Why are you just telling us now?"

"Because it is taking every fiber of my being to keep me here," Roslyn responded. "I wanted to leave Hyena City that day for home, but what is happening here is just as important. I need all of my friends to help me, to make sure I get through this."

"Of course we will help you," Heath told her. "You know you can count on us."

Roslyn smiled at him and squeezed his hand. "Thank you," she told them. "Now that that is out of the way, let's eat, shall we?"

Chapter Four

Heath was walking to his tent when Kavan called to him from outside of one of the houses of Karina's village. Heath stopped in his tracks and turned to walk towards Kavan who had started walking to him. Solana ran along beside him, bouncing slightly as she exercised her wings.

"Can we talk?" Kavan asked him.

"Of course," Heath answered him. "Why don't you show me around up here while we talk? I hear there was a sinkhole?"

"Yeah, sure, it's this way," Kavan said, and he directed him towards the path to the mountain and where the shrine of the Dragon Clan had been. Kavan explained what had happened with the earthquake that made the sinkhole as they went, and then he got quiet as they got closer to what remained of the hole. Solana sniffed around the area as the two men stood there by the edge.

"Roslyn filled it in most of the way," Kavan said quietly as they looked down into the hole.

"What's wrong?" Heath looked at his friend with concern.

"What did you want to talk about?"

"I am backing out of wooing Roslyn," Kavan blurted out.

"What?" Heath was taken aback. "Why?"

"As a werewolf, even with this pendant keeping me from changing, I will no longer age," Kavan explained.

"So take the cure," Heath admonished him.

"I do not want to."

Heath looked speechless, and then he realized something. "You like the power too much," Heath said as he shook his head with disdain.

"Remember the garrison?" Kavan asked Heath, who nodded in response. "I could do nothing to save my friends. With this new power though?"

"I understand, but I don't want to win Roslyn by default," Heath said finally. "Have you said anything to her yet?"

Kavan shook his head, and told him, "Not yet."

"Don't tell her yet," Heath pleaded. "Just give her some distance for now so I can have more opportunities to win her heart."

"I can do that," Kavan assured him. "Just try not to get shot again, hm?"

That made Heath laugh, and he answered, "I will do my best."

"This is quite the mountain though," Heath commented, looking up the trail. "This is where it happened? Roslyn finding her familiar and you being turned into a werewolf?"

Kavan nodded. "Alexander was living up here for a long time, all alone."

"It's too bad he thought making his own army to fight Edwin was the only way to go," Heath said with a sigh. "You would not be in this mess."

"Well, it happened, and I have made my decision," Kavan told him firmly. "She would be better off with you anyways. It would solidify the alliance between the Archipelago, and your familiars are similar."

"She doesn't want that kind of marriage though, and you know it," Heath told him.

"I know. I still think you are the better option," Kavan replied with a sideways smile. "Come on, let's head back. I think I have a plan for getting you more time with Roslyn before you head below ground."

***

Cypress knocked on the frame of the entrance to Roslyn's tent. He looked concerned as she told him to enter. She was sitting at her desk going over the list of supplies she would need, Leaf curled up in a large ball next to her feet.

"What is it?" she asked the orc warrior.

"The rest of the orcs are coming," Cypress informed her. "Avis is concerned that some of the warriors will challenge you."

"Why does she think that?"

"She is down below arguing with them right now," Cypress explained. "The centaurs are keeping their distance, but I can tell they are unsettled by the presence of these orcs."

"That cannot be good," Roslyn said with a sigh as she stood up. Leaf uncurled herself and stretched, twitching her tail back and forth like a cat. "How do they want to challenge me?"

"A fight," Cypress informed her. She nodded and went over to her weapons stand to pick out what she should use.

"What weapon does their champion use, did you see?" Roslyn asked Cypress.

"Two handed sword."

Roslyn nodded, biting her lower lip as she thought about it.

"Would I be allowed to wear armour?"

"Neither of you can wear armour," Cypress told her. "Not in the kind of challenge he wants to make."

"I see. Well then…" Roslyn finally picked up her frishna sword. "All right, let's go." She put her sheath on her belt and sheathed the sword before following Cypress out of the tent. She found her Honour Guard, and Karina, waiting with their horses. Tiffany gave her a smile and told her, "Show them what you can do, but just be careful."

"I will do my best," Roslyn assured her as she mounted her horse Sage. "Where are Heath and Kavan?"

"They went for a walk," Karina informed her. "I saw them not too long ago walking on the path to the mountain."

"Oh, okay then. Teddy, would you please go get them? This business with the orcs cannot wait."

Teddy nodded and turned her horse towards the path to the mountain, nudging her horse into a run. Roslyn motioned to Leaf who jumped up onto her lap and draped herself across the front of the saddle. Roslyn and the rest of her Honour Guard headed for the tunnel that went down through the plateau to the land below at a run.

As they left the tunnel Roslyn could see the centaurs huddled together by the tree she had planted near the entrance of the tunnel. Avis had the new group of orcs settled just outside the walls of Base Town, and Roslyn was surprised at the size of the group. There must be a few hundred orcs milling about the makeshift tent city that they had put up.

Roslyn dismounted and handed the reins to Tiffany, Leaf jumping down from the horse's neck. As she walked towards Avis who was waiting in the open gate of the town, Cypress at her side, Kavan joined them.

"Heath is coming," Kavan told her. "He's just a little slower than I am."

Roslyn chuckled at the joke and greeted Avis.

"My Queen," Avis greeted her, bowing her head deeply. "Thank you for coming so quickly."

"Of course. Thank you for dealing with the issue until I could be here. What is going on?"

"Farrow is one of our Chiefs," Avis started to explain as she nodded towards a rather large orc leaning on his two handed sword in front of his tent. A dozen more orc warriors stood around him. "He is not happy with this new arrangement, arguing that you must have bewitched the ancestors into accepting you. He wishes to challenge you."

"What did you say to him?" Roslyn asked Avis.

"I told him that the ancestors cannot be magically persuaded, but he is stubborn."

"That seems to be a common trait," Roslyn joked as she started stretching.

"So he will underestimate you," Tiffany told her as she and the rest of the Honour Guard joined them after settling their horses. "Just like Grau."

"Grau was not much of a warrior," Roslyn reminded her. "This Farrow looks like he knows how to use that sword."

"He does," Avis told her. "He is one of our best warriors."

"Introduce us please, Avis?" Roslyn asked the elder.

"My pleasure, My Queen," Avis told her with a smile before they stepped out from between the gates of Base Town and walked towards where Farrow was standing. Leaf walked next to Roslyn, her eyes narrowing in on the orc who dared to challenge Roslyn.

Roslyn could tell by the change in Farrow's expression that he had not believed that her familiar was a dragon. The other warriors started pointing at Leaf and a crowd of orcs gathered to look at her. As Roslyn, Avis, and Leaf approached Farrow,

Roslyn could see him looking at the tribal tattoo the orc ancestors had marked her with. Roslyn noticed that Farrow had the same tattoo on his arm.

"Chief Farrow, this is your Queen, Roslyn Amelie," Avis started to introduce them. "My Queen, your Chief Farrow."

Farrow growled as Avis called Roslyn his Queen and then again when she said Farrow was Roslyn's Chief.

"You are not a puny human like I thought," Farrow said, looking down at Roslyn. He must be a good head or more taller than her, bigger than Cypress even. "What is so special about you, hm? How did you get our ancestors to accept you?"

Roslyn shrugged and told him, "I do not know what made them decide to accept me; I showed them who I am and they seemed to like me. I do know that I honour them by bringing your people into my home and under my protection. You would go against the wishes of your ancestors by challenging me?"

"I would," Farrow snarled at her.

"Then I accept your challenge," Roslyn told him as she backed away to find an open space. She motioned for everyone to move back and a large circle was formed around them. Avis and Leaf left her side as she began to stretch again.

Roslyn saw Heath standing next to Kavan out of the corner of her eye. Heath looked worried, but Kavan seemed to be assuring him of something. Avis and Leaf both joined Kavan and Heath, Leaf sitting next to Solana as they watched.

Farrow approached Roslyn as he hefted This sword in his hands. He was just wearing his tunic which was made of furs, and rough spun breeches, his feet bare. Roslyn drew her sword as he advanced towards her and she blocked his initial swing at her chest before deftly moving back and out of his way. He swung again at her and she moved around it. Sometimes being smaller than the opponent had its advantages, since Roslyn was able to move a little faster than the large orc.

Heath looked up from the fight as he noticed large angry looking clouds move over them. He nudged Kavan and pointed to the sky as a loud crack of thunder roared over them followed by lightning striking the field not too far from where Roslyn and Farrow were fighting.

Roslyn stepped back from Farrow as he moved to swing at her again, another grumble of thunder moving over them. She put her sword down and knelt as another strike of lightning hit just inches away from Farrow.

Farrow's face had turned as white as it could as the hair on top of his head stood up from the static. He turned to look at Avis who was smirking.

"What is going on?" Heath asked Avis.

"The ancestors are telling him to stop," Avis explained. "In the plainest way they can."

Farrow threw his sword down and knelt as another strike of lightning hit again in the exact same spot just in front of him.

"Fine!" Farrow yelled up to the storm. "Since it is the wish of the ancestors, I yield!"

The orcs around them were all whispering about what was happening, and Roslyn was actually slightly disappointed that she would not be able to show Farrow what kind of warrior she was. Well, there would be plenty of time to prove to him in the future at least.

A wisp of wind moved around her, urging her to stand. She looked up and saw the ghostly form of one of the orc ancestors standing in front of her. She heard the gasps of the orcs around them, and Farrow looked up, his mouth hanging open and his eyes wide.

"Chief Farrow, you go against the wishes of your ancestors," the ghostly form spoke in a very disappointed voice. "You are hereby stripped of your status as Chief. I would banish you as well, but I believe Roslyn may need you in the future."

Farrow looked down, his shoulders slumped.

"Where is warrior Stane?" the ancestor asked the crowd of orcs. Orcs moved aside in one section to reveal a young orc not much smaller than Farrow. "Stane, you are the new Chief of your Clan. Serve Queen Roslyn well."

With another rumble of thunder the ancestor's ghost disappeared.

Roslyn picked up her sword and sheathed it before going to pick up Farrow's sword. She did so with little effort, and then she offered it to him.

"I do not like you," Farrow told her. "But I will do as my ancestors say and serve you."

"I know," she responded as he accepted his sword back. "I look forward to sparring with you in the future."

Chapter Five

Heath found Roslyn in her tent after she was done meeting with the orcs. The orcs were going to stay down in their makeshift tent city for now until homes could be built. Leaf was just outside exercising her wings again, and Solana chose to join the dragon instead of going into the tent with Heath.

"You just missed Kavan," Roslyn commented as she looked up to find him in the opening of her tent. "He wants to go make sure all of the redcaps and dwarves are making it to Bella Vale, and he wants to take the centaurs there too."

"Oh?" Heath commented, figuring that this was Kavan's plan to give them some time together.

"I told him to take McKenna and a few of the other warriors with him. My mother can take command here while we go underground."

That was a little easier than Heath thought it would be for Kavan to give them space, but maybe she wanted to have more alone time with Heath? He hoped so anyway. He felt nervous for the first time in a long time about their relationship, and he was unsure about what lay ahead. The one thing he did know though after being apart from her for so long, was that he loved Roslyn and wanted a future with her.

"I made this for you," Heath started to say as he advanced on her desk and took something out of his pocket. Roslyn looked up from her papers and found a crystalized seashell dangling from a silver cord. She smiled sweetly at him and moved her hair so he could put it around her neck. He did so, lightly touching her shoulder with his pinky finger as he closed the clasp. She shivered slightly at his touch.

"I love it," Roslyn told him as she looked at it. "Thank you!"

A Descent into the Roots

"I made it while I was on the island of Kyprago," Heath told her. "Nadim helped me to find the perfect one for you."

"I will have to thank him the next time I see him," Roslyn said with a smile, and he felt his chest tighten at the warmth of her smile. He loved that smile, and her laugh.

"Do you want to go for a picnic?" he asked her. "I got the cooks to put some things together. We could watch the sunset."

"I would love that," Roslyn told him as she pushed herself away from the table and the papers on it. "Where did you have in mind?"

"Karina suggested a couple of places," he told her, earning a lopsided grin from Roslyn.

Roslyn followed him out of her tent to find her horse, Sage, and Heath's horse both saddled and waiting there. Leaf looked at her with her head cocked slightly and she got up from where she was playing with Solana to follow them as they both mounted their horses. Solana ran to catch up as Heath led Roslyn to a place on the edge of the plateau where they could watch the sun set.

There was a small grouping of lilac trees that had bloomed and Roslyn inhaled their scent as Heath laid out a blanket for them to sit on. Leaf and Solana climbed one of the lilac trees and chittered at each other while Heath pulled out a bottle of wine from his saddlebag as well as two cups, and brought over a basket that had been on the other side of his saddle. He placed the basket down and offered her a cup before opening the bottle and pouring her some wine.

The view that greeted them was the west side of the plateau looking down at the rest of the land of Jay'Al below. On the horizon the sun was beginning to set, and the sky was starting to turn different hues of red.

"This is lovely," Roslyn commented as she sipped her wine. She remembered their first picnic together, and her cheeks turned a little pink as she remembered swimming with him in the hot spring.

Heath smiled at her, showing his dimples, and opened the picnic basket. He brought out a small platter of roasted boar with roasted potatoes, carrots, and a bowl of gravy, along with two plates and cutlery. He saw her smile get bigger when she saw the gravy, which was still steaming, and he chuckled. They each took what they wanted, Heath letting Roslyn have the gravy first.

"I have been waiting for some alone time with you ever since I got back," Heath commented as they leaned against each other while sipping their wine, Heath with his arm around her. "I missed you *so* much while I was gone."

"I missed you too," she whispered back. "I was so happy to find out you were still alive."

Heath hugged her then as she sighed deeply, and she raised her glass to ask for more wine. He topped up her cup and his own and then returned to holding her in his arms. He could feel her heart beating fast against him. She reached out her hand and entwined their hands together, giving him a light squeeze.

Roslyn liked that his hands were slightly callused, and how he smelled of cedar. The muscles in his arms were comfortable and warm to lean into, making her feel safe and secure while being held. It felt right to be in his arms.

"What do you think we will find below ground?" Roslyn asked him, showing that she was slightly worried about what they would find.

"Hopefully nothing too big," Heath joked, earning a chuckle from her. "More dark elves, and whatever the behemoths are. We will figure things out and then get the hell out of there as fast as we can."

Roslyn tilted her head up to look at him, moving her cup of wine out of the way. Heath smiled down at her and put his hand on her chin, leaning down and kissing her gently. She returned his kiss, and the gentility turned to heat as they continued. Roslyn put her cup down without looking and turned her body more towards him. She pulled away reluctantly and rested her head against his chest.

"Can we just sit here for a while?" she asked him quietly. "Just with your arms around me?"

"Of course," was his gruff reply, and he wrapped his arms around her, resting his chin on her head. Together they breathed in the scent of the lilac and watched the stars as they began to shine.

***

Tiffany smiled as she watched Heath and Roslyn return to Roslyn's tent, Heath bidding Roslyn goodnight. Heath turned to give Tiffany a smile and a wink before he and Solana went to their own lodgings for the night.

Tiffany had seen Kavan leave earlier with McKenna and a handful of both orc and Jay'Alian warriors. When she asked Aidan about it he had told her that Kavan was leaving to make sure the redcaps and dwarves had made it to Bella Vale, and to escort the centaurs there as well. Tiffany wondered why he suddenly decided to do that since it was Kavan that Roslyn had wanted to take care of things while they went below ground.

"Roz said her mother can take care of things," Aidan had explained with a shrug. "I did not ask any further."

Now Tiffany wondered about the two men and their plans to win Roslyn's heart. The timing of Kavan leaving was too convenient for what was going on right now, at least that was what Tiffany thought. Tiffany knew that Kavan did not want to take the cure to become human again, and she had talked to Alexander about it before. They had all stopped aging the day they were turned into werewolves. So Kavan would remain young while Roslyn grew older, and Tiffany realized that Kavan knew that. There was no possible way he could have a relationship with her unless he took the cure, but now Tiffany understood that Kavan had graciously stepped back to allow Heath alone time with Roslyn. Was that why they had gone for a walk earlier that day?

Tiffany realized that Heather was saying something to her and she blinked and looked at the young woman. "Sorry?"

"The stars look really nice tonight," Heather repeated, looking up at the very clear sky and the hundreds of bright shining stars. Heather pointed at a grouping of stars and said, "Look, Karina told me that one is called The Wolf."

Tiffany had to squint to see it but she had to admit it did look kind of canine like.

"Come on," Tiffany said to Heather and the others of the Honour Guard. "Let's go get some hot cocoa and sit around the fire for a bit. Leaf will watch over Roslyn tonight."

***

Roslyn awoke to the smell of fresh bacon as Heath put a platter of food on her table. She smiled at him and looked at the breakfast he had brought her, all of her favourite things: bacon, blueberry scones, fruit turnovers, and the special wake-up drink made just how she liked it.

"Breakfast in bed?" she asked, sitting up with her blanket covering her upper body. "How thoughtful of you."

"Anything for you, my sweet," he told her as he leaned in and kissed her cheek.

"I think Tiffany wants to talk with you about something so you better get dressed," he told her. "She is waiting patiently outside."

"Ah, well then. I will get dressed, you can tell her to come in a minute. Thank you for breakfast," she told him again as he turned to leave. He winked at her and left the tent.

Roslyn dressed quickly in a simple long tunic and breeches, and she was doing up her leather boots when Tiffany entered her tent.

"The girls and I were talking last night," Tiffany started to say, and she walked over to the table where the breakfast platter was sitting and picked up a scone, taking a bite of it. She swallowed and then continued, "We think we should be called your 'Queen's Guard' now."

"Why is that?"

"According to Deirdre, your father used the 'Honour Guard' name to placate some of the crusty old nobles. Now you are no longer under the eye of Ellsgrove we think it is time to change it."

"Sounds good to me," Roslyn answered as she sat down at her desk and took a bite of bacon. "Do you know where Oswick is? I haven't seen him since we got back."

"He is helping Judd with the stones for building the lower city," Tiffany told her. "I thought you knew."

Roslyn shook her head. "He must be feeling a little left out right now so he is trying to help any way he can," Roslyn explained. "That is what he is like."

"As a merchant in the middle of a new country where all of the trading agreements have been put in place now, I can only imagine how bored he is," Tiffany commented.

"That, and Judd is his type," Roslyn replied with a smile. "I am sure Oswick is enjoying himself."

Tiffany hid a smile and then told her, "Avis and the rest of the elders wanted to talk with you about where their homes and fields will be. I think Avis also wants to apologize for the actions of Farrow yesterday."

"Not everyone is going to like me," Roslyn said with a wave of her hand. "I accepted that a long time ago. As long as he respects his ancestors' wishes and does not cause trouble again, I am happy. The Elders and the rest of the orcs we have been travelling with will soon spread the word of what kind of person I am and there should be no more issues, hopefully." Roslyn sipped from her cup and then took a bite of one of the other scones as Tiffany finished the one she had taken. "Where are Avis and the other Elders now? Are they down below still or are they up here?"

"Down below. Cypress brought the message just a little while ago."

"Did he stay down there?"

"Yes, he felt he needed to talk to the warriors after what happened with Farrow," Tiffany explained. "He spent the night down there to do so."

"All right, can you get Aidan to meet me at the entrance to the tunnel in a bit with the city plans? I would like to talk to the Elders."

"Of course," Tiffany responded, bowing her head and turning to leave. "It was a really nice night last night, eh? The sky was so very clear."

Roslyn almost choked on her drink as Tiffany laughed and quickly left the tent.

Chapter Six

Edmond was sitting at his desk in his study reading papers when Alara entered, her guard behind her. He greeted her with a smile, taking in how nice she looked that afternoon. She had been busy all morning with her spy network and had been unable to have breakfast with him.

"I received a communication from Rafi this morning," Alara told him as she sat down in one of the chairs on the other side of his desk. "He is down south at his family estate which is near Count Gresham's. He was able to get a couple of our spies smuggled into the Count's estate."

"That is very good news," Edmond commented. "Do we know if the Count is there yet?"

"He is not," Alara responded. "Which is odd. We have searched the city and have not found any more evidence that he is still here."

"So he is somewhere between here and there," Edmond suggested with a smirk, earning a sideways smile from Alara. "We know he is not still here in the Capital. Does he have ties in any other cities between here and his estate?"

"A few, which we are following up on," Alara assured him.

"He will be found," Edmond told her. "My father is having 'Wanted' posters sent all over the kingdom. There is a price on his head, even with the threat of the mercenaries. The conservatives will think twice if we catch him and put him to the block."

"Do you know where Cassidy and Kai are this afternoon?" Alara asked him.

"I believe they went to the Mage's College," Edmond responded as his stomach growled. "Cassidy wanted to get a few books on our way of magic from there."

"Anything in particular?"

"She wanted to learn how to make those freeze bombs and other things,"

Edmond explained. "Roslyn was too busy learning the ways of the shamans to teach her anything."

"She could have asked me," Alara commented, feeling a little hurt.

"I think it has more to do with it being where Roslyn went to school," Edmond told her. "She misses her sister right now, and wants to feel some connection."

"I can understand that," Alara conceded. "Her Honour Guard is with her?"

"Yes, Sully and the others went with her. She is well protected."

Alara leaned forward and he put down the papers he had just picked up to read. "How are your siblings doing?"

"It finally hit Robert," Edmond told her, his eyes sad as he thought about his younger brother crying over their mother. "Eliza and Poppy are pretending to be strong for him but I see their red eyes."

Alara reached her hands over and took his hands in hers.

"And you, darling?"

Edmond could feel the tears coming forth as she quickly got up from her chair and went around his desk to hold him as he cried.

"She was your mother, you are allowed to mourn her, there is no shame in crying," Alara whispered to him as she held him. He leaned into her and she could feel him shudder with sobs. She ran her fingers through his dark blond hair and kissed his forehead. "Everything will be okay, Ed. I promise."

***

Cassidy stared at the portrait of the King of Ellsgrove, her father, with his family. Queen Elle's smile had been captured beautifully, and Roslyn's aloofness as well. The younger siblings all looked happy in the portrait, though she could tell that Robert was bored from having to sit for the painting.

The portrait hung in the main entrance of the Mage's College, and she felt a pain in her heart seeing Elle's smile there. It also made her miss Roslyn even more.

The Mage's College was a large multi-winged stone building in the city of Guerrier, a mere one hour horse ride north-east from the Capital. She and Kai, along with Sully and the Honour Guard, had left the palace late in the morning to get there and had stopped at an inn for lunch before going to the College.

Crick chirped at her from near her ankles, and Cassidy looked down at her familiar with a sad smile. "I know Crick," she responded. "I will be alright."

"Duchess Cassidy?" a woman in grey robes approached them as a group of students in their mage robes walked by them into the school. The woman was several inches shorter than Cassidy with dark brown hair that hung past her shoulders. Under her robes she wore a dark blue silk blouse and dark brown breeches, knee high black leather boots adorning her feet. "Ah yes, you do look exactly like Roslyn," the woman commented as she looked Cassidy up and down. "It's the eyes that are the difference, I can see that. The King sent me a message this morning saying that you were coming. I am Headmistress Dake, how may I be of service to you today?"

"I was hoping I could find someone to teach me how to make freeze bombs and the like," Cassidy explained. "Roslyn had no time to go over things with me."

"Yes, I believe I can find you a professor or two who can be of service," Headmistress Dake told her. "Please, follow me."

The halls were tiled with plain gray tiles, the walls stone with some tapestries hanging here and there. Mage lights lit up niches as they went, windows sparse except for the Conservatory that the Headmistress walked them through. There was finally a sign for the 'East Wing: Alchemy' hanging on the wall before a set of double wooden doors.

Some students stared at Cassidy, whispering that she looked like the princess Roslyn. Cassidy heard some people correct them, telling them she was Roslyn's twin sister who had grown up in Jay'Al–how they knew that, Cassidy had no idea, unless word had spread already from the Capital to the students.

"Lady Jessica has been back to the College since the incident," Headmistress Dake explained to Cassidy. "She takes care of one of our dorms. Word of your arrival in Ellsgrove came from her, and of your relation to Roslyn."

"Is she doing okay? She was injured in the attack."

"She is healing well, thank you for asking," Headmistress Dake responded with a smile. She finally stopped in front of a room at the end of the hall that had the words 'Combustibles and Corrosives' written on a plaque above the door.

Dake opened the door and ushered their group in, smiling lightly at the sight of the two familiars. "How adorable. You will have to explain to me how familiars work for you. Jessica could only explain a little."

"When a shaman comes of age they are matched with a familiar," Cassidy explained. "Sometimes it does not happen right away, it can even take months. They help us channel our magic more, and even store some of our magic, as well as connect us to the land."

"And you can understand them?"

Cassidy nodded.

"Intriguing," Dake commented, looking thoughtful. Someone in the room cleared their throat and Dake turned to find the professor she was looking for standing at her large wooden desk on the other side of the room; between them and the professor were dozens of alchemy stations like the one Roslyn had. "Ah, sorry, this is Professor Reed, she will instruct you on how to make what you were asking about."

Professor Reed was a curvy woman in her early thirties with brown skin and curly dark brown hair that she wore cut short. She wore the same kind of outfit as Dake did, though her blouse was dark green and her boots brown leather, her mage robe being a dark orange colour.

"Professor, this is Duchess Cassidy from Jay'Al, our Princess Roslyn's sister," Dake introduced them. "And her companions."

"Pleased to meet you," Professor Reed greeted them. "How can I help you today?"

"I want to learn how to make freeze bombs and fire bombs," Cassidy explained. "I figured this was the best place."

"My afternoon class is about to start, so why don't you all join us?" Professor Reed asked them. "No better way to learn than hands-on experience!"

Chapter Seven

Kavan kept pace with the centaurs on foot along with Terran, Louran, and Pine. McKenna and a few other Jay'Alian warriors rode along beside them on their horses. They had left the plateau shortly after the incident Roslyn had with Farrow, and had camped late in the night at the edge of where the savannah met the plains. He used some of Roslyn's crystals to protect the camp during the night.

Kavan remembered the look on her face when he asked her about leaving. She had looked slightly confused, but he had a good point about making sure that the creatures made it safely to Bella Vale. At least she had let him go, he had been unsure if she would let him because of the dangers that could be out there. What if more dekellians came above ground? Well, that was something he would have to deal with if it happened, but he could not stay there on the plateau with Roslyn.

Alexander and Edwin had chosen to stay on the plateau.

Alexander had given him a knowing look when Kavan had explained that he was leaving. Kavan slightly resented Alexander for giving him these powers. He was choosing them over Roslyn. At the same time, he was glad he had the powers; Heath had his magic, but Kavan was just an orphan who was particularly good with a sword.

Kavan shook his head, forcing himself to stop thinking about it. They were heading north still, now in the forest, and he could smell the redcaps in the distance, along with other scents that were similar. He could also smell other centaurs in the area, which he informed Malvin of.

"It will be good to meet more of us," Malvin commented to his brother.

"Yes, it will be. I am enjoying the fresh air up here, and the sunlight," Samman told him. "We can *live* up here."

"We can raise a family up here," Malvin's wife, Bei, said. Malvin smiled at her.

"Did you want us to go find them now?" Kavan asked them, halting. "I think it will be better to gather them now rather than later."

"Yes, I think so too," Malvin replied.

Kavan looked at McKenna and pointed in the general direction he smelled the centaurs in and together they changed course.

The forest they were riding through was not very dense, with mostly maples and pine trees, a few birch scattered here and there. There were dozens of bird noises, and squirrels chittering in the trees above, that Kavan had to filter out. He could even hear the centaurs in the distance walking and talking.

As they approached the area where the other centaurs were, Kavan put his hand up to signal that they halt. He turned to Malvin and indicated that he should come with him. Malvin nodded and together they walked through some cedar bushes into the clearing on the other side where there was a group of centaurs resting.

The centaurs had heard the rustling in the bushes and all stood at attention, some of them wielding polearms, others bows and arrows. When they saw another centaur they relaxed a bit, though Kavan's presence still had them wary as one of the centaurs greeted them.

"Good evening," the centaur, an older male who looked like he was in his fifties, was the one to greet them. "From where do you come?"

"My family and I were slaves to the dark elves," Malvin explained. "We escaped during the earthquakes and came to the surface where we found a group of humans to help us. They are taking us somewhere safe."

"How do you know that for sure?" the other centaur asked him, folding his arms across his chest. He wore what looked to be an undyed wool jacket. His dark blond hair was cut short to his head.

"The Queen of Jay'Al has offered sanctuary," Kavan spoke up. "I am Kavan, I work for Queen Roslyn. I am gathering all of the magical creatures we can find and taking them north to a safe place."

"Jay'Al has a Queen now?" the older centaur asked. "When did that happen? Our stories of the above-ground told of warring clans."

"Roslyn has been Queen for only a few months, but she has united both the human clans and the orc clans under her banner," Kavan explained.

"She is also a mage," Malvin further explained. "She healed our eyes so the sun no longer hurts us."

"Interesting," the centaur commented. "Well, I am Lorimer," he introduced himself. Malvin told him his name in return as Kavan looked at the rest of the group of centaurs, of which there were fifteen including Lorimer. There were a few others that looked as old as Lorimer, but the rest looked like they were in their early twenties or younger.

"Well met, Lorimer," Kavan told the centaur. "Would you like to join the sanctuary that Queen Roslyn has offered?"

Lorimer looked at the other centaurs in his group to gauge their feelings before looking at Kavan again. "I think we would like to see what your Queen has to offer, yes."

***

The redcaps were easily found after Lorimer and his centaurs joined Kavan's group. The redcap that Roslyn had given her crystals to was leading the group, and he recognized McKenna. They were grateful for the added protection.

"Sleeping under the stars is scary," Darton, the redcap with the crystals, explained to McKenna and Kavan. "Even with the crystals to protect us during the night. During the day, though, there are too many sounds coming from the forest. The above-ground is scary."

"What was it like, underground?" Kavan asked him.

"There were large caverns, several of them, where we all lived," Darton explained. "The dark elves were in several caverns further down, and they did not stray far from them usually. Us redcaps, and the dwarves, were able to live together somewhat peacefully, along with the centaurs, until all of this mess started."

"How many slaves did the dark elves take?" Kavan asked, thinking about Malvin and his family.

"It was mostly centaurs they would take, but if they could get a hand on any of us, they did," Darton explained. "We have no idea how many," he added with a shrug.

"Let's camp for the night here, shall we?" McKenna suggested a large clearing near a stream just ahead of them. "Now that we have caught up with the redcaps and dwarves we do not need to hurry. We might be able to find others as well."

"One big happy party of magical creatures," Kavan commented with a chuckle. "This should be interesting."

"You're human," Darton butted in, earning a raised eyebrow from Kavan and a grin from McKenna and the rest of their group.

"I, little redcap, am a werewolf," Kavan informed him, smiling inwardly as he watched the redcap's eyes grow wide. "Now, let's start setting up camp and getting food prepared. I am getting a little *peckish*."

Chapter Eight

Roslyn knocked on the door frame of the house that the remaining werewolves had been given to live in. Nearly half of the werewolves had chosen to take the cure, but Edwin and Alexander had managed to talk the rest of them into just using the pendants for now because Roslyn might need them in the coming weeks to help defend Jay'Al.

The house they were staying in was one of the larger ones with two stories, the previous family having moved down to the surface. After a moment Alexander opened the simple wooden door and gave her a welcoming smile.

"My Queen, to what do I owe the pleasure of this visit?" Alexander asked her as he beckoned her to come inside. "We are just settling in for supper, care to join us?"

"I think that will depend on what you are eating," Roslyn half-joked as she followed him into the common room where a dozen people were sitting on cushions and pillows around a short, long table.

Alexander chuckled and told her, "Just some roasted chickens and potatoes. We also have gravy, which I hear you love."

"I would love to, but I already promised Tiffany I would eat with her tonight. I just wanted to talk with you about something," Roslyn told him, adding after a pause, "In private."

"Oh, ok…uhm…" Alexander looked around and gestured to the door on the other side of the common room that led to a greenhouse of sorts attached to the house. He opened the door and let her go through before closing it behind them.

"How is everyone settling in?" Roslyn asked him. Alexander noted that she was wringing her hands, and she looked unsettled.

"They are fine," Alexander answered her. "Those who took the cure were mostly from the Beaver Clan and they have all returned home. That's not why you asked to speak with me in private though, is it?"

"Is Kavan planning on taking the cure after all of this is over? He asked me to make him the pendant, but I assumed he just wanted to keep his strength in case it was needed."

Alexander sighed and looked away from her, pinching his nose as he thought about what to say. "I think you know the answer already."

He saw her face drop, and he could hear her heart beat faster out of agitation.

"He likes the power more," Roslyn heard herself saying, slightly numb now that she had the confirmation.

"He knows he will not age," Alexander told her. "That is why he left."

"Why did he not tell me outright?" Roslyn wanted to know, leaning against one of the workbenches that still had some half empty potting jars on it.

"I suspect he wanted you to choose Heath of your own accord," Alexander informed her. "They are friends after all. He wants you to be happy, and he knows that he cannot be what you need now."

"I see," was all she could bring herself to say.

"All you all right?" Alexander asked her. "I understand you had feelings for Kavan, and this must not be easy to hear."

"He chose the powers you gave him over me, clearly he would not be a good choice," Roslyn managed to say, straightening herself and crossing her arms across her chest. "Thank you for telling me the truth Alexander."

"I am sorry it had to come from me," Alexander went to her and put a hand on her shoulder. "You are a good woman, Roslyn. You will be a great Queen to our people."

She gave him a weak smile and excused herself, bidding the rest of the werewolves a good night as she left the house. She looked around at her Queen's Guard who were waiting nearby, and Leaf who was sitting at Tiffany's feet.

"Everything OK?" Tiffany asked her.

"Yeah, I just…I need to take a walk. By myself. And Leaf."

"Of course. You should be safe up here anyways," Tiffany said, understanding that Roslyn needed some time to herself right now. Tiffany did not know what Roslyn had wanted to talk to Alexander about, but whatever it was, it had ruffled some feathers.

Roslyn nodded and Leaf joined her as she started walking towards the mountain.

"What do you think, Leaf?" Roslyn asked her familiar as they walked. She shivered and looked up at the clouds that threatened rain. There was a rumble of thunder.

"I think you knew his choice as soon as he asked you about making a pen-

dant instead of the cure for him," Leaf told her. *"He is not the one for you."*

Roslyn stopped and looked down at the silver dragon that now came up to above her knees, her tail nearly as long as her body. Her wings had grown even more, and she had spent a lot of time lately strengthening them. She felt some drops of water on her head and she looked up as the rain clouds opened up. Instead of shielding herself from the rain she let herself get soaked.

"I know it is not easy to hear this, I know you were fond of him," Leaf told her.

"No, it is not; but I know that Heath chose me, above everything. He could have stayed in the Archipelago, but he came back to make sure I was safe."

Leaf rubbed up against her legs and then looked up at her with wide eyes. Roslyn could feel the love coming from her familiar and it helped warm her up a little bit inside.

"Come on," Leaf said to her, turning to head back to the village. *"You should get warmed up and change into dry clothes before you catch a cold."*

"You sound like my…" she was about to say Mother Elle but stopped, remembering that she would never see her stepmother again.

Leaf stood on her back legs and rested her front paws on Roslyn's chest, looking her in the eyes. *"This too shall pass,"* Leaf told her. *"I know it hurts still, but you will get through this."*

Roslyn sighed deeply and looked into her dragon's eyes, seeing stars in their depths. Something in Leaf's eyes made her feel better, and she kissed the dragon's head in thanks. With that Leaf got down and led her back to the village.

***

Roslyn watched the group of men and orcs mill about the area where her palace was going to be built. Oswick was there beside Judd at his table, helping to direct the workers as they went about placing markers. Roslyn felt a little bad for displacing the villagers, something she had really hoped not to do, but Karina's father Lou had assured her that his people were extremely happy to be able to have farms on the ground below the plateau and that they were looking forward to growing their herds and expanding to other animals.

"One can only eat alpaca and chicken for so long," Karina had whispered to her during the meeting they had had with the orc clans about the building of the city. "I told him about lamb and boar, and he is looking forward to it."

Over a sennight had passed since Kavan had left, and Roslyn's talk with Alexander. She had not been able to find any alone time with Heath since their picnic, but he was always there at her side for breakfast and to offer his advice during meetings.

Aidan was busy trying to gather everything Roslyn and her group would need for their expedition, and she rarely saw much of him beyond breakfast. Karina was usually busy training with the Queen's Guard and the orc warriors.

Roslyn missed Cassidy and Rafi, even Kai in those moments during meetings. Her mother Amelia was with her a lot, learning what she would need to do for when Roslyn would leave. Amelia's presence, and that of her other sisters, Leona and Sawyer, helped calm her nerves about the expedition ahead.

Roslyn turned around and went back inside her tent where her council was waiting, sitting around a table. Her council consisted of Aidan, Heath, Amelia, Leona, Sawyer, Tiffany, Karina, Cypress, and the new orc chief Stane. This was the first time in several days that all of her council was available to meet since they all had important things to do. All of the familiars, Leaf, Solana, Ecko, and Mister Scruffy, were huddled in a cuddle pile near the hearth. The sight of them made Roslyn smile.

"Maeve will be arriving soon with the seeds we will need for planting," Aidan started talking. "We have the fields marked out. Willow has sent word that their warriors will be arriving soon, and we have confirmation from the other Chiefs that their warriors are being gathered along with supplies."

Aidan turned to Heath, who was sitting on Roslyn's right side and nodded to him.

"The training with the guns is going well," Heath informed the group. "We have weeded out the worst shots, and those who have a good eye have gone on to aim at smaller targets. Our blacksmiths are also working hard to make more bullets, as per the instructions that the Archipelago's gunsmiths have provided."

"The orc warriors have blended in well with the Jay'Alian warriors that the Fox Clan sent us," Tiffany spoke up next. "Karina, Cypress, and especially Stane, have been a huge help in smoothing things over between the two groups. A fun rivalry has even started."

"Your Ellsgrovian soldiers were a key to that," Karina interjected. "A lot of them have seen me with you, and they accepted me quickly since you trusted me. They have gotten to know a lot of the orc warriors since Cypress and his men joined us, so I think that helped the Jay'Alian warriors accept them as well."

"I am glad to hear that," Roslyn commented. "I would hate to leave on my expedition if there were any signs of animosity between the groups."

"I think I can deal with any issues if they should arise," Amelia commented. "I will have Cypress here to help out if that were to happen."

Roslyn ducked her head to cover a smile: ever since Cypress had saved them from the werewolf attack in the mountains Amelia had been very fond of the big orc warrior.

"When do you think we should be able to leave for the expedition?" Roslyn asked Aidan.

"As soon as the rest of the supplies get here with Maeve," Aidan responded. "Which will be any day now."

"Alright, I want scouts out waiting for Maeve," Roslyn told him. "I want to know before she gets here."

Aidan inclined his head and ushered to one of the messengers waiting by the door of the tent. The messenger left after a moment to go have scouts sent out.

"Anything else that needs to be discussed before the meeting ends?" Roslyn asked the group. The response she got was shaken heads so she smiled and stood up from her seat, stretching.

"Think the cooks have a snack ready for me to eat?" Roslyn asked as the council started to disperse.

"They should," Heath commented, "they know you pretty well by now."

Roslyn stuck her tongue out at him and exited her tent, Heath following behind. The familiars extricated themselves one by one from the cuddle pile and followed their masters out of the tent. Solana and Leaf stretched their wings and fluttered them before running after Heath and Roslyn who were heading for the house where the cooks worked. One of the cooks met them at the door of the house with a platter of scones and cookies, a large smile on his face. Roslyn thanked him and accepted the platter, offering a scone to Heath.

"Are you anxious to leave on the expedition?" Heath asked her as they walked together around the area the builders were marking off for the palace.

"I worry about what the behemoths are doing," she commented. "And the dark elves."

"Have you searched again for them?" Heath wanted to know.

Roslyn nodded and told him, "I can sense they are there, but I cannot see them. I think they are guarding their location with magic of some kind."

"Are you sure it will be wise to go underground still?" Heath asked her. "We have no idea what these behemoths really are."

"The reason for the expedition is to learn what they are," Roslyn reminded him.

"I still don't think it is safe for you to be the one leading the expedition."

"I know. As I have said, I will not be a ruler who will let others go into danger. It is my choice," she reminded him.

"You also have a responsibility to your people to remain safe," Heath told her. "The ancestors chose *you*, not your mother, not your sister; *you*, Roslyn. You should stay here, above ground. Let me go underground and find out what the behemoths are."

Roslyn had had this conversation with friends and family a few times in the last couple of weeks.

"I would be an absolute wreck waiting for you to return," she told Heath. "I would be worried sick about all of you."

A Descent into the Roots

"We can take care of ourselves," Heath reminded her. "You can send along some special spells and such, but you should be staying here."

Roslyn looked down at Leaf who cocked her head to the side, and she heard her familiar in her mind: *"He is right and you know it."*

"Whose side are you on here?" Roslyn asked her familiar, putting her hands on her hips.

Heath chuckled as Solana told him what Leaf said. "See? Even Leaf agrees with me!"

"Let me think about it, OK?" she told him finally after swallowing the bite of scone she had just taken.

"What will it take for you to see that staying here is the best option for your people? You are sending an expedition to find out what the behemoths are, that is good. But you are their Queen now, you should not be going into dangerous places needlessly. You have warriors and mages for that."

"I said I would think about it, OK?!" Roslyn told him, stopping short and raising her voice a little. "Can you please give me some time?!"

Heath smiled sheepishly at her. "Sorry," he told her. "I'll uhh…go talk to Oswick about how the building is going."

Roslyn sighed as he and Solana walked towards where Oswick and Judd were standing.

"He loves you and needs you to be safe," Leaf told Roslyn as they continued walking. *"If you have doubts about what you should do, maybe you should ask the ancients."*

Roslyn gave a resigned sigh and changed course to the area where the Dragon Shrine had been. She had been meaning to rebuild it, so now seemed like as good a time as any. She had partially filled in the sinkhole after she and Karina had resurfaced, so she sat at the edge of the hole that remained with Leaf sitting beside her, one paw resting on her knee.

Roslyn called out to her magic and that of the ground beneath her. She reached down with her magic and called on the roots, weaving them together to create a bubble of sorts around where the shrine had been underground. Using her magic she called on rocks to build a stairway, and she found the dragon statue buried beneath the rubble that she now moved up beside her. Once the bubble and stairs were done she moved the roots from the great cedar tree up the mountain to run through the new shrine.

Now she covered the bubble in soil, willing the grass to grow again to solidify the outside of the shrine. Next she recreated the spot where the opening was, placing the dragon statue near to where it had been before. The enchantments that connected the statue to the shrine had been broken when the sinkhole had happened, so now she replaced them, urging the door to open for her. When it did she looked down at Leaf with a smile and together the two of them descended into the new shrine.

The shrine of course looked different than the last time she had been down there, more of an oval shaped room, the walls still covered in the glowing moss. The roots of the great cedar tree came from the roof of the room and descended down into the rest of the plateau from there. The roots thrummed ever so slightly as she approached the woven column, taking her small knife out of its sheath and made a small cut on her pointer finger, letting a drop of blood fall onto the roots.

"Never have we been awakened so much as this past year," a feminine voice echoed around the shrine. *"Our dear Roslyn, what wisdom do you seek now?"*

Roslyn could not help but roll her eyes. Were the ancestors giving her sass now?

"Heath is trying to convince me to stay above ground rather than go below on the expedition to find the behemoths," she explained.

"Smart fellow you have there," a male voice spoke up. *"My, my, my, how stubborn our Roslyn is. We have tried telling you that you do not need to shoulder everything yourself. You have friends you can count and depend on. Let them do their part."*

Roslyn looked down, embarrassed that they were chiding her so. "Well excuse me," Roslyn said, "Sorry that I care so much about them."

"Everyone has a part to play. Yours is not down below," the first feminine voice told her.

"Fine," Roslyn told them. "But I do not like it."

"You will make many decisions as a ruler that you do not completely like," the male voice told her. *"That is part of being Queen. Thank you for rebuilding the shrine; took you long enough."*

The roots stopped thrumming and Roslyn looked at Leaf with a raised eyebrow. "Well, someone gave them an extra dose of sass this morning," she commented to her familiar as she headed for the staircase. "I guess my mother will be happy to hear that I am staying here now instead of going underground on the expedition."

"Heath will be happy too," Leaf reminded her.

"I will have to make something he can use to make tunnels underground," Roslyn mused to herself. "I think I have a few ideas in mind."

Chapter Nine

The servants of the palace moved out of Cassidy's way as she and Kai headed for Edmond's study at a fast pace. He had summoned them quite suddenly while they were eating a late breakfast together in the kitchen. Sully followed behind them; the rest of the Honour Guard were in training that morning with some other young noblewomen who had expressed their desires of learning how to use a sword. Crick and Tej each sat on their respective shaman's shoulders.

Cassidy opened the door to Edmond's study and ushered Kai through before closing the door behind them. They turned to find Edmond at his desk talking with a person who sat in one of the chairs on the other side of his desk. This person was not Alara, but Rafi.

"I thought you were supposed to be down south," Cassidy said. "What are you doing back?"

"Hello to you too," Rafi answered. "I wish it was under better circumstances, but I felt the information I had was too valuable to be sent by any courier."

"And what is that?" Kai asked Rafi.

"Count Gresham is at his estate," Rafi told them, looking at Edmond. "And more mercenaries arrived from Tellemeracus."

Edmond sat up straighter. "Do you think King Jordan has a part in this?" he asked, concerned with this new information.

Rafi shrugged, saying, "You did choose Alara over his daughter, but I do not think he is part of this. The mercenaries are only known for having their base in Tellemeracus, not having any kind of true allegiance to the king. He tolerates them, has even used them on a few occasions, but they do not answer to him."

"So what does that bring his army to?" Cassidy asked them as she took the other seat next to Rafi. Kai stood behind her.

"Almost five thousand," Edmond said with a wince. "I wonder how he is paying for all of this."

"Has the King called in his army?" Rafi asked Edmond.

"Yes, more soldiers arrive each day, but I do not have a confirmed count yet," Edmond told him.

"Okay, give me an estimate," Cassidy pressed him.

"Fifteen thousand, maybe a little more," Edmond responded. "That does not include the several hundred mages who have responded to the call to muster though."

"The mages could be a huge part of the army, if they can supply us with the right armaments," Cassidy commented. "Fire bombs and the like, certain traps."

"I am sure father will be able to utilize the mages…" Edmond started to say, but he saw the look in Cassidy's eye, so much like Roslyn when she had an idea. "What is it?"

"Could you ask father if I can lead the mages? I think between myself and Headmistress Dake we can come up with a lot of things to help the army."

"I will suggest it to him at the meeting today," Edmond assured her. "I know you have different forms of magic than the other mages that could come in use."

Cassidy had several ideas in mind, and a lot of it could be put to good use to help the Ellsgrovian army. Even if there were mages with the mercenaries they would not know her spells as a shaman from Jay'Al. Hopefully their father would see that she would be a good choice to lead the mages.

"When is the meeting?" Cassidy asked him.

"Just after lunch," Edmond told her.

"While you wait, care to join me at my family estate?" Rafi asked her and Kai. "Some of Alara's people have made it their base in town."

"That was quite generous of you," Edmond commented, giving Rafi a knowing look. "I know some of her spies are grateful for the rooms."

Rafi put his hands up and shrugged, telling them, "I am just doing my part." Cassidy could see his roguish smile though and knew that he must have found one of Alara's spies more than agreeable.

About time he found someone else, Cassidy thought in her mind. She knew that he and Roslyn had remained friends, but she also knew that he had had a hard time letting her go to begin with. Cassidy still thought they would have made an odd pair, but then again, Cassidy did not know Roslyn during that time; she might have been completely different than the Roslyn she had come to know in the last year.

"We would love some time out of the palace," Cassidy told Rafi. "Thank you."

A Descent into the Roots

Kai looked at Cassidy and smiled, nodding his agreement. "How about something to drink this afternoon? I remember Roslyn talking about a tavern that had really good ale."

***

Cassidy took in the brick house that Rafi led them to. They had eaten lunch at a tavern and were now heading to Rafi's estate. There was a main gate at the street that Rafi had unlocked with a key before leading them up a cobbled pathway. There were a few flower beds of sprouting spring flowers, and Cassidy could smell fresh lavender nearby.

Servants met them at the door, taking Rafi's jacket and bringing them each a glass of wine. Rafi led his friends into his study, where Cassidy took in his messy desk and cluttered bookshelves.

"Is it just you who lives here?" Cassidy asked as she sat down in a plump chaise. Crick jumped up beside her, and Kai sat in the chaise next to her, Tej at his ankles.

"I'm letting some of Alara's agents stay here," Rafi answered as he sipped his wine while leafing through some of the papers on top of his desk. "They use it as a checkpoint throughout the day."

"Food delivery!" someone called from the main entrance, and Rafi looked up from his papers with a smile on his face.

"Bring it in my study please," Rafi told his servant, and Cassidy watched as they pushed a trolley with a large crate on it into the study. Rafi waved his servants away and went to open the crate, earning a raised eyebrow from Cassidy.

Rafi opened the top of the crate and a young woman stood up, stretching as she did so. She looked at Rafi with a grateful smile and accepted his hand in helping her out of the crate. She was dressed as a laundress, her chestnut colour hair pulled back in a tight bun. Cassidy could not help but notice that the woman's hands were very dry.

She must be one of Alara's spies, Cassidy thought to herself and Crick.

"Cassidy, Kai, this is Nova," Rafi introduced them, and the young woman looked at them with dark emerald eyes.

"Pleased to meet you," Nova commented with a slight curtsey. "I have heard much about you, your highness."

"Do you always enter houses this way?" Cassidy asked her with amusement, peering over the side of the crate to see a folded up blanket for added comfort.

"To avoid being followed we sometimes ship ourselves to certain destinations," Nova explained. "I was in our neighbouring city when I had information to bring in, but I was being watched. If they are looking for you at the gates they will not see you in the crates."

"And they cannot exactly open shipping crates," Rafi added. "Do you need to go see Alara right away?" he asked Nova.

Nova smiled sweetly at him and leaned in to kiss him on the cheek. "I do, but it will be a quick visit. I will come straight back."

"I will be here," he assured her, and he watched her head out the back door of the house, grabbing a coat as she went.

"I see why you are letting Alara's agents work out of your house," Cassidy commented as she sipped her wine. "Nova is nearly as beautiful as Alara."

Rafi ducked his head and looked at the door that Nova had gone out of. "She keeps me on my toes," he told them.

"I am sure she does," Kai mused, before changing the subject by asking, "Can I have some more wine?"

***

Lucius looked thoughtful as the meeting adjourned, Edmond collecting his papers into his satchel as Sir Sullivan left the king's study.

"You think Cassidy is up to the task?" he asked his son.

"I do not think she would have said anything if she was not," Edmond told him. "Helping Alara was not what she is best at. Dealing with magic though? I think she will surprise us, just like Roslyn has."

"Very well. I will have to talk with her about it myself, along with the Headmistress. We will have to figure out what resources they will need and get ahead of that."

"I will send a message to Headmistress Dake," Edmond informed him.

"Thank you. You said Cassidy and Kai went with Rafi into the city?" Edmond nodded. "Have her come see me when she gets back then."

"Yes, sir," Edmond told him with a smile before he left the room, his guards leaving the ones stationed outside the door and following him.

Lucius stood up from his desk and went to the door, eager to go see his younger children. His guards surrounded him, two of them walking ahead with the rest around and behind him. The palace had become very quiet, with only the most loyal of his nobles staying within the palace walls. He understood that the rest of the nobles were scared after the attack that had killed Elle, but he was about ready to push them into assuring him of their loyalty by inviting them all for a special dinner. Alara's spies had confirmed Count Gresham's main conspirators and they had been arrested, so the nobles should no longer be worried.

Lucius reached the door to his children's suite of rooms, it being guarded by two soldiers and a mage. The guards covered their hearts with their fists and bowed slightly as he walked by them, his personal guards staying outside with the other guards as Lucius went through the door.

Poppy and Eliza greeted him from the table where they were working on their needlework, and Robert from where he was sitting in a chair reading. Roland smiled at him from where he sat next to Eliza.

"How are you all today?" Lucius asked his younger children as he went to Robert first, ruffling the boys' blonde hair slightly. "How was your practice this morning?"

"Very well, father," Eliza answered him without looking up from her stitching.

"Eliza threw our instructor today!" Poppy exclaimed excitedly. "He said she might be able to stand up to Roslyn someday!"

Lucius watched as his almost fifteen year old daughter's face turned slightly red.

"Good for you, Eliza," Lucius praised her. "I know Roslyn would be proud to hear that."

"I miss her," Eliza whispered. "It's so weird having Cassidy here: she looks like Roz, but it's just not her."

"Roslyn would be here if she could," Lucius assured her, squeezing her shoulder. "She is dealing with a lot of things in Jay'Al right now."

"Is it true that there are actual werewolves?" Robert piped up, looking up from his book.

"Yes," Lucius responded with a smile, moving to sit in a chair next to Robert. "But they are working with Roslyn now."

"How dangerous is a werewolf?" Poppy asked him. "Are they like the ones in the stories?"

"Hard to say," Lucius answered her. "They were dangerous at first, but now since Roslyn has helped them they are on her side. Their curse spreads by bite, just like the old stories, but the only thing that can kill one is the frishna metal."

"I'm glad Roslyn found a cure for them," Poppy commented. "It's scary to think of werewolves running rampant around the countryside."

Robert laughed at Poppy and she stuck her tongue out at him.

"Yes, it is a very good thing they did not spread out of Jay'Al centuries ago," Lucius commented. "If they had spread to our continent...I do not want to think about what might have been."

That made his children stop and think for a moment. He watched Poppy frown as she continued her needlework. Eliza was looking at him with raised eyebrows.

"I wonder what it was like back then, in Jay'Al," Eliza commented. "The Clans were at their peak, right? It was after the Werewolf wars that the Clans became so divided."

"You've been reading the history Cassidy brought with her," Lucius said with a grin. "Yes, it would be very interesting to see how Jay'Al was back then. From what Cassidy has told me, Hyena City is the only city that remains from that time. All of the others were either abandoned or destroyed."

"Maybe Roslyn can go to all of the Clans and get all of their written histories together," Robert commented. "I am sure there are some scholars dying for the chance to accumulate the history of Jay'Al."

"I am sure she has thought of that herself," Lucius told him.

Roland gestured to Lucius as the butler stood up, and Lucius followed him into another room.

"What is it?" he asked his butler.

"They did very good today, all of them," Roland told him. "Poppy's form is improving immensely. Robert was even a bit more lively today."

"The past couple of weeks have been hard on them," Lucius commented. "Especially Robert."

"They will get through this," Roland said. "They are strong, like their father and older sister."

Lucius smiled weakly at his butler, thinking of Elle. Did his butler know that he still slept with her pillow next to him? Probably not, and he was not about to say anything.

"Your Majesty," came a voice from the door to the suite of rooms. "Duchess Cassidy is here to see you."

"Let her in," Lucius called out, and he walked to the door to meet Cassidy. He could see Kai waiting outside with the rest of the Honour Guard.

"How was the city?" Lucius asked her. "I hope Rafi showed you some good places other than his own house."

"He did, and it was good," Cassidy assured him. "Did Edmond talk with you?"

"He did," Lucius assured her with a smile. "You will be in charge of the Mages in the army," he added. "I have sent word to Headmistress Dake, but you might want to follow up with her yourself."

Cassidy smiled broadly and hugged her father. "Thank you, father. I will not let you down."

Lucius held onto his second born tightly before letting her go. "I know you won't. Now, why don't you invite Kai in and we can spend some time together?"

Chapter Ten

Kavan stared at the empty village of Bella Vale. It had taken them a sennight to reach the village from the plateau. The outlying farms, Roslyn's Uncle Grigori's and some of the alpaca farms, were still there for they were not about to pack up and leave to join Roslyn's capital just yet. The village seemed a little eerie to Kavan with its people gone, but soon it would liven up again with the redcaps, Dwarves and centaurs that were about to take residence.

Kavan had sent McKenna ahead to talk to the farmers so he was waiting for them at the gate to the village. Grigori was with him, his eyes wide with astonishment at seeing the magical creatures.

"Well, isn't this something," Grigori said as they opened the gates for the magical creatures and let them into the village. "Never in my life did I ever think I would see any of these creatures. I've seen pictures in some of our old books, but this is something else."

"Oy, what are you staring at?" Darton asked Grigori as he walked by the man.

"Careful Darton, this is Queen Roslyn's uncle," Kavan warned him. "You will have to get used to the stares. I know you cannot help that you were all underground for a couple hundred years, but still."

"My apologies," Darton said to Grigori, ducking his head and hurrying past.

"You have to be careful with redcaps," Kavan reminded Grigori.

"Oh, I know. They'll just as easily stab you as help you," Grigori responded. "I remember the tales my father would tell me as a child."

"Yes, well, hopefully they remain safe here in Bella Vale," Kavan said as the two older men followed him into the village along with the magical creatures. "I am going to put the crystal around the village to keep them safe, and we will have lookouts out and about looking for more of them."

"This will be something," Kavan heard Grigori say to McKenna. "Redcaps, dwarves, centaurs…I wonder what else we will see?"

"Hopefully we do not see any dark elves any time soon," Kavan said to him. Grigori's eyes widened.

"Dark elves? By the ancestors, them coming back is not good."

"You're telling me," Kavan shook his head. "Heath faced some in the isles, and Roslyn even sent some running a few weeks ago."

Grigori shook his head and then changed the subject, saying, "Our new residents will need food."

"We brought some provisions," Kavan assured him. "But we will hunt for some more meat today."

"Sounds like a plan. As long as they stay away from my horses, and the alpacas on the other farms, then we will be good," Grigori commented.

"They will," Kavan assured him again.

"Come on Grigori," McKenna spoke up. "Stop giving Kavan a hard time. We are here to protect them and you, you have nothing to worry about."

Grigori gave a 'harumph' and then bade them farewell for now before heading back to his farm.

McKenna chuckled and looked at Kavan. "He does not like change all that much," McKenna told him. "Come on, let's get them settled and then go hunting."

***

After placing the last crystal around the village that evening, Kavan finished the enchantment with a word and watched as the protective barrier went up. He turned to look around, the din of the village reaching his ears. The creatures had settled in nicely, rejoicing at the fact that they had a roof over their heads again instead of having to sleep under the night sky. The centaurs had more of an issue with finding a place that worked for them, and they ended up moving into the stables for now. Kavan realized that someone would have to make a centaur friendly home, but what would they need?

Kavan walked back to the Chief's house where he and the others were staying. McKenna was sitting by the hearth with Louran and Terren, while the others were in the kitchen preparing food for the evening.

"We should come up with a schedule," Kavan told McKenna as he joined him by the hearth. "Of lookouts and scouts," he continued.

"Agreed," McKenna answered him. "I think we need some of the centaurs to help though, in case we find more of them."

"The dwarves will likely help," Louran spoke up. "I have heard them say that there are more of them out there. They would be eager to bring them here."

"Do you think the redcaps will stay out of trouble?" Kavan asked McKenna.

"I think with you here watching over them, they will be sure to," McKenna told him with a chuckle. "Though I think some of them are wondering if you really *are* a werewolf or if you were just saying that to scare them."

"Well I am not going to take my pendant off and change just to show them," Kavan said with a shake of his head. "They will just have to wait and see what else I can do."

"Well, none of them have seen you run yet," Terren commented with a laugh. "That would convince me."

"You should see me take down a wild boar," Kavan told him, earning a respectful nod from the orc.

"That would be a sight, I am sure," Terren said.

The others brought the food out to them and they ate together, sitting on the floor in front of the hearth.

Chapter Eleven

Heath peered through his looking glass at the ground below, smiling as he took in the convoy of wagons that was coming from the south. Maeve had finally arrived with their supplies and seeds, and he was eager to see her again. It was late afternoon, nearing sundown, and there were no clouds in the sky.

Solana rubbed up against his legs as he stood there, and he looked down at her. His gryphon familiar had grown again and she was nearly as big as Leaf now. The two creatures had been spending a lot of time strengthening their wings together, and Heath knew it was just a matter of time before both of them were flying. Heath marvelled at how fast the gryphon was growing; he knew that if Selene ever met the gryphon, that his normal cat would be dwarfed by the magical creature. Thinking of Selene made him sad, but Solana butted his hand with her head. He scratched her head as she began to purr, making him feel a little better. Hearing footsteps, he turned to see Roslyn coming towards him.

"Maeve is almost here," Heath told her. "I'd like to go down and meet them."

"I will join you," Roslyn commented. "Would you get the horses ready? Leaf is eating, and I know she will want to go as well."

"I'll meet you at the tunnel," Heath told her as she turned to go back to her tent to retrieve her familiar.

Leaf was finishing up her meal when Roslyn got to her tent, and the dragonling stretched like a cat before testing her wings. Leaf looked at Roslyn, reading her thoughts, and bounded towards her with excitement.

"What has you so excited?" Roslyn asked the dragon as they headed for the tunnel, meeting Heath with their horses along the way. Solana and Leaf sniffed each other and flapped their wings excitedly, both of them taking off

594

of the ground for a few moments.

"Will not be long now," Roslyn commented as she mounted her horse. "They will be flying soon."

"How much bigger do you think they will get?" Heath asked her as they rode down the tunnel, the two familiars following beside them.

"I have no idea," Roslyn told him with a shrug. "Leaf has mentioned that some dragons got very big, but I have no idea how big a gryphon gets."

"It will be interesting to see," Heath commented. "A fully grown gryphon. Do you think I could ride on her back?"

Again Roslyn shrugged. "Maybe."

"What about you riding on Leaf's back?" Heath asked her. "Have you thought about that? Do you think she will be able to breathe fire?"

"She will be able to breathe fire," Roz told him, "when she is fully mature. I *should* be able to ride on her back."

"That will be a sight to see," Heath said as they rode. "You would be a magnificent vision."

Roslyn chuckled at the image that sprang to her mind of herself on the back of a grown-up Leaf, flying through the air. What would it be like, indeed?

They reached the bottom of the tunnel and rode out of Base Town. The orcs had started to repair some of the buildings, the elders taking over some of the houses while the rest of them had their tents fanned out around the town. Roslyn greeted many of the orcs and people of Karina's Clan that were milling about, smiling as they called out their own greetings. Their new chief, Stane, had been working with Aidan to mark house lots and streets, as well as farms outside the city. Roslyn could see the workers laying street posts and marking lots.

The orc blacksmiths had even built their own smithy with the help of the human blacksmiths, and together they were hard at work making items that were needed for the new buildings that were being planned. Other orcs were busy in the quarry getting stone ready.

Roslyn, Heath, and their familiars met with Maeve's group a short ride away from the plateau near a small grouping of trees. Maeve had her golden brown hair tied back in a braid and was dressed much like Heath, her leather boots covered in a layer of dust. Beside her rode Kasimir, the merchant Roslyn and company had found in the underground cavern after being shipwrecked. Behind them were a group of wagons laden with barrels and bags.

"Well met," Maeve spoke as she waved at them. "We met no dangers on our way here."

"I am glad to hear that…" Roslyn started to say, but at that moment a small bird fluttered over from the nearby trees and flew to Maeve, fluttering around the woman's head.

"Hey!" Maeve said as she tried to shoo it away, but she stopped suddenly as she looked it in the eyes. The bird calmed down and landed on the horn of Maeve's saddle, looking up at her with its round yellow eyes.

"It's a pygmy owl," Maeve said with surprise. The bird was small and compact, with a large circular head. It was brown overall, with fine white speckles on the head and white spots on its back. Its beak was as yellow as its eyes.

The owl chattered at her and hopped up and down a few times before it flew up to her shoulder and started preening the loose hair from her braid.

"Oh wow," Maeve whispered as she felt the presence of the owl in her mind.

Heath chuckled and told her, "I think you just found your familiar."

"Did you add your blood to the tree on Mast as well?" Roslyn asked Maeve, surprised that yet another non-Jay'Alian had bonded with a familiar. Maeve nodded as she reached up and preened the owl's feathers on its head.

"Well then, whatever I did with those trees changed *something*," Roslyn commented. "I just wish I knew *what* I had done."

"Well, no need to worry about it right now," Maeve told her. "I think this is really nifty. It's a female, and I think I will name her…Luma."

"That is a good, solid name," Heath told her. He turned to the pale skinned, red haired Kasimir and said, "I hope your travels this time have been uneventful."

Heath had gotten to know Kasimir during their short stay in Hyena City, learning how Roslyn and her company had found him and about his travels home.

"Very uneventful," Kasimir responded. "It was quite a relief, after the last time."

"Good. Come, join us at our fires," Roslyn told them. "We welcome you."

Chapter Twelve

Alara awoke in her suite of rooms, feeling slightly off. She got out of bed and looked out the window that faced the east. The sun was just starting to rise over the Royal Forest. She felt a need to go out to the forest and walk through the morning dew, so she got dressed quickly and called on her guards who were just changing shifts.

"Your highness?" her female guard Esra inquired as the rest gathered around her door.

"I want to go for a morning walk through the forest," she told them. "Would Prince Edmond be awake yet?"

"I saw him go into his study not too long ago," another guard, Baris, told her.

"Would you ask him to join me?" she asked Baris. He nodded and went to do as she asked.

"Come, let us make our way down to the Royal Forest, shall we? I am sure my prince will not be far behind," Alara told her guard, and after locking her rooms they headed towards the stairs that would take them to the main floor of the palace. Edmond and his guards joined them on the way down the stairs.

"What is it?" Edmond asked her, noticing a look in her eyes.

"I just feel a need to go out to the forest this morning," she told him. "I cannot explain it."

"Have you eaten anything yet?" Edmond asked her, and she noticed he had a small platter of breakfast turnovers in his hand that he was offering to her. She smiled at him and grabbed one of the fruit turnovers that was glazed with a bit of icing.

Edmond's guards opened the doors to the Royal Forest ahead of them, with Alara's bringing up the rear as they went through the doorway. They walked by several fountains on their way to the forest, and when they got to the grass Alara took her shoes off and stepped off the path. She absorbed the dew through her skin, feeling her body wake up slightly. Something was tugging at her though, a presence at the back of her mind.

A ray of sunlight broke through some of the branches, making Alara look at where it landed. There was a grouping of rocks near a small pond that the ray of light illuminated, and on one of those rocks was a tiger salamander that was mostly black but for some dark green spots. Alara stepped towards it, and as she got closer it moved its head up to look at her with its wide protruding eyes. Alara knelt before the rocks and offered her hand to the salamander, and after a moment of sniffing it moved onto her hand. Instantly Alara felt her arm hairs stand on end, and she felt a magical presence in the back of her mind.

"What just happened?" Edmond asked her, noticing her arm hairs standing up.

"I think…I think I just found my familiar," Alara told him.

"I thought…I wondered…after hearing the reports from Mast about Heath getting a familiar because of the tree Roslyn gave them, I wondered if something like this might happen to me."

"Well, whatever she did, it seems to be spreading then," Edmond commented. "First Mast, now here? I wonder if anyone else has found themselves bonding with familiars."

"There should not be anyone else here," Alara informed him. "So far as I know, I am the only mage to have added their blood to the tree."

"Let's talk to Cassidy about this," Edmond told her. "She and Kai should be in the training yards by now."

***

The palace of the Capital of Ellsgrove was oddly quiet as Cassidy and Kai, along with their familiars and their guards, walked through it. Alara and Edmond had just left them after their morning workouts in the training yard, and now they were headed to the South Wing of the palace. The South Wing was an abandoned area that Lucius had told them would be a good spot to meet with the Mages who would be under her command. Her brother had sent word to Headmistress Dake days ago, and she in turn had given him a list of names of volunteers that was impressively long; as well as a list of supplies they would need to prepare magical weapons and defenses.

Cassidy had personally sent out the requests to each mage on the list, and the majority of them had started arriving early that morning.

Sully opened the double doors that led to the South Wing, and Cassidy noted that someone had started cleaning it already. Lucius had shown it to her when he had mentioned it, and there had been a lot of cobwebs. Her father explained that it had been abandoned since the sickness, but it would be tidied up before she made use of it. It was a relief at least not to have to worry about dust and cobwebs while trying to plan magical defenses.

She could hear the people talking from down the corridor as they approached the room they were using. The door was open and light from inside the room illuminated part of the hallway. Cassidy thought they could use more lanterns in the corridor and made a mental note to bring that up with her father.

The talking stopped as Cassidy appeared in the doorway. She took in the group of thirty people whose ages ranged from around her own age to into the forties, both men and women. She recognized Jessica, Tiffany's cousin, who had a splint on her arm where she had been injured during the assassination attempt that had taken Elle's life. She also saw Professor Reed, and another Professor she had met at the University before, Professor Rhiannon. The second professor was a woman in her late thirties with sandy-blonde hair and blue eyes, her mage robes a light blue colour.

"Well met," Cassidy greeted them all. "I am Cassidy, thank you all for volunteering and coming here today."

"Thank you for having us," Professor Reed responded. "We are eager to help defend our kingdom."

Cassidy looked around at the tables that were set up and the ingredients that were arrayed on them. "Shall we get to work?" she asked them. "We have no idea how much time we have, and when the enemy strikes we have to move fast."

"Are these people really that dumb, to go up against the throne?" someone asked, and Cassidy looked for the speaker.

It was a person not that much younger than Cassidy who was standing near Professor Rhiannon. They had their golden blonde hair cut short, the tips dyed black, and wore clothes that were gender-fluid: breeches and a simple tunic with a vest over top, their light blue mage robes over top.

"After everything King Lucius has done for the kingdom, and furthering the women's cause, we should be grateful. These idiots think they can do a better job at rebuilding the kingdom after the sickness? I doubt it. Lucius has done more in his short time as king than his cousin did. We have an alliance with Jay'Al, the Archipelago, Kyprago, and Raistminestine now," the young person continued.

"The alliance with Jay'Al was only possible because of King Lucius' cousin's actions," Sully spoke up. "All of the other pieces fell into place after that."

"Well I still think we are better off with King Lucius, not those conservative pricks in the south," the person said next.

Professor Rhiannon put a hand on the young person's shoulder and told them to shush.

"My apologies for my child, they are very outspoken when it comes to people's rights," Rhiannon explained.

"No apologies needed. What is your name?" Cassidy asked them.

"Astra, your highness," they replied.

"A strong name," Cassidy responded with a smile. "And you can just call me Cassidy here. I look forward to working with you all."

They worked together for hours going over the city wall plans and figuring out where the best defensible positions were, and where it would be a good spot to set up magical defenses outside of the city.

"Roslyn had these enchanted crystals that put up a protective barrier around our campsites. Could we do something like that with the city? Would it stop things shot by catapults?"

"That kind of barrier only works if they don't know it's there. It cloaks them in a sort of invisibility barrier as well as a protective barrier," Dake told her. "A giant city being covered by such a barrier would take a lot of magic, but huge rocks thrown at it will hurt the barrier more and it will not last. They know there is a city here, it's not like we can just move the whole city."

"Ah, ok." Cassidy looked a little disappointed. "Is there a way we can change the enchantment to just be a shield?"

"I don't see why not," Rhiannon told her. "We have spells for such shield barriers, I do not see why we cannot use it with the crystals."

"They would have to just be in certain areas, like the most vulnerable. Do we have a plan of evacuating the part of the city closest to the wall?" Professor Reed inquired.

"Yes, my father has a plan in place," Cassidy answered.

"Okay, so protective barriers would be best placed at the gates and sections of the outer wall that have weak points," Sully piped up. "That's where I would put them."

"Sounds like a plan," Cassidy said. "Let us do that then. We should split off into groups so we can cover more ground."

Cassidy looked out the window and saw how late in the day it was. She turned to Sully and asked, "We went right through lunch?" He nodded in reply.

"How about we take a break in the Royal Forest and have lunch there?" Cassidy inquired of the group. "Sully, would you send a messenger to the kitchens to bring our food out there to the pavilion? We will need tables."

Sully nodded and went to the messenger that was waiting in the hallway. The young page took off at a run.

"Let's make our way out there now, shall we?" Cassidy asked the group as they started to pack up their things. "Leave everything where it is. I have a spell to protect this room."

As they filed out the door and down the hallway following Sully to the doors that would lead them out to Royal Forest, Cassidy closed the door and cast her spell. The runes she had written around the doorway lit up briefly before disappearing. Satisfied that the door was locked and bespelled, she followed the mages out of the wing and did the same with the double doors there. Kai, Tej, and Crick were waiting for her there, and together they followed Sully and the mages out to the Royal Forest.

The pavilion was in a clearing not too far from the gazebo where she, Edmond and Alara had taken lunch before an assassin had interrupted. To get to the pavilion they had to walk by the tree that Roslyn had sent her father, and Cassidy had an idea after what happened that morning with Alara.

"Everyone, if you would take a moment as you walk by this tree here, give an offering of your blood to it. A drop will do on the roots," Cassidy told them, getting ahead of them and stopping at the tree. "This is the tree Queen Roslyn sent as an alliance gift. I have a hunch that it might help strengthen us."

"How so?" one of the female mages in her late twenties asked her, raising a delicate brow at her over spectacles. The woman wore her mahogany coloured hair pulled back in a single braid, and she wore yellow and black robes. She gazed at the tree with blue eyes before looking at Cassidy again. "How did this grow so fast?" she inquired.

"Lexi, was it?" Cassidy tried to remember the woman's name. She nodded.

"Magic," Cassidy told her with a smile. "Humor me, please?"

Lexi shrugged, and along with Professor Rhiannon, and Astra, they each pricked a finger and let a drop of blood land on one of the protruding roots. The rest of the mages followed suit as they passed by the tree.

"I'm starving," Astra said, earning a laugh from their mother and Cassidy.

"Come, young Astra," Sully called to them. "Lunch is being served." The knight indicated the row of servants who were bringing out food for them on carts.

Kai stood next to Cassidy and raised an eyebrow at her. "Do you think more mages will bond with familiars here?"

"First Heath…now Alara? Why not? Whatever my sister did to the trees, it has changed things. I think this might help us."

Chapter Thirteen

Kavan watched with amusement as Darton tried to notch an arrow in his bow. He was trying to teach the redcaps how to use bows for hunting, but it was not going overly well. Both the redcaps, and the few dwarves who had joined them, just had too short of arms to be able to use the normal bows properly.

"We might need to get crossbows made special for them," McKenna commented from where he was leaning on a tree nearby. "With shorter bolts that they can more easily shoot with."

"Great," Darton commented. "How will we hunt once you fellas are gone?"

"The centaurs are handy with bows," Louran spoke up. "And you can set traps."

"So someone will teach us how to set traps then?" Darton asked next.

Kavan smiled at him wolfishly and told him, "Yes, I will take a group of you out tonight to show you."

He watched as Darton swallowed, a slight glint of fear in his eyes.

"It's not a full moon, is it?" Darton turned his head to ask McKenna. Kavan could tell that McKenna was having a hard time holding in his laughter.

"I do not believe so," McKenna answered after a moment of suppressing his amusement.

Darton still looked nervous, but Kavan reassured him by saying, "You would be a little too chewy for my taste, little redcap. There are meatier things out there for me to eat."

"I do not know whether to be insulted or grateful," Darton commented with a slight chuckle. "How long would it take for a special crossbow to be made?"

"We would have to talk to the blacksmiths about it and see if they can do anything," Kavan answered. "It might take a little bit of time. We will start you on trapping for now. Go ahead and go about your day, we will meet this evening after dinner and go out."

Darton and the other redcaps, and dwarves, handed over their bows and arrows to Kavan and McKenna before heading back into the village.

"Terren and Louran are out with the centaurs getting scouting routes set up," McKenna told Kavan as they walked towards the village gates. "Several of them volunteered for it, which was nice to see. They are glad to be doing their part to help secure their new home, it seems. They talk of Roslyn to the others, telling them how she helped them see in the sun and protected them. It is good to have someone with unbiased first-hand experience with our Queen so that these newcomers will know it is true."

"Agreed," Kavan responded as they reached the small gatehouse where they kept what little armory they had. Together they hung up the bows and put the arrows in a large quiver that hung from the wall. They had left the targets out there in the treed area for when they worked with the centaurs next.

"Well, I should prepare all of the trapping gear for tonight," Kavan told McKenna after they left the gatehouse. "Where will you be?"

"I am going to help Grigori get his horses ready for travel to the plateau. He thinks it will be the safest place for the Spring Market this year, and the other Clans agreed."

"When is he planning on leaving?" Kavan inquired. He had not thought there would still be a Spring Market with everything that was going on, but with the warriors of Jay'Al amassing at the plateau, it would both be the safest place and the best place to sell horses that were trained for battle.

"In a few days," came the reply as McKenna started walking towards the trail that would take him out to Grigori's farm. "The alpaca farmers are planning on heading out with him. Grigori was hoping you had some extra crystals to spare to help protect them all."

"I should, though maybe Terren and the orcs should go with them as added protection."

"We will talk about that tonight after you get back from showing Darton and company how to trap," McKenna called behind him. "Till later!"

***

Darton shuffled from foot to foot as Kavan approached the small group of redcaps that were waiting at the gate of the village, a handful of dwarves with them. Kavan carried a sack over his shoulder which had equipment to be used for trapping in it; at his waist was his sword. The redcaps and dwarves had found some clothing in one of the houses and they altered them to fit them. They also had bathed and looked much better than when Kavan first met them.

Kavan looked over at Terren who was leaning against a tree while sharpening a knife. Terren nodded at the group and asked, "You need some help with the traps?"

"I will not say no," Kavan replied. "Thank you."

Terren huffed and joined the group of redcaps and dwarves, the small magical creatures craning their necks to look up at the orc. Terren was dressed in leather and frishna armour, and he had a broadsword strapped to his back.

"I know the area pretty well," Terren commented. "I can suggest some good spots to place some traps."

"Sounds like a plan," Kavan told him. "Come on group, let's head out. If we catch anything tonight we will show you how to clean them in the morning."

The redcaps and dwarves followed behind Kavan and Terren as they left the village, heading out to the forest. Terren pointed Kavan to an area closer to the mountains, citing that there should be abundant hares in the area.

Kavan took in the scent of the forest, of the still thawing ground and the new buds on the trees. He could hear squirrels moving about on branches, and birds flitting through the trees. He tuned out the excess noise as he walked; it could get overwhelming if he let it.

Terren chose a few areas to set up snares with bait, showing the redcaps how to set them. He had them each try it several times before he was satisfied with their work. Finally as the sun began to set Darton commented that he was hungry and ready to head back to Bella Vale.

"Supper should be ready by now," Kavan told him. "Louran has been preparing a deer since this morning."

"I am growing to like venison," Darton told Kavan. "We ate a lot of mushrooms, cave lizards, and fish down below."

"I can only imagine what eating so many mushrooms would be like–" Kavan stopped talking and stood still as he heard a branch snap nearby. He turned around and inhaled sharply as he saw a dekellian staring at him from a distance. Mounted on the creature's back was a dark elf, its eyes narrowed as they watched them.

"Terren, get them out of here," Kavan told the orc as he drew his sword.

"Roslyn would never forgive me if I left you here," Terren told him as he looked at Darton and the rest of the redcaps and dwarves. "Run!" he told them. "Get the crystals up around the village!"

Kavan took his eyes off of the dekellian for a moment to watch the redcaps and dwarves run off towards the village. When he looked at the dekellian and dark elf again the dekellian was in a position to pounce. Beside him, Terren drew his broadsword.

The dark elf urged the dekellian forward and it came at them at a run, its teeth barred. The creature wove its way through the trees to get to them. Terren leapt back and swung his sword at the dekellian's head as it reached them, striking it across its left eye. Blood sprayed out of the wound and the dekellian screeched, rearing back. The dark elf held on to the halter, but Kavan took the opportunity to jump up behind the dark elf as the dekellian put its front down again. Kavan beheaded the dark elf, grimacing as blood got on his shirt. As the body of the dark elf fell off of the dekellian, and the dekellian registered that its rider was no longer in the saddle, Terren stabbed his broadsword into the dekellian's eye. The orc put his weight onto the sword and the dekellian jerked as the blade entered its brain. Kavan jumped down as the dekellian collapsed.

"Well, that was effective," Kavan commented, and Terren grinned at him as he went to pull his sword out of the dekellian's head.

As Terren grabbed hold of the hilt of his sword another dekellian appeared from the shadows of the forest and latched on to Terren's right arm. Terren screamed in pain and surprise as the dekellian tossed its head like a dog with a chew toy, chomping down on Terren's arm as it did so.

Kavan pulled Terren's broadsword out of the first dekellian's head and shouted at the second one, "Hey lizard brain!" The dekellian stopped its chewing and tossing to regard Kavan with curiosity. With one last chomp accompanied by the sound of bone breaking, Terren fell to the ground, his arm dangling from the creature's mouth. The dekellian tossed the arm away and snarled at Kavan, digging its back legs into the ground to pounce on him.

The dekellian leapt at him but he swiftly moved out of the way, slashing at its front leg with Terren's sword. He had maimed it some with that strike, so it was limping now as it turned to attack him again. Kavan could see no saddle on its back or any other dark elves.

It charged at him again, swiping at him with its other front paw. The claws struck his arm, and he gritted his teeth from the pain as he moved away from it. The dekellian stalked behind him.

"I hate these things," Kavan said under his breath as he faced the dekellian. As it jumped at him again he struck the same leg and kept striking until he had hacked its leg in half. More blood sprayed onto him as the dekellian screeched and fell over. He saw his opportunity and plunged Terren's sword into the dekellian's chest. The dekellian jerked a couple of times before it finally stayed still.

Kavan ran to the unconscious orc and used his sword belt to make a tourniquet on what was left of Terren's arm. He felt for a pulse in Terren's neck and was thankful that he found one. He lifted the orc up and slung him over his shoulder like a sack of potatoes and carried him back to the village.

"Hang on, Terren. You will be alright."

Kavan could see Bella Vale ahead, and that the redcaps and dwarves had made it ahead of him. Behind him, though, he thought he could hear another dekellian running through the trees. The gates of the village opened ahead of him, and he could see McKenna rushing out with his sword at hand, Louran behind him.

"Get back inside!" Kavan yelled at them as he ran, but as McKenna stopped to turn something shot past Kavan.

Kavan barely registered it at first until he saw McKenna's body go slack and fall to the ground as he ran towards him. He saw Louran gather McKenna up in his arms and drag him inside the gate as Kavan came to the gates.

"Put up the protection!" Kavan screamed, and somewhere nearby he heard Darton swear and then the sparkle of magic erupted in a dome over the village.

Kavan put Terren down as Grigori and some of the other redcaps came running to help. He turned to look at Louran who was staring down at McKenna, a sad expression on his face. Kavan looked down and his face went white.

Sticking out of McKenna's chest was a four foot long spike that had impaled him completely. McKenna stared up at him blankly, blood trickling from his mouth and down to his chest to join in the pool of blood below his body. Kavan knelt and closed McKenna's eyes, saying a small prayer to the gods as he did so.

"Is there a healer who could see to Terren?" he heard himself asking Louran and Grigori. Grigori shook himself as he stared down at McKenna's body.

"I think one of the redcaps has some healing magic," Louran told him as he picked up his friend's unconscious body.

"Take him to him," Kavan ordered him as he stood and looked at the wall of the village. He went to the stairs and climbed up to the walkway so he could try to see what had killed McKenna. There, sitting in the middle of the path, was a dekellian with a dark elf mounted on its back, a contraption in the dark elf's hands that looked like it could throw a spike. Kavan could just barely make out a long scar on the dark elves' face, from its brow down the side of its cheek ending under its chin.

"You'll be dead soon!" Kavan shouted. "You have no idea what you have just done!"

He heard the dark elf laugh and it turned the dekellian away before urging it back up the path and into the darkness.

"We will have to keep a look out for them now," Grigori said as Kavan came back down. Kavan saw that Grigori had covered his brother-in-law's body with a blanket. "It's going to be dangerous."

"We have to send word to Roslyn," Kavan told him. "More dark elves have come to the surface."

Chapter Fourteen

Roslyn watched as they unloaded the bags of seeds from the wagons. They were back at the top of the plateau with Maeve and those who had come with her. These sacks would be divided between the many farms that were being established at the base of the plateau. Maeve also had brought with her several chickens and a few roosters, several turkey hens and toms, and some heifers with a bull so they could breed cattle. The capital was slowly growing. It just needed a name still.

She thought it was amusing, how the capital of Ellsgrove was called The Capital; she did not want that for her capital of Jay'Al. She really needed to come up with a name for her new city.

"Dragon City," Roslyn voiced aloud. Leaf looked up at her from where she was standing by her feet, and Heath grinned because he understood what was going through her mind. Karina, who was also standing nearby, said, "Huh?"

"The name of the city," Roslyn explained. "Dragon City. You were the Dragon Clan, and this is now going to be Dragon City."

"I like it," Karina commented.

"Agreed," Heath added. "It honours Karina's people and brings everyone together."

"Then that is what it will be called," Roslyn confirmed. "I need to tell Aidan."

"Tell Aidan what?" Aidan asked as he joined them.

"I have named my capital," Roslyn explained. "Dragon City."

"I will have a sign made," Aidan assured her.

"This city will grow," Heath commented. He looked at Roslyn. "*Your* city will grow. I can see it thriving."

Roslyn reached over and took Heath's hand, and he squeezed hers lightly.

She felt him rub his thumb along the side of her hand and she closed her eyes for a moment, imagining his hands on other parts of her. As her cheeks started turning red she distracted herself by looking at the sacks of seeds again.

"The orcs will be happy to finally start planting," she commented to Maeve who stood nearby, watching her with amusement. "They have been preparing their fields for days now."

Maeve reached up to her shoulder and scratched her familiar's chin. The pygmy owl on her shoulder, Luma, closed her eyes as she enjoyed the scratching.

"Happy to help," Maeve told her. "Though as Heath has mentioned, we have a mission ahead of us."

Roslyn looked at the ground and then back up at Maeve. "It was supposed to be me leading the mission," she explained. "They talked me out of it."

"Ah, I see," Maeve commented, looking at Heath. "It does make sense that the new Queen of Jay'Al does not put herself in unnecessary danger."

"Yes, well, I still do not like it," Roslyn said, gripping Heath's hand a little tighter. He smiled at her and leaned in to kiss her brow.

"With Maeve and the rest of them we will discover what we need and return immediately," he assured her. "You need not worry about us."

"You know I will worry no matter what," Roslyn told him. "I care about all of you. I worry I will never see you again."

"Then believe in me," Heath said, pulling her closer. "We *will* return."

Roslyn looked up into his green eyes and smiled, enjoying how he was looking at her. "I will hold you to that," she told him. She looked at Maeve and told her, "I trust you to bring him back to me in one piece."

"You have my word, Your Majesty," Maeve assured her with a grin. "Who all will be going?"

"You two, Heather, Karina, Edwin and Alexander," Roslyn informed her. "I have a few enchantments I want to make for you before you leave though. Some things to help keep you safe."

"The werewolves are coming with us?" Heath asked, surprised.

"I think it would be a good idea," Roslyn told him. "I have mentioned it to Alexander; he was supposed to talk to Edwin about it. I thought having someone who had an enhanced sense of smell, hearing, and sight would work well as scouts."

Maeve shrugged and commented, "Makes sense."

"Or you could make an enchantment for us so we have enhanced hearing, sight, and smell," Heath spoke up. "Not that I don't trust Alexander and Edwin..."

"I might be able to come up with something," Roslyn told him as she thought about it. "I will have to go through mom's book of spells and enchantments, and my own spells, before I can say for sure."

A Descent into the Roots

"*You can do anything you put your mind to*," Leaf told her. Roslyn looked down at her dragonling familiar and smiled.

"Thank you for the encouragement," she mused.

"Does she talk in your head?" Maeve asked Roslyn, indicating the dragon. "I hear Luma in my mind, a whisper in the back of my head."

"Same with Solana," Heath told her. "It was strange at first, the extra presence there in the back of my mind, but I have grown accustomed to her now." Heath looked at the gryphon who was stretched out on a rock nearby, grooming herself. "She can be sassy sometimes."

"So can Leaf," Roslyn told him with a smirk.

Roslyn looked behind her shoulder as she heard someone call her name. It was Tiffany letting her know that their supper was ready.

"A nice meal has been prepared for your arrival," Roslyn told Maeve. "Let us go and eat together."

***

Cypress found them as they were finishing up their meal, sitting around the fire pit and drinking ale together. The large orc was wearing his armour, the sword Roslyn had given him strapped to his back. Roslyn's Queen's Guard were sitting nearby as well, with Aidan, Oswick, Tiffany, Karina, Alexander, Edwin, Maeve, and Kasimir. All of the Queen's Guard were wearing their light armour with their weapons with them.

"Your Majesty," he greeted Roslyn with a slight bow of the head. "I hope you are doing well this evening."

Roslyn looked taken aback at his formality and looked up at him and then around to her friends.

Maybe he thought he had to be more formal with her around people he did not know? She thought that might be it.

"Cypress, this is Maeve and Kasimir," Roslyn introduced him to the sailor, and merchant.   "Maeve is one of Heath's lieutenants, and Kasimir is a merchant. Friends, this is Cypress, one of my best warriors."

Maeve waved at Cypress in greeting, and Kasimir nodded to him.

"Did you need something, Cypress?" Roslyn asked him.

"Stane and a few of the others wished to speak with you tonight," Cypress explained. "Do you have some time?"

"Yes, I think I can tonight," she told him after a moment. Leaf, who was lying on her feet, chirped as Roslyn stood up.

"Sorry to displace you," Roslyn told her familiar. "We have things to do."

"I will accompany you," Heath told her, but she told him to stay and relax with Maeve. He shrugged and allowed her to fill his mug with more ale before she turned to go.

Tiffany and the rest of the Queen's Guard stood up as well, and followed Roslyn to the stables. Roslyn looked behind her to see Teddy down the rest of her drink and give a sweet smile to Maeve before the knight hurried after her Queen. Teddy saw Roslyn looking at her and she blushed, but Roslyn just winked at her and continued to the stables. Once there they quickly got their horses ready and then were riding down the tunnel to the encampment below with Cypress. Leaf decided she wanted to fly her way down the tunnel, mostly gliding her way down ahead of them.

"Show off," Roslyn muttered as she watched Leaf glide ahead of them, earning a chuckle from all of her companions.

By the time they had ridden to the encampment below the sun had nearly completely set, leaving just a sliver of light on the horizon.

Roslyn could see that Aidan's hard work of sectioning off the city and giving out claims had worked well. To the east of the main encampment of Base Town, which was to be used as the inside defence of the whole city, Karina's Clan had staked their claims on lots. To the west, Cypress' Clan had chosen theirs. Strings of lights had been placed along the streets, held up by posts that had recently been laid. Families had put up their tents in their new lots and were eating supper around their respective fires.

Roslyn followed Cypress to the Elders' tent. They had left behind their log building when they followed Roslyn and so had to make do with a large round tent until a proper building could be built. They had set it up right next to where the western wall would be built.

Inside the tent had been decorated with the same things as the log building had been, and the door was covered with the same bearskin. In the centre of the tent was a fire pit, the smoke trailing through an opening in the ceiling; around the fire were five tree stumps that they had brought with them. The Elders were sitting on the tree stumps talking when Roslyn entered the tent, leaving her Queen's Guard outside.

"Good evening," Roslyn greeted the Elders as she took a seat on the empty stump. Leaf settled at her feet. "What was it you wanted to discuss?"

"Chief Stane here," Avis motioned to the young orc who had replaced the former chief, who was standing behind her, "Wished to talk with you about the role the orc warriors will play."

"I was going to have a sign-up sheet for those who wanted to be palace guards or work as city guards," Roslyn informed them. "It was something I had not gotten to yet, with everything that has been going on lately."

Avis nodded, as if she knew the answer already and looked at Stane with a half-smile. "What would the Chief want his role to be?" she asked Stane.

"Head of the city guard, if it would please Her Majesty," Stane commented, bowing his head. "I would be honoured to protect your city."

"It shall be done," Roslyn told him with a smile. "I will leave it with you to gather the right warriors to be under your command. Though I do suggest that some of the part-orcs should definitely be included in your ranks."

"I have already talked to Lou about some of their warriors," Stane assured her. "Karina's brothers are on my list."

"That pleases me," Roslyn commented. "Was there anything else you wished to discuss?"

"We also wanted to know about what is to be done about the dark elves," Avis piped up. "From what Cypress has told us you are planning an expedition to discover what the behemoths are?"

"Yes, that is the plan," Roslyn replied. "I have a small group leaving in a few days. Karina is one of them."

"I hope it goes well," Avis told her. "I think that is all we needed to discuss, sorry for taking up your evening."

"It is a fine night," Roslyn said as she waved her hand, thinking in her mind, *This meeting could have been a missive.* "The days are getting warmer, and the stars will be nice to see."

"Maybe you could spend the night down here," Cypress mentioned as she left the tent, Leaf at her heels. "My family has a nice spot, and I made some pecan pasties today."

"I would love to," Roslyn told him as she looked at her Queen's Guard. Teddy was yawning, and Tiffany was looking up at the stars. "Do you have any ale as well?"

Cypress grinned and nodded, saying, "I have prepared for a visit from you, My Queen, in hopes you would honour me with another visit."

Roslyn found herself blushing slightly, but she was thankful for the darkness that hid it. "Then I would be pleased to spend an evening with you and your family."

"Follow me," Cypress told her, and he started leading them down the marked street.

"Anda and Ulmer have been asking about you," Cypress explained as they walked. "I confess, when Stane mentioned him wanting to talk with you, I took the opportunity to invite you down to the encampment."

"Cypress, you do not need an excuse to ask me to visit," Roslyn explained to him. "You are one of my allies, and you have proven your loyalty already. You would have a title, my friend."

"I want to fight by your side, My Queen," Cypress told her. "I will be one of your greatest warriors."

"I accept your allegiance," Roslyn told him with a smile as they got to Cypress's plot of land. She could see Anda and Ulmer sitting next to the fire and she smiled at them.

Roslyn stopped in her tracks as she heard shouting from the scouts outside of the encampment. They were giving the alarm: something was out there.

Together Roslyn and Cypress turned and started running to the perimeter, her Guard steps behind her.

"What is going on?" Roslyn asked one of the sentries, one of her Ellsgrovian soldiers.

"Something was spotted, might be a dekellian and a dark elf," the soldier explained. "Not sure how many."

Roslyn swore and drew her sword, wishing she had her armour.

"Roz," Tiffany started to stay, but she shook her head.

"I'm not leaving my people right now," Roslyn told her. She turned to the sentry and said, "Call them all in, and sound the call to get the warriors gathered."

The sentry nodded and pulled out a horn, blowing it to indicate an attack. Roslyn closed her eyes and pushed her astral form up to the top of the plateau, to where Alexander and Edwin were still eating with Heath, Maeve, and the others.

"There is an attack," Roslyn told them, and they jumped because they were not expecting her. "Edwin, Alexander, I need the werewolves down here."

"Right away," Alexander told her, and together he and Edwin sped out of the house. Heath looked up at her with wide eyes.

"I should have gone with you," Heath told her, angry at himself.

"Too late for that now," Roslyn told him. "I have Cypress and the orc warriors down here, as well as most of the soldiers. We should be alright."

Roslyn pulled herself back to her body, not happy with leaving Heath up on the plateau. There was nothing to be done right now, he would never make it down in time unlike the werewolves.

"We are here," she heard Alexander behind her, followed by Edwin and the rest of the werewolves. "What is happening?"

"Dark elves," she told them. She could see the sentries coming in, and one that she knew, Finn, was nearby.

"Three dekellians, all with dark elves on their backs," Finn confirmed.

Roslyn swore and looked to her soldiers and warriors who were now gathering. "Leaf," she said as she turned to look at her dragon familiar. "Help me deal with these things."

Leaf laid a paw on her leg and she felt the magic grow inside her. She felt her power melt into the ground and go forth, seeking the enemy. She felt like she was in the ground, moving along with the tendrils of her magic as it sought out the dark elves and their mounts. She felt disembodied, not unlike when she used her astral form just…light as a feather.

She could sense them, the three creatures with their masters riding on their backs, above her. She reached out with her magic, forming a giant hand made of roots, reached out and grabbed hold of one the dekellians, squishing it and the dark elf within her fist. In the back of her mind she could hear yelling, as if someone was trying to get her attention. She felt someone shaking her shoulders and she brought her consciousness back into her body.

Tiffany was shaking her shoulders, and when Roslyn opened her eyes she stopped.

"Great job, but there are more!" Tiffany explained, pointing to the east. "They are surrounding us!"

"I cannot be on both sides at once," Roslyn said, panic in her voice.

"Good thing you have an army here," Cypress told her, hoisting his sword up. "Let us do our job, My Queen."

"Do it," Roslyn responded, holding her breath. "Stay safe." She watched him nod and he called out to his orc warriors before heading to the eastern side of the encampment.

Roslyn looked at Tiffany and her Queen's Guard, and the werewolves waiting for her command.

"You should not wear yourself thin," Alexander told her. "You have us. Use us."

"Do you think you can go up against them? Edwin lost several men."

"They caught us by surprise," Edwin retorted. "They will not stand a chance against us this time."

"Do your worst," Roslyn told them, "but try your best to come back."

Alexander and Edwin looked at each other and nodded, then they both looked at her and smiled. Together they turned and ordered their werewolves in human form to follow them as they advanced on one of the dekellians and dark elves that was coming at them from the west.

That left one on that side for Roslyn to deal with. She looked down at Leaf and asked, "Can we do what we did before?" Meaning grabbing the dekellian with the roots. Leaf shrugged.

"This was the first time you did extensive magic with me aiding you", Leaf told her. *"I have no idea what you can do."*

"Well, let's test the waters," Roslyn commented as she closed her eyes, reaching out with her magic again. "Tiffany, protect me."

"Will do," she heard Tiffany say before her consciousness delved back into the roots. She focused on the dekellian that was not fighting against the werewolves, stabbing it with roots and grabbing hold of its paws to pull it down. She could feel it in her hand, the squirming and then the warmth as she crushed down on it. Pulling herself back into her body she started retching at the sensation she had just felt. A cool hand, Heather's, touched her back and kept her from throwing up again.

"Thank you," Roslyn whispered, wishing she had never had to feel that to begin with. Why had it been so different the first time? Was it because Tiffany had tried to get her attention at the same time and so she had not been able to feel it all? She had no idea.

She took in her surroundings. She could see Alexander and the werewolves fighting the dekellian and the dark elf on its back. She watched as they dragged the dark elf out of its saddle and killed it before getting to the dekellian. On the other side she watched Cypress and the orc warriors battling the other dekellians and their masters. With their frishna swords they cut their way through the dekellians until the dark elves were on their feet fighting against the orcs, their mounts dead.

As she watched Cypress kill the dark elves she paused as a shadow crossed behind them, another dekellian creeping up, its eyes on Cypress. With a shout she ran towards them, brandishing her sword. Cypress turned in surprise as the dekellian launched itself off of the ground. Cypress brought his sword up to meet the dekellian only to be knocked back by its front paw, its claws raking his right arm. Blood streamed down Cypress' arm as Roslyn reached him, the dekellian snarling at her.

The dekellian snapped its head back and turned its body like a cat advancing on its prey. Roslyn could feel Leaf's presence nearby and urged her through their link to stay safe. The dragon reluctantly complied, so Roslyn was able to focus on the dekellian as it now seemed intent on her.

Roslyn drew her sword, still wishing she had her armour on. She readied herself, setting her feet in a stance that would keep her balanced. The dekellian snarled and gnashed at her but she moved out of the way, swinging her sword at its head. She felt it connect, and then her sword was wrenched out of her hands. She stared in shock as her sword, which was embedded in the dekellian's skull now, moved out of her reach.

She reached into her magic, extending into the ground to siphon more magic from the land. An astral hand formed in front of the dekellian and using it she grabbed hold of its snout and held it down, its body convulsing as it ran out of air. Roslyn turned away as the dekellian stopped breathing, and she focused on Cypress. Throwing the body of the dekellian away she ran to Cypress and put a hand on his bleeding arm.

"I got you," Roslyn told him, looking around to make sure there were no more dekellians and dark elves. She saw Tiffany nearby and her knight nodded to her as the rest of the Guard closed in. Roslyn started a healing spell on Cypress' arm, waiting till it was all healed to be satisfied, then letting his arm go.

"Are they all dealt with?" Roslyn asked Tiffany. She saw Tiffany nod her head. "Any idea on the casualties?" This time Tiffany shook her head.

"There are definitely a few werewolves hurt," Tiffany told her. "I have no idea how many or which ones though."

"Find out for me, will you?" Roslyn asked her, and she saw Tiffany nod before turning to go do so. She looked up at Heather and asked, "Is it all over?"

Heather looked around for a moment and then turned to her with a smile.

A Descent into the Roots

"I believe so, yes."

Chapter Fifteen

assidy looked at the room of mages with slightly raised eyebrows. Every single mage who had added their blood to the tree that Roslyn had gifted Ellsgrove now had a familiar. Lexi had a wolf-dog with bright blue eyes, though it was significantly smaller than most wolves. Professor Rhiannon's was a red fox, her youth's a hedgehog. The mage Stephanie also had a fox. Headmistress Dake had a feline familiar, as did Professor Reed. Dake's cat was a tortoiseshell. Reed's was a tricolour cat; both were larger cats than normal, much like Amelia's familiar Ecko.

"I had hoped it would work," Cassidy finally spoke after taking in all of the new familiars. "But this…this is something else."

"How will this help us?" Astra asked her, holding her hedgehog familiar in their hands.

"For us shamans of Jay'Al it connects us to the land and allows us more access to the magic around us, making us stronger. Our familiars can also store magic for us, and help us control it better," Cassidy explained. "You now have further access to the magic of Ellsgrove, and your familiars will help you in the same way mine does."

"Can you hear yours talking in the back of your mind too?" Headmistress Dake asked her. The professor was sitting with her cat familiar curled up on her lap.

Cassidy smiled and nodded. "Yes, you can communicate with your familiars in your minds, and spoken aloud. They can be your eyes and ears, you seeing through them, as well."

"How long do they live for?" Astra asked next.

A Descent into the Roots

"Once they reach maturity they will no longer age: they will live as long as you do," Cassidy explained.

"What if someone kills a familiar?" Astra inquired.

"Familiars are highly regarded in Jay'Al, and the killing of one is punishable by death," Cassidy told them. "I only know that if a shaman dies, the familiar will continue to live out its days as normal."

"So you've never heard of, say, a hawk killing a pine marten familiar?" Astra continued her questions.

"As a magical part of the land, the rest of the animals know that the familiar is sacred and would never kill one as prey," Cassidy assured them.

Astra seemed content with the answers as they looked down at the hedgehog in their hands. "Ok, good," Cassidy heard Astra say quietly before they hugged the hedgehog against their chest lightly. Cassidy found herself smiling at the youth, remembering the first time her own mother had explained familiars to her when she was young.

"Well, now that that is out of the way, we need to get started on the defences we talked about the other day," Cassidy spoke up, looking over at Kai and Tej who were sitting on one of the desks in their meeting room. "We've had word that Count Gresham has made it to his home estate, and the mercenaries are growing in number. They also seem to be preparing to embark. We cannot delay any longer."

The group of mages split up, each heading to a part of the city wall that they had flagged as weak places or important spots to protect. Cassidy, Kai, Headmistress Dake, and her Honour Guard headed for the main gates of the city where they were going to put their enchantments up.

They rode on horseback through the city, their familiars riding on the front of their saddles. Cassidy discovered that she knew the city better now and could recognize buildings, including remembering where her favourite bakeries were. She mentioned to Sully about a cinnamon roll and he smiled knowingly, agreeing to stop to grab one for her. Once she had her sweet they continued on their way towards the gate.

The city was lively for mid-morning, and Cassidy saw Rafi come out of a clothing shop with a package in hand.

"Good morning, Rafi!" She called out to him, and he looked at her with a smile.

"Where are you off to this morning?" he asked her as he walked towards them, Cassidy slowing her horse down to a walk.

"We are starting our protection enchantments on the city gate today," Cassidy told him as she stopped her horse in front of him. Crick chirped at him in greeting.

"Mind if I join you?" Rafi inquired. "I'll run this package home and meet you there?"

"By all means," she responded with a smile. "We shall see you there."

Rafi nodded and went over to where his horse was tethered outside the shop and they watched as he rode away.

"What do you think of him and that spy of Alara's?" Sully asked her as they continued on their way. "I've seen them together several times after meetings."

"I have not had much time to spend with her," Cassidy explained as they rode. "I have been with Eliza and Poppy a lot."

"Oh?"

"When you are with the king, I am with my sisters teaching them how to throw daggers," Cassidy told him. "Eliza is quite proficient at it."

"I learn something new every day," Sully said with a chuckle. "I am glad the princesses have you to teach them."

"Roslyn had done a lot already with them," Cassidy assured him. "And my father has made sure they know how to use other weapons. Throwing daggers, however, is a very different skill."

They arrived at the city's main gate and a soldier came to take their horses to the stables nearby. Sully led the group to a door that took them to the walkway above the city gate. Once up there Cassidy turned to look at the Capital of Ellsgrove, taking in how big the city was and the palace at its centre on a hill. What would it have been like to grow up in Ellsgrove? She knew she and Roslyn thought a lot the same, but would she have turned out just like Roslyn if their roles had been reversed? She would have lived not knowing her mother was out there, and she would not have found Crick as a familiar.

"Let's get started, shall we?" Roslyn asked Headmistress Dake. The woman nodded and they went about laying down the crystals and enchantments on that section of the gate. While they were working, Rafi joined them.

"Lovely day," Rafi commented as he handed her a lamb kebab from one of the street vendors nearby. "I figured you would be hungry."

"Thank you," Cassidy told him as she accepted it, taking a bite out of the piece of meat at the top. "I haven't had much to eat today really. Though that cinnamon roll I had was very good."

"So what all are you doing?" Rafi asked her. "I know tidbits, but not the whole thing."

"Protecting the city," she simplified her answer in case there were spies listening. "That is all you need to know."

He grinned, understanding why she was being so vague. He changed the subject, saying, "Want to come to my house for supper tonight?"

"I think I should be able to," she replied with a smile. "Do you have plans for this afternoon?"

"Nova was going to stop by later, but otherwise I have no plans as of yet."

"Thank you for everything you have done in getting us the information we needed," Cassidy said to him as she worked. She was embedding crystals in the wall with her magic and casting enchantments on the area.

"This is my home," Rafi told her. "And I am loyal to my King. I will do whatever I can to help. Elle was always good to me. That the usurpers tried to kill the whole family…I was furious. I wish I could shoot Count Gresham myself."

Cassidy stopped what she was doing and turned to look at Rafi. "I understand your frustration," she told him. "I would like nothing more than to wring his neck myself."

"You strangle him, I'll shoot him," Rafi told her with a wry grin. "That way we know for sure he is dead."

Cassidy chuckled and continued with the enchantments. Finally she and Dake met at the middle, both of them done with that section of the wall.

"Let's go to the next section on our list," Cassidy said to the group. "We have a few stops to make today."

***

Roland, King Lucius' butler, entered the King's study to prepare the room for the King's next meeting. The curtains of the windows were still drawn and the room had no lighting, so he went to open the curtains. He looked back through the door and saw Lucius coming down the hall with his guards, his two younger daughters with him. Quickly he went to pull the curtain open but stopped short as a darker shadow appeared in his vision in the shape of a man. He was about to call out when he felt something grab hold of the front of his smock and pull him close, and then there was an icy feeling against his throat before it turned red hot. He gasped and reached for his neck with one hand, reaching out for the curtain with his other. He pulled the curtain down as he fell, making enough noise that Lucius stopped in the doorway with wide eyes.

The sunlight in the room now revealed a person dressed all in black, a black mask over their head. Lucius looked down at Roland who was lying prone, blood pooling from his neck where his throat had been cut. As the assassin reached for one of the many knives at their belt, Lucius felt himself pushed out of the way.

"Not my father too!" Lucius heard Eliza shout as she pushed him down, and he heard the guards behind them shout. Next thing he knew one of the guards was helping him to his feet, though the soldier was looking at something else. Lucius followed the soldier's gaze and his eyes went wide.

Eliza stood there, half of her hair a mess where she had seemingly pulled one of the sticks that had been keeping her hair up. The assassin's body was laying there next to Roland, a dagger that looked similar to what was in Eliza's hair sticking out of their chest.

"Eliza?" Lucius spoke, and Eliza turned to look at him, tears in her eyes.

"You're safe, papa," she told him. "No one will take you from me, I promise."

Lucius pulled his daughter close as Poppy hugged him from behind. The guards went to the assassin's body.

"Where did you learn to throw like that?" Lucius asked Eliza.

"Cassidy has been teaching me," she explained. "She gave me these dagger-pins for my hair."

"Fantastic job, darling," Lucius told her. "I am so proud of you. Thank you."

She sniffed and wiped her face with the sleeve of her dress. "When will this end, papa? When will we be safe?"

Lucius' eyes darkened and he hugged them tighter. "Soon, sweethearts, soon."

Chapter Sixteen

Kavan ran through the darkness, using his enhanced sight and speed to get him to the plateau in only a few hours. He had just left Bella Vale after the attack; he was the only one fast enough who could get a message to Roslyn in time. He was thankful that the dark elves had left Bella Vale alone for now. He was worried about leaving the creatures there even though they had Roslyn's protection stones.

He smelled blood.

Kavan stopped just short of the plateau and the encampment at its base. He had been too late to warn them about the dark elves, for clearly they had been attacked at the same time. Using his enhanced vision he scoured the groups of people cleaning up the areas of battle, people using light crystals carrying wounded on stretchers into the encampment. He spotted a group of knights he recognized by a fire and headed there.

"Roslyn," Kavan spoke as he stepped into the light of the fire. "Is everyone all right?"

Roslyn startled slightly at his sudden appearance, as did a few of the knights.

"By the gods Kavan, do we need to put a bell on you?" Tiffany joked as her heart raced from the shock of his sudden arrival. A few of the knights chuckled.

"Alexander was hurt but he should survive," Roslyn told him. "A few soldiers as well, but no fatalities. Why are you here?"

"The dark elves attacked Bella Vale at, seemingly, the same time they attacked you," he explained, "Three of them. Roz…McKenna was killed."

He watched as she closed her eyes and lowered her head, her hand pressing against her forehead as the words sunk in. He noticed that she was not wearing her armour, and was glad that she had not been hurt during the fighting.

"Damnit," Tiffany said. "Any other fatalities?"

Kavan shook his head and then told her, "Terren lost an arm, but he will live."

"How did they know to attack you there?" Tiffany asked.

Kavan shrugged and told her, "No idea. Maybe they were following a scent? They could have been after the centaurs."

"Is Bella Vale safe?" Roslyn asked as she opened her eyes again. "Uncle Grigori and the rest of the farmers?"

"For now, yes," he replied. "Grigori and the other farmers were preparing to come here soon."

"The only way it will be safe is if they have a magical guard," Roslyn commented with a sigh. "We will have to plan something, coordinate *something…*" her voice trailed off as she turned her head to look at the tunnel that led up to the plateau. "I'm going to have to tell mother."

"Do they know that everyone down here is all right?" Kavan inquired, waving a hand to indicate the encampment.

"Edwin took word," Tiffany responded. "Roslyn was just about to set up a magical perimeter for the night to keep everyone safe."

"Where is Heath?" Kavan asked her.

"He stayed above while we came down to talk to the orcs. It was then that the attack came," Tiffany explained.

"Ah." Kavan turned to look at Cypress, who was walking towards them; he had a newly healed wound on his own arm.

"Cyp," Kavan called as he walked towards the orc.

"What news do you bring?" Cypress asked him.

"We were attacked in Bella Vale as well," Kavan explained. "Terren was mauled, he lost an arm but he will live."

Cypress growled and swore. "These dark elves need to be taken out," Cypress said with a huff.

"McKenna was killed," Kavan continued, and he watched Cypress look over at Roslyn who was trying not to cry.

"This is a sad day indeed," Cypress told him. "It is unfair."

"Kavan," Roslyn called to him. "Will you stay the night here? Tomorrow we can figure something out to bring the farmers from Bella Vale here. If the magical creatures do not feel safe there, they might as well come here as well."

"I will run back to Bella Vale to let them know, and hopefully they can come to a consensus while I am gone," Kavan replied. "I will be back as soon as I can."

"Be safe!" Roslyn called after him as he sped off, heading back to Bella Vale.

A Descent into the Roots

Kavan hurried back the way he came, vigilant of anything around him to make sure that no more dark elves were out there. From what he saw at the encampment, no dark elves or dekellians were left alive. One dark elf and its mount survived the attack on Bella Vale, one enemy to take word back to the rest of them. He should have gone after that dark elf, but warning Roslyn had been more important.

"Should you take McKenna's body back with you?" Grigori asked him after he returned to Bella Vale.

"No, Roslyn wants to bring all of you to the plateau. Talk to the centaurs and the others, try to convince them. She will send a guard to bring you, I'm guessing most likely all of the werewolves and some enchantments," Kavan explained. "I will be back tomorrow sometime with them."

"I will do my best," Grigori responded. "I will talk to Louran about it."

"How is Terren?" Kavan thought to ask before leaving again.

"Awake, and annoyed at his missing arm," Grigori answered. "He is happy to be alive though, and he knows he has you to thank for that."

"Cypress will be happy that he is all right. Keep the crystals up till I return tomorrow. No one goes outside of the village," Kavan told him. He saw Grigori nod and then he sped away again, feeling the enchantment going back into place after the gates of the village were closed once again.

When he returned to the plateau he found the battlefield empty, mounds of burning dekellians and dark elves on the outskirts of the encampment. A shout went up as he was seen in the crystal-light, and then a soldier beckoned him through a small opening in the enchantment that protected the encampment. The soldier closed the opening behind them as he placed a crystal back on the ground.

"Queen Roslyn is at the base of the plateau," the soldier informed him. Kavan nodded and headed through the marked streets at a slow run–he did not want to startle anyone else–taking in the strings of lights that had been put up along the streets. He could see the very raw beginning of a city in how everything was marked out, and he could not wait to see how it would look when it was done.

Roslyn was sitting near the willow tree near the opening of the tunnel, her knights arrayed around her. There were crystals hanging in the tree branches giving off light, giving the area an ethereal seeming. Cypress was sitting next to Roslyn, letting her lean on him as she yawned. The wounded were on makeshift cots nearby, having been seen to by either Roslyn, Heather, or Karina.

"There you are," Roslyn said as she spotted him coming towards them. She yawned again, stifling it with her hand. "I was trying to stay awake till you returned."

"Have you told your mother?" Kavan asked as he sat down on her other side.

She shook her head. "I want to do it in person," she explained. "Not in astral form. I want to be there to comfort her."

Kavan thought about when she found out that her stepmother Elle had been killed and understood. He nodded and looked over at Tiffany.

"Where are we sleeping tonight?" he asked her.

"Here," Roslyn responded, and he felt a sudden cushioning underneath him. He looked down and found a very plush layer of moss underneath them, and he knew that she had grown it for them. Lou, Karina's father, brought over some blankets for them, and Kavan grabbed one to put over Roslyn. She smiled at him weakly before she yawned again, and a pillow made of moss appeared under her head. Cypress tucked her blanket in on his side, and Kavan did the same on his own. He watched as she quickly fell asleep.

Kavan looked up at the lights in the tree, thinking how magical they looked in the dark. He looked over to see Lou lighting some small braziers to give them all heat, and he mouthed a 'thank you' to the part orc. Lou nodded his head and left them as slowly more snoring could be heard from the group.

***

Kavan awoke to the smell of cooking food nearby. He looked over at Roslyn who was still nestled in her blanket cocoon, Cypress still on her other side. Sitting up he found that the sun was just barely peeking over the horizon to the east, and there were only a handful of bedrolls empty.

He followed the smell of food to a building where Karina and her parents were working together to get a breakfast made. Kavan offered to help but Dacey, Karina's mother, just handed him a cup of the wake up drink along with some sugar and milk before sending him back outside.

Kavan wandered a little, taking in the posts of the marked streets and the tents put up on the properties. When he came back to the tree he found Roslyn awake, sitting up and looking around. She smiled warmly at him when she saw him approaching.

"I am very glad you are here," she told him. "Thank you for protecting Bella Vale."

He lowered his eyes, saying, "I did not do the greatest job of it."

"You did not kill McKenna," Roslyn reminded him. "It is not your fault. It is the dark elves' fault."

Kavan reached down and took hold of her hand to help her stand. "I know," he told her. "I tried to tell him to stay inside the gate but it was too late."

"He wanted to help you," Roslyn commented. "That is the McKenna I knew. Ever since I have been here he was so accommodating and helpful. He had hoped the day would come when I returned. He was a father to Cassidy when our father was not able to be there. It will break my heart even more to tell my mother what happened."

"Let me do it," Kavan told her. "Please."

"No, I want it to be me," Roslyn replied, and he could tell how hard it was for her to say it. "It needs to be me."

They were almost done eating the breakfast that Karina and her parents had made for them when Roslyn's family, Heath, Oswick, Aidan and a few of the other soldiers that had been left above on the plateau rode into the encampment from the tunnel.

Kavan watched as Roslyn went to them. He saw Amelia look over the group and see him there. He could hear her ask why he was there. He tried not to listen but it was hard not to: Roslyn told her mother that there was an attack on Bella Vale at the same time they were attacked. He heard her tell her mother that McKenna had been killed. Kavan watched as Roslyn caught her mother in her arms, her mother sobbing. He could hear Roslyn's siblings cry out, and he felt it in his heart. He could watch no longer, looking away as the family continued to mourn.

Chapter Seventeen

Roslyn held her mother in her arms as she cried, and she reached out to grab hold of her younger sister Leona's hands. Her two brothers, Oko and Quinn, were holding Sawyer.

"You make the dark elves pay for this," Leona told her. "You need to stop them from taking any more people."

Roslyn looked up at Heath who had just put a hand on her shoulder to offer his comfort and she smiled at him through her tears. She used her sleeve to wipe her face and gestured to Leona to take her place in holding their mother.

"Get the expedition ready," Roslyn told Heath. "We cannot wait any longer. I will quickly make you some enchantments while you prepare. Alexander and Edwin will go with you, as will Cypress."

Heath nodded and went to go do as she asked. She turned to Aidan and told him, "We need to bring the creatures and farmers from Bella Vale here. I will make enchantments for wagons to protect them, and the werewolves will guard them."

Aidan nodded before pulling her into a hug.

"I'm so sorry," he told her, almost a whisper. He let her go and she smiled weakly at him before he turned and walked away, heading to do his job.

It was Oswick's turn to hug her, and his hug was strong. When he pulled away he looked at her deeply and then kissed her brow like he would his sisters. "What do you need me to do?" he asked her.

"I need an area for the creatures set up," she told him. "Can you work with Stane to find an area and get some tents prepared?"

"I can do that," Oswick assured her. He let her go and went to find Stane.

Roslyn turned back to look at her family. Amelia was looking at her now, her tears stopped for the moment.

"They will pay for this," Roslyn assured her. She looked over at Kavan as she added, "Kavan saw the dark elf who did it. If and when we cross paths, there will be nothing left of him."

"I know," Amelia spoke, her voice cracking. She cleared her throat. "I know you will avenge him."

***

Roslyn had Kavan bring her alchemy table down to the encampment so she could work on her enchantments. She was set up in a tent beside the willow tree sitting on a stool working on them; Leaf sat in the doorway. For the wagons she just had to tweak one part of the enchantments from when they were guarding against the werewolves, which was relatively easy.

For the expedition, Roslyn had to take a moment to think about what would be most useful for them. They had her protective crystals for when they would sleep, but they would also need something to help them see in the dark; except for the werewolves, of course, who already were able to do that. She already had warmth charms for them at least.

"What do you think you will need?" Roslyn asked Heath when he came to check on her; she stood up and stretched. "I have charms to help you see in the dark, and we already have the warmth charms. You'll have the protective crystals as well."

"I think that should be fine," Heath told her as he took her into his arms and held her tightly. "I don't want to leave you after what just happened."

She nuzzled into his shoulder, taking in his scent; he smelled like cedar.

"I appreciate that, but I need you with the expedition," she spoke quietly. She didn't want him to let go of her so she clung to him now, hearing his heart racing against his chest. "Just come back to me, all right?"

"Nothing could keep me from you," she heard him say as she closed her eyes, her face buried in his tunic. "You should know that by now, darling."

She felt his hand on her chin and she opened her eyes as he tilted her face up. He peered into her eyes, searching for something, and then he finally leaned in and kissed her. She felt his warm hands on her lower back as she responded, enjoying the heat of him against her and the *need* in his kiss.

"*Kavan incoming,*" Roslyn heard Leaf's voice in her mind and reluctantly pulled away from Heath.

"We have company," she told him, and she stepped out of the tent to greet Kavan.

"The werewolves are ready to go, just waiting on you," Kavan informed her.

"I won't be much longer," Roslyn assured him. Heath stepped out of the tent after her. Solana, who had been beside Leaf, went to rub up against her master's legs.

Kavan looked from Heath to Roslyn and smiled, happy to see them together. Kavan wondered if she noticed him distancing himself, and he had realized last night that she had not attempted to cuddle with him while they slept next to each other. He closed his eyes for a moment, remembering the last time they had slept together, and he felt a pang in his chest. It had been his decision, his choice to choose the powers he had as a werewolf rather than be with Roslyn. She deserved someone better than him, someone less selfish, and that person was definitely Heath.

"Heath, gather your party here then and get the enchanted charms I have for you," Roslyn told Heath. "I will take you to the swamp where we found Darton and reopen the pathway underground for you to go down."

"Sounds like a plan. I will go get them," Heath responded, leaning in and kissing her on the cheek before turning to leave. Solana followed him, testing her wings. The gryphon had gone through another growth spurt and it would not be long till she was flying beside Leaf.

"We will be waiting at the edge of the encampment," Kavan informed her before he too left.

Roslyn returned to her tent and finished the enchantments in time for Heath and the rest of the expedition party to gather there. She gave Edwin and Alexander warmth charms just in case, and Cypress and Karina as well. Cypress and Karina also got a charm to help them see in the dark, as did the rest of the humans.

"Everyone is ready?" Roslyn asked the party. They all had their packs with them and weapons. Maeve's pygmy owl familiar Luma sat on her shoulder. Heather looked a little anxious, but she was in good spirits.

"Heather, were you able to make some of those potions and bombs?" Roslyn asked the knight-mage. Heather nodded and showed her her bag with everything in it. "Very good," Roslyn told her, pleased.

Roslyn checked to make sure Heath had his guns on him. His smaller gun was in its holster at his waist, his longer one strapped to his back. He even had a sword on his other hip. Cypress had the sword Roslyn had given him, and Maeve had her guns as well. Edwin and Alexander both had armour and swords. Karina and Heather both carried baskets of food. Roslyn hoped it would be enough to last them several days, if not longer.

"Let's head out then," Roslyn said as she led the way to their horses. Together with the rest of her Queen's Guard they rode out to the swamp where the redcaps and dwarves had come to the surface which was just a short ride from the encampment. Leaf flew along beside them, Solana laying across the front of Heath's saddle. Once there, Roslyn dismounted from Sage and handed her reins to Heath. She took a few steps towards where the tunnel had been and reached out with her magic, creating a new entrance and fortifying the tunnel at the same time. Way underneath them she could sense a series of tunnels built of rocks that led to a giant underground cavern. At least they were in the right spot, and hopefully the expedition would find some answers.

A Descent into the Roots

Roslyn sighed as Heath turned to her, the rest of the group heading towards the opening.

"Stay safe," Roslyn reiterated. He smiled at her before pulling her close for a kiss.

"You as well, darling," he said as he pulled away, his voice a little husky. With one last glance at her he turned and led the way down into the tunnel, Solana at his heels.

Maeve nodded to Roslyn before following Heath. Karina, who had Mister Scruffy in a sling across her body, waved, as did Heather, and Cypress smiled at her before they descended together. Edwin and Alexander looked at each other and then at Roslyn.

"We will keep Heath safe," Alexander assured her. "All of them."

"I know," she responded. "May the ancestors watch over you."

***

Roslyn and her Queen's Guard returned to the encampment, each of them with one of the party's horses reins attached to their saddles. Tiffany took the reins of Heath's horse from Roslyn so she could go meet with Kavan and the rest of the werewolves who were going to Bella Vale. She handed Kavan the enchantments that would be put on the wagons.

"The enchantments will put up a protective barrier around the wagons, and also give the horses more energy and speed," she explained to him. "Uncle Grigori and the farmers should have enough wagons."

"And the livestock?" Kavan inquired, thinking of the alpacas and horses.

"The enchantments will give them speed and energy as well. Here are some more protective crystals for you when you stop for the night," Roslyn told him as she handed him a pouch. "There should be enough to encircle a large caravan."

"If everything goes to plan, we should be back in just a couple days," Kavan told her.

Roslyn nodded and watched as he and the other werewolves took off, a blur in her eye as they used their enhanced speed to run. She turned to find Tiffany standing nearby.

"That never gets old," Tiffany commented. "Seeing them run like that."

"It sure is something," Roslyn agreed as she walked beside her, Leaf following at her heels. Together the three of them headed back towards the plateau.

"How are you doing?" Tiffany asked her.

"McKenna's death did not hit me as hard as Elle's, I've only known him for six months, but I am sad for my mother and my siblings," Roslyn explained. "I know Cassidy will take it hard. I still have to tell her."

Tiffany understood, and she put a hand on Roslyn's shoulder to comfort her, saying, "Seeing your sister go through what you did will be hard, no doubt."

"How did this happen? How did assassins get into the palace? How did the damned dark elves know where to go? Why did the gods, and the ancestors, let this happen?!"

"The gods roll their dice in their realm, and down here someone dies," Tiffany said with a shrug. "The ancestors might have some sway, but they are nothing against the schemes of the gods."

"Well the gods need to see how it feels when someone we love dies," Roslyn commented. "Do they even have hearts?"

Tiffany shushed her, "Do not heckle the gods. You have the attention of your ancestors, you don't need the gods interested in you too." Tiffany thought about it for a moment. "Are there gods in Jay'Al? You have the ancients, but are there gods above them, or are the ancients a sort of god?"

"That is a very good question," Roslyn told her. "I will have to look through the shaman's books to see, and maybe ask. I never thought about that before. We have gods we worship in Ellsgrove, but they would have their own versions in different kingdoms."

"What about the orcs?" Tiffany asked her. "They worshipped the dragons, did they not? Is there a dragon god?"

Roslyn looked down at Leaf, who was watching them and listening to their conversation.

There are dragon gods," Leaf told Roslyn. "*Roopa and her mate Gozol.*"

Roslyn passed the information on to Tiffany who found it intriguing. "So the orcs worship the dragon gods?"

"Maybe we should ask Avis," Roslyn suggested. "Now I am interested in finding that out."

Roslyn headed for the Elder's Tent, Tiffany following her. They went into the tent and Leaf followed behind, and found Avis sitting alone by the fire. The female orc was wrapped in furs, her one missing tusk glimmering in the firelight.

"My Queen, to what do I owe the pleasure of this visit?" Avis asked her as she stood up to greet them. She looked down at Leaf and smiled at the dragon. "Hello there, beauty."

"Tiffany and I were discussing deities and wondered if you worshipped the dragon gods," Roslyn told her.

"Yes, we worship Roopa and Gozol," Avis informed her. "They are the ones who created the orcs."

"That's interesting," Roslyn commented. "Thank you, Avis."

"Anytime," Avis told her, bowing her head slightly as Roslyn turned to leave. "I am sorry to hear about McKenna," Avis added. "He was very helpful to us when we first came here."

Roslyn halted and turned back, "Thank you. It was quite a shock."

630

A Descent into the Roots

"I will pray to the gods that his soul finds peace," Avis added. Roslyn nodded and smiled her thanks before leaving the tent with Tiffany and Leaf.

"Who should we ask about the Jay'Alian gods?" Tiffany asked her.

"I do not want to bother mother about it right now," Roslyn told her. "Willow should be arriving soon with her army. I will ask her then. In the meantime, I need to brew an astral potion so I can tell Cassidy about McKenna. Also, I want to go back under the plateau to those tunnels Karina and I found."

"Is that wise right now, with everything that is going on?" Tiffany asked her with a serious tone. She looked at Leaf. "Should she?"

"*We might learn some more about the people who built it,*" Leaf said to Roslyn, and she told Tiffany that.

Tiffany sighed and said, "Fine, but your Queen's Guard is going with you."

Chapter Eighteen

Heath stared in wonder at the massive tunnels they were now traversing. Solana stayed close to him, and he could feel her discomfort at
being underground. He reached a hand down and scratched her head,
earning a purr from her as they walked.

Roslyn's charms worked at least. They did not need anything to light their
way underground since they could see in the dark. That would come in handy
if they were trying to avoid any dark elves or dekellians.

When they first came upon an intersection they had to choose which way
to go. Karina left a magical mark shaped like an 'x' on the path they chose not
to go down as they continued. They agreed they should not split up for safety
reasons, but Heath still felt like it would be easier to do so.

"Could we maybe send Luma down the other tunnel to scout?" Heath suggested at the next fork in the tunnels.

Maeve looked at her pygmy owl and they seemed to be speaking to each
other through their minds. After a moment, Luma took flight and headed
down the other tunnel. A few minutes later she returned.

"It's a dead end," Maeve told him.

"Well that saved us time," Heath commented as they went the other way.
They had to turn back though when they discovered that the tunnel had caved
in.

"Back to the first fork?" Heather suggested, and so they did.

This tunnel had moss growing on its walls that they discovered glowed in
the dark, and as they walked down it from the other tunnel Edwin noticed
carvings underneath the moss.

"This is interesting," Edwin noted as he cleared the moss from the carvings. "These are old."

"How can you tell?" Heath asked him, peering at the carvings that looked like they might be a language.

"This dialect has not been spoken since before my time," Edwin informed him. "Someone came down here. I wonder why."

"Do you think they left carvings on good tunnels?" Karina asked him. "Or can you read it?"

"I would say your assumption is correct," Edwin answered. "If my memory is correct, it seems like a marker to remember where they came from."

"Well, that sounds promising then," Heath said. "Let's get a move on."

When they came to other forks, sometimes three of them, Edwin would check for carvings that continued to lead them down into the earth. Finally they came to a large cavern with what looked like hot springs in them, and crystals in the ceiling that lit the room.

"Perfect place to stop for a rest and a bite to eat," Heath commented as he leaned against the wall of the cavern. He grabbed his water pouch from his belt and took a swig.

"How will we know if the water down here is any good?" Cypress asked them, eyeing the pools.

"You have two water mages with you," Heath told him, "Do you not think we can tell if water is no good?"

"You can *actually* do that?" Cypress asked him.

"Yes," Heath and Maeve said in unison, earning a chuckle from Karina and Heather. Karina let Mister Scruffy out of the sling to explore a little, and both Luma and Solana joined him.

"Well that is handy then. Is this water good then?" Cypress asked them both.

"Yes," Heath assured him. "Hopefully we find some cold springs as well, hot springs like this usually taste heavily of minerals."

They rested for a little while longer before continuing on, Maeve sending Luma on ahead; Mister Scruffy and Solana also ventured ahead, using their combined sense of smell to try to figure out the tunnels. Alexander kept a notebook with a roughly drawn map of the tunnels and the markings, and Karina left hers.

They reached a rather large cave that looked like it had been partially carved out, several smaller caves that seemed like rooms leading off of it; there were two different pools on either side, one a hotspring the other a cool pool that was fed from somewhere above. Glowing moss covered part of the cave, and there were smaller crystals in the other caves that provided light.

"Seems as good a place as any to stop for the night," Heath commented as they checked out the cave. "Refill our water skeins in the cold pool."

"Do you think someone used to live here?" Maeve asked the group as she watched the three familiars examine around the caves. "It looks too clean to have been abandoned for long."

"Maybe some of the creatures that went up to the surface?" Heather responded. "Though you would think they were in too much of a hurry to leave it like this."

"My thoughts exactly," Edwin commented. "I do not smell anything odd."

"Well, it is still a good place to stop for a rest," Heath reiterated. He and Solana headed to one of the smaller caves and he set up his bedroll. "Heather, will you put the crystals up?"

"Yes, sir," Heather responded as she took the protective crystals out of a pouch at her waist and she went about laying them out at the entrances of the big cave.

***

Heath awoke to the sound of something scuttling in the wall of the cave-room he had claimed. He looked over at Solana who was poised at attention, her eyes wide and watching the wall behind him. She clacked her beak once loudly and then started to growl. The scuttling sound stopped suddenly.

"What's going on?" he heard Maeve ask sleepily from where she was sleeping just a few feet away.

"Something in the wall," he responded in a whisper. "Solana does not like it."

"What did it sound like?" she whispered back.

"Kind of like a crab scuttling along rocks," Heath responded in kind. He got out of his bedroll and saw that she was doing the same. Luma was perched on her shoulder. Karina also peeked around the corner from where she had been sleeping, Mister Scruffy at her feet.

"I heard it too," Karina told them quietly. "Mister Scruffy does not like it either."

The sound started again, this time heading back seemingly the way it had come, getting quieter as they went.

"That is *so* creepy," Maeve whispered, goosebumps going up her spine.

Maeve turned to look at the rest of their party, whom were all stirring in their bedrolls, and noticed that Cypress was missing.

"Cyp?" She called out, going to where he had been keeping watch before she had fallen asleep, near the opening to the next section of tunnels. She looked down at the crystals and found that the protective barrier was still up.

"What's wrong?" Heath asked her.

"Cypress is missing."

"What? Do you think he just wandered off?" Heath joined her at the barrier.

"Heath," Karina called his attention to two empty bedrolls.

"Where are Edwin and Alexander?" She asked. "They were both here when I fell asleep."

A Descent into the Roots

Heath looked at their bedrolls and his gaze caught sight of something else: there were splash marks on the ground around the cold spring, which were right near where the two werewolves had placed their bedrolls. Heath went to the side of the spring and Maeve joined him there with a raised eyebrow.

"What are you thinking?" Maeve asked him as he used his magic to probe the water.

"There is an opening in the pool that was not there before. Something came through here, probably whatever I heard on the other side of the stone."

"And it took Edwin, Alexander, *and* Cypress? Why?" Karina asked him, looking nervous. He could tell that she really did not like being underground, especially with so many unknowns out there.

He shrugged and responded, "Edwin and Alexander were closest to the spring, but Cypress…unless he saw it happen or maybe he was getting a drink? I have no idea."

"Do you think *it* was on its way back for the rest of us when Solana scared it away?" Maeve asked Heath as he thought about what to do next. He was not about to abandon Cypress, nor Alexander and Edwin. Besides, who knew if this was a faster way to finding the Behemoths?

Karina shivered and hugged her familiar, eyes wide as she thought about what could have taken her friends.

"What are we going to do?" Karina asked Heath. "We can't just leave them to whatever fate the creature has for them." Thinking about them being eaten made her stomach churn.

"I am going to go after them," Heath explained. "Solana and I will go after them. Maeve, you continue on. I should be able to sense your magic and find you after."

"Are you sure? Roz would never forgive me if something happened to you," Maeve reminded him.

"Very sure," he told her. "Let's all break camp together before I head into the water. I will take their packs with me for when I find them."

"Do you want to take some of the crystals with you?" Heather asked him as she helped roll up Edwin and Alexander's bedrolls.

"I should," he replied. "I'll take a handful. Here," Heath pulled Alexander's map out of the bag. "You'll need this. Keep an eye out for the runes, and maybe continue the map if you can."

"I will," Heather assured him. "Be careful."

"You as well." Heath looked at Solana and then back up at his travelling companions, giving them a wry smile. "Let's go. Maeve, the crystals?"

Maeve collected the crystals, feeling the magical barrier come down around them. She handed some to Heath and he put them in a pouch on his belt. He checked his pistol, making sure it was loaded and ready to go just in case he needed it. He adjusted his sword next, and then hoisted the packs he carried over his shoulder.

"Come on, Solana, let's go find our friends," he told his familiar as he headed towards the pool. Using his magic he created a tunnel through the water to the opening near the bottom and he jumped in, Solana diving in after him. The opening was definitely big enough for an orc to go through, and there were scratch marks on the sides as if something had clawed its way through. The opening led into a small sub chamber of water that had a ledge above it that led to a tunnel that seemed to run parallel to the caves they had slept in. There was a loose boulder sitting at the bottom of the chamber.

Heath pulled himself up onto the ledge, feeling something slimy under his hands. He cringed as he stood up, feeling his leather boots settle into the slime. He attempted to rub off some of the slime onto the rock wall as Solana investigated the slime, sniffing it. He took a handkerchief out of his pocket and used it to get rid of the rest of the slime on his hands, discarding the cloth in the tunnel. He could see the slime trailing down the tunnel.

"Well that seems to be the right direction," he told Solana as he started following, trying his best to avoid the slime trail.

"*The smell…*" he heard Solana in his mind, "*I do not like it.*"

"Well nothing we can do about that now," he teased her. "We have to save our friends."

It seemed like ages that he had been going down the tunnel when he came upon a fork, though he followed the slime trail still down the left one. Solana walked along beside him, her talons clicking ever so slightly on the stone. She seemed to be at constant alert as they went, and he could hear her muttering in the back of his mind about being underground. She missed the open air, even if they had only been down there a day.

They came to an opening in the tunnel that was big enough for two people to pass through, and the trail led inside. Heath peeked his head in cautiously and found a cavern with stalactites and stalagmites, with what looked like several large cocoons on several of them in the middle of the cavern.

"Oh, I definitely do NOT like this," Heath whispered to Solana. "What can you see?"

"*There is definitely something in those cocoons,*" she told him, shifting from paw to paw.

"*I can smell Cypress close by.*"

"Do you think he is in one of those cocoons?" Heath asked her.

"*Could be.*"

He sighed deeply and took a step into the cavern. He made his way slowly towards the centre of the cavern, Solana right beside him. He noted that there was no glowing moss on the walls or any kind of crystals in the ceiling. As he looked up he could see a few openings in the ceilings but that was it. He made out a few piles of bones on the ground here and there, making him feel even more uneasy as he kept going. Was he too late?

He reached the cocoons on the stalagmites in the centre. There were five of them, two more than companions he was missing. One was clearly bigger than the others so he went to it first, drawing his dagger to use to cut it open. He did so carefully since he did not want to cut the person inside.

He could tell it was Cypress inside after the first couple cuts, so he started to pull the cocoon apart. From the ever so slight rise and fall of Cypress' chest he could tell he was still breathing, and he let out a sigh of relief. Finally he pulled enough of the material away that he had to catch Cypress as he fell, nearly falling over with the weight of him. He laid him down on the stone, noticing what looked like a welt on the orc's neck.

Wondering what that was from, he went to the next cocoon while Solana nudged Cypress' face with her beak.

The second cocoon had Edwin inside, and he was already waking up while Heath was extracting him.

"Hey, careful, it's me Heath," he said so Edwin would not lash out. "I don't know what the hells happened but I am getting you out."

"Alexander—"

"I think he is in the next cocoon," Heath told him.

"Cocoon?!" Edwin opened his eyes and looked around before he stretched out his arms and ripped himself out of the rest of the material. He jumped down and landed next to Cypress who was slowly waking up now. Heath could see a welt on Edwin's neck as well but it was healing already.

Mumbling came from the next cocoon and Edwin rushed over to it, tearing the cocoon off of Alexander. He fell into Edwin's arms, and Edwin placed him carefully on the floor.

"Are you hurt?" Edwin asked Alexander, examining him and finding a welt on his neck.

Alexander reached up and touched the welt on Edwin's neck.

"You will heal," Heath told them. "You all have the same mark, presumably from the creature that took you."

"Where are the others?" Edwin asked him as he stood up and looked around the cavern.

"We split up. We will find them after we get out of here."

"Where is here?" Cypress asked with a groan as he sat up, holding his head in his hands.

"The creature's lair," Heath told them. "Though I have not seen it yet."

"It smells in here," Alexander noted, and his gaze stopped on the other two cocoons.

"Who is in those?"

"None of our people," Heath told him.

"Should we not rescue them as well?" Cypress asked him.

Heath shrugged and went to the farthest cocoon, using his dagger to cut it open, stopping short when he saw what was inside: a dark elf. It looked like it had been there for a while, and had clearly been fed upon. It was not breathing.

"Dark elf, and it's long gone," Heath told them as he turned to the last cocoon. He was about to start cutting it open when he heard a scuttling noise above them. He turned his head to look up, the others and Solana following his gaze.

Above them, clinging to the ceiling with its multiple feet, was something akin to a centipede but a thousand times bigger and with clear fangs hanging out of its mouth. It chittered at them loudly and angrily before twirling around a stalactite to the ground where it started moving around them in a circle.

"Oh, that thing is so ugly," Heath found himself saying aloud, earning a half-hearted laugh from Alexander.

Solana soared in from above the creature, scratching at its eyes with her talons. It reared its head back and roared, giving Heath the time he needed to pull his pistol and shoot at it, aiming for its head. The bullet hit the side of its head. He quickly reloaded and shouted at Solana to get out of the way—she had swooped down again to tear its one eye out. She flew away as he fired again, and this time the bullet struck it right between the eyes. The creature collapsed, its multiple legs twitching erratically as it died.

"Hells that thing was huge," Cypress commented as they stood there watching its death throes.

"I really hope there aren't more of those," Heath told them. "But there probably is because the girth of that thing was way too big to get through the cold spring."

The others looked at him in slight horror.

"Last thing I remember before waking up here was getting a drink," Cypress told him.

"Edwin and I were talking, then I felt a sting on my neck, and then I awoke in the cocoon," Alexander added.

Heath was about to say something when he heard another scuttling sound. They all looked up again but this time instead of one of those creatures, there were at least a dozen staring down at them now from the holes in the ceiling.

"Do you have enough bullets for them all?" Cypress asked Heath.

"NO," Heath scoffed. "Time to go! Solana!"

Heath led them to the way he came into the cavern as the creatures came down to the ground. They were closing in on the group when they reached the opening, and Heath took something out of his bag: it was one of Roslyn freeze bombs. He tossed it into the oncoming fray of creatures and then followed the others out into the tunnel. Next he took a different bomb, a gun powder one, and tossed it against the side of the opening as something hit him in the shoulder. It erupted as it hit the stone and caused what Heath hoped was a massive cave-in.

They stood there in the dust for a moment until Heath used his magic to move the dust along. He turned to look at Edwin when he started feeling woozy, and he could not feel his hands. He was about to say something when he collapsed and everything went dark.

Cypress rushed towards Heath, catching him as he fell. A small spike the size of his finger was sticking out of Heath's shoulder.

"Quick, pull it out!" Edwin advised him, and Cypress did. The end dripped with some kind of paralytic. Cypress wrapped it in cloth and put it in his bag as Alexander attempted to heal Heath.

"The paralytic needs to leave his system before it will let me heal him," Alexander said with a shake of his head. "I will bandage it up quickly and then we should get going." He turned to Solana who was pawing at Heath's other shoulder. "Solana, do you think you can lead us to Maeve and the others?"

Solana looked down at Heath and then back up at Alexander before she gave him what he accepted as a nod before he picked Heath up and put him over his shoulder like a sack of potatoes.

"All right Solana, lead the way."

Chapter Nineteen

The mages gathered in the wing of the palace that had been designated as theirs. Cassidy watched with amusement as she noted all of the new familiars that were there. Mage Stephanie's fox familiar was enjoying a good stomach scratch, its laughter filling up the room.

"I cannot say I am surprised anymore," Alara whispered to Cassidy. "I cannot wait to meet your sister, see what else she can do."

Cassidy smiled at her and called attention to the room.

"You have all done a wonderful job at getting the city's protections up," Cassidy told them. They had been busy the last couple of days putting the spells and crystals up around the city walls. Some of them had also helped evacuate the citizens that lived close to the city wall. They had received intelligence that told them that Count Gresham's forces were heading to the capitol. Anyone in range of a catapult was sent further into the city, and King Lucius had made plans to bring in enough supplies for the city in case of a minor siege. Alara had suggested they set up an underground passage out of the city in case they needed to take people out of the city or bring more food in. That was now on the agenda for the day.

"We have a long day ahead of us." Cassidy told the room. "We will be building a tunnel out of the city using our magic. We need a short path to a destination that will be undercover, in case we need to smuggle people out of the city and food in. King Lucius has decided that the best place to start inside the city is the Lightning Inn, and the other end will be a farmhouse just outside the city to the north."

Murmurs filled the room and Cassidy let them talk.

"I know this may seem extreme, but in the event of a siege we need to think about everything. We have mustered our forces, soldiers and mages, and we have higher odds than the enemy. We are still routing out spies within the city, so we need to plan for any event," Cassidy continued. "We will work together to get the tunnel made over several shifts the next couple of days."

The youth Astra was the first to speak, "We will do what is needed to protect our people."

The rest of the mages seemed to follow their lead and they all agreed. Cassidy smiled at Astra and nodded her thanks.

Astra had their hedgehog familiar in their hands, and it reminded Cassidy of just how much had changed in the last couple of weeks. She had gone through losing Mother Elle, and then the magic of Jay'Al showed up in Ellsgrove to bring the people together in what could be their most trying time with the coming civil war. Somehow Ellsgrove got lucky with having Roslyn as its Princess. Destiny, it seemed, had a funny way of doing things.

Cassidy separated the mages into different shifts and had dismissed them with the first shift heading to the Inn, when she spotted Roslyn out of the corner of her eye. She was a ghost-like form, Cassidy knew that it was Roslyn using her astral-projection. She waited for the room to empty and found just herself, Kai, and Alara, along with their familiars left.

"Hello!" Alara greeted Roslyn. "It is good to 'see' you under better circumstances, Roslyn."

Roslyn looked pained at that, and Alara took a step back.

"Please, Alara, may we have the room?" Roslyn asked her.

"Wh–what has happened?" Cassidy asked, understanding Roslyn's facial expression.

"It's McKenna," Roslyn told her as Alara left her and Kai in the room. "He had gone with Kavan and the magical creatures back to Bella Vale. They were attacked by dark elves and their dekellians."

"No," Cassidy whispered, and Kai took hold of her hand.

"McKenna was killed by the dark elves," Roslyn told her, and she could tell that her sister had been crying over it. "I'm so sorry."

"How is mother?" was all Cassidy could think to ask.

"She is strong, and she has her family. Our younger siblings feel it harder," Roslyn told her. "Kavan has gone back to evacuate Bella Vale and bring them to me."

"I see."

"The dark elves will pay for what they have done," Roslyn assured her.

"I know," Cassidy whispered. "Just as Count Gresham already has a noose around his neck."

Roslyn gave her a grim look but she nodded her understanding. "Kai," Roslyn called to Cassidy's partner. "Let her cry, and hold her close," Roslyn advised. "There is a lot to grieve."

Kai nodded solemnly and pulled Cassidy against his chest where she gave in to the tears.

Katie M. Thornton

***

King Lucius was in his study when an apparition of his eldest daughter appeared. If he had not seen her before in this form he would have been scared, but he smiled at her until he saw the serious look on her face.

"What is it, Roz?" he asked her, concerned.

She told him about McKenna, and how he had died. When he wanted to go to Cassidy, Roslyn assured him that Kai was there.

"She will need you in the morning," Roslyn told him.

"How is your family holding up?" Lucius asked her.

"Amelia is strong, and is handling it. My siblings–it hit them as hard as my other siblings."

"Do you have your friends to help you?"

"Everyone is a little scattered right now," Roslyn told him. "Kavan has gone to evacuate Bella Vale, and Heath is leading an expedition underground to try to find out what the Behemoths are. I have Tiffany though, and my Queen's Guard."

"Tiffany was always good for you," Lucius commented. "I am glad you found her."

Roslyn gave him a wry smile and then seemed to look off at something else that he could not see.

"I have to go, father," she told him. "I love you. Please let Edmond, Eliza, Poppy, and Robert know that I am thinking of them daily, and that I love them too."

"I will, darling, I will. I love you too."

He watched as her form faded away into nothing. He looked up at his guard that was standing in the doorway; they were to watch him at all times after the last assassination attempt. At least the soldier had known Roslyn and had met Cassidy, so seeing her astral form now was not a huge shock to him.

"I need to see my children," Lucius told them as he stood up. "Let's go."

***

Cassidy awoke the next morning with her eyes crusty from crying. Kai had stayed with her the whole night, holding her and letting her cry. It was worse now after losing Mother Elle, and seeing her siblings go through that loss. Now she could not be there for her other siblings during their father's death and she felt at a loss. She wanted to go back to Jay'Al but she knew that she was doing so much there in Ellsgrove. Now she knew how Roslyn had felt, and she was sad that they both had to go through the same thing.

She washed her face in the bathroom, the cold water helping to wake her faster. Crick jumped beside the bowl and rubbed against her face, some of the pine marten's hair sticking to her. With a wry smile, Cassidy washed her face again and then used a cloth to quickly dry herself. Crick watched her, and she knew that her familiar was there to offer her her strength. She felt a pit in her stomach just thinking about her step-father.

"Thank you," she told Crick as she reached out to pet her chin. Feeling more resolve, she squared her shoulders and went to get dressed. She left the room as Kai and Tej still slept.

Cassidy found Edmond and Alara in Edmond's study. They both stopped talking when she entered, and they stood together and went to her with their arms open, pulling her into a hug. She held back her tears and gave them a shaky smile when they pulled back.

"I'm okay," she told them. "I will be, anyways."

"Do you need anything from us?" Alara asked her as they went to sit back down. Alara offered her a biscuit. Cassidy shook her head as she took the biscuit, taking a seat.

"Not right now. Just your presence is enough. Now, is there any new word?"

Cassidy meant news about the Count and his forces that were coming towards the Capital.

"Count Gresham and his mercenaries come closer every day," Alara told her. "We have weeded out more spies from the city though, and the digging of the tunnel is going as planned. The mages are doing an exemplary job."

"I want to go see the tunnel," Cassidy told them. "I should be there."

"They all know what happened," Alara told her quietly. "They do not blame you for not being there right now."

"It will do me good to keep busy right now," Cassidy assured her.

"Very well," Edmond said, "Alara will take you after we eat breakfast. Where is Kai?"

"He was still asleep when I left our room," she replied.

"Go get him for breakfast then," Edmond told her.

***

Cassidy marveled at the work the mages had gotten done since the day before. They had worked in shifts, as planned, and they were nearly to the city wall already. It would not take much longer for them to get to the end destination outside of the city.

The mages, led by Headmistress Dake, stepped aside for Cassidy to view their work. Cassidy nodded at the group that was currently working, which consisted of Dake, Reed, Rhiannon, Astra, and Stephanie. Astra's hedgehog familiar, whom they had named Moonstone, peeked out at Cassidy from the front pocket of the youth's mage robe, making her smile. The hedgehog was white in colour, something that Cassidy thought was unusual in a hedgehog.

"How are you?" Headmistress Dake asked Cassidy as they walked back out of the tunnel together, with Alara and Kai just behind them. Sully and the Honour Guard had waited above ground in the inn for them.

"Good, considering," Cassidy told her truthfully. "Thank you for asking."

They reached the area that joined with the inn and went up the stairs, two guards opening the trap door for them after they knocked. Cassidy took in the mostly empty inn except for her Honour Guard, and noticed that Rafi had joined them.

"Hey," Rafi greeted her gently. "McKenna was a good man," Rafi told her, and since he was the only other one besides herself and Kai who even remotely knew her stepfather, it made her a little emotional. Rafi reached out to hug her when Cassidy heard a warning shout from a familiar voice: Nova, one of Alara's spies who was pretending to be a serving wench in the inn, moved to leap in front of Cassidy.

For Cassidy the adrenaline seemed to make time slow down. She saw the dart heading towards her, and knew that Nova would be too late. Then she felt someone push her aside and she saw Rafi in front of her, his eyes filled with pain as his body shook with the impact of the dart.

"Rafi!" Cassidy cried out at the same time that Nova threw her own dart at the assassin who was dressed as a porter; Nova found her mark and the woman went down quickly.

Cassidy moved to Rafi's side, horrified to see the amount of blood pouring out of him. She looked up at Alara and Nova as she tried to use her magic to heal him, but was unsuccessful.

"Something is not right," Cassidy told them, "I cannot heal him."

Nova took the dart out of Rafi's side and sniffed it. "Poison. This one gets in the way of magic healing."

"Do you know its counter?" Cassidy demanded of the spy.

"Yes!" Nova told her as she took something out of her pocket. "Rafi, chew this, quickly!" Nova put the item in Rafi's mouth and she could tell that he did not like the taste.

"I know it tastes horrible, but it will save your life!" Nova told him.

Cassidy watched in a panic as he chewed the herb that Nova had given him. She looked at Nova who nodded and Cassidy applied her healing magic once more, this time finding no resistance.

Chapter Twenty

Kavan sighed in relief when he and the other werewolves reached Bella Vale with no hostility from the dark elves or their dekellians. It was even more of a relief when Grigori told him that everyone was ready to go with him.

"Terren is fierce," Grigori told him. "He has held on. Louran has been a voice to the other creatures, telling them that they will be safer with Roslyn. They are ready to go. Tell us what we need to do."

"Everyone needs to get in the wagons," Kavan told everyone gathered by the gates. "Roslyn has enchanted them to keep everyone safe. Once everyone is loaded in, we will get going."

"What about us?" Malvin the centaur asked.

"Roslyn told me that once you are within the field of the enchantments you will be able to run as fast as me," Kavan told him. "We should reach Roslyn in a matter of hours with her enchantments."

"Then what are we waiting for?!" Malvin asked him, motioning for his fellow centaurs to gather close. Kavan could

hear him explain to the other centaurs what they needed to do and went to go talk to the dwarves and redcaps. Kavan looked at the handful of other werewolves that Roslyn had sent with him; they had been the ones who had chosen the amulet to keep their shifting at bay instead of the cure so they could fight for Roslyn. There were only five of them, all men who were as old as Edwin and Alexander. They all had their red hair cut short to varying degrees, and several of them had facial scars that must have occurred before they were turned.

"I believe everyone is ready," Grigori told him from the front of the wagon he was driving.

Kavan raised his hand and waited for them to notice and quiet down. Malvin nodded his understanding and directed the rest of the centaurs closer to the wagons.

"Move out!" Kavan shouted, and together the wagons got rolling forward and the horses, spurred on by the magical enchantments that Roslyn had made, moved as fast as Kavan did when he used his werewolf strength.

To Kavan's surprise the dark elves still did not show themselves as their company ran through the forest towards the plateau. It made him feel uneasy; where were the dark elves now?

***

They reached the plateau without any issues to find that the orcs and humans had worked very hard to get the beginnings of the outer wall started with stones from a nearby quarry. Aidan met them at what Kavan assumed would be the front gates and directed them to some large tents that had been put up for the magical creatures.

"There are bathing tubs as well–with running water! Also, our seamstresses are prepared to make you new clothing," Aidan told the redcaps and dwarves as they hopped out of the wagons and gathered around him. "There will be fresh bread and stew for you as well after you are settled in."

Darton made a sound that Kavan thought was almost a groan–did redcaps prefer to be dirty? But then the redcap led the others towards where Aidan was pointing. The centaurs waited patiently to be directed to where they were to go.

"I was unsure what a centaur would need," Aidan confessed to Kavan and Malvin. "If you wish to clean yourselves we put together some shower units. The largest tents we set up are for you."

"Our thanks, Aidan," Malvin told him. "We do eat meat still, mostly fish and chicken though."

"The stew has alpaca meat in it," Aidan told him. "And lamb."

"That is acceptable," Malvin responded with a smile. "Again, my thanks."

Kavan and Aidan watched the group of centaurs head to the larger tents, seeing a few of them break off to check out the shower stalls nearby.

"You got all of this done in the few hours I was gone?" Kavan asked him, impressed.

"The things you can get done with some good help," Aidan explained, motioning to Karina's family who were in charge of the stew. Since the dining hall had been damaged by the werewolves they had moved the cooking stoves outside under a large awning and had several large pots over the coals. "Lou and Dacey helped me rig up the showers, and their boys got the orcs to set all of the tents up. Cypress' siblings got in on it as well."

"It's nice to see everyone working together," Kavan commented. "You have made a lot of progress with other things as well." Kavan indicated the rough beginnings of the city wall.

"Roslyn wanted to get that done first," Aidan explained. "A lot of the orcs will have farms to tend outside of the wall, but for now it will be safer for them to have homes inside the city walls. I am sure sometime in the near future they will have homesteads out there, and a few inns."

Kavan thought about the inn that his mother had run when he was young, before he was orphaned. He could not remember what the inn had been called. That was going to bother him.

"It would be nice to retire, and run an inn," Kavan commented as they started walking down the marked off main street that led to the opening up to the plateau. As they had talked, someone had come and taken the horses and wagons away, and Grigori and the other farmers had taken their animals away as well. Terren and Louran and rejoined with their tribe.

"Where is Roslyn? Above?" Kavan asked Aidan.

"Uh, sort of," Aidan responded. "Probably below, by now."

"Excuse me?" Kavan stopped in his tracks to glare at Aidan. "You don't mean to tell me that she went back underground to those passages, do you?"

Aidan made a face that told Kavan that that was exactly what he meant and he should have known better than to think that Roslyn's curiosity would not take her back down there.

"Her Queen's Guard are with her," Aidan assured him as he started walking again, this time at a quicker pace.

"I still do not like that," Kavan told him. "If anything were to happen to her…"

"You'll what?" Aidan asked him. "You chose to stay a werewolf rather than be with her, Kavan. You don't get to be this overly protective of her."

Kavan stopped walking and whipped his head back around to glare at Aidan, who did not back down at his feral gaze.

"She knows, too," Aidan continued. He stood there, his feet grounded and his shoulders squared as Kavan continued to glare. Aidan, the quiet quartermaster, telling Kavan off? He was impressed again.

Kavan's shoulders slumped as he heard Aidan's words. He dropped his glare, looking at the ground.

"It does not mean I still do not love her," Kavan told him. "Did you hear about the East Garrison, Aidan?"

Aidan thought for a moment before nodding.

"I was one of the few survivors," Kavan explained. "There was nothing I could do to save my friends that day. Now though, with these powers? I can be of some use in this war to come, to *help* Roslyn, to keep her *safe*."

"What about after the war?" Aidan wanted to know. "When everything is settled? You would watch her be with Heath?"

Kavan looked away from his friend, but he could not help but smile. "What, you think I would be better for her?"

"I just did not think you would give up so easily," Aidan told him. "I was disappointed. I understand, but still."

"I keep my powers so I can protect her, because I love her," Kavan told him. "Now, I am going to go find her and make sure she has not gotten herself into trouble."

"Then why did you leave in the first place, with the centaurs?" Aidan wanted to know.

"To give her and Heath some time alone, so she would pick him."

Aidan shook his head. "Wow, okay then. I'm going to go talk with the orcs, you do what you have to do."

Kavan watched him go, slightly amused and slightly disturbed at the same time. If Aidan thought that of him, just what did Roslyn think?

He looked at the tunnel and shrugged before running towards it and up to the top of the plateau.

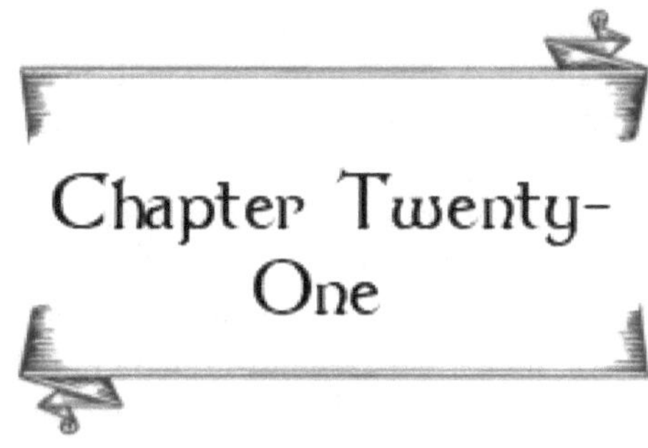

Chapter Twenty-One

Roslyn watched Leaf sniff around the cave that had the remains of the aerie in it. Tiffany was wandering around the other side of the cavern, with the rest of her Queen's Guard spanned out between her and the door to the corridor they had come down.

"Roslyn!" Tiffany called out, waving her over. "There's a door back here!"

Roslyn made her way around the pillars towards Tiffany, wondering why she had not noticed the stone door the first time she was down there; though admittedly they had not really looked around much after she had climbed up to one of the nests. It did not take much effort for the two of them to push it open to reveal another corridor that was decorated with images of gryphons and other magical creatures painted along it. Special runes painted on the walls glowed with a magic light to illuminate the corridor.

"Well, let's see where this goes," Roslyn said as she stepped through the door into the corridor, Tiffany following behind her. The lady knights followed, and Leaf sniffed along as they went. The corridor seemed to lead them downhill for quite a ways until finally they found the end of the corridor. There was a wooden door inlaid with silver, with what looked like a design of feathered wings on it. On each side of the door were two oil lamps that were unlit. Roslyn noted that the oil had long since dried up.

Roslyn reached to pull on the latch for the door but Tiffany stopped her.

"Let me," Tiffany told her. "Just to be safe."

Roslyn sighed and said, "Fine."

Tiffany opened the door and stepped into the room beyond, gasping at the sight she found. Roslyn followed her through, her eyes widening at what she saw. Before them was a large underground cavern with a giant crystal in its roof, much like the one where they had found themselves after going down the whirlpool months before. Instead of large mushrooms, however, there was a forest of trees before them. A small group of giant birds flew above the forest, and there were what looked like smaller birds flitting about the boughs of the branches of the closest trees.

Roslyn squinted up at the giant birds for a moment. "Those are gryphons!" she exclaimed with excitement to her companions.

The lady knights surrounded her as several gryphons broke off from their aerial acrobatics to come investigate the newcomers to their home.

Leaf leapt into the air and flew to the gryphons, making a crooning noise as she did. Roslyn watched in amazement as the gryphons greeted the dragonling with chirps, all the while hearing Leaf assuring her that she was safe.

"It's okay," Roslyn told her guard. "Leaf says it is safe."

One of the larger gryphons broke away from Leaf to glide towards Roslyn. She motioned for her guard to stand back and give it room, smiling at the size of it while thinking that Solana would one day get that big.

"Hello there, you beauty," Roslyn greeted the gryphon, noting its light fawn coloured fur and matching feathers.

Roslyn felt a presence touch her mind, one not unlike Leaf's.

"*The dragon says you are Queen Roslyn of Jay'Al, and that she is your familiar,*" the gryphon spoke with its mind to Roslyn. From the reaction of her companions she could tell that they heard the gryphon in their minds as well. "*I am the leader of these gryphons, you may call me Hawk.*"

"I am very pleased to meet you," Roslyn told Hawk. "Would you like to soar in the skies above ground?"

The gryphon seemed to bristle with excitement, its tail swishing back and forth. "*We have waited centuries to be able to do so again!*" Hawk told her. "*Bring us to the surface, and we will owe you a great debt.*"

"What else is down here?" Roslyn asked Hawk, looking past her wings to what she had thought had been birds flitting about the trees. Somehow, though, now that she was looking directly at them, she realized that they were *not,* in fact, birds.

"*Pixies,*" Hawk told her. "*They are magical beings who can create small spells and enchantments. They look like tiny humans with wings, and pointed ears.*"

Roslyn walked towards the trees, Hawk going with her. As she got closer, a small group of pixies noticed her and one of them broke off to greet them. The pixie did indeed look like a small human, about the length of Roslyn's hand, with luminescent wings that sparkled. Magic surrounded the pixie like a shimmering light. Roslyn held out her hand to the pixie, who looked to be female and was wearing their stark white hair in a braid. The pixie wore a dress that seemed to be woven from spider silk.

A Descent into the Roots

"'Ello there!" The pixie's voice was high pitched and tiny, which was just what Roslyn expected. She had to stifle a laugh, though she did hear one of her companions let out a giggle. "Where di' ye come from?"

"The surface," Roslyn told her, trying not to speak too loud.

"The surface?!" the pixie squealed, very excited. The pixie shot up into the air and went to its fellows, coming back with the whole hoard of them to fly around Roslyn. The first pixie returned to Roslyn's hand, who was looking really amused at the sounds of excitement coming from the dozens of pixies that were flying around her.

"Ar' ye taking the gryphons t' the surface?" the pixie asked her. "Will ye take us too?"

"What is your name?" Roslyn asked the pixie.

"Chiye," the pixie told her.

"I am Queen Roslyn, of Jay'Al," she told Chiye. "I would be very happy to bring you to the surface with us."

"*Queen* Roslyn, eh?" The pixie looked surprised. "What ar' ye doin' down 'ere, your majesty?"

Roslyn smiled at the pixie and replied, "Getting my hands dirty, like always. I don't quite have a throne yet, I'm newly crowned and my capital city is still under construction, so I might as well go on a few outings, hm? We found some tunnels after an earthquake, which led us here."

"Ah, yes, we felt the groun' shake too," Chiye told her.

Roslyn was distracted at that moment by the sound of a gryphon shriek somewhere in the forest.

"*Not again,*" she heard Hawk say in her mind.

"What is it?" Roslyn looked at the gryphon for an explanation.

"*Ever since that last earthquake we have had these giant centipede type creatures encroaching on our cavern,*" Hawk told her. "*Not that I am complaining, they have tasty flesh compared to the fish in our underground lake. They are relatively easy to kill if you have a few gryphons on hand.*"

"Show me?" Roslyn asked Hawk, and the gryphon dipped its head and took flight, leading her into the forest. From that angle, Roslyn could tell that Hawk was a female gryphon.

"Spread the word," Roslyn told Chiye, "to the rest of your brethren: you are going to the surface! Meet back here?"

Chiye nodded her head and took off again, this time disappearing into the forest with the others who had been flying around them.

"How did you come to be down here?" Roslyn asked Hawk as she ran to catch up. Her guard followed after her.

"*I was born here,*" Hawk told her. "*My parents told me that the path above had been blocked and we were stuck down here. This is a large cavern,*" *and we figured out another passage that led to another one of equal size some time ago. We have not bred much though, so as not to over-populate."*

Roslyn reached out to the trees with her magic, feeling them calling back to her. Something moved out of one of the trees and Roslyn turned in surprise to see what she could only assume was a dryad, a forest spirit. Cassidy had described them to her before but she had not seen one yet. It was a magical being that was barely perceptible but for the shape of it: it was made up of what Roslyn could only think of as some kind of pollen that made its shape and features, almost like a ghost.

Roslyn hurried after Hawk and found herself stopping short as she saw the carcass of a giant centipede type creature lying there next to a hole in the ground that it had obviously come from. A couple other gryphons were picking away at it.

"Well then," Roslyn said as she took in the creature. "I guess we should block them from being able to get up here so the surface is safe."

As she stepped towards the hole the ground began to rumble and another large centipede creature emerged, rearing its front at them. Roslyn drew her frishna sword and swiftly cut its head off, splattering the ground and the nearby gryphons with the creature's blood.

"I think now would be as good a time as any to get it closed up," Hawk told her. Did the gryphon almost sound amused? Roslyn thought to herself as she cleaned off her sword before sheathing it. She turned to find her lady knights looking at her with both amusement and slight horror on their faces.

"You'll find a lot of different things here in Jay'Al," Roslyn told them. "You have already seen dekellians and dark elves, what's a giant centipede?"

"Did you say dark elves?" Hawk asked her. Roslyn nodded. *"They have found their way up to the surface?"*

"Yes. You know the dark elves?"

"Some time ago some dark elves came in and took some of our eggs, and captured a few of my brethren," Hawk told her. *"I only knew of them from what my parents had told me."*

"We have been fighting them, scrimmages mostly, nothing serious yet but it is only a matter of time," Roslyn told Hawk. "My friend Heath found a gryphon egg that had been in the possession of the dark elves, and it hatched for him and became his familiar."

"Truly?" Hawk asked her. *"It will be interesting to meet them."*

Roslyn used her magic to fill in the tunnel, solidifying the earth into something that could not be dug through. As she finished, what she had just done gave her an idea.

"Well, time to go I guess?" Roslyn said to her companions and the gryphons. Hawk nodded her head and took flight, calling out to the gryphons as a bird would. Within moments there were nearly fifty gryphons of varying sizes and colours flying alongside Hawk. They reached the spot where the stone door was, only to find Kavan coming through the door.

"Here you are," Kavan said to her as he took her and the gryphons in. "Oh wow! More gryphons!"

"What are you doing down here?" Roslyn asked him. "When did you get back?"

"Not too long ago, and just making sure you are safe," Kavan responded. "The dark elves did not even bother us one bit," Kavan added before Roslyn could ask.

"That is odd," Roslyn commented, "seeing as how much trouble they have been lately. I hope they aren't up to something."

"That was my worry, and then when I found out you were down here…"

"You were worried about me," Roslyn commented, and she could not help but smile warmly at him. "I appreciate that, Kavan."

It confused her too, though.

"What are the–oh!" Kavan stopped talking as Chiye flew up to stop right in front of his face. "Hello there. What are you?"

"I'm a pixie!" Chiye told him in her high pitched voice. "What are ye? Ye don't smell like a human."

Kavan winced slightly before answering, "I'm technically a werewolf. My name is Kavan, and I serve Queen Roslyn."

"She has werewolves on her side?" Chiye asked, looking at Roslyn. "I suppose I know whose good side I be stayin' on."

Roslyn laughed at that before saying, "Just get along with
the people and you should be fine, though I would stay in Jay'Al until the rest of the world knows you are out and about again. Sometimes people can be ignorant of new things."

"We shall stay with ye," Chiye told her.

"Well, Kavan, we are heading up to the surface, all of us. Care to lead the way?" Roslyn asked Kavan, and he smiled and turned towards the door, making sure it was opened all the way so the gryphons could fit through. Hawk, who was the biggest, had to duck a little bit, but otherwise the rest of them went through with ease.

"To the surface!" Roslyn exclaimed, motioning for Kavan to keep going. He smiled at her and turned to lead the way back up the corridor and the path that Roslyn had made to get down there, the gryphons and pixies following behind.

***

Above ground the gryphons took to the air, flying in large circles over the top of the plateau. The pixies took to the trees, scaring off the birds who had never seen them before. Roslyn realized that there must be a couple hundred pixies or more, and was slightly worried what the pixies would make of the surface. Roslyn could hear the orcs and humans who were working on the foundation of the palace exclaim in surprise and wonder at the gryphons that flew overhead. Many of them had seen Solana before Heath had left on his mission, but to see a fully grown gryphon was another sight in itself.

"Roslyn!" She turned to find Oswick and the stonemason Judd coming towards them, both of them looking up at the gryphons. She started walking towards them, meeting them half-way.

"I see you actually found something this time," Oswick mused as they watched the gryphons. "This just keeps getting more interesting by the day!"

"My question," Judd spoke up, "Is 'What will they eat?'"

"They eat fish," Roslyn told him, "Just like Solana. Giant bugs. We will have to talk to them about what livestock are out of bounds, I suppose."

"That's all of them?" Oswick asked her. She nodded. "So they don't breed that much?"

"Actually, Hawk, their leader, said they made sure not to over breed so they would not get crowded down there. Now that they are above ground, they will most likely find roosts and have more young," Roslyn explained. "I might be able to make them a nice aerie somewhere with an abundance of good food for them, actually."

"It will be interesting seeing so many gryphons flying about," Judd commented. "Come on, Oz, enough gawking. Let's get back to work."

Roslyn smiled knowingly at her friend who gave her a sheepish smile before following the stonemason back to their project.

"I have something I want to try," Roslyn told Kavan and Tiffany, who were standing just behind her. "Down below, with the city walls."

"Oh? What is it this time?" Tiffany asked her, raising an eyebrow.

"You shall see," Roslyn teased, and she headed for the horses. As she mounted Sage she reached down with her magic and enclosed the tunnels below again, turning the earth into solid matter.

Once below the plateau on the ground, Roslyn approached the beginnings of the city wall. She had the idea from when she closed up the bug-creatures path, and it would save them a lot of time. Leaf sat next to her, one paw touching her leg so she could channel her magic through her familiar, and from the land better.

"Get everyone to stand back," Roslyn told Aidan, who was supervising the construction of the wall. Aidan sent word out and then went to stand next to Roslyn. Together they watched as the builders backed away from the wall. Roslyn's guard stood just behind her, and Kavan leaned against a nearby tree to watch.

Roslyn reached out with her magic, feeling the stones that had already been prepared for the city wall. She sent her magic below and out, calling up earth and stones and shaping them into her vision of what the city wall would look like

Tiffany stiffened as she watched the ground beyond the city limits move like tremors on the water, and then the ground moved upwards at the wall. Earth and stone seemed almost liquid-like as it moved up to form a city wall that was at least a hundred feet in height. Once it solidified she could see that there were staircases at certain intervals, and what looked like a walkway at the top of the wall along with crenellations on the outside part of the wall. There were several openings where gates would go.

Kavan's mouth hung open as he turned around, seeing the wall form along the entire marked out section along the entirety of what would be Dragon City, all the way to the plateau on both sides. He imagined that it looked like a giant 'C' from atop the plateau. He turned back to Roslyn in time to see her sway, and he rushed to catch her as she nearly fainted.

"Thank you," Roslyn said quietly, slightly out of breath. "I think I need to have a nap now."

Roslyn checked her nose and was grateful that it was not bleeding. She looked at Leaf who seemed to be smiling up at her.

"See what you can do when you use your familiar correctly," she heard Leaf say in her mind.

"I will take you up to your bed," Kavan told her, and Tiffany nodded to him. He lifted Roslyn up into his arms, she putting her arms around his neck. He held her close to his chest as he swiftly ran her up to her tent atop the plateau. Kavan placed her gently onto her bed, covering her with her blanket. She fell asleep instantly.

Leaf had flown up the plateau alongside them, and she curled up next to Roslyn's bed.

"That was amazing," Kavan commented to Leaf. "Did you know she could do that?"

Leaf nodded her head and seemed to smile at him.

"I will stand watch outside," Kavan told Leaf, "until her Queen's Guard get up here."

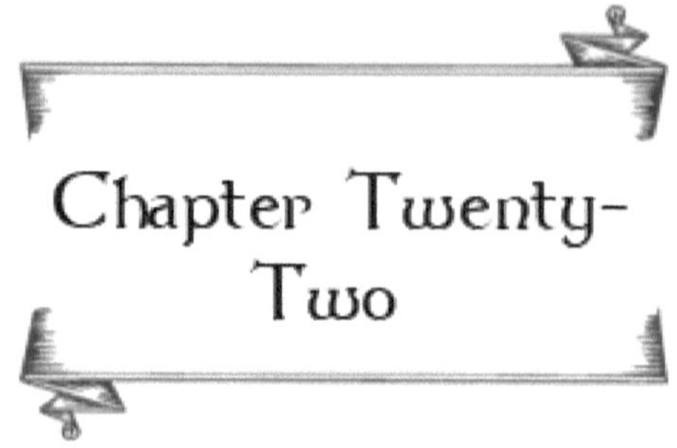

Chapter Twenty-Two

Heath woke up laying on his stomach. He tried to turn over but hands kept him down. His mind was a little fuzzy, but the last thing he remembered was running from giant centipede creatures, and blowing them up.

"Gods can you just stay still," he heard Karina's voice, and he turned his head to look up at her.

They were in a small cave somewhere underground, and Maeve was looking down at him with worry.

"About time you woke up," she told him.

Something nuzzled his left hand and he looked down to find Solana, who he could tell from their link was equally as worried as Maeve.

"How long?" he asked as he realized he was not wearing a shirt. He glanced back at the wound in his shoulder and turned away again.

"A couple of days," Karina answered. "I have been leeching the poison out of your blood so I can heal you. I did the same with Edwin and Alexander already, though since they are werewolves their bodies had already started breaking down the poison…somehow you got a slightly bigger dose than they did."

"If I knew how to heal," Maeve commented, "I would have been able to help."

"Well *sorry* we haven't had the time for me to teach you," Heath retorted. "We've been a little busy with other things."

"Not the time," Karina chided them. Mister Scruffy chirped at them, and Solana made a couple chirping noises back at the feline familiar. "We have been lucky with the enchantments, and that those creatures were either killed or blocked off from coming after you. We still have a mission, remember?"

"Where is my shirt?" Heath asked, shivering slightly.

"I will grab one from your bag as soon as Karina is done," Maeve told him. "We need you in top form. I don't want to be the one telling Roslyn that you died of an infected wound."

Heath had to laugh at that, and he winced as it made the wound hurt.

"For the love of the ancestors, stop moving!" Karina told him again. "Please!"

"All right, all right!" Heath laid back down on his stomach and let Karina finish what she was doing. Finally she told him he could sit up and Maeve handed him one of the tunics from his bag.

Cypress handed him some smoked sausages and cheese to eat, and Alexander gave him water.

"Anything happen while I was out?" Heath asked his companions.

"Not a thing, surprisingly," Edwin responded. "We have seen no more creatures, nor been pursued by anything."

"I do not know what to make of that," Heath commented as he ate. "Did you move any further into the tunnels while I was out?"

"Slightly," Maeve told him. "We had you on a stretcher for a day while Karina worked on Cypress. Edwin and Alexander just needed some blood–which they got from some fish in the water–and they were perfectly fine."

"All right, so we have not come any closer yet to these Behemoths," he said to no one in particular. "For all we know, around the next corner we will find what we are looking for."

"I hate you," Maeve told him as she rolled her eyes. "You just jinxed us!"

"I did not!" he retorted. "If I had jinxed us I would have said 'Well we'll go a little further and we won't find anything at all'!"

Maeve gave Karina a look and the part-orc could not help but laugh at it, making Maeve laugh as well.

"What?!" Heath asked them. "What did I say that was *so* funny?"

That only made them laugh harder, and finally Heath turned to Edwin, Alexander, and Cypress, all of whom looked equally perplexed.

"Some help you are," Heath muttered as he finished eating. "We will get going as soon as I am done, all right?"

Maeve and Karina stopped laughing long enough to nod in acknowledgment before going to sort out their things.

Edwin and Alexander exchanged pitying looks with him, but Cypress seemed almost amused.

"The werewolves have a higher immune system," Cypress reminded Heath. "You and I are just normal beings."

"Don't tell Solana that," Heath told him with a wink as he petted his gryphon familiar.

Cypress chuckled and held up his hand as if surrendering before going to get his own things gathered up.

They travelled further underground for several more days, with no more signs of the giant centipede creatures or of any other magical creature what-so-ever. Edwin and Alexander still mapped out where they went.

"Are we sure these behemoths are still underground?" Karina whispered to Heath.

"I think that if any such creatures made their way above ground, Roslyn would have found a way to tell us," he answered. "Or we would have felt an earthquake of some sort."

"And neither of those things have occurred," Karina said with resignation.

"So deeper down we go," Heath replied with a sigh. "I know, I don't like it either. Neither does Solana. But this is part of our mission." He had to keep reminding himself of that; they were on a mission, sent by Roslyn, one of the most important people in the world to him. He did not want to let her down, and it was actually an important mission: the behemoths were a threat to eve-ryone above ground and they had to be dealt with.

They came across underground rivers that had fish in them, which they caught and ate. More giant caverns with crystals in the ceiling that mimicked the sun, but there was nothing more than normal sized bugs left living there. Was it where the centaurs, redcaps, and dwarves used to live though? Maybe. They found some traces of occupancy in the caverns but nothing more.

Finally after several more days they entered an enormous cavern that was shaped like a bowl, with giant mushrooms and trees growing in it. The crystal in the ceiling of the cavern gave off a warm light, just like the others they had come across. Heath and his companions stood in the opening they had come through, looking down at the cavern before them.

Where they stood was like the lip of the bowl, and they could barely see the other side.

"This is the biggest one yet," Heath commented quietly. "Anything could be down there and we would not know it."

"There," Edwin said quietly, pointing down towards a grouping of rocks. "I saw something big move."

Heath squinted, and Alexander stepped forward to take a better look.

"I see it too," Alexander whispered. "It's big, whatever it is."

"How about you and I get a closer look?" Edwin asked Alexander, looking at Heath for permission.

"Just be careful," Heath told them. The two werewolves nodded and using their supernatural speed they made their way down amongst the forest of trees and mushrooms. They looked like a blur to Heath.

Solana rubbed up against Heath's leg, telling him, *"Something feels off."*

"You sense something?" Heath asked her, looking down at the gryphon.

Solana nodded without saying anything more, and moved to sharpen her nails on a nearby tree.

A Descent into the Roots

Mister Scruffy joined Solana in sharpening nails, and Luma flitted up to land on a branch above the two familiars. The pygmy owl started looking for bugs to eat. Maeve and Karina both moved to sit on two stocky looking short mushrooms, and Cypress leaned against another tree. Heath stayed where he was, watching for any more movement below.

They did not have long to wait before Alexander and Edwin returned.

"How did Roslyn describe the behemoths again?" Edwin asked Heath.

"The dark elf described it like a dinosaur type creature," Heath told him.

"So a giant lizard-type creature then?" Edwin asked. "I've never seen a dinosaur."

"Yes."

"I think we found them then," Edwin told him. "That definitely describes the creatures down there. But they are not alone, there's something that I would describe as a mix between a lizard and a dark elf but bigger? It's like the behemoths are their creatures."

"Oh great," Heath muttered. "This just gets better and better."

"The dark elf never mentioned anything about them, I take it?" Edwin inquired, earning a head shake from Heath.

"It's entirely possible that the dark elves have no idea that someone is behind the behemoth's movements," Heath contemplated aloud. "Whatever those things are, they used the behemoths to push the dark elves and all of the other magical creatures above ground, but to what end? And why have they not come to the surface yet?"

"And why did the dark elves say they were after the magic of the land?" Edwin continued Heath's train of thought. "You were worried they were after Roslyn, which the dark elves certainly are interested in her magic, but whatever is controlling the behemoths? What do *they* want?"

"Can we risk revealing ourselves and just ask them?" Karina spoke up.

"We should watch them first," Heath told his companions. "See what we can find out."

"They were heading this way," Edwin told him. "They seemed to have come from the other side of the cavern where there was a giant hole. We found abandoned houses, too, so I think we found where most of the magical creatures lived."

"All right, let's find someplace to watch them from," Heath told them. "How big were the behemoths? Were they trampling down trees or anything?"

Edwin and Alexander both shook their heads.

"Okay then, I'm going to climb a tree," Heath commented before he headed into the forest. The others followed him and they each chose a tree to climb. Each of them found a sturdy branch part way up that had a good amount of leaves to partially hide them. Each of the familiars stayed close to their mage.

Heath grimaced at the sap stuck to his hand as he tried to get in a better position. Of course the tree he picked had to be a pine; it was his own doing. He sighed and tried his best to wipe the sap off, to no avail.

Finally after what seemed like hours, Maeve signalled to Heath that the behemoths and their masters were coming that way.

Heath watched as the large lizard-like creatures moved through the forest towards them; the biggest one was almost as long as a whale, and its eyes were set at the front of its skull. Their legs held them up off the ground by several feet, and their heads brushed against the branches of the trees. Heath could see their sharp teeth, and the claws looked equally as sharp.

Walking between the creatures were the beings that Edwin spoke of. They walked on two legs, and had two arms, but they looked lizard-like themselves with a snout on their face. Their ears were pointed, and their skin looked scaly. Their eyes were lizard-like and yellow. They wore rough spun clothing and some kind of armour.

There were eight of these beings with the five behemoths, and they headed out of the cavern the way that Heath and his companions had entered it.

Heath climbed down the pine tree after waiting a few minutes to make sure there were no others lagging behind. His companions joined him on the ground as well.

"I think those were kobolds," Heath told Edwin. "Do you remember them?"

"I think the description fits, though they were well before my time," Edwin replied.

"I've only read about them in storybooks," Maeve commented. "Are you sure they were kobolds?"

"What else could they be? It's like there's creatures just magically popping up out of the ground these days," Heath told her, half muttering.

"That cannot be all of them though, right?" Edwin piped up. "The behemoths not only drove the dark elves above ground but all of the other magical creatures fled as well."

"He had to say it," Maeve whispered, putting her palm to her forehead.

"Even if he had not, I'm sure this was just a forward party," Heath told her. "The dark elves came from further underground, pushing everything out ahead of the behemoths."

Heath looked to Edwin and Alexander and told them, "Would you please go check that hole in the ground you saw? I'm betting there is an army on the other side."

Maeve shook her head, and Luma settled on her shoulder to preen her hair as Edwin and Alexander took off again.

A Descent into the Roots

"If there is an army behind us, we are stuck between their forward party and them," Maeve told Heath.

"Oh I know," Heath told her. "We are going to have to be very careful getting back up to the surface again."

"Very careful," Maeve scoffed. "Are you kidding me right now?"

"We have a map, they do not," Heath explained. He held up the map that Edwin and Alexander had made. "We know there is a small tunnel that goes around this cavern here," he pointed to an area that was two caverns up from where they currently were. "We can get around them here; and maybe snag a prisoner to bring back with us."

Edwin and Alexander returned at that moment, and they both nodded to Heath but it was Alexander who spoke: "You were right. There is an army on the other side of that hole. At least five hundred more kobolds and a few dozen more behemoths."

"Time to go," Heath told them, heading towards the tunnel they had come from. "We should stay as close to the forward party as we can without being seen."

"I assume you have a plan," Edwin commented dryly, and Heath pointed to the tunnel on the map. "I suppose that will work."

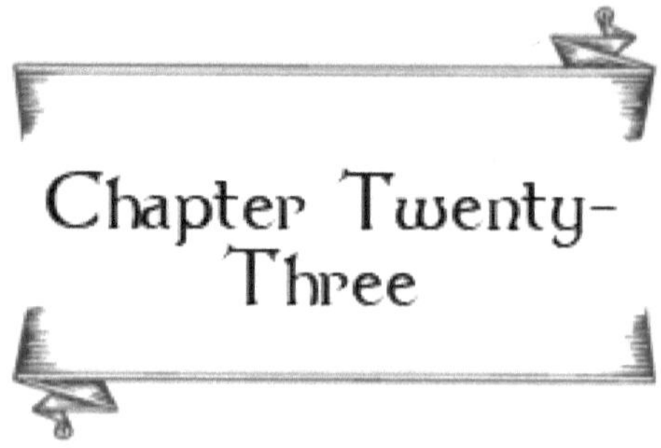

Chapter Twenty-Three

"You wanted to see me?" Cassidy asked King Lucius from the doorway of his study. Two soldiers stood on either side of him and there were two more at the door.

King Lucius looked up at her, weariness showing in his demeanor. "How is Rafi doing?" he asked her after a moment.

"He has been stuck to his bed for the last few days because he is still weak," Cassidy told him. "He is lucky to be alive."

"Yes, indeed. If Alara's spy had not known the counter for the poison used he would not be with us. It is troubling that they should target you with such a weapon," Lucius told her. "I am worried about you."

Cassidy smiled warmly at her father. "Alara was able to capture an assassin just after the incident and interrogated him. She believes they have found the rest of the spies and assassins in the city."

"I hope so, but I plan on sending Eliza, Poppy, and Robert back to Wardgrove for their safety," Lucius informed her. "I was hoping you and your Guard would see them there safely."

"But the mercenaries are on their way here," Cassidy argued. "I can't leave now."

"You have done a lot to make sure the city is protected, Cassidy. Our soldiers stand at the ready, and the people have been moved to safer locations. However, I need my youngest children someplace safer if there is to be a siege, and I want you to see them there. There are people I trust up north to protect them once you get them there, and you can come right back."

"All right, I will do this for you, father," Cassidy told him. He breathed a sigh of relief.

"Thank you. I want you to leave this afternoon, please."

A Descent into the Roots

"I will go tell my Guard and we will be ready by just after lunch," Cassidy assured him.

He nodded and watched her leave before glancing down at the stain that had been left from when his butler had been killed by an assassin. He did not want to chance that happening again with his children there. Those words his daughter Eliza had said after she had killed the assassin haunted him: *When will this end, papa? When will we be safe?*

He remembered seeing Roland's body on the floor, his life blood draining from the cut on his throat. He shivered, thinking about how Roland had been one of his closest friends and advisors since he was Roslyn's age. Another casualty of the damned insurrectionists who had killed his wife and kept threatening the rest of his family.

Lucius knew that Roslyn had placed enchantments all over Wardgrove to keep her family safe, and he had his local knights that he knew were loyal to him and his family. Eliza, Poppy, and Robert would be safe up there and we would not worry as much for their safety.

Edmond came into his father's study just then, seeing him eyeing the stain on the floor.

"Father?" He called his father's attention to him.

"Edmond, how are you this morning?" Lucius asked his oldest son, shaking off the feeling he had.

"I'm doing okay," Edmond responded. "You asked to see me?"

"I'm having Cassidy escort your brother and sisters back to Wardgrove, they are leaving this afternoon," he told Edmond. "They will be safer up there until all of this is over."

"I think that is a good decision, father," Edmond told him. "Did you need anything else? Alara and I were going to a meeting with the Quartermaster about the wedding."

"Also, unless you have a sizable guard, I would prefer you all stay inside the palace for the time being," Lucius told him. "I know Alara says they rooted out all the assassins and spies, but I just want to be careful."

"Of course, father. We will let you know if we need to go out into the city, and of course we will take a large guard with us," Edmond assured him.

"Go see the Quartermaster," Lucius told him, waving him off with a smile. Edmond grinned at him and left, his personal guard who had been waiting outside of the study following after him.

***

Cassidy and Kai met with Sully and their part of the Honour Guard in the stables just after the city clock struck noon. They had prepared everything beforehand for their departure, and their horses were saddled and waiting. They found Eliza, Poppy and Robert there with Lucius. The two princesses and the prince were all wearing peasant clothing, and the two girls had even gone as far as putting some straw into their hair to help with the disguise. Robert's hair was a mess and he had a streak of dirt across his cheek.

"You'll go in a merchant wagon," Lucius informed them. "And you will act as the guard." He waved towards a large wagon at the back of the stables that had a thick canvas, and a team of four horses. "You will leave through the Supply Gate, and then out of the city through the Merchant's Gate. Sully can lead you north to Wardgrove. Once you are sure no one is following you, leave the wagon at any farm you can and just take them and ride as fast as you can."

"I will send a message once we get there," Cassidy assured him.

Lucius looked down at Eliza and nearly plucked the straw from her hair.

"You listen to Cassidy," he told her, and he looked at Poppy and Robert too. "All of you. You used to camp out all the time with Roslyn, this will be no different than that."

Eliza nodded and then threw herself into her father's arms, and the other two followed suit.

"I want to stay," Eliza told him. "Who will protect you?"

Lucius stifled a half-choke-half-laugh at her words, and he felt his eyes growing wet.

"Nonsense, sweetie, we have stepped up the security. I need you, Poppy, and Robert to be safe," Lucius told them. "Please do this for me."

"Okay, poppa," Eliza finally said, and she pulled away and wiped her tears on her sleeve. "We will listen."

"Good. I will see you all when this settles down," he assured his youngest children, and he watched as they got into the back of the wagon. Cassidy hugged her father as well, and he kissed her on the cheek.

"Ride swiftly," he told her as they parted. She nodded and turned to her Honour Guard and gave them the cue to mount their horses. Sully drove the wagon, his horse on a lead behind the wagon.

Cassidy rode beside the wagon, Crick on her shoulder, the other lady knights going ahead or behind. Kai rode just behind her. She was not wearing her frishna armour but a plain set of armour that a merchant's guard would wear. She had her sword at her waist still, and her bow and arrows just behind her saddle. They were let out of the double gate that was the Supply Gate, the doors closing right behind them as they went. Sully directed them towards the Merchant's Gate where they were let through, and out into the countryside they went. They headed east a little bit on the road and then took the first northern road.

"Anything?" Cassidy asked Kai, and he glanced behind them. "No one is following us so far."

"We will stay this way as long as we can and then stop at night-fall," Cassidy spoke to the whole group. "Tomorrow we will see what happens."

A Descent into the Roots

At nightfall they set up tents, and Cassidy used the crystals that Roslyn had made to set up a protective perimeter around their campsite. Eliza and Poppy helped brush down the horses and Robert helped Sully gather wood for a fire.

"We always helped Roz and Edmond with the fire," Robert told Cassidy as they sat around the fire while the sun continued setting.

"You would camp a lot?" Cassidy asked him. They each had a blanket around their shoulders for late spring in Ellsgrove could still get a little cool in the evenings.

Eliza smiled and answered, "Yes, we would go out to the forest and Roz would catch a few rabbits. We would cook them over the fire and eat them for supper. Then we would sleep under the stars."

"Can we do that tonight?" Robert asked Cassidy, his eyes hopeful.

"I don't think so, it is already a cool evening and will get even colder," Cassidy told him.

"Sleeping under the stars is best for the summer," Eliza told her brother. "We can do it then."

They ate some smoked sausages and cheese along with some crackers before heading to bed. Sully took the first watch even though they had the protective barrier.

"Gotta make sure we weren't followed," Sully told her. "I'll wake you in a few hours for your turn."

True to his word, Sully awoke Cassidy sometime during the night to take watch.

"Nothing so far," Sully told her. "Everything seems pretty quiet."

"Sounds good," she replied, and she got out of her tent and went to sit by the fire with her blanket and sword.

The best part of the protection enchantment that Roslyn did with the crystals was that anyone on the outside would not be able to see, hear, or smell anything from inside. The people inside, however, could see and hear the outside.

Sometime after taking over for Sully, the jangle of a horse's tack caught Cassidy's attention. Then she heard a horse chuff from outside the barrier. She stood up slowly, turning in the direction of the sound, making Crick, who was sleeping at her feet, stand at attention as well.

"*A horse and a man*, Crick told Cassidy. *No, three horses and three men.*"

Cassidy and her group had set up camp a stone's throw from the road, but looking through Crick's eyes she could tell that these three men were riding just slightly off of the road on their side, all of them looking for something.

"If they came this way we would have found them by now," one of the men hissed at his companions.

"Why would they *not* go north?" the one at the back asked.

"I don't like this," the first one said.

"One of them is a mage, they probably have their camp hidden," the one in the middle spoke up.

"What magic can hide a group that big?" The first man wanted to know.

"Something that could whoop your ass back to last week, I'm sure," the middle man told him.

Cassidy let out a small chuckle at the man's remark, and she watched as they kept riding by. Someone *had* followed after them, but now they had successfully avoided them. She would have to keep an eye out in the morning before taking up their protective barrier, send out a scout in to make sure the men were not around.

"*I can follow them for a bit,* Crick told Cassidy. *I can follow my nose back to you.*"

"I will send you after them in the morning. Do you have their scent right now?"

"*Yes.*"

"That will do. I know how good your nose is."

Cassidy looked up at the stars and wondered where Roslyn was. How long had it been since Roslyn asked her to go to Ellsgrove? A month or two? She was unsure. What did the gryphon look like? Where was everyone at that moment?

Cassidy reached out with her magic, knowing that it would not work but still hoping in the back of her mind. She called to her twin sister who was on the other side of the world, feeling her magic seep into the ground and the roots of the nearby trees.

"*Is everything okay?*" She heard Roslyn's voice and looked up, finding her sister's astral form standing in front of her. She was wearing her nightclothes, and had a blanket around her shoulders. "*How did you do that? I heard your call through the tree roots.*"

"I have absolutely no idea, I was just trying to see if it would work," Cassidy told her sheepishly.

Roslyn looked around them, and then back at Cassidy. "*Why are you camping? Where are you?*"

"Father asked me to escort Eliza, Poppy, and Robert to Wardgrove," Cassidy explained. "An attempt was made on my life a few days ago–"

"*What?!*"

"I am uninjured," Cassidy assured her sister. "Rafi got in the way."

"*Is he okay?!*"

"Yes, he will be. The dart was poisoned against magic, but one of our spies was there and she knew the counter for it. He will be bedridden for a couple more days," Cassidy told her, before continuing with, "Not long before that though, another attempt was made on father, and his butler was killed. Eliza got rid of the assassin that time though."

"*What happened?*"

"The assassin was in father's study but Roland went in just ahead of father. I had been teaching Eliza how to use throwing knives, and I had gifted her a set that doubled as hairpins. She used them to kill the assassin."

"*Oh, wow,*" was all Roslyn could say. "*Gods I wish I could be there.*"

"This is why you sent me, sister," Cassidy reminded her.

"You are now the Queen of Jay'Al and are dealing with your own problems there. I am free to be here, protecting our family."

"*How are* you *doing?*" Roslyn asked her.

"I grieve just as you do," Cassidy told her with a grim smile. "Mom?"

"*She has our other siblings to help her,*" Roslyn responded. "*I've been busy with all of the gryphons and pixies, or else I would have more time to spend with her.*"

"The *what* now?!"

"*After you left there was an earthquake on the plateau, and a sinkhole opened up. Karina and I were in the shrine when it happened and we found ourselves underground. This happened not long before we made peace with the werewolves. I decided the other day I wanted to explore a little more of what we found: an aerie that could belong to gryphons. On the other side of this room we found a hidden door that led to a hallway with more paintings, and then there was a cavern like the one we found Kasimir in, and a bunch of gryphons and pixies. We brought them to the surface.*"

"By the ancestors," Cassidy said as she shook her head. "That is amazing! Where are the others?"

"*Kavan is here, and the rest of the magical creatures. Heath, Maeve, Cypress, Karina, Heather, Edwin and Alexander are underground trying to find the behemoths.*"

"Edwin and Alexander are the werewolves right?"

"*Yes. Alexander was the one that turned Kavan; he thought the only way to fight Edwin was with an army of his own. I have been able to create a cure, and a pendant that keeps them from changing and passing on the curse.*"

"I see. *Wow.* That's a lot to take in. But, seeing you made me feel a lot better, and it was *very* good to see you, Roz. Give my love to the family."

"*And mine to the family there,*" Roslyn told her with a smile before her astral form faded away.

Cassidy sat there with Crick by the fire until pre-dawn, and she started cooking breakfast. Just simple honeyed oatmeal and fruit. Eliza was the first one to join her at the fire and accepted a bowl with a smile. One by one the lady knights woke up and came to the fire with their empty bowls for their breakfast. Poppy, Robert, and Sully were the last ones up.

"You've gotten efficient at this," Eliza commented. "Breakfast ready before anyone wakes.”

“We have had some time to get used to this,” Cassidy told her. “We travelled for several weeks together like this.”

“Better Cassidy making breakfast than Sully,” one of the lady knights commented, and Sully, who was half asleep still, looked up as he rubbed his eyes.

“Oy, who said that?” he asked, earning a chuckle from the knights.

“You burn the oatmeal,” Cassidy told him. “It’s terrible.”

“Oh,” Sully responded. “Sorry. Why didn’t you say anything before?”

“They wanted to spare your feelings,” Cassidy said. “I tried telling them that just switching us wouldn’t work because what if something happened and you were the one making breakfast again? You know now.” Cassidy shrugged and continued eating.

“Sorry, my knights. I will try not to burn the oatmeal if I am ever on breakfast duty again,” Sully promised them.

“Go brush your hair, your morning curls are out of control,” Cassidy told him with a smirk, and he sighed before going back to his tent to brush his hair, taking his bowl of oatmeal with him. He came back moments later with his hair properly kept.

“Three men passed by the camp just off the road last night,” Cassidy told Sully. “They were trying to find us. Crick got their scent, so we should be able to tell if they are anywhere nearby still. I would like to send out a couple scouts though before we break camp, just in case.”

“Of course,” Sully responded. “Baylee, Kallista?”

“On it,” Baylee responded as she finished what was in her bowl. “Kallista, I will get the horses ready while you finish up.”

“Thank you,” Kallista answered; she was a slow eater, and everyone knew it.

“I also spoke with Roslyn last night,” Cassidy continued. “She found an underground cavern beneath the plateau that had more gryphons, and pixies in it, and brought them to the surface.”

“That must be a sight to see,” Sully commented. “What is a pixie?”

“Like a sprite,” Eliza told him. “Same thing, just different name.”

“Ah, ok. They were part of our fairy tales,” Sully told Cassidy.

“And mine, just as pixies,” Cassidy teased.

“How is your family doing?” Sully asked her.

“Roz says they are dealing. Just like we are,” Cassidy answered, reaching out and putting an arm around Eliza, who was sitting next to her.

“I miss dad,” Robert whispered, and Eliza took his hand.

“We will see dad again,” Eliza assured him. “Cassidy will see us to Wardgrove and then she will go right back to him.”

“Yes, I will do just that,” Cassidy told him. “Now hurry up and finish eat ing so we can start packing up."

Sully let the two scouts out of the barrier when they were almost ready to get on the road again. The two scouts headed north ahead of their group. Crick sat on Cassidy's saddle and sniffed the air.

"*Nothing*," Crick told Cassidy. "*They are not nearby.*"

"Crick says the men are not nearby," Cassidy informed Sully.

"Let's head out then," Sully told the group. "We will see how things are at the closest farm, and if all is good then we leave the wagon and just ride as fast as we can."

About an hour later, Kallista and Baylee returned to them after scouting ahead and around them.

"Not many travellers out," Kallista told them. "We talked to a few farmers and they know about the army heading for the capital, so I think that is why there aren't many people out and about. We found no camps, and saw no men. They may have continued on or doubled back."

"How far is the nearest farm?" Sully asked them.

"Half an hour at most," Baylee replied.

"We head there then. Baylee, ride behind us a mile. Kallista, a mile ahead," Sully ordered them. Both women nodded and did as he bid them.

It started off as a warm morning, but as the day progressed the clouds came in looking dark , and the wind picked up. They left the wagon at the farm, Eliza riding with Cassidy, Poppy with Sully, and Robert with Kai.

"Are you sure it is wise to leave the wagon when it looks like rain?" Cassidy asked Sully as they started to ride away from the farm.

"There's a military outpost not far from here that we can stop at if it gets too bad," Sully informed her. "King Lucius gave me a letter to use in case we needed to go to one."

"If you're sure," she told him, knowing that he knew Ellsgrove way better than she did.

The rain held off for several hours as they made great headway, and only once they had reached the outpost did the rain come pouring down. Both Kallista and Baylee had rejoined them. Sully led them to the gates of the outpost where a sentry talked to him; the soldier left and came back shortly with the commanding officer who took a look at the letter Sully had. He quickly let them in, and showed them to a room where they could dry off by a cozy fire.

"I will have hot food sent to you," the commanding officer, who had introduced himself as Commander Raoul and was a hulk of a man, told them before he left them in the room.

"At least we do not have to bother with brushing down the horses, they have people in the stables for that," Baylee commented as they took seats in front of the fire.

"Yes, they will be well looked after," Sully agreed.

"How much longer will this journey be?" Poppy asked Cassidy. Cassidy looked at Sully for the answer.

"Do you remember how long it took you when you came to the Capital from Wardgrove last year?" Sully asked her. She nodded.

"Half that time, hopefully," he told her. "Why don't Robert and I go check the place out while you girls change into some dryer clothes?"

Chapter Twenty-Four

alking out of his tent, Kavan noticed a peculiar sight near the kitchen that Lou and Dacey worked out of. The two part-orcs were watching something from just outside the door to the kitchen, but Kavan could not see it from there. He walked over, and Dacey glanced up at him, smiling in greeting.

"What is going on?" he asked them.

"The pixies have decided they want to help cook," Dacey informed him. "Which I suppose would be fine, if they knew how to use our cooking devices."

Kavan peeked in and saw that the handful of pixies that were in there were not doing a very good job, so he went inside to talk to them.

"Excuse me?" Kavan used a normal voice first, but after a moment they had not turned to him so he channeled his inner werewolf and repeated himself, letting out a half snarl as he did so. *That* got the pixie's attention. Each of them landed on the table, looking sheepish.

"If you really want to help Dacey and Lou, let them show you what you can do. *Do not* take over their kitchen. Do you understand?" Kavan asked them. "They can teach you. I know you guys can adapt to life up here. Show me you can."

Kavan turned to walk back out, but then had an idea. "You guys can make little spells and potions right?" One of the pixies nodded. "Anything useful? Luck, anti-stress, energy type potions?"

Several of the pixies showed excitement with the prospects he was revealing to them.

"I bet you guys would make a lot of money selling potions like that," he told them. "Just make sure you tell the users how long the effects last and such, right?"

"Oh, we will make sure they know everything," one of the pixies told him, and they talked quickly amongst themselves before taking off, leaving a mess for Dacey and Lou to clean up.

"Thank you," Dacey said to him.

Kavan smiled at her and Lou, and told them, "I will help you clean up. What's on the menu today?"

***

Kavan went in search of Roslyn after he was done helping Karina's parents. He found her helping to install the front gate of the city, and he could not help but marvel still at her display of power in the making of the wall. He was willing to bet that she could build her own palace with her magic instead of waiting for it to be built.

Leaf was sitting under a tree watching Roslyn and the builders work as she ate. Kavan could tell that she had gone through another growth spurt because she was definitely bigger than she had been a few days ago: she was the size of a horse now.

"How big are you going to get?" Kavan asked the dragon as he neared her.

"Probably at least a few times bigger," Roslyn told him as she joined the two of them.

"How are you feeling?" Kavan asked her, looking for any signs of fatigue or overuse of magic. Her fainting after creating the wall reminded him that she may be powerful, but she was still only human.

"Much better after all of the sleep I got. I didn't get a good look at the wall the other day but I went for a walk on it this morning and I cannot believe *I* created *this*," Roslyn told him, making a flourish with her hand to encompass the wall.

"Have you thought about building your own palace like you did the wall?" Kavan asked her, watching her think about it. He enjoyed watching her think, noting the way she bit her lower lip.

"A wall was easy; yes I added some stairs and the walkway, but a guard-house will need to be built off of the wall. A palace would have *hundreds* of rooms," Roslyn told him finally. "I could maybe make an outer shell with floors, and the rest would just be framing the rooms maybe? I don't know."

"That's an idea," Kavan told her. "Maybe we should talk to Oswick and Judd about it?"

"I suppose we could," she replied, turning to look up at the plateau. "Would you carry me up there?" She turned back to him with a sly smile on her face.

Kavan grinned at her and moved to pick her up, with her putting her arm around his shoulder. He inhaled her scent, cedar wood, and he felt his breath catch before he shook his head and focused on running. Her warmth against his chest was very distracting, and her hair tickled his nose slightly. They were at the top of the plateau within moments, and Kavan stopped in front of where Oswick and Judd had their little headquarters tent where they oversaw the building of the palace. Behind the tent was the foundation of the palace, and the builders were working away at it.

He put her down gently, and she turned her face to smile at him, her eyes shining. He couldn't help himself, he put his hand on her chin and leaned down, pressing his lips against hers. At first she seemed surprised but then she kissed him back eagerly.

Someone clearing their throat nearby surprised them both, and they both took a step back while their faces turned a little red.

Oswick was leaning on the frame of the tent door, his expression one of amusement. "Sorry to uhm…interrupt," Oswick told them. "To what do we owe the pleasure of your visit, Your Majesty?"

"Don't start with that again," Roslyn told him.

"It's just I haven't seen you for a while, thought you forgot about us up here," Oswick joked. "I see you have been busy though."

"Have the gryphons been bothering you at all?" Kavan asked as he looked up to see a few gryphons flying overhead.

"Not really, some of them have gone off exploring but many have started to make nests up in the mountain or on the side of the plateau," Oswick informed him. "The pixies, though, are another thing."

"Yes, I have dealt with a few myself," Kavan told him.

"They are very curious little buggers," Oswick said, and Kavan agreed with him.

"What did they do?" Roslyn asked them both.

"Caused a mess in the kitchen. I had a talk with the ones who did it," Kavan told her.

"Yeah, pretty much the same thing with our blueprints," Oswick said next. "I made them clean it up. They have made several nest-type things in the trees in the area."

"I see. Let me know if anything else happens, please," Roslyn told them both. "Now," she continued, "Kavan thinks I could make a palace like I did the city wall."

"I see," Oswick said after a moment. "I think our builders would be a little disappointed if you did, honestly."

"It would just be the outer shell and floors," Kavan told him. "The rooms would need to be made still, and staircases and such."

"I will talk with Judd about it and let you know by tonight," Oswick replied, though he still did not look happy about the idea. "Judd got a little moody about the wall, he was looking forward to building it."

"Apologize to him for me, please," Roslyn told him. "With the threat of the dark elves I did not think it was safe to wait."

"I don't think it'll be safe for you to make the palace," Oswick told her. "You slept for two days after the wall. What if there is an attack while you recuperate?"

"A very valid point. I will leave the palace to your men then. The foundation looks pretty good already," Roslyn told him.

"We are about to start the front staircase and the main doors," Oswick informed her. "Then we have to dig out a little bit to make the basement level a little deeper before we start framing for the first floor."

"I look forward to seeing it completed," Roslyn said as smiled at her friend. "Thank you, Oswick."

He nodded with a smile and went back inside his tent.

"Speaking of dark elves, we should have scouts out," Kavan commented as he gestured for them to walk together.

"We have a few scouting the immediate area, but the dekellians are so fast I don't want to put people in danger by having them go too far," Roslyn told him.

Kavan looked up at Hawk the gryphon who was flying towards them, and he pointed out the gryphon to her. "What about them? We can put scouts on gryphons and they can fly overhead looking for the enemy."

"Well, let's see what Hawk thinks," Roslyn replied, and she waved Hawk down to them.

"*Yes, Your Majesty?*" Hawk asked as she landed in front of them. Roslyn told her Kavan's idea.

"*The gryphons would be honoured to help you in this way. We might be able to imprint on a few people, a bond not unlike your familiars,*" Hawk told them. "*Having that connection will help both flyers in the air.*"

"I will get some volunteers together if you can find some adult gryphons willing to help," Roslyn said.

"The group should have a name," Kavan commented as Hawk took off to gather some more adult gryphons.

"How about…'Feathers'?" Roslyn asked him.

"Or 'The Queen's Feathers'?" Kavan shot back.

"Too long. 'Feathers' seems right," Roslyn replied.

"Sounds good to me," Kavan said with a smile, and he found himself thinking about their kiss. He really wanted to kiss her again. "Have you eaten breakfast yet?"

"I have not, no."

"Care to join me on a picnic?" he asked her.

"I would love that."

***

Roslyn had sent word out to her scouts and soldiers to see if anyone was interested in scouting from the air on the backs of gryphons. Since it was such an interesting new thing over thirty people volunteered to see if they could bond with a gryphon.

Since the gryphons were as interested in the idea as the humans were, there were enough of them to match the volunteers.

Roslyn was not surprised to see four of her scouts in the line-up: Myles and Len, both Jay'Alian; Finn, an Ellsgrovian; and Trys, a female orc. She was, however, surprised to see her own brother Quinn, Karina's brother Jaco, and Cypress' brother Ulmer. There were also two other people from the Dragon Clan who Karina had introduced her to, Ceska, and Castor, who were both part orc. There were several other Jay'Alians and orcs/part orcs as well that Roslyn did not know.

Hawk instructed all of the human volunteers to blindfold themselves after sitting on the ground. They were at the bottom of the plateau, just next to the tree that Roslyn had grown. Each of them dutifully got down on their bums, crossing their legs and putting their hands on their knees to wait patiently.

"My brethren will go around and sniff each of you," Hawk told the group. *"If they choose you, they will rub up against you."*

"I've been meaning to ask," Roslyn whispered to Hawk as the group of volunteer gryphons started to make their rounds. "Can all gryphons mind-speak?"

"It starts at adolescence," Hawk told her. *"Our very young cannot do it."*

"Ah, so that explains how Solana cannot mind-speak yet," Roslyn commented. "That is Heath's gryphon familiar."

"Once she reaches a year old she will be able to start. As a   familiar, though, she will be able to communicate with her mage right away. My parents told me several things about being a familiar."

"So what do you expect the outcome of this to be?" Roslyn asked the gryphon, nodding at the gryphons going around the seated humans. Several of them had chosen already, and Roslyn was again surprised when her brother Quinn was chosen by a dark grey coloured gryphon.

"Honestly, I have no idea. I just know that this can happen, from what my parents told me. We have to trust the process."

Roslyn chuckled at that, but she sobered when there were fifteen people chosen: besides Quinn, Myles, Finn, Trys, and Len were chosen, as were Ulmer and Jaco, Ceska and Castor. Those she had not known previously were: Harcourt, an Ellsgrovian; Holly, part orc; Mucio, a Jay'Alian; Colby, an Ellsgrovian; Alistair, another Ellsgrovian; and Keenan, a part orc. Fifteen in total.

"Well, I'll be damned," Roslyn whispered. "Can they ride without saddles?"

"For now," Hawk told her. *"You can start making some, though. They will need to be dressed warmly, it gets colder the further up they get."*

"I have just the thing for that," Roslyn responded, a sly smile on her face.

Chapter Twenty-Five

Heath sat next to a low fire, staring across the small flames at their prize: they had managed to get ahead of the kobolds' advance party, and had captured one of their scouts. They had left nothing to chance and had basically ran out of the tunnels, leaving as many traps as they could as they went. Now they were above ground. Heather had filled in the entrance of the tunnel using her magic.

Edwin and Alexander had gone out to scout not too long ago, leaving Karina, Maeve, Heather, and Cypress there with Heath to guard the kobold. It was a warm evening, for summer was getting closer.

The kobold looked at Heath with intelligence in its reptilian eyes. Heath had bound the kobold's hands together with both rope and magic, and they had gagged it with a piece of someone's shirt. From what Heath could tell the kobold was a male, and was wearing crude armour over rough spun clothing. The sword that they had taken from it looked impressive though.

The kobold flexed his hands, not paying much mind to the rope that bound them together. Heath thought that the claws the kobold had on both hands would make good weapons too. Though Heath had to wonder, with the scale-like skin the kobold had, why did it need the armour?

Karina sat down next to Heath, Mister Scruffy rubbing up against Solana who was curled up at Heath's side.

"What do you think?" Karina asked Heath. "What do you think the kobolds want?"

"Well if what the dark elf said is true, they want the magic of the land. Could they have not done something underground to take it? Siphon it? Or do they need something else, like say, the most magical person who is connected with the land?"

"And we know who that is," Karina whispered her answer. If the kobolds didn't know who it was they were after, she was going to make sure they would not find out any time soon.

"I'm going to contact Roslyn and let her know where we are," Heath told Karina as he stood up. Solana got up and stretched as well. Karina nodded her understanding and stayed there to stand watch on their prisoner.

Heath walked off a little ways, still within their protective barrier. He closed his eyes and concentrated on his astral form, sending it to the plateau and where he could feel Roslyn's magic. He opened his eyes through his magical form and found himself on top of the plateau amongst several lantern posts that led up to the foundation of the palace. Heath was not surprised to see how far along the construction was coming.

A large campfire not too far away drew his attention, as did the group of people around it. He could see Roslyn in her large throne-like chair that her grandfather had made her for her birthday. There was no mistaking Tiffany either. Aidan was there, as was Kavan next to Roslyn. Oswick sat on the ground next to the fire, leaning against a man who Heath only briefly met, the stonemason Judd.

Leaf was the one to notice Heath first, and she stood up from where she was curled up behind Roslyn. Leaf nudged Roslyn and Roslyn turned towards him. Her face broke out in a huge smile and she jumped up from her seat. Heath met her half way.

"Heath! Where are you? Is everything alright?" Roslyn asked him, stopping before him. He could tell that she wanted to hug him but with him being an astral projection she could not.

"*We just reached the surface again tonight,*" Heath explained. "*We found the behemoths: they belong to an army of kobolds.*"

Roslyn swore.

"*We were able to capture one of their forward scouts,*" Heath continued. "*We blocked the entrance to the tunnel as well, and left as many traps behind as we could on our way back to the surface.*"

"I will send Kavan and the rest of the werewolves to guard you tonight," Roslyn told him.

"*No need, we have your protective crystals,*" he told her.

"Then in the morning we will ride out to meet you," Roslyn replied.

"*I can't wait to kiss you again,*" Heath told her. He could see the blush in her cheeks as his form faded away.

Opening his eyes again in his human form he looked around in the darkness beyond the protective barrier. He could see both Edwin and Alexander approaching the camp at a slow jog, and he hoped that they had good news. He opened the barrier for them by lifting a crystal, replacing it once they were inside.

"Everything seems quiet," Alexander told him. "No sign of the dark elves or their dekellians."

"Not sure whether that's a comfort or not," Heath replied. "Will you two take watch tonight?"

They nodded their heads to say that they would, and Heath crawled into his bedroll with Solana curling up beside his head.

***

It was a few hours past dawn when Edwin spotted Roslyn and the group with her. They had been walking towards the plateau, with both werewolves scouting around them as they went. Now Edwin dropped back to let Heath know, and he decided to wait where they were near a little stream for Roslyn to get to them. He heard a screech somewhere above them, and he shielded his eyes from the sun to look. Solana, who had been walking along beside, let out an excited noise as she flapped her wings and took off.

"What is that?" Heath heard Maeve ask as she too looked up. A shadow fell over them and Heath could see what looked like a gryphon with a person riding on its back.

"Well I'll be damned," Heath commented as he watched Solana fly around the other gryphon. "Where did they come from? And who is riding it?"

"Ulmer!" Cypress let out a shout as the orc recognized the gryphon rider as they descended to them. "That's my brother!"

"Cypress!" Ulmer shouted his own greeting as the gryphon he was riding landed, Solana not far behind. "It is good to see you in one piece, brother."

"Where did you get that gryphon?" Heath asked him as he watched Solana prance around the adult gryphon.

"Roslyn found a bunch of gryphons under the plateau, and some pixies," Ulmer explained as he dismounted. "I'm one of fifteen gryphon riders called 'Feathers'. We are scouts for Her Majesty." The gryphon he was riding looked down at Solana and then began washing the younger gryphon.

"*Little sister*," Heath heard the gryphon's voice in his head as it talked to Solana. "*It is good to see that you were rescued from the dark elves.*"

"Wait, what?" Heath asked, confused.

"Roslyn can explain it better than I can," Ulmer told him as he took something out of his pocket and squeezed it.

"What's that?" Cypress asked him.

"Roslyn came up with a few things for us riders," Ulmer explained, showing him the crystal in his hand. "This links to an item that Roslyn has. I just triggered it, meaning I have found you and it will lead her here."

"Fascinating," Karina commented. "Using the gryphons as scouts was a good idea."

"They are coming," Ulmer nodded towards where Heath could now see Roslyn riding towards them. Behind her came her Queen's Guard as well as Kavan. They had extra horses with them for Heath and his companions to ride, and a wagon with a large cage in the back to put their prisoner. The kob-old had not given them any trouble, seemingly resigned to its fate of being a prisoner.

"I will speak with you later," Ulmer told his brother as he remounted his gryphon. "Dasan and I have work to do."

"Be safe, little brother!" Cypress called after him as they took off.

Heath walked up to Roslyn as she approached and dismounted, a wide smile on his face; she smiled back at him, her eyes shining with delight to see him well. "You made good timing," he told her.

"When Kavan went to bring the magical creatures to us I made a charm for haste to help them get back faster. We used it to reach you," she told him as she hugged him. "You will have time to report once we get back, let's get the kobold in the cell and head out: our scouts tell us the dark elves are on the move from the east where they have been biding their time."

"Then let *us* make haste," Heath answered, letting go of the hug; she smelled of cinnamon and lilac, with a faint bit of cedar. He nodded to Cypress who had hold of the kobold's bindings and Cypress ushered the kobold to the cell in the back of the wagon. It got in without any argument.

Kavan brought Heath his horse, which he mounted while thanking him.

"It's good to see you," Kavan told Heath. "We were starting to get wor-ried."

Heath grunted, and said, "I bet you were. I saw how close you were sitting to her last night."

"Jealous?" Kavan teased him.

"You back in the running, my friend?" Heath asked him, curious if Kavan had indeed changed his mind about courting Roslyn.

"Maybe," Kavan told him with a wink before he nudged his horse into a gallop to catch up with Roslyn and the others.

Chapter Twenty-Six

ully showed Robert around the outpost as much as he could without going into the soldier's quarters themselves. They took the time to change into their own dry clothes in one of the bathing rooms. The soldiers paid them no mind, just nodding to Sully. When they returned from the walk around, all of the women were changed into dry clothes, and there was some warm soup available for them to eat. A warm fire crackled in the hearth, and thunder rolled loudly above them. They could see a flash of lightning through the windows of the room they were in. They could hear the heavy rain on the roof.

"Everything alright?" Cassidy asked him as she handed Sully a bowl of the potato and bacon soup.

"The outpost is fairly quiet. They are on alert because of the army coming north but otherwise everything is fine," Sully told her. "We should be safe here tonight."

"Would it be bad of me if I still used the crystals to protect this room?" Cassidy asked him. "I really don't want to take any chances."

"The protective barrier will work inside a room?" Sully asked her.

Cassidy shrugged and told him, "Honestly, I have no idea."

"Better safe than sorry, I suppose. We can try it."

When it came time for them to set up their bedrolls around the room, with the three royal children sleeping in the middle of the room, Cassidy put the crystals at each corner of the room. She could feel the barrier there, and knowing that it was there put her at ease.

Cassidy got into her bedroll next to Eliza; Crick settled in next to her head. Kai slept on her other side. Sully was sleeping in front of the door, and Baylee by the window.

Eliza rolled over to look at Cassidy, her face showing her worry as more thunder rolled above them.

"Are we safe here?" Eliza asked her. "I have this feeling in my gut that something is going to go wrong."

"The protective barrier is up, we will be safe in here tonight," Cassidy assured her. "Then we will be on our way to Wardgrove again in the morning."

"OK," she replied, though Cassidy could tell that she was still unsure.

"Get some sleep, Eliza," Cassidy told her. "We *will* reach Wardgrove in a few days."

***

Cassidy stared at the broken bridge in anger. All of the rain that had fallen had swollen the river so much that it poured over the wooden bridge, and it could not handle the swell.

She looked at Sully and asked, "Where is the next crossing?"

"A day's ride east," he responded.

She swore under her breath. "Of course it is."

"And it's another two days west," Sully told her. "Honestly, they should build more bridges."

"We can mention that when we get back," Eliza spoke up, looking slightly bemused.

"East it is then," Cassidy said after a moment, and Sully urged his horse to keep going down the road. The rest of the group followed.

After a few hours they stopped at a farm to water their horses and eat something. Sully sent Baylee and Kallista out to scout while they rested.

"My home is not too far from here," Sully told Cassidy. "I know your father wants them in Wardgrove, but I trust my soldiers to keep your brother and sister safe."

"How far away?" Cassidy asked him.

"We would be there tomorrow, just on the other side of the next bridge basically," he told her.

"We can stop there so you can see your other sister," Cassidy told him. "But I have to get them to Wardgrove like my father wanted."

Sully sighed and said, "Then we should not linger too much longer. I can see her after this is all over."

"No, no I think it would be good to check in on your sister," Cassidy told him. "I've met Deirdre, what is your other sister's name?"

"Adrienne," he told her. "I haven't seen her in almost a year."

"Then let's go see her."

They reached Sir Sullivan's fief the next day, and his sister Adrienne met them at the gates. She looked to be around fourteen, and had the same blonde curly hair that Sully had but longer. She was wearing breeches and a tunic, something that made Cassidy smile.

"Brother!" Adrienne greeted them from atop the walkway.

A Descent into the Roots

"It is good to see you!" She motioned to someone to open the gate and the double wooden gates that led up to the castle opened.

"You as well," Sully told her as he urged his horse forward. "We cannot stay long; I just wanted to check in on you while we head north."

"Is everything alright?" she asked him as she took in his travelling companions. "Is that her? Princess Roslyn?"

Sully cleared his throat and shook his head, telling her, "This is Roslyn's twin sister, Cassidy. We are heading north on a mission."

"Oh. Well, come on everyone, the midday meal will be ready soon," Adrienne told them, directing them up to the castle as she joined them on the cobblestone path. "I received your last letter just this week."

"Are all of our soldiers prepared if I call them to join the fighting?" Sully asked her as he dismounted his horse, and the two siblings shared a quick hug.

"Of course they are," Adrienne told him as soldiers let them into the castle. "I know how to run things."

Cassidy stifled a laugh as she walked behind them, her siblings just behind her, followed by the rest of their guard. Sully gave her a half-smile when he saw the expression on her face.

"Thank you, sister," Sully told Adrienne. "I had no doubts that you could do it."

"Mmmmhmmm…" was all Cassidy heard Adrienne say next as she led them into the dining hall. Adrienne then told one of the servants that they would need more plates, and to inform the kitchens of the additions to the meal.

"So what brings you all this way?" Adrienne asked them as they each took a seat at the long wooden table in the dining hall. Above them was a large chandelier made from wood and metal, with large oil lamps on it that were unlit; the large windows on the one side of the dining room were enough to light the space during the day.

"I told you, a mission," Sully spoke, slight irritation in his voice. "That is all you need to know."

"It is not you," Cassidy interjected in a whisper, "but possible spies that we do not want to know about what is going on." She turned to Sully and whispered, "No need to antagonize your *sister*."

Sully looked properly chastised, and Adrienne leaned back in her chair with crossed arms to look at the group.

"What have you brought here, brother? What dangers are there?"

Sully leaned into his sister's ear and told her in a quiet voice, "Princesses Eliza and Poppy, and Prince Robert of Ellsgrove are under our protection."

Adrienne quickly glanced at the three younger people at the table and then back at her brother. "Shit," she whispered. "Gale!" This second word came at a shout.

The person she called for came, a guardsman, and there were whispered words exchanged. The guard left and Adrienne regarded her brother coolly. "Proper accommodations are being made, you *will* spend the night. With all of this rain I can only imagine what you all have gone through. Cook has prepared a fine meal, we are more than happy to share it with you all."

"Adrien–" Sully started, but his sister broke him off with a sharp shake of her head.

"It is *so* good to have you and your friends here, brother,"

Adrienne told him, and he shut his mouth as he finally understood what the problem was. "Do tell me of your travels to Jay'Al?"

***

It was not until they were done eating and Adrienne was showing them to their rooms when Sully was able to talk to his sister without servants or guards around.

"What is going on?" Cassidy heard Sully ask quietly as they walked through the castle.

"Yesterday a few men came by, looking for people who match *their* descriptions, if they were cleaned up properly," Adrienne whispered back; Cassidy understood that Adrienne meant Eliza, Poppy, and Robert were the ones who the men were looking for. "I was told they moved on, but if they knew you were with *them* then it is no coincidence that they showed up here."

"Double the guards tonight, and keep an eye out for them if they return," Sully told his sister. "We do have a way of protecting ourselves, but we want to keep them off our trail still."

"It will be done. I assume Cassidy is a mage just like Roslyn?" Adrienne asked him, glancing at Cassidy.

"I am," Cassidy responded for Sully.

"I had hoped so. I might need your help tonight to keep the castle safe. Only loyal servants and guards are allowed to work for us, but lately we have had some questionable sicknesses that I was hoping you could take a look at," Adrienne told her. "The people who took over for them have been heavily watched."

"Of course. If I can be of any help to you, I will do it," Cassidy assured her. She turned to Sully and told him, "Get my brother and sisters to a safe place. My guard will stay with you." She turned to Kai who was walking just behind her. "You with me?" she asked him.

"Always," he answered her with a smile, and Tej his familiar chirped up as well. From under Cassidy's hair on her shoulder, Crick chirped as well.

Cassidy smiled and looked at Adrienne, saying, "Take us to them."

***

Adrienne took her and Kai out of the castle into the village below it, having first disguised them as servants. The first house they went to there was a young woman sick in bed with a fever. Cassidy examined her before heading to the next house where another young woman was sick with the same symptoms. The sun was getting close to setting over the village.

"How many?" Cassidy asked her after the third person she saw, this one a young man.

"Five in total," Adrienne answered.

"None of their sicknesses are natural," Cassidy told her. "The people who took their places inside the castle are either spies or assassins, or both."

Adrienne swore and urged Cassidy back to the castle.

"What is it?" Cassidy asked her.

"They are all night-time servants," Adrienne told her. "They will be on the castle grounds *now*."

They all hurried back up to the castle as the street lamps in the village were being lit for the night. Guardsmen responded to Adrienne's orders to have the grounds searched for the replacement servants as they hurried to where Sully and the rest of the guard were with the princesses and the prince on the main floor. They reached the room to find that both Sully and Robert were missing.

"What is it?" Baylee asked them when Cassidy asked where the two had gone. Cassidy quickly explained it.

"They went to find something else for Robert to wear," Eliza told them. "Sully told him he had some old clothes that should fit him."

Adrienne grabbed hold of Cassidy's hand and led her to the stairs, telling her, "Sully's room is on the third floor."

Kai followed as they ran up the stairs, heading for the third floor stairs. They stopped at the bottom of the steps as they found Sully lying prone on the stairs. Cassidy panicked and told Kai to see to Sully as she heard a shout from somewhere on the second floor that sounded like Robert. She headed towards a large double door and kicked it open, finding a library lit with lanterns and candles on the other side and a man dressed as a servant who had a hold of Robert and a knife to the young prince's throat.

"Don't take another step," the spy told her as he glanced at the prince, "or he'll have a nice scar."

Cassidy could see the panicked look on Robert's face as he felt the cool steel of the man's knife against his throat. She also saw her familiar, Crick, who had somehow gotten into the library and behind the man holding her brother hostage.

"*Distract him*," Cassidy told Crick, and a moment later Crick used her teeth to bite the man's inner thigh. He jerked, releasing Robert–Robert ran towards Cassidy, holding the side of his neck–and Cassidy since she had no throwing knives on her she used a spell she learned from Roslyn to shoot a ball of flames at the spy. Crick ran towards her as the man was engulfed in flames, his screams tapering off suddenly as he died.

Cassidy took Robert into her arms and noticed his neck bleeding from a slight cut. She put her hand over it and healed it as he cried into her tunic.

"I've got you, little brother," Cassidy told him as she held him. She heard someone call her name and she turned to see Kai and Adrienne supporting Sully, who was holding onto the back of his head. She nodded to them and told them, "He is safe." Reaching out towards the body of the burning man, she cast a water spell to put the fire out–no need to burn the library down, the man was already dead.

"The servant came up behind me and knocked me out," Sully told her with a wince. "I'm so sorry this happened in my home."

"We should never have stopped," Cassidy answered. "This is my fault. Hopefully the guards have rooted out the rest of the spies. We stay in groups of four if we leave the protected room. We will leave at first light."

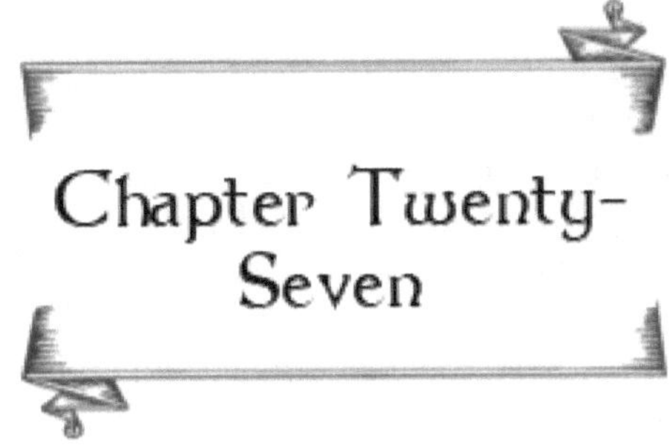

Chapter Twenty-Seven

R oslyn observed the kobold in the cage from a distance under the tree she grew near the plateau. They had made it back to Dragon City that morning with no incidents, though their scouts kept relaying information to them about the progress of the dark elves and dekellians: they were slowly getting closer to the city. Whether the kobold army with their behemoths were extremely delayed because of what Heath and his party did below ground they would only know if Roslyn herself used her astral form to do some reconnaissance. She wanted to try to talk to the kobold first though.

As she sat there, Myles and his gryphon landed next to the tree. They still had no saddle, but Myles had a warmth charm that she had made to keep him warm in the air. He had a Jay'Alian flag that Aidan had made that had a silver dragon on it that was attached to his belt. His gryphon had orange fur and orange-red feathers, and Roslyn had heard that his name was Sargam. Leaf went to confer with the gryphon while Myles came to make his report.

"Your Majesty," Myles addressed her with a half-bow before straightening to give his report. "Chief Willow's war party is approaching from the west, and Chief Erick's war party is just to the south of us. There has also been an army seen coming from the south-west that is flying a Kypragon flag."

Roslyn sat up at that information. "King Ullas has sent us an army to help?" she asked aloud. "Myles, will you go to them and talk to whomever is leading this Kypragon army?"

"Of course, Your Majesty," Myles answered with another half-bow and he went back to Sargam and mounted the gryphon, taking flight after a few moments of conference between the two of them. Leaf rejoined Roslyn under the tree, flapping her wings.

"When do you think we could take to the air together?" Roslyn asked her familiar.

"We could try right now, if you want to," Leaf told her, kneeling down to give her access to her back.

Roslyn shrugged and got up, being careful of Leaf's wings as she mounted just before them. Leaf was about the size of a horse now, and she had been exercising her wings a lot lately, flying up and down the plateau. Now was as good a time as any to see if she was ready for Roslyn to ride on her back,

"You comfortable?" Leaf asked her, and Roslyn told her it was fine. Roslyn felt her gather herself and felt her jump into the air as she flapped her wings, feeling the rush of air in her ears as they ascended to the clouds above them. It seemed that Leaf was more than ready to fly with her, something that made Roslyn very happy. Now once Solana caught up she could carry Heath, and they could go flying together.

Roslyn thought about Heath, and of Kavan. She had thought Kavan was pulling away because of his wanting to keep his werewolf abilities, and therefore him staying a werewolf, but now she was not sure after that kiss the other day. Heath, however, had always remained a constant since he had first started wooing her. She was as confused still as she had been after Kavan's first morning picnic on her nineteenth birthday.

Leaf flew her up above the plateau, circling the mountain where she had found Leaf. Several of the gryphons called out to them and came to fly with them, leaving again after a little while. It was surreal to Roslyn to be flying so high, and to see so far across the countryside. As she looked down at the start of her capital city she felt a great pride in the work of her people. They would be a united people once more, and her kingdom would thrive again.

She saw another Feather flying towards her and saw that it was her brother Quinn. She urged Leaf to hover so that Quinn could relay his message to her.

"It's about time you two took to the sky," Quinn told her with a smile. "The dark elves and their dekellians have stopped at the giant fissure in the ground. They have made camp there."

"Thank you! You should go get some food and rest now," she told him. "Mother will be worrying about you."

Quinn grinned and nodded, letting his gryphon Curran circle down to Dragon City below.

Roslyn let Leaf fly them around the area a little bit longer until Solana came up to join them.

"She says it is not fair that we are up here together and she cannot carry Heath yet," Leaf told Roslyn.

"You have a few more growth spurts in you before you will be able to, I think," Roslyn assured Solana. "It won't be too much longer, I am sure."

Solana seemed to huff at her words but she soared with them a little bit before heading back down to Heath, who Roslyn assumed was watching the whole time.

"Let's go down to them, Leaf," Roslyn finally told her familiar, and they started their descent back down to the city. Heath met them when they landed, with Solana beside him. Heath helped her to dismount, and as she moved towards him he pulled her into a kiss.

She eagerly kissed him back, feeling the heat of it as it continued. She could feel something catch in her chest, and wanted more of him than just a kiss. As he pulled back, leaving her almost breathless, she realized that her body had not responded like that to Kavan's last kiss. She would have to think about that later, for Myles had returned with a message from the leader of the Kypragon army.

"A man named Nadim is the general," Myles told her, handing her a note. "He said that Heath knows him."

"He's the merman that saved my life," Heath explained. "How many soldiers does he bring?"

"Almost two thousand," Roslyn told him, reading the note. "That adds a substantial amount to our army. We should stand a pretty good chance now against the dark elves, as long as the kobolds do not arrive too soon. Thank you, Myles. Please tell Nadim we are very happy he is here."

Myles nodded and gave her a half-bow before leaving on his gryphon again.

"Speaking of kobolds, I need to do some reconnaissance," Roslyn told Heath.

"I think that will have to wait," Heath interjected, putting his arm around her. "With the armies converging like this you need to be there to greet everyone. The recon can wait a little bit."

Roslyn leaned in and kissed him again, feeling giddy as he ardently kissed her back. They parted for breath and Roslyn had to take a step back to keep from kissing him more, because it was only making her want him more.

Heath was smiling at her slyly now, definitely out of breath.

"I've missed kissing you," he told her.

Roslyn wasn't sure she could speak at that moment so all she could do was smile.

"Your Majesty!" another Feather had landed with their gryphon, and Roslyn had to remember the person's name. It was Harcourt, one of her Ellsgrovian soldiers. "Chief Erick will be arriving shortly!"

"Tell Aidan to have a tent set up at the gates for me to greet everyone in," Roslyn told him. "And Harcourt, we will need refreshments!"

"Yes, Your Majesty!" The pair took off again, heading for the area of the wall that had been turned into an area where the Feathers could land and report to Aidan, who could either send out runners with the information or direct the Feather straight to her.

"Well," Roslyn said with regret. "No more time for kissing right now." She could see the sparkle in his green eyes and knew that he wanted more of her as well. It took a lot for her to take another step away from him and say, "I need to go be a Queen now. There's an army that needs to be greeted and incorporated with the rest of our soldiers."

"Of course, Your Majesty," Heath told her in a teasing way, his eyes shining. "Let's head to the gate together, shall we?"

He reached out his hand to hold hers and she took it. Solana and Leaf walked on either side of them as they walked through the makeshift city streets towards the double gates. By the time they got there Aidan's people were already working at erecting a tent for the meeting. Roslyn also noted that a few casks of her uncle Martin's ale had been brought from his wagon.

Aidan came out of the Feather's Nest–which was what he had taken to calling it–to meet them at the tent with a couple of his people bringing chairs along with them. The sides of the tent were open so Leaf could sit with them. Some soldiers brought a couple tables over for them as well.

"Willow is not too far out as well," Aidan told them. "Both Chiefs are camping their armies on either side of the city, and they will both meet us here. Nadim is about an hour behind them."

"What do we have to offer them for food?" Roslyn asked him. "I see the refreshments have been taken care of already."

"Lou and Dacey have a lot of smoked meats they are bringing down, and we have cheese and fresh bread," Aidan answered her. "A proper meal will be prepared for tonight. Your soldiers' cooks have already started making stews for their people."

"And my orcs are preparing food as well, in case the Kypragons do not have time to cook anything," Cypress told them as he joined them. "How far out are the enemy? Will we have time to entertain today?"

Roslyn chuckled at that. "The dark elves have camped by the gaping hole in the ground," she told him. "Our scouts will keep us well appraised of their positions throughout the afternoon."

Karina and Mister Scruffy had joined them in time to hear Roslyn tell them where the dark elves were.

"Roz, can they get into the underground tunnels below the plateau from there?" Karina asked her, worried.

"I collapsed them after we brought the gryphons and pixies up," Roslyn assured her. "The dark elves will not know that until they try to go down there. I also left a few traps, just in case."

Karina was satisfied with that answer and she took a seat. She watched as Aidan unrolled a map of the area so they would be able to plan offensive maneuvers once Willow, Erick, and Nadim were there. Karina smiled at her mother who she saw was bringing a large platter of smoked meats to them.

A Descent into the Roots

"The cheese and bread will be here shortly," Dacey informed them. "Is there anything else you need?"

"Have the pixies been giving you any more trouble?" Karina asked her mother.

"Thankfully no," Dacey told her with a chuckle. "I think Kavan scared them pretty good. They have been minding their own business in their little houses, brewing special potions for people. They handed out little flyers the other day with potions they can make."

"Is this something I should be worried about?" Roslyn asked Dacey.

"Unsure. A lot of the potions are harmless: courage, luck, energy. Stuff like that."

"I see. Thank you, Dacey."

Dacey gave her a half-curtsy before sharing a smile with her daughter and turning to go.

Edwin and Alexander joined them, as did Maeve and the new orc chief Stane. Roslyn looked around the group, feeling Cassidy's absence more in that moment. What would her sister have to say about the dark elves and kobolds?

We have werewolves and merfolk again, why not dark elves and kobolds too?! That was what Roslyn imagined her sister saying, and she chuckled to herself. She hoped Cassidy was safe still on her mission to take their siblings north, and that their father was still safe in the palace.

"Where is Kavan?" Roslyn asked Edwin and Alexander. They both shrugged.

"I haven't seen him in a few hours," Alexander told her. "You?"

"I haven't seen him since we got back this morning," Roslyn replied. "I wonder where he is."

"Do you want me to go look for him?" Alexander asked her, standing up. "I will be quick."

Roslyn nodded and in the blink of an eye Alexander was gone.

"Never gets old," she heard Karina say, and she looked at the part orc who was smiling. "How fast they move," Karina added.

Willow and Erick arrived at the same time in front of the gate and were let in. Willow was the chief of the Beaver Clan, and Erick the chief of the Hyena Clan–and also Kai's uncle. Willow had her hair held back in tight braids, and she wore frishna armour similar to what Roslyn had back in her tent. Erick wore frishna armour as well, his red hair cut short to his head.

Both chiefs dismounted and handed their reins to a couple soldiers, walking towards the tent.

"My Queen," Erick said as he went down to one knee before the tent. "The start of your city is amazing."

"Thank you, Chief Erick," Roslyn greeted him with a smile and bade him to rise. Chief Willow gave her a half-bow with a smile in greeting.

"Our scouts tell us we have some time to prepare still," Willow told them.

"The Kypragon Army is an hour away, should we wait for them before we start?" Roslyn asked them as she offered them seats. "We have some chilled ale and smoked meat, cheese and fresh bread as we wait."

At that moment Dacey arrived with a cart of fresh buns and a platter of cheese that she left next to the table that had the casks and smoked meat on it. Roslyn's nostrils flared at the smell of the fresh bread and her stomach rumbled a little bit. She realized she had not eaten since that morning.

"I think some food should be the first order of the meeting," Willow told her with a smile. "My soldiers are setting up their camps on the west side of the wall, and our scouts are out still."

"I should introduce everyone," Roslyn said after a moment as she noticed Willow looking around the group she had there. "Chiefs Willow and Erick, this is Edwin the leader of the werewolves, and Cypress, one of my orc generals. I believe you know everyone else who is here with us."

"It is good to meet you," Willow told Edwin. "I grew up on stories about werewolves. I am glad you are on our side."

Edwin grinned wolfishly at her and told her, "I agree. If you are anything like your ancestor you would be a formidable foe. We can be thankful to Roslyn for rescuing us from the dekellians and showing us that we can be saved from ourselves."

"Only a handful of werewolves chose to stay and fight," Roslyn interjected. "But one werewolf can fight with the strength of ten men."

"Who wants some ale?" Aidan asked everyone. "This ale was made by Roslyn's uncle, and has been nicely chilled for us on this hot afternoon as we await the Kypragons."

Chapter Twenty-Eight

Kavan had helped brush down the horses they had used that morning and feed them in the stables near the gate of the city. Then he went to help Dacey and Lou in their smokehouse that they had built onto their kitchen: some of the meat, like the boar he had helped hunt the day before, was too heavy for the part orcs to lift. Kavan was happy to help in any way he could.

It was just after midday when Kavan went in search of Roslyn, finding her and Leaf flying above the city. He decided to wait on the city wall nearby for them to come back down.

When they did, though, Heath was already there so Kavan hung back, watching from the nearby wall. He saw how they interacted, how they kissed. He bristled, knowing that she had never kissed him like that, and he knew at that moment that she would not pick him. His original plan to stay away so she would pick Heath had worked, he supposed. Now that he had wanted to fight for her, he had already lost. He slumped his shoulders and looked away from the pair. He had to get away from there.

He ran up to the plateau, and up the mountain to where Alexander had lived in exile. He remembered waking up there after the avalanche. He should have died in the snow, but Alexander had dug him out and bitten him. It was up that mountain where he had transformed into a werewolf. He had chosen to keep those powers, and in so doing he had lost Roslyn.

When Alexander found him, he found his former home a mess. Kavan was leaning against the wall with his eyes closed, breathing heavily.

"What happened?" Alexander asked him.

"I lost my temper," Kavan answered him apologetically.

"Do you want to talk about it?" Alexander asked him,

Kavan sighed and opened his eyes, turning to look at Alexander. "Just coming to terms with certain things," Kavan told him. "What brings you up here?"

"Looking for you," Alexander answered. "Chiefs Willow and Erick are here, and there is a Kypragon army coming to join us as well. They should be outside the city within the hour. Roslyn has gathered her inner circle to meet with them, but we couldn't find you."

"Let's not keep them waiting then, shall we?" Kavan told him as he headed for the door. Alexander nodded and together they ran back down the mountain and tunnel through the plateau to the city below.

Kavan found Tiffany sitting next to Roslyn at a long table, with Karina on her other side. Heath was sitting across from Roslyn with Aidan and Cypress on either side. Maeve and the orc chief Stane were sitting next to Cypress. Chief Willow and Chief Erick were both sitting at the far end of the table, with Edwin and three empty chairs at the other end of the table. Each of them had a tankard of ale in their hand, and a small plate of smoked meat and cheese in front of them. Alexander and Kavan took the empty seats and Dacey brought them a filled tankard of ale and a plate of the food.

Spread out on the table was a map of the area, with a few small icons sitting on top of it that Kavan knew Aidan used to place troops.

"What did we miss?" Alexander asked the group.

"Not much," Roslyn told him. "Willow was praising Dacey's smoked meat though, it is delicious. I cannot wait to try the blueberry mead she is making too. They'll have the finest eatery and brewery in the city, I just know it!"

"Blueberry mead sounds good," Kavan commented, making himself look at Roslyn. She was too busy looking at some notes that Aidan had just given her to notice him at the moment. Edwin and Alexander were talking about how exciting it was to finally meet a merman, so he sat back in his chair and snacked on the plate of food in front of him.

***

Heath greeted Nadim at the gate, taking his horse's reins for him. The Kypragon army had chosen to camp on the other side of Chief Erick's forces. The dust was still settling a bit as Nadim dismounted from his horse and greeted Heath in turn with a hug.

"You look well, my friend!" Nadim told him. The merman was in his human form, his dark brown dreadlocks pulled back from his face with a leather thong. His frishna armour gleamed in the sunlight.

"Thank you, you do as well. How is your family?" Heath asked him as he led the man to the awaiting party under the tent.

"They miss me, as I do them, but they know that what I am doing is important," Nadim answered. He turned to Roslyn and greeted her with a, "It is good to finally meet you, Queen Roslyn. I have heard a lot about you."

A Descent into the Roots

"And I you, Nadim," Roslyn answered as she stood to shake his hand in greeting. "Please come join us." She indicated the empty chair next to Kavan and introduced everyone to Nadim at the same time.

"Would you like some ale?" Dacey asked Nadim as she offered him a tankard and a plate of the smoked meats and cheese. He accepted both with a smile and took a hearty swig, clearly enjoying the refreshment.

"How did you chill it?" Nadim inquired of Dacey, and Dacey looked up at Heath who chuckled. "Ah," Nadim caught on, "Heath used his magic to chill it! Very useful."

"Now, down to business," Roslyn spoke up, and everyone turned to look at her. "Our scouts say the dark elf army numbers almost three thousand, including the dekellians. With the forces we have gathered here we nearly match them. We will make our stand here, at Dragon City, which is the most defensible position we have. I'm sending all of the civilians up to the plateau in the morning, and we will bring all of our forces inside the wall to camp." Roslyn moved three of the icons to inside the part of the map that had the city wall on it. "We will dig trenches here," Roslyn placed sticks in several places outside the city, some with many trenches in a row; there were several clear paths between each section.. "And put up defensive barriers before and after them, and cover the trenches. We will need logs and spikes for these." She placed pinecones in those spots. "Since the Archipelago gave us firearms to use, our shooters will be on the walls with the archers."

"And the army itself?" Tiffany asked her, looking down at the map.

"Half of the army will be spread out in the front, here," Roslyn replied, indicating the area in front of the barriers. "Some soldiers will be in the trenches with polearms to kill dekellians. The rest of the army will be behind the trenches. The forward army meets the enemy first and then withdraws back, drawing the enemy closer to the walls and the traps between."

"We should have some trenches with oil in them, set some of them on fire if they fall in," Heath suggested.

"Now that's an idea," Roslyn said contemplatively as she looked around the table. "Anyone else have any ideas?"

***

They talked for hours and only broke up the meeting to eat supper together. Messengers had come and gone, relaying more information on the dark elves and their scouts. More planning had been made during the course of the afternoon, and Roslyn felt somewhat confident that they could defeat the dark elves.

Nadim approached Roslyn as she was finishing up her plate of food.

"Heath tells me they captured a kobold," Nadim began, "Have you interrogated it yet?"

Roslyn shook her head no as she swallowed her last bite of food. "I have not had the time, no."

"I would very much like to see the kobold, and maybe help with the interrogation," Nadim told her.

"Sure, I will take you to him," Roslyn responded, getting up and handing her empty plate to Dacey. She thanked Karina's mother for the meal and then led Nadim to where they had the kobold in a cage near the tunnel up to the plateau. Leaf chose to stay behind in the tent because she was still eating a large bowl of meat. There were four soldiers keeping guard around the cage.

"Fascinating," Nadim commented as he took in the kobold. "Has he said anything?"

Roslyn looked at one of the guards who shook his head, but then said, "He has taken food and eaten it without complaint. He has said nothing though."

Roslyn let Nadim approach the kobold, and was surprised when Nadim started making some kind of guttural sound. She was even more surprised when the kobold perked up and seemed to actually understand what the merman was saying to it. The kobold then replied with the same kind of sounds.

Nadim looked at Roslyn with a satisfied smile as he turned to her.

"You know how to speak their language?" Roslyn asked him, surprise showing in her voice.

"For most of the world it is a lost language, but some of us merfolk still know it. He says his name is Lo'Lir, and he was a scout for his leader's army. He only knows that his leader is after some kind of magic that it first felt several months ago. His leader is a High Priest, someone who uses magic. There are very few kobolds who can use magic, and those who do usually end up being the leaders," Nadim informed her.

"How long ago did his High Priest feel this new magic?" Roslyn asked him. Nadim turned to the kobold and used the guttural language to ask the question.

After the kobold replied, Nadim told her, "About nine months ago, give or take."

"That's around the time I joined with Jay'Al after returning," Roslyn told him. "Heath thought they were after me because of my connection to Jay'Al making my powers stronger."

"It could be," Nadim answered her with a shrug. "Unfortunately, he was just a scout and not privy to the High Priests' motivations."

"Thank you for your assistance," Roslyn told Nadim as they headed back over to the main city gate and the tent where a few of her companions were still sitting and talking; Kavan and Aidan were both not there. "And thank you for saving Heath."

"He is a very good man," Nadim told her. "You are very important to him. All he wanted was to get back to you."

Roslyn felt something squeeze her heart and she looked at Heath who was still sitting there talking to Maeve, a tankard in his hand that he was drinking from.

"He's very important to me too," Roslyn whispered to Nadim. She cleared her throat and thanked him again, going over to the empty chair next to Heath and sitting down. She reached out slowly and took his hand in hers as he talked to Maeve, and he squeezed it before giving her a sweet smile.

Solana went over to Leaf, who was done eating, and nudged her before looking at Roslyn and Heath. Leaf followed the gryphon's gaze and sighed as she felt Roslyn's feelings through their bond.

"*I guess that's that,*" Leaf told Solana. "*We'll be spending a lot of time together in the future, Solana.*"

Solana seemed to like that, for she curled up against Leaf's side and started washing her. Leaf felt a little tickled but she was enjoying the grooming.

"*I like you too, little one,*" Leaf said to the gryphon, and she used her one wing to cover the gryphon who then started purring as she fell asleep next to the dragon.

Chapter Twenty-Nine

assidy looked at the city wall of Wardgrove and thought about growing up there as Roslyn had. Poppy pointed out certain buildings as they made their way through the city to the family castle. When they got to the castle a guard approached her.

"Well I'll be, King Lucius told me you would look exactly like Roz but seeing it is something else," the guard told her. "I grew up with Roz, your highness. You can call me Ned."

"A pleasure to meet you, Ned," Cassidy greeted him. "I think Roslyn told me about you, and the antics you would get up to as children."

Ned seemed pleased to hear that as he ordered stable boys to come get their horses. "Poppy, Eliza, Robert, it is good to see you again. I hope your travels weren't too much."

"That would be an understatement," Eliza commented as she dismounted and stretched her back. "It is good to be home though, Ned."

"Sir Sullivan, here is a report for you," Ned said as he gave Sully some papers. "King Lucius sent a few mages to us over the last month to get the castle ready, and we have been keeping track of who has come and gone from the city. We rooted out a couple of spies who were shipped to the northern outpost prison. If you and the Duchess want to double-check the castle before you leave I would completely understand."

"Thank you, Ned. I think that is just what I am going to do," Cassidy told him as she dismounted and handed the reins of her horse to a stable boy. "Have there been any servants sick lately?"

"No, ma'am. No new faces working in the castle either. Everyone inside was handpicked by Roland's replacement, who was handpicked himself by the King. The mages he sent were friends of your sister."

"Show us around the castle and tell us what they did," Sully told him as he quickly went over the notes. Satisfied, he put the notes in his bag.

"Come this way," Ned said as he gestured for them to follow him.

"Kai, stay with them please," Cassidy told Kai who nodded. "And the rest of the guard."

The lady knights nodded and handed over the reins of their horses as well before closing in to make a tight circle around the three royals.

"We will make a quick pass through the castle," Cassidy assured Eliza before going inside.

***

Cassidy hugged her younger siblings tightly before leaving them with Ned and the rest of the soldiers who were patrolling the castle. She had been satisfied with the protective measures put into place by the mages and the soldiers, so she knew they would be safe. Cassidy even added a few more protective spells of her own as they did their walk-through.

"I will be back for you once everything is safe again," Cassidy promised her siblings. "Maybe you could travel with me to Jay'Al, hm?"

"I'd like that," Eliza told her. "Be safe, Cass."

"Be safe, Cass," the other two echoed as they hugged her tightly back.

"Now go on inside, and mind Ned, ok?" Cassidy said as she urged them to let go. They did so reluctantly, and she walked down the steps to where Sully, Kai, and the lady knights were waiting with the horses.

Cassidy mounted her horse and turned to look at where her siblings were watching from one of the windows. She could tell Poppy was trying not to cry, and Robert was holding his chin up trying not to cry either. Eliza was standing straight, her hand up in a wave.

"Let's move out," Cassidy told her companions. "We need to get back to my father as fast as we can."

***

Five days of hard riding brought them to just outside of the Capital just after dawn. They rode up a hill and stopped to stare at the city below them. They could see the camped mercenary forces just on the other side of the city, but it looked like the city as of yet went untouched.

"The fighting has not started yet," Sully commented as he looked through his spyglass. "We won't be able to enter the city through the gates."

"Good thing we built that tunnel," Cassidy told him. "Come on, we have no more time to waste."

They found the farmhouse just to the north of the city, finding it empty but for a few tables and chairs. The storm doors of the basement had been replaced with large double-doors that were locked with a large lock built into it, and magic. Cassidy said the magic word to unlock the magic, and produced a key to unlock the lock. It took both her and Sully to open the large doors, re-vealing a sloping tunnel that they would be able to ride their horses through. Cassidy urged everyone ahead of her and Sully, and together they closed the doors from the inside with the key, and she replaced the magic that kept it safe.

It was a short ride into the city where they had to unlock another door that led them into the stables outside of the tavern. There were two entrances to the tunnel, one in the stables for those with horses and wagons, and another one with a ladder that went into the basement of the tavern. Soldiers guarded the stables, but upon seeing Cassidy and Sully they stood down.

"Report," Sully told the first soldier. "When did the mercenaries arrive?"

"Yesterday," the soldier told him.

"Any terms demanded?" Sully asked next.

"No one has approached the city yet with any terms," the soldier respond-ed.

"Which means they are going to attack soon," Sully commented. "Do you know where our King is?"

"He should be in the palace," the soldier told him.

Sully turned to Cassidy, and said, "Come on, we need to find out what he knows."

They rode through the city up to the palace where stable boys immediately met them to take their horses. Guards let them inside with a nod and a fist over their hearts.

They found Lucius in the War Room with a few of his generals and Headmistress Dake. Lucius looked relieved to see them as they entered the room. Kai waited outside with the lady knights.

Cassidy looked at her father and noticed his rumpled clothes and his barely brushed hair. When was the last time he had slept, or bathed? She went right up to him and hugged him. As she pulled back she looked at the generals and dismissed them. They left without a comment.

"What did you do that for?" Lucius asked her, half-amused.

"When did you sleep last?" Cassidy asked him. "Bathe? Eat?"

Lucius half-chuckled, and said, "You sound like Roslyn."

Cassidy rolled her eyes and moved him to a seat, and he sank into it slow-ly. "Eliza, Poppy, and Robert are safe in Wardgrove with Ned. You can relax a little more now."

"That is good to hear. Ned was always very loyal, I know he will keep them safe," Lucius commented quietly.

"Father, I want you to go eat something and then have a hot bath before a nap," Cassidy told him. "Do you hear me?"

"Yes, yes, alright, alright," Lucius told her as he stood up again. "My gen-erals can fill you in, they should be waiting outside still."

A Descent into the Roots

Cassidy watched her father leave the room, and his three generals came back in.

"He wouldn't listen to us," the one general, Weyland, told her. Weyland was her father's age, and one of his trusted friends. He wore his armour, a sword at his waist as well as a pistol. "It's good to see you back."

"Fill me in, please," Cassidy told them, and she nodded to Sully who closed the door to the War Room after stepping inside.

"They arrived the other day and made camp. No terms have been made yet. Their numbers are the same as we were informed before, nearly five thousand," General Weyland told them. "The citizens living closest to the walls have been evacuated to the inner circle of the city."

"Siege engines?" Sully asked them.

"They have catapults, and a few ballistae," the other general, Locke, informed them. This man was in his early thirties with dark blonde hair. He was also wearing his armour, and had a longsword strapped to his back.

"When do you think they will start their attack?" Cassidy asked them.

"Anytime now, really. They might still make terms before they start, or they might wait till after they see us vulnerable before they make terms," Weyland told them with a shrug.

"Our soldiers are ready?" Cassidy asked them. All three of them nodded.

"Get them ready at the wall. Archers, cannons and guns," Sully told them. "Once the King is awake we will send word. Send your reports to us here."

The generals nodded and left them in the War Room. Cassidy sighed and leaned against the table.

"At least we made it in time," Sully commented as Kai came into the room with Tej. Crick chirped from her place on Cassidy's shoulder.

"I'm going to go make sure Father is doing as he was told," Cassidy said with a chuckle. "I'll meet you back here," she told Sully.

Together with Kai she went to her father's suite of rooms. The guards let them in and they found Lucius eating a bowl of oatmeal with fruits.

"I may be stubborn, but I'm not *that* stubborn," Lucius told them when he saw them. "I know when to concede to a woman."

That made Cassidy laugh, and she sat down next to her father at the small table he was sitting at.

"The generals have gone to the wall to prepare the soldiers," Cassidy told him.

"Good. Once I'm done eating I am going to nap. When I wake up I will shower, it will help," Lucius told her. "Now go, I'll be fine."

Cassidy and Kai left him then. As she closed the door, she turned to one of the guards and told them, "I want to know when he is awake again, ok?"

The guard nodded his understanding. Satisfied, Cassidy and Kai went back to the War Room where they found Sully drinking the wake-up drink that

Heath was so fond of.

"Got any more of that?" Cassidy asked him. "I think we are going to need it today."

Chapter Thirty

awn started to light up the sky as Roslyn watched from the city wall. She had had trouble sleeping so she had decided to get up to watch the sunrise.

"What are you doing up so early?"

She turned to find Kavan standing a stone's throw down the walkway.

"Me? What about you?" she asked him.

"I don't need as much sleep as I used to," Kavan told her. "I've been patrolling the wall for most of the night."

"Oh."

"Well?" he asked her.

"I need to talk to you," she told him after a moment of watching the sun rise.

"I know," he told her. She looked at him with surprise. "I see it. You're in love with Heath. I concede. I know you will be very happy together."

"I'm sorry."

He grinned crookedly at her and told her, "You have nothing to be sorry about, Roz. Your heart picked for you. I will always be your friend, that will never change."

"Thank you," she told him, relieved.

"Where is Leaf?" he asked her. "Your shadow is not with you?"

"I think she is having another growth spurt," Roslyn told him. "She sleeps heavier when she does."

"How did it feel flying with her yesterday?" Kavan inquired of her, leaning against the side of the walkway.

"It was amazing," she replied. "I know I will be doing it a lot more."

"Is it comfortable without a saddle? I imagine her scales are hard."

Roslyn shrugged and told him, "It's not too bad. I might have a small saddle made up though."

"The Feathers seem to be doing well," Kavan commented as he looked up to see a gryphon with a rider flying above them.

"Quinn says they have soft backs," Roslyn informed her. "He does wish he had a saddle though, something to hold him in place in case they have to do maneuvers."

"That's a great idea," Kavan commented, thinking. "I think I have something in mind. If you will excuse me, I am going to go talk to the blacksmith about a saddle. I will see you later."

"Till later," she called after him as he headed for the nearest stairs.

Thinking of Heath, she looked for his tent. Finding it, she headed for it. Solana lifted her head from where she was sleeping next to Heath's bedroll when Roslyn opened the flap of the tent. Solana made a chirping noise, waking Heath up slightly–he opened an eye to look at the gryphon and then noticed Roslyn. Solana got up, stretched, and left the tent. Was it Roslyn's imagination, or had the gryphon given her a knowing look?

Heath lifted up his blanket and moved over a little bit to give her more room as she crawled into bed with him. He put an arm around her, pulling her close against him; he smelled of the cedar soap they had in the bathing house, and she knew he had bathed the night before. She kissed him, and he kissed her back, sleepily at first but then he began to wake up more as the kisses became more heated. Her hands went to his tunic, pulling it up, and he helped her take it off of him. As he pulled the tunic over his head he heard her say, "I want you Heath."

He smiled at her as he brought his hands down to touch her face. "Does that mean?"

"You are the one I want," she told him. He leaned in happily and kissed her again, and as their hands wandered he pulled back and looked to the door of the tent.

Roslyn chuckled and lifted her hand, casting a spell around the tent. "No one will be able to hear us," Roslyn assured him.

"If you say so," Heath said with a grin, and he started kissing her again, this time not stopping his hands from wandering further.

***

Aidan found Roslyn and Heath eating breakfast together in Lou and Dacey's kitchen. The pair were sitting close to each other, and were acting just a little giddy.

"Morning reports," Aidan told them as he handed some papers to Roslyn. He accepted a plate of bacon and eggs from Dacey and took a seat at the table across from Roslyn and Heath.

"You have way too many things on your hands," Roslyn told Aidan as she looked at the reports. "How exactly did you become the one the Feathers reported to?"

Aidan shrugged, "It just happened? I have no idea. I deal with the normal scouts, so I guess they thought they should report to me?"

"Heath," Roslyn said as she looked up at her partner, "I know you haven't had the chance to actually fly yet, but you should be the leader of the Feathers."

"I accept if it's alright with you," Heath said as he looked at Aidan.

Aidan breathed a sigh of relief. "Thank you. Here," he handed Heath a set of keys. "These are to the Feathers Nest. I'll let them know after I'm done eating."

"The scribes are helping you too, right?" Roslyn asked Aidan.

"Yes, yes, of course. They have been very helpful. Just between everything…I fear I have spread myself a little thin."

"What else can we help you with?" Heath asked him. "We might have some ideas to lighten your load."

"Between the city planning and farm planning, I've been swamped," Aidan admitted.

"Well, that planning might have to wait until we get rid of the dark elves," Roslyn told him. "The outline you have made of the city already is amazing. You tactfully put magical creatures in a good place, and worked with the orc Elders to make sure they had a proper area as well. I couldn't have done it better myself."

"It is gratifying to hear you say that, Roz," Aidan told her. "I will take a break for now, and let Heath take the reins of the Feathers."

"Please do rest," Roslyn told him. "I don't need any of you to burn yourselves out."

***

When Roslyn and Heath left Lou and Dacey's after eating, they discovered Hawk and Solana waiting outside for them.

"*Solana tells me you need to learn to fly with a gryphon,*" Hawk told Heath. "*I would like to help.*"

"Are you related to Solana?" Heath asked Hawk. "Ulmer's gryphon called her 'little sister'."

"*She is my grandchild,*" Hawk told him. "*Dark Elves came and stole some of our eggs.*"

"I wondered about that," Roslyn commented.

"Thank you for the offer," Heath told Hawk. "I accept."

Hawk knelt down for Heath to mount her back, and as Heath climbed on Roslyn saw Leaf coming towards them with an eager bounce in her step.

"*We can fly together!*" Leaf said excitedly to Roslyn. "*Come on, climb on!*"

Roslyn chuckled and mounted Leaf as Hawk and Heath took to the air, with Solana following. Within moments they had joined the gryphon and her rider in flying above the city. Roslyn noticed the clouds in the sky as they flew up and made circles, and she thought she could smell rain.

"*A storm is coming*," Leaf agreed.

"It's a good thing the dark elves have stayed put for now," Roslyn told her, thinking of the reports that Aidan had given her.

Hawk and Heath flew along beside them, with Solana flying on Leaf's other side, as they went up to the plateau and circled the palace. Oswick and Judd, who had come out of their tent, waved up at them. Roslyn saw the clouds growing darker and she suggested they go back down to the city.

When they landed Roslyn was pleased to find that the civilians had packed up their belongings and were heading up the tunnel to the plateau as she had ordered to be done. Aidan did not seem very happy that his early plans and markings were being taken down to make room for their army to come inside the city walls but he knew it had to be done. Roslyn made a mental note to get something for Aidan as a 'thank you' for everything he had helped her with.

The soldiers began setting up their tents in neat rows as thunder rolled overhead, and lightning flashed in the distance. Roslyn peered up at the sky, waiting for the rain to come. She had an idea to keep the rain off the soldiers, so she grabbed some of her crystals and headed up to the walkway of the city wall. She placed her crystals at certain intervals on the outside part of the wall, and when she was done she activated the spell just in time. As the angry clouds above them let loose their rain a protective magical dome went up over the area below. Water ran down the outside of the dome and down the city wall like a waterfall.

Peering down the side of the outer wall, Roslyn used her magic to make a small aqueduct to capture the water, and she made a small cistern to collect the water in. A water reserve would definitely come in handy if there was going to be a battle or a siege there. She doubted it would come to that, but she wanted to plan for different outcomes, just in case.

Heath had gone to the Feathers Nest, and Roslyn could see many gryphon riders coming back in out of the rain, landing on the outside deck of the Nest and going through its doors. Roslyn knew that the gryphons would be able to sense her magical barrier and avoid it, so they were all heading for the Nest. Roslyn hoped there was enough room in there for them all. As she headed towards the Nest she saw a large door open on the inside of the city and the gryphons and their riders walked out that way into the city. Relieved, Roslyn watched as her brother Quinn came running towards hers.

"The dark elves are on the move," Quinn informed her. "They are heading this way."

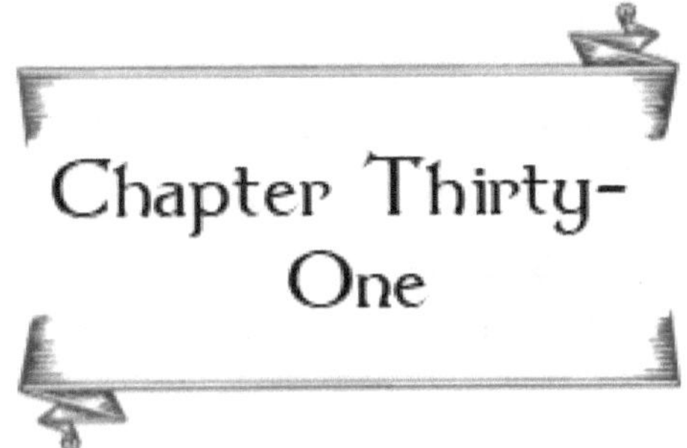

Chapter Thirty-One

King Lucius looked at the paper in front of him. Count Gresham had sent terms finally after two days of being camped outside the Capital. Lucius scoffed and threw the paper on the war table. Cassidy picked it up and read it as the three generals waited their turn. Cassidy handed the paper to General Weyland and the other two generals leaned over his shoulder to read it with him. Cassidy watched her father for any sign of his thoughts.

"This is insane," Weyland commented. "He cannot expect you to give in to these demands."

"And he knows I won't," Lucius told him. "I will not give him the throne, nor will I hand over my daughter to him."

"He's really going to attack the city?" Edmond asked, looking at the paper; Alara read it over his shoulder. He looked up at Cassidy and watched her expression.

"He tried assassinating us," Cassidy said, "and that didn't work. So this is what he will do next."

"We knew this was coming," Weyland told Edmond. "You know that. There was no way we were ever going to surrender to his terms. The future of your kingdom is at stake. The future of our sisters, our daughters, is at stake."

"I knew I liked you for a reason," Cassidy commented to Weyland. "Though I would advise you to speak better to Edmond. He knows *exactly* what is at stake, for he has fought for that future as well."

"My apologies," Weyland said to her and Edmond. "I'm more angry at the Count than anything."

Lucius grabbed another piece of paper and a writing utensil to write his reply. He rolled it up and poured wax on the lip of the paper, using his signet ring to seal it and leave his mark. He handed the reply to a messenger who was waiting at the door. The messenger took it and ran off to deliver it to the soldier who had brought the note of terms to the gate only hours before.

"Make sure our soldiers are ready," Lucius told his generals. "Once they get my reply, the attack on the city will start."

General Weyland nodded his head and stood at attention, putting his right fist over his heart. "Yes, my King," he responded, and the other two generals followed suit. Lucius dismissed them with a nod, and he, Cassidy, Edmond, and Alara watched the generals leave the room. Alara looked down at the map of the city on the table.

"Hopefully all of our preparations will mean something," Alara commented. Edmond took her hand in a reassuring way and then looked up at his father.

"Are you OK, da?" he asked his father.

"I never wanted this," Lucius told him. "I was never supposed to be on the throne. Now look at what is happening."

Cassidy took hold of her father's shoulders and he looked at her with surprise. "No," she told him. "You were born to be on this throne, do not forget that father. Your changes to the kingdom have meant something to *a lot* of people. Do not forget that. You are doing what is right. Count Gresham is doing this for his own power."

"Thank you, Cassidy," Lucius told her as he hugged her. "You give me strength." He looked at Edmond and said, "Both of you do."

"I should head down to the wall," Cassidy told her father. "Sully and Kai are waiting for me."

"I will protect your father and brother," Alara told her. Cassidy hugged her brother and Alara quickly before leaving the room.

Cassidy was joined by her lady knights as she left the War Room and headed for her suite. There Baylee helped her get her frishna armour on. The lady knights were already in their armour and ready. Crick got up on her shoulder. Together the group of women walked through the palace for the stables; the nobles who were still in the palace watched them go, some of the noblewomen cheering for them. Cassidy held her head high and smiled her appreciation for the women who cheered.

Their horses were ready and waiting. Together they rode for the wall through eerily empty streets. Word had spread of an impending attack so everyone was ordered to stay indoors. The whole first ring of the city had been evacuated already, and there was a message system in place, just iin case the second ring needed to be evacuated as well.

Sully and Kai met them, a soldier taking their horses to a nearby stable. Up the wall they went, and Cassidy was surprised to see the enemy soldiers in their formations, just waiting. Several catapults were moved forward, and Cassidy could tell that they were still trying to bring the catapults to the right range–there were a few boulders in the ground a good thousand meters away from the wall. Cassidy had her barrier in place for such an event, all she had to do was activate it.

Headmistress Dake joined them at the wall, along with the rest of the mages who had been helping Cassidy over the last few weeks. All of them were wearing their mage robes over armour, and their familiars were with them as well. The Headmistress had a bag slung over her shoulder where her feline familiar poked its head out of.

"I want someone to double check the defenses we set up," Cassidy told the Headmistress. "I need to make sure everything is still in place before I call up the barrier."

"Of course," the Headmistress replied, and within short order several mages left to go do that. A little while later Headmistress Dake came back to her to let her know that everything was still in place.

In that time Cassidy had watched the enemy test out two more boulders in the catapults, getting significantly closer each time. She was preparing to bring the barrier up any moment.

Kai reached out and took her hand, squeezing it. "Are you ready for this?" he asked her. "I've never been in any kind of battle before."

"Me neither," Cassidy replied. "I will *not* let this city fall."

Kai smiled before leaning in and kissing her. "I am by your side," he told her when they parted.

"As are we," Headmistress Dake piped up from where she was standing nearby with the mages, waiting to take orders. Cassidy smiled at the mages and then looked back out at the enemy in time to watch them launch another boulder. This one soared farther than the others had, and Cassidy quickly brought up the barrier. The boulder struck the barrier and broke apart, dust and debris falling to the ground outside of the city.

"That'll piss them off," one of the mages, Lexi, commented with a grin. Her wolf-dog familiar was at her feet, seemingly grinning herself.

"They'll most likely test a few more boulders at different intervals along the wall," Cassidy commented. "They'll get even more pissed off, I'm sure."

The group watched as more catapults were brought forward and adjusted, only for the boulders to hit the invisible barrier and break up into bits. The barrage went on for another hour or so until they stopped loading the catapults all together.

"What are they doing now?" the mage Stephanie asked as there was moved in the enemy lines.

"They'll try their hand at getting through a gate with a battering ram," Sully told them. "If they can get close enough. They need to bring their siege towers closer to protect the battering ram and the people using it. They'll also try to bring their soldiers over the wall with them."

"Will the barrier protect against soldiers trying to get over the wall?" Stephanie asked Cassidy.

"Oh yes," Cassidy said with a wicked grin. "They'll feel like they hit a stone wall."

"Technically their bridges won't even be able to connect with the wall, so they won't be able to even make it across," Sully commented. "So, still yes."

"Thanks, Sully," was all Cassidy could say to that, earning a chuckle from the mages. Sully shook his head and looked at Kai.

"Hitting a stone wall was more fun," Kai told him with a shrug.

"More dramatic!" Astra piped up, making everyone laugh again.

Cassidy looked at the enemy with her spyglass and saw that they were putting together their siege towers. There were at least fifteen of them going up quickly, and the soldiers were reforming to get ready to move them forward.

"Sully, are the cannons prepared?" Cassidy asked the knight.

"Yes, ma'am," he replied. "All of the cannons are manned and waiting."

A runner came with a message from the generals, who were in the gatehouse over the main gate a few wall sections away from where Cassidy and her people were.

"They are getting the soldiers prepared to go out to meet them once their siege towers fail," Cassidy told Sully and Kai. "I can't wait to see the look on Count Gresham's face."

***

It took only a few hours more for the siege towers to be moved close enough, and within range of the cannons. Cassidy didn't realize how close one of them was until it went off, startling her and Crick, as well as the other mages and familiars.

The cannonball that was shot missed the siege tower it was aimed at by the tiniest amount, but it took out a group of soldiers as it did so.

The catapults were moved to aim at the cannons, which were some areas that were not completely protected by the barrier for obvious reasons. Cassidy hoped the small opening she gave them would not be found by the catapults, though she knew it would take a miracle for them to hit the right spot. Thankfully when the catapults threw their next boulders they were misses, several of them aimed at cannons but none of them found their marks. It did not take long for whomever ran the catapults to give that up as well.

Archers and gunmen moved to sections of the wall where Cassidy had a special barrier around the crenellations so they could still fire at the enemy. As the enemy grew within range Cassidy could hear gunfire pop here and there.

Cassidy watched a group of enemy soldiers with shields over their heads break off from the main group that was getting closer to the wall. These soldiers were heading for one of the lesser gates not too far away from where Cassidy and her companions were. They were carrying something big with them.

"Aim for those soldiers heading for that gate!" Cassidy shouted, and several gunmen nearby heard her and switched their target to the group of soldiers. The soldiers closed their shields more around them and moved slower but still with purpose towards the gate. Cassidy was about to head over there when she saw them toss what they had in their hands and then break and run.

"Everybody down!" Cassidy yelled, but it was too late. An explosion destroyed the gate and the crystals above it, throwing and killing any soldiers that were on that section of the wall. Cassidy and her companions were thrown to the walkway in the aftershock of the explosion. As she lay there on the walkway, coughing in the smoke and debris, she could feel her barrier coming down.

"Mages!" Cassidy yelled as she struggled to get up. "We need to combine our strength and put up our own barrier!"

The whine of a projectile whizzing through the air caught her attention and she felt Kai grab hold of her and pull her out of the way. Cassidy used a gust of air to throw the other mages back out of the way as a boulder broke the wall where they had just been standing.

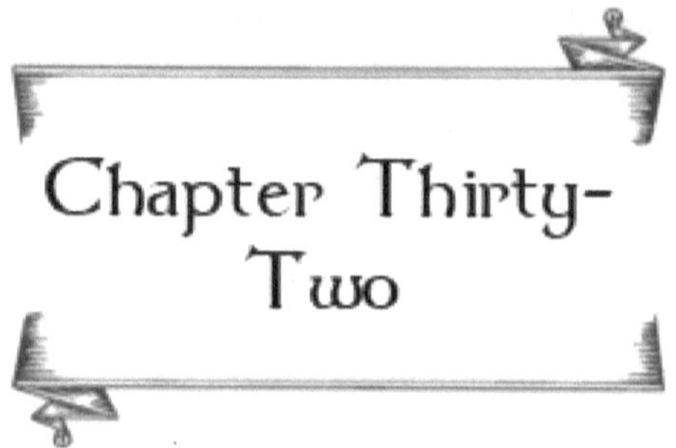

Chapter Thirty-Two

The rain did not hinder the movement of the dark elves. They advanced on Dragon City as the lightning cracked above them, the aftershock of thunder following closely. Roslyn looked through her spyglass at them, seeing dark elves riding on the backs of the dekellians, many of them holding large gun-like weapons that she could only assume from their description was what was used to kill McKenna.

Between the enemy and the city walls were the defenses she had had her people put up or dig: trenches, and sharp barriers to catch dekellians on.

"All Feathers should be grounded in this weather," Roslyn told Heath, who was standing beside her on the wall of the city.

"Already done," Heath replied coolly. "Quinn was the last one in."

"I need to make sure the kobolds are not going to join in on the attack," Roslyn told Heath after a moment. "We cannot take on both forces if they do arrive now," she added as she saw him about to protest.

Heath grimaced, knowing full well that they definitely would not be able to hold off against both armies. "As long as you are quick about it," Heath told her. "We have done a lot to prepare for this, but we might need you."

"I will do my best," Roslyn said as she turned to find the best spot to sit down. They were safe from the rain and the storm under her barrier, so she chose to go to the willow tree near the plateau.

Sitting down cross legged with Leaf beside her, Roslyn closed her eyes and willed her astral form to come out. She felt her body separate into two pieces, her human form sitting on the moss under the tree, and her astral form, light and corporeal. She moved underground, finding the tunnels that she had caved in and following them out towards where Heath had been underground. She could sense Maeve's and Karina's magic in the tunnels and knew that she was in the right place.

Heath had described the underground caverns to her a few times but she still marvelled at them. Who had made all of those caverns, with their crystals that imitated the sun? There were too many of them to be a coincidence, she thought, remembering the one they had found Kasimir in and which had been utilized by Alexander to trap the werewolves in centuries ago.

She saw up ahead a group of kobolds, at least fifteen of them, and she made herself blend in with the mushrooms and trees. The group moved past her, carrying digging materials towards the sections that were caved in. By the looks of it they had already dug out a few sections, but they were still underground. All of them wore the same kind of armour that Lo'Lir had when he was captured.

About to head back up to her body, Roslyn felt a tug of magic that drew her down the tunnels further. She tried to resist it but it was a different magic that called her, something she could not stop. She found herself curious, so she let it pull her further.

She moved through the underground forest, hidden from the groups of kobolds that were camped there waiting to get to the surface. She saw the behemoths, a group of twenty of them, exactly how Heath had described them, off to the side of the kobold's camp. There were a few groups of kobolds who looked like they had been digging already, and she figured they were digging in shifts. None of them took notice of her or made any indication that they saw her ghostly form.

Finally she stopped moving outside of what looked an awful lot like a shaman's tent, with talismans hanging from the doorway. The tent was made of some kind of hide, and wooden poles. A faint aroma of smoke came through the doorway, and some kind of spice that Roslyn could not place.

She felt something probe her mind, something that surprised her.

"*Come on in,*" she heard the voice inside her head, strange and intrusive.

Steeling herself, Roslyn entered the tent. Sitting in front of a fire was someone whom Roslyn could only guess was the High Priest the captured kobold scout had told her about. This kobold though looked somehow more humanoid than the others she had seen, or maybe it was the shorter snout it had and the less claw-like fingers that greeted her. The High Priest looked at her with slightly slanted eyes that were set in the front of his head, eyes very different from the rest of the kobolds.

"*I have felt your presence, here and there, over the weeks,*" the voice inside her mind told her. "*Please take a seat.*" The High Priest gestured to a chair on her side of the fire. In a moment she was sitting down in the chair, though how she was doing so in her astral form she had no idea. She feared that the High Priest could manipulate her somehow this way.

"How do you know my language?" Roslyn asked him first.

"*I learned it from your mind, though I can only speak it in mine. My mouth was not made for your words,*" he told her. "*I've been waiting to meet you.*"

"Can't say I feel the same," Roslyn retorted. "You have caused a lot of trouble."

Something that sounded like a low laugh tickled the back of her mind as the High Priest stirred the fire with a metal poker.

"*That is the biggest understatement I have ever heard,*" he told her. "*Tell me, what is your name?*"

"Tell me yours first," she hissed at him. She was starting to grow tired of his games.

"*You may call me Raktim,*" he told her as he half-bowed to her, flourishing his arms outward. The fire flickered a little at his movements.

"Roslyn," she told him. "Queen Roslyn, of Jay'Al."

"Queen *Roslyn,*" he repeated. "*I've been waiting for you.*"

Roslyn felt a shiver run down her spine, and she was sure that if she was in her human form she would have goosebumps running up her arms.

"*I felt a stirring in the earth when you joined with the land,*" he told her. "*It was too enticing to ignore. You were too enticing to ignore. Do you know how much power you yield?*"

"I have a vague idea," she whispered.

"*A* vague *idea,*" he scoffed. "*You have a dragon as a familiar. That has not happened since the founding of Jay'Al. Your existence changes the very course of the world, and it has already started, whether you know it or not.*"

Roslyn felt something around her wrists and she looked down to find magical tendrils coming up from the floor to wrap around her wrists like manacles. She felt the same things around her ankles and looked down to find that the tendrils were coming from the High Priest. She tried to pull herself back to her body but she found that she was stuck there in that chair.

"What are you doing? How are you doing this?" she demanded as she strained against her bonds.

The High Priest stood up, and she took in his form: he was tall, over six feet, wearing robes made of spider silk. He walked towards her, reaching out to touch her face.

"*You will be my guest here for a while,*" he told her.

***

Tiffany had followed Roslyn to the tree and waited patiently for her to return. She scratched Leaf's chin and fed the dragon some fish as she watched the rain hit the invisible dome above and then slide down the sides. Leaf had grown a lot more during her last growth spurt and was now much bigger than a horse, her wingspan twice the size as Hawk's.

Leaf startled her by standing up straight, staring at Roslyn and growling low. Roslyn's body had stiffened, and goosebumps ran up her arms. Then she started to try to move her hands but they stayed in place as if bound by something.

"Karina!" Tiffany called for the part-orc shaman. Karina came running, Mister Scruffy at her side.

A Descent into the Roots

"Something is wrong," Tiffany told Karina. Mister Scruffy went over to Leaf, who was still growling, and seemed to talk to the dragon.

"Leaf says something has hold of Roslyn's astral form," Karina informed her. "Leaf is afraid for Roslyn."

"Get Heath," Karina told Tiffany. "He needs to see this."

Tiffany ran to get Heath, who was waiting on the wall for Roslyn to return; the enemy had started formations but had yet to advance on them.

Heath and Solana came at a run, worry evident in Heath's face. He knelt next to Roslyn and could tell that she was scared.

"What's happening?" he asked Karina.

"Someone has hold of her astral form," Karina told him.

"How can someone do that?" Heath wanted to know, aggravation showing in his voice. "That should not be possible."

"Can you go after her, see if you can find out what is going on?" Tiffany asked him.

"We cannot risk Heath being caught in the same thing," Karina interjected. "Not when the dark elves are poised to attack us."

"We need Roslyn too though," Tiffany argued, but Heath took a step back to look at both of them.

"Karina is right," Heath told her. "Roslyn is strong enough that she can get out of whatever it is herself, and she would tell us the same thing. You know that, Tiffany."

Tiffany looked at Leaf, who was still bristling, and then to Karina and back at Heath. "Fine, you are right. Karina, will you stay with her, and let us know if anything changes?"

"I will," Karina assured them.

Heath put a hand on Roslyn's shoulder, feeling her shiver. "Come back to me," he told her before turning and leading both Solana and Tiffany back to the wall.

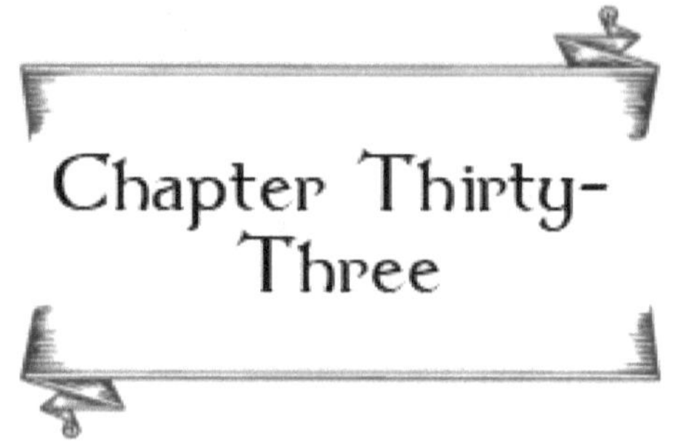

Chapter Thirty-Three

After the dust settled, Cassidy could see that the group of mages, though dishevelled, were all alive still. She breathed a sigh of relief as Kai helped her to stand. Crick, who was on her shoulder, chirped at her. She heard Tej whine, and Kai picked his familiar up. Behind them, Sully and the rest of the lady knights were getting up and dusting themselves off.

"Mistress Dake!" Cassidy called over the hole in the wall. She saw the Headmistress look up, and she realized there was blood on the woman's face.

"I'm alright!" she called over to her. Astra helped her to stand.

"I want you all to pull back!" Cassidy told them.

"But—"

"That's an order!" Cassidy shouted. "Now!"

Cassidy watched as the Headmistress nodded and she gathered up the mages on her side of the walkway and they headed for the nearest stairs at a run. Another boulder flew over them to land in an abandoned house not too far away in the city.

Cassidy blocked the next boulder that flew towards the city, angry now. She tossed the boulder back the way it had come, not thinking that it would actually go, but she was surprised when it flew back through the air to hit the very catapult that had thrown it. Kai looked at her with surprise, and Crick made a confused sound.

"I know," Cassidy said to Crick, "That should not have happened."

"What's wrong?" Kai asked her.

"My magic, something just spiked in it," Cassidy told him. She felt goosebumps go up her arms as she knew instantly that something was wrong.

"Something is wrong with Roslyn," Cassidy whispered. Her breath caught in

716

her chest. "Something is *very* wrong with Roslyn."

Kai blocked the next boulder, letting it fall outside the city. "I am not sure how you can tell, but if you can feel it from this far away then it must be serious," Kai commented, worry in his voice.

Cassidy shook herself and watched as the cannons destroyed a few of the siege towers. The enemies were moving their siege towers faster now, spurred on by their generals now that the barrier protecting the city was down. Several of the traps they had placed outside of the city went off, triggering explosions and freeze bombs. Many of the soldiers scattered, breaking rank only to be directed back by their generals.

"What do you sense?" Sully asked Cassidy.

"Something has taken hold of Roslyn," Cassidy told him, "I can't explain it, I just *know*."

"That doesn't bode well," Sully commented as he looked out over the approaching enemy. "But we cannot lose focus on this battle right now."

"I know that," Cassidy said with exasperation. "We have done all we can here for now," Cassidy told Sully. "We need to pull back to the palace and fortify it in case they make it into the city."

"No, we need to stay here to make sure that doesn't happen," Sully told her. "We need to do something about the breach in the wall."

Cassidy felt magic surge through her again, but this time the ground shook and they watched as large rocks came out of the ground where the small gate used to be. Cassidy stood there in shock, as did her companions.

"Well, that's new," Kai commented.

"It wasn't me, not really," Cassidy responded. "I can feel that Roslyn is afraid."

Both Sully and Kai looked at her with worry.

Crick nuzzled against her cheek, "*She will be alright.*"

"We have to focus," Sully reminded her.

Another boulder flew through the air, and this time Cassidy threw it back with her magic again. Soldiers scattered as it hit a catapult.

Cassidy looked down to see the generals ready to ride out to meet the enemy soldiers. General Weyland looked up at her and saluted before placing his clenched fist over his heart. She heard him give the order and the great gate was opened to let them through before they rode through it.

Cassidy watched as the soldiers on the walls utilized the freeze bombs she had the mages make for if the siege towers came too close, or if anyone tried to raise a ladder to get up the wall. Enemy soldiers were frozen where they stood close to the wall, and siege towers froze to the ground. From the wall the Ellsgrovian soldiers threw oil on the siege engines and lit them on fire. She could hear the screams of the enemy soldiers from where they were standing.

"We should fall back to the palace," Cassidy reiterated. "The generals have it from here. Count Gresham's army is being decimated."

They watched as general Weyland and his troops plowed down the mercenary soldiers as the cannons continued to fire at the other siege towers that were left. Some of the general's men had lances that they used to dismount enemy officers, and there were sharpshooters who took care of the ones at the back of the army.

"Fine, let's pull back to the palace," Sully finally agreed.

They went down the closest staircase and a soldier brought them their horses. They mounted and headed for the palace. Halfway there they came across Headmistress Dake and the mages heading in the same direction.

"Need a lift?" Cassidy asked Dake, and she offered the older woman a hand up. She took it and Cassidy pulled her up to sit behind her. Sully and her lady knights each took up a mage and then they were back on their way up to the palace.

***

Lucius, Edmond, and Alara met them at the doors to the palace. The soldiers guarding the palace were watching the fighting on the outside of the city now, and many of them asked Cassidy and Sully how the fighting was going.

"Count Gresham will be pushed back by the end of the day if General Weyland has anything to say about it," Cassidy told them. She turned to Headmistress Dake and said, "Take everyone to the infirmary, they'll be bringing the wounded up soon."

Dake gathered her mages and headed in the direction of the infirmary. Cassidy could see that several carts of wounded were already on their way up to the infirmary. She had visited it on her tour of the palace after she had first arrived, and she knew there was plenty of room for the wounded to be treated by healers and mages alike.

"What happened at the wall?" her father asked her as they headed for the War Room. A runner came and handed the king the latest report. He opened it and smiled as he read it. "General Weyland has routed the enemy forces and pushed them into a retreat. His officers are trying to find the Count."

"What do you mean, 'trying'?" Sully asked him. "The Count should have been with the commanders of the mercenaries."

Cassidy stopped in her tracks, making everyone else stop. They were only a stone's throw away from the War Room, and Cassidy could not see the guards who had stood there earlier in the day.

"Sully," she nodded to the doors ahead. Sully looked and nodded, meaning he understood what she meant. Sir Sullivan moved in front of the king, Cassidy's lady knights motioning to Edmond and Alara to move back as Cassidy and Sullivan advanced on the doors slowly. Cassidy motioned for Kai to stay with her father and brother.

A Descent into the Roots

Cassidy took hold of the door knob and started turning it.

Heat erupted from the room, and it was only her quick reflexes that saved her and Sully–and maybe a little bit of Roslyn's magic as well. She threw up a shield around them both as they were thrown backwards in the explosion; they landed just shy of where their companions were standing. The explosion brought soldiers running.

"He has to be in the castle," Cassidy hissed as she stood up. "Crick, do you smell anything different?"

Crick sniffed the air and jumped down from her shoulders. She went to one of the rooms nearby and sniffed around the door. Sully opened it, revealing a storage closet where the two dead guards had been stashed. Crick sniffed around their bodies for a few moments before looking up at Cassidy and telling her, "*I have the scent of their killer.*"

"Then lead me to him," Cassidy told her familiar, and with that Crick was off running down the hallway that led past the War Room. Kai and Sully followed her, with Cassidy shouting back to her knights to stay with the king.

They were in the servants wing after a few turns, where washerwomen cleaned clothes and the servants had their quarters. The scent led Crick through there and out the back of the palace near the entrance to the garden and forest. Crick's attention was caught by a man who was walking away from the palace at a quickened pace, but not too quick to arouse suspicion. Cassidy saw him try to hide his face and she instantly knew that it was him.

Using the fireball spell she had learned from Roslyn, she threw one to land just in front of the man. He wheeled in surprise, and she was gratified to see that it was indeed the man who had killed Elle and countless more innocent people. He tried to lift his pistol to shoot at her but she was too quick for him: he was engulfed in flames before he got the shot off. The gun fired from the heat, the bullet hitting a nearby tree.

"He won't be trying to assassinate anyone soon," Cassidy said as she turned and started back towards the palace.

Chapter Thirty-Four

The rain did not bother the dark elves as they moved into formation before the city walls. Heath watched them through his spy glass, Solana standing beside him with her front paws on the crenellations so she could get a good look at what was going on outside the wall. Above them, more thunder cracked and lightning flashed as the rain droned on.

"What can we expect, do you think?" Heath asked Tiffany.

"No clue," she told him. "Has Kavan been informed of what happened?"

Heath nodded and gestured to where Kavan was standing with Alexander and Edwin; Kavan was turned to look at Roslyn who was still under the tree, unmoving.

"We are all worried," Tiffany commented. "I am going to go talk to him."

Heath nodded his understanding and then ordered his gunmen to double check their weapons before loading. Below them, the gates opened up to let Willow and Erick ride out with their soldiers.

Solana shifted from one back paw to the other, flapping her wings with irritation. Heath could hear the rest of the gryphons that were inside the dome flap their wings as well, and they all let out the same kind of growling noise that made the hairs on the back of his neck stand up.

"What's gotten into you all?" Heath asked Solana as he reached over and petted her.

"*We want to fight,*" Solana told him. "*Rip and shred.*"

"I see," Heath said after a moment. He had heard her voice in his mind before but somehow she seemed different, a little more mature than before.

A Descent into the Roots

Willow and Erick's soldiers took the formation that Roslyn had planned. The dark elves advanced, several of them shooting off their weapons. Heath watched in trepidation as the Jay'Alian soldiers put forth their frishna shields to protect themselves–the spikes did not go through them, though they did seem to dent them a little bit. Several of Erick's soldiers had guns and Heath could hear them open fire. He had advised them on where the dark elves were vulnerable and was gratified when a dozen or more dark elves who were advancing fell to the bullets.

Heath could hear the two armies clash together, as they screamed and yelled. The clank of sword against sword was almost drowned out by the rain and thunder though as the storm seemed to get worse.

"Do you think frishna metal is conductive?" Kavan asked him as he joined him and Solana. "I really hope none of our people get struck by lightning."

"Not sure," Heath said after a moment. Tiffany followed Kavan over.

"Any news?" Kavan inquired, and Heath knew that he meant Roslyn. At that moment a messenger came to them and told them, "No change with Her Majesty."

All three of them sighed and turned to look back at the fighting. Heath looked down to Nadim who was waiting for the signal; Heath instructed Solana to shriek like a hawk and she did so, loud enough that everyone in the vicinity had to cover their ears. It was also at a certain pitch that it made the dark elves stagger, which was an unexpected outcome but not an unwelcome one.

Willow and Erick ordered their men back behind the trenches, drawing the dark elves closer to the wall. As Heath ordered his men to take aim, he thought he felt a drop of water on his head. He looked up, as did those around him, as Roslyn's magical barrier came down bringing the rain with it. There was no time to think more beyond that, for Heath yelled, "FIRE!" and his gunmen set loose a volley of bullets into the dark elves and dekellians. Dekellians who tried to jump over the barriers found their feet sinking into the mud and in turn they fell onto the barriers, impaling themselves.

Nadim and his merfolk soldiers used the rain and mud to their advantage. Several of the dark elves found themselves drowning in a puddle of water. One of the trenches was full of water by now so Heath used that to pull dark elves into and then he froze it quickly. Chaos ensued on the battlefield as more and more dark elves fell to either a blade or were frozen solid.

"Heath," Kavan got his attention as he pointed to a dark elf that sat on top of a dekellian, watching the fray from the other side of the barrier; there were a handful of dark elves that hung back there.

"Must be the officers," Heath joked.

"No, Heath, that's the one that killed McKenna," Kavan told him.

"You're sure?"

"I would recognize that ugly scarred bastard anywhere," Kavan assured him.

Heath cracked his knuckles and sought out some water close to the dark elves that hung back. There was a puddle just behind them, and Heath used his magic to make the puddle bigger and deeper, calling in rain water as he did so. Finally he peeked at Kavan and told him, "Think you can shoot his dekellian out from under him?"

"Do you have a gun that can reach that far?" Kavan asked him. "Or do you want me to get as close as I can to do it?"

"As close as you can," was the response as Heath handed him his pistol. "Right between the eyes should do it. I put frishna bullets in it."

"And when his dekellian is down?" Kavan asked him, checking to make sure the pistol was ready.

"The bastard drowns," Heath replied, and Kavan grinned at him.

Heath watched the blur that was Kavan leave the city and head for their target. He barely had to slow down to make the shot, and the next thing the dark elf knew was his mount was rearing back, blood trailing from a wound on its head. Heath reached out with his magic and the puddle of water grabbed hold of the dark elf. The dark elf thrashed and turned, trying to get out, and the rest of the officers panicked. Heath held the dark elf under the water until he was sure there was no more air in his lungs before letting go.

Kavan took the opportunity to shoot the rest of the dark elf officers, and the dark elves who were fighting panicked and broke, running away from the fighting.

"Heath!" Heath turned to find Karina running towards them. "Something is happening!"

***

"*You shouldn't struggle so much,*" Raktim admonished her. Somehow the magical manacles he had her in were chafing her skin and making her bleed as she tried to get out of them.

"Why are you doing this," she asked him again. He had not answered before, she was not sure why he would now.

"*For too long my people have been underground, left to rot in the underbelly of the earth. We used to be feared above ground before the dark elves got us all banished,*" Raktim told her, surprising her. "*We delved deep and built a small kingdom for ourselves, but gradually we forgot the feel of the sun on our skin and the feel of the wind. We diminished to a sick form of our former glory. I would take the lands above for us!*"

"The lands above belong to people already," Roslyn hissed at him, and she found herself growing weaker. She already knew that her barrier over the city had come down, for she felt the rain on her human form above. "I will not let you take it!"

A Descent into the Roots

"*You will not have much to say about it once I take your powers,*" Raktim told her with a wave of his hand.

Roslyn looked inside herself and found her magic waning, being drained. She reached out with her mind and what little magic she had left for the roots in the ground around them. There, at the edge of the senses, she felt something coming towards her.

"You think I will give up so easily?" she asked him. "You think I don't understand the power I wield? That I am ignorant of what my ancestors and the gods gave me?"

A root tendril wrapped around her ankle and she felt herself grow strong again as she fought to regain what he had stolen from her.

His eyes widened and he stood up, shouting, "*How are you doing this?!*"

Her astral form broke free of the magical bonds and then was absorbed into the root, carrying her away from the High Priest and out of the reach of his magic.

***

"What the–" was all Heath could say as they got to where Roslyn had been. The willow tree she had grown had somehow reached out with its roots to grab hold of her and it was now seemingly absorbing her into itself.

"Roslyn!" Heath yelled before he could no longer see her.

"Her wrists had started to bleed," Karina told him. "She was struggling against something. I felt her magic in the tree spike and then it started to move, but I didn't think *this* would happen."

The willow tree pulsed in front of them and seemed to grow three times bigger as it did so. They all took several steps back. Heath looked at Leaf and was relieved to see that she was no longer upset, but rather thoughtful looking.

"*She has descended into the roots of the tree to be rejoined with her astral form,*" Solana told him. "*That is what Leaf says. Something happened down below. She seeks to keep something from coming up.*"

Below them the earth rumbled and Heath reached out with his magic. He could tell that the roots of the tree were growing exponentially in size and being joined by other trees to form *something* underground. He could not tell what though.

"So how long until she comes back out?" Heath asked Leaf, who seemed to shrug her shoulders.

"*Much was taken from her,*" Solana passed on what Leaf had to say. "*She could return to us in minutes, or days, I have no idea. I just know that she is safe now.*"

Heath's shoulders slumped and he put his hand against the tree, feeling it pulsing almost like a heartbeat. He looked up at the sound of a horse coming towards them to find Erick and Willow, bloodied and covered in mud.

"Those of the dark elves that are not dead have fled," Willow told him. "What has happened here?"

Heath looked at Karina and she nodded before taking the two chiefs away to tell them what had been going on. He stood there, eyes closed, with his hand against the tree as the rain finished falling; someone had put a blanket over his shoulders at some point. Kavan sent Quinn up to the plateau to inform Amelia and the rest of Roslyn's family about what had happened.

It was nightfall when Kavan went to Heath and talked him into sitting down to eat. They gathered chairs next to the tree and someone made a fire. Kavan put a tankard of ale in Heath's hand and then made sure he had something to eat.

"Come on Heath, Dacey roasted a nice boar today," Kavan told him. "There's potatoes and gravy too."

"Gravy?" he whispered, finding his throat dry. He took a swig of the ale and then cleared his throat.

"She's alive," Kavan reminded him. "Leaf would tell us if something was wrong."

Heath ate, though he still felt her absence as something cold in his chest. When it came nighttime he put his sleeping roll next to the willow tree. As he climbed into his sleeping roll he saw Tiffany and Karina coming with their sleeping rolls too.

"We will stay with you," Karina told him.

Solana curled up next to him, her body keeping him warm. Mister Scruffy snuggled up against the gryphon, with Karina there next to her familiar. Tiffany slept on Karina's other side.

"Looks like we all had the same idea," Kavan said as he and Aidan joined them. "This reminds me of when Grau had captured her and we gathered in the kitchen because we could not sleep."

"She told me about that," Heath commented. "Being kidnapped by Grau and how she met Karina."

"She saved my life," Karina told Heath.

"I'm pretty sure that at *some time* over the last year she has saved all of our lives," Tiffany spoke up, earning a chuckle from the group.

As it grew darker around them small lights that were lightning bugs lit up in the dangling branches of the willow, and Heath almost thought that the moss beneath his sleeping roll grew softer. He fell asleep thinking of holding Roslyn against his body.

Chapter Thirty-Five

King Lucius looked at the destruction of the city wall. It could have been much worse, he thought. Much, much worse.

Edmond and Alara were with him as he surveyed the damage. Cassidy and her lady knights were escorting them around the city so that everyone could see that the last assassination attempt had not only been unsuccessful, but that it would be the very last one.

Word spread through the city when the King's Generals had come back after the battle with the mercenary leader in shackles as well as the Count's son who had been with the officers. The city could be at ease again; for the last several months the assassination attempts had put everyone on edge. Now they could live normally again.

Cassidy watched her father closely as he walked along the section of the wall where she had been standing several days before. Had it really been three days since the battle?

The last couple of days had been a blur: she remembered killing Count Gresham, and Kai taking her up to their suite of rooms to clean themselves up. She hadn't realized it during the fighting but when the boulder hit their walkway a small piece of wood had lodged itself in an unprotected part of her arm near the elbow. Kai had removed the splinter and healed it, but there had been quite a bit of blood. She had slept for nearly the whole next day, dreaming of kobolds and tree roots.

She knew her father had been busy with getting Count Gresham's estate under his control as well as sending the mercenary army packing. The people of the city had spent the last few days cleaning up the debris from the catapult boulders that had made it into the city and had already started to rebuild.

"Excuse me," a young woman a few years older than Cassidy, with dark skin and dark hair, got her attention. From the way she was dressed Cassidy could tell that she was a courtesan.

"Yes?" Cassidy dismounted and went to her. "Can I help you?"

"So it's true, Princess Roslyn has a twin sister," the woman commented. "Roslyn knew me. She helped me a few times over the years."

"I'm Cassidy," she introduced herself.

"Damaris," the courtesan returned the favour. "I had heard the rumours, and I saw you fighting the other day so I wasn't quite sure they were true, but here you are. Thank you for fighting for the city."

"How did you know Roslyn?" Cassidy asked her.

"She helped me and my girls out at our brothel," Damaris told her. "Anti-pregnancy charms, and healings. When the nobles were trying to go against the King's reforms, it was my idea to close our legs to them."

Cassidy grinned widely. "I had heard about that," she told her. "Thank you for backing her up."

"Can you tell me something?" Damaris asked her. Cassidy raised an eyebrow to her and nodded. "Did you travel with a man named Kavan?"

Now Cassidy was curious. "I did, yes."

"He was an orphan, yeah?"

Cassidy nodded.

"Word at the orphanage was that he was with Roslyn in Jay'Al," Damaris told her. "I grew up in the Girl's Orphanage, right across the street from the Boy's Orphanage. I knew him. The Masters said he had survived the war. I just hadn't seen him since he left for it, you see. We weren't sure if he had survived or not."

"Well he is alive," Cassidy assured her. "He's one of Roslyn's inner circle."

"He is?" Damaris beamed. "Orphan Kavan, close friends with the new Queen of Jay'Al. Who'd have thought!"

"Cassidy!" Edmond called to her then.

"You had better go," Damaris told her. "Thanks again for fighting for us."

***

Cassidy and Edmond joined their father and Alara in the King's Study that evening because Alara had gotten a message from one of her contacts in Jay'Al. Alara made sure they were all seated before she started.

"It seems Roslyn's forces faced the dark elves and defeated them," Alara told them once they were all seated. "Though something happened with Roslyn and her magic before the fighting started. My contact is not sure what all happened, but somehow her magic made her…how do I word this…become absorbed with a tree? Like she is inside the tree."

"Come again?" Cassidy heard her father ask after a moment. She herself could not make herself speak after hearing that.

"From what my contact has found out, Roslyn is alive and possibly regenerating inside the tree, inside its roots," Alara told them.

"Tree roots," Cassidy muttered, thinking of her dream of being in tree roots. Had she seen through Roslyn's eyes inside the roots of the willow tree? Did Roslyn even know where she was?

"Apparently Heath has barely left the tree's side," Alara continued. "He waits for her to come back out."

"I…" Lucius still could not find the words to say. He leaned back in his chair and raised both his eyebrows. "Inside a *tree?*"

Cassidy couldn't help but laugh at the expression on her father's face. He looked at her with bewilderment for a moment but then he too started to laugh.

Edmond looked from his sister to his father, and then to his betrothed. "Have they lost their minds?" Edmond asked Alara, and she nearly started laughing too.

"Only Roslyn would have that happen to her," Cassidy said as she tried to stop laughing. "I know she is alive and well, I have had dreams of being inside a tree. I think whatever happened with my magic that day connected us somehow."

"Do you think that when you go to bed tonight you might be able to connect with her again?" Edmond asked her.

"I can try?" she replied, uncertain. "I don't know if I can do it on purpose, I don't know how this kind of magic works. Roslyn changed *so* many things with her trees."

"She changed *a lot* of things," Edmond commented.

"I will do my best," Cassidy assured them. "I'm going to go start getting ready for bed, I think I know what to try."

***

Kai helped Cassidy get into the hot tub; she was wearing her undergarments still, for even though they had seen each other naked before she didn't think her sister would like to see her naked in her dreams–Cassidy sure didn't.

Crick and Tej watched from the door to the room.

"You sure this will work?" Kai asked her as he handed her a phial.

"Edmond said she gave this to him to help him sleep," Cassidy told him. "It's very similar to the one I made for all of us after she was taken by Grau."

"Ok," he said as he handed it to her and watched her swallow the contents. She gave him the empty phial back and then rested against the back of the tub. In her other hand she held a piece of crystal called spectrolite that would help her take control of her subconscious mind, so once she was asleep she might be able to direct herself.

It was not long before she was asleep, the warmth of the tub helping the potion work through her body faster.

"Cassidy?" the voice in her mind was Roslyn's. She opened her dream-eyes and found herself floating in what she could only describe as some kind of pod filled with liquid. Roslyn was floating there in front of her corporeal form, still wearing her set of armour.

"Hey, sister," she used her mind to talk to her.

"How are you here?" Roslyn asked her, confusion showing on her face. *"Are you dead too?"*

"I don't think you're dead, Roslyn," Cassidy told her hurriedly, hoping that it wasn't true. Did Roslyn not know what had happened to her?

"The High Priest was taking my magic," Roslyn told her, almost sleepily. *"I went into the tree to escape him. I had to stop him from coming after me."*

"Roslyn!" Cassidy waved her hands in front of her sister's face to get her attention. Roslyn's eyes snapped open and she looked more awake now. *"Listen to me: you are alive! I want you to listen in here, feel with your magic. I bet you Heath is right outside this tree waiting for you to come back."*

"Heath?" that perked her up.

"Yes, Heath is waiting for you," she told her again.

Something in her dream changed and she thought she heard Heath's voice say, *"Come back to me."*

Roslyn stirred, seemingly waking up more. She looked around with wide eyes at her surroundings and then started to swim up to what looked like some sort of tunnel that glowed green. She looked back at Cassidy and smiled.

"Thank you, sister," she said to Cassidy before she continued to swim up.

Cassidy awoke with a start back in the bathtub. Kai grabbed hold of her and reassured her that she was safe.

"I saw her," Cassidy told Kai. "She was asleep. I think I woke her up and she's getting out of *wherever* she was."

"Amazing," Kai said as he hugged her. "Now can I get you into our bed where it's nice and dry?"

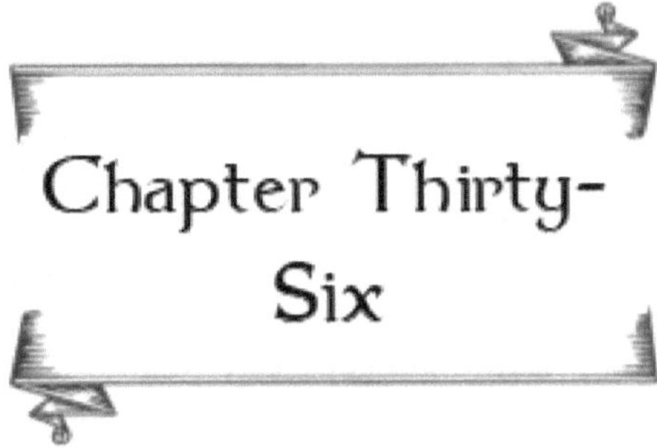

Chapter Thirty-Six

The ground shook, startling Heath who was sitting next to the willow tree with one hand on it. He had bathed quickly earlier that morning and changed clothes, a simple tunic and breeches. He had dozed off slightly, Solana curled up at his feet. Leaf lay on the other side of the tree, her tail slightly touching the tree.

As Heath watched, the tree opened up and spewed Roslyn out in a heap of fluid. She was still wearing her armour, and her hair was slightly matted. She lay there on the mossy ground breathing heavily until Heath broke out of his shock and said her name.

"Roslyn," he whispered, relief evident in his voice. He got up and went to her, not caring about the wet ground as he knelt down beside her. She looked up at him with her two different eyes, squinting in the sunlight in order to see him better. Leaf had gotten up and was prancing around like an excited puppy, gathering the attention of the soldiers who were camped nearby. One of the soldiers ran off to inform certain people that Roslyn was back.

"I'm not dead," she told him as she propped herself up with an elbow. "Cassidy told me I wasn't dead, and I'm not!"

Heath looked perplexed now but he reached out and touched her face. "You feel alive to me," he told her.

"How long was I gone for?" she asked him as he helped her up.

"Just over three days," he told her.

"The dark elves?"

"Beaten back," he replied. "Kavan and I even got the one that killed McKenna."

"Sorry I missed it," she told him, but then he pulled her into a tight hug. She looked up at him and before she could say anything else he was kissing her.

Someone cleared their throat nearby and they parted to find their friends gathering around them, smiles on their faces.

"You're a sight for sore eyes," Tiffany told her, crossing her arms over her chest. "Took you long enough to come back."

"It is good to see you well," Cypress spoke up.

"What happened?" Heath asked her, and she started to tell them. A soldier brought chairs and Dacey handed her a plate of food as she told them about Raktim and what had happened. After she finished telling them about escaping him, she looked at her wrists: there was raw skin there where the magical shackles had been.

"Well the kobolds haven't invaded. Whatever you did worked," Aidan commented.

"I...I used the roots of the trees to trap them underground," Roslyn told them. "All of the Clan trees, I wove them together with magic to keep them from coming up."

"*Amazing,*" Karina said.

"You said you saw Cassidy?" Heath inquired of her after she took a drink of water from Dacey.

"Yes, in my dream, though I don't think it was really a dream..." Roslyn told him, but she got distracted because she could see her mother and other siblings coming quickly down the tunnel from the plateau on horseback.

"Looks like someone told them you were back," Kavan commented, and a gryphon's shadow passed over them. The group looked up and they found Quinn and his gryphon getting ready to land.

Amelia took her daughter in her arms and the rest of Roslyn's siblings joined the hug as well.

"You had us worried," Amelia told her, tears coming to her eyes. "By the ancestors, what happened?"

Roslyn repeated what she told her friends, her mother and siblings marvelling at her power. They finally let her go, and Roslyn wrinkled her nose.

"I smell like tree sap," she said.

"Come," Tiffany told her, grabbing her hand. "Let's get you out of that armour and into a bath."

***

After bathing and washing her hair, Roslyn left her tent in a clean dress that had slits up both sides, and leggings underneath. She went first for the wall to survey any damages, and was glad to see that the enemy dead had been buried already.

Leaf, who was now too big to walk on the wall with her, waited for her below.

All of the soldiers who saw her expressed their happiness at seeing her, and she thanked them shyly. Tiffany had told her how Heath had stayed by the tree the whole time she was in it, and she also told her that her soldiers were despondent with her absence as well. She was grateful for all of them, and she knew she needed to show them that. She would have to plan a feast for everyone soon.

She turned to look at the plateau, marvelling at how much bigger the willow tree was now. She noticed that all of the soldiers had moved their tents outside of the city again, and Aidan's people had remarked the streets. The orcs and centaurs had also put their huts back up. Roslyn wondered what it would look like with actual houses and cobblestone streets, and she found herself excited at the prospect of a finished city.

"My Queen," one of her messengers approached her, bowing and placing a clenched fist over his heart. "The Chiefs, and General Nadim, wish an audience with you."

"Of course," she replied, following the messenger to the nearest stairs and out the city gate to where Willow, Erick, and Nadim were waiting under a tent. Willow was wearing her armour, but the men were in relaxed clothes.

"It is good to see you are well," Willow greeted her, "my Queen."

"Tiffany gave me your reports," she told them. "I have not had the time to go through them yet."

"It's understandable," Erick told her. "What you accomplished the other day must have used a lot of magic. You need time to recuperate after that."

"Yes, well three days inside a tree should be enough," Roslyn commented with a chuckle. "The magic of Jay'Al itself saved me. If the kobold High Priest had taken my magic I am not sure what would have happened to everyone."

"Destruction," Nadim told her. "The kobolds would have come to the surface and waged war on all of us. They would have destroyed Jay'Al. You did the ultimate duty as Queen to protect both your people and your kingdom. I commend you for it."

"We will be leaving today," Willow said, motioning to the tents outside the city. "We were just waiting for you to return before we left."

"I appreciate it. Once my palace is done I will have a grand ball for all of you," Roslyn told them. "I look forward to seeing you all then."

"My men and I will be leaving with Erick as well," Nadim said. "My King is eager to hear of everything. He will want to plan a visit with Jay'Al in the near future."

"I look forward to meeting him," Roslyn told him. "Thank you for fighting with us."

Nadim lowered his head and gave her a smile. "My pleasure," he told her with a bow. "I was wondering…could I take the kobold with me back to Kyprago? He cannot return underground, and there is no place for him here."

"That should be fine," Roslyn told him. "I am sure he will just like being above ground."

"My thoughts as well. Fare thee well, Queen Roslyn."

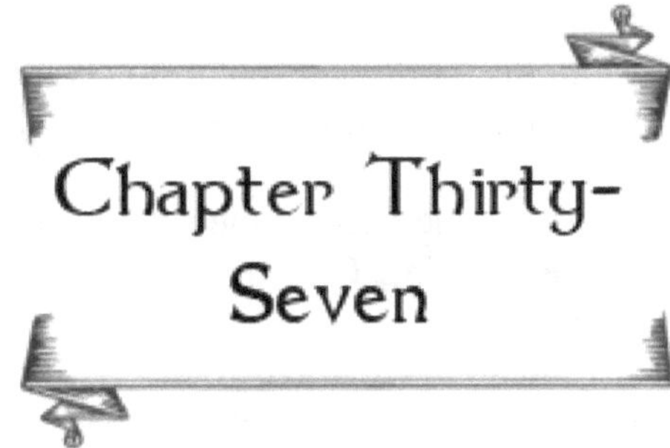

Chapter Thirty-Seven

Edmond and Alara walked into Lucius' study together. The King was sitting at his desk looking over some papers, but he set them down as his son and future daughter-in-law came in. Alara's familiar was on her shoulder, the tiger salamander looking at everything it could.

"Ah, good timing," he told them. He gestured to the chairs in front of his desk. "Please take a seat."

"What is it, father?" Edmond asked as they sat down.

"Your eighteenth birthday is tomorrow," Lucius commented. "And you two are getting married in a couple of days."

"Yes," Edmond answered, confused as to why his father had wanted to talk to them both. "What of it?"

"I've had to make a decision," Lucius spoke gravely. "I wanted to tell you both first."

Edmond raised an eyebrow at his father. "What is it?"

"I am abdicating the throne to you," Lucius told him. Alara gasped and Edmond's eyes went wide.

"What? Why?" Edmond asked incredulously.

"I have done my part as king, and paved the way for you both," Lucius explained. "I am going to teach Eliza how to run Wardgrove and be a Countess. Then I might do some travelling."

"I was not expecting to be king so soon," Edmond told him. "I don't think I am ready yet, father."

"Alara will be a lot of help," Lucius told him, and Alara reached out to take Edmond's hand in hers. "And you will have your advisors, whomever you choose."

"I–I don't know what to say," Edmond spoke slowly, and then he looked at Alara who smiled encouragingly at him. "I was definitely not expecting this."

"After everything we have gone through the past few months…I had to take a step back to look at everything. Cassidy said I was born for this, but it was the actions of a few that gave me the crown. We have dealt with the old conservatives. The next generation will have you to look up to as their king and queen," Lucius told them. "Alara is a mage and has connections. You can use that to your advantage."

"We will not let you down," Alara assured Lucius.

He smiled at her and nodded his head. "I know you won't."

***

Cassidy mounted her horse and turned to look up the steps of the palace. Crick, who was on her shoulder, chirped in her ear. Alara and Edmond were hugging Lucius good-bye. Edmond's birthday, and their wedding, had come and gone. Lucius had handed his crown over to Edmond as well.

"Cassidy," she turned to find Rafi and Nova coming towards her. Rafi had taken a little longer than expected to recover from being poisoned, but he was looking in better health than he had been the last time Cassidy had seen him.

Cassidy greeted the pair with a warm smile. "I was hoping to see you before we left."

"Sully told us about your plans," Rafi told her. "I wanted to see you off."

"Will you be coming to Jay'Al in the fall?" Cassidy asked him. "Roslyn is hoping to have us all there."

"Yes, I have started making plans for it," Rafi answered.

"Good. Nova, keep him out of trouble, hm?"

The young woman nodded her head and smiled, saying, "I will do my best."

Cassidy turned to see Kai, Sully, and her lady knights coming to join her with their horses, plus a horse for her father.

"It will be a more leisurely ride this time," Sully told Cassidy. "And we can stay at inns."

"What, you don't want to camp under the stars?" Cassidy teased him.

"I just don't want to burn breakfast," Sully replied, earning a chuckle from the knights. "Besides, I think we've earned a comfortable journey."

"I suppose," Cassidy said, and she smiled at Kai and Tej. "Some more privacy would be nice."

"Safe travels," Rafi told them as he and Nova went to go talk to Edmond and Alara. Lucius greeted Rafi as he came to join Cassidy.

"We all set?" Lucius asked the group. "I'm eager to get back to Wardgrove."

A Descent into the Roots

"We were waiting on you, father," Cassidy teased him as she nudged her horse to start going. "Good-bye Edmond! Good-bye Alara!"

Edmond and Alara waved their good-byes before heading inside the palace with Rafi and Nova.

"My apologies," he said with a grin as he mounted his horse. The group started heading out of the city.

As they rode up a hill north of the city Lucius stopped and looked back down at the palace.

Cassidy stopped beside him and watched her father's face as he thought.

"The first memory I have of the palace was when I was five years old," Lucius told her. "My grandfather, the king, loved having us visit. I miss that old man."

"You will return someday," Cassidy reminded him.

"Will I?" Lucius mused. "Yes, I will miss Edmond so I suppose I will be back. There will be some grandchildren running around there soon enough. I want them to know me."

"Between Jay'Al and Ellsgrove, you'll have a lot of travelling to do," Cassidy commented. "I would get tired of so much travel."

"You don't think you'll be back to visit your brother?" Lucius questioned him.

"Of course I will," Cassidy told him. "I'll have to make a schedule though."

That made Lucius laugh, and together they continued after their travelling companions.

***

Roslyn watched from the gates as a patrol returned. The dark elves had been defeated but there was still a small group of them left above ground and they were trying to find them. Her Feathers kept an eye out as they flew over the country-side, but there were plenty of places where the dark elves could hide. At least all of their dekellians were dead. She wondered if they had headed north to the mountains; that's what she would do if she were in their place.

"Jackson is on his way here," a messenger told her. "He and the rest of the sailors."

"Heath will be happy to see him again," Roslyn commented. "Thank you."

Leaf was waiting for her at the bottom of the stairs and together they walked down the main street of Dragon City. Houses had gone up quickly in the last couple of weeks, many of them in a mix of styles: there was a lot of architecture similar to Hyena City, with open courtyards; and the orc influence could clearly be seen in a lot of houses. Roslyn loved it. Outside the city the farms were thriving and growing. Her uncle Grigori had established his new horse farm next to the plateau outside the city wall, and he had a lot of new workers to help him.

They turned down a street and she stopped in front of a stone building that was still being constructed. Judd was overseeing the building, with a lot of orcs helping.

"The University is coming along nicely," Roslyn said to Leaf as they continued past the building. "I cannot wait to see it done."

The smell of food led them to Dacey's Eatery, a large wooden building that Cypress had built so Dacey could have a proper kitchen. The Eatery took up almost one full side of the city square. Leaf waited outside as Roslyn went into the eatery to grab a fresh bun with butter on it. She also grabbed a bowl of cooked meat for Leaf, which the dragon eagerly ate up.

The other three sides of the city square were comprised of the Law Office, and a large stables; several shops, one of which was a potions shop where pixie's sold potions; and a large stone building that had a marketplace inside. They had started a trade route with several other cities to keep produce and other things moving, and once it came harvest they could sell a lot of their crops or use it to trade. Roslyn was satisfied with how far her capital was coming, and she knew that the people living there were happy with it as well.

Eating her fresh bun, Roslyn and Leaf headed for the willow tree and the tunnel up to the plateau. People in the streets greeted them warmly, riders moving out of the way so Leaf could pass.

"Pretty soon you'll be too big to walk the streets with me," Roslyn commented to Leaf as they got to the clearing with the willow tree. Leaf leaned down so Roslyn could climb onto her back, and within moments they were in the air above the city.

"*You are the Queen of Jay'Al, you should not be walking the streets anyways,*" Leaf reminded her. "*It would not be safe unless you had your Queen's Guard with you.*"

"And they will be with me the next time, they are just busy right now," Roslyn retorted as they circled over the city before heading up to the palace.

Roslyn had talked Judd into letting her make the outside shell of the palace. She had promised him the University build in exchange, and he grudgingly took it. With the outer shell and the floors done, she also included the plumbing, using clay to create the pipes, all that was left was to put up the walls and doors. With all of the builders working together over the last couple of weeks the interior of the palace was almost completed–it was the top floor of the palace that was Roslyn's suite that was still being finished. The floor below her suite was where her knights had their rooms, and they were currently adding some finishing touches to them before moving their things in.

Leaf landed on a balcony that led into a giant room built specifically for the dragon. It had large double doors on the outside that swung in so she could get inside easily, and high vaulted ceilings. There was a large pillow for her to use, and a giant food bowl. Roslyn left Leaf there and went through the door into the palace.

Magical lanterns lit the hallways. The walls were painted to look like stones, making it seem like it was all built from stone. Human, part-orc, and full orc servants bowed to her as she passed them, and she greeted them. The palace was pretty quiet now, but soon it would be bustling with life.

Roslyn headed up a flight of stairs and then another, until she came to the level of the palace that had a merman statue. The floor was tiled in a herring-bone style and there were paintings of the ocean and large galleons along the hallways. She smiled, knowing that Maeve and Heath had chosen to decorate their floor as a homage to the archipelagos and sea life. She approached Heath's room, which he had moved into the day before, and knocked on the door.

Heath opened it, smiling when he saw her. He was wearing a loose white tunic and black breeches, with his calf-high leather boots still on.

"Hello, sweetheart," Heath greeted her, and he motioned for her to come inside. He closed the door behind her and she sat on one of the sofas. Solana greeted her with a chirp from the balcony where she was sunbathing. The double doors that led out to the balcony were wide open to allow the gryphon full access to the suite. The room was decorated much like the hallway, painted in hues of blue and with a sea theme.

"Jackson will be here soon," Roslyn told him. "Where did you get this sofa?"

"I had Erick send me some things," Heath told her. "And you as well."

"Oh?"

"I can't wait to show you your room," Heath told her. "Oswick and Aidan have been working hard to get it together for you."

"I can't wait to have a proper bed to sleep in again," Roslyn commented. "My cot in my tent just doesn't cut it."

Heath looked at her slyly and said, "It'll be nice to have a bed to be in together."

Roslyn looked up at him and he leaned in to kiss her.

"Will you go for a walk with me by the lake?" Heath asked her when they parted.

"Sure, I haven't had time to see the lake yet," Roslyn answered. "We should have some time before Jackson gets here."

Heath held her hand as they walked out of the palace together through a back entrance. A garden had been started behind the palace but it was still early. There was a cobbled path that led them to the lake. Above them gryphons soared through the air. A slight breeze moved through the grass and trees, and over the surface of the lake. Someone had built a pier that jutted out into the lake.

"This looks nice," Roslyn commented as she took in the lake. "I can't wait to stock it with fish."

Roslyn turned to look at Heath and her breath caught in her chest as she saw him holding up a ring. The gem was topaz, and its blue and green colours glimmered in the sunlight.

"Will you do me the honour of marrying me, Roslyn?" Heath asked her as he knelt before her. "I want to spend the rest of my days with you."

"*Yes*," she told him, and he eagerly put the ring on her finger. When he stood up he pulled her in for a kiss.

"My Queen," he whispered when their lips parted, "I love you, Roz."

She smiled sweetly at him and told him, "I love you too, Heath. Now come on, I know how much you have missed Selene and I know Jackson is bringing her."

Heath's smile grew bigger and he grabbed her hand before they headed back to the palace together.

Epilogue

Cassidy looked up at the walls of Dragon City and wondered how it had been made. Beside her, her father had the same expression of wonder on his face.

"This has Roslyn written all over it," Sully commented behind them, making the knights laugh.

"You're not wrong," Kavan said as he leaned against the gate in front of them. "We've been expecting you."

"Sorry, bit of a delay through the Archipelago, but we are here!" Cassidy told him. "This place looks amazing!"

"Did Roslyn really make the wall?" Eliza asked from her seat on the wagon behind them. Poppy and Robert were looking up at the wall with wide eyes.

"She did," Kavan answered. "Welcome to Dragon City!"

Cassidy could not believe how the area had changed in the months since she had been there. There were cobbled streets, and *so* many houses. Signs along the streets gave them directions to the City Square, and once they were there she saw Dacey's Eatery. She was looking forward to eating there.

"What happened in the Archipelago?" Kavan asked them. He had walked alongside their horses as they went into the city.

"Commandant Mortimer wanted to host us for a couple days, and have several feasts," Lucius answered him. "It was quite the event."

"Well it is very good to have you here," Kavan told him. "Roslyn has been waiting for you."

Kavan led them to the tunnel and watched the young royals stare around in wonder as they rode up it. "Roslyn made this tunnel with her magic," Kavan told them. "Before the tunnel, there was a giant staircase up the side of the plateau that took several days to climb."

"Have you heard from Rafi?" Cassidy asked Kavan.

"Our Feather scouts saw his party a day's ride away," Kavan answered.

"What's a 'Feather'?" Eliza asked him.

"Gryphon riders," Kavan told her. "They are special scouts."

"I heard Heath has a gryphon," Eliza commented. "Will we get to meet her?"

"Of course," Kavan responded. "Solana and Heath are nearly inseparable."

"And the dragon?" Lucius asked.

"Leaf will be around," Kavan answered. "She has gotten so big that she can't go everywhere with Roslyn anymore."

Finally they made it to the top of the plateau, coming out of the tunnel into the sunlight.

"Did Roslyn help make the palace too?" Cassidy asked with amusement as she took in the structure before them.

"She did," Kavan told her with a chuckle.

"It's amazing," Lucius commented. Stable boys came to take their horses as they dismounted in front of the palace.

Kavan led them through the huge double doors of the palace. The main entrance had high ceilings and a double staircase up to the next level.

"The main floor is where the scribes and quartermaster work," Kavan explained as they looked around the foyer. "There is a lower level for food storage and such."

Aidan came out of one of the rooms off of the foyer and Cassidy went to hug him.

"Where is Kai?" Aidan asked Cassidy as they hugged.

"He is a little behind us. Chief Erick had some things for Roslyn's room and Kai wanted to be the one to bring it," Cassidy explained.

"It is good to see you again," Lucius greeted Aidan. "I hope the scribes I sent you are earning their keep."

"Yes, sir, they certainly are," Aidan told him with a grin. "We have had a lot to do in the last couple of weeks."

Aidan walked with them as Kavan led them up the stairs to the next level.

"I saw the Law Office in the city square," Lucius commented. "Do you have a sheriff?"

Kavan chuckled and told him, "Edwin and Alexander run the constabulary."

"The werewolves?" Sully asked.

"Yes. At first Roslyn wanted the werewolves to be part of the Royal Guard but Alexander suggested the need for the law service in such a big city and it kind of went from there," Kavan told him. "The two of them have taken their new responsibility very seriously."

A Descent into the Roots

"I can't wait to meet them," Cassidy told Kavan. "I've heard so much about them."

"They should be at dinner later," Kavan assured her.

Kavan led them up another few flights of stairs until they got to the level with the statue of a merman. "The ambassador suites are down here," Kavan told them. "We have rooms set up for you."

Lucius had his own room at the end of the hall, with Eliza and Poppy sharing a room across the hall from him. Robert got a room next to his father's.

"Cassidy, there is a room for you on the top level, and the second top level has rooms for the knights," Kavan told her after showing Lucius and his children to their rooms and leaving them there. He told them he would be back to collect them for dinner soon.

"I can show them up there," Aidan told Kavan. "If you don't mind."

"Of course," Kavan replied. "I have a few things to do before dinner still."

Aidan led Cassidy, Sully, and the lady knights up another level where Deirdre met them. Sully hugged his sister in greeting and Deirdre offered to show the knights to their rooms for Aidan. Aidan then led Cassidy up another set of stairs.

"You definitely get your exercise here," Cassidy mused as they got to the top of the stairs.

"Were you able to get it?" Aidan asked her in a whisper as he led her down the hallway.

"I was wondering when you were going to ask," Cassidy said with a chuckle as she produced a jewelry box from her bag. Crick chirped at her, making her smile. "Commandant Mortimer was very happy to make these for them."

"Can I see them?" Aidan asked, excitement showing in his tone.

Cassidy chuckled and opened the box, revealing the two rings inside that were made of frishna metal. There was a band in the middle of the rings that was made of wood.

"Everett took the wood from a tree on their home island," Cassidy explained. "A little piece of the archipelago for them."

"Roslyn's going to love them," Aidan said with feeling. "I love weddings."

"Oh come on, I know you were rooting for Kavan," Cassidy teased him as she closed the box and put it back away.

"I may have wanted the underdog to win–no pun intended–but I know Heath loves Roslyn. They make a very good pair," Aidan informed her.

"Is Everett coming?" Aidan asked her as they stopped in front of a door that was painted a dark green colour.

"Yes, he should be here in a few days," Cassidy answered as he opened the door to the room and motioned for her to go in. "It's too bad that Edmond and Alara can't be here."

Inside the suite Cassidy found a sitting area, her own bathing room, and a nice large bed with a fireplace in the corner. Crick jumped down from her shoulder and went to the bed, curling up on it.

"Where is my mother?" Cassidy asked Aidan as she placed her bag on the foot of the bed.

"She has a home in the city," Aidan informed her. "She will be at dinner though."

"Oh. I thought she would be living in the palace," Cassidy commented as she petted Crick.

"She didn't want to," Aidan told her. "Roslyn didn't press it."

Cassidy went over to the doors to her balcony and opened them, marveling at the gryphons that were flying over the palace.

"Amazing," Cassidy said with awe. "They are beautiful."

Aidan joined her on the balcony to watch the gryphons. "They really are. But just wait till you meet the pixies, they are something else."

"I'm sure they are," Cassidy said with amusement. "I can't wait."

"Kavan actually talked some pixies into selling potions," Aidan told her. "They have a shop on the square."

"Really? Huh. That'd be interesting."

"Well, you get ready for dinner. I'm going to check in on Roslyn and then I'll collect you on the way back down?"

"Sure. Is her suite that big set of doors in the middle of the hallway?"

"Yes."

"I'll definitely need a guide around the palace until I get used to it," Cassidy commented as he headed for the door. "It'd be too easy to get lost in here."

"I keep joking to Roz that we need a map on each level," Aidan replied. "See you in a bit."

***

The Dining Hall had high vaulted ceilings with wooden accents, two large chandeliers lit with mage lights hanging from the ceiling. The south side of the room was mostly all glass windows but for a door that led out to a balcony. The one table in the room was made of oak and looked big enough for fifty people or more to sit at. Cassidy noticed that there were placemats and chairs for twenty people.

Movement on the balcony made her look, and she found Roslyn and Leaf out there. Cassidy went to the door and opened it, walking out onto the balcony as Roslyn climbed down off of Leaf's back. Roslyn had her hair braided in two braids and she wore the diadem that the ancestors had given her. She wore a beautiful dark green coloured dress, the front cut just low enough.

Roslyn smiled in greeting at her twin sister and went to hug her.

"It is good to have you home again," Roslyn told her. They parted and

A Descent into the Roots

Roslyn inspected Cassidy's outfit, a dark blue silk blouse and dark brown breeches. "Did Alara give you that blouse?"

"Yes, the silk from her kingdom is very nice," Cassidy informed her. "I wish you could have been there for the wedding."

"Me too," Roslyn told her as she led her back inside, leaving Leaf to bask in the sun on the balcony.

"She sure has gotten big," Cassidy commented, nodding to the silver dragon who was now three-times the size of a draft horse.

"She doesn't like not being able to go everywhere with me anymore, but she deals with it well," Roslyn told her. "Looks like we are the first ones to arrive for dinner." Roslyn approached the table and sat in the chair at the head of the table, motioning for her to take the seat on the side of the table beside her. Cassidy noticed that there were name tags on each plate, and that seat was indeed hers.

"Aidan brought me down and went to go get dad and the family," Cassidy told her. "Where is Heath?"

"He should be arriving any moment," Roslyn replied, turning to look out at the balcony. "See?"

Cassidy looked to find Heath riding on the back of a gryphon who had a calico coat. They landed, and Heath dismounted before coming inside the Dining Hall. The gryphon went over to Leaf and nuzzled up against the dragon. Heath was wearing a fine velvet blouse that was crimson red, and black velvet breeches with his leather calf-high boots. He had his dark hair tied back.

"Cassidy!" Heath greeted her with enthusiasm, his green eyes shining. "Welcome home!"

Cassidy grinned at him as he took his seat next to Roslyn at the head of the table. "This palace is amazing," Cassidy told them. "You did a good job."

"Careful planning with Judd, and a model, made it easier than when I made the wall," Roslyn told her. "Everything has been coming together."

Cassidy looked to the doorway to find Kai. He must have arrived not too long ago, but he had had time to change for dinner. Alara had given him some silk shirts too, and Cassidy was amused to see that they were wearing matching colours.

Roslyn watched as Kai took his seat next to Cassidy. She was happy that her sister had found someone. Maybe there would be more weddings in their future.

She was nervous. It had been a year since she saw her father and younger siblings; and her mother was going to be there as well with the rest of her siblings.

Aidan and Kavan arrived with Lucius, Eliza, Poppy, and Robert. Roslyn stood and went to hug her father and siblings. Eliza nearly squealed with excitement upon seeing her, running into her sister's arms. As they parted Eliza caught sight of Leaf and Solana on the balcony and she gasped.

"They are beautiful," Eliza said, and Poppy and Robert quickly hugged Roslyn before following Eliza over to the door.

"Can we?" Eliza asked Roslyn, nodding to the balcony.

"Go ahead," she told them, and she watched as they went out and introduced themselves to Leaf and Solana. The gryphon rolled over and offered her belly to be rubbed, and Leaf let them touch her wings before Lucius called them back in.

"We are here for dinner," Lucius reminded his youngest children. He looked at Roslyn and pulled her in for a hug. "It is very good to see you again," he told her as she hugged him tightly back.

"I'm so happy you're here," Roslyn whispered as they parted. "I hope your journey was well."

"Very uneventful, thankfully," Lucius told her as he went to the table and found his seat which was on the side of the table next to Heath.

Karina and Cypress joined them in the Dining Hall, taking their seats at the table. Roslyn watched with amusement as her younger siblings took in the part-orc and full orc. Tiffany came in next with Oswick, and then Amelia with Roslyn's other siblings.

Lucius stood up when he saw Amelia enter the Dining Hall. She was wearing one of Roslyn's dresses, and even with the burn scars she looked beautiful. Lucius went to her and the two shared a hug before Amelia introduced him to her other children. In turn Lucius introduced his three youngest to them before they all sat at the table.

Oswick and Judd joined them in the Dining Hall at the same time as Alexander and Edwin.

A servant brought wine and juice out, filling cups as Roslyn introduced everyone to her father and younger siblings. Roslyn sat back in her chair and watched both sides of her siblings talking and getting to know each other. Then she looked at everyone at the table and felt a deep sense of comfort and happiness inside. Heath took her hand and kissed it, and she smiled at him.

Roslyn looked at her mother and father. It had been almost twenty years since they had last seen each other. If it was not for them she would not be there, and now they were reunited again.

Almost everyone close to her was sitting at the table with her. She felt at ease to have them there, the people she loved the most. In a few days she and Heath would be married, and they had the rest of their lives ahead of them to rule over Jay'Al together. She looked forward to the future.

A group of servants brought out the food for them, and one of them brought a gravy boat to Roslyn.

A Descent into the Roots

"Gravy, Your Majesty?" the servant asked her.

"Best leave the boat there with her," Lucius told the servant. "She loves her gravy."

A chuckle went around the table and the servant left the gravy boat next to Roslyn's plate.

"It's good to have you all here," Roslyn told them. "Thank you for being here with me."

Kavan raised a glass of wine and the rest of her companions followed suit. "To Queen Roslyn," Kavan said, and everyone echoed him.

"To you, my friends," Roslyn said as she raised her own glass. "I could not have gotten here without you."

Cast of Characters

<u>ELLSGROVE</u>
King Lucius of Ellsgrove: Roslyn's father
Queen Elle of Ellsgrove: Roslyn's step-mother
Roslyn: known as Roz, Queen of Jay'Al
Edmond: Roslyn's younger half-brother
Eliza: Roslyn's younger half-sister
Poppy: Roslyn's younger half-sister
Robert: Roslyn's younger half-brother
Roland: the king's butler
Rupert: Edmond's valet
Kasimir de Lauritia: merchant
Judd: stonemason
Oswick: merchant friend of Roslyn
Rafi: merchant friend of Roslyn
Kavan: Master at Arms, friend of Roslyn's
Heath: captain, former pirate, friend of Roz
Maeve: Heath's lieutenant
Jackson: Heath's lieutenant
Count Gersham: Conservative noble who wants to depose Lucius

<u>WOLF CLAN</u>
Amelia: Roslyn's birth mother
McKenna: Roslyn's step-father
Cassidy: Roslyn's twin sister
Sawyer: Roslyn's younger half-sister
Leona: Roslyn's younger half-sister
Quinn: Roslyn's younger half-brother
Oko: Roslyn's younger half-brother
Jessamine: frishna blacksmith
Chief Rotho: Roslyn's grandfather
Tanner: Roslyn's uncle
Martin: Roslyn's uncle
Joss: Roslyn's uncle
Grigori: Roslyn's uncle
Anna: Roslyn's aunt, Amelia's twin sister

<u>BEAVER CLAN</u>
Willow: the Chief of the Beaver Clan, head Shaman

<u>FOX CLAN</u>
Daron: Shaman of the Fox Clan

<u>BEAR CLAN</u>
Jerred: Shaman of the Bear Clan

<u>HYENA CLAN</u>
Kai: Shaman of the Hyena Clan
Erick: Chief of the Hyena Clan, Kai's uncle
Gabe: Erick's son, Kai's cousin
Keaton: Erick's son, Kai's cousin
Layne: Kai's father

<u>DRAGON CLAN</u>
Lou: Karina's father, Chief of the Dragon Clan
Dacey: Karina's mother, Lou's wife
Karina: Shaman of the Dragon Clan
Jaco: Karina's brother
Fadi: Karina's brother
Davin: Karina's brother
Jarrod: half-orc warrior

<u>FAMILIARS</u>
Ecko: Amelia's feline familiar
Crick: Cassidy's familiar, a pine marten
Tej: Kai's familiar, a fennec fox
Mister Scruffy: Karina's feline familiar
Leaf: Roslyn's silver dragon familiar
Solana: Heath's gryphon familiar
Luma: Maeve's pygmy owl familiar
Yara: Alara's tiger salamander familiar

<u>ROSLYN'S HONOUR GUARD</u>
Sir Sullivan: known as Sully, a knight of Ellsgrove
Deirdre: Sully's sister, lady knight of Ellsgrove
Baylee: lady knight of Ellsgrove
Isobel: lady knight of Ellsgrove
Kallista: lady knight of Ellsgrove
Maia: lady knight of Ellsgrove
Nadia: lady knight of Ellsgrove
Paula: lady knight of Ellsgrove

Perdita: lady knight of Ellsgrove
Saffron: lady knight of Ellsgrove
Kris: lady knight of Ellsgrove
Heather: lady knight of Ellsgrove, also a mage
Dara: lady knight of Ellsgrove
Theodora: lady knight of Ellsgrove
Vera: lady knight of Ellsgrove
Harriet: lady knight of Ellsgrove

<u>ORCS OF THE NORTH SNOW CLAN</u>
Terren: orc warrior, former member of Grau's group
Louran: orc warrior, former member of Grau's group
Anda: Cypress' sister
Ulmer: Cypress' brother
Tirren: orc warrior
Loua: orc warrior
Resba: orc warrior
Avis: orc elder
Malen: orc elder
Bhag: orc elder
Delon: orc elder
Leib: orc elder

<u>WEREWOLVES</u>
Glendon
Edwin: the first werewolf
Alexander: werewolf who can change at will
Mack
Ari
Nav
Selig
Waylon

<u>MERFOLK</u>
Nadim: the merman who saved Heath's life
Ullas: King of the mermen

<u>Raistminestine people:</u>
Alara: princess and mage
Eren: king of Raistminestine
Mira: Alara's handmaiden

Gabor: Alara's uncle and the ambassador

<u>Tribes of Archipelago</u>
Graydon: Heath's older brother
Sofia: Heath's mother
Mortimer: Commandant of the Archipelago
Jonah: Ambassador to Jay'Al
Matteo: Heath's father
Lorenzo: Maeve's brother
Everett: Heath's younger brother

About the Author

Katie grew up in the nineties, watching Star Trek, Xena, Stargate, Andromeda, and Charmed. She was an avid reader from the start, and it was Patricia C. Wrede's Enchanted Forest Chronicles that got her into reading fantasy novels.

Katie grew up on a farm in small community in Huron County, Ontario. The youngest of three girls, she was also the tallest. While picking stones in the fields Katie would find fossils and shards of pottery that got her interested in archaeology.

When she was around twelve Katie discovered Tamora Pierce's Song of the Lioness Quartet, and was sucked into the world of Tortall. Katie was inspired to write her own female heroes for future generations and started writing then.

Katie had started at Laurier for Archeology and Medieval Studies in 2009, and even participated in a dig on a native site in Ontario. After two years though she went home to get a job to pay off her student debt and met her husband. Eleven years and three kids later, Katie is still writing.

Katie is also a gamer, enjoying Dragon Age, Baldur's Gate, Mass Effect, and Greedfall.

A Note from the Author

This journey of bringing Roslyn's story out started all the way back in 2020. I wanted a female hero that was unique and not afraid to be herself, so Roslyn was created. I styled her after the character Starfire from the show Titans, and of course she needed some love interests that were not the main part of the story.

It has been quite a journey getting this far. My beta readers have been amazing and supportive, and my own family as well.

I especially want to thank my editors: Laura, Anna and Lexi; and Erika, Sarah, Colin, and Cordelia for their amazing support! This trilogy is only here because of you and I am SO very thankful for you all!

www.ingramcontent.com/pod-product-compliance
Lightning Source LLC
Chambersburg PA
CBHW051305190726
48290CB00001B/5